AGATHA CHRISTIE

Five Complete Novels
of Murder and Detection

About the Author

AGATHA CHRISTIE's enormous success as a detective story writer and the excellence of her work caused her to be honored by Queen Elizabeth II of England as a Dame of the British Empire in 1971.

She knew, and described with humor and deadly accuracy, the world of culture, wealth, and breeding, laying bare, with devastating effectiveness, the passions that dwelt there, turning otherwise attractive men and women into killers. Her devilishly complex and daring plots have baffled and delighted mystery fans throughout the world for more than half a century.

After her marriage to the archaeologist Max Mallowan, she spent part of each year in the Middle East, which provided the exotic settings for several of her popular mysteries.

At the time of her death in 1976, Agatha Christie had written a total of 87 published works, over fifty of them mysteries, and had been translated more widely than any other British author, not excepting Shakespeare.

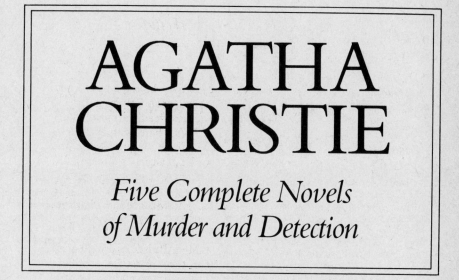

AGATHA CHRISTIE

*Five Complete Novels
of Murder and Detection*

PERIL AT END HOUSE
THE MURDER AT HAZELMOOR
EASY TO KILL
TEN LITTLE INDIANS
EVIL UNDER THE SUN

WINGS BOOKS
New York • Avenel, New Jersey

This Omnibus edition was previously published in separate volumes under the titles: *Peril at End House,* Copyright 1931, 1932 by Agatha Christie, Copyright renewed © 1959 by Agatha Christie Mallowan; *The Murder at Hazelmoor,* Copyright 1931 by Agatha Christie, Copyright renewed © 1959 by Agatha Christie Mallowan; *Easy to Kill,* Copyright 1938, 1939 by Agatha Christie Mallowan; Copyright renewed © 1967 by Agatha Christie Mallowan; *Ten Little Indians,* Copyright 1939, 1940 by Agatha Christie Mallowan, Copyright renewed © 1967 by Agatha Christie Mallowan; *Evil Under the Sun,* Copyright 1940, 1941 by Agatha Christie Mallowan, Copyright renewed © 1969 by Agatha Christie Mallowan.

Ten Little Indians has also been published as *And Then There Were None*

This edition is published by Wings Books,
distributed by Random House Value Publishing, Inc.,
40 Engelhard Avenue, Avenel, New Jersey 07001,
by arrangement with Dodd, Mead and Company, Inc.

Printed and Bound in the United States of America

Library of Congress Cataloging-in-Publication Data
Christie, Agatha, 1890–1976.
[Selections. 1991]
Five complete novels of murder and detection / Agatha Christie.
p.   cm.
Contents: Peril at end house — The murder at Hazelmoor — Easy to
kill — Ten little Indians — Evil under the sun.
ISBN 0-517-03750-5
1. Detective and mystery stories, English.   I. Title.   II. Title:
5 complete novels of murder and detection.
[PR6005.H66A6   1991]
823'.912 — dc20   90-26594   CIP

8   7   6   5

CONTENTS

PERIL
AT
END
HOUSE

To

E D E N   P H I L L P O T T S

To whom I shall always be grateful for his
friendship and the encouragement he
gave me many years ago

Contents

1
The Majestic Hotel

NO SEASIDE TOWN in the south of England is, I think, as attractive as St.
Loo. It is well named the Queen of Watering Places and reminds one
forcibly of the Riviera. The Cornish coast is to my mind every bit as
fascinating as that of the south of France.

I remarked as much to my friend, Hercule Poirot.

"So it said on our menu in the restaurant car yesterday, *mon ami.*
Your remark is not original."

"But don't you agree?"

He was smiling to himself and did not at once answer my question. I
repeated it.

"A thousand pardons, Hastings. My thoughts were wandering.
Wandering indeed to that part of the world you mentioned just now."

"The south of France?"

"Yes. I was thinking of that last winter that I spent there and of the
events which occurred."

I remembered. A murder had been committed on the Blue Train,
and the mystery—a complicated and baffling one—had been solved by
Poirot with his usual unerring acumen.

"How I wish I had been with you," I said with deep regret.

"I too," said Poirot. "Your experience would have been invaluable
to me."

I looked at him sideways. As a result of long habit, I distrust his
compliments but he appeared perfectly serious. And after all, why not?
I have a very long experience of the methods he employs.

"What I particularly missed was your vivid imagination, Hastings,"
he went on dreamily. "One needs a certain amount of light relief. My
valet, Georges, an admirable man with whom I sometimes permitted
myself to discuss a point, has no imagination whatever."

7

This remark seemed to me quite irrelevant.

"Tell me, Poirot," I said. "Are you never tempted to renew your activities? This passive life—"

"Suits me admirably, my friend. To sit in the sun—what could be more charming? To step from your pedestal at the zenith of your fame—what could be a grander gesture? They say of me, 'That is Hercule Poirot!—the great—the unique! There was never anyone like him, there never will be!' *Eh bien*—I am satisfied. I ask no more. I am modest."

I should not myself have used the word modest. It seemed to me that my little friend's egotism had certainly not declined with his years. He leaned back in his chair, caressing his mustache and almost purring with self-satisfaction.

We were sitting on one of the terraces of the Majestic Hotel. It is the biggest hotel in St. Loo and stands in its own grounds on a headland overlooking the sea. The gardens of the hotel lay below us freely interpersed with palm trees. The sea was of a deep and lovely blue, the sky clear and the sun shining with all the single-hearted fervor an August sun should (but in England so often does not) have. There was a vigorous humming of bees, a pleasant sound—and altogether nothing could have been more ideal.

We had only arrived last night, and this was the first morning of what we proposed should be a week's stay. If only these weather conditions continued, we should indeed have a perfect holiday.

I picked up the morning paper which had fallen from my hand and resumed my perusal of the morning's news. The political situation seemed unsatisfactory but uninteresting, there was trouble in China, there was a long account of a rumored City swindle but on the whole there was no news of a very thrilling order.

"Curious thing, this parrot disease," I remarked as I turned the sheet.

"Very curious."

"Two more deaths at Leeds, I see."

"Most regrettable."

I turned a page.

"Still no news of that flying fellow, Seton, in his round-the-world flight. Pretty plucky, these fellows. That amphibian machine of his, the *Albatross,* must be a great invention. Too bad if he's gone west. Not that they've given up hope yet. He may have made one of the Pacific islands."

"The Solomon Islanders are still cannibals, are they not?" inquired Poirot pleasantly.

"Must be a fine fellow. That sort of thing makes one feel it's a good thing to be an Englishman after all."

"It consoles for the defeats at Wimbledon," said Poirot.

"I—I didn't mean," I began.

My friend waved my attempted apology aside gracefully.

"Me," he announced, "I am not amphibian, like the machine of the poor Captain Seton, but I am cosmopolitan. And for the English I have always had, as you know, a great admiration. The thorough way, for instance, in which they read the daily paper."

My attention had strayed to political news.

"They seem to be giving the Home Secretary a pretty bad time of it," I remarked with a chuckle.

"The poor man. He has his troubles, that one. Ah! yes. So much so that he seeks for help in the most improbable quarters."

I stared at him.

With a slight smile, Poirot drew from his pocket his morning's correspondence, neatly secured by a rubber band. From this he selected one letter which he tossed across to me.

"It must have missed us yesterday," he said.

I read the letter with a pleasurable feeling of excitement.

"But, Poirot," I cried. "This is most flattering!"

"You think so, my friend?"

"He speaks in the warmest terms of your ability."

"He is right," said Poirot, modestly averting his eyes.

"He begs you to investigate this matter for him—puts it as a personal favor."

"Quite so. It is unnecessary to repeat all this to me. You understand, my dear Hastings, I have read the letter myself."

"It's too bad," I cried. "This will put an end to our holiday."

"No, no, *calmez-vous*—there is no question of that."

"But the Home Secretary says the matter is urgent."

"He may be right—or again he may not. These politicians they are easily excited. I have seen myself, in the Chambre des Deputés in Paris—"

"Yes, yes, but, Poirot, surely we ought to be making arrangements? The express to London has gone—it leaves at twelve o'clock. The next—"

"Calm yourself, Hastings, calm yourself, I pray of you! Always the excitement, the agitation. We are not going to London today—nor yet tomorrow."

"But this summons—"

"Does not concern me. I do not belong to your police force, Hastings. I am asked to undertake a case as a private investigator. I refuse."

"You refuse?"

"Certainly. I write with perfect politeness, tender my regrets, my

apologies, explain that I am completely desolated—but what will you?
I have retired—I am finished."

"You are not finished," I exclaimed warmly.

Poirot patted my knee.

"There speaks the good friend—the faithful dog. And you have
reason, too. The grey cells, they still function—the order, the
method—it is still there. But when I have retired, my friend, I have
retired! It is finished! I am not a stage favorite who gives the world a
dozen farewells. In all generosity I say: Let the young men have a
chance. They may possibly do something creditable. I doubt it, but
they may. Anyway they will do well enough for this doubtless tiresome
affair of the Home Secretary's."

"But, Poirot, the compliment!"

"Me, I am above compliments. The Home Secretary, being a man
of sense, realizes that if he can only obtain my services all will be
successful. What will you? He is unlucky. Hercule Poirot has solved
his last case."

I looked at him. In my heart of hearts I deplored his obstinacy. The
solving of such a case as was indicated might add still further luster to
his already world-wide reputation. Nevertheless I could not but admire
his unyielding attitude.

Suddenly a thought struck me and I smiled.

"I wonder," I said, "that you are not afraid. Such an emphatic
pronouncement will surely tempt the gods."

"Impossible," he replied, "that anyone should shake the decision of
Hercule Poirot."

"Impossible, Poirot?"

"You are right, *mon ami,* one should not use such a word. *Eh, ma
foi,* I do not say that if a bullet should strike the wall by my head, I
would not investigate the matter! One is human after all!"

I smiled. A little pebble had just struck the terrace beside us, and
Poirot's fanciful analogy from it tickled my fancy. He stooped now and
picked up the pebble as he went on.

"Yes—one is human. One is the sleeping dog—well and good, but
the sleeping dog can be roused. There is a proverb in your language
that says so."

"In fact," I said, "if you find a dagger planted by your pillow
tomorrow morning—let the criminal who put it there beware!"

He nodded, but rather absently.

Suddenly, to my surprise, he rose and descended the couple of steps
that led from the terrace to the garden. As he did so, a girl came into
sight hurrying up towards us.

I had just registered the impression that she was a decidedly pretty girl when my attention was drawn to Poirot who, not looking where he was going, had stumbled over a root and fallen heavily. He was just abreast of the girl at the time and she and I between us helped him to his feet. My attention was naturally on my friend, but I was conscious of an impression of dark hair, an impish face and big dark blue eyes.

"A thousand pardons," stammered Poirot. "Mademoiselle, you are most kind. I regret exceedingly—ouch!—my foot, he pains me considerably. No, no, it is nothing really—the turned ankle, that is all. In a few minutes all will be well. But if you could help me, Hastings—you and Mademoiselle between you, if she will be so very kind. I am ashamed to ask it of her."

With me on the one side and the girl on the other we soon settled Poirot in a chair on the terrace. I then suggested fetching a doctor, but this my friend negatived sharply.

"It is nothing, I tell you. The ankle turned, that is all. Painful for the moment, but soon over." He made a grimace. "See, in a little minute I shall have forgotten. Mademoiselle, I thank you a thousand times. You were most kind. Sit down, I beg of you."

The girl took a chair.

"It's nothing," she said. "But I wish you would let it be seen to."

"Mademoiselle, I assure you, it is a *bagatelle*! In the pleasure of your society the pain passes already."

The girl laughed.

"That's good."

"What about a cocktail?" I suggested. "It's just about the time."

"Well—" she hesitated, "thanks very much."

"Martini?"

"Yes, please—dry Martini."

I went off. On my return, after having ordered the drinks, I found Poirot and the girl engaged in animated conversation.

"Imagine, Hastings," he said, "that house there—the one on the point—that we have admired so much, it belongs to Mademoiselle here."

"Indeed?" I said, though I was unable to recall having expressed any admiration. In fact I had hardly noticed the house. "It looks rather eerie and imposing standing there by itself far from anything."

"It's called End House," said the girl. "I love it—but it's a tumble-down old place. Going to rack and ruin."

"You are the last of an old family, Mademoiselle?"

"Oh! we're nothing important. But there have been Buckleys here for two or three hundred years. My brother died three years ago, so I'm the last of the family."

"That is sad. You live there alone, Mademoiselle?"

"Oh! I'm away a good deal and when I'm at home there's usually a cheery crowd coming and going."

"That is so modern. Me, I was picturing you in a dark mysterious mansion, haunted by a family curse."

"How marvelous! What a picturesque imagination you must have. No, it's not haunted. Or if so, the ghost is a beneficent one. I've had three escapes from sudden death in as many days so I must bear a charmed life."

Poirot sat up alertly.

"Escapes from death? That sounds interesting, Mademoiselle."

"Oh! they weren't very thrilling. Just accidents, you know." She jerked her head sharply as a wasp flew past. "Curse these wasps. There must be a nest of them round here."

"The bees and the wasps—you do not like them, Mademoiselle? You have been stung—yes?"

"No—but I hate the way they come right past your face."

"The bee in the bonnet," said Poirot, "your English phrase."

At that moment the cocktails arrived. We all held up our glasses and made the usual inane observations.

"I'm due in the hotel for cocktails really," said Miss Buckley. "I expect they're wondering what has become of me."

Poirot cleared his throat and set down his glass.

"Ah! for a cup of good rich chocolate," he murmured. "But in England they make it not. Still, in England you have some very pleasing customs. The young girls, their hats they come on and off—so prettily—so easily—"

The girl stared at him.

"What do you mean? Why shouldn't they?"

"You ask that because you are young—so young, Mademoiselle. But to me the natural thing seems to have a coiffure high and rigid—so—and the hat attached with many hatpins—là—là—là et là."

He executed four vicious jabs in the air.

"But how frightfully uncomfortable!"

"Ah! I should think so," said Poirot. No martyred lady could have spoken with more feeling. "When the wind blew it was the agony—it gave you the *migraine*."

Miss Buckley dragged off the simple wide-brimmed felt she was wearing and cast it down beside her.

"And now we do this," she laughed.

"Which is sensible and charming," said Poirot with a little bow.

I looked at her with interest. Her dark hair was ruffled and gave her an elfin look. There was something elfin about her altogether. The small vivid face, pansy shaped, the enormous dark blue eyes, and something else—something haunting and arresting. Was it a hint of recklessness? There were dark shadows under the eyes.

The terrace on which we were sitting was a little used one. The main terrace where most people sat was just round the corner at a point where the cliff shelved directly down to the sea.

From round this corner now there appeared a man, a red-faced man with a rolling carriage who carried his hands half clenched by his side. There was something breezy and carefree about him—a typical sailor.

"I can't think where the girl's got to," he was saying in tones that easily carried to where we sat. "Nick—Nick."

Miss Buckley rose.

"I knew they'd be getting in a state. Attaboy—George—here I am."

"Freddie's frantic for a drink. Come on, girl."

He cast a glance of frank curiosity at Poirot who must have differed considerably from most of Nick's friends.

The girl performed a wave of introduction.

"This is Commander Challenger—er—"

But to my surprise Poirot did not supply the name for which she was waiting. Instead he rose, bowed very ceremoniously and murmured, "Of the English Navy. I have a great regard for the English Navy."

This type of remark is not one that an Englishman acclaims most readily. Commander Challenger flushed and Nick Buckley took command of the situation.

"Come on, George. Don't gape. Let's find Freddie and Jim."

She smiled at Poirot.

"Thanks for the cocktail. I hope the ankle will be all right."

With a nod to me she slipped her hand through the sailor's arm and they disappeared round the corner together.

"So that is one of Mademoiselle's friends," murmured Poirot thoughtfully. "One of her cheery crowd. What about him? Give me your expert judgment, Hastings. Is he what you call a good fellow—yes?"

Pausing for a moment to try and decide exactly what Poirot thought I should mean by a "good fellow," I gave a doubtful assent.

"He seems all right—yes," I said. "So far as one can tell by a cursory glance."

"I wonder," said Poirot.

The girl had left her hat behind. Poirot stooped to pick it up and twirled it round absentmindedly on his finger.

"Has he a *tendresse* for her? What do you think, Hastings?"

"My dear Poirot! How can I tell? Here—give me that hat. The lady will want it. I'll take it to her."

Poirot paid no attention to my request. He continued to revolve the hat slowly on his finger.

"*Pas encore. Ça m'amuse.*"

"Really, Poirot!"

"Yes, my friend, I grow old and childish, do I not?"

This was so exactly what I was feeling that I was somewhat disconcerted to have it put into words. Poirot gave a little chuckle, then, leaning forward, he laid a finger against the side of his nose.

"But no—I am not so completely imbecile as you think! We will return the hat—but assuredly—but later. We will return it to End House and thus we shall have the opportunity of seeing the charming Miss Nick again."

"Poirot," I said, "I believe you have fallen in love."

"She is a pretty girl—eh?"

"Well—you saw for yourself. Why ask me?"

"Because alas! I cannot judge. To me, nowadays, anything young is beautiful. *Jeunesse—jeunesse*. . . . It is the tragedy of my years. But you—I appeal to you? Your judgment is not up to date, naturally, having lived in the Argentine so long. You admire the figure of five years ago, but you are at any rate more modern than I am. She is pretty—yes? She has the appeal to the sexes?"

"One sex is sufficient, Poirot. The answer, I should say, is very much in the affirmative. Why are you so interested in the lady?"

"Am I interested?"

"Well—look at what you've just been saying."

"You are under a misapprehension, *mon ami*. I may be interested in the lady—yes—but I am much more interested in her hat."

I stared at him, but he appeared perfectly serious.

He nodded his head at me.

"Yes, Hastings, this very hat." He held it towards me. "You see the reason for my interest?"

"It's a nice hat," I said bewildered. "But quite an ordinary hat. Lots of girls have hats like it."

"Not like this one."

I looked at it more closely.

"You see, Hastings?"

"A perfectly plain fawn felt. Good style—"

"I did not ask you to describe the hat. It is plain that you do *not* see. Almost incredible, my poor Hastings, how you hardly ever *do* see! It amazes me every time anew! But regard, my dear old imbecile—it is not necessary to employ the grey cells—the eyes will do. Regard—regard—"

And then at last I saw to what he had been trying to draw my attention. The slowly turning hat was revolving on his finger, and that finger was stuck neatly through a hole in the brim of the hat. When he saw that I had realized his meaning, he drew his finger out and held the hat towards me. It was a small neat hole, quite round, and I could not imagine its purpose, if purpose it had.

"Did you observe the way Mademoiselle Nick flinched when a bee flew past? The bee in the bonnet—the hole in the hat."

"But a bee couldn't make a hole like that."

"Exactly, Hastings! What acumen! It could not. But a bullet could, *mon cher*!"

"A bullet?"

"*Mais oui*! A bullet like this."

He held out his hand with a small object in the palm of it.

"A spent bullet, *mon ami.* It was that which hit the terrace just now when we were talking. A spent bullet!"

"You mean—?"

"I mean that one inch of difference and that hole would be not through the hat but through the head. Now do you see why I am interested, Hastings? You were right, my friend, when you told me not to use the word 'impossible.' Yes—one is human! Ah! but he made a grave mistake, that would-be murderer, when he shot at his victim within a dozen yards of Hercule Poirot! For him, it is indeed *la mauvaise chance*. But you see now why we must make our entry into End House and get into touch with Mademoiselle? Three near escapes from death in three days. That is what she said. We must act quickly, Hastings. The peril is very close at hand."

2
End House

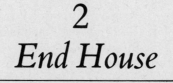

"POIROT," I SAID, "I have been thinking."

"An admirable exercise, my friend. Continue it."

We were sitting facing each other at lunch at a small table in the window.

"This shot must have been fired quite close to us. And yet we did not hear it."

"And you think that in the peaceful stillness, with the rippling waves the only sound, we should have done so?"

"Well, it's odd."

"No, it is not odd. Some sounds—you get used to them so soon that you hardly notice they are there. All this morning, my friend, speedboats have been making trips in the bay. You complained at first—soon, you did not even notice. But, *ma foi*, you could fire a machine gun almost and not notice it when one of those boats is on the sea."

"Yes, that's true."

"Ah! *voilà*," murmured Poirot. "Mademoiselle and her friends. They are to lunch here, it seems. And therefore I must return the hat. But no matter. The affair is sufficiently serious to warrant a visit all on its own."

He leaped up nimbly from his seat, hurried across the room, and presented the hat with a bow just as Miss Buckley and her companions were seating themselves at table.

They were a party of four, Nick Buckley, Commander Challenger, another man and another girl. From where we sat we had a very imperfect view of them. From time to time the Naval man's laugh boomed out. He seemed a simple likable soul, and I had already taken a fancy to him.

My friend was silent and distrait during our meal. He crumbled his bread, made strange little ejaculations to himself and straightened everything on the table. I tried to talk, but meeting with no encouragement, soon gave it up.

He continued to sit at the table long after he had finished his cheese. As soon as the other party had left the room, however, he too rose to his feet. They were just settling themselves at a table in the lounge when Poirot marched up to them in his most military fashion, and addressed Nick directly.

"Mademoiselle, may I crave one little word with you."

The girl frowned. I realized her feelings clearly enough. She was afraid that this queer little foreigner was going to be a nuisance. I could not but sympathize with her, knowing how it must appear in her eyes. Rather unwillingly, she moved a few steps aside.

Almost immediately I saw an expression of surprise pass over her face at the low hurried words Poirot was uttering.

In the meantime, I was feeling rather awkward and ill at ease. Challenger with ready tact came to my rescue, offering me a cigarette and making some commonplace observation. We had taken each other's measure and were inclined to be sympathetic to each other. I fancied that I was more his own kind than the man with whom he had been lunching. I now had the opportunity of observing the latter. A tall, fair, rather exquisite young man, with a somewhat fleshy nose and overemphasized good looks. He had a supercilious manner and a tired drawl. There was a sleekness about him that I especially disliked.

Then I looked at the woman. She was sitting straight opposite me in a big chair and had just thrown off her hat. She was an unusual type—a weary Madonna describes it best. She had fair, almost colorless hair, parted in the middle and drawn straight down over her ears to a knot on the neck. Her face was dead white and emaciated—yet curiously attractive. Her eyes were very light grey with large pupils. She had a curious look of detachment. She was staring at me. Suddenly she spoke.

"Sit down—till your friend has finished with Nick."

She had an affected voice, languid and artificial—yet which had withal a curious attraction—a kind of resonant lingering beauty. She impressed me, I think, as the most tired person I had ever met. Tired in mind, not in body, as though she had found everything in the world to be empty and valueless.

"Miss Buckley very kindly helped my friend when he twisted his ankle this morning," I explained, as I accepted her offer.

"So Nick said." Her eyes considered me, still detachedly. "Nothing wrong with his ankle now, is there?"

I felt myself blushing.

"Just a momentary sprain," I explained.

"Oh! well—I'm glad to hear Nick didn't invent the whole thing. She's the most heaven-sent little liar that ever existed, you know. Amazing—it's quite a gift."

I hardly knew what to say. My discomfiture seemed to amuse her.

"She's one of my oldest friends," she said, "and I always think loyalty's such a tiresome virtue, don't you? Principally practiced by the Scotch—like thrift and keeping the Sabbath. But Nick is a liar, isn't she, Jim? That marvelous story about the brakes of the car—and Jim says there was nothing in it at all."

The fair man said in a soft rich voice, "I know something about cars."

He half turned his head. Outside amongst other cars was a long red car. It seemed longer and redder than any car could be. It had a long gleaming bonnet of polished metal. A super car!

"Is that your car?" I asked on a sudden impulse.

He nodded.

"Yes."

I had an insane desire to say, "It would be!"

Poirot rejoined us at that moment. I rose, he took me by the arm, gave a quick bow to the party and drew me rapidly away.

"It is arranged, my friend. We are to call on Mademoiselle at End House at half past six. She will be returned from the motoring by then. Yes, yes, surely she will have returned—in safety."

His face was anxious and his tone was worried.

"What did you say to her?"

"I asked her to accord me an interview—as soon as possible. She was a little unwilling—naturally. She thinks—I can see the thoughts passing through her mind—'Who is he—this little man? Is he the bounder, the upstart, the moving-picture director?' If she could have refused she would—but it is difficult—asked like that on the spur of the moment, it is easier to consent. She admits that she will be back by six-thirty. *Ça y est!*"

I remarked that that seemed to be all right then, but my remark met with little favor. Indeed Poirot was as jumpy as the proverbial cat. He walked about our sitting room all afternoon, murmuring to himself and ceaselessly rearranging and straightening the ornaments. When I spoke to him, he waved his hands and shook his head.

In the end we started out from the hotel at barely six o'clock.

"It seems incredible," I remarked as we descended the steps of the terrace, "to attempt to shoot anyone in a hotel garden. Only a madman would do such a thing."

"I disagree with you. Given one condition, it would be quite a reasonably safe affair. To begin with, the garden is deserted. The people who come to hotels are like a flock of sheep. It is customary to sit on the terrace overlooking the bay—*eh bien*, so everyone sits on the terrace. Only I who am an original sit overlooking the garden. And even then, I *saw* nothing. There is plenty of cover, you observe—trees, groups of palms, flowering shrubs. Anyone could hide himself comfortably and be unobserved whilst he waited for Mademoiselle to pass this way. And she would come this way. To come round by the road from End House would be much longer. Mademoiselle Nick Buckley, she would be of those who are always late and taking the short cut!"

"All the same, the risk was enormous. He might have been seen—and you can't make shooting look like an accident."

"Not like an accident—no."

"What do you mean?"

"Nothing—a little idea. I may or may not be justified. Leaving it aside for a moment, there is what I mentioned just now—an essential condition."

"Which is?"

"Surely you can tell me, Hastings."

"I wouldn't like to deprive you of the pleasure of being clever at my expense!"

"Oh! The sarcasm! The irony! Well, what leaps to the eye is this: the motive cannot be obvious. If it were—why then truly the risk would indeed be too great to be taken! People would say: 'I wonder if it were So and So. Where was So and So when the shot was fired?' No, the murderer—the would-be murderer, I should say—cannot be obvious. And that, Hastings, is why I am afraid! Yes, at this minute I am afraid. I reassure myself. I say—'There are four of them.' I say—'Nothing can happen when they are all together.' I say—'It would be madness!' And all the time I am afraid. These 'accidents'—I want to hear about them!"

He turned back abruptly.

"It is still early. We will go the other way by the road. The garden has nothing to tell us. Let us inspect the orthodox approach to End House."

Our way led out of the front gate of the hotel, up a sharp hill to the right, and at the top of it a small lane with a notice on the wall: *To End House Only*.

We followed it and after a few hundred yards the lane gave an abrupt turn and ended in a pair of dilapidated entrance gates, which would have been the better for a coat of paint.

Inside the gates, to the right, was a small lodge. This lodge presented a piquant contrast to the gates and to the condition of the grass-grown drive. The small garden round it was spick-and-span, the window frames and sashes had been lately painted and there were clean bright curtains at the windows.

Bending over a flower bed was a man in a faded Norfolk jacket. He straightened up as the gate creaked and turned to look at us. He was a man of about sixty, six feet at least with a powerful frame and a weather-beaten face. His head was almost completely bald. His eyes were a vivid blue and twinkled. He seemed a genial soul.

"Good afternoon," he observed as we passed.

I responded in kind, and as we went on up the drive I was conscious of those blue eyes raking our backs inquisitively.

"I wonder," said Poirot thoughtfully.

He left it at that without vouchsafing any explanation of what it was that he wondered.

The house itself was large and rather dreary looking. It was shut in by trees, the branches of which actually touched the roof. It was clearly in bad repair. Poirot swept it with an appraising glance before ringing the bell—an old-fashioned bell that needed a Herculean pull to produce any effect and which once started, echoed mournfully on and on.

The door was opened by a middle-aged woman—"a decent woman

in black," so I felt she should be described. Very respectable, rather mournful, completely uninterested.

Miss Buckley, she said, had not yet returned. Poirot explained that we had an appointment. He had some little difficulty in gaining his point, she was the type that is apt to be suspicious of foreigners. Indeed I flatter myself that it was my appearance which turned the scale. We were admitted and ushered into the drawing room to await Miss Buckley's return.

There was no mournful note here. The room gave on the sea and was full of sunshine. It was shabby and betrayed conflicting styles— ultramodern of a cheap variety superimposed on solid Victorian. The curtains were of faded brocade, but the covers were new and gay and the cushions were positively hectic. On the walls were hung family portraits. Some of them, I thought, looked remarkably good. There was a gramophone and some records lying idly about. There was a portable wireless, practically no books and one newspaper flung open on the end of the sofa. Poirot picked it up—then laid it down with a grimace. It was the *St. Loo Weekly Herald and Directory*. Something impelled him to pick it up a second time and he was glancing at a column when the door opened and Nick Buckley came into the room.

"Bring the ice, Ellen," she called over her shoulder, then addressed herself to us.

"Well, here I am—and I've shaken off the others. I'm devoured with curiosity. Am I the long-lost heroine that is badly wanted for the films? You were so very solemn" (she addressed herself to Poirot) "that I feel it can't be anything else. Do make me a handsome offer."

"Alas! Mademoiselle—" began Poirot.

"Don't say it's the opposite," she begged him. "Don't say you paint miniatures and want me to buy one. But no—with that mustache and staying at the Majestic which has the nastiest food and the highest prices in England—no, it simply can't be."

The woman who had opened the door to us came into the room with ice and a tray of bottles. Nick mixed cocktails expertly, continuing to talk. I think at last Poirot's silence (so unlike him) impressed itself upon her. She stopped in the very act of filling the glasses and said sharply: "Well?"

"That is what I wish it to be—well, Mademoiselle." He took the cocktail from her hand. "To your good health, Mademoiselle—to your continued good health." The girl was no fool. The significance of his tone was not lost on her.

"Is—anything the matter?"

"Yes, Mademoiselle. This . . ."

He held out his hand to her with the bullet on the palm of it. She picked it up with a puzzled frown.

"You know what that is?"

"Yes, of course I know. It's a bullet."

"Exactly. Mademoiselle—it was not a wasp that flew past your face this morning—it was this bullet."

"Do you mean—was some criminal idiot shooting bullets in a hotel garden?"

"It would seem so."

"Well, I'm damned," said Nick frankly. "I do seem to bear a charmed life. That's number four."

"Yes," said Poirot. "That is number four. I want, Mademoiselle, to hear about the other three—accidents."

She stared at him.

"I want to be very sure, Mademoiselle, that they were—accidents."

"Why, of course! What else could they be?"

"Mademoiselle, prepare yourself, I beg, for a great shock. What if someone is attempting your life?"

All Nick's response to this was a burst of laughter. The idea seemed to amuse her hugely.

"What a marvelous idea! My dear man, who on earth do you think would attempt my life? I'm not the beautiful young heiress whose death releases millions. I wish somebody was trying to kill me—that would be a thrill if you like—but I'm afraid there's not a hope!"

"Will you tell me, Mademoiselle, about those accidents?"

"Of course—but there's nothing in it. They were just stupid things. There's a heavy picture hangs over my bed. It fell in the night. Just by pure chance I had happened to hear a door banging somewhere in the house and went down to find it and shut it—and so I escaped. It would probably have bashed my head in. That's number one."

Poirot did not smile.

"Continue, Mademoiselle. Let us pass to number two."

"Oh! that's weaker still. There's a scrambly cliff path down to the sea. I go down that way to bathe. There's a rock you can dive off. A boulder got dislodged somehow and came roaring down just missing me. The third thing was quite different. Something went wrong with the brakes of the car—I don't know quite what—the garage man explained but I didn't follow it. Anyway if I'd gone through the gate and down that hill, they wouldn't have held and I suppose I'd have gone slap into the Town Hall and there would have been the devil of a smash. Slight defacement of the Town Hall, complete obliteration of Me. But owing to my always leaving something behind, I turned back and merely ran into the laurel hedge."

"And you cannot tell me what the trouble was?"

"You can go and ask them at Mott's Garage. They'll know. It was something quite simple and mechanical that had been unscrewed, I think. I wondered if Ellen's boy—(my stand-by who opened the door to you has got a small boy)—had tinkered with it. Boys do like messing about with cars. Of course Ellen swore he'd never been near the car. I think something must just have worked loose in spite of what Mott said."

"Where is your garage, Mademoiselle?"

"Round the other side of the house."

"Is it kept locked?"

Nick's eyes widened in surprise.

"Oh! no. Of course not."

"Anyone could tamper with the car unobserved?"

"Well—yes—I suppose so. But it is so silly."

"No, Mademoiselle. It is not silly. You do not understand. You are in danger—grave danger. I tell it to you. I! And you do not know who I am?"

"No?" said Nick breathlessly.

"I am Hercule Poirot."

"Oh!" said Nick in rather a flat tone. "Oh! yes."

"You know my name, eh?"

"Oh! yes."

She wriggled uncomfortably. A hunted look came into her eyes. Poirot observed her keenly.

"You are not at ease. That means, I suppose, that you have not read my books."

"Well—no—not all of them. But I know the name, of course."

"Mademoiselle, you are a polite little liar." (I started, remembering the words spoken at the Majestic Hotel that day after lunch.) "I forgot—you are only a child—you would not have heard. So quickly does fame pass. My friend there—he will tell you."

Nick looked at me. I cleared my throat, somewhat embarrassed.

"Monsieur Poirot is—er—was—a great detective," I explained.

"Ah! my friend," cried Poirot. "Is that all you can find to say? *Mais dis donc*! Say then to Mademoiselle that I am a detective unique, unsurpassed, the greatest that ever lived!"

"That is now unnecessary," I said coldly. "You have told her yourself."

"Ah! yes, but it is more agreeable to have been able to preserve the modesty. One should not sing one's own praises."

"One should not keep a dog and have to bark oneself," agreed Nick with mock sympathy. "Who is the dog, by the way? Dr. Watson, I presume."

"My name is Hastings," I said coldly.

"Battle of—1066," said Nick. "Who said I wasn't educated? Well, this is all too, too marvelous! Do you think someone really wants to do away with me? It would be thrilling. But of course that sort of thing doesn't really happen. Only in books. I expect Monsieur Poirot is like a surgeon who's invented an operation or a doctor who's found an obscure disease and wants everyone to have it."

"*Sacré tonnerre!*" thundered Poirot. "Will you be serious? You young people of today, will nothing make you serious? It would not have been a joke, Mademoiselle, if you had been lying in the hotel garden a pretty little corpse with a nice little hole through your head instead of your hat. You would not have laughed then—eh?"

"Unearthly laughter heard at a *séance*," said Nick. "But seriously, Monsieur Poirot—it's very kind of you and all that, but the whole thing must be an accident."

"You are as obstinate as the devil!"

"That's where I get my name from. My grandfather was popularly supposed to have sold his soul to the devil. Everyone round here called him Old Nick. He was a wicked old man—but great fun. I adored him. I went everywhere with him and so they called us Old Nick and Young Nick. My real name is Magdala."

"That is an uncommon name."

"Yes, it's a kind of family one. There have been lots of Magdalas in the Buckley family. There's one up there." She nodded at a picture on the wall.

"Ah!" said Poirot. Then, looking at a portrait hanging over the mantelpiece, he said: "Is that your grandfather, Mademoiselle?"

"Yes, rather an arresting portrait, isn't it? Jim Lazarus offered to buy it, but I wouldn't sell. I've got an affection for Old Nick."

"Ah!" Poirot was silent for a minute, then he said very earnestly: "*Revenons à nos moutons*. Listen, Mademoiselle. I implore you to be serious. You are in danger. Today, somebody shot at you with a Mauser pistol—"

"A Mauser pistol?"

For the moment she was startled.

"Yes, why? Do you know of anyone who has a Mauser pistol?"

She smiled.

"I've got one myself."

"You have?"

"Yes—it was Dad's. He brought it back from the War. It's been knocking round here ever since. I saw it only the other day in that drawer."

She had indicated an old-fashioned bureau. Now, as though suddenly struck by an idea, she crossed to it and pulled the drawer open. She turned rather blankly. Her voice held a new note.

"Oh!" she said. "It's—it's gone."

3

Accidents?

IT WAS FROM that moment that the conversation took on a different tone. Up to now, Poirot and the girl had been at cross purposes. They were separated by a gulf of years. His fame and reputation meant nothing to her—she was of the generation that knows only the great names of the immediate moment. She was, therefore, unimpressed by his warnings. He was to her only a rather comic elderly foreigner with an amusingly melodramatic mind.

And this attitude baffled Poirot. To begin with, his vanity suffered. It was his constant dictum that all the world knew Hercule Poirot. Here was someone who did not. Very good for him, I could not but feel—but not precisely helpful to the object in view!

With the discovery of the missing pistol, however, the affair took on a new phase. Nick ceased to treat it as a mildly amusing joke. She still treated the matter lightly, because it was her habit and her creed to treat all occurrences lightly, but there was a distinct difference in her manner.

She came back and sat down on the arm of a chair frowning thoughtfully.

"That's odd," she said.

Poirot whirled round on me.

"You remember, Hastings, the little idea I mentioned? Well, it was correct, my little idea! Supposing Mademoiselle had been found shot lying in the hotel garden? She might not have been found for some hours—few people pass that way. And beside her hand—just fallen from it—is her own pistol. Doubtless the good Madame Ellen would identify it. There would be suggestions, no doubt, of worry or of sleeplessness—"

Nick moved uneasily.

"That's true. I have been worried to death. Everybody's been telling me I'm nervy. Yes—they'd say all that . . ."

"And bring in a verdict of suicide. Mademoiselle's fingerprints conveniently on the pistol and nobody else's—but yes, it would be very simple and convincing."

"How terribly amusing!" said Nick, but not, I was glad to note, as though she were terribly amused.

24

Poirot accepted her words in the conventional sense in which they were uttered.

"*N'est-ce pas*? But you understand, Mademoiselle, there must be no more of this. Four failures—yes—but the fifth time there may be a success."

"Bring out your rubber-tired hearses," murmured Nick.

"But we are here, my friend and I, to obviate all that!"

I felt grateful for the we. Poirot has a habit of sometimes ignoring my existence.

"Yes," I put in. "You mustn't be alarmed, Miss Buckley. We will protect you."

"How frightfully nice of you," said Nick. "I think the whole thing is perfectly marvelous. Too, too thrilling."

She still preserved her airy detached manner, but her eyes, I thought, looked troubled.

"And the first thing to do," said Poirot, "is to have the consultation."

He sat down and beamed upon her in a friendly manner.

"To begin with, Mademoiselle, a conventional question—but—have you any enemies?"

Nick shook her head rather regretfully.

"I'm afraid not," she said apologetically.

"*Bon*. We will dismiss that possibility then. And now we ask the question of the cinema, of the detective novel—who profits by your death, Mademoiselle?"

"I can't imagine," said Nick. "That's why it all seems such nonsense. There's this beastly old barn, of course, but it's mortgaged up to the hilt, the roof leaks and there can't be a coal mine or anything exciting like that hidden in the cliff."

"It is mortgaged—*hein*?"

"Yes. I had to mortgage it. You see there were two lots of death duties—quite soon after each other. First my grandfather died—just six years ago, and then my brother. That just about put the lid on the financial position."

"And your father?"

"He was invalided home from the War, then got pneumonia and died in 1919. My mother died when I was a baby. I lived here with Grandfather. He and Dad didn't get on (I don't wonder), so Dad found it convenient to park me and go roaming the world on his own account. Gerald—that was my brother—didn't get on with Grandfather either. I dare say I shouldn't have got on with him if I'd been a boy. Being a girl saved me. Grandfather used to say I was a chip of the old block and had inherited his spirit." She laughed. "He was an awful old rip, I believe. But frightfully lucky. There was a saying round here that everything he touched turned to gold. He was a gambler, though, and gambled it away again. When he died he left hardly anything beside the house and land. I was sixteen when he died and Gerald was twenty-two. Gerald was killed in a motor accident just three years ago and the place came to me.''

"And after you, Mademoiselle? Who is your nearest relation?''

"My cousin, Charles. Charles Vyse. He's a lawyer down here. Quite good and worthy but very dull. He gives me good advice and tries to restrain my extravagant tastes.''

"He manages your affairs for you—eh?''

"Well—yes, if you like to put it that way. I haven't many affairs to manage. He arranged the mortgage for me and made me let the lodge.''

"Ah!—the lodge. I was going to ask you about that. It is let?''

"Yes—to some Australians. Croft their name is. Very hearty, you know—and all that sort of thing. Simply oppressively kind. Always bringing up sticks of celery and early peas and things like that. They're shocked at the way I let the garden go. They're rather a nuisance really—at least he is. Too terribly friendly for words. She's a cripple, poor thing, and lies on a sofa all day. Anyway they pay the rent and that's the great thing.''

"How long have they been here?''

"Oh! about six months.''

"I see. Now beyond this cousin of yours—on your father's side or your mother's by the way?''

"Mother's. My mother was Amy Vyse.''

"*Bien*! Now beyond this cousin, as I was saying, have you any other relatives?''

"Some very distant cousins in Yorkshire—Buckleys.''

"No one else?''

"No.''

"That is lonely.''

Nick stared at him.

"Lonely? What a funny idea. I'm not down here much, you know. I'm usually in London. Relations are too devastating as a rule. They fuss and interfere. It's much more fun to be on one's own.''

"I will not waste the sympathy. You are a modern, I see, Mademoiselle. Now—your household.''

"How grand that sounds! Ellen's the household. And her husband who's a sort of a gardener—not a very good one. I pay them frightfully little because I let them have the child here. Ellen does for me when I'm down here and if I have a party we get in who and what we can to help. I'm giving a party on Monday. It's Regatta Week, you know.''

"Monday—and today is Saturday. Yes. Yes. And now, Mademoiselle, your friends—the ones with whom you were lunching today, for instance?"

"Well, Freddie Rice—the fair girl—is practically my greatest friend. She's had a rotten life. Married to a beast of a man who drank and drugged and was altogether a queer of the worst description. She had to leave him a year or two ago. Since then she's drifted round. I wish to goodness she'd get a divorce and marry Jim Lazarus."

"Lazarus? The art dealer in Bond Street?"

"Yes. Jim's the only son. Rolling in money, of course. Did you see that car of his? And he's devoted to Freddie. They go about everywhere together. They are staying at the Majestic over the weekend and are coming to me on Monday."

"And Mrs. Rice's husband?"

"The mess? Oh! he's dropped out of everything. Nobody knows where he is. It makes it horribly awkward for Freddie. You can't divorce a man when you don't know where he is."

"*Evidemment!*"

"Poor Freddie," said Nick pensively. "She's had rotten luck. The thing was all fixed once. She got hold of him and put it to him, and he said he was perfectly willing, but he simply hadn't got the cash to take a woman to a hotel. So the end of it all was she forked out—and he took it and off he went and has never been heard of from that day to this. Pretty mean, I call it."

"Good heavens," I exclaimed.

"My friend Hastings is shocked," remarked Poirot. "You must be more careful, Mademoiselle. He is out of date, you comprehend. He has just returned from those great clear open spaces, etc., and he has yet to learn the language of nowadays."

"Well, there's nothing to get shocked about," said Nick opening her eyes very wide. "I mean, everybody knows, don't they, that there are such people. But I call it a lowdown trick all the same. Poor old Freddie was so damned hard up at the time that she didn't know where to turn."

"Yes, yes, not a very pretty affair. And your other friend, Mademoiselle. The good Commander Challenger?"

"George? I've known George all my life—well, for the last five years anyway. He's a good scout, George."

"He wishes you to marry him—eh?"

"He does mention it now and again. In the small hours of the morning or after the second glass of port."

"But you remain hard-hearted."

"What would be the use of George and me marrying one another?

We've neither of us got a bean. And one would get terribly bored with George. That 'playing for one's side,' 'good old school' manner. After all, he's forty if he's a day."

The remark made me wince slightly.

"In fact he has one foot in the grave," said Poirot. "Oh! do not mind me, Mademoiselle. I am a grandpapa—a nobody. And now, tell me more about these accidents. The picture, for instance?"

"It's been hung up again—on a new cord. You can come and see it if you like."

She led the way out of the room and we followed her. The picture in question was an oil painting in a heavy frame. It hung directly over the bed head.

With a murmured, "You permit, Mademoiselle," Poirot removed his shoes and mounted upon the bed. He examined the picture and the cord and gingerly tested the weight of the painting. With an eloquent grimace he descended.

"To have that descend on one's head—no, it would not be pretty. The cord by which it was hung, Mademoiselle, was it, like this one, a wire cable?"

"Yes, but not so thick. I got a thicker one this time."

"That is comprehensible. And you examined the break—the edges were frayed?"

"I think so—but I didn't notice particularly. Why should I?"

"Exactly. As you say, why should you? All the same, I should much like to look at that piece of wire. Is it about the house anywhere?"

"It was still on the picture. I expect the man who put the new wire on just threw the old one away."

"A pity. I should like to have seen it."

"You don't think it was just an accident after all? Surely it couldn't have been anything else."

"It may have been an accident. It is impossible to say. But the damage to the brakes of your car—that was not an accident. And the stone that rolled down the cliff—I should like to see the spot where that accident occurred."

Nick took us out in the garden and led us to the cliff edge. The sea glittered blue below us. A rough path led down the face of the rock. Nick described just where the accident occurred and Poirot nodded thoughtfully. Then he asked, "How many ways are there into your garden, Mademoiselle?"

"There's the front way—past the lodge. And a tradesman's entrance—a door in the wall halfway up that lane. Then there's a gate just along here on the cliff edge. It leads out onto a zigzag path that runs up from that beach to the Majestic Hotel. And then of course you can go straight through a gap in the hedge into the Majestic garden—that's the way I went this morning. To go through the Majestic garden is a short cut to the town anyway."

"And your gardener—where does he usually work?"

"Well, he usually potters round the kitchen garden, or else he sits in the potting shed and pretends to be sharpening the shears."

"Round the other side of the house, that is to say?"

"Yes."

"So that if anyone were to come in here and dislodge a boulder he would be very unlikely to be noticed."

Nick gave a sudden little shiver.

"Do you—do you really think that is what happened?" she asked. "I can't believe it somehow. It seems so perfectly futile."

Poirot drew the bullet from his pocket again and looked at it.

"That was not futile, Mademoiselle," he said gently.

"It must have been some madman."

"Possibly. It is an interesting subject of after-dinner conversation—are all criminals really madmen? There may be a malformation in their little grey cells—yes, it is very likely. That, it is the affair of the doctor. For me—I have different work to perform. I have the innocent to think of, not the guilty—the victim, not the criminal. It is you I am considering, Mademoiselle, not your unknown assailant. You are young and beautiful, and the sun shines and the world is pleasant, and there is life and love ahead of you. It is all that of which I think, Mademoiselle. Tell me, these friends of yours, Mrs. Rice and Mr. Lazarus—they have been down here, how long?"

"Freddie came down on Wednesday to this part of the world. She stopped with some people near Tavistock for a couple of nights. She came on here yesterday. Jim has been touring round about, I believe."

"And Commander Challenger?"

"He's at Devonport. He comes over in his car whenever he can—weekends mostly."

Poirot nodded. We were walking back to the house. There was a silence and then he said suddenly: "Have you a friend whom you can trust, Mademoiselle?"

"There's Freddie."

"Other than Mrs. Rice."

"Well, I don't know. I suppose I have. Why?"

"Because I want you to have a friend to stay with you—immediately."

"Oh!"

Nick seemed rather taken aback. She was silent a moment or two thinking. Then she said doubtfully: "There's Maggie. I could get hold of her, I expect."

"Who is Maggie?"

"One of my Yorkshire cousins. There's a large family of them. He's a clergyman, you know. Maggie's about my age and I usually have her to stay sometime or other in the summer. She's no fun, though—one of those painfully pure girls, with the kind of hair that has just become fashionable by accident. I was hoping to get out of having her this year."

"Not at all. Your cousin, Mademoiselle, will do admirably. Just the type of person I had in mind."

"All right," said Nick with a sigh. "I'll wire her. I certainly don't know who else I could get hold of just now. Everyone's fixed up. But if it isn't the Choirboys' Outing or the Mothers' Beanfeast she'll come all right."

"Could you arrange for her to sleep in your room?"

"I suppose so."

"She would not think that an odd request?"

"Oh! no, Maggie never thinks. She just does—earnestly, you know. Christian works—with faith and perserverance. All right, I'll wire her to come on Monday."

"Why not tomorrow?"

"With Sunday trains? She'll think I'm dying if I suggest that. No, I'll say Monday. Are you going to tell her about the awful fate hanging over me?"

"*Nous verrons*. You still make a jest of it? You have courage, I am glad to see."

"It makes a diversion anyway," said Nick.

Something in her tone struck me and I glanced at her curiously. I had a feeling that there was something she had left untold. We had re-entered the drawing room. Poirot was fingering the newspaper on the sofa.

"You read this, Mademoiselle?" he asked suddenly.

"The *St. Loo Herald*? Not seriously. I opened it to see the tides. It gives them every week."

"I see. By the way, Mademoiselle, have you ever made a will?"

"Yes, I did. About six months ago. Just before my op."

"*Qu'est-ce que vous dites*? Your *op*?"

"Operation. For appendicitis. Someone said I ought to make a will, so I did. It made me feel quite important."

"And the terms of that will?"

"I left End House to Charles. I hadn't much else to leave but what there was I left to Freddie. I should think probably the what do they call them—liabilities—would have exceeded the assets, really."

Poirot nodded absently.

"I will take my leave now. *Au revoir*, Mademoiselle. Be careful."

"What of?" asked Nick.

"You are intelligent. Yes, that is the weak point—in which direction are you to be careful? Who can say? But have confidence, Mademoiselle. In a few days I shall have discovered the truth."

"Until then beware of poison, bombs, revolver shots, motor accidents and arrows dipped in the secret poison of the South American Indians," finished Nick glibly.

"Do not mock yourself, Mademoiselle," said Poirot gravely.

He paused as he reached the door.

"By the way," he said. "What price did M. Lazarus offer you for the portrait of your grandfather?"

"Fifty pounds."

"Ah!" said Poirot.

He looked earnestly back at the dark saturnine face above the mantelpiece.

"But, as I told you, I don't want to sell the old boy."

"No," said Poirot thoughtfully. "No, I understand."

4

There Must Be Something!

"POIROT," I SAID as soon as we were out upon the road, "there is one thing I think you ought to know."

"And what is that, *mon ami*?"

I told him of Mrs. Rice's version of the trouble with the motor.

"*Tiens! C'est intéressant, ça.* There is, of course, a type, vain, hysterical, that seeks to make itself interesting by having marvelous escapes from death and which will recount to you surprising histories that never happened! Yes, it is well known, that type there. Such people will even do themselves grave bodily injury to sustain the fiction."

"You don't think that—"

"That Mademoiselle Nick is of that type? No, indeed. You observed, Hastings, that we had great difficulty in convincing her of her danger. And right to the end she kept up the farce of a half-mocking disbelief. She is of her generation, that little one. All the same, it is interesting—what Madame Rice said. Why should she say it? Why say it even if it were true? It was unnecessary—almost *gauche*."

"Yes," I said. "That's true. She dragged it into the conversation neck and crop for no earthly reason that I could see."

"That is curious. Yes, that is curious. The little facts that are curious, I like to see them appear. They are significant. They point the way."

"The way—where?"

"You put your finger on the weak spot, my excellent Hastings. Where? Where indeed! Alas, we shall not know till we get there."

"Tell me, Poirot," I said. "Why did you insist on her getting this cousin to stay?"

Poirot stopped and waved an excited forefinger at me.

"Consider," he cried. "Consider for one little moment, Hastings. How are we handicapped! How are our hands tied! To hunt down a murderer after a crime has been committed—*c'est tout simple*! Or at least it is simple to one of my ability. The murderer has, so to speak, signed his name by committing the crime. But here there is no crime—and what is more we do not want a crime. To detect a crime before it has been committed—that is indeed of a rare difficulty.

"What is our first aim? The safety of Mademoiselle. And that is not easy. No, it is not easy, Hastings. We cannot watch over her day and night—we cannot even send a policeman in big boots to watch over her. We cannot pass the night in a young lady's sleeping chamber. The affair bristles with difficulties.

"But we can do one thing. We can make it more difficult for our assassin. We can put Mademoiselle upon her guard and we can introduce a perfectly impartial witness. It will take a very clever man to get around those two circumstances."

He paused and then said in an entirely different tone of voice:

"But what I am afraid of, Hastings—"

"Yes?"

"What I am afraid of is—that he is a very clever man. And I am not easy in my mind. No, I am not easy at all."

"Poirot," I said, "you're making me feel quite nervous."

"So am I nervous. Listen, my friend, that paper the *St. Loo Weekly Herald*. It was open and folded back at—where do you think? A little paragraph which said, '*Among the guests staying at the Majestic Hotel are M. Hercule Poirot and Captain Hastings*.' Supposing—just supposing that someone had read that paragraph. They know my name—everyone knows my name—"

"Miss Buckley didn't," I said with a grin.

"She is a scatterbrain—she does not count. A serious man—a criminal—would know my name. And he would be afraid! He would wonder! He would ask himself questions. Three times he has attempted the life of Mademoiselle and now Hercule Poirot arrives in the neighborhood. 'Is that coincidence?' he would ask himself. And he would fear that it might *not* be a coincidence. What would he do then?"

"Lie low and hide his tracks," I suggested.

"Yes—yes—or else—if he had real audacity, he would strike quickly—without loss of time. Before I had time to make the inquiries—*pouf*, Mademoiselle is dead. That is what a man of audacity would do."

"But why do you think that somebody read that paragraph other than Miss Buckley?"

"It was not Miss Buckley who read that paragraph. When I mentioned my name it meant nothing to her. It was not even familiar. Her face did not change. Besides she told us she opened the paper to look at the tides—nothing else. Well, there was no tide table on that page."

"You think someone in the house—"

"Someone in the house or who had access to it. And that last is easy—the window stands open. Without doubt Miss Buckley's friends pass in and out."

"Have you any idea? Any suspicion?"

Poirot flung out his hands.

"Nothing. Whatever the motive, it is, as I predicted, not an obvious one. That is the would-be murderer's security—that is why he could act so daringly this morning. On the face of it, no one seems to have any reason for desiring the little Nick's death. The property? End House? That passes to the cousin—but does he particularly want a heavily mortgaged and very dilapidated old house? It is not even a family place so far as he is concerned. He is not a Buckley, remember. We must see this M. Charles Vyse, certainly, but the idea seems fantastic.

"Then there is Madame—the bosom friend—with her strange eyes and her air of a lost Madonna—"

"You felt that too?" I asked startled.

"What is her concern in the business? She tells you that her friend is a liar. *C'est gentille, ca*! Why does she tell you? Is she afraid of something that Nick may say? Is that something connected with the car? Or did she use that as an instance and was her real fear of something else? Did anyone tamper with the car, and if so, who? And does she know about it?

"Then the handsome blond M. Lazarus. Where does he fit in? With his marvelous automobile and his money. Can he possibly be concerned in any way? Commander Challenger—"

"He's all right," I put in quickly. "I'm sure of that. A real pukka sahib."

"Doubtless he has been to what you consider the right school. Happily, being a foreigner, I am free from these prejudices, and can make investigations unhampered by them. But I will admit that I find it hard to connect Commander Challenger with the case. In fact I do not see that he can be so connected."

"Of course he can't," I said warmly.

Poirot looked at me meditatively.

"You have an extraordinary effect on me, Hastings. You have so strongly the *flair* in the wrong direction that I am almost tempted to go by it! You are that wholly admirable type of man, honest, credulous, honorable, who is invariably taken in by any scoundrel. You are the type of man who invests in doubtful oil fields, and non-existent gold mines. From hundreds like you, the swindler makes his daily bread. Ah well—I shall study this Commander Challenger. You have awakened my doubts."

"My dear Poirot," I cried angrily. "You are perfectly absurd. A man who has knocked about the world like I have—"

"Never learns," said Poirot sadly. "It is amazing—but there it is."

"Do you suppose I'd have made a success of my ranch out in the Argentine if I was the kind of credulous fool you make out?"

"Do not enrage yourself, *mon ami.* You have made a great success of it—you and your wife."

"Bella," I said, "always goes by my judgment."

"She is as wise as she is charming," said Poirot. "Let us not quarrel, my friend. See, there ahead of us, it says Mott's Garage. That, I think, is the garage mentioned by Mademoiselle Buckley. A few inquiries will soon give us the truth of that little matter."

We duly entered the place and Poirot introduced himself by explaining that he had been recommended there by Miss Buckley. He made some inquiries about hiring a car for some afternoon drives and from there slid easily into the topic of the damage sustained by Miss Buckley's car not long ago.

Immediately the garage proprietor waxed voluble. Most extraordinary thing he'd ever seen. He proceeded to be technical. I, alas, am not mechanically minded. Poirot, I should imagine, is even less so. But certain facts did emerge unmistakably. The car had been tampered with. And the damage had been something quite easily done occupying very little time.

"So that is that," said Poirot as we strolled away. "The little Nick was right, and the rich M. Lazarus was wrong. Hastings, my friend, all this is very interesting."

"What do we do now?"

"We visit the post office and send off a telegram if it is not too late."

"A telegram?" I said hopefully.

"Yes," said Poirot thoughtfully. "A telegram."

The post office was still open. Poirot wrote out his telegram and dispatched it. He vouchsafed me no information as to its contents. Feeling that he wanted me to ask him, I carefully refrained from doing so.

"It is annoying that tomorrow is Sunday," he remarked as we strolled back to the hotel. "We cannot now call upon M. Vyse till Monday morning."

"You could get hold of him at his private address."

"Naturally. But that is just what I am anxious not to do. I would prefer, in the first place, to consult him professionally and to form my judgment of him from that aspect."

"Yes," I said thoughtfully. "I suppose that would be best."

"The answer to one simple little question, for instance, might make a great difference. If M. Charles Vyse was in his office at twelve-thirty this morning, then it was not he who fired that shot in the garden of the Majestic Hotel."

"Ought we not to examine the alibis of the three at the hotel?"

"That is much more difficult. It would be easy enough for one of them to leave the others for a few minutes, a hasty egress from one of the innumerable windows—lounge, smoking room, drawing room, writing room—quickly under cover to the spot where the girl must pass, the shot fired and a rapid retreat. But as yet, *mon ami*, we are not even sure that we have arrived at all the *dramatis personae* in the drama. There is the respectable Ellen—and her so far unseen husband. Both inmates of the house and possibly, for all we know, with a grudge against our little Mademoiselle. There are even the unknown Australians at the lodge. And there may be others, friends and intimates of Miss Buckley's whom she has no reason for suspecting and consequently has not mentioned. I cannot help feeling, Hastings, that there is something behind this—something that has not yet come to light. I have a little idea that Miss Buckley knows more than she told us."

"You think she is keeping something back?"

"Yes."

"Possibly with an idea of shielding whoever it is?"

Poirot shook his head with the utmost energy.

"No, no. As far as that goes, she gave me the impression of being utterly frank. I am convinced that as regards these attempts on her life, she was telling all she knew. But there is something else—something that she believes has nothing to do with that at all. And I should like to know what that something is. For I—I say it in all modesty—am a great deal more intelligent than *une petite comme ca*. I, Hercule Poirot, might see a connection where she sees none. It might give me the clue I am seeking. For I announce to you, Hastings, quite frankly and humbly, that I am as you express it, all on the sea. Until I can get some glimmering of the reason behind all this, I am in the dark. There must be something—some factor in the case that I do not grasp. What is it? *Je me demande ça sans cesse. Qu'est-ce que c'est?*"

"You will find out," I said soothingly.

"So long," he said somberly, "as I do not find out too late."

5

Mr. and Mrs. Croft

THERE WAS DANCING that evening at the hotel. Nick Buckley dined there with her friends and waved a gay greeting to us.

She was dressed that evening in floating scarlet chiffon that dragged on the floor. Out of it rose her white neck and shoulders and her small impudent dark head.

"An engaging young devil," I remarked.

"A contrast to her friend—eh?"

Frederica Rice was in white. She danced with a languorous weary grace that was as far removed from Nick's animation as anything could be.

"She is very beautiful," said Poirot suddenly.

"Who? Our Nick?"

"No—the other. Is she evil? Is she good? Is she merely unhappy? One cannot tell. She is a mystery. She is, perhaps, nothing at all. But I tell you, my friend, she is an *allumeuse*."

"What do you mean?" I asked curiously.

He shook his head smiling.

"You will feel it sooner or later. Remember my words."

Presently to my surprise, he rose. Nick was dancing with George Challenger. Frederica and Lazarus had just stopped and had sat down at their table. Then Lazarus got up and went away. Mrs. Rice was alone. Poirot went straight to her table. I followed him.

His methods were direct and to the point.

"You permit?" He laid a hand on the back of a chair, then slid into it. "I am anxious to have a word with you while your friend is dancing."

"Yes?" Her voice sounded cool, uninterested.

"Madame, I do not know whether your friend has told you. If not, I will. Today her life has been attempted."

Her great grey eyes widened in horror and surprise. The pupils, dilated black pupils, widened too.

"What do you mean?"

"Mademoiselle Buckley was shot at in the garden of this hotel."

She smiled suddenly—a gentle pitying incredulous smile.

"Did Nick tell you so?"

"No, Madame, I happened to see it with my own eyes. Here is the bullet."

He held it out to her and she drew back a little.

"But then—but then—"

"It is no fantasy of Mademoiselle's imagination, you understand. I vouch for that. And there is more. Several very curious accidents have happened in the last few days. You will have heard—no, perhaps you will not. You only arrived yesterday, did you not?"

"Yes—yesterday."

"Before that you were staying with friends, I understand. At Tavistock."

"Yes."

"I wonder, Madame, what were the names of the friends with whom you were staying."

She raised her eyebrows.

"Is there any reason why I should tell you that?" she asked coldly.

Poirot was immediately all innocent surprise.

"A thousand pardons, Madame. I was most *maladroit*. But I myself, having friends at Tavistock, fancied that you might have met them there . . . Buchanan—that is the name of my friends."

Mrs. Rice shook her head.

"I don't remember them. I don't think I can have met them." Her tone now was quite cordial. "Don't let us talk about boring people. Go on about Nick. Who shot at her? Why?"

"I do not know who—as yet," said Poirot. "But I shall find out. Oh! yes, I shall find out. I am, you know, a detective. Hercule Poirot is my name."

"A very famous name."

"Madame is too kind."

She said slowly: "What do you want me to do?"

I think she surprised us both there. We had not expected just that.

"I will ask you, Madame, to watch over your friend."

"I will."

"That is all."

He got up, made a quick bow and we returned to our own table.

"Poirot," I said, "aren't you showing your hand very plainly?"

"*Mon ami*, what else can I do? It lacks subtlety, perhaps, but it makes for safety. I can take no chances. At any rate one thing emerges plain to see."

"What is that?"

"Mrs. Rice was not at Tavistock. Where was she? Ah! but I will find out. Impossible to keep information from Hercule Poirot. See—the handsome Lazarus has returned. She is telling him. He looks over at us. He is clever, that one. Note the shape of his head. Ah! I wish I knew—"

"What?" I asked as he came to a stop.

"What I shall know on Monday," he returned ambiguously.

I looked at him but said nothing. He sighed.

"You have no longer the curiosity, my friend. In the old days—"

"There are some pleasures," I said coldly, "that it is good for you to do without."

"You mean—?"

"The pleasure of refusing to answer questions."

"Ah, *c'est malin*."

"Quite so."

"Ah, well, well," murmured Poirot. "The strong silent man beloved of novelists in the Edwardian age."

His eyes twinkled with their old glint.

Nick passed our table shortly afterwards. She detached herself from her partner and swooped down on us like a gaily colored bird.

"Dancing on the edge of death," she said lightly.

"It is a new sensation, Mademoiselle?"

"Yes. Rather fun."

She was off again with a wave of her hand.

"I wish she hadn't said that," I said slowly. "Dancing on the edge of death. I don't like it."

"I know. It is too near the truth. She has courage, that little one. Yes, she has courage. But unfortunately it is not courage that is needed at this moment. Caution, not courage—*voilà ce qu'il nous faut!*"

The following day was Sunday. We were sitting on the terrace in

front of the hotel and it was about half past eleven when Poirot
suddenly rose to his feet.

"Come, my friend. We will try a little experiment. I have ascertained that M. Lazarus and Madame have gone out in the car and
Mademoiselle with them. The coast is clear."

"Clear for what?"

"You shall see."

We walked down the steps and across a short stretch of grass to
where a gate gave onto the zigzag path leading down to the sea. A
couple of bathers were coming up it. They passed us laughing and
talking.

When they had gone, Poirot walked to the point where an
inconspicuous small gate, rather rusty on its hinges, bore the words in
half-obliterated letters *End House. Private*. There was no one in sight.
We passed quietly through.

In another minute we came out on the stretch of lawn in front of the
house. There was no one about. Poirot strolled to the edge of the cliff
and looked over. Then he walked towards the house itself. The French
windows onto the veranda were open and we passed straight into the
drawing room. Poirot wasted no time there. He opened the door and
went out into the hall. From there he mounted the stairs, I at his heels.
He went straight to Nick's bedroom—sat down on the edge of the bed
and nodded to me with a twinkle.

"You see, my friend, how easy it is. No one has seen us come. No
one will see us go. We could do any little affair we had to do in perfect
safety. We could, for instance, fray through a picture wire so that it
would be bound to snap before many hours had passed. And supposing
that by chance anyone did happen to be in front of the house and see us
coming. Then we would have a perfectly natural excuse—providing
that we were known as friends of the house."

"You mean that we can rule out a stranger?"

"That is what I mean, Hastings. It is no stray lunatic who is at the
bottom of this. We must look nearer home than that."

He turned to leave the room and I followed him. We neither of us
spoke. We were both, I think, troubled in mind.

And then, at the bend of the staircase, we both stopped abruptly. A
man was coming up.

He, too, stopped. His face was in shadow but his attitude was of one
completely taken aback. He was the first to speak, in a loud rather
bullying voice.

"What the hell are you doing here, I'd like to know?"

"Ah!" said Poirot. "Monsieur—Croft, I think?"

"That's my name, but what—"

"Shall we go into the drawing room to converse? It would be better, I think."

The other gave way, turned abruptly and descended, we following close on his heels. In the drawing room, with the door shut, Poirot made a little bow.

"I will introduce myself. Hercule Poirot, at your service."

The other's face cleared a little.

"Oh!" he said slowly. "You're the detective chap. I've read about you."

"In the *St. Loo Herald*?"

"Eh? I've read about you way back in Australia. French, aren't you?"

"Belgian. It makes no matter. This is my friend, Captain Hastings."

"Glad to meet you. But look, what's the big idea? What are you doing here? Anything—wrong?"

"It depends what you call—wrong."

The Australian nodded. He was a fine-looking man in spite of his bald head and advancing years. His physique was magnificent. He had a heavy, rather underhung face—a crude face, I called it to myself. The piercing blue of his eyes was the most noticeable thing about him.

"See here," he said. "I came round to bring little Miss Buckley a handful of tomatoes and a cucumber. That man of hers is no good—bone idle—doesn't grow a thing. Lazy hound. Mother and I—why, it makes us mad and we feel it's only neighborly to do what we can! We've got a lot more tomatoes than we can eat. Neighbors should be matey, don't you think? I came in, as usual, through the window and dumped the basket down. I was just going off again when I heard footsteps and men's voices overhead. That struck me as odd. We don't deal much in burglars round here—but after all it was possible. I thought I'd just make sure everything was all right. Then I met you two on the stairs coming down. It gave me a bit of a surprise. And now you tell me you're a bonza detective. What's it all about?"

"It is very simple," said Poirot, smiling. "Mademoiselle had a rather alarming experience the other night. A picture fell above her bed. She may have told you of it?"

"She did. A mighty fine escape."

"To make all secure I promised to bring her some special chain—it will not do to repeat the occurrence, eh? She tells me she is going out this morning but I may come and measure what amount of chain will be needed. *Voilà*—it is simple."

Croft drew a deep breath.

"So that's all it is?"

"Yes—you have had the scare for nothing. We are very law-abiding citizens, my friend and I."

"Didn't I see you yesterday?" said Croft slowly. "Yesterday evening it was. You passed our little place."

"Ah! yes, you were working in the garden and were so polite as to say good afternoon when we passed."

"That's right. Well—well. And you're the M. Hercule Poirot I've heard so much about. Tell me, are you busy, Mr. Poirot? Because if not, I wish you'd come back with me now—have a cup of morning tea, Australian fashion, and meet my old lady. She's read all about you in the newspapers."

"You are too kind, M. Croft. We have nothing to do and shall be delighted."

"That's fine."

"You have the measurements correctly, Hastings?" asked Poirot turning to me.

I assured him that I had the measurements correctly and we accompanied our new friend.

Croft was a talker, we soon realized that. He told us of his home near Melbourne, of his early struggles, of his meeting with his wife, of their combined efforts and of his final good fortune and success.

"Right away we made up our minds to travel," he said. "We'd always wanted to come to the old country. Well, we did. We came down to this part of the world—tried to look up some of my wife's people—they came from round about here. But we couldn't trace any of them. Then we took a trip on the Continent—Paris, Rome, the Italian Lakes, Florence—all those places. It was while we were in Italy that we had the train accident. My poor wife was badly smashed up. Cruel, wasn't it? I've taken her to the best doctors and they all say the same—there's nothing for it but time—time and lying up. It's an injury to the spine."

"What a misfortune!"

"Hard luck, isn't it? Well, there it was. And she'd only got one kind of fancy—to come down here. She kind of felt if we had a little place of our own—something small—it would make all the difference. We saw a lot of messy-looking shacks, and then by good luck we found this. Nice and quiet and tucked away—no cars passing, or gramophones next door. I took it right away."

With the last words we had come to the lodge itself. He sent his voice echoing forth in a loud "Cooee" to which came an answering "Cooee."

"Come in," said Mr. Croft. He passed through the open door and up the short flight of stairs to a pleasant bedroom. There, on a sofa, was a stout middle-aged woman with pretty grey hair and a very sweet smile.

"Who do you think this is, Mother?" said Mr. Croft. "The extraspecial world-celebrated detective, Mr. Hercule Poirot. I brought him right along to have a chat with you."

"If that isn't too exciting for words," cried Mrs. Croft, shaking Poirot warmly by the hand. "Read about that Blue Train business, I did, and you just happening to be on it, and a lot about your other cases. Since this trouble with my back, I've read all the detective stories that ever were, I should think. Nothing else seems to pass the time away so quick. Bert dear, call out to Edith to bring the tea along."

"Right you are, Mother."

"She's a kind of nurse attendant, Edith is," Mrs. Croft explained. "She comes along each morning to fix me up. We're not bothering with servants. Bert's as good a cook and a house-parlor-man as you'd find anywhere, and it gives him occupation—that and the garden."

"Here we are," cried Mr. Croft reappearing with a tray. "Here's the tea. This is a great day in our lives, Mother."

"I suppose you're staying down here, Mr. Poirot?" Mrs. Croft asked as she leaned over a little and wielded the tea pot.

"Why yes, Madame, I take the holiday."

"But surely I read that you had retired—that you'd taken a holiday for good and all."

"Ah! Madame, you must not believe everything you read in the papers."

"Well, that's true enough. So you still carry on business?"

"When I find a case that interests me."

"Sure you're not down here on work?" inquired Mr. Croft shrewdly. "Calling it a holiday might be all part of the game."

"You mustn't ask him embarrassing questions, Bert," said Mrs. Croft. "Or he won't come again. We're simple people, Mr. Poirot, and you're giving us a great treat coming here today—you and your friend. You really don't know the pleasure you're giving us."

She was so natural and so frank in her gratification that my heart quite warmed to her.

"That was a bad business about that picture," said Mr. Croft.

"That poor little girl might have been killed," said Mrs. Croft with deep feeling. "She is a live wire. Livens the place up when she comes down here. Not much liked in the neighborhood, so I've heard. But that's the way in these stuck-up English places. They don't like life and gaiety in a girl. I don't wonder she doesn't spend much time down here. And that long-nosed cousin of hers has no more chance of persuading her to settle down here for good and all than—than—well, I don't know what."

"Don't gossip, Milly," said her husband.

"Aha," said Poirot. "The wind is in that quarter. Trust the instinct of Madame! So M. Charles Vyse is in love with our little friend?"

"He's silly about her," said Mrs. Croft. "But she won't marry a country lawyer. And I don't blame her. He's a poor stick anyway. I'd like her to marry that nice sailor—what's his name, Challenger. Many a smart marriage might be worse than that. He's older than she is, but what of that? Steadying—that's what she needs. Flying about all over the place, the Continent even, all alone or with that queer-looking Mrs. Rice. She's a sweet girl, Mr. Poirot—I know that well enough. But I'm worried about her. She's looked none too happy lately. She's had what I call a haunted kind of look. And it worries me! I've got my reasons for being interested in that girl, haven't I, Bert?"

Mr. Croft got up from his chair rather suddenly.

"No need to go into that, Milly," he said. "I wonder, Mr. Poirot, if you'd care to see some snapshots of Australia?"

The rest of our visit passed uneventfully. Ten minutes later we took our leave.

"Nice people," I said. "So simple and unassuming, typical Australians."

"You liked them?"

"Didn't you?"

"They were very pleasant—very friendly."

"Well, what is it then? There's something, I can see."

"They were, perhaps, just a shade too 'typical,' " said Poirot thoughtfully. "That cry of 'Cooee'—that insistence on showing us snapshots—was it not perhaps playing a part just a little too thoroughly?"

"What a suspicious old devil you are!"

"You are right, *mon ami*. I am suspicious of everyone—of everything. I am afraid, Hastings—afraid."

6

A Call Upon Mr. Vyse

POIROT CLUNG FIRMLY to the Continental breakfast. To see me consuming eggs and bacon upset and distressed him—so he always said. Consequently he breakfasted in bed upon coffee and rolls and I was free to start the day with the traditional Englishman's breakfast of bacon and eggs and marmalade.

I looked into his room on Monday morning as I went downstairs. He was sitting up in bed arrayed in a very marvelous dressing gown.

"*Bonjour*, Hastings. I was just about to ring. This note that I have written, will you be so good as to get it taken over to End House and delivered to Mademoiselle at once."

I held out my hand for it. Poirot looked at me and sighed.

"If only—if only, Hastings, you would part your hair in the middle instead of at the side! What a difference it would make to the symmetry of your appearance. And your mustache. If you *must* have a mustache, let it be a real mustache—a thing of beauty such as mine."

Repressing a shudder at the thought, I took the note firmly from Poirot's hand and left the room.

I had rejoined him in our sitting room when word was sent up to say Miss Buckley had called. Poirot gave the order for her to be shown up.

She came in gaily enough, but I fancied that the circles under her eyes were darker than usual. In her hand she held a telegram which she handed to Poirot.

"There," she said, "I hope that will please you!"

Poirot read it aloud.

"Arrive 5:30 today Maggie."

"My nurse and guardian!" said Nick. "But you're wrong, you know. Maggie's got no kind of brains. Good works is about all she's fit for. That and never seeing the point of jokes. Freddie would be ten times better at spotting hidden assassins. And Jim Lazarus would be better still. I never feel one has got to the bottom of Jim."

"And the Commander Challenger?"

"Oh! George! He'd never see anything till it was under his nose. But he'd let them have it when he did see. Very useful when it came to a showdown, George would be."

She tossed off her hat and went on.

"I gave orders for the man you wrote about to be let in. It sounds mysterious. Is he installing a dictaphone or something like that?"

Poirot shook his head.

"No, no, nothing scientific. A very simple little matter of opinion, Mademoiselle. Something I wanted to know."

"Oh, well," said Nick, "it's all great fun, isn't it?"

"Is it, Mademoiselle?" asked Poirot gently.

She stood for a minute with her back to us, looking out of the window. Then she turned. All the brave defiance had gone out of her face. It was childishly twisted awry, as she struggled to keep back the tears.

"No," she said. "It—it isn't really. I'm afraid—I'm afraid. Hideously afraid. And I always thought I was brave."

"So you are, *mon enfant*, so you are. Both Hastings and I, we have both admired your courage."

"Yes, indeed," I put in warmly.

"No," said Nick, shaking her head. "I'm not brave. It's—it's the waiting. Wondering the whole time if anything more's going to happen. And how it'll happen! And expecting it to happen."

"Yes, yes—it is the strain."

"Last night I pulled my bed out into the middle of the room. And I fastened my window and bolted my door. When I came here this morning, I came round by the road. I couldn't—I simply couldn't come through the garden. It's as though my nerve had gone all of a sudden. It's this thing coming on top of everything else."

"What do you mean exactly by that, Mademoiselle? On top of everything else?"

There was a momentary pause before she replied.

"I don't mean anything particular. What the newspapers call 'the strain of modern life,' I suppose. Too many cocktails, too many cigarettes—all that sort of thing. It's just that I've got into a ridiculous—sort of—of state."

She had sunk into a chair and was sitting there, her small fingers curling and uncurling themselves nervously.

"You are not being frank with me, Mademoiselle. There is something."

"There isn't—there really isn't."

"There is something you have not told me."

"I've told you every single smallest thing."

She spoke sincerely and earnestly.

"About these accidents—about the attacks upon you, yes."

"Well—then?"

"But you have not told me everything that is in your heart—in your life. . . ."

She said slowly:

"Can anyone do that. . . ?"

"Ah! then," said Poirot with triumph. "You admit it!"

She shook her head. He watched her keenly.

"Perhaps," he suggested shrewdly, "it is not your secret?"

I thought I saw a momentary flicker of her eyelids. But almost immediately she jumped up.

"Really and truly, M. Poirot, I've told you every single thing I know about this stupid business. If you think I know something about someone else, or have suspicions, you are wrong. It's having no suspicions that's driving me mad! Because I'm not a fool. I can see that if these 'accidents' weren't accidents, they must have been engineered by somebody very near at hand—somebody who—knows me. And that's what is so awful. Because I haven't the least idea—not the very least—who that somebody might be."

She went over once more to the window and stood looking out. Poirot signed to me not to speak. I think he was hoping for some further revelation, now that the girl's self-control had broken down.

When she spoke, it was in a different tone of voice, a dreamy far away voice.

"Do you know a queer wish I've always had? I love End House. I've always wanted to produce a play there. It's got an—an atmosphere of drama about it. I've seen all sorts of plays staged there in my mind. And now it's as though a drama were being acted there. Only I'm not producing it . . . I'm in it! I'm right in it! I am, perhaps, the person who—dies in the first act."

Her voice broke.

"Now, now, Mademoiselle." Poirot's voice was resolutely brisk and cheerful. "This will not do. This is the hysteria."

She turned and looked at him sharply.

"Did Freddie tell you I was hysterical?" she asked. "She says I am, sometimes. But you mustn't always believe what Freddie says. There are times, you know, when—when she isn't quite herself."

There was a pause, then Poirot asked a totally irrelevant question.

"Tell me, Mademoiselle," he said. "Have you ever received an offer for End House?"

"To sell it, do you mean?"

"That is what I meant."

"No."

"Would you consider selling it if you got a good offer?"

Nick considered for a moment.

"No, I don't think so. Not, I mean, unless it was such a ridiculously good offer that it would be perfectly foolish not to."

"*Précisément.*"

"I don't want to sell it, you know, because I'm fond of it."

"Quite so. I understand."

Nick moved slowly towards the door.

"By the way, there are fireworks tonight. Will you come? Dinner at eight o'clock. The fireworks begin at nine-thirty. You can see them splendidly from the garden where it overlooks the harbor."

"I shall be enchanted."

"Both of you, of course," said Nick.

"Many thanks," I said.

"Nothing like a party for reviving the drooping spirits," remarked Nick. And with a little laugh she went out.

"*Pauvre enfant*," said Poirot.

He reached for his hat and carefully flicked an infinitesimal speck of dust from its surface.

"We are going out?" I asked.

"*Mais oui*, we have legal business to transact, *mon ami*."

"Of course, I understand."

"One of your brilliant mentality could not fail to do so, Hastings."

The offices of Messrs. Vyse, Trevannion & Wynnard were situated in the main street of the town. We mounted the stairs to the first floor and entered a room where three clerks were busily writing. Poirot asked to see Mr. Charles Vyse.

A clerk murmured a few words down a telephone, received, apparently, an affirmative reply, and remarking that Mr. Vyse would see us now, he led us across the passage, tapped on a door and stood aside for us to pass in.

From behind a large desk covered with legal papers, Mr. Vyse rose up to greet us.

He was a tall young man, rather pale, with impassive features. He was going a little bald on either temple and wore glasses. His coloring was fair and indeterminate.

Poirot had come prepared for the encounter. Fortunately he had with him an agreement, as yet unsigned, and on some technical points in connection with this, he wanted Mr. Vyse's advice.

Mr. Vyse, speaking carefully and correctly, was soon able to allay Poirot's alleged doubts, and to clear up some obscure points of the wording.

"I am very much obliged to you," murmured Poirot. "As a foreigner, you comprehend, these legal matters and phrasing are most difficult."

It was then that Mr. Vyse asked who had sent Poirot to him.

"Miss Buckley," said Poirot promptly. "Your cousin, is she not? A most charming young lady. I happened to mention that I was in perplexity and she told me to come to you. I tried to see you on Saturday morning—about half past twelve—but you were out."

"Yes, I remember. I left early on Saturday."

"Mademoiselle your cousin must find that large house very lonely? She lives there alone, I understand."

"Quite so."

"Tell me, M. Vyse, if I may ask, is there any chance of that property being in the market?"

"Not the least, I should say."

"You understand, I do not ask idly. I have a reason! I am in search myself, of just such a property. The climate of St. Loo enchants me. It is true that the house appears to be in bad repair, there has not been, I gather, much money to spend upon it. Under those circumstances, is it not possible that Mademoiselle would consider an offer?"

"Not the least likelihood of it," Charles Vyse shook his head with the utmost decision. "My cousin is absolutely devoted to the place. Nothing would induce her to sell, I know. It is, you understand, a family place."

"I comprehend that, but—"

"It is absolutely out of the question. I know my cousin. She has a fanatical devotion to the house."

A few minutes later we were out in the street again.

"Well, my friend," said Poirot. "And what impression did this M. Charles Vyse make upon you?"

I considered.

"A very negative one," I said at last. "He is a curiously negative person."

"Not a strong personality, you would say?"

"No, indeed. The kind of man you would never remember on meeting him again. A mediocre person."

"His appearance is certainly not striking. Did you notice any discrepancy in the course of our conversation with him?"

"Yes," I said slowly. "I did. With regard to the selling of End House."

"Exactly. Would you have described Mademoiselle Buckley's attitude towards End House as one of 'fanatical devotion'?"

"It is a very strong term."

"Yes—and M. Vyse is not given to using strong terms. His normal attitude—a legal attitude—is to under-rather than over-state. Yet he says that Mademoiselle has a fanatical devotion to the house of her ancestors."

"She did not convey that impression this morning," I said. "She spoke about it very sensibly, I thought. She's obviously fond of the place—just as anyone in her position would be—but certainly nothing more."

"So, in fact, one of the two is lying," said Poirot thoughtfully.

"One would not suspect Vyse of lying."

"Clearly a great asset if one has any lying to do," remarked Poirot. "Yes, he has quite the air of a George Washington, that one. Did you notice another thing, Hastings?"

"What was that?"

"He was not in his office at half past twelve on Saturday."

7
Tragedy

THE FIRST PERSON we saw when we arrived at End House that evening was Nick. She was dancing about the hall wrapped in a marvelous kimono covered with dragons.

"Oh! it's only you!"

"Mademoiselle—I am desolated!"

"I know. It did sound rude. But you see, I'm waiting for my dress to arrive. They promised—the brutes—promised faithfully!"

"Ah! if it is a matter of *la toilette*! There is a dance tonight, is there not?"

"Yes. We are all going on to it after the fireworks. That is, I suppose we are."

There was a sudden drop in her voice. But the next minute she was laughing.

"Never give in! That's my motto. Don't think of trouble and trouble won't come! I've got my nerve back tonight. I'm going to be gay and enjoy myself."

There was a footfall on the stairs. Nick turned.

"Oh! here's Maggie. Maggie, here are the sleuths that are protecting me from the secret assassin. Take them into the drawing room and let them tell you about it."

In turn we shook hands with Maggie Buckley and as requested she took us into the drawing room. I formed an immediate favorable opinion of her.

It was, I think, her appearance of calm good sense that so attracted me. A quiet girl, pretty in the old-fashioned sense—certainly not smart. Her face was innocent of makeup and she wore a simple, rather shabby, black evening dress. She had frank blue eyes, and a pleasant slow voice.

"Nick has been telling me the most amazing things," she said. "Surely she must be exaggerating? Who ever would want to harm Nick? She can't have an enemy in the world."

Incredulity showed strongly in her voice. She was looking at Poirot in a somewhat unflattering fashion. I realized that to a girl like Maggie Buckley, foreigners were always suspicious.

"Nevertheless, Miss Buckley, I assure you that it is the truth," said Poirot quietly.

She made no reply but her face remained unbelieving.

"Nick seems quite fey tonight," she remarked. "I don't know what's the matter with her. She seems in the wildest spirits."

That word—fey! It sent a shiver through me. Also, something in the intonation of her voice had set me wondering.

"Are you Scotch, Miss Buckley?" I asked abruptly.

"My mother was Scottish," she explained.

She viewed me, I noticed, with more approval than she viewed Poirot. I felt that my statement of the case would carry more weight with her than Poirot's would.

"Your cousin is behaving with great bravery," I said. "She's determined to carry on as usual."

"It's the only way, isn't it?" said Maggie. "I mean—whatever one's inward feelings are—it is no good making a fuss about them. That's only uncomfortable for everyone else." She paused and then added in a soft voice, "I'm very fond of Nick. She's been very good to me always."

We could say nothing more for at that moment Frederica Rice drifted into the room. She was wearing a gown of Madonna blue and looked very fragile and ethereal. Lazarus soon followed her and then Nick danced in. She was wearing a black frock and round her was wrapped a marvelous old Chinese shawl of vivid lacquer red.

"Hullo, people," she said. "Cocktails."

We all drank and Lazarus raised his glass to her.

"That's a marvelous shawl, Nick," he said. "It's an old one, isn't it?"

"Yes—brought back by Great-Great-Great-Uncle Timothy from his travels."

"It's a beauty—a real beauty. You wouldn't find another to match it if you tried."

"It's warm," said Nick. "It'll be nice when we're watching the fireworks. And it's gay. I—I hate black."

"Yes," said Frederica. "I don't believe I've ever seen you in a black dress before, Nick. Why did you get it?"

"Oh! I don't know." The girl flung aside with a petulant gesture, but I had caught a curious curl of her lips as though of pain. "Why does one do anything?"

We went into dinner. A mysterious manservant had appeared—hired, I presume for the occasion. The food was indifferent. The champagne, on the other hand, was good.

"George hasn't turned up," said Nick. "A nuisance his having to go back to Plymouth last night. He'll get over this evening some time or other, I expect. In time for the dance, anyway. I've got a man for Maggie. Presentable, if not passionately interesting."

A faint roaring sound drifted in through the window.

"Oh! curse that speedboat," said Lazarus. "I get so tired of it."

"That's not the speedboat," said Nick. "That's a seaplane."

"I believe you're right."

"Of course I'm right. The sound's quite different."

"When are you going to get your Moth, Nick?"

"When I can raise the money," laughed Nick.

"And then, I suppose, you'll be off to Australia like that girl—what's her name?"

"I'd love to—"

"I admire her enormously," said Mrs. Rice in her tired voice. "What marvelous nerve! All by herself too."

"I admire all these flying people," said Lazarus. "If Michael Seton had succeeded in his flight round the world he'd have been the hero of the day—and rightly so. A thousand pities he's come to grief. He's the kind of man England can't afford to lose."

"He may still be all right," said Nick.

"Hardly. It's a thousand to one against by now. Poor Mad Seton."

"They always called him Mad Seton, didn't they?" asked Frederica. Lazarus nodded.

"He comes of rather a mad family," he said. "His uncle, Sir Matthew Seton who died about a week ago—he was as mad as a hatter."

"He was the mad millionaire who ran bird sanctuaries, wasn't he?" asked Frederica.

"Yes. Used to buy up islands. He was a great woman hater. Some girl chucked him once, I believe, and he took to Natural History by way of consoling himself."

"Why do you say Michael Seton is dead?" persisted Nick. "I don't see any reason for giving up hope—yet."

"Of course, you knew him, didn't you?" said Lazarus. "I forgot."

"Freddie and I met him at Le Touquet last year," said Nick. "He was too marvelous, wasn't he, Freddie?"

"Don't ask me, darling. He was your conquest, not mine. He took you up once, didn't he?"

"Yes—at Scarborough. It was simply too wonderful."

"Have you done any flying, Captain Hastings?" Maggie asked of me in polite conversational tones.

I had to confess that a trip to Paris and back was the extent of my acquaintance with air travel.

Suddenly, with an exclamation, Nick sprang up.

"There's the telephone. Don't wait for me. It's getting late. And I've asked lots of people."

She left the room. I glanced at my watch. It was just nine o'clock.

Dessert was brought, and port. Poirot and Lazarus were talking art. Pictures, Lazarus was saying, were a great drug in the market just now. They went on to discuss new ideas in furniture and decoration.

I endeavored to do my duty by talking to Maggie Buckley, but I had to admit that the girl was heavy in hand. She answered pleasantly but without throwing the ball back. It was uphill work.

Frederica Rice sat dreamily silent, her elbows on the table and the smoke from her cigarette curling round her fair head. She looked like a meditative angel.

It was just twenty past nine when Nick put her head round the door. "Come out of it, all of you! The animals are coming in two by two."

We rose obediently. Nick was busy greeting arrivals. About a dozen people had been asked. Most of them were rather uninteresting. Nick, I noticed, made a good hostess. She sunk her modernisms and made everyone welcome in an old-fashioned way. Amongst the guests I noticed Charles Vyse.

Presently we all moved out into the garden to a place overlooking the sea and the harbor. A few chairs had been placed there for the elderly people, but most of us stood. The first rocket flamed to Heaven.

At that moment, I heard a loud familiar voice and turned my head to see Nick greeting Mr. Croft.

"It's too bad," she was saying, "that Mrs. Croft can't be here too. We ought to have carried her on a stretcher or something."

"It's bad luck on poor Mother altogether. But she never complains—that woman's got the sweetest nature—Ha! that's a good one." This as a shower of golden rain showed up in the sky.

The night was a dark one—there was no moon—the new moon being due in three days' time. It was also, like most summer evenings, cold. Maggie Buckley, who was next to me, shivered.

"I'll just run in and get a coat," she murmured.

"Let me."

"No, you wouldn't know where to find it."

She turned towards the house. At that moment Frederica Rice's voice called.

"Oh! Maggie, get mine too. It's in my room."

"She didn't hear," said Nick. "I'll get it, Freddie. I want my fur one—this shawl isn't nearly hot enough. It's this wind."

There was, indeed, a sharp breeze blowing off the sea.

Some set pieces started down on the quay. I fell into conversation with an elderly young lady standing next me who put me through a rigorous catechism as to life, career, tastes and probable length of stay.

Bang! A shower of green stars filled the sky. They changed to blue, then red, then silver.

Another and yet another.

"'Oh!' and then 'Ah!' that is what one says," observed Poirot suddenly close to my ear. "At the end it becomes monotonous, do you not find? Brrr! The grass, it is damp to the feet! I shall suffer for this—a chill. And no possibility of obtaining a proper *tisane*!"

"A chill? On a lovely night like this?"

"A lovely night! A lovely night! You say that, because the rain it does not pour down in sheets! Always when the rain does not fall, it is a lovely night. But I tell you, my friend, if there were a little thermometer to consult you would see."

"Well," I admitted. "I wouldn't mind putting on a coat myself."

"You are very sensible. You have come from a hot climate."

"I'll bring yours."

Poirot lifted first one, then the other foot from the ground with a catlike motion.

"It is the dampness of the feet I fear. Would it, think you, be possible to lay the hands on a pair of galoshes?"

I repressed a smile.

"Not a hope," I said. "You understand, Poirot, that it is no longer done."

"Then I shall sit in the house," he declared. "Just for the Guy Fawkes show, shall I want only *enrhumer* myself? And catch, perhaps, a *fluxion de poitrine*?"

Poirot still murmuring indignantly, we bent our footsteps towards the house. Loud clapping drifted up to us from the quay below where another set piece was being shown—a ship, I believe, with WELCOME TO OUR VISITORS displayed across it.

"We are all children at heart," said Poirot thoughtfully. "*Les Feux d'Artifices*, the Party, the games with balls—yes, and even the conjuror, the man who deceives the eye, however carefully it watches—*mais qu'est-ce que vous avez*?"

I had caught him by the arm, and was clutching him with one hand while with the other I pointed.

We were within a hundred yards of the house and just in front of us, between us and the open French window, *there lay a huddled figure wrapped in a scarlet Chinese shawl. . . .*

"*Mon Dieu!*" whispered Poirot. "*Mon Dieu. . . .*"

8

The Fatal Shawl

I SUPPOSE it was not more than forty seconds that we stood there, frozen with horror, unable to move, but it seemed like an hour. Then Poirot moved forward shaking off my hand. He moved stiffly like an automaton.

"It has happened," he murmured, and I can hardly describe the anguished bitterness of his voice. "In spite of everything—in spite of my precautions it has happened. Ah! miserable criminal that I am, why did I not guard her better? I should have foreseen, yes—I should have foreseen. Not for one instant should I have left her side."

"You mustn't blame yourself," I said.

My tongue stuck to the roof of my mouth and I could hardly articulate.

Poirot only responded with a sorrowful shake of his head. He knelt down by the body.

And at that moment we received a second shock.

For Nick's voice rang out, clear and gay, and a moment later Nick appeared in the square of the window silhouetted against the lighted room behind.

"Sorry I've been so long, Maggie," she said. "But—"

Then she broke off—staring at the scene before her.

With a sharp exclamation Poirot turned over the body on the lawn and I pressed forward to see.

I looked down into the dead face of Maggie Buckley.

In another minute Nick was beside us. She gave a sharp cry.

"Maggie—Oh! Maggie—it—it can't—"

Poirot was still examining the girl's body. At last very slowly he rose to his feet.

"Is she—is—" Nick's voice broke off.

"Yes, Mademoiselle. She is dead."

"But why? But why? Who could have wanted to kill her?"

Poirot's reply came quickly and firmly.

"It was not her they meant to kill, Mademoiselle! It was you! They were misled by the shawl."

A great cry broke from Nick.

"Why couldn't it have been me?" she wailed. "Oh! why couldn't it have been me? I'd so much rather. I don't want to live—now. I'd be glad—willing—happy—to die."

She flung up her arms wildly and then staggered slightly. I passed an arm around her quickly to support her.

"Take her into the house, Hastings," said Poirot. "Then ring up the police."

"The police?"

"*Mais oui*! Tell them someone has been shot. And afterwards stay with Mademoiselle Nick. On no account leave her."

I nodded comprehension of these instructions, and supporting the half-fainting girl, made my way through the drawing room window. I laid the girl on the sofa there, with a cushion under her head, and then hurried out into the hall in search of the telephone.

I gave a slight start on almost running into Ellen. She was standing there with a most peculiar expression on her meek respectable face. Her eyes were glittering and she was passing her tongue repeatedly over her dry lips. Her hands were trembling, as though with excitement. As soon as she saw me, she spoke.

"Has—has anything happened, sir?"

"Yes," I said curtly. "Where's the telephone?"

"Nothing—nothing wrong, sir?"

"There's been an accident," I said evasively. "Somebody hurt. I must telephone."

"Who has been hurt, sir?"

There was a positive eagerness in her face.

"Miss Buckley. Miss Maggie Buckley."

"Miss Maggie? Miss Maggie? Are you sure, sir—I mean are you sure that—that it's Miss Maggie?"

"I'm quite sure," I said. "Why?"

"Oh!—nothing, I—I thought it might be one of the other ladies. I thought perhaps it might be—Mrs. Rice."

"Look here," I said. "Where's the telephone?"

"It's in the little room here, sir." She opened the door for me and indicated the instrument.

"Thanks," I said. And as she seemed disposed to linger, I added, "That's all I want, thank you."

"If you want Dr. Graham—"

"No, no," I said. "That's all. Go, please."

She withdrew reluctantly, as slowly as she dared. In all probability she would listen outside the door, but I could not help that. After all, she would soon know all there was to be known.

I got the police station and made my report. Then, on my own initiative, I rang up the Dr. Graham Ellen had mentioned. I found his number in the book. Nick, at any rate, should have medical attention, I felt—even though a doctor could do nothing for that poor girl lying out there. He promised to come at once and I hung up the receiver and came out into the hall again.

If Ellen had been listening outside the door she had managed to disappear very swiftly. There was no one in sight when I came out. I went back into the drawing room. Nick was trying to sit up.

"Do you think—could you get me—some brandy?"

"Of course."

I hurried into the dining room, found what I wanted and came back. A few sips of the spirit revived the girl. The color began to come back into her cheeks. I rearranged the cushion for her head.

"It's all—so awful." She shivered. "Everything—everywhere."

"I know, my dear, I know."

"No, you don't! You can't! And it's all such a waste. If it only were me. It would be all over. . . ."

"You mustn't," I said, "be morbid."

She only shook her head, reiterating: "You don't know! You don't know!"

Then, suddenly, she began to cry. A quiet, hopeless sobbing like a child. That, I thought, was probably the best thing for her, so I made no effort to stem her tears.

When their first violence had died down a little, I stole across to the window and looked out. I had heard an outcry of voices a few minutes before. They were all there by now, a semicircle round the scene of the tragedy, with Poirot like a fantastical sentinel, keeping them back.

As I watched, two uniformed figures came striding across the grass. The police had arrived.

I went quietly back to my place by the sofa. Nick lifted her tearstained face.

"Oughtn't I to be doing something?"

"No, my dear. Poirot will see to it. Leave it to him."

Nick was silent for a minute or two, then she said: "Poor Maggie. Poor dear old Maggie. Such a good sort who never harmed a soul in her life. That this should happen to her. I feel as though I'd killed her—bringing her down in the way that I did."

I shook my head sadly. How little one can foresee the future. When Poirot insisted on Nick's inviting a friend, how little did he think that he was signing an unknown girl's death warrant.

We sat in silence. I longed to know what was going on outside but I loyally fulfilled Poirot's instructions and stuck to my post.

It seemed hours later when the door opened and Poirot and a police inspector entered the room. With them came a man who was evidently Dr. Graham. He came over at once to Nick.

"And how are you feeling, Miss Buckley? This must have been a terrible shock." His fingers were on her pulse. "Not too bad."

He turned to me.

"Has she had anything?"

"Some brandy," I said.

"I'm all right," said Nick bravely.

"Able to answer a few questions, eh?"

"Of course."

The police inspector moved forward with a preliminary cough. Nick greeted him with the ghost of a smile.

"Not impeding the traffic this time," she said.

I gathered they were not strangers to each other.

"This is a terrible business, Miss Buckley," said the inspector. "I'm very sorry about it. Now Mr. Poirot here whose name I'm very familiar with (and proud we are to have him with us, I'm sure) tells me that to the best of his belief you were shot at in the grounds of the Majestic Hotel the other morning?"

Nick nodded.

"I thought it was just a wasp," she explained. "But it wasn't."

"And you'd had some rather peculiar accidents before that?"

"Yes—at least it was odd their happening so close together."

She gave a brief account of the various circumstances.

"Just so. Now how came it that your cousin was wearing your shawl tonight?"

"We came in to fetch her coat—it was rather cold watching the fireworks. I flung off the shawl on the sofa here. Then I went upstairs and put on the coat I'm wearing now—a light nutria one. I also got a wrap for my friend Mrs. Rice out of her room. There it is on the floor by the window. Then Maggie called out that she couldn't find her coat. I said it must be downstairs. She went down and called up she still couldn't find it. I said it must have been left in the car—it was a tweed coat she was looking for—she hasn't got an evening furry one—and I said I'd bring her down something of mine. But she said it didn't matter—she'd take my shawl if I didn't want it. And I said of course but would that be enough? And she said Oh! yes, because she really didn't feel it particularly cold after Yorkshire. She just wanted something. And I said all right, I'd be out in a minute. And when I did—did come out—"

She stopped, her voice breaking . . .

"Now, don't distress yourself, Miss Buckley. Just tell me this: Did you hear a shot—or two shots?"

Nick shook her head.

"No—only just the fireworks popping and the squibs going off."

"That's just it," said the inspector. "You'd never notice a shot with all that going on. It's no good asking you, I suppose, if you've any clue to who it is making these attacks upon you?"

"I haven't the least idea," said Nick. "I can't imagine."

"And you wouldn't be likely to," said the inspector. "Some homicidal maniac—that's what it looks like to me. Nasty business. Well, I won't need to ask you any more questions tonight, Miss. I'm more sorry about this than I can say."

Dr. Graham stepped forward.

"I'm going to suggest, Miss Buckley, that you don't stay here. I've been talking it over with M. Poirot. I know of an excellent nursing home. You've had a shock, you know. What you need is complete rest—"

Nick was not looking at him. Her eyes had gone to Poirot.

"Is it—because of the shock?" she asked.

He came forward.

"I want you to feel safe, *mon enfant*. And *I* want to feel, too, that you are safe. There will be a nurse there—a nice practical unimaginative nurse. She will be near you all night. When you wake up and cry out—she will be there, close at hand. You understand?"

"Yes," said Nick. "I understand. But you don't. I'm not afraid any longer. I don't care one way or another. If anyone wants to murder me, they can."

"Hush, hush," I said. "You're overstrung."

"You don't know. None of you know!"

"I really think M. Poirot's plan is a very good one," the doctor broke in soothingly. "I will take you in my car. And we will give you a little something to ensure a good night's rest. Now what do you say?"

"I don't mind," said Nick. "Anything you like. It doesn't matter."

Poirot laid his hand on hers.

"I know, Mademoiselle. I know what you must feel. I stand before you ashamed and stricken to the heart. I, who promised protection, have not been able to protect. I have failed. I am a miserable. But believe me, Mademoiselle, my heart is in agony because of that failure. If you knew what I am suffering, you would forgive me, I am sure."

"That's all right," said Nick, still in the same dull voice. "You mustn't blame yourself. I'm sure you did the best you could. Nobody could have helped it—or done more, I'm sure. Please don't be ·unhappy."

"You are very generous, Mademoiselle."

"No, I—"

There was an interruption. The door flew open and George Challenger rushed into the room.

"What's all this?" he cried. "I've just arrived. To find a policeman at the gate and a rumor that somebody's dead. What is it all about? For God's sake, tell me. Is it—is it—Nick?"

The anguish in his tone was dreadful to hear. I suddenly realized that Poirot and the doctor between them completely blotted out Nick from his sight.

Before anyone had time to answer, he repeated his question.

"Tell me—it can't be true—Nick isn't dead?"

"No, *mon ami*," said Poirot gently. "She is alive."

And he drew back so that Challenger could see the little figure on the sofa.

For a moment or two Challenger stared at her incredulously. Then, staggering a little, like a drunken man, he muttered: "Nick—Nick."

And suddenly dropping on his knees beside the sofa and hiding his head in his hands, he cried in a muffled voice, "Nick—my darling—I thought that you were dead."

Nick tried to sit up.

"It's all right, George. Don't be an idiot. I'm quite safe."

He raised his head and looked around wildly.

"But somebody's dead? The policeman said so."

"Yes," said Nick. "Maggie. Poor old Maggie. Oh!—"

A spasm twisted her face. The doctor and Poirot came forward. Graham helped her to her feet. He and Poirot, one on each side, helped her from the room.

"The sooner you get to your bed the better," remarked the doctor. "I'll take you along at once in my car. I've asked Mrs. Rice to pack a few things ready for you to take."

They disappeared through the door. Challenger caught my arm.

"I don't understand. Where are they taking her?"

I explained.

"Oh! I see. Now then, Hastings, for God's sake give me the hang of this thing. What a ghastly tragedy! That poor girl."

"Come and have a drink," I said. "You're all to pieces."

"I don't mind if I do."

We adjourned to the dining room.

"You see," he explained as he put away a stiff whisky and soda, "I thought it was Nick."

There was very little doubt as to the feelings of Commander George Challenger. A more transparent lover never lived.

9

A. to J.

I DOUBT IF I shall ever forget the night that followed. Poirot was a prey to such an agony of self-reproach that I was really alarmed. Ceaselessly he strode up and down the room heaping anathemas on his own head and deaf to my well-meant remonstrances.

"What is it to have too good an opinion of oneself? I am punished—yes, I am punished. I, Hercule Poirot. I was too sure of myself."

"No, no," I interpolated.

"But who would imagine—who could imagine—such unparalleled audacity? I had taken, as I thought, all possible precautions. I had warned the murderer—"

"Warned the murderer?"

"*Mais oui*. I had drawn attention to myself. I had let him see that I suspected—someone. I had made it, or so I thought, too dangerous for him to dare to repeat his attempts at murder. I had drawn a cordon round Mademoiselle. And he slips through it! Boldly—under our very eyes almost, he slips through it! In spite of us all—of everyone being on the alert, he achieves his object."

"Only he doesn't," I reminded him.

"That is the chance only! From my point of view, it is the same. A human life has been taken, Hastings—whose life is nonessential?"

"Of course," I said, "I didn't mean that."

"But on the other hand, what you say is true. And that makes it worse—ten times worse. For the murderer is still as far as ever from achieving his object. Do you understand, my friend? The position is changed—for the worse. It may mean that not one life—but two—will be sacrificed."

"Not while you're about," I said stoutly.

He stopped and wrung my hand.

"*Merci, mon ami! Merci!* You still have confidence in the old one—you still have the faith. You put new courage into me. Hercule Poirot will not fail again. No second life shall be taken. I will rectify my error—for, see you, there must have been an error! Somewhere there has been a lack of order and method in my usually so well-arranged ideas. I will start again. Yes, I will start at the beginning. And this time—I will not fail."

"You really think, then," I said, "that Nick Buckley's life is still in danger?"

"My friend, for what other reason did I send her to this nursing home?"

"Then it wasn't the shock—"

"The shock! Pah! One can recover from shock as well in one's own home as in a nursing home—better for that matter. It is not amusing there, the floors of green linoleum, the conversation of the nurses—the meals on trays, the ceaseless washing. No, no, it is for safety and safety only. I take the doctor into my confidence. He agrees. He will make all arrangements. No one, *mon ami*, not even her dearest friend, will be admitted to see Miss Buckley. You and I are the only ones permitted. *Pour les autres—eh bien*! 'Doctor's orders,' they will be told. A phrase very convenient and one not to be gainsaid."

"Yes," I said. "Only—"

"Only what, Hastings?"

"That can't go on forever."

"A very true observation. But it gives us a little breathing space. And you realize, do you not, that the character of our operations has changed."

"In what way?"

"Our original task was to ensure the safety of Mademoiselle. Our task now is a much simpler one—a task with which we are well acquainted. It is neither more nor less than the hunting down of a murderer."

"You call that simpler?"

"Certainly it is simpler. The murderer has, as I said the other day, signed his name to the crime. He has come out into the open."

"You don't think—" I hesitated, then went on. "You don't think that the police are right? That this is the work of a madman, some wandering lunatic with homicidal mania?"

"I am more than ever convinced that such is not the case."

"You really think that—"

I stopped. Poirot took up my sentence, speaking very gravely.

"That the murderer is someone in Mademoiselle's own circle? Yes, *mon ami*, I do."

"But surely last night must almost rule out that possibility. We were all together and—"

He interrupted.

"Could you swear, Hastings, that any particular person had never left our little company there on the edge of the cliff? Is there any one person there whom you could swear you had seen all the time?"

"No," I said slowly, struck by his words. "I don't think I could. It was dark. We all moved about, more or less. On different occasions I noticed Mrs. Rice, Lazarus, you, Croft, Vyse—but all the time—no."

Poirot nodded his head.

"Exactly. It would be a matter of a very few minutes. The two girls go to the house. The murderer slips away unnoticed, hides behind that sycamore tree in the middle of the lawn. Nick Buckley, or so he thinks, comes out of the window, passes within a foot of him, he fires three shots in rapid succession—"

"Three?" I interjected.

"Yes. He was taking no chances this time. We found three bullets in the body."

"That was risky, wasn't it?"

"Less risky in all probability than one shot would have been. A Mauser pistol does not make a great deal of noise. It would resemble more or less the popping of the fireworks and blend in very well with the noise of them."

"Did you find the pistol?" I asked.

"No. And there, Hastings, lies to my mind the undisputable proof that no stranger is responsible for this. We agree, do we not, that Miss Buckley's own pistol was taken in the first place for one reason only—to give her death the appearance of suicide."

"Yes."

"That is the only possible reason, is it not? But now, you observe, there is no pretense of suicide. The murderer knows that we should not any longer be deceived by it. He knows, in fact, what we know!"

I reflected, admitting to myself the logic of Poirot's deduction.

"What did he do with the pistol do you think?"

Poirot shrugged his shoulders.

"For that, it is difficult to say. But the sea was exceedingly handy. A good toss of the arm, and the pistol sinks, never to be recovered. We cannot, of course, be absolutely sure—but that is what *I* should have done."

His matter-of-fact tone made me shiver a little.

"Do you think—do you think he realized that he'd killed the wrong person?"

"I am quite sure he did not," said Poirot grimly. "Yes, that must have been an unpleasant little surprise for him when he learned the truth. To keep his face and betray nothing—it cannot have been easy."

At that moment I bethought me of the strange attitude of the maid, Ellen. I gave Poirot an account of her peculiar demeanor. He seemed much interested.

"She betrayed surprise, did she, that it was Maggie who was dead?"

"Great surprise."

"That is curious. And yet, the fact of a tragedy was clearly not a surprise to her. Yes, there is something there that must be looked into. Who is she, this Ellen? So quiet, so respectable in the English manner? Could it be she who—?" He broke off.

"If you're going to include the accidents," I said, "surely it would take a man to have rolled that heavy boulder down the cliff."

"Not necessarily. It is very largely a question of leverage. Oh, yes! It could be done."

He continued his slow pacing up and down the room.

"Anyone who was at End House last night comes under suspicion. But those guests—no, I do not think it was one of them. For the most part, I should say, they were mere acquaintances. There was no intimacy between them and the young mistress of the house."

"Charles Vyse was there," I remarked.

"Yes, we must not forget him. He is, logically, our strongest suspect." He made a gesture of despair and threw himself into a chair opposite mine. "*Voilà*—it is always that we come back to! Motive! We must find the motive if we are to understand this crime. And it is there, Hastings, that I am continually baffled. Who can possibly have a motive for doing away with Mademoiselle Nick? I have let myself go to the most absurd suppositions. I, Hercule Poirot, have descended to the most ignominious flights of fancy. I have adopted the mentality of the cheap thriller. The grandfather—the 'Old Nick'—he who is supposed to have gambled his money away. Did he really do so, I have asked myself? Did he, on the contrary, hide it away? Is it hidden somewhere in End House? Buried somewhere in the grounds? With that end in view (I am ashamed to say it) I inquired of Mademoiselle Nick whether there had ever been any offers to buy the house."

"Do you know, Poirot," I said, "I call that rather a bright idea. There may be something in it."

Poirot groaned.

"You would say that! It would appeal, I knew, to your romantic but slightly mediocre mind. Buried treasure—yes, you would enjoy the idea."

"Well—I don't see why not—"

"Because, my friend, the more prosaic explanation is nearly always the more probable. Then Mademoiselle's father—I have played with even more degrading ideas concerning him. He was a traveler. Supposing, I say to myself, that he has stolen a jewel—the eye of a god. Jealous priests are on his track. Yes, I, Hercule Poirot, have descended to depths such as these.

"I have had other ideas concerning this father," he went on. "Ideas at once more dignified and more probable. Did he, in the course of his wanderings, contract a second marriage? Is there a nearer heir than M. Charles Vyse? But again, that leads nowhere, for we are up against the same difficulty that there is really nothing of value to inherit.

"I have neglected no possibility. Even that chance reference of Mademoiselle Nick's to the offer made her by M. Lazarus. You remember? The offer to purchase her grandfather's portrait. I telegraphed on Saturday for an expert to come down and examine that picture. He was the man about whom I wrote to Mademoiselle this morning. Supposing, for instance, it were worth several thousand pounds?"

"You surely don't think a rich man like young Lazarus—?"

"Is he rich? Appearances are not everything. Even an old established firm with palatial showrooms and every appearance of prosperity may rest on a rotten basis. And what does one do then? Does one run about crying out that times are hard? No, one buys a new and luxurious car. One spends a little more money than usual. One lives a little more ostentatiously. For credit, see you, is everything! But sometimes a monumental business has crashed—for no more than a few thousand pounds—of ready money.

"Oh! I know," he continued forestalling my protests. "It is farfetched—but it is not so bad as revengeful priests or buried treasure. It bears, at any rate, some relationship to things as they happen. And we can neglect nothing—nothing that might bring us nearer the truth."

With careful fingers he straightened the objects on the table in front of him. When he spoke, his voice was grave and, for the first time, calm.

"Motive!" he said. "Let us come back to that, and regard this problem calmly and methodically. To begin with, how many kinds of motive are there for murder? What are the motives which lead one human being to take another human being's life?

"We exclude for the moment homicidal mania. Because I am absolutely convinced that the solution of our problem does not lie there. We also exclude killing done on the spur of the moment under the impulse of an ungovernable temper. This is a cold-blooded deliberate murder. What are the motives that actuate such a murder as that?

"There is, first, Gain. Who stood to gain by Mademoiselle Buckley's death? Directly or indirectly. Well, we can put down Charles Vyse. He inherits a property that, from the financial point of view, is probably not worth inheriting. He might, perhaps, pay off the mortgage, build small villas on the land and eventually make a small profit. It is possible. The place might be worth something to him if he had any deeply cherished love of it—if it were, for instance, a family place. That is, undoubtedly an instinct very deeply implanted in some human beings, and it has, in cases I have known, actually led to crime. But I cannot see any such motive in M. Vyse's case.

"The only other person who would benefit at all by Mademoiselle Buckley's death is her friend, Madame Rice. But the amount would clearly be a very small one. Nobody else, as far as I can see, gains by Mademoiselle Buckley's death.

"What is another motive? Hate—or love that has turned to hate. The *crime passionnel*. Well, there again we have the word of the observant Madame Croft that both Charles Vyse and Commander Challenger are in love with the young lady."

"I think we can say that we have observed the latter phenomenon for ourselves," I remarked with a smile.

"Yes—he tends to wear his heart on his sleeve, the honest sailor. For the other, we rely on the word of Madame Croft. Now, if Charles Vyse felt that he was supplanted, would he be so powerfully affected that he would kill his cousin rather than let her become the wife of another man?"

"It sounds very melodramatic," I said doubtfully.

"It sounds, you would say, un-English. I agree. But even the English have emotions. And a type such as Charles Vyse is the most likely to have them. He is a repressed young man. One who does not show his feelings easily. Such often have the most violent feelings. I would never suspect the Commander Challenger of murder for emotional reasons. No, no, he is not the type. But with Charles Vyse—yes, it is possible. But it does not entirely satisfy me.

"Another motive for crime—Jealousy. I separate it from the last, because Jealousy may not, necessarily, be a sexual emotion. There is envy—envy of possession—of supremacy. Such a jealousy as drove the Iago of your great Shakespeare to one of the cleverest crimes (speaking from the professional point of view) that has ever been committed."

"Why was it so clever?" I asked, momentarily diverted.

"*Parbleu*—because he got others to execute it. Imagine a criminal nowadays on whom one was unable to put the handcuffs because he had never done anything himself. But this is not the subject we were discussing. Can jealousy, of any kind, be responsible for this crime? Who has reason to envy Mademoiselle? Another woman? There is only Madame Rice, and as far as we can see, there was no rivalry between the two women. But again, that is only 'as far as we can see.' There may be something there.

"Lastly—Fear. Does Mademoiselle Nick, by any chance, hold

somebody's secret in her power? Does she know something which, if it were known, might ruin another life? If so, I think we can say very definitely, that she herself is unaware of it. But that might be, you know. That might be. And if so, it makes it very difficult. Because, whilst she holds the clue in her hands, she holds it unconsciously and will be quite unable to tell us what it is."

"You really think that is possible?"

"It is a hypothesis. I am driven to it by the difficulty of finding a reasonable theory elsewhere. When you have eliminated other possibilities you turn to the one that is left and say—since the other is not—this must be so. . . ."

He was silent a long time.

At last, rousing himself from his absorption, he drew a sheet of paper towards him and began to write.

"What are you writing?" I asked curiously.

"*Mon ami*, I am composing a list. It is a list of people surrounding Mademoiselle Buckley. Within that list, if my theory is correct, there must be the name of the murderer."

He continued to write for perhaps twenty minutes—then shoved the sheets of paper across to me.

"*Voilà, mon ami*. See what you make of it."

The following is a reproduction of the paper.

A. Ellen.
B. Her gardener husband.
C. Their child.
D. Mr. Croft.
E. Mrs. Croft.
F. Mrs. Rice.
G. Mr. Lazarus.
H. Commander Challenger.
I. Mr. Charles Vyse.
J. ?

REMARKS:

A.   *Ellen*. Suspicious circumstances. Her attitude and words on hearing of the crime. Best opportunity of anyone to have staged accidents and to have known of pistol *but* unlikely to have tampered with car, and general mentality of crime seems above her level.
Motive. None—unless Hate arising out of some incident unknown.

Note. Further inquiries as to her antecedents and general relations with N. B.

B. *Her husband*. Same as above. More likely to have tampered with car.
    Note. Should be interviewed.

C. *Child*. Can be ruled out.
    Note. Should be interviewed. Might give valuable information.

D. *Mr. Croft*. Only suspicious circumstance: the fact that we met him mounting the stair to bedroom floor. Had ready explanation which may be true. But it may not! Nothing known of antecedents.
    Motive. None.

E. *Mrs. Croft*. Suspicious circumstances: none.
    Motive. None.

F. *Mrs. Rice*. Suspicious circumstances. Full opportunity. Asked N. B. to fetch wrap. Has deliberately tried to create impression that N. B. is a liar and her account of "accidents" not to be relied on. Was not at Tavistock when accidents occurred. Where was she?
    Motive. *Gain*? Very slight. *Jealousy*? Possible, but nothing known. *Fear*? Also possible, but nothing known.
    Note. Converse with N. B. on subject. See if any light is thrown upon matter. Possibly something to do with F. R.'s marriage.

G. *Mr. Lazarus*. Suspicious circumstances. General opportunity. Offer to buy picture. Said brakes of car were quite all right (according to F. R.). May have been in neighborhood prior to Friday.
    Motive. None—unless profit on picture. *Fear*?—unlikely.
    Note. Find out where J. L. was before arriving at St. Loo. Find out financial position of Aaron Lazarus and Son.

H. *Commander Challenger*. Suspicious circumstances: none. Was in neighborhood all last week, so opportunity for "accidents" good. Arrived half an hour after murder.
    Motive. None.

I. *Mr. Vyse*. Suspicious circumstances. Was absent from office at time when shot was fired in garden of hotel. Opportunity good. Statement about selling of End House open to doubt. Of a repressed temperament. Would probably know about pistol.
    Motive. *Gain*? Slight. *Love or hate*? Possible with one of his temperament. *Fear*? Unlikely.
    Note. Find out who held mortgage. Find out position of Vyse's firm.

J. *?* There *could* be a J.: e.g., an outsider. *But* with a link in the form of one of the foregoing. If so, probably connected with A., D. and E. or F. The existence of J. would explain (1) Ellen's lack of surprise at crime and her pleasurable satisfaction. (But that might be due to natural pleasurable excitement of her class over deaths.) (2) The reason for Croft and his wife coming to live in lodge. (3) Might supply motive for F. R.'s *fear* of secret being revealed or for *jealousy*.

Poirot watched me as I read.

"It is very English, is it not?" he remarked with pride. "I am more English when I write than when I speak."

"It's an excellent piece of work," I said warmly. "It sets all the possibilities out most clearly."

"Yes," he said thoughtfully, as he took it back from me. "And one name leaps to the eye, my friend. Charles Vyse. He has the best opportunities. We have given him the choice of two motives. *Ma foi*—if that was a list of racehorses, he would start favorite, *n'est-ce pas?*"

"He is certainly the most likely suspect."

"You have a tendency, Hastings, to prefer the least likely. That, no doubt, is from reading too many detective stories. In real life, nine times out of ten, it is the most likely and the most obvious person who commits the crime."

"But you don't really think that is so this time?"

"There is only one thing that is against it. The boldness of the crime! That has stood out from the first. Because of that, as I say, the motive cannot be obvious."

"Yes, that is what you said at first."

"And that is what I say again."

With a sudden brusque gesture he crumpled the sheet of paper and threw it on the floor.

"No," he said, as I uttered an exclamation of protest. "That list has been in vain. Still, it has cleared my mind. Order and method! That is the first stage. To arrange the facts with neatness and precision. The next stage—"

"Yes?"

"The next stage is that of the psychology. The correct employment of the little grey cells! I advise you, Hastings, to go to bed."

"No," I said. "Not unless you do. I'm not going to leave you."

"Most faithful of dogs! But see you, Hastings, you cannot assist me to think. That is all I am going to do—think."

I still shook my head.

"You might want to discuss some point with me."

"Well—well—you are a loyal friend. Take at least, I beg of you, the easy chair."

That proposal I did accept. Presently the room began to swim and dip. The last thing I remember was seeing Poirot carefully retrieving the crumpled sheet of paper from the floor and putting it away tidily in the waste-paper basket.

Then I must have fallen asleep.

10

Nick's Secret

IT WAS DAYLIGHT when I awoke.

Poirot was still standing where he had been the night before. His attitude was the same, but in his face was a difference. His eyes were shining with that queer catlike green light that I knew so well.

I struggled to an upright position, feeling very stiff and uncomfortable. Sleeping in a chair is a proceeding not to be recommended at my time of life. Yet one thing at least resulted from it—I awoke not in that pleasant state of lazy somnolence but with a mind and brain as active as when I fell asleep.

"Poirot," I cried. "You have thought of something."

He nodded. He leaned forward tapping the table in front of him.

"Tell me, Hastings, the answer to these three questions. Why has Mademoiselle Nick been sleeping badly lately? Why did she buy a black evening dress—she never wears black? Why did she say last night, 'I have nothing to live for—now'?"

I stared. The questions seemed beside the point.

"Answer those questions, Hastings, answer them!"

"Well—as to the first—she said she had been worried lately."

"Precisely. What has she been worried about?"

"And the black dress—well, everybody wants a change sometimes."

"For a married man, you have very little appreciation of feminine psychology. If a woman thinks she does not look well in a color, she refuses to wear it."

"And the last—well, it was a natural thing to say after that awful shock."

"No, *mon ami*, it was not a natural thing to say. To be horror-struck by her cousin's death, to reproach herself for it—yes, all that is natural enough. But the other, no. She spoke of life with weariness—as of a thing no longer dear to her. Never before had she displayed that attitude. She had been defiant—yes, she had snapped the fingers, yes—and then, when that broke down, she was afraid. Afraid, mark you, because life was sweet and she did not wish to die. But weary of life—no! That never! Even before dinner that was not so. We have there, Hastings, a *psychological change*. And that is interesting. What was it caused her point of view to change?"

"The shock of her cousin's death?"

"I wonder. It was the shock that loosed her tongue. But suppose the change was before that. Is there anything else could account for it?"

"I don't know of anything."

"Think, Hastings. Use your little grey cells."

"Really—"

"What was the last moment we had the opportunity of observing her?"

"Well, actually, I suppose, at dinner."

"Exactly. After that, we only saw her receiving guests, making them welcome—purely a formal attitude. What happened at the end of dinner, Hastings?"

"She went to telephone," I said slowly.

"*À la bonheur*. You have got there at last. She went to telephone. And she was absent a long time. Twenty minutes at least. That is a long time for a telephone call. Who spoke to her over the telephone? What did they say? Did she really telephone? We have got to find out, Hastings, what happened in that twenty minutes. For there, or so I fully believe, we shall find the clue we seek."

"You really think so?"

"*Mais oui, mais oui*! All along, Hastings, I have told you that Mademoiselle has been keeping something back. She doesn't think it has any connection with the murder—but I, Hercule Poirot, know better! It must have a connection. For all along, I have been conscious that there is a factor lacking. If there were not a factor lacking—why then, the whole thing would be plain to me! And as it is not plain to me—*eh bien*—then the missing factor is the keystone of the mystery! I know I am right, Hastings.

"I must know the answer to those three questions. And then—and then—I shall begin to see. . . ."

"Well," I said, stretching my stiffened limbs. "I think a bath and a shave are indicated."

By the time I had had a bath and changed into day clothing I felt better. The stiffness and weariness of a night passed in uncomfortable conditions passed off. I arrived at the breakfast table feeling that one drink of hot coffee would restore me to my normal self.

I glanced at the paper, but there was little news in it beyond the fact that Michael Seton's death was now definitely confirmed. The intrepid airman had perished. I wondered whether, tomorrow, new headlines would have sprung into being. "GIRL MURDERED DURING FIREWORK PARTY. MYSTERIOUS TRAGEDY." Something like that.

I had just finished breakfast when Frederica Rice came up to my table. She was wearing a plain little frock of black marocain with a little soft pleated white collar. Her fairness was more evident than ever.

"I wanted to see M. Poirot, Captain Hastings. Is he up yet, do you know?"

"I will take you up with me now," I said. "We shall find him in the sitting room."

"Thank you."

"I hope," I said, as we left the dining room together, "that you didn't sleep too badly?"

"It was a shock," she said in a meditative voice. "But of course I didn't know the poor girl. It's not as though it had been Nick."

"I suppose you'd never met this girl before?"

"Once—at Scarborough. She came over to lunch with Nick."

"It will be a terrible blow to her father and mother," I said.

"Dreadful."

But she said it very impersonally. She was, I fancied, an egotist. Nothing was very real to her that did not concern herself.

Poirot had finished his breakfast and was sitting reading the morning paper. He rose and greeted Frederica with all his customary Gallic politeness.

"Madame," he said. "*Enchanté!*"

He drew forward a chair.

She thanked him with a very faint smile and sat down. Her two hands rested on the arms of the chair. She sat there very upright looking straight in front of her. She did not rush into speech. There was something a little frightening about her stillness and aloofness.

"M. Poirot," she said at last. "I suppose there is no doubt that this—sad business last night was all part and parcel of the same thing? I mean—that the intended victim was really Nick?"

"I should say, Madame, that there was no doubt at all."

Frederica frowned a little.

"Nick bears a charmed life," she said.

There was some curious undercurrent in her voice that I could not understand.

"Luck, they say, goes in cycles," remarked Poirot.

"Perhaps. It is certainly useless to fight against it."

Now there was only weariness in her tone. After a moment or two, she went on.

"I must beg your pardon, M. Poirot. Nick's pardon, too. Up till last night I did not believe. I never dreamed that the danger was—serious."

"Is that so, Madame?"

"I see now that everything will have to be gone into—carefully. And I imagine that Nick's immediate circle of friends will not be immune from suspicion. Ridiculous, of course, but there it is. Am I right, M. Poirot?"

"You are very intelligent, Madame."

"You asked me some questions about Tavistock the other day, M. Poirot. As you will find out sooner or later, I might as well tell you the truth now. I was not at Tavistock."

"No, Madame?"

"I motored down to this part of the world with Mr. Lazarus early last week. We did not wish to arouse more comment than necessary. We stayed at a little place called Shellacombe."

"That is, I think, about seven miles from here, Madame?"

"About that—yes."

Still that quiet faraway weariness.

"May I be impertinent, Madame?"

"Is there such a thing—in these days?"

"Perhaps you are right, Madame. How long have you and M. Lazarus been friends?"

"I met him six months ago."

"And you—care for him, Madame?"

Frederica shrugged her shoulders.

"He is—rich."

"Oh! *là, là*," cried Poirot. "That is an ugly thing to say."

She seemed faintly amused.

"Isn't it better to say it myself—than to have you say it for me?"

"Well—there is always that, of course. May I repeat, Madame, that you are very intelligent."

"You will give me a diploma soon," said Frederica and rose.

"There is nothing more you wish to tell me, Madame?"

"I do not think so—no. I am going to take some flowers round to Nick and see how she is."

"Ah, that is very *aimable* of you. Thank you, Madame, for your frankness."

She glanced at him sharply, seemed about to speak, then thought better of it and went out of the room, smiling faintly at me as I held the door open for her.

"She is intelligent," said Poirot. "Yes, but so is Hercule Poirot!"

"What do you mean?"

"That it is all very well and very pretty to force the richness of M. Lazarus down my throat—"

"I must say that rather disgusted me."

"*Mon cher*, always you have the right reaction in the wrong place. It is not, for the moment, a question of good taste or otherwise. If Madame Rice has a devoted friend who is rich and can give her all she needs—why then obviously Madame Rice would not need to murder her dearest friend for a mere pittance."

"Oh!" I said.

"*Précisément!* 'Oh!' "

"Why didn't you stop her going to the nursing home?"

"Why should I show my hand? Is it Hercule Poirot who prevents Mademoiselle Nick from seeing her friends? *Quelle idée!* It is the doctors and the nurses. Those tiresome nurses! So full of rules and regulations and 'doctor's orders.' "

"You're not afraid that they may let her in after all? Nick might insist."

"Nobody will be let in, my dear Hastings, but you and me. And for that matter, the sooner we make our way there, the better."

The sitting room door flew open and George Challenger barged in. His tanned face was alive with indignation.

"Look here, M. Poirot," he said. "What's the meaning of this? I rang up that damned nursing home where Nick is. Asked how she was and what time I could come round and see her. And they say the doctor won't allow any visitors. I want to know the meaning of that? To put it plainly, is this your work? Or is Nick really ill from shock?"

"I assure you, Monsieur, that I do not lay down rules for nursing homes. I would not dare. Why not ring up the good doctor—what was his name now?—Ah! yes, Graham."

"I have. He says she's going on as well as could be expected—usual stuff. But I know all the tricks—my uncle's a doctor. Harley Street. Nerve specialist. Psychoanalysis—all the rest of it. Putting relations and friends off with soothing words. I've heard about it all, I don't believe Nick isn't up to seeing anyone. I believe you're at the bottom of this, M. Poirot."

Poirot smiled at him in a very kindly fashion. Indeed, I have always observed that Poirot has a kindly feeling for a lover.

"Now listen to me, *mon ami*," he said. "If one guest is admitted, others cannot be kept out. You comprehend? It must be all or none. We want Mademoiselle's safety, you and I, do we not? Exactly. Then, you understand—it must be none."

"I get you," said Challenger slowly. "But then—"

"Chut! We will say no more. We will forget even what we have said."

"I can hold my tongue," said the sailor quietly.

He turned away to the door, pausing as he went out to say: "No embargo on flowers, is there? So long as they are not white ones."

Poirot smiled.

"And now," he said as the door shut behind the impetuous Challenger. "Whilst M. Challenger and Madame and perhaps M. Lazarus all encounter each other in the flower shop, you and I will drive quietly to our destination."

"And ask for the answer to the three questions?" I said.

"Yes. We will ask. Though, as a matter of fact, I know the answer."

"What?" I exclaimed.

"Yes."

"But when did you find out?"

"Whilst I was eating my breakfast, Hastings. It stared me in the face."

"Tell me."

"No, I will leave you to hear it from Mademoiselle."

Then, as if to distract my mind, he pushed an open letter across to me.

It was a report by the expert Poirot had sent to examine the picture of old Nicholas Buckley. It stated definitely that the picture was worth at most twenty pounds.

"So that is one matter cleared up," said Poirot.

"No mouse in that mousehole," I said remembering a metaphor of Poirot's on one past occasion.

"Ah! you remember that? No, as you say, no mouse in that mousehole. Twenty pounds and M. Lazarus offered fifty. What an error of judgment for a seemingly astute young man. But there, there, we must start on our errand."

The nursing home was set high on a hill overlooking the bay. A white-coated orderly received us. We were put into a little room downstairs and presently a brisk-looking nurse came to us.

One glance at Poirot seemed to be enough. She had clearly received her instructions from Dr. Graham together with a minute description of the little detective. She even concealed a smile.

"Miss Buckley has passed a very fair night," she said. "Come up, will you?"

In a pleasant room with the sun streaming into it, we found Nick. In the narrow iron bed, she looked like a tired child. Her face was white and her eyes were suspiciously red, and she seemed listless and weary.

"It's good of you to come," she said in a flat voice.

Poirot took her hand in both of his.

"Courage, Mademoiselle. There is always something to live for."

The words startled her. She looked up in his face.

"Oh!" she said. "Oh!"

"Will you not tell me now, Mademoiselle, what it was that has been worrying you lately? Or shall I guess? And may I offer you, Mademoiselle, my very deepest sympathy."

Her face flushed.

"So you know. Oh! well, it doesn't matter who knows now. Now that it's all over. Now that I shall never see him again."

Her voice broke.

"Courage, Mademoiselle."

"I haven't got any courage left. I've used up every bit in these last weeks. Hoping and hoping and—just lately—hoping against hope."

I stared. I could not understand one word.

"Regard the poor Hastings," said Poirot. "He does not know what we are talking about."

Her unhappy eyes met mine.

"Michael Seton, the airman," she said. "I was engaged to him—and he's dead."

11

The Motive

I WAS DUMBFOUNDED.

I turned on Poirot.

"Is that what you meant?"

"Yes, *mon ami*. This morning—I knew."

"How did you know? How did you guess? You said it stared you in the face at breakfast."

"So it did, my friend. From the front page of the newspaper. I remembered the conversation at dinner last night—and I saw everything."

He turned to Nick again.

"You heard the news last night?"

"Yes. On the wireless. I made an excuse about the telephone. I wanted to hear the news alone—in case. . . ." She swallowed hard. "And I heard it. . . ."

"I know. I know." He took her hand in both of his.

"It was—pretty ghastly. And all the people arriving. I don't know how I got through it. It all felt like a dream. I could see myself from outside—behaving just as usual. It was queer somehow."

"Yes, yes, I understand."

"And then, when I went to fetch Freddie's wrap—I broke down for a minute. I pulled myself together quite quickly. But Maggie kept calling up about her coat. And then at last she took my shawl and went, and I put on some powder and some rouge and followed her out. And there she was—dead. . . ."

"Yes, yes, it must have been a terrible shock."

"You don't understand. I was angry! I wished it had been me! I wanted to be dead—and there I was—alive and perhaps to live for years! And Michael dead—drowned far away in the Pacific."

"*Pauvre enfant.*"

"I don't want to be alive. I don't want to live, I tell you!" she cried rebelliously.

"I know—I know. To all of us, Mademoiselle, there comes a time when death is preferable to life. But it passes—sorrow passes and grief. You cannot believe that now, I know. It is useless for an old man like me to talk. Idle words—that's what you think—idle words."

"You think I'll forget—and marry someone else. Never!"

She looked rather lovely as she sat up in bed, her two hands clenched and her cheeks burning.

Poirot said gently, "No, no. I am not thinking anything of the kind. You are very lucky, Mademoiselle. You have been loved by a brave man—a hero. How did you come to meet him?"

"It was at Le Touquet—last September. Nearly a year ago."

"And you became engaged—when?"

"Just after Christmas. But it had to be a secret."

"Why was that?"

"Michael's uncle—old Sir Matthew Seton. He loved birds and hated women."

"*Ah, ce n'est pas raisonnable!*"

"Well—I don't mean quite that. He was a complete crank. Thought women ruined a man's life. And Michael was absolutely dependent on him. He was frightfully proud of Michael and it was he who financed the building of the *Albatross* and the expenses of the round-the-world flight. It was the dearest dream of his life as well as of Michael's. If Michael had pulled it off—well, then he could have asked his uncle anything. And even if old Sir Matthew had still cut up rough, well, it wouldn't have really mattered. Michael would have been made—a kind of world hero. His uncle would have come round in the end."

"Yes, yes, I see."

"But Michael said it would be fatal if anything leaked out. We must keep it a dead secret. And I did. I never told anyone—not even Freddie."

Poirot groaned.

"If only you had told me, Mademoiselle."

Nick stared at him.

"But what difference would it have made? It couldn't have anything to do with these mysterious attacks on me? No, I'd promised Michael—and I kept my word. But it was awful—the anxiety, wondering and getting in a state the whole time. And everyone saying one was so nervy. And being unable to explain."

"Yes, I comprehend all that."

"He was missing once before, you know. Crossing the desert on the way to India. That was pretty awful, and then after all, it was all right. His machine was damaged, but it was put right, and he went on. And I kept saying to myself that it would be the same this time. Everyone said he must be dead—and I kept telling myself that he must be all right really. And then—last night . . ."

Her voice trailed away.

"You had hoped up till then?"

"I don't know. I think it was more that I refused to believe. It was awful never being able to talk to anyone."

"Yes, I can imagine that. Were you never tempted to tell Madame Rice, for instance."

"Sometimes I wanted to frightfully."

"You do not think she—guessed?"

"I don't think so." Nick considered the idea carefully. "She never said anything. Of course she used to hint things sometimes. About our being great friends and all that."

"You never considered telling her when M. Seton's uncle died? You knew that he died about a week ago?"

"I know. He had an operation or something. I suppose I might have told anybody then. But it wouldn't have been a nice way of doing it, would it? I mean it would have seemed rather boastful—to do it just then—when all the papers were full of Michael. And reporters would have come and interviewed me. It would all have been rather cheap. And Michael would have hated it."

"I agree with you, Mademoiselle. You could not have announced it publicly. I only meant that you could have spoken of it privately to a friend."

"I did sort of hint to one person," said Nick. "I—thought it was only fair. But I don't know how much he—the person took in."

Poirot nodded.

"Are you on good terms with your cousin, M. Vyse?" he asked with a rather abrupt change of subject.

"Charles? What put him into your head?"

"I was just wondering—that was all."

"Charles means well," said Nick. "He's a frightful stick, of course. Never moves out of his place. He disapproves of me, I think."

"Oh! Mademoiselle, Mademoiselle. And I hear that he has laid all his devotion at your feet!"

"Disapproving of a person doesn't keep you from having a pash for them. Charles thinks my mode of life is reprehensible and he disapproves of my cocktails, my complexion, my friends and my conversation. But he still feels my fatal fascination. He always hopes to reform me, I think."

She paused and then said, with a ghost of a twinkle, "Who have you been pumping to get the local information?"

"You must not give me away, Mademoiselle. I had a little conversation with the Australian lady, Madame Croft."

"She's rather an old dear—when one has time for her. Terribly sentimental. Love and home and children—you know the sort of thing."

"I am old-fashioned and sentimental myself, Mademoiselle."

"Are you? I should have said that Captain Hastings was the sentimental one of you two."

I blushed indignantly.

"He is furious," said Poirot eyeing my discomfiture with a good deal of pleasure. "But you are right, Mademoiselle. Yes, you are right."

"Not at all," I said angrily.

"Hastings has a singularly beautiful nature. It has been the greatest hindrance to me at times."

"Don't be absurd, Poirot."

"He is, to begin with, reluctant to see evil anywhere, and when he does see it his righteous indignation is so great that he is incapable of dissembling. Altogether a rare and beautiful nature. No, *mon ami*, I will not permit you to contradict me. It is as I say."

"You've both been very kind to me," said Nick gently.

"*Là, là,* Mademoiselle. That is nothing. We have much more to do. To begin with, you will remain here. You will obey orders. You will do what I tell you. At this juncture I must not be hampered."

Nick sighed wearily.

"I'll do anything you like. I don't care what I do."

"You will see no friends for the present."

"I don't care. I don't want to see anyone."

"For you the passive part—for us the active one. Now, Mademoiselle, I am going to leave you. I will not intrude longer upon your sorrow."

He moved towards the door, pausing with his hand on the handle to say over his shoulder:

"By the way, you once mentioned a will you made. Where is it, this will?"

"Oh! it's knocking round somewhere."

"At End House?"

"Yes."

"In a safe? Locked up in your desk?"

"Well, I really don't know. It's somewhere about." She frowned. "I'm frightfully untidy, you know. Papers and things like that would be mostly in the writing table in the library. That's where most of the bills are. The will is probably with them. Or it might be in my bedroom."

"You permit me to make the search—yes?"

"If you want to—yes. Look at anything you like."

"*Merci*, Mademoiselle. I will avail myself of your permission."

12

Ellen

POIROT SAID NO WORD till we had emerged from the nursing home into the outer air. Then he caught me by the arm.

"You see, Hastings? You see? Ah! *Sacré tonnerre!* I was right! I was right! Always I knew there was something lacking—some piece of the puzzle that was not there. And without that missing piece the whole thing was meaningless."

His almost despairing triumph was double Dutch to me. I could not see that anything very epoch-making had occurred.

"It was there all the time. And I could not see it. But how should I? To know there is *something*—that, yes—but to know what that something is. *Ah!—c'est bien plus difficile*."

"Do you mean that this has some direct bearing on the crime?"

"*Ma foi*, do you not see?"

"As a matter of fact, I don't."

"Is it possible? Why, it gives us what we have been looking for—the motive—the hidden obscure motive!"

"I may be very dense, but I can't see it. Do you mean jealousy of some kind?"

"Jealousy? No, no, my friend. The usual motive—the inevitable motive. Money, my friend, money!"

I stared. He went on, speaking more calmly.

"Listen, *mon ami*. Just over a week ago Sir Matthew Seton dies. And Sir Matthew Seton was a millionaire—one of the richest men in England."

"Yes, but—"

"*Attendez*. One step at a time. He has a nephew whom he idolizes and to whom, we may safely assume, he has left his vast fortune."

"But—"

"*Mais oui*—legacies, yes, an endowment to do with his hobby, yes, but the bulk of the money would go to Michael Seton. Last Tuesday, Michael Seton is reported missing—*and on Wednesday the attacks on Mademoiselle's life begin*. Supposing, Hastings, that Michael Seton made a will before he started on this flight, and that in that will he left all he had to his fiancée."

"That's pure supposition."

"It is supposition—yes. But it must be so. Because, if it is not so, there is no meaning in anything that has happened. It is no paltry inheritance that is at stake. It is an enormous fortune."

I was silent for some minutes turning the matter over in my mind. It seemed to me that Poirot was leaping at conclusions in a most reckless manner, and yet I was secretly convinced that he was right. It was his extraordinary flair for being right that influenced me. Yet it seemed to me that there was a good deal to be proved still.

"But if nobody knew of the engagement," I argued.

"Pah! Somebody did know. For the matter of that, somebody always does know. If they do not know, they guess. Madame Rice suspected. Mademoiselle Nick admitted as much. She may have had means of turning those suspicions into certainties."

"How?"

"Well, for one thing, there must have been letters from Michael Seton to Mademoiselle Nick. They had been engaged some time. And her best friend could not call that young lady anything but careless. She leaves things here and there, and everywhere. I doubt if she has ever locked up anything in her life. Oh! yes, there would be means of making sure."

"And Frederica Rice would know about the will that her friend had made?"

"Doubtless. Oh! yes, it narrows down now. You remember my list—a list of persons numbered from A. to J. It has narrowed down to only two persons. I dismiss the servants. I dismiss the Commander Challenger—even though he did take one hour and a half to reach here from Plymouth—and the distance is only thirty miles. I dismiss M. Lazarus who offered fifty pounds for a picture that was only worth twenty. I dismiss the Australians—so hearty and so pleasant. I keep two people on my list still."

"One is Frederica Rice," I said slowly.

I had a vision of her face, the golden hair, the white fragility of the features.

"Yes. She is indicated very clearly. However carelessly worded Mademoiselle's will may have been, she would be plainly indicated as a residuary legatee. Apart from End House, everything was to go to her. If Mademoiselle Nick instead of Mademoiselle Maggie had been shot last night, Madame Rice would be a rich woman today."

"I can hardly believe it!"

"You mean that you can hardly believe that a beautiful woman can be a murderess? One often has a little difficulty with members of a jury on that account. But you may be right. There is still another suspect."

"Who?"

"Charles Vyse."

"But he only inherits the house."

"Yes—but he may not know that. Did he make Mademoiselle's will for her? I think not. If so, it would be in his keeping, not 'knocking around somewhere' or whatever the phrase was that Mademoiselle used. So, you see, Hastings, it is quite probable that he knows nothing about that will. He may believe that she has never made a will and that, in that case, he will inherit as next of kin."

"You know," I said. "That really seems to be much more probable."

"That is your romantic mind, Hastings. The wicked solicitor! A familiar figure in fiction. If as well as being a solicitor he has an impassive face, it makes the matter almost certain. It is true that, in some ways, he is more in the picture than Madame. He would be more likely to know about the pistol and more likely to use one."

"And to send the boulder crashing down."

"Perhaps. Though, as I have told you, much can be done by leverage. And the fact that the boulder was dislodged at the wrong minute, and consequently missed Mademoiselle, is more suggestive of feminine agency. The idea of tampering with the interior of a car seems masculine in conception—though many women are as good mechanics as men nowadays. On the other hand, there are one or two gaps in the theory against M. Vyse."

"Such as—?"

"He is less likely to have known of the engagement than Madame. And there is another point. His action was rather precipitate."

"What do you mean?"

"Well, until last night there was no certitude that Seton was dead. To act rashly, without due assurance, seems very uncharacteristic of the legal mind."

"Yes," I said. "A woman would jump to conclusions."

"Exactly. *Ce que femme veut, Dieu veut.* That is the attitude."

"It's really amazing the way Nick has escaped. It seems almost incredible."

And suddenly I remembered the tone in Frederica's voice as she had said: "Nick bears a charmed life."

I shivered a little.

"Yes," said Poirot thoughtfully. "And I can take no credit to myself. Which is humiliating."

"Providence," I murmured.

"Ah! *mon ami*, I would not put on the shoulders of the good God the burden of men's wrongdoing. You say that in your Sunday morning voice of thankfulness—without reflecting that what you are really saying is that *le bon Dieu* has killed Miss Maggie Buckley."

"Really, Poirot!"

"Really, my friend! But I will not sit back and say '*le bon Dieu* has arranged everything, I will not interfere.' Because I am convinced that *le bon Dieu* created Hercule Poirot for the express purpose of interfering. It is my *métier*."

We had been slowly ascending the zigzag path up the cliff. It was at this juncture that we passed through the little gate into the grounds of End House.

"*Pouf*," said Poirot. "That ascent is a steep one. I am hot. My mustaches are limp. Yes, as I was saying just now, I am on the side of the innocent. I am on the side of Mademoiselle Nick because she was attacked. I am on the side of Mademoiselle Maggie because she has been killed."

"And you are against Frederica Rice and Charles Vyse."

"No, no, Hastings. I keep an open mind. I say only that at the moment one of those two is indicated. Chut!"

We had come out on the strip of lawn by the house and a man was driving a mowing machine. He had a long stupid face and lackluster eyes. Beside him was a small boy of about ten, ugly but intelligent looking.

It crossed my mind that we had not heard the mowing machine in action, but I presumed that the gardener was not overworking himself. He had probably been resting from his labors, and had sprung into action on hearing our voices approaching.

"Good morning," said Poirot.

"Good morning, sir."

"You are the gardener, I suppose. The husband of Madame who works in the house."

"He's my dad," said the small boy.

"That's right, sir," said the man. "You'll be the foreign gentleman, I take it, that's really a detective. Is there any news of the young mistress, sir?"

"I come from seeing her at the immediate moment. She has passed a satisfactory night."

"We've had policemen here," said the small boy. "That's where the lady was killed. Here by the steps. I seen a pig killed once, haven't I, Dad?"

"Ah!" said his father unemotionally.

"Dad used to kill pigs when he worked on a farm. Didn't you, Dad? I seen a pig killed. I liked it."

"Young 'uns like to see pigs killed," said the man, as though stating one of the unalterable facts of nature.

"Shot with a pistol, the lady was," continued the boy. "She didn't have her throat cut. No."

We passed on to the house, and I felt thankful to get away from the ghoulish child.

Poirot entered the drawing room, the windows of which were open, and rang the bell. Ellen, neatly attired in black, came in answer to the bell. She showed no surprise at seeing us.

Poirot explained that we were here by permission of Miss Buckley to make a search of the house.

"Very good, sir."

"The police have finished?"

"They said they had seen everything they wanted, sir. They've been about the garden since very early in the morning. I don't know whether they've found anything."

She was about to leave the room when Poirot stopped her with a question.

"Were you very surprised last night when you heard Miss Buckley had been shot?"

"Yes, sir, very surprised. Miss Maggie was a nice young lady, sir. I can't imagine anyone being so wicked as to want to harm her."

"If it had been anyone else, you would not have been so surprised—eh?"

"I don't know what you mean, sir."

"When I came into the hall last night," I said, "you asked at once whether anyone had been hurt. Were you expecting anything of the kind?"

She was silent. Her fingers pleated a corner of her apron. She shook her head and murmured:

"You gentlemen wouldn't understand."

"Yes, yes," said Poirot, "I would understand. However fantastic what you may say, I would understand."

She looked at him doubtfully, then seemed to make up her mind to trust him.

"You see, sir," she said, "this isn't a good house."

I was surprised and a little contemptuous. Poirot, however, seemed to find the remark not in the least unusual.

"You mean it is an old house."

"Yes, sir, not a good house."

"You have been here long?"

"Six years, sir. But I was here as a girl. In the kitchen as kitchen maid. That was in the time of old Sir Nicholas. It was the same then."

Poirot looked at her attentively.

"In an old house," he said, "there is sometimes an atmosphere of evil."

"That's it, sir," said Ellen eagerly. "Evil. Bad thoughts and bad deeds too. It's like dry rot in a house, sir, you can't get it out. It's a sort of feeling in the air. I always knew something bad would happen in this house, someday."

"Well, you have been proved right."

"Yes, sir."

There was a very slight underlying satisfaction in her tone, the satisfaction of one whose gloomy prognostications have been shown to be correct.

"But you didn't think it would be Miss Maggie."

"No, indeed, I didn't, sir. Nobody hated her—I'm sure of it."

It seemed to me that in those words was a clue. I expected Poirot to follow it up, but to my surprise he shifted to quite a different subject.

"You didn't hear the shots fired?"

"I couldn't have told with the fireworks going on. Very noisy they were."

"You weren't out watching them?"

"No, I hadn't finished clearing up dinner."

"Was the waiter helping you?"

"No, sir, he'd gone out into the garden to have a look at the fireworks."

"But you didn't go."

"No, sir."

"Why was that?"

"I wanted to get finished."

"You don't care for fireworks?"

"Oh, yes, sir, it wasn't that. But you see, there's two nights of them, and William and I get the evening off tomorrow and go down into the town and see them from there."

"I comprehend. And you heard Mademoiselle Maggie asking for her coat and unable to find it?"

"I heard Miss Nick run upstairs, sir, and Miss Buckley call up from the front hall saying she couldn't find something and I heard her say, all right—she'd take the shawl—"

"Pardon—" Poirot interrupted. "You did not endeavor to search for the coat for her—or get it from the car where it had been left."

"I had my work to do, sir."

"Quite so—and doubtless neither of the two young ladies asked you because they thought you were out looking at the fireworks?"

"Yes, sir."

"So that, other years, you have been out looking at the fireworks?"

A sudden flush came into her pale cheeks.

"I don't know what you mean, sir. We're always allowed to go out into the garden. If I didn't feel like it this year, and would rather get on with my work and go to bed, well, that's my business, I imagine."

"*Mais oui. Mais oui.* I did not intend to offend you. Why should you not do as you prefer? To make a change, it is pleasant."

He paused and then added: "Now another little matter in which I wonder whether you can help me. This is an old house. Are there, do you know, any secret chambers in it?"

"Well—there's a kind of sliding panel—in this very room. I remember being shown it as a girl. Only I can't remember just now where it is. Or was it in the library? I can't say, I'm sure."

"Big enough for a person to hide in?"

"Oh! no, indeed, sir! A little cupboard place—a kind of niche. About a foot square, sir, not more than that."

"Oh! that is not what I meant at all."

The blush rose to her face again.

"If you think I was hiding anywhere—I wasn't! I heard Miss Nick run down the stairs and out and I heard her cry out—and I came into the hall to see if—if anything was the matter. And that's the gospel truth, sir. That's the gospel truth."

13

Letters

HAVING SUCCESSFULLY got rid of Ellen, Poirot turned a somewhat thoughtful face towards me.

"I wonder now—did she hear those shots? I think she did. She heard them, she opened the kitchen door. She heard Nick rush down the stairs and out and she herself came into the hall to find out what had happened. That is natural enough. But why did she not go out and watch the fireworks that evening? That is what I should like to know, Hastings."

"What was your idea in asking about a secret hiding place?"

"A mere fanciful idea that, after all, we might not have disposed of J."

"J.?"

"Yes. The last person on my list. The problematical outsider. Supposing for some reason connected with Ellen that J. had come to the house last night. He (I assume a he) conceals himself in a secret chamber in this room. A girl passes through whom he takes to be Nick. He follows her out—and shoots her. *Non—c'est idiot!* And anyway, we know that there is no hiding place. Ellen's decision to remain in the kitchen last night was a pure hazard. Come, let us search for the will of Mademoiselle Nick."

There were no papers in the drawing room. We adjourned to the library, a rather dark room looking out on the drive. Here there was a large old-fashioned walnut bureau writing table.

It took us some time to go through it. Everything was in complete confusion. Bills and receipts were mixed up together. Letters of invitation, letters pressing for payment of accounts, letters from friends.

"We will arrange these papers," said Poirot sternly, "with order and method."

He was as good as his word. Half an hour later, he sat back with a pleased expression on his face. Everything was neatly sorted, docketed and filed.

"*C'est bien, ça.* One thing is at least to the good. We have had to go through everything so thoroughly that there is no possibility of our having missed anything."

"No, indeed. Not that there's been much to find."

"Except possibly this."

He tossed across a letter. It was written in large sprawling handwriting, almost indecipherable.

> Darling,
> Party was too, too marvelous. Feel rather a worm today. You were wise not to touch that stuff—don't ever start, darling. It's too damned hard to give up. I'm writing the boy friend to hurry up the supply. What Hell life is.
>
> > Yours,
> > Freddie.

"Dated last February," said Poirot thoughtfully. "She takes drugs, of course, I knew that as soon as I looked at her."

"Really? I never suspected such a thing."

"It is fairly obvious. You have only to look at her eyes. And then there are her extraordinary variations of mood. Sometimes she is all on edge, strung up—sometimes she is lifeless—inert."

"Drug-taking affects the moral sense, does it not?"

"Inevitably. But I do not think Mrs. Rice is a real addict. She is at the beginning—not the end."

"And Nick?"

"There are no signs of it. She may have attended a dope party now and then for fun, but she is no taker of drugs."

"I'm glad of that."

I remembered suddenly what Nick had said about Frederica that she was not always herself. Poirot nodded and tapped the letter he held.

"This is what she was referring to, undoubtedly. Well, we have drawn the blank, as you say, here. Let us go up to Mademoiselle's room."

There was a desk in Nick's room also, but comparatively little was kept in it. Here again, there was no sign of a will. We found the registration book of her car and a perfectly good dividend warrant of a month back. Otherwise there was nothing of importance.

Poirot sighed in an exasperated fashion.

"The young girls—they are not properly trained nowadays. The order, the method, it is left out of their bringing up. She is charming, Mademoiselle Nick, but she is a featherhead. Decidedly she is a featherhead."

He was now going through the contents of a chest of drawers.

"Surely, Poirot," I said with some embarrassment, "those are underclothes."

He paused in surprise.

"And why not, my friend?"

"Don't you think—I mean—we can hardly—"

He broke into a roar of laughter.

"Decidedly, my poor Hastings, you belong to the Victorian era. Mademoiselle Nick would tell you so if she were here. In all probability she would say that you had the mind like the sink! Young ladies are not ashamed of their underclothes nowadays. The camisole, the cami-knicker, it is no longer a shameful secret. Every day, on the beach, all these garments will be discarded within a few feet of you. And why not?"

"I don't see any need for what you are doing."

"*Écoutez*, my friend. Clearly, she does not lock up her treasures, Mademoiselle Nick. If she wished to hide anything from sight—where would she hide it? Underneath the stockings and the petticoats. Ah! what have we here?"

He held up a packet of letters tied with a faded pink ribbon.

"The love letters of M. Michael Seton, if I mistake not."

Quite calmly, he untied the ribbon and began to open out the letters.

"Poirot," I cried, scandalized. "You really can't do that. It isn't playing the game."

"I am not playing a game, *mon ami*." His voice rang out suddenly harsh and stern. "I am hunting down a murderer."

"Yes, but private letters—"

"May have nothing to tell me—On the other hand, they may. I must take every chance, my friend. Come, you might as well read them with me. Two pairs of eyes are no worse than one pair. Console yourself with the thought that the staunch Ellen knows them by heart."

I did not like it. Still I realized that in Poirot's position he could not afford to be squeamish, and I consoled myself by the quibble that Nick's last words had been "Look at anything you like."

The letters spread over several dates, beginning last winter. New Year's Day.

Darling,
The New Year is in and I'm making good resolutions. It seems too wonderful to be true—that you should actually love me. You've made all the difference to my life. I believe we both knew—from the very first moment we met. Happy New Year, my lovely girl.

Yours for ever,
Michael

FEB. 8th
Dearest Love,
How I wish I could see you more often. This is pretty rotten, isn't it? I hate all this beastly concealment but I explained to you how things are. I know how much you hate lies and concealment. I do too. But honestly, it might upset the whole apple cart. Uncle Matthew has got an absolute bee in his bonnet about early marriages and the way they wreck a man's career. As though you could wreck mine, you dear angel.
Cheer up, darling. Everything will come right.

Yours,
Michael

MARCH 2nd
I oughtn't to write to you two days running, I know. But I must. When I was up yesterday I thought of you. I flew over Scarborough. Blessed, blessed, blessed Scarborough—the most wonderful place in the world. Darling, you don't know how I love you.

Yours,
Michael

APRIL 18th
Dearest,
The whole thing is fixed up. Definitely. If I pull this off (and I shall pull it off) I shall be able to take a firm line with Uncle Matthew—and if he doesn't like it—well, what do I care? It's adorable of you to be so interested in my long technical descriptions of the *Albatross*. How I long to take you up in her. Someday! Don't for goodness sake, worry about me. The thing isn't half so risky as it sounds, I simply couldn't get killed now that I know you care for me. Everything will be all right, sweetheart. Trust your

Michael

APRIL 20th

You angel—every word you say is true and I shall treasure that letter always. I'm not half good enough for you. You are so different from everybody else. I adore you.

Yours,
Michael

The last was undated.

Dearest,

Well—I'm off tomorrow. Feeling tremendously keen and excited and absolutely certain of success. The old *Albatross* is all tuned up. She won't let me down.

Cheer up, sweetheart, and don't worry. There's a risk, of course, but all life's a risk really. By the way, somebody said I ought to make a will (tactful fellow—but he meant well) so I have—on a half sheet of notepaper and sent it to old Whitfield. I'd no time to go round there. Somebody once told me that a man made a will of three words, "All to Mother," and it was legal all right. My will was rather like that—I remembered your name was really Magdala which was clever of me! A couple of the fellows witnessed it.

Don't take all this solemn talk about wills to heart, will you? (I didn't mean that pun. An accident.) I shall be as right as rain. I'll send you telegrams from India and Australia and so on. And keep up heart. *It's going to be all right.* See?

Good night and God bless you,
Michael

Poirot folded the letters together again.

"You see, Hastings? I had to read them—to make sure. It is as I told you."

"Surely you could have found out some other way?"

"No, *mon cher*, that is just what I could not do. It had to be this way. We have now some very valuable evidence."

"In what way?"

"We now know that the fact of Michael's having made a will in favor of Mademoiselle Nick is actually recorded in writing. Anyone who had read those letters would know the fact. And with letters carelessly hidden like that, anyone could read them."

"Ellen?"

"Ellen, almost certainly, I should say. We will try a little experiment on her before passing out."

"There is no sign of the will."

"No, that is curious. But in all probability it is thrown on top of a bookcase, or inside a China jar. We must try to awaken Mademoiselle's memory on that point. At any rate, there is nothing more to be found here."

Ellen was dusting the hall as we descended.

Poirot wished her good morning very pleasantly as we passed. He turned back from the front door to say: "You knew, I suppose, that Miss Buckley was engaged to the airman, Michael Seton?"

She stared.

"What? The one there's all the fuss in the papers about?"

"Yes."

"Well, I never. To think of that. Engaged to Miss Nick."

"Complete and absolute surprise registered very convincingly," I remarked as we got outside.

"Yes. It really seemed genuine."

"Perhaps it was," I suggested.

"And that packet of letters reclining for months under the *lingerie*? No, *mon ami*."

"All very well," I thought to myself. "But we are not all Hercule Poirots. We do not all go nosing into what does not concern us."

But I said nothing.

"This Ellen—she is an enigma," said Poirot. "I do not like it. There is something here that I do not understand."

14

The Mystery of the Missing Will

WE WENT STRAIGHT back to the nursing home.

Nick looked rather surprised to see us.

"Yes, Mademoiselle," said Poirot, answering her look. "I am like the Jack in the Case. I pop up again. To begin with I will tell you that I have put the order in your affairs. Everything is now neatly arranged."

"Well, I expect it was about time," said Nick unable to help smiling. "Are you very tidy, M. Poirot?"

"Ask my friend Hastings here."

The girl turned an inquiring gaze at me.

I detailed some of Poirot's minor peculiarities—toast that had to be made from a square loaf—eggs matching in size—his objection to golf as a game "shapeless and haphazard" whose only redeeming feature was the tee boxes! I ended by telling her the famous case which Poirot had solved by his habit of straightening ornaments on the mantelpiece.

Poirot sat by, smiling.

"He makes the good tale of it, yes," he said when I had finished. "But on the whole it is true. Figure to yourself, Mademoiselle, that I never cease trying to persuade Hastings to part his hair in the middle instead of on the side. See what an air—lopsided and unsymmetrical—it gives him."

"Then you must disapprove of me, M. Poirot," said Nick. "I wear a side parting. And you must approve of Freddie who parts her hair in the middle."

"He was certainly admiring her the other evening," I put in maliciously. "Now I know the reason."

"*C'est assez*," said Poirot. "I am here on serious business. Mademoiselle, this will of yours, I find it not."

"Oh!" She wrinkled her brows. "But does it matter so much? After all, I'm not dead. And wills aren't really important till you are dead, are they?"

"That is correct. All the same, I interest myself in this will of yours. I have various little ideas concerning it. Think, Mademoiselle. Try to remember where you placed it—where you saw it last?"

"I don't suppose I put it anywhere particular," said Nick. "I never do put things in places. I probably shoved it into a drawer."

"You did not put it in the secret panel by any chance?"

"The secret what?"

"Your maid, Ellen, says that there is a secret panel in the drawing room or the library."

"Nonsense," said Nick. "I've never heard of such a thing. Ellen said so?"

"*Mais oui*. It seems she was in service at End House as a young girl. The cook showed it to her."

"It's the first I've ever heard of it. I suppose Grandfather must have known about it, but, if so, he didn't tell me. And I'm sure he would have told me. M. Poirot, are you sure Ellen isn't making it all up?"

"No, Mademoiselle, I am not at all sure! *Il me semble* that there is something—odd about this Ellen of yours."

"Oh! I wouldn't call her odd. William's a half-wit, and the child is a nasty little brute, but Ellen's all right. The essence of respectability."

"Did you give her leave to go out and see the fireworks last night, Mademoiselle?"

"Of course. They always do. They clear up afterwards."

"Yet she did not go out."

"Oh! yes, she did."

"How do you know, Mademoiselle?"

"Well—well—I suppose I don't know. I told her to go and she thanked me—and so of course I assumed that she did go."

"On the contrary—she remained in the house."

"But—how very odd!"

"You think it odd?"

"Yes, I do. I'm sure she's never done such a thing before. Did she say why?"

"She did not tell me the real reason—of that I am sure."

Nick looked at him questioningly.

"Is it—important?"

Poirot flung out his hands.

"That is just what I cannot say, Mademoiselle. *C'est curieux.* I leave it like that."

"This panel business too," said Nick reflectively. "I can't help thinking that's frightfully queer—and unconvincing. Did she show you where it was?"

"She said she couldn't remember."

"I don't believe there is such a thing."

"It certainly looks like it."

"She must be going batty, poor thing."

"She certainly recounts the histories! She said also that End House was not a good house to live in."

Nick gave a little shiver.

"Perhaps she's right there," she said slowly. "Sometimes I've felt that way myself. There's a queer feeling in that house. . . ."

Her eyes grew large and dark. They had a fated look. Poirot hastened to recall her to other topics.

"We have wandered from our subject, Mademoiselle. The will. The last will and testament of Magdala Buckley."

"I put that," said Nick with some pride. "I remember putting that, and I said pay all debts and testamentary expenses. I remembered that out of a book I'd read."

"You did not use a will form, then?"

"No, there wasn't time for that. I was just going off to the nursing home, and besides Mr. Croft said will forms were very dangerous. It was better to make a simple will and not try to be too legal."

"M. Croft. He was there?"

"Yes. It was he who asked me if I'd made one. I'd never have thought of it myself. He said if you died in—in—"

"Intestate," I said.

"Yes, that's it. He said if you died intestate, the Crown pinched a lot and that would be a pity."

"Very helpful, the excellent M. Croft!"

"Oh! he was," said Nick warmly. "He got Ellen in and her husband to witness it. Oh! of course! What an idiot I've been!"

We looked at her inquiringly.

"I've been a perfect idiot. Letting you hunt round End House. Charles has got it, of course! My cousin, Charles Vyse."

"Ah! so that is the explanation."

"Mr. Croft said a lawyer was the proper person to have charge of it."

"*Très correct, ce bon M. Croft.*"

"Men are useful sometimes," said Nick. "A lawyer or the bank—that's what he said. And I said Charles would be best. So we stuck it in an envelope and sent it off to him straight away."

She lay back on her pillows with a sigh.

"I'm sorry I've been so frightfully stupid. But it is all right now. Charles has got it, and if you really want to see it, of course he'll show it to you."

"Not without an authorization from you," said Poirot, smiling.

"How silly."

"No, Mademoiselle. Merely prudent."

"Well, I think it's silly." She took a piece of paper from a little stack that lay beside her bed. "What shall I say? Let the dog see the rabbit?"

"*Comment?*"

I laughed at his startled face.

He dictated a form of words, and Nick wrote obediently.

"Thank you, Mademoiselle," said Poirot as he took it.

"I'm sorry to have given you such a lot of trouble. But I really had forgotten. You know how one forgets things almost at once?"

"With order and method in the mind one does not forget."

"I'll have to have a course of some kind," said Nick. "You're giving me quite an inferiority complex."

"That is impossible. *Au revoir*, Mademoiselle." He looked round the room. "Your flowers are lovely."

"Aren't they? The carnations are from Freddie and the roses from George and the lilies from Jim Lazarus. And look here—"

She pulled the wrapping from a large basket of hot-house grapes by her side.

Poirot's face changed. He stepped forward sharply.

"You have not eaten any of them?"

"No. Not yet."

"Do not do so. You must eat nothing, Mademoiselle, that comes in from outside. You comprehend?"

"Oh!"

She stared at him, the color ebbing slowly from her face.

"I see. You think—you think it isn't over yet. You think that they're still trying?" she whispered.

He took her hand.

"Do not think of it. You are safe here. But remember—nothing that comes in from outside."

I was conscious of that white frightened face on the pillow as we left the room.

Poirot looked at his watch.

"*Bon*. We have just time to catch M. Vyse at his office before he leaves it for lunch."

On arrival we were shown into Charles Vyse's office after the briefest of delays.

The young lawyer rose to greet us. He was as formal and unemotional as ever.

"Good morning, M. Poirot. What can I do for you?"

Without more ado Poirot presented the letter Nick had written. He took it and read it, then gazed over the top of it at us in a perplexed manner.

"I beg your pardon. I really am at a loss to understand—"

"Has not Mademoiselle Buckley made her meaning clear?"

"In this letter," he tapped it with his fingernail, "she asks me to hand over to you, a will made by her and entrusted to my keeping in February last."

"Yes, Monsieur."

"But, my dear sir, no will has been entrusted to my keeping."

"*Comment*?"

"As far as I know my cousin never made a will. I certainly never made one for her."

"She wrote this herself, I understand, on a sheet of notepaper and posted it to you."

The lawyer shook his head.

"In that case all I can say is that I never received it."

"Really, M. Vyse—"

"I never received anything of the kind, M. Poirot."

There was a pause, then Poirot rose to his feet.

"In that case, M. Vyse, there is nothing more to be said. There must be some mistake."

"Certainly there must be some mistake."

He rose also.

"Good day, M. Vyse."

"Good day, M. Poirot."

"And that is that," I remarked when we were out in the street once more.

"*Précisément.*"

"Is he lying, do you think?"

"Impossible to tell. He has the good poker face, M. Vyse, besides looking as though he had swallowed one. One thing is clear, he will not budge from the position he has taken up. He never received the will. That is his point."

"Surely Nick will have a written acknowledgement of its receipt."

"*Cette petite*, she would never bother her head about a thing like that. She dispatched it. It was off her mind. *Voilà*. Besides, on that very day, she went into a nursing home to have her appendix out. She had her emotions, in all probability."

"Well, what do we do now?"

"*Parbleu*, we go and see M. Croft. Let us see what he can remember about this business. It seems to have been very much his doing."

"He didn't profit by it in any way," I said thoughtfully.

"No. No, I cannot see anything in it from his point of view. He is probably merely the busybody—the man who likes to arrange his neighbor's affairs."

Such an attitude was indeed typical of Mr. Croft, I felt. He was the kindly know-all who causes so much exasperation in this world of ours.

We found him busy in his shirt sleeves over a steaming pot in the kitchen. A most savory smell pervaded the little lodge.

He relinquished his cookery with enthusiasm being clearly eager to talk about the murder.

"Half a jiffy," he said. "Walk upstairs. Mother will want to be in on this. She'd never forgive us for talking down here. Cooee—Milly. Two friends coming up."

Mrs. Croft greeted us warmly and was eager for news of Nick. I liked her much better than her husband.

"That poor dear girl," she said. "In a nursing home, you say? Had a complete breakdown, I shouldn't wonder. A dreadful business, Mr. Poirot—perfectly dreadful. An innocent young girl like that shot dead. It doesn't bear thinking about—it doesn't indeed. And no lawless wild part of the world either. Right here in the heart of the old country. Kept me awake all night, it did."

"It's made me nervous about going out and leaving you, old lady," said her husband, who had put on his coat and joined us. "I don't like to think of your having been left all alone here yesterday evening. It gives me the shivers."

"You're not going to leave me again, I can tell you," said Mrs. Croft. "Not after dark, anyway. And I'm thinking I'd like to leave this part of the world as soon as possible. I shall never feel the same about it. I shouldn't think poor Nicky Buckley could ever bear to sleep in that house again."

It was a little difficult to reach the object of our visit. Both Mr. and Mrs. Croft talked so much and were so anxious to know all about everything. Were the poor dead girl's relations coming down? When was the funeral? Was there to be an inquest? What did the police think? Had they any clue yet? Was it true that a man had been arrested in Plymouth?

Then, having answered all these questions, they were insistent on offering us lunch. Only Poirot's mendacious statement that we were obliged to hurry back to lunch with the Chief Constable saved us.

At last a momentary pause occurred and Poirot got in the question he had been waiting to ask.

"Why, of course," said Mr. Croft. He pulled the blind cord up and down twice, frowning at it abstractedly. "I remember all about it. Must have been when we first came here. I remember. Appendicitis—that's what the doctors said—"

"And probably not appendicitis at all," interrupted Mrs. Croft. "These doctors—they always like cutting you up if they can. It wasn't the kind you have to operate on anyhow. She'd had indigestion and one thing and another and they'd X-rayed her and they said out it had better come. And there she was, poor little soul, just going off to one of those nasty homes."

"I just asked her," said Mr. Croft, "if she'd made a will. More as a joke than anything else."

"Yes?"

"And she wrote it out then and there. Talked about getting a will form at the post office—but I advised her not to. Lot of trouble they cause sometimes, so a man told me. Anyway, her cousin is a lawyer. He could draw her out a proper one afterwards if everything was right—as of course I knew it would be. This was just a precautionary matter."

"Who witnessed it?"

"Oh! Ellen, the maid, and her husband."

"And afterwards? What was done with it?"

"Oh! we posted it to Vyse. The lawyer, you know."

"You know that it was posted?"

"My dear M. Poirot, I posted it myself. Right in this box here by the gate."

"So if M. Vyse says he never got it—"

Croft stared.

"Do you mean that it got lost in the post? Oh! but surely that's impossible."

"Anyway, you are certain that you posted it."

"Certain sure," said Mr. Croft heartily. "I'll take my oath on that any day."

"Ah! well," said Poirot. "Fortunately it does not matter. Mademoiselle is not likely to die just yet awhile."

We made our escape.

"*Et voilà!*" said Poirot when we were out of earshot and walking down to the hotel. "Who is lying? M. Croft? Or M. Charles Vyse? I must confess I see no reason why M. Croft should be lying. To suppress the will would be of no advantage to him—especially when he had been instrumental in getting it made. No, his statement seems clear enough and tallies exactly with what was told us by Mademoiselle Nick. But all the same—"

"Yes?"

"All the same, I am glad that M. Croft was doing the cooking when we arrived. He left an excellent impression of a greasy thumb and first finger on a corner of the newspaper that covered the kitchen table. I managed to tear it off unseen by him. We will send it to our good friend Inspector Japp of Scotland Yard. There is just a chance that he might know something about it."

"Yes?"

"You know, Hastings, I cannot help feeling that our genial M. Croft is a little too good to be genuine.

"And now," he added. "*Le déjeuner.* I faint with hunger."

15

Strange Behavior of Frederica

POIROT'S INVENTIONS about the Chief Constable were proved not to have been so mendacious after all. Colonel Weston called upon us soon after lunch.

He was a tall man of military carriage with considerable good looks.

He had a suitable reverence for Poirot's achievements with which he seemed to be well acquainted.

"Marvelous piece of luck for us having you down here, M. Poirot," he said again and again.

His one fear was that he should be compelled to call in the assistance of Scotland Yard. He was anxious to solve the mystery and catch the criminal without their aid. Hence his delight at Poirot's presence in the neighborhood.

Poirot, so far as I could judge, took him completely into his confidence.

"Deuced odd business," said the Colonel. "Never heard of anything like it. Well, the girl ought to be safe enough in a nursing home. Still, you can't keep her there forever!"

"That, M. le Colonel, is just the difficulty. There is only one way of dealing with it."

"And that is?"

"We must lay our hands on the person responsible."

"If what you suspect is true, that isn't going to be so easy."

"*Ah! je le sais bien.*"

"Evidence! Getting evidence is going to be the devil."

He frowned abstractedly.

"Always difficult, these cases, where there's no routine work. If we could get hold of the pistol—"

"In all probability it is at the bottom of the sea. That is, if the murderer had any sense."

"Ah!" said Colonel Weston. "But often they haven't. You'd be surprised at the fool things people do. I'm not talking of murderers—we don't have many murders down in these parts, I'm glad to say—but in ordinary police court cases. The sheer damn foolishness of these people would surprise you."

"They are of a different mentality, though."

"Yes—perhaps. If Vyse is the chap, well, we'll have our work cut out. He's a cautious man and a sound lawyer. He'll not give himself away. The woman—well, there would be more hope there. Ten to one she'll try again. Women have no patience."

He rose.

"Inquest tomorrow morning. Coroner will work in with us and give away as little as possible. We want to keep things dark at present."

He was turning towards the door when he suddenly came back.

"Upon my soul, I'd forgotten the very thing that will interest you most, and that I want your opinion about."

Sitting down again, he drew from his pocket a torn scrap of paper with writing on it and handed it to Poirot.

"My police found this when they were searching the grounds. Not far from where you were all watching the fireworks. It's the only suggestive thing they did find."

Poirot smoothed it out. The writing was large and straggling.

"—must have money at once. If not you—
—what will happen. I'm warning you"

Poirot frowned. He read and re-read it.

"That is interesting," he said. "I may keep it?"

"Certainly. There are no fingerprints on it. I'll be glad if you can make anything of it."

Colonel Weston got to his feet again.

"I really must be off. Inquest tomorrow, as I said. By the way, you are not being called as witness—only Captain Hastings. Don't want the newspaper people to get wise to your being on the job."

"I comprehend. What of the relations of the poor young lady?"

"The father and mother are coming from Yorkshire today. They'll arrive about half past five. Poor souls, I'm heartily sorry for them. They are taking the body back with them the following day."

He shook his head.

"Unpleasant business. I'm not enjoying this, M. Poirot."

"Who could, M. le Colonel? It is, as you say, an unpleasant business."

When he had gone, Poirot examined the scrap of paper once more.

"An important clue?" I asked.

He shrugged his shoulders.

"How can one tell? There is a hint of blackmail about it. Some one of our party that night was being pressed for money in a very unpleasant way. Of course, it is possible that it was one of the strangers."

He looked at the writing through a little magnifying glass.

"Does this writing look at all familiar to you, Hastings?"

"It reminds me a little of something—ah! I have it—that note of Mrs. Rice's."

"Yes," said Poirot slowly. "There are resemblances. Decidedly there are resemblances. It is curious. Yet I do not think that this is the writing of Madame Rice. Come in," he said as a knock came at the door.

It was Commander Challenger.

"Just looked in," he explained. "Wanted to know if you were any further forward."

"*Parbleu*," said Poirot. "At this moment I am feeling that I am considerably further back. I seem to progress *en reculant*."

"That's bad. But I don't really believe it, M. Poirot. I've been hearing all about you and what a wonderful chap you are. Never had a failure, they say."

"That is not true," said Poirot. "I had a bad failure in Belgium in 1893. You recollect, Hastings? I recounted it to you. The affair of the box of chocolates."

"I remember," I said.

And I smiled, for at the time that Poirot told me that tale, he had instructed me to say "chocolate box" to him if ever I should fancy he was growing conceited! He was then bitterly offended when I used the magical words only a minute and a quarter later.

"Oh! well," said Challenger. "That is such a long time ago it hardly counts. You are going to get to the bottom of this, aren't you?"

"That I swear. On the word of Hercule Poirot. I am the dog who stays on the scent and does not leave it."

"Good. Got any ideas?"

"I have suspicions of two people."

"I suppose I mustn't ask who they are?"

"I should not tell you! You see, I might possibly be in error."

"My alibi is satisfactory, I trust," said Challenger with a faint twinkle.

Poirot smiled indulgently at the bronzed face in front of him. "You left Devonport at a few minutes past 8:30. You arrived here at five minutes past ten—twenty minutes after the crime had been committed. But the distance from Devonport is only just over thirty miles and you have often done it in an hour since the road is good. So, you see, your alibi is not good at all!"

"Well, I'm—"

"You comprehend, I inquire into everything. Your alibi, as I say, is not good. But there are other things beside alibis. You would like, I think, to marry Mademoiselle Nick?"

The sailor's face flushed.

"I've always wanted to marry her," he said huskily.

"Precisely. *Eh bien*—Mademoiselle Nick was engaged to another man. A reason, perhaps, for killing the other man. But that is unnecessary—he dies the death of a hero."

"So it is true—that Nick was engaged to Michael Seton? There's a rumor to that effect all over the town this morning."

"Yes—it is interesting how soon news spreads. You never suspected it before?"

"I knew Nick was engaged to someone—she told me so two days ago. But she didn't give me a clue as to who it was."

"It was Michael Seton. *Entre nous*, he has left her, I fancy, a very pretty fortune. Ah! assuredly, it is not a moment for killing Mademoiselle Nick—from your point of view. She weeps for her lover now, but the heart consoles itself. She is young. And I think, Monsieur, that she is very fond of you. . . ."

Challenger was silent for a moment or two.

"If it should be . . ." he murmured.

There was a tap on the door.

It was Frederica Rice.

"I've been looking for you," she said to Challenger. "They told me you were here. I wanted to know if you'd got my wrist watch back yet."

"Oh! yes, I called for it this morning."

He took it from his pocket and handed it to her. It was a watch of rather an unusual shape—round, like a globe, set on a strap of plain black moiré. I remembered that I had seen one much the same shape on Nick Buckley's wrist.

"I hope it will keep better time now."

"It's rather a bore. Something is always going wrong with it."

"It is for beauty, Madame, and not for utility," said Poirot.

"Can't one have both?" She looked from one to the other of us. "Am I interrupting a conference?"

"No, indeed, Madame. We were talking the gossip—not the crime. We were saying how quickly news spreads—how that everyone now knows that Mademoiselle Nick was engaged to that brave airman who perished."

"So Nick was engaged to Michael Seton!" exclaimed Frederica.

"It surprises you, Madame?"

"It does a little. I don't know why. Certainly I did think he was very taken with her last autumn. They went about a lot together. And then, after Christmas, they both seemed to cool off. As far as I know, they hardly met."

"The secret, they kept it very well."

"That was because of old Sir Matthew, I suppose. He was really a little off his head, I think."

"You had no suspicion, Madame? And yet Mademoiselle Nick was such an intimate friend."

"Nick's a close little devil when she likes," murmured Frederica. "But I understand now why she's been so nervy lately. Oh! and I ought to have guessed from something she said only the other day."

"Your little friend is very attractive, Madame."

"Old Jim Lazarus used to think so at one time," said Challenger with his loud rather tactless laugh.

"Oh! Jim—" She shrugged her shoulders, but I thought she was annoyed.

She turned to Poirot.

"Tell me, M. Poirot, did you—?"

She stopped. Her tall figure swayed and her face turned whiter still. Her eyes were fixed on the center of the table.

"You are not well, Madame."

I pushed forward a chair, helped her to sink into it. She shook her head, murmured: "I'm all right," and leaned forward, her face between her hands. We watched her awkwardly.

She sat up in a minute.

"How absurd! George darling, don't look so worried. Let's talk about murders. Something exciting. I want to know if M. Poirot is on the track."

"It is early to say, Madame," said Poirot noncommittally.

"But you have ideas—yes?"

"Perhaps. But I need a great deal more evidence."

"Oh!" She sounded uncertain.

Suddenly she rose.

"I've got a head. I think I'll go and lie down. Perhaps tomorrow they'll let me see Nick."

She left the room abruptly. Challenger frowned.

"You never know what that woman's up to. Nick may have been fond of her, but I don't believe she was fond of Nick. But there, you can't tell with women. It's darling—darling—darling—all the time—and 'damn you' would probably express it much better. Are you going out, M. Poirot?" For Poirot had risen and was carefully brushing a speck off his hat.

"Yes, I am going into the town."

"I've got nothing to do. May I come with you?"

"Assuredly. It will be a pleasure."

We left the room. Poirot, with an apology, went back.

"My stick," he explained as he rejoined us.

Challenger winced slightly. And indeed the stick, with its embossed gold band, was somewhat ornate.

Poirot's first visit was to a florist.

"I must send some flowers to Mademoiselle Nick," he explained.

He proved difficult to suit.

In the end he chose an ornate gold basket to be filled with orange carnations. The whole to be tied up with a large blue bow.

The shopwoman gave him a card and he wrote on it with a flourish, "With the Compliments of Hercule Poirot."

"I sent her some flowers this morning," said Challenger. "I might send her some fruit."

"*Inutile!*" said Poirot.

"What?"

"I said it was useless. The eatables—it is not permitted."

"Who says so?"

"I say so. I have made the rule. It has already been impressed on Mademoiselle Nick. She understands."

"Good Lord!" said Challenger.

He looked thoroughly startled. He stared at Poirot curiously.

"So that's it, is it?" he said. "You're still—afraid."

16

Interview with Mr. Whitfield

THE INQUEST was a dry proceeding—mere bare bones. There was evidence of identification, then I gave evidence of the finding of the body. Medical evidence followed.

The inquest was adjourned for a week.

The St. Loo murder had jumped into prominence in the daily press. It had, in fact, succeeded "SETON STILL MISSING. UNKNOWN FATE OF MISSING AIRMAN."

Now that Seton was dead and due tribute had been paid to his memory, a new sensation was due. The St. Loo Mystery was a godsend to papers at their wits' end for news in the month of August.

After the inquest, having successfully dodged reporters, I met Poirot and we had an interview with the Rev. Giles Buckley and his wife.

Maggie's father and mother were a charming pair, completely unworldly and unsophisticated.

Mrs. Buckley was a woman of character, tall and fair and showing very plainly her northern ancestry. Her husband was a small man, grey-headed, with a diffident appealing manner.

Poor souls, they were completely dazed by the misfortune that had overtaken them and robbed them of a well-loved daughter, "our Maggie" as they called her.

"I can scarcely realize it even now," said Mr. Buckley. "Such a dear child, M. Poirot. So quiet and unselfish—always thinking of others. Who could wish to harm her?"

"I could hardly understand the telegram," said Mrs. Buckley. "Why it was only the morning before that we had seen her off."

"In the midst of life we are in death," murmured her husband.

"Colonel Weston has been very kind," said Mrs. Buckley. "He assures us that everything is being done to find the man who did this thing. He must be a madman. No other explanation is possible."

"Madame, I cannot tell you how I sympathize with you in your loss—and how I admire your bravery!"

"Breaking down would not bring Maggie back to us," said Mrs. Buckley sadly.

"My wife is wonderful," said the clergyman. "Her faith and courage are greater than mine. It is all so—so bewildering, M. Poirot."

"I know—I know, Monsieur."

"You are a great detective, M. Poirot?" said Mrs. Buckley.

"It has been said, Madame."

"Oh! I know. Even in our remote country village we have heard of you. You are going to find out the truth, M. Poirot?"

"I shall not rest until I do, Madame."

"It will be revealed to you, M. Poirot," quavered the clergyman. "Evil cannot go unpunished."

"Evil never goes unpunished, Monsieur. But the punishment is sometimes secret."

"What do you mean by that, M. Poirot?"

Poirot only shook his head.

"Poor little Nick," said Mrs. Buckley. "I am really sorriest of all for her. I had a most pathetic letter. She says she feels she asked Maggie down here to her death."

"That is morbid," said Mr. Buckley.

"Yes, but I know how she feels. I wish they would let me see her. It seems so extraordinary not to let her own family visit her."

"Doctors and nurses are very strict," said Poirot evasively. "They make the rules—so—and nothing will change them. And doubtless they fear for her the emotion—the natural emotion—she would experience on seeing you."

"Perhaps," said Mrs. Buckley doubtfully. "But I don't hold with nursing homes. Nick would do much better if they let her come back with me—right away from this place."

"It is possible—but I fear they will not agree. It is long since you have seen Mademoiselle Buckley?"

"I haven't seen her since last autumn. She was at Scarborough. Maggie went over and spent the day with her and then she came back and spent a night with us. She's a pretty creature—though I can't say I like her friends. And the life she leads—well, it's hardly her fault, poor child. She's had no upbringing of any kind."

"It is a strange house—End House," said Poirot thoughtfully.

"I don't like it," said Mrs. Buckley. "I never have. There's something all wrong about that house. I disliked old Sir Nicholas intensely. He made me shiver."

"Not a good man, I'm afraid," said her husband. "But he had a curious charm."

"I never felt it," said Mrs. Buckley. "There's an evil feeling about that house. I wish we'd never let our Maggie go there."

"Ah! wishing," said Mr. Buckley and shook his head.

"Well," said Poirot. "I must not intrude upon you any longer. I only wished to proffer to you my deep sympathy."

"You have been very kind, M. Poirot. And we are indeed grateful for all you are doing."

"You return to Yorkshire—when?"

"Tomorrow. A sad journey. Goodby, M. Poirot, and thank you again."

"Very simple delightful people," I said after we had left.

Poirot nodded.

"It makes the heart ache, does it not, *mon ami*? A tragedy so useless—so purposeless. *Cette jeune fille*—Ah! but I reproach myself bitterly. I, Hercule Poirot, was on the spot and I did not prevent the crime!"

"Nobody could have prevented it."

"You speak without reflection, Hastings. No ordinary person could have prevented it—but of what good is it to be Hercule Poirot with grey cells of a finer quality than other people's, if you do not manage to do what ordinary people cannot?"

"Well, of course," I said. "If you are going to put it like that—"

"Yes, indeed. I am abashed, downhearted—completely abased."

I reflected that Poirot's abasement was strangely like other people's conceit, but I prudently forbore making any remark.

"And now," he said. "*En avant*. To London."

"London?"

"*Mais oui*. We shall catch the two o'clock train very comfortably. All is peaceful here. Mademoiselle is safe in the nursing home. No one can harm her. The watchdogs therefore can take leave of absence. There are one or two little pieces of information that I require."

Our first proceeding on arriving in London was to call upon the late Captain Seton's solicitors, Messrs. Whitfield, Pargiter & Whitfield.

Poirot had arranged for an appointment beforehand, and although it was past six o'clock, we were soon closeted with Mr. Whitfield, the head of the firm.

He was a very urbane and impressive person. He had in front of him a letter from the Chief Constable and another from some high official at Scotland Yard.

"This is all very irregular and unusual, M.—ah—Poirot," he said, as he polished his eyeglasses.

"Quite so, M. Whitfield. But then murder is also irregular—and I am glad to say, sufficiently unusual."

"True. True. But rather farfetched—to make a connection between this murder and my late client's bequest—eh?"

"I think not."

"Ah! you think not. Well—under the circumstances—and I must admit that Sir Henry puts it very strongly in his letter—I shall be—er—happy to do anything that is in my power."

"You acted as legal adviser to the late Captain Seton?"

"To all the Seton family, my dear sir. We have done so—our firm has done so, I mean—for the last hundred years."

"*Parfaitement*. The late Sir Matthew Seton made a will?"

"We made it for him."

"And he left his fortune—how?"

"There were several bequests—one to the Natural History Museum, but the bulk of his large—his, I may say, very large, fortune he left to Captain Michael Seton absolutely. He had no other near relations."

"A very large fortune you say?"

"The late Sir Matthew was the second richest man in England," replied Mr. Whitfield composedly.

"He had somewhat peculiar views, had he not?"

Mr. Whitfield looked at Poirot severely.

"A millionaire, M. Poirot, is allowed to be eccentric. It is almost expected of him."

Poirot received this correction meekly and asked another question.

"His death was unexpected, I understand?"

"Most unexpected. Sir Matthew enjoyed remarkably good health. He had an internal growth, however, which no one had suspected. It reached a vital tissue and an immediate operation was necessary. The operation was, as always on these occasions, completely successful. But Sir Matthew died."

"And his fortune passed to Captain Seton."

"That is so."

"Captain Seton had, I understand, made a will before leaving England?"

"If you can call it a will—yes," said Mr. Whitfield with strong distaste.

"Is it legal?"

"It is perfectly legal. The intention of the testator is plain and it is properly witnessed. Oh! yes, it is legal."

"But you do not approve of it?"

"My dear sir, what are we for?"

I had often wondered. Having once had occasion to make a perfectly simple will myself, I had been appalled at the length and verbiage that resulted from my solicitor's office.

"The truth of the matter was," continued Mr. Whitfield, "that at the time Captain Seton had little or nothing to leave. He was dependent on the allowance he received from his uncle. He felt, I suppose, that Anything would Do."

And he thought correctly, I whispered to myself.

"And the terms of this will?" asked Poirot.

"He leaves everything of which he dies possessed to his affianced wife, Miss Magdala Buckley, absolutely. He names me as his executor."

"Then Miss Buckley inherits?"

"Certainly Miss Buckley inherits."

"And if Miss Buckley had happened to die last Monday?"

"Captain Seton having predeceased her, the money would go to whoever she had named in her will as residuary legatee—or failing a will, to her next of kin."

"I may say," added Mr. Whitfield with an air of enjoyment, "that the death duties would have been enormous. Enormous! Three deaths, remember, in rapid succession." He shook his head. "Enormous!"

"But there would have been something left?" murmured Poirot meekly.

"My dear sir, as I told you, Sir Matthew was the second richest man in England."

Poirot rose.

"Thank you, Mr. Whitfield, very much for the information that you have given me."

"Not at all. Not at all. I may say that I shall be in communication with Miss Buckley—indeed I believe the letter has already gone. I shall be happy to be of any service I can to her."

"She is a young lady," said Poirot, "who could do with some sound legal advice."

"There will be fortune hunters, I am afraid," said Mr. Whitfield, shaking his head.

"It seems indicated," agreed Poirot. "Good day, Monsieur."

"Goodby, M. Poirot. Glad to have been of service to you. Your name is—ah!—familiar to me."

He said this kindly—with an air of one making a valuable admission.

"It is all exactly as you thought, Poirot," I said when we were outside.

"*Mon ami*, it was bound to be. It could not be any other way. We will go now to the Cheshire Cheese where Japp meets us for an early dinner."

We found Inspector Japp of Scotland Yard awaiting us at the chosen rendezvous. He greeted Poirot with every sign of warmth.

"Years since I've seen you, Moosior Poirot! Thought you were growing vegetable marrows in the country."

"I tried, Japp, I tried. But even when you grow vegetable marrows you cannot get away from murder."

He sighed. I knew of what he was thinking—that strange affair at Fernley Park. How I regretted that I had been far away at that time.

"And Captain Hastings too," said Japp. "How are you, sir?"

"Very fit, thanks," I said.

"And now there are more murders?" continued Japp facetiously.

"As you say—more murders."

"Well, you mustn't be depressed, old cock," said Japp. "Even if you can't see your way clear—well—you can't go about at your time of life and expect to have the success you used to do. We all of us get stale as the years go by. Got to give the young 'uns a chance, you know."

"And yet the old dog is the one who knows the tricks," murmured Poirot. "He is cunning. He does not leave the scent."

"Oh! well—we're talking about human beings, not dogs."

"Is there so much difference?"

"Well, it depends how you look at things. But you're a caution, isn't he, Captain Hastings? Always was. Looks much the same—hair a bit thinner on top but the face fungus fuller than ever."

"Eh?" said Poirot. "What is that?"

"He's congratulating you on your mustaches," I said soothingly.

"They are luxuriant, yes," said Poirot complacently caressing them.

Japp went off into a roar of laughter.

"Well," he said, after a minute or two. "I've done your bit of business. These fingerprints you sent me—"

"Yes?" said Poirot eagerly.

"Nothing doing. Whoever the gentleman may be—he hasn't passed through our hands. On the other hand I wired to Melbourne and nobody of that description or name is known there."

"Ah!"

"So there may be something fishy after all. But he's not one of the lads.

"As to the other business," went on Japp.

"Yes?"

"Lazarus and Son have a good reputation. Quite straight and honorable in their dealings. Sharp, of course—but that's another matter. You've got to be sharp in business. But they're all right.

They're in a bad way, though—financially, I mean."

"Oh!—is that so?"

"Yes—the slump in pictures has hit them badly. And antique furniture too. All this modern continental stuff coming into fashion. They built new premises last year and—well—as I say, they're not far from Queer Street."

"I am much obliged to you."

"Not at all. That sort of thing isn't my line, as you know. But I made a point of finding out as you wanted to know. We can always get information."

"My good Japp, what should I do without you?"

"Oh! that's all right. Always glad to oblige an old friend. I let you in on some pretty good cases in the old days, didn't I?"

This, I realized, was Japp's way of acknowledging indebtedness to Poirot who had solved many a case which had baffled the Inspector.

"They were the good days—yes."

"I wouldn't mind having a chat with you now and again even in these days. Your methods may be old-fashioned but you've got your head screwed on the right way, M. Poirot."

"What about my other question. The Dr. MacAllister?"

"Oh! him. He's a woman's doctor. I don't mean a gynecologist. I mean one of these nerve doctors—tell you to sleep in purple walls and an orange ceiling—talk to you about your libido whatever that is—tells you to let it rip. He's a bit of a quack if you ask me—but he gets the women all right. They flock to him. Goes abroad a good deal—does some kind of medical work in Paris, I believe."

"Why Dr. MacAllister?" I asked bewildered. I had never heard of the name. "Where does he come in?"

"Dr. MacAllister is the uncle of Commander Challenger," explained Poirot. "You remember he referred to an uncle who was a doctor?"

"How thorough you are," I said. "Did you think he had operated on Sir Matthew?"

"He's not a surgeon," said Japp.

"*Mon ami*," said Poirot, "I like to inquire into everything. Hercule Poirot is a good dog. The dog follows the scent, and if, regrettably, there is no scent to follow, he noses around—seeking always something that is not very nice. So also, does Hercule Poirot. And often—oh! so often—does he find it!"

"It's not a nice profession, ours," said Japp. "Stilton, did you say? I don't mind if I do. No, it's not a nice profession. And yours is worse than mine—not official, you see, and therefore a lot more worming yourself into places in underhand ways."

"I do not disguise myself, Japp. Never have I disguised myself."

"You couldn't," said Japp. "You're unique. Once seen, never forgotten."

Poirot looked at him rather doubtfully.

"Only my fun," said Japp. "Don't mind me. Glass of port? Well, if you say so. . . ."

The evening became thoroughly harmonious. We were soon in the middle of reminiscences. This case, that case, and the other. I must say that I, too, enjoyed talking over the past. Those had been good days. How old and experienced I felt now!

Poor old Poirot. He was perplexed by this case—I could see that. His powers were not what they were. I had the feeling that he was going to fail—that the murderer of Maggie Buckley would never be brought to book.

"Courage, my friend," said Poirot slapping me on the shoulder. "All is not lost. Do not pull the long face, I beg of you."

"That's all right. I'm all right."

"And so am I. And so is Japp."

"We're all all right," declared Japp hilariously.

And on this pleasant note we parted.

The following morning we journeyed back to St. Loo. On arrival at the hotel Poirot rang up the nursing home and asked to speak to Nick.

Suddenly I saw his face change—he almost dropped the instrument.

"*Comment*? What is that? Say it again, I beg."

He waited for a minute or two listening. Then he said, "Yes, yes, I will come at once."

He turned a pale face to me.

"Why did I go away, Hastings? *Mon Dieu*! Why did I go away?"

"What has happened?"

"Mademoiselle Nick is dangerously ill. Cocaine poisoning. They have got at her after all. *Mon Dieu, mon Dieu*, why did I go away?"

17

A Box of Chocolates

ALL THE WAY to the nursing home Poirot murmured and muttered to himself. He was full of self-reproach.

"I should have known," he groaned. "I should have known! And yet, what could I do? I took every precaution. It is impossible—impossible. No one could get to her! Who has disobeyed my orders?"

At the nursing home we were shown into a little room downstairs and after a few minutes Dr. Graham came to us. He looked exhausted and white.

"She'll do," he said. "It's going to be all right. The trouble was knowing how much she's taken of the damned stuff."

"What was it?"

"Cocaine."

"She will live?"

"Yes, yes, she'll live."

"But how did it happen? How did they get at her? Who has been allowed in?" Poirot fairly danced with impotent excitement.

"Nobody has been allowed in."

"Impossible."

"It's true."

"But then—"

"It was a box of chocolates."

"Ah, *sacré*. And I told her to eat nothing—nothing—that came from outside."

"I don't know about that. It's hard work keeping a girl from a box of chocolates. She only ate one, thank goodness."

"Was there cocaine in all the chocolates?"

"No. The girl ate one. There were two others in the top layer. The rest were all right."

"How was it done?"

"Quite clumsily. Chocolate cut in half—the cocaine mixed with the filling and the chocolate stuck together again. Amateurishly. What you might call a homemade job."

Poirot groaned.

"Ah! if I knew—if I knew. Can I see Mademoiselle?"

"If you come back in an hour I think you can see her," said the doctor. "Pull yourself together, man. She isn't going to die."

For another hour we walked the streets of St. Loo. I did my best to distract Poirot's mind—pointing out to him that all was well, that, after all, no mischief had been done.

But he only shook his head, and repeated at intervals:

"I am afraid, Hastings, I am afraid. . . ."

And the strange way he said it made me, too, feel afraid.

Once he caught me by the arm.

"Listen, my friend. I am all wrong. I have been all wrong from the beginning."

"You mean it isn't the money. . . ."

"No, no, I am right about that. Oh! yes. But those two—it is too simple—too easy, that. There is another twist still. Yes, there is something!"

And then in an outburst of indignation:

"*Ah! cette petite!* Did I not forbid her? Did I not say—'Do not touch anything from outside'? And she disobeys me—me, Hercule Poirot. Are not four escapes from death enough for her? Must she take a fifth chance? *Ah, c'est inouï!*"

At last we made our way back. After a brief wait we were conducted upstairs.

Nick was sitting up in bed. The pupils of her eyes were widely dilated. She looked feverish and her hands kept twitching violently.

"At it again," she murmured.

Poirot experienced real emotion at the sight of her. He cleared his throat and took her hand in his.

"Ah! Mademoiselle—Mademoiselle."

"I shouldn't care," she said defiantly, "if they had got me this time. I'm sick of it all—sick of it!"

"*Pauvre petite!*"

"Something in me doesn't like to give them best!"

"That is the spirit—*le sport*—you must be the good sport, Mademoiselle."

"Your old nursing home hasn't been so safe after all," said Nick.

"If you had obeyed orders, Mademoiselle—"

She looked faintly astonished.

"But I have."

"Did I not impress upon you that you were to eat nothing that came from outside?"

"No more I did."

"But these chocolates—"

"Well, they were all right. You sent them."

"What is that you say, Mademoiselle?"

"You sent them!"

"Me? Never. Never anything of the kind."

"But you did. Your card was in the box."

"What?"

Nick made a spasmodic gesture towards the table by the bed. The nurse came forward.

"You want the card that was in the box?"

"Yes, please, nurse."

There was a moment's pause. The nurse returned to the room with it in her hand.

"Here it is."

I gasped. So did Poirot. For on the card, in flourishing handwriting, were written the same words that I had seen Poirot inscribe on the card that accompanied the basket of flowers: "With the Compliments of Hercule Poirot."

"*Sacré tonnerre!*"

"You see," said Nick accusingly.

"I did not write this!" cried Poirot.

"What?"

"And yet," murmured Poirot, "and yet it is my handwriting."

"I know. It's exactly the same as the card that came with the orange carnations. I never doubted that the chocolates came from you."

Poirot shook his head.

"How should you doubt? Oh! the devil! The clever cruel devil! To think of that! Ah! but he has genius, this man, genius! '*With the Compliments of Hercule Poirot.*' So simple. Yes, but one had to think of it. And I—I did not think. I omitted to foresee this move."

Nick moved restlessly.

"Do not agitate yourself, Mademoiselle. You are blameless— blameless. It is I that am to blame, miserable imbecile that I am! I should have foreseen this move. Yes, I should have foreseen it."

His chin dropped on his breast. He looked the picture of misery.

"I really think—" said the nurse.

She had been hovering nearby, a disapproving expression on her face.

"Eh? Yes, yes, I will go. Courage, Mademoiselle. This is the last mistake I will make. I am ashamed, desolated—I have been tricked, outwitted—as though I were a little schoolboy. But it shall not happen again. No. I promise you. Come, Hastings."

Poirot's first proceeding was to interview the matron. She was, naturally, terribly upset over the whole business.

"It seems incredible to me, M. Poirot, absolutely incredible. That a thing like that should happen in my nursing home."

Poirot was sympathetic and tactful. Having soothed her sufficiently, he began to inquire into the circumstances of the arrival of the fatal packet. Here, the matron declared, he would do best to interview the orderly who had been on duty at the time of its arrival.

The man in question, whose name was Hodd, was a stupid but honest-looking young fellow of about twenty-two. He looked nervous and frightened. Poirot put him at his ease, however.

"No blame can be attached to you," he said kindly. "But I want you to tell me exactly when and how this parcel arrived."

The orderly looked puzzled.

"It's difficult to say, sir," he said slowly. "Lots of people come and inquire and leave things for the different patients."

"The nurse says this came last night," I said. "About six o'clock."

The lad's face brightened.

"I do remember, now, sir. A gentleman brought it."

"A thin-faced gentleman—fair-haired?"

"He was fair-haired—but I don't know about thin-faced."

"Would Charles Vyse bring it himself?" I murmured to Poirot.
I had forgotten that the lad would know a local name.

"It wasn't Mr. Vyse," he said. "I know him. It was a bigger gentleman—handsome-looking—came in a big car."

"Lazarus," I exclaimed.

Poirot shot me a warning glance and I regretted my precipitance.

"He came in a large car and he left this parcel. It was addressed to
Miss Buckley?"

"Yes, sir."

"And what did you do with it?"

"I didn't touch it, sir. Nurse took it up."

"Quite so, but you touched it when you took it from the gentleman,
n'est-ce pas?"

"Oh! that, yes, of course, sir. I took it from him and put it on the
table."

"Which table? Show me if you please."

The orderly led us into the hall. The front door was open. Close to it,
in the hall, was a long marble-topped table on which lay letters and
parcels.

"Everything that comes is put on here, sir. Then the nurses take
things up to the patients."

"Do you remember what time this parcel was left?"

"Must have been about five-thirty, or a little after. I know the post
had just been, and that's usually at about half-past five. It was a pretty
busy afternoon, a lot of people leaving flowers and coming to see
patients."

"Thank you. Now, I think, we will see the nurse who took up the
parcel."

This proved to be one of the probationers, a fluffy little person all
agog with excitement. She remembered taking the parcel up at six
o'clock when she came on duty.

"Six o'clock," murmured Poirot. "Then it must have been twenty
minutes or so that the parcel was lying on the table downstairs."

"Pardon?"

"Nothing, Mademoiselle. Continue. You took the parcel to Miss
Buckley?"

"Yes, there were several things for her. There was this box and some
flowers also—sweet peas—from a Mr. and Mrs. Croft, I think. I took
them up at the same time. And there was a parcel that had come by

post—and curiously enough that was a box of Fuller's chocolates also."

"*Comment*? A second box?"

"Yes, rather a coincidence. Miss Buckley opened them both. She said: 'Oh! what a shame. I'm not allowed to eat them.' Then she opened the lids to look inside and see if they were both just the same, and your card was in one and she said, 'Take the other impure box away, nurse. I might get them mixed up.' Oh! dear, whoever would have thought of such a thing? Seems like an Edgar Wallace, doesn't it?"

Poirot cut short this flood of speech.

"Two boxes, you say? From whom was the other box?"

"There was no name inside."

"And which was the one that came—that had the appearance of coming—from me? The one by post or the other?"

"I declare now—I can't remember. Shall I go up and ask Miss Buckley?"

"If you would be so amiable."

She ran up the stairs.

"Two boxes," murmured Poirot. "There is confusion for you."

The nurse returned breathless.

"Miss Buckley isn't sure. She unwrapped them both before she looked inside. But she thinks it wasn't the box that came by post."

"Eh?" said Poirot a little confused.

"The box from you was the one that didn't come by post. At least she thinks so, but she isn't quite sure."

"*Diable*!" said Poirot as we walked away. "Is no one ever quite sure? In detective books—yes. But life—real life—is always full of muddle. Am I sure, myself, about anything at all? No, no—a thousand times, no."

"Lazarus," I said.

"Yes, that is a surprise, is it not?"

"Shall you say anything to him about it?"

"Assuredly. I shall be interested to see how he takes it. By the way, we might as well exaggerate the serious condition of Mademoiselle. It will do no harm to let it be assumed that she is at death's door. You comprehend? The solemn face—Yes, admirable. You resemble closely an undertaker. *C'est tout à fait bien*."

We were lucky in finding Lazarus. He was bending over the bonnet of his car outside the hotel.

Poirot went straight up to him.

"Yesterday evening, M. Lazarus, you left a box of chocolates for Mademoiselle," he began without preamble.

Lazarus looked rather surprised.

"Yes?"

"That was very amiable of you."

"As a matter of fact they were from Freddie, from Mrs. Rice. She asked me to get them."

"Oh! I see."

"I took them round there in the car."

"I comprehend."

Poirot was silent for a minute or two and then said: "Madame Rice, where is she?"

"I think she's in the lounge."

We found Frederica having tea. She looked up at us with an anxious face.

"What is this I hear about Nick being taken ill?"

"It is a most mysterious affair, Madame. Tell me, did you send her a box of chocolates yesterday?"

"Yes. At least she asked me to get them for her."

"She asked you to get them for her?"

"Yes."

"But she was not allowed to see anyone. How did you see her?"

"I didn't. She telephoned."

"Ah! And she said—what?"

"Would I get her a two-pound box of Fuller's chocolates."

"How did her voice sound—weak?"

"No—not at all. Quite strong. But different somehow. I didn't realize it was she speaking at first."

"Until she told you who she was?"

"Yes."

"Are you sure, Madame, that it was your friend?"

Frederica looked startled.

"I—I—why, of course it was. Who else could it have been?"

"That is an interesting question, Madame."

"You don't mean—"

"Could you swear, Madame, that it was your friend's voice—apart from what she said?"

"No," said Frederica slowly. "I couldn't. Her voice was certainly different. I thought it was the phone—or perhaps being ill. . . ."

"If she had not told you who she was, you would not have recognized her?"

"No, no, I don't think I should. Who was it, M. Poirot? Who was it?"

"That is what I mean to know, Madame."

The graveness of his face seemed to awaken her suspicions.

"Is Nick—has anything happened?" she asked breathlessly.

Poirot nodded.

"She is ill—dangerously ill. Those chocolates, Madame—were poisoned."

"The chocolates *I* sent her? But that's impossible—impossible!"

"Not impossible, Madame, since Mademoiselle is at death's door."

"Oh! my God." She hid her face in her hands, then raised it white and quivering. "I don't understand—I don't understand. The other, yes, but not this. They couldn't be poisoned. Nobody ever touched them but me and Jim. You're making some dreadful mistake, M. Poirot."

"It is not I that made a mistake—even though my name was in the box."

She stared at him blankly.

"If Mademoiselle Nick dies—" he said, and made a threatening gesture with his hand.

She gave a low cry.

He turned away, and taking me by the arm, went up to the sitting room.

He flung his hat on the table.

"I understand nothing—but nothing! I am in the dark. I am a little child. Who stands to gain by Mademoiselle's death? Madame Rice. Who buys the chocolates and admits it and tells a story of being rung up on the telephone that cannot hold water for a minute? Madame Rice. It is too simple—too stupid. And she is not stupid—no."

"Well, then—"

"But she takes cocaine, Hastings. I am certain she takes cocaine. There is no mistaking it. And there was cocaine in those chocolates. And what does she mean when she said, 'The other, yes, but not this.' It needs explaining, that! And the sleek M. Lazarus—what is he doing in all this? What does she know, Madame Rice? She knows something. But I cannot make her speak. She is not of those you can frighten into speech. But she knows something, Hastings. Is her tale of the telephone true, or did she invent it? If it is true, whose voice was it?

"I tell you, Hastings, this is all very black—very black."

"Always darkest before dawn," I said reassuringly.

He shook his head.

"Then the other box—that came by post. Can we rule that out? No, we cannot, because Mademoiselle is not sure. It is an annoyance, that!"

He groaned.

I was about to speak when he stopped me.

"No, no. Not another proverb. I cannot bear it. If you would be the good friend—the good helpful friend—"

"Yes," I said eagerly.

"Go out, I beg of you, and buy me some playing cards."

I stared.

"Very well," I said coldly.

I could not but suspect that he was making a deliberate excuse to get rid of me.

Here, however, I misjudged him. That night, when I came into the sitting room about ten o'clock, I found Poirot carefully building card houses—and I remembered!

It was an old trick of his—soothing his nerves. He smiled at me.

"Yes—you remember. One needs the precision. One card on another—so—in exactly the right place and that supports the weight of the card on top and so on, up and up. Go to bed, Hastings. Leave me here, with my house of cards. I clear the mind."

It was about five in the morning when I was shaken awake.

Poirot was standing by my bedside. He looked pleased and happy.

"It was very just what you said, *mon ami*—Oh! it was very just. More, it was *spirituel*!"

I blinked at him, being imperfectly awake.

"Always darkest before dawn—that is what you said. It has been very dark—and now it is dawn."

I looked at the window. He was perfectly right.

"No, no, Hastings. In the head! The mind! The little grey cells!"

He paused and then said quietly:

"You see, Hastings, Mademoiselle is dead."

"What?" I cried, suddenly wide awake.

"Hush—hush. It is as I say. Not really—*bien entendu*—but it can be arranged. Yes, for twenty-four hours it can be arranged. I arrange it with the doctors, with the nurses.

"You comprehend, Hastings? The murderer has been successful. Four times he has tried and failed. The fifth time he has succeeded.

"And now, we shall see what happens next. . . .

"It will be very interesting."

18

The Face at the Window

THE EVENTS OF the next day are completely hazy in my memory. I was unfortunate enough to awake with fever on me. I have been liable to these bouts of fever at inconvenient times ever since I once contracted malaria.

In consequence, the events of that day take on in my memory the semblance of a nightmare—with Poirot coming and going as a kind of fantastic clown, making a periodic appearance in a circus.

He was, I fancy, enjoying himself to the full. His pose of baffled despair was admirable. How he achieved the end he had in view and which he had disclosed to me in the early hours of the morning, I cannot say. But achieve it, he did.

It cannot have been easy. The amount of deception and subterfuge involved must have been colossal. The English character is averse to lying on a wholesale scale and that, no less, was what Poirot's plan required. He had, first, to get Dr. Graham converted to the scheme. With Dr. Graham on his side, he had to persuade the Matron and some members of the staff of the nursing home to conform to the plan. There again, the difficulties must have been immense. It was probably Dr. Graham's influence that turned the scale.

Then there was the Chief Constable and the police. Here, Poirot would be up against officialdom. Nevertheless he wrung at last an unwilling consent out of Colonel Weston. The Colonel made it clear that it was in no way his responsibility. Poirot and Poirot alone was responsible for the spreading abroad of these lying reports. Poirot agreed. He would have agreed to anything so long as he was permitted to carry out his plan.

I spent most of the day dozing in a large armchair with a rug over my knees. Every two or three hours or so, Poirot would burst in and report progress.

"*Comment ça va, mon ami*? How I commiserate you. But it is as well, perhaps. The farce, you do not play it as well as I do. I come this moment from ordering a wreath—a wreath immense—stupendous. Lilies, my friend—large quantities of lilies. '*With heartfelt regret. From Hercule Poirot.*' Ah! what a comedy."

He departed again.

"I come from a most poignant conversation with Madame Rice," was his next piece of information. "Very well dressed in the black, that one. Her poor friend—what a tragedy! I groan sympathetically. Nick, she says, was so joyous, so full of life. Impossible to think of her as dead. I agree. 'It is,' I say, 'the irony of death that it takes one like that. The old and useless are left.' Oh! *là là* I groan again."

"How you are enjoying this," I murmured feebly.

"*Du tout.* It is part of my plan, that is all. To play the comedy successfully, you must put the heart into it. Well, then, the conventional expressions of regret over, Madame comes to matters nearer home. All night she has lain awake wondering about those sweets. It is impossible—impossible. 'Madame,' I say. 'It is not impossible. You can see the analyst's report.' Then she says, and her voice is far from steady, 'It was—cocaine, you say?' I assent. And she says, 'Oh! my God. I don't understand.' "

"Perhaps that's true."

"She understands well enough that she is in danger. She is intelligent. I told you that before. Yes, she is in danger, and she knows it."

"And yet it seems to me that for the first time you don't believe her guilty."

Poirot frowned. The excitement of his manner abated.

"It is profound what you say there, Hastings. No—it seems to me that—somehow—the facts no longer fit. These crimes—so far what has marked them most—the subtlety, is it not? And here is no subtlety at all—only the crudity, pure and simple. No, it does not fit."

He sat down at the table.

"*Voilà*—let us examine the facts. There are three possibilities. There are the sweets bought by Madame and delivered by M. Lazarus. And in that case the guilt rests with one or the other or both. And the telephone call, supposedly from Mademoiselle Nick, that is an invention pure and simple. That is the straightforward—the obvious solution.

"Solution 2. The other box of sweets—that which came by post. Anyone may have sent those. Any of the suspects on our list from A. to J. (You remember? A very wide field.)But, if that were the guilty box, what is the point of the telephone call? Why complicate matters with a second box?"

I shook my head feebly. With a temperature of 102°, any complication seemed to me quite unnecessary and absurd.

"Solution 3. A poisoned box was substituted for the innocent box bought by Madame. In that case the telephone call is ingenious and understandable. Madame is to be what you call the kitten's paw. She is to pull the roasting chestnuts out of the fire. So Solution 3 is the most logical—but, alas, it is also the most difficult. How be sure of substituting a box at the right moment? The orderly might take the box straight upstairs—a hundred and one possibilities might prevent the substitution being effected. No, it does not seem sense."

"Unless it were Lazarus," I said.

Poirot looked at me.

"You have the fever, my friend. It mounts, does it not?"

I nodded.

"Curious how a few degrees of heat should stimulate the intellect. You have uttered there an observation of profound simplicity. So simple, was it, that I had failed to consider it. But it would suppose a very curious state of affairs. M. Lazarus, the dear friend of Madame, doing his best to get her hanged. It opens up possibilities of a very curious nature. But complex—very complex."

I closed my eyes. I was glad I had been brilliant, but I did not want to think of anything complex. I wanted to go to sleep.

Poirot, I think, went on talking, but I did not listen. His voice was vaguely soothing. . . .

It was late afternoon when I saw him next.

"My little plan, it has made the fortune of the flower shops," he announced. "Everybody orders wreaths. M. Croft, M. Vyse, Commander Challenger—"

The last name awoke a chord of compunction in my mind.

"Look here, Poirot," I said. "You must let him in on this. Poor fellow, he will be distracted with grief. It isn't fair."

"You have always the tenderness for him, Hastings."

"I like him. He's a thoroughly decent chap. You've got to take him into the secret."

Poirot shook his head.

"No, *mon ami*. I do not make the exceptions."

"But you don't suspect him of having anything to do with it?"

"I do not make the exceptions."

"Think how he must be suffering."

"On the contrary, I prefer to think of what a joyful surprise I prepare for him. To think the loved one dead—and find her alive! It is a sensation unique—stupendous."

"What a pig-headed old devil you are. He'd keep the secret all right."

"I am not so sure."

"He's the soul of honor. I'm certain of it."

"That makes it all the more difficult to keep a secret. Keeping a secret is an art that requires many lies magnificently told, and a great aptitude for playing the comedy and enjoying it. Could he dissemble, the Commander Challenger? If he is what you say he is, he certainly could not."

"Then you won't tell him?"

"I certainly refuse to imperil my little idea for the sake of the sentiment. It is life and death we play with, *mon cher*. Anyway, the suffering, it is good for the character. Many of your famous clergymen have said so—even a bishop if I am not mistaken."

I made no further attempt to shake his decision. His mind, I could see, was made up.

"I shall not dress for dinner," he murmured. "I am too much the broken old man. That is my part, you understand. All my self-confidence has crashed—I am broken. I have failed. I shall eat hardly any dinner—the food untasted on the plate. That is the attitude, I think. In my own apartment I will consume some brioches and some chocolate éclairs (so called) which I had the foresight to buy at a confectioner's. *Et vous?*"

"Some more quinine, I think," I said sadly.

"Alas, my poor Hastings. But courage, all will be well tomorrow."

"Very likely. These attacks often last only twenty-four hours."

I did not hear him return to the room. I must have been asleep.

When I awoke, he was sitting at the table writing. In front of him was a crumpled sheet of paper smoothed out. I recognized it for the paper on which he had written that list of people—A. to J.—which he had afterwards crumpled up and thrown away.

He nodded in answer to my unspoken thought.

"Yes, my friend, I have resurrected it. I am at work upon it from a different angle. I compile a list of questions concerning each person. The questions may have no bearing on the crime—they are just things that I do not know—things that remain unexplained and for which I seek to supply the answer from my own brain."

"How far have you got?"

"I have finished. You would like to hear? You are strong enough?"

"Yes, as a matter of fact, I am feeling a great deal better."

"*À la bonheur!* Very well, I will read them to you. Some of them, no doubt, you will consider puerile."

He cleared his throat.

"A. *Ellen.* Why did she remain in the house and not go out to see fireworks? (Unusual, as Mademoiselle's evidence and surprise make clear.) What did she think or suspect might happen? Did she admit anyone (J. for instance) to the house? Is she speaking the truth about the secret panel? If there is such a thing why is she unable to remember where it is? (Mademoiselle seems very certain there is no such thing—and she would surely know.) If she invented it, why did she invent it? Had she read Michael Seton's love letters or was her surprise at Mademoiselle Nick's engagement genuine?

"B. *Her husband.* Is he as stupid as he seems? Does he share Ellen's knowledge whatever it is, or does he not? Is he, in any respect, a mental case?

"C. *The child.* Is his delight in blood a natural instinct common to his age and development, or is it morbid, and is that morbidity inherited from either parent? Has he ever shot with a toy pistol?

"D. *Who is Mr. Croft?* Where does he really come from? Did he post the will as he swears he did? What motive could he have in not posting it?

"E. *Same as above.* Who are Mr. and Mrs. Croft? Are they in hiding for some reason—and if so, what reason? Have they any connection with the Buckley family?

"F. *Mrs. Rice.* Was she really aware of the engagement between Nick and Michael Seton? Did she merely guess it, or had she actually read the letters which passed between them? (In that case she would know Mademoiselle was Seton's heir.) Did she know that she herself was Mademoiselle's residuary legatee? (This, I think, is likely. Mademoiselle would probably tell her so, adding perhaps that she would not get much out of it.) Is there any truth in Commander Challenger's suggestion that Lazarus was attracted by Mademoiselle Nick? (This might explain a certain lack of cordiality between the two friends which seems to have shown itself in the last few months.) Who is the 'boy friend' mentioned in her note as supplying the drug? Could this possibly be J.? Why did she turn faint one day in this room? Was it something that had been said—or was it something she *saw*? Is her account of the telephone message asking her to buy chocolates correct—or is it a deliberate lie? What did she mean by 'I can understand the other—but not this'? If she is not herself guilty, what knowledge has she got that she is keeping to herself?

"You perceive," said Poirot, suddenly breaking off, "that the questions concerning Madame Rice are almost innumerable. From beginning to end, she is an enigma. And that forces me to a conclusion. Either Madame Rice is guilty, or she knows—or shall we say, thinks she knows—who is guilty. But is she right? Does she know or does she merely suspect? And how is it possible to make her speak?"

He sighed.

"Well, I will go on with my list of questions.

"G. *Mr. Lazarus*. Curious—there are practically no questions to ask concerning him—except the crude one, 'Did he substitute the poisoned sweets?' Otherwise I find only one totally irrelevant question. But I have put it down. 'Why did M. Lazarus offer fifty pounds for a picture that was only worth twenty?' "

"He wanted to do Nick a good turn," I suggested.

"He would not do it that way. He is a dealer. He does not buy to sell at a loss. If he wished to be amiable he would lend her money as a private individual."

"It can't have any bearing on the crime, anyway."

"No, that is true—but all the same, I should like to know. I am a student of the psychology, you understand.

"Now we come to H.

"H. *Commander Challenger*. Why did Mademoiselle Nick tell him she was engaged to someone else? What necessitated her having to tell him that? She told no one else. Had he proposed to her? What are his relations with his uncle?"

"His uncle, Poirot?"

"Yes, the doctor. That rather questionable character. Did any private news of Michael Seton's death come through to the Admiralty before it was announced publicly?"

"I don't quite see what you're driving at, Poirot. Even if Challenger knew beforehand about Seton's death, it does not seem to get us anywhere. It provides no earthly motive for killing the girl he loved."

"I quite agree. What you say is perfectly reasonable. But these are just things I should like to know. I am still the dog, you see, nosing about for the things that are not very nice!

"I. *Mr. Vyse*. Why did he say what he did about his cousin's fanatical devotion to End House? What possible motive could he have in saying that? Did he, or did he not, receive the will? Is he, in fact, an honest man—or is he not an honest man?

"And now J. *Eh bien*, J. is what I put down before—a giant question mark. Is there such a person, or is there not—

"*Mon Dieu*! my friend, what have you?"

I had started from my chair with a sudden shriek. With a shaking hand I pointed at the window.

"A face, Poirot!" I cried. "A face pressed against the glass. A dreadful face! It's gone now—but I saw it."

Poirot strode to the window and pushed it open. He leant out.

"There is no one there now," he said thoughtfully. "You are sure you did not imagine it, Hastings?"

"Quite sure. It was a horrible face."

"There is a balcony, of course. Anyone could reach there quite easily if they wanted to hear what we were saying. When you say a dreadful face, Hastings, just what do you mean?"

"A white staring face, hardly human."

"*Mon ami*, that is the fever. A face, yes. An unpleasant face, yes. But a face hardly human—no. What you saw was the effect of a face pressed closely against the glass—that allied to the shock of seeing it there at all."

"It was a dreadful face," I said obstinately.

"It was not the face of—anyone you knew?"

"No, indeed."

"Mm—it might have been, though! I doubt if you would recognize it under these circumstances. I wonder now—yes, I very much wonder. . . ."

He gathered up his papers thoughtfully.

"One thing at least is to the good. If the owner of that face overheard our conversation we did not mention that Mademoiselle Nick was alive and well. Whatever else our visitor may have heard, that at least escaped him."

"But surely," I said, "the results of this—er—brilliant maneuver of yours have been slightly disappointing up to date. Nick is dead and no startling developments have occurred!"

"I did not expect them yet awhile. Twenty-four hours, I said. *Mon ami*, tomorrow, if I am not mistaken, certain things will arise. Otherwise I am wrong from start to finish. There is the post, you see. I have hopes of tomorrow's post."

I awoke in the morning feeling weak but with the fever abated. I also felt hungry. Poirot and I had breakfast served in our sitting room.

"Well?" I said maliciously, as he sorted his letters. "Has the post done what you expected of it?"

Poirot, who had just opened two envelopes which patently contained bills, did not reply. I thought he looked rather cast down and not his usual cock-a-hoop self.

I opened my own mail. The first was a notice of a Spiritualist meeting.

"If all else fails, we must go to the Spiritualists," I remarked. "I often wonder that more tests of this kind aren't made. The spirit of the victim comes back and names the murderer. That would be a proof."

"It would hardly help us," said Poirot absently. "I doubt if Maggie Buckley knew whose hand it was shot her down. Even if she could speak she would have nothing of value to tell us. *Tiens*, that is odd."

"What is?"

"You talk of the dead speaking, and at that moment I open this letter."

He tossed it across to me. It was from Mrs. Buckley.

Langley Rectory

Dear M. Poirot,

On my return here I found a letter written by my poor child on her arrival at St. Loo. There is nothing in it of interest to you, I'm afraid, but I thought perhaps you would care to see it.

Thanking you for your kindness,

Yours sincerely,
Jean Buckley

The enclosure brought a lump to my throat. It was so terribly commonplace and so completely untouched by any apprehension of tragedy.

Dear Mother,

I arrived safely. Quite a comfortable journey. Only two other people in the carriage all the way to Exeter.

It is lovely weather here. Nick seems very well and gay—a little restless perhaps, but I cannot see why she should have telegraphed for me in the way she did. Tuesday would have done just as well.

No more now. We are going to have tea with some neighbors. They are Australians and have rented the lodge. Nick says they are kind but rather awful. Mrs. Rice and Mr. Lazarus are coming to stay. He is the art dealer. I will post this in the box by the gate, then it will catch the post. Will write tomorrow.

Your loving daughter,
Maggie

P.S. Nick says there is a reason for her wire. She will tell me after tea. She is very queer and jumpy.

"The voice of the dead," said Poirot quietly. "And it tells us—nothing."

"The box by the gate," I remarked idly. "That's where Croft said he posted the will."

"Said so—yes. I wonder. How I wonder!"

"There is nothing else of interest among your letters?"

"Nothing, Hastings, I am very unhappy. I am in the dark. Still in the dark. I comprehend nothing."

At that moment the telephone rang. Poirot went to it.

Immediately I saw a change come over his face. His manner was very restrained, nevertheless he could not disguise from my eyes his intense excitement.

His own contributions to the conversation were entirely non-committal so that I could not gather what it was all about.

Presently, however, with a "*Très bien. Je vous remercie*," he put back the receiver and came back to where I was sitting. His eyes were sparkling with excitement.

"*Mon ami*," he said. "What did I tell you? Things have begun to happen."

"What was it?"

"That was M. Charles Vyse on the telephone. He informs me that this morning, through the post, he has received a will signed by his cousin, Miss Buckley, and dated the 25th of February, last."

"What? *The* will?"

"*Évidemment.*"

"It has turned up?"

"Just at the right moment, *n'est-ce pas*?"

"Do you think he is speaking the truth?"

"Or do I think he has had the will all along? Is that what you say? Well, it is all a little curious. But one thing is certain. I told you that if Mademoiselle Nick was supposed to be dead, we should have developments—and sure enough here they are!"

"Extraordinary," I said. "You were right. I suppose this is the will making Frederica Rice residuary legatee?"

"M. Vyse said nothing about the contents of the will. He was far too correct. But there seems very little reason to doubt that this is the same will. It is witnessed, he tells me, by Ellen Wilson and her husband."

"So we are back at the old problem," I said. "Frederica Rice."

"The enigma!"

"Frederica Rice," I murmured inconsequently. "It's a pretty name."

"Prettier than what her friends call her. Freddie"—he made a face—"*ce n'est pas jolie*—for a young lady."

"There aren't many abbreviations of Frederica," I said. "It's not like Margaret where you can have half a dozen—Maggie, Margot, Madge, Peggie—"

"True. Well, Hastings, are you happier now? That things have begun to happen?"

"Yes, of course. Tell me—did you expect this to happen?"

"No—not exactly. I had formulated nothing very precise to myself. All I had said was that given a certain result, the causes of that result must make themselves evident."

"Yes," I said respectfully.

"What was it that I was going to say just as that telephone rang?" mused Poirot. "Oh! yes, that letter from Mademoiselle Maggie. I wanted to look at it once again. I have an idea in the back of my mind that something in it struck me as rather curious."

I picked it up from where I had tossed it, and handed it to him.

He read it over to himself. I moved about the room, looking out of the window and observing the yachts racing on the bay.

Suddenly an exclamation startled me. I turned around.

Poirot was holding his head in his hands and rocking himself to and fro apparently in an agony of woe.

"Oh!" he groaned, "but I have been blind—blind."

"What's the matter?"

"Complex, I have said? Complicated? *Mais non.* Of a simplicity extreme—extreme. And miserable one that I am, I saw nothing—nothing."

"Good gracious, Poirot, what is this light that has suddenly burst upon you?"

"Wait—wait—do not speak. I must arrange my ideas. Rearrange them in the light of this discovery so stupendous."

Seizing his list of questions, he ran over them silently, his lips moving busily. Once or twice he nodded his head emphatically.

Then he laid them down and leaning back in his chair he shut his eyes. I thought at last that he had gone to sleep.

Suddenly he sighed and opened his eyes.

"But yes!" he said. "It all fits in! All the things that have puzzled me. All the things that have seemed to me a little unnatural. They all have their place."

"You mean—you know everything?"

"Nearly everything. All that matters. In some respects I have been right in my deductions. In other ways ludicrously far from the truth. But now it is all clear. I shall send today a telegram asking two questions—but the answers to them I know already—I know here!" He tapped his forehead.

"And when you receive the answers?" I asked curiously.

He sprang to his feet.

"My friend, do you remember that Mademoiselle Nick said she wanted to stage a play at End House? Tonight, we stage such a play in End House. But it will be a play produced by Hercule Poirot. Mademoiselle Nick will have a part to play in it." He grinned suddenly. "You comprehend, Hastings, there will be a ghost in this play. Yes, a ghost. End House has never seen a ghost. It will have one tonight. No—" as I tried to ask a question. "I will say no more. Tonight, Hastings, we will produce our comedy—and reveal the truth. But now, there is much to do—much to do."

He hurried from the room.

19

Poirot Produces a Play

IT WAS A curious gathering that met that night at End House.

I had hardly seen Poirot all day. He had been out for dinner but had left me a message that I was to be at End House at nine o'clock. Evening dress, he had added, was not necessary.

The whole thing was like a rather ridiculous dream.

On arrival I was ushered into the dining room, and when I looked round I realized that every person on Poirot's list from A. to I. (J. was necessarily excluded, being in the Mrs. Harris-like position of "there ain't no sich person") was present.

Even Mrs. Croft was there in a kind of invalid chair. She smiled and nodded at me.

"This is a surprise, isn't it?" she said cheerfully. "It makes a change for me, I must say. I think I shall try and get out now and again. All M. Poirot's idea. Come and sit by me, Captain Hastings. Somehow I feel this is rather a gruesome business—but Mr. Vyse made a point of it."

"Mr. Vyse?" I said rather surprised.

Charles Vyse was standing by the mantelpiece. Poirot was beside him talking earnestly to him in an undertone.

I looked round the room. Yes, they were all there. After showing me in (I had been a minute or two late) Ellen had taken her place on a chair just beside the door. On another chair, sitting painfully straight and breathing hard, was her husband. The child, Alfred, squirmed uneasily between his father and mother.

The rest sat round the dining-table. Frederica in her black dress, Lazarus beside her, George Challenger and Croft on the other side of the table. I sat a little away from it near Mrs. Croft. And now Charles Vyse with a final nod of the head took his place at the head of the table and Poirot slipped unobtrusively into a seat next to Lazarus.

Clearly the producer, as Poirot had styled himself, did not propose to take a prominent part in the play. Charles Vyse was apparently in charge of the proceedings. I wondered what surprises Poirot had in store for him.

The young lawyer cleared his throat and stood up. He looked just the same as ever, impassive, formal and unemotional.

"This is rather an unconventional gathering we have here tonight," he said. "But the circumstances are very peculiar. I refer, of course, to the circumstances surrounding the death of my cousin, Miss Buckley. There will have, of course, to be an autopsy—there seems to be no doubt that she met her death by poison, and that that poison was administered with the intent to kill. This is police business and I need not go into it. The police would doubtless prefer me not to do so.

"In an ordinary case, the will of a deceased person is read after the funeral, but in deference to M. Poirot's especial wish, I am proposing to read it before the funeral takes place. In fact, I am proposing to read it here and now. That is why everyone has been asked to come here. As I said just now, the circumstances are unusual and justify a departure from precedent.

"The will itself came into my possession in a somewhat unusual manner. Although dated last February, it only reached me by post this morning. However, it is undoubtedly in the handwriting of my cousin—I have no doubt on that point, and though a most informal document, it is properly attested."

He paused and cleared his throat once more.

Every eye was upon his face.

From a long envelope in his hand, he drew out an enclosure. It was, as we could see, an ordinary piece of End House notepaper with writing on it.

"It is quite short," said Vyse. He made a suitable pause, then began to read.

"This is the last Will and Testament of Magdala Buckley. I direct that all my funeral expenses should be paid and I appoint my cousin

Charles Vyse as my executor. I leave everything of which I die possessed to Mildred Croft in grateful recognition of the services rendered by her to my father Philip Buckley which services nothing can ever repay.

"*Signed Magdala Buckley*
"*Witnesses Ellen Wilson*
       "*William Wilson*"

I was dumbfounded! So I think was everyone else. Only Mrs. Croft nodded her head in quiet understanding.

"It's true," she said quietly. "Not that I ever meant to let on about it. Philip Buckley was out in Australia, and if it hadn't been for me—well, I'm not going into that. A secret it's been and a secret it had better remain. She knew about it, though. Nick did, I mean. Her father must have told her. We came down here because we wanted to have a look at the place. I'd always been curious about this End House Philip Buckley talked of. And that dear girl knew all about it, and couldn't do enough for us. Wanted us to come and live with her, she did. But we wouldn't do that. And so she insisted on our having the lodge—and not a penny of rent would she take. We pretended to pay it, of course, so as not to cause talk, but she handed it back to us. And now—this! Well, if anyone says there is no gratitude in the world, I'll tell them they're wrong! This proves it."

There was still an amazed silence. Poirot looked at Vyse.

"Had you any idea of this?"

Vyse shook his head.

"I knew Philip Buckley had been in Australia. But I never heard any rumors of a scandal there."

He looked inquiringly at Mrs. Croft.

She shook her head.

"No, you won't get a word out of me. I never have said a word and I never shall. The secret goes to the grave with me."

Vyse said nothing. He sat quietly tapping the table with a pencil.

"I presume, M. Vyse"—Poirot leaned forward—"that as next of kin, you could contest that will? There is, I understand, a vast fortune at stake which was not the case when the will was made."

Vyse looked at him coldly.

"The will is perfectly valid. I should not dream of contesting my cousin's disposal of her property."

"You're an honest fellow," said Mrs. Croft approvingly, "and I'll see you don't lose by it."

Charles shrank a little from this well-meant but slightly embarrassing remark.

"Well, Mother," said Mr. Croft, with an elation he could not quite keep out of his voice. "This is a surprise! Nick didn't tell me what she was doing."

"The dear sweet girl," murmured Mrs. Croft putting her handkerchief to her eyes. "I wish she could look down and see us now. Perhaps she does—who knows?"

"Perhaps," agreed Poirot.

Suddenly an idea seemed to strike him. He looked round.

"An idea! We are all here seated round a table. Let us hold a *séance*."

"A *séance*?" said Mrs. Croft somewhat shocked. "But surely—"

"Yes, yes, it will be most interesting. Hastings, here, has pronounced mediumistic powers." (Why fix on me, I thought.) "To get through a message from the other world—the opportunity is unique! I feel the conditions are propitious. You feel the same, Hastings?"

"Yes," I said resolutely, playing up.

"Good. I knew it. Quick, the lights."

In another minute he had risen and switched them off. The whole thing had been rushed on the company before they had the energy to protest, had they wanted to do so. As a matter of fact they were, I think, still dazed with astonishment over the will.

The room was not quite dark. The curtains were drawn back and the window was open for it was a hot night, and through those windows came a faint light. After a minute or two, as we sat in silence, I began to be able to make out the faint outlines of the furniture. I wondered very much what I was supposed to do and cursed Poirot heartily for not having given me my instructions beforehand.

However, I closed my eyes and breathed in a rather stertorous manner.

Presently Poirot rose and tiptoed to my chair. Then returning to his own, he murmured: "Yes, he is already in a trance. Soon—things will begin to happen."

There is something about sitting in the dark, waiting, that fills one with unbearable apprehension. I know that I myself was a prey to nerves and so, I am sure, was everyone else. And yet I had at least an idea of what was about to happen. I knew the one vital fact that no one else knew.

And yet in spite of all that, my heart leapt into my mouth as I saw the dining-room door slowly opening. It did so quite soundlessly (it must have been oiled) and the effect was horribly grisly. It swung slowly open and for a minute or two that was all. With its opening a cold blast of air seemed to enter the room. It was, I suppose, a common or garden draft owing to the open window, but it felt like the icy chill mentioned in all the ghost stories I have ever read.

And then we all saw it! Framed in the doorway was a white shadowy figure. Nick Buckley. . . .

She advanced slowly and noiselessly—with a kind of floating ethereal motion that certainly conveyed the impression of nothing human. . . .

I realized then what an actress the world had missed. Nick had wanted to play a part at End House. Now she was playing it, and I felt convinced that she was enjoying herself to the core. She did it perfectly.

She floated forward into the room—and the silence was broken.

There was a gasping cry from the invalid chair beside me. A kind of gurgle from Mr. Croft. A startled oath from Challenger. Charles Vyse drew back his chair, I think. Lazarus leaned forward. Frederica alone made no sound or movement.

And then a scream rent the room. Ellen sprang up from her chair.

"It's her!" she shrieked. "She's come back. She's walking! Them that's murdered always walks. It's her! It's her!"

And then, with a click the lights went on.

I saw Poirot standing by them, the smile of the ringmaster on his face. Nick stood in the middle of the room in her white draperies.

It was Frederica who spoke first. She stretched out an unbelieving hand—touched her friend.

"Nick," she said. "You're—you're real!"

It was almost a whisper.

Nick laughed. She advanced.

"Yes," she said. "I'm real enough. Thank you so much for what you did for my father, Mrs. Croft. But I'm afraid you won't be able to enjoy the benefit of that will just yet."

"Oh! my God," gasped Mrs. Croft. "Oh! my God." She twisted to and fro in her chair. "Take me away, Bert. Take me away. It was all a joke, my dear—all a joke, that's all it was. Honest."

"A queer sort of joke," said Nick.

The door had opened again and a man had entered so quietly that I had not heard him. To my surprise I saw that it was Japp. He exchanged a quick nod with Poirot as though satisfying him of something. Then his face suddenly lit up and he took a step forward towards the squirming figure in the invalid chair.

"Hullo-ullo-ullo," he said. "What's this? An old friend! Milly Merton, I declare! And at your old tricks again, my dear."

He turned round in an explanatory way to the company,

disregarding Mrs. Croft's shrill protests.

"Cleverest forger we've ever had, Milly Merton. We knew there had been an accident to the car they made their last getaway in. But there! Even an injury to the spine wouldn't keep Milly from her tricks. She's an artist, she is!"

"Was that will a forgery?" said Vyse.

He spoke in tones of amazement.

"Of course it was a forgery," said Nick scornfully. "You don't think I'd make a silly will like that, do you? I left you End House, Charles, and everything else to Frederica."

She crossed as she spoke and stood by her friend, and just at that moment *it happened*!

A spurt of flame from the window and the hiss of a bullet. Then another and the sound of a groan and a fall outside. . . .

And Frederica on her feet with a thin trickle of blood running down her arm. . . .

20

J.

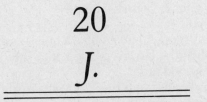

IT WAS ALL so sudden that for a moment no one knew what had happened.

Then, with a violent exclamation, Poirot ran to the window. Challenger was with him.

A moment later they reappeared, carrying with them the limp body of a man. As they lowered him carefully into a big leather armchair and his face came into view, I uttered a cry. "The face—the face at the window."

It was the man I had seen looking in on us the previous evening. I recognised him at once. I realized that when I had said he was hardly human I had exaggerated as Poirot had accused me of doing.

Yet there was something about his face that justified my impression. It was a lost face—the face of one removed from ordinary humanity.

White, weak, depraved, it seemed a mere mask—as though the spirit within had fled long ago.

Down the side of it there trickled a stream of blood.

Frederica came slowly forward till she stood by the chair.

Poirot intercepted her.

"You are hurt, Madame?"

She shook her head.

"The bullet grazed my shoulder—that is all."

She put him aside with a gentle hand and bent down.

The man's eyes opened and he saw her looking down at him.

"I've done for you this time, I hope," he said, in a low vicious snarl, and then, his voice changing suddenly till it sounded like a child's, "Oh! Freddie, I didn't mean it. I didn't mean it. You've always been so decent to me. . . . "

"It's all right—"

She knelt down beside him.

"I didn't mean—"

His head dropped. The sentence was never finished.

Frederica looked up at Poirot.

"Yes, Madame, he is dead," he said gently.

She rose slowly from her knees and stood looking down at him. With one hand she touched his forehead—pitifully, it seemed. Then she sighed and turned to the rest of us.

"He was my husband," she said quietly.

"J.," I murmured.

Poirot caught my remark and nodded a quick assent.

"Yes," he said softly. "Always I felt that there was a J. I said so from the beginning, did I not?"

"He was my husband," said Frederica again. Her voice was terribly tired. She sank into a chair that Lazarus brought for her. "I might as well tell you everything—now.

"He was—completely debased. He was a drug fiend. He taught me to take drugs. I have been fighting the habit ever since I left him. I think—at last—I am nearly cured. But it has been—difficult. Oh! so horribly difficult. Nobody knows how difficult!

"I could never escape from him. He used to turn up and demand money—with threats. A kind of blackmail. If I did not give him money he would shoot himself. That was always his threat. Then he took to threatening to shoot me. He was not responsible. He was mad—crazy. . . .

"I suppose it was he who shot Maggie Buckley. He didn't mean to shoot her, of course. He must have thought it was me.

"I ought to have said, I suppose. But after all, I wasn't sure. And those queer accidents Nick had—that made me feel that perhaps it wasn't him after all. It might have been someone quite different.

"And then—one day—I saw a bit of his handwriting on a torn piece of paper on M. Poirot's table. It was a part of a letter he had sent me. I knew then that M. Poirot was on the track.

"Since then I have felt that it was only a matter of time. . . .

"But I don't understand about the sweets. He wouldn't have wanted to poison Nick. And anyway, I don't see how he could have had anything to do with that. I've puzzled and puzzled."

She put both hands to her face, then took them away and said with a queer pathetic finality:

"That's all. . . . "

21

The Person—K.

LAZARUS CAME QUICKLY to her side.

"My dear," he said. "My dear."

Poirot went to the sideboard, poured out a glass of wine and brought it to her, standing over her while she drank it.

She handed the glass back to him and smiled.

"I'm all right now," she said. "What—what had we better do next?"

She looked at Japp, but the Inspector shook his head.

"I'm on a holiday, Miss Rice. Just obliging an old friend—that's all I'm doing. The St. Loo police are in charge of the case."

She looked at Poirot.

"And M. Poirot is in charge of the St. Loo police?"

"Oh! *quelle idée, Madame!* I am a mere humble adviser."

"M. Poirot," said Nick, "can't we hush it up?"

"You wish that, Mademoiselle?"

"Yes. After all—I'm the person most concerned. And there will be no more attacks on me—now."

"No, that is true. There will be no more attacks on you now."

"You're thinking of Maggie. But, M. Poirot, nothing will bring Maggie back to life again. If you make all this public, you'll only bring a terrible lot of suffering and publicity on Frederica—and she hasn't deserved it."

"You say she has not deserved it?"

"Of course she hasn't! I told you right at the beginning that she had a brute of a husband. You've seen tonight—what he was. Well, he's dead. Let that be the end of things. Let the police go on looking for the man who shot Maggie. They just won't find him, that's all."

"So that is what you say, Mademoiselle? Hush it all up."

"Yes. Please. Oh! please. Please, dear M. Poirot."

Poirot looked slowly round.

"What do you all say?"

Each spoke in turn.

"I agree," I said as Poirot looked at me.

"I too," said Lazarus.

"Best thing to do," from Challenger.

"Let's forget everything that's passed in this room tonight." This very determinedly from Croft.

"You would say that!" interpolated Japp.

"Don't be hard on me, dearie," his wife sniffed to Nick, who looked at her scornfully but made no reply.

"Ellen?"

"Me and William won't say a word, sir. Least said, soonest mended."

"And you, M. Vyse?"

"A thing like this can't be hushed up," said Charles Vyse. "The facts must be made known in the proper quarter."

"Charles," cried Nick.

"I'm sorry, dear. I look at it from the legal aspect."

Poirot gave a sudden laugh.

"So you are seven to one. The good Japp is neutral."

"I'm on holiday," said Japp with a grin. "I don't count."

"Seven to one. Only M. Vyse holds out—on the side of law and order! You know, M. Vyse, you are a man of character!"

Vyse shrugged his shoulders.

"The position is quite clear. There is only one thing to do."

"Yes—you are an honest man. *Eh bien*—I, too, range myself on the side of the minority. I, too, am for the truth."

"M. Poirot!" cried Nick.

"Mademoiselle—you dragged me into the case. I came into it at your wish. You cannot silence me now."

He raised a threatening forefinger in a gesture that I knew well.

"Sit down, all of you, and I will tell you—the truth."

Silenced by his imperious attitude, we sat down meekly and turned attentive faces towards him.

"*Écoutez*! I have a list here—a list of persons connected with the crime. I numbered them with the letters of the alphabet including the letter J. J. stood for a person unknown—linked to the crime by one of the others. I did not know who J. was until tonight, but I knew that there was such a person. The events of tonight have proved that I was right.

"But yesterday, I suddenly realized that I had made a grave error. I had made an omission. I added another letter to my list. The letter K."

"Another person unknown?" asked Vyse with a slight sneer.

"Not exactly. I adopted J. as the symbol for a person unknown. Another person unknown would be merely another J. K. has a different significance. It stands for a person who should have been included in the original list, but who was overlooked."

He bent over Frederica.

"Reassure yourself, Madame. Your husband was not guilty of murder. It was the person K. who shot Mademoiselle Maggie."

She stared.

"But who is K.?"

Poirot nodded to Japp. He stepped forward and spoke in tones reminiscent of the days when he had given evidence in police courts.

"Acting on information received, I took up a position here early in the evening, having been introduced secretly into the house by M. Poirot. I was concealed behind the curtains in the drawing room. When everyone was assembled in this room, a young lady entered the drawing room and switched on the light. She made her way to the fireplace, and opened a small recess in the paneling that appeared to be operated with a spring. She took from the recess a pistol. With this in her hand she left the room. I followed her and opening the door a crack I was able to observe her further movements. Coats and wraps had been left in the hall by the visitors on arrival. The young lady carefully wiped the pistol with a handkerchief and then placed it in the pocket of a grey wrap, the property of Mrs. Rice—"

A cry burst from Nick.

"This is untrue—every word of it!"

Poirot pointed a hand at her.

"*Voilà!*" he said. "*The person K.! It was Mademoiselle Nick who shot her cousin, Maggie Buckley.*"

"Are you mad?" cried Nick. "Why should I kill Maggie?"

"In order to inherit the money left to her by Michael Seton! Her name too was Magdala Buckley—and it was to her he was engaged —not you."

"You—you—"

She stood there trembling—unable to speak. Poirot turned to Japp.

"You telephoned to the police?"

"Yes, they are waiting in the hall now. They've got the warrant."

"You're all mad!" cried Nick contemptuously. She moved swiftly to Frederica's side. "Freddie, give me your wrist watch as—as a souvenir, will you?"

Slowly Frederica unclasped the jeweled watch from her wrist and handed it to Nick.

"Thanks. And now—I suppose we must go through with this perfectly ridiculous comedy."

"The comedy you planned and produced in End House. Yes—but you should not have given the star part to Hercule Poirot. That, Mademoiselle, was your mistake—your very grave mistake."

22

The End of the Story

"YOU WANT ME to explain?"

Poirot looked round with a gratified smile and the air of mock humility I knew so well.

We had moved into the drawing room and our numbers had lessened. The domestics had withdrawn tactfully, and the Crofts had been asked to accompany the police. Frederica, Lazarus, Challenger, Vyse and I remained.

"*Eh bien*—I confess it—I was fooled—fooled completely and absolutely. The little Nick, she had me where she wanted me, as your idiom so well expresses it. Ah! Madame, when you said that your friend was a clever little liar—how right you were! How right!"

"Nick always told lies," said Frederica composedly. "That's why I didn't really believe in these marvelous escapes of hers."

"And I—imbecile that I was—did!"

"Didn't they really happen?" I asked. I was, I admit, still hopelessly confused.

"They were invented—very cleverly—to give just the impression they did."

"What was that?"

"They gave the impression that Mademoiselle Nick's life was in danger. But I will begin earlier than that. I will tell you the story as I have pieced it out—not as it came to me imperfectly and in flashes.

"At the beginning of the business then, we have this girl, this Nick Buckley, young and beautiful, unscrupulous, and passionately and fanatically devoted to her home."

Charles Vyse nodded.

"I told you that."

"And you were right. Mademoiselle Nick loved End House. But she had no money. The house was mortgaged. She wanted money—she wanted it feverishly—and she could not get it. She met this young Seton at Le Touquet, he is attracted by her. She knows that in all probability he is his uncle's heir and that that uncle is worth millions. Good, her star is in the ascendant, she thinks. But he is not really seriously attracted. He thinks her good fun, that is all. They meet at Scarborough, he takes her up in his machine and then—the catastrophe occurs. He meets Maggie and falls in love with her at first sight.

"Mademoiselle Nick is dumbfounded. Her cousin Maggie whom she has never even considered pretty! But to young Seton she is 'different.' The one girl in the world for him. They become secretly engaged. Only one person knows—has to know. That person is Mademoiselle Nick. The poor Maggie—she is glad that there is one person she can talk to. Doubtless she reads to her cousin parts of her fiancé's letters. So it is that Mademoiselle gets to hear of the will. She pays no attention to it at the time. But it remains in her mind.

"Then comes the sudden and unexpected death of Sir Matthew Seton and hard upon that the rumors of Michael Seton's being missing. And straight away an outrageous plan comes into our young lady's head. Seton does not know that her name is Magdala also. He only knows her as Nick. His will is clearly quite informal—a mere mention of a name. But in the eyes of the world Seton is her friend! It is with her that his name has been coupled. If she were to claim to be engaged to him, no one would be surprised. But to do that successfully Maggie must be out of the way.

"Time is short. She arranges for Maggie to come and stay in a few days' time. Then she has her escapes from death. The picture whose cord she cuts through. The brake of the car that she tampers with. The boulder—that perhaps was natural and she merely invented the story of being underneath on the path.

"And then—she sees my name in the paper (I told you, Hastings, everyone knew Hercule Poirot!) and she has the audacity to make me an accomplice! The bullet through the hat that falls at my feet. Oh! the pretty comedy. And I am taken in! I believe in the peril that menaces her! *Bon*! She has got a valuable witness on her side. I play into her hands by asking her to send for a friend.

"She seizes the chance and sends for Maggie to come a day earlier.

"How easy the crime is actually. She leaves us at the dinner table and after hearing on the wireless that Seton's death is a fact, she starts to put her plan into action. She has plenty of time then to take Seton's letters to Maggie—look through them and select the few that will answer her purpose. These she places in her own room. Then, later, she and Maggie leave the fireworks and go back to the house. She tells her cousin to put on her shawl. Then stealing out after her, she shoots her. Quick, into the house, the pistol concealed in the secret panel (of whose existence she thinks nobody knows). Then upstairs. There she waits till voices are heard. The body is discovered. It is her cue.

"Down she rushes and out through the window.

"How well she played her part! Magnificently! Oh! yes, she staged a fine drama here. The maid, Ellen, said this was an evil house. I am inclined to agree with her. It was from the house that Mademoiselle took her inspiration."

"But those poisoned sweets," said Frederica. "I still don't understand about that."

"It was all part of the same scheme. Do you not see that if Nick's life was attempted after Maggie was dead that absolutely settled the question that Maggie's death had been a mistake.

"When she thought the time was ripe she rang up Madame Rice and asked her to get her a box of chocolates."

"Then it was her voice?"

"But, yes! How often the simple explanation is the true one! *N'est-ce pas*? She made her voice sound a little different—that was all. So that you might be in doubt when questioned. Then, when the box arrived—again how simple. She fills three of the chocolates with cocaine (she had cocaine with her, cleverly concealed), eats one of them and is ill—but not too ill. She knows very well how much cocaine to take and just what symptoms to exaggerate.

"And the card—my card! Ah! *Sapristi*—she has a nerve! It was my card—the one I sent with the flowers. Simple, was it not? Yes, but it had to be thought of. . . ."

There was a pause and then Frederica asked, "Why did she put the pistol in my coat?"

"I thought you would ask that, Madame. It was bound to occur to you in time. Tell me—had it ever entered your head that Mademoiselle Nick no longer liked you? Did you ever feel that she might—hate you?"

"It's difficult to say," said Frederica slowly. "We lived an insincere life. She used to be fond of me."

"Tell me, M. Lazarus—it is not a time for false modesty, you understand—was there anything between you and her?"

"No," Lazarus shook his head. "I was attracted to her at one time. And then—I don't know why—I went off her."

"Ah!" said Poirot nodding his head sagely. "That was her tragedy. She attracted people—and then they 'went off her.' Instead of liking her better and better you fell in love with her friend. She began to hate Madame—Madame who had a rich friend behind her. Last winter when she made a will, she was fond of Madame. Later it was different.

"She remembered that will. She did not know that Croft had suppressed it—that it had never reached its destination. Madame (or so the world would say) had got a motive for desiring her death. So it was to Madame she telephoned asking her to get the chocolates. Tonight, the will would have been read, naming Madame her residuary legatee—and then the pistol would be found in her coat—the pistol with which Maggie Buckley was shot. If Madame found it, she might incriminate herself by trying to get rid of it."

"She must have hated me," murmured Frederica.

"Yes, Madame. You had what she had not—the knack of winning love, and keeping it."

"I'm rather dense," said Challenger, "but I haven't quite fathomed the will business yet."

"No? That's a different business altogether—a very simple one. The Crofts are lying low down here. Mademoiselle Nick has to have an operation. She has made no will. The Crofts see a chance. They persuade her to make one and take charge of it for the post. Then, if anything happens to her—if she dies—they produce a cleverly forged will—leaving the money to Mrs. Croft with a reference to Australia and Philip Buckley whom they know once visited that country.

"But Mademoiselle Nick has her appendix removed quite satisfactorily so the forged will is no good. For the moment, that is. Then the attempts on her life begin. The Crofts are hopeful once more. Finally, I announce her death. The chance is too good to be missed. The forged will is immediately posted to M. Vyse. Of course, to begin with, they naturally thought her much richer than she is. They knew nothing about the mortgage."

"What I really want to know, M. Poirot," said Lazarus, "is how you actually got wise to all this. When did you begin to suspect?"

"Ah! there I am ashamed. I was so long—so long—There were things that worried me—yes. Things that seemed not quite right. Discrepancies between what Mademoiselle Nick told me and what other people told me. Unfortunately, I always believed Mademoiselle Nick.

"And then, suddenly, I got a revelation. Mademoiselle Nick made one mistake. She was too clever. When I urged her to send for a friend she promised to do so—and suppressed the fact that she had already sent for Mademoiselle Maggie. It seemed to her less suspicious—but it was a mistake.

"For Maggie Buckley wrote a letter home immediately on arrival and in it she used one innocent phrase that puzzled me. '*I cannot see why she should have telegraphed for me in the way she did. Tuesday would have done just as well.*' What did that mention of Tuesday mean? It could only mean one thing. Maggie had been coming to stay on Tuesday anyway. But in that case Mademoiselle Nick had lied—or had at any rate suppressed the truth.

"And for the first time I looked at her in a different light. I criticized her statements. Instead of believing them, I said, 'Suppose this were not true.' I remembered the discrepancies. 'How would it be if every time it was Mademoiselle Nick who was lying and not the other person?'

"I said to myself, 'Let us be simple. What has really happened?'

"And I saw that what had really happened was that Maggie Buckley had been killed. Just that! But who could want Maggie Buckley dead?

"And then I thought of something else—a few foolish remarks that Hastings had made not five minutes before. He said that there were plenty of abbreviations for Margaret—Maggie, Margot, etc. And it suddenly occurred to me to wonder what was Mademoiselle Maggie's real name?

"Then, *tout d'un coup*, it came to me! Supposing her name was *Magdala*! It was a Buckley name, Mademoiselle Nick had told me so. Two Magdala Buckleys. Supposing. . . .

"In my mind I ran over the letters of Michael Seton's that I had read. Yes—there was nothing impossible. There was a mention of Scarborough—but Maggie had been in Scarborough with Nick—her mother had told me so.

"And it explained one thing which had worried me. Why were there so few letters? If a girl keeps her love letters at all, she keeps all of them. Why these select few? Was there any peculiarity about them?

"And I remembered that there was no name mentioned in them. They all began differently—but they began with a term of endearment. Nowhere in them was there the name—*Nick*.

"And there was something else, something that I ought to have seen at once—that cried the truth aloud."

"What was that?"

"Why—this. Mademoiselle Nick underwent an operation for appendicitis on February 27th last. There is a letter of Michael Seton's dated March 2nd, and no mention of anxiety, of illness or anything unusual. That ought to have shown me that the letters were written to a different person altogether.

"Then I went through a list of questions that I had made. And I answered them in the light of my new idea.

"In all but a few isolated questions the result was simple and convincing. And I answered, too, another question which I had asked myself earlier. *Why did Mademoiselle Nick buy a black dress*? The answer was that she and her cousin had to be dressed alike, with the scarlet shawl as an additional touch. That was the true and convincing answer, not the other. A girl would not buy mourning before she knew her lover was dead. She would be unreal—unnatural.

"And so I, in turn, staged my little drama. And the thing I hoped for happened! Nick Buckley had been very vehement about the question of a secret panel. She had declared there was no such thing. But if there were—and I did not see why Ellen should have invented it—Nick must know of it. Why was she so vehement? Was it possible that she had hidden the pistol there? With the secret intention of using it to throw suspicion on somebody later?

"I let her see that appearances were very black against Madame. That was as she had planned. As I foresaw, she was unable to resist the crowning proof. Besides it was safer for herself. That secret panel might be found by Ellen and the pistol in it!

"We are all safely in here. She is waiting outside for her cue. It is absolutely safe, she thinks, to take the pistol from its hiding place and put it in Madame's coat. . . .

"And so—at the last—she failed. . . ."

Frederica shivered.

"All the same," she said, "I'm glad I gave her my watch."

"Yes, Madame."

She looked up at him quickly.

"You know that too?"

"What about Ellen?" I asked, breaking in. "Did she know or suspect anything?"

"No. I asked her. She told me that she decided to stay in the house that night because in her own phrase she 'thought something was up.' Apparently Nick urged her to see the fireworks rather too decisively. She had fathomed Nick's dislike of Madame. She told me that 'she felt in her bones something was going to happen' but she thought it was going to happen to Madame. She knew Miss Nick's temper, she said, and she was always a queer little girl."

"Yes," murmured Frederica. "Yes, let us think of her like that. A queer little girl. A queer little girl who couldn't help herself. . . . I shall—anyway."

Poirot took her hand and raised it gently to his lips.

Charles Vyse stirred uneasily.

"It's going to be a very unpleasant business," he said quietly. "I must see about some kind of defense for her, I suppose."

"There will be no need, I think," said Poirot gently. "Not if I am correct in my assumptions."

He turned suddenly on Challenger.

"That's where you put the stuff, isn't it?" he said. "In those wrist watches."

"I—I—" the sailor stammered—at a loss.

"Do not try and deceive me—with your hearty goodfellow manner. It has deceived Hastings—but it does not deceive *me*. You make a good thing out of it, do you not—the traffic in drugs—You and your uncle in Harley Street."

"M. Poirot!"

Challenger rose to his feet.

My little friend blinked up at him placidly.

"You are the useful 'boy friend.' Deny it if you like. But I advise you if you do not want the facts put in the hands of the police—to go."

And to my utter amazement, Challenger did go. He went from the room like a flash. I stared after him open-mouthed.

Poirot laughed.

"I told you so, *mon ami*. Your instincts are always wrong. *C'est épatant!*"

"Cocaine was in the wrist watch—" I began.

"Yes, yes. That is how Mademoiselle Nick had it with her so conveniently at the nursing home. And having finished her supply in the chocolate box she asked Madame just now for hers which was full."

"You mean she can't do without it?"

"*Non, non.* Mademoiselle Nick is not an addict. Sometimes—for fun—that is all. But tonight she needed it for a different purpose. It will be a full dose this time."

"You mean—?" I gasped.

"It is the best way. Better than the hangman's rope. But pst! we must not say so before M. Vyse who is all law and order. Officially I know nothing. The contents of the wrist watch—it is the merest guess on my part."

"Your guesses are always right, M. Poirot," said Frederica.

"I must be going," said Charles Vyse, cold disapproval in his attitude as he left the room.

Poirot looked from Frederica to Lazarus.

"You are going to get married—eh?"

"As soon as we can."

"And indeed, M. Poirot," said Frederica, "I am not the drug taker you think. I have cut myself down to a tiny dose. I think now—with happiness in front of me—I shall not need a wrist watch any more."

"I hope you will have happiness, Madame," said Poirot gently. "You have suffered a great deal. And in spite of everything you have suffered, you have still the quality of mercy in your heart. . . ."

"I will look after her," said Lazarus. "My business is in a bad way but I believe I shall pull through. And if I don't—well, Frederica does not mind being poor—with me."

She shook her head smiling.

"It is late," said Poirot, looking at the clock.

We all rose.

"We have spent a strange night in this strange house," Poirot went on. "It is, I think, as Ellen says, an evil house. . . ."

He looked up at the picture of old Sir Nicholas.

Then, with a sudden gesture, he drew Lazarus aside.

"I ask your pardon, but, of all my questions, there is one still unanswered. Tell me, why did you offer fifty pounds for that picture? It would give me much pleasure to know—so as, you comprehend, to leave nothing unanswered."

Lazarus looked at him with an impassive face for a minute or two. Then he smiled.

"You see, M. Poirot," he said, "I am a dealer."

"Exactly."

"That picture is not worth a penny more than twenty pounds. I knew if I offered Nick fifty, she would immediately suspect it was worth more and would get it valued elsewhere. Then she would find that I had offered her far more than it was worth. The next time I offered to buy a picture she would not have got it valued."

"Yes, and then?"

"The picture on the far wall is worth at least five thousand pounds," said Lazarus dryly.

"Ah!" Poirot drew a long breath.

"Now I know everything," he said happily.

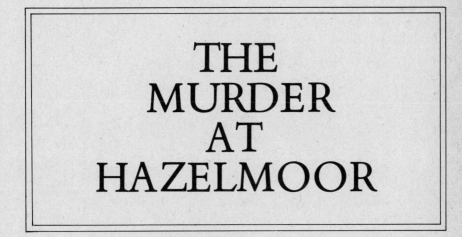

THE
MURDER
AT
HAZELMOOR

To

M E M

With whom I discussed the plot of this
book, to the alarm of those around us

Contents

1

Sittaford House

Major Burnaby drew on his gum boots, buttoned his overcoat collar round his neck, took from a shelf near the door a hurricane lantern, and cautiously opened the front door of his little bungalow and peered out.

The scene that met his eyes was typical of the English countryside as depicted on Xmas cards and in old-fashioned melodramas. Everywhere was snow, deep drifts of it—no mere powdering an inch or two thick. Snow had fallen all over England for the last four days, and up here on the fringe of Dartmoor it had attained a depth of several feet. All over England householders were groaning over burst pipes, and to have a plumber friend (or even a plumber's mate) was the most coveted of all distinctions.

Up here, in the tiny village of Sittaford, at all times remote from the world, and now almost completely cut off, the rigors of winter were a very real problem.

Major Burnaby, however, was a hardy soul. He snorted twice, grunted once, and marched resolutely out into the snow.

His destination was not far away. A few paces along a winding lane, then in at a gate, and so up a drive partially swept clear of snow to a house of some considerable size built of granite.

The door was opened by a neatly clad parlormaid. The Major was divested of his British Warm, his gum boots and his aged scarf.

A door was flung open and he passed through it into a room which conveyed all the illusion of a transformation scene.

Although it was only half past three the curtains had been drawn, the electric lights were on and a huge fire blazed cheerfully on the hearth. Two women in afternoon frocks rose to greet the stanch old warrior.

"Splendid of you to turn out, Major Burnaby," said the elder of the two.

"Not at all, Mrs. Willett, not at all. Very good of you to ask me." He shook hands with them both.

"Mr. Garfield is coming," went on Mrs. Willett, "and Mr. Duke, and Mr. Rycroft *said* he would come—but one can hardly expect him at his age in such weather. Really, it is *too* dreadful. One feels one *must* do something to keep oneself cheerful. Violet, put another log on the fire."

The Major rose gallantly to perform this task.

155

"Allow me, Miss Violet."

He put the log expertly in the right place and returned once more to the armchair his hostess had indicated. Trying not to appear as though he were doing so, he cast surreptitious glances round the room. Amazing how a couple of women could alter the whole character of a room—and without doing anything very outstanding that you could put your finger on.

Sittaford House had been built ten years ago by Captain Joseph Trevelyan, R.N., on the occasion of his retirement from the Navy. He was a man of substance, and he had always had a great hankering to live on Dartmoor. He had placed his choice on the tiny hamlet of Sittaford. It was not in a valley like most of the villages and farms, but perched right on the shoulder of the moor under the shadow of Sittaford Beacon. He had purchased a large tract of ground, had built a comfortable house with its own electric light plant and an electric pump to save labor in pumping water. Then, as a speculation, he had built six small bungalows, each in its quarter acre of ground, along the lane.

The first of these, the one at his very gates, had been allotted to his old friend and crony, John Burnaby—the others had by degrees been sold, there being still a few people who from choice or necessity like to live right out of the world. The village itself consisted of three picturesque but dilapidated cottages, a forge, and a combined post office and sweet shop. The nearest town was Exhampton, six miles away, a steady descent which necessitated the sign, "Motorists engage your lowest gear," so familiar on the Dartmoor roads.

Captain Trevelyan, as has been said, was a man of substance. In spite of this—or perhaps because of it—he was a man who was inordinately fond of money. At the end of October a house-agent in Exhampton wrote to him asking if he would consider letting Sittaford House. A tenant had made inquiries concerning it, wishing to rent it for the winter.

Captain Trevelyan's first impulse was to refuse, his second to demand further information. The tenant in question proved to be a Mrs. Willett, a widow with one daughter. She had recently arrived from South Africa and wanted a house on Dartmoor for the winter.

"Damn it all, the woman must be mad," said Captain Trevelyan. "Eh, Burnaby, don't you think so?"

Burnaby did think so, and said so as forcibly as his friend had done.

"Anyway, you don't want to let," he said. "Let the fool woman go somewhere else if she wants to freeze. Coming from South Africa too!"

But at this point Captain Trevelyan's money complex asserted itself. Not once in a hundred times would you get a chance of letting your house in midwinter. He demanded what rent the tenant was willing to pay.

An offer of twelve guineas a week clinched matters. Captain Trevelyan went into Exhampton, rented a small house on the outskirts at two guineas a week, and handed over Sittaford House to Mrs. Willett, half the rent to be paid in advance.

"A fool and her money are soon parted," he growled.

But Burnaby was thinking this afternoon as he scanned Mrs. Willett covertly, that she did not look a fool. She was a tall woman with a rather silly manner—but her physiognomy was shrewd rather than foolish. She was inclined to overdress, had a distinct Colonial accent, and seemed perfectly content with the transaction. She was clearly very well off and that—as Burnaby had reflected more than once, really made the whole affair more odd. She was not the kind of woman one would credit with a passion for solitude.

As a neighbor she had proved almost embarrassingly friendly. Invitations to Sittaford House were rained on everybody. Captain Trevelyan was constantly urged to "Treat the house as though we hadn't rented it." Trevelyan, however, was not fond of women. Report went that he had been jilted in his youth. He persistently refused all invitations.

Two months had passed since the installation of the Willetts and the first wonder at their arrival had passed away.

Burnaby, naturally a silent man, continued to study his hostess, oblivious to any need for small talk. Liked to make herself out a fool, but wasn't really. So he summed up the situation. His glance shifted to Violet Willett. Pretty girl—scraggy, of course—they all were nowadays. What was the good of a woman if she didn't look like a woman? Papers said curves were coming back. About time too.

He roused himself to the necessity of conversation.

"We were afraid at first that you wouldn't be able to come," said Mrs. Willett. "You said so, you remember. We were so pleased when you said that after all you would."

"Friday," said Major Burnaby, with an air of being explicit.

Mrs. Willett looked puzzled.

"Friday?"

"Every Friday go to Trevelyan's. Tuesday he comes to me. Both of us done it for years."

"Oh! I see. Of course, living so near—"

"Kind of habit."

"But do you still keep it up? I mean now that he is living in Exhampton—"

"Pity to break a habit," said Major Burnaby. "We'd both of us miss those evenings."

"You go in for competitions, don't you?" asked Violet. "Acrostics and crosswords and all those things."

Burnaby nodded.

"I do crosswords. Trevelyan does acrostics. We each stick to our own line of country. I won three books last month in a crossword competition," he volunteered.

"Oh! really. How nice. Were they interesting books?"

"Don't know. Haven't read them. Looked pretty hopeless."

"It's the winning them that matters, isn't it?" said Mrs. Willett vaguely.

"How do you get to Exhampton?" asked Violet. "You haven't got a car."

"Walk."

"What? Not really? Six miles."

"Good exercise. What's twelve miles? Keeps a man fit. Great thing to be fit."

"Fancy! Twelve miles. But both you and Captain Trevelyan were great athletes, weren't you?"

"Used to go to Switzerland together. Winter sports in winter, climbing in summer. Wonderful man on ice, Trevelyan. Both too old for that sort of thing nowadays."

"You won the Army Racquets Championship, too, didn't you?" asked Violet.

The Major blushed like a girl.

"Who told you that?" he mumbled.

"Captain Trevelyan."

"Joe should hold his tongue," said Burnaby. "He talks too much. What's the weather like now?"

Respecting his embarrassment, Violet followed him to the window. They drew the curtain aside and looked out over the desolate scene.

"More snow coming," said Burnaby. "A pretty heavy fall too, I should say."

"Oh! how thrilling," said Violet. "I do think snow is so romantic. I've never seen it before."

"It isn't romantic when the pipes freeze, you foolish child," said her mother.

"Have you lived all your life in South Africa, Miss Willett?" asked Major Burnaby.

Some of the girl's animation dropped away from her. She seemed almost constrained in her manner as she answered.

"Yes—this is the first time I've ever been away. It's all most frightfully thrilling."

Thrilling to be shut away like this in a remote moorland village? Funny idea. He couldn't get the hang of these people.

The door opened and the parlormaid announced:

"Mr. Rycroft and Mr. Garfield."

There entered a little, elderly, dried-up man and a fresh-colored, boyish young man. The latter spoke first.

"I brought him along, Mrs Willett. Said I wouldn't let him be buried in a snowdrift. Ha, ha. I say, this all looks simply marvelous. Yule logs burning."

"As he says, my young friend very kindly piloted me here," said Mr. Rycroft as he shook hands somewhat ceremoniously. "How do you do, Miss Violet? Very seasonable weather—rather too seasonable, I fear."

He moved to the fire talking to Mrs. Willett. Ronald Garfield buttonholed Violet.

"I say, can't we get up any skating anywhere? Aren't there some ponds about?"

"I think path digging will be your only sport."

"I've been at it all the morning."

"Oh! you he-man!"

"Don't laugh at me. I've got blisters all over my hands."

"How's your aunt?"

"Oh! she's always the same—sometimes she says she's better and sometimes she says she's worse, but I think it's all the same really. It's a ghastly life, you know. Each year, I wonder how I can stick it—but there it is—if one doesn't rally round the old bird for Xmas—why, she's quite capable of leaving her money to a Cat's Home. She's got five of them, you know. I'm always stroking the brutes and pretending I dote upon them."

"I like dogs much better than cats."

"So do I. Any day. What I mean is a dog is—well, a dog's a dog, you know."

"Has your aunt always been fond of cats?"

"I think it's just a kind of thing old maids grow into. Ugh! I hate the brutes."

"Your aunt's very nice, but rather frightening."

"I should think she was frightening. Snaps my head off sometimes. Thinks I've got no brains, you know."

"Not really?"

"Oh! look here, don't say it like that. Lots of fellows look like fools and are laughing underneath."

"Mr. Duke," announced the parlormaid.

Mr. Duke was a recent arrival. He had bought the last of the six bungalows in September. He was a big man, very quiet and devoted to gardening. Mr. Rycroft, who was an enthusiast on birds and who lived next door to him, had taken him up, overruling the section of thought which voiced the opinion that of course Mr. Duke was a very nice man, quite unassuming, but was he, after all, quite—well, quite? Mightn't he, just possibly, be a retired tradesman?

But nobody liked to ask him—and indeed it was thought better not to know. Because if one did know, it might be awkward, and really in such a small community it was best to know everybody.

"Not walking to Exhampton in this weather?" he asked of Major Burnaby.

"No, I fancy Trevelyan will hardly expect me tonight."

"It's awful, isn't it?" said Mrs. Willett with a shudder. "To be buried up here, year after year—it must be ghastly."

Mr. Duke gave her a quick glance. Major Burnaby too stared at her curiously.

But at that moment tea was brought in.

2

The Message

AFTER TEA, Mrs. Willett suggested bridge.

"There are six of us. Two can cut in."

Ronnie's eyes brightened.

"You four start," he suggested. "Miss Willett and I will cut in."

But Mr. Duke said that he did not play bridge.

Ronnie's face fell.

"We might play a round game," said Mrs. Willett.

"Or table turning," suggested Ronnie. "It's a spooky evening. We spoke about it the other day, you remember. Mr. Rycroft and I were talking about it this evening as we came along here."

"I am a member of the Psychical Research Society," explained Mr. Rycroft in his precise way. "I was able to put my young friend right on one or two points."

"Tommy rot," said Major Burnaby very distinctly.

"Oh! but it's great fun, don't you think?" said Violet Willett. "I mean, one doesn't believe in it or anything. It's just an amusement. What do you say, Mr. Duke?"

"Anything you like, Miss Willett."

"We must turn the lights out, and we must find a suitable table. No—not that one, Mother. I'm sure it's much too heavy."

Things were settled at last to everyone's satisfaction. A small round table with a polished top was brought from an adjoining room. It was set in front of the fire and everyone took his place round it with the lights switched off.

Major Burnaby was between his hostess and Violet. On the other side of the girl was Ronnie Garfield. A cynical smile creased the Major's lips. He thought to himself:

"In my young days it was Up Jenkins." And he tried to recall the name of a girl with fluffy fair hair whose hand he had held beneath the table at considerable length. A long time ago that was. But Up Jenkins had been a good game.

There were all the usual laughs, whispers, stereotyped remarks.

"The spirits are a long time."

"Got a long way to come."

"Hush—nothing will happen unless we are serious."

"Oh! do be quiet—everyone."

"Nothing's happening."

"Of course not—it never does at first."

"If only you'd all be quiet."

At last, after some time, the murmur of talk died away.

A silence.

"This table's dead as mutton," murmured Ronnie Garfield disgustedly.

"Hush."

A tremor ran through the polished surface. The table began to rock.

"Ask it questions. Who shall ask? You, Ronnie."

"Oh—er—I say—what do I ask it?"

"Is a spirit present?" prompted Violet.

"Oh! Hullo—is a spirit present?"

A sharp rock.

"That means yes," said Violet.

"Oh! er—who are you?"

No response.

"Ask it to spell its name."

"How can it?"

"We count the number of rocks."

"Oh! I see. Will you please spell your name."

The table started rocking violently.

"A B C D E F G H I—I say, was that I or J?"

"Ask it. Was that I?"

One rock.

"Yes. Next letter, please."

The spirit's name was Ida.

"Have you a message for anyone here?"

"Yes."

"Who is it for? Miss Willett?"

"No."

"Mrs. Willett?"

"No."

"Mr. Rycroft?"

"No."

"Me?"

"Yes."

"It's for you, Ronnie. Go on. Make it spell it out."

The table spelt "Diana."

"Who's Diana? Do you know anyone called Diana?"

"No, I don't. At least—"

"There you are. He does."

"Ask her if she's a widow."

The fun went on. Mr. Rycroft smiled indulgently. Young people must have their jokes. He caught one glance of his hostess's face in a sudden flicker of the firelight. It looked worried and abstracted. Her thoughts were somewhere far away.

Major Burnaby was thinking of the snow. It was going to snow again this evening. Hardest winter he ever remembered.

Mr. Duke was playing very seriously. The spirits, alas, paid very little attention to him. All the messages seemed to be for Violet and Ronnie.

Violet was told she was going to Italy. Someone was going with her. Not a woman. A man. His name was Leonard.

More laughter. The table spelt the name of the town. A Russian jumble of letters—not in the least Italian.

The usual accusations were leveled.

"Look here, Violet" ("Miss Willett" had been dropped). "You are shoving."

"I'm not. Look, I take my hands right off the table and it rocks just the same."

"I like raps. I'm going to ask it to rap. Loud ones."

"There should be raps." Ronnie turned to Mr. Rycroft. "There ought to be raps, oughtn't there, sir?"

"Under the circumstances, I should hardly think it likely," said Mr. Rycroft drily.

There was a pause. The table was inert. It returned no answer to questions.

"Has Ida gone away?"

One languid rock.

"Will another spirit come, please?"

Nothing. Suddenly the table began to quiver and rock violently.

"Hurrah. Are you a new spirit?"

"Yes."

"Have you a message for someone?"

"Yes."

"For me?"

"No."

"For Violet?"

"No."

"For Major Burnaby?"

"Yes."

"It's for you, Major Burnaby. Will you spell it out please."

The table started rocking slowly.

"T R E V—are you sure it's V? It can't be. T R E V—it doesn't make sense."

"Trevelyan, of course," said Mrs. Willett. "Captain Trevelyan."

"Do you mean Captain Trevelyan?"

"Yes."

"You've got a message for Captain Trevelyan?"

"No."

"Well, what is it then?"

The table began to rock—slowly, rhythmically. So slowly that it was easy to count the letters.

"D—" a pause. "E—A D."

"Dead."

"Somebody is dead?"

Instead of Yes or No, the table began to rock again till it reached the letter T.

"T—do you mean Trevelyan?"

"Yes."

"You don't mean Trevelyan is dead?"

"Yes."

A very sharp rock. "Yes."

Somebody gasped. There was a faint stir all round the table.

Ronnie's voice as he resumed his questions held a different note—an awed uneasy note.

"You mean—that Captain Trevelyan is dead?"

"Yes."

There was a pause. It was as though no one knew what to ask next, or how to take this unexpected development.

And in the pause, the table started rocking again.

Rhythmically and slowly. Ronnie spelled out the letters aloud . . .
M-U-R-D-E-R . . . .

Mrs. Willett gave a cry and took her hands off the table.

"I won't go on with this. It's horrible. I don't like it."

Mr. Duke's voice rang out, resonant and clear. He was questioning
the table.

"Do you mean—that Captain Trevelyan has been murdered?"

The last word had hardly left his lips when the answer came. The
table rocked so violently and assertively that it nearly fell over. One
rock only.

"Yes . . ."

"Look here," said Ronnie. He took his hands from the table. "I call
this a rotten joke." His voice trembled.

"Turn up the lights," said Mr. Rycroft.

Major Burnaby rose and did so. The sudden glare revealed a
company of pale uneasy faces.

Everyone looked at each other. Somehow—nobody quite knew
what to say.

"All rot, of course," said Ronnie, with an uneasy laugh.

"Silly nonsense," said Mrs. Willett. "Nobody ought to—to make
jokes like that."

"Not about people dying," said Violet. "It's—oh! I don't like it."

"I wasn't shoving," said Ronnie, feeling unspoken criticism leveled
at him. "I swear I wasn't."

"I can say the same," said Mr. Duke. "And you, Mr. Rycroft?"

"Certainly not," said Mr. Rycroft warmly.

"You don't think I'd make a joke of that kind, do you?" growled
Major Burnaby. "Rotten bad taste."

"Violet dear—"

"I didn't, Mother. Indeed I didn't. I wouldn't do such a thing."

The girl was almost tearful.

Everyone was embarrassed. A sudden blight had come over the
cheerful party.

Major Burnaby pushed back his chair, went to the window and
pulled aside the curtain. He stood there looking out with his back to the
room.

"Twenty-five minutes past five," said Mr. Rycroft glancing up at the
clock. He compared it with his own watch and somehow everyone felt
that the action was significant in some way.

"Let me see," said Mrs. Willett with forced cheerfulness. "I think
we'd better have cocktails. Will you ring the bell, Mr. Garfield?"

Ronnie obeyed.

Ingredients for cocktails were brought and Ronnie was appointed mixer. The situation grew a little easier.

"Well," said Ronnie, raising his glass. "Here's how."

The others responded—all but the silent figure by the window.

"Major Burnaby. Here's your cocktail."

The Major roused himself with a start. He turned slowly.

"Thank you, Mrs. Willett. Not for me." He looked once more out into the night then came slowly back to the group by the fire. "Many thanks for a very pleasant time. Good night."

"You're not going?"

"Afraid I must."

"Not so soon. And on a night like this."

"Sorry, Mrs. Willett—but it's got to be done. If there were only a telephone."

"A telephone?"

"Yes—to tell you the truth—I'm—well, I'd like to be sure that Joe Trevelyan's all right. Silly superstition and all that—but there it is. Naturally, I don't believe in this tommy rot—but—"

"But you can't telephone from anywhere. There's not such a thing in Sittaford."

"That's just it. As I can't telephone, I'll have to go."

"Go—but you couldn't get a car down that road! Elmer wouldn't take his car out on such a night."

Elmer was the proprietor of the sole car in the place, an aged Ford, hired at a handsome price by those who wished to go into Exhampton.

"No, no—car's out of the question. My two legs will take me there, Mrs. Willett."

There was a chorus of protest.

"Oh! Major Burnaby—it's *impossible*. You said yourself it was going to snow."

"Not for an hour—perhaps longer. I'll get there, never fear."

"Oh! you can't. We can't allow it."

She was seriously disturbed and upset.

But argument and entreaty had no more effect on Major Burnaby than if he were a rock. He was an obstinate man. Once his mind was made up on any point, no power on earth could move him.

He had determined to walk to Exhampton and see for himself that all was well with his old friend, and he repeated that simple statement half a dozen times.

In the end they were brought to realize that he meant it. He wrapped himself up in his overcoat, lighted the hurricane lantern, and stepped out into the night.

"I'll just drop into my place for a flask," he said cheerily, "and then push straight on. Trevelyan will put me up for the night when I get there. Ridiculous fuss, I know. Everything sure to be all right. Don't worry, Mrs. Willett. Snow or no snow—I'll get there in a couple of hours. Good night."

He strode away. The others returned to the fire.

Rycroft had looked up at the sky.

"It *is* going to snow," he murmured to Mr. Duke. "And it will begin long before he gets to Exhampton. I—I hope he gets there all right."

Duke frowned.

"I know. I feel I ought to have gone with him. One of us ought to have done so."

"Most distressing," Mrs. Willett was saying. "Most distressing. Violet, I will not have that silly game ever played again. Poor Major Burnaby will probably plunge into a snowdrift—or if he doesn't he'll die of the cold and exposure. At his age, too. Very foolish of him to go off like that. Of course, Captain Trevelyan is perfectly all right."

Everyone echoed:

"Of course."

But even now they did not feel really too comfortable.

Supposing something *had* happened to Captain Trevelyan . . .

Supposing . . .

3

Five and Twenty Past Five

TWO AND A HALF HOURS LATER, just before eight o'clock, Major Burnaby, hurricane lantern in hand, his head dropped forward so as not to meet the blinding drive of the snow, stumbled up the path to the door of "Hazelmoor," the small house tenanted by Captain Trevelyan.

The snow had begun to fall about an hour ago—great blinding flakes of it. Major Burnaby was gasping, emitting the loud sighing gasps of an utterly exhausted man. He was numbed with cold. He stamped his feet, blew, puffed, snorted and applied a numbed finger to the bell push.

The bell trilled shrilly.

Burnaby waited. After a pause of a few minutes, as nothing happened, he pushed the bell again.

Once more there was no stir of life.

Burnaby rang a third time. This time he kept his finger on the bell.

It trilled on and on—but there was still no sign of life in the house.

There was a knocker on the door. Major Burnaby seized it and worked it vigorously, producing a noise like thunder.

And still the little house remained silent as the dead.

The Major desisted. He stood for a moment as though perplexed— then he slowly went down the path and out at the gate, continuing on the road he had come towards Exhampton. A hundred yards brought him to the small police station.

He hesitated again, then finally made up his mind and entered.

Constable Graves, who knew the Major well, rose in astonishment.

"Well, I never, sir, fancy you being out on a night like this."

"Look here," said Burnaby curtly. "I've been ringing and knocking at the Captain's house and I can't get any answer."

"Why, of course, it's Friday," said Graves who knew the habits of the two pretty well. "But you don't mean to say you've actually come down from Sittaford on a night like this? Surely the Captain would never expect you."

"Whether he's expected me or not, I've come," said Burnaby testily. "And as I'm telling you, I can't get in. I've rung and knocked and nobody answers."

Some of his uneasiness seemed to communicate itself to the policeman.

"That's odd," he said, frowning.

"Of course, it's odd," said Burnaby.

"It's not as though he's likely to be out—on a night like this."

"Of course he's not likely to be out."

"It *is* odd," said Graves again.

Burnaby displayed impatience at the man's slowness.

"Aren't you going to do something?" he snapped.

"Do something?"

"Yes, do something."

The policeman ruminated.

"Think he might have been taken bad?" His face brightened. "I'll try the telephone." It stood at his elbow. He took it up and gave the number.

But to the telephone, as to the front door bell, Captain Trevelyan gave no reply.

"Looks as though he *had* been taken bad," said Graves as he replaced the receiver. "And all alone in the house, too. We'd best get hold of Dr. Warren and take him along with us."

Dr. Warren's house was almost next door to the police station. The doctor was just sitting down to dinner with his wife and was not best pleased at the summons. However, he grudgingly agreed to accompany them, drawing on an aged British Warm and a pair of rubber boots and muffling his neck with a knitted scarf.

The snow was still falling.

"Damnable night," murmured the doctor. "Hope you haven't brought me out on a wild goose chase. Trevelyan's as strong as a horse. Never has anything the matter with him."

Burnaby did not reply.

Arriving at Hazelmoor once more, they again rang and knocked, but elicited no response.

The doctor then suggested going round the house to one of the back windows.

"Easier to force than the door."

Graves agreeing, they went round to the back. There was a side door which they tried on the way, but it too was locked, and presently they emerged on the snow-covered lawn that led up to the back windows. Suddenly, Warren uttered an exclamation.

"The window of the study—it's open."

True enough, the window, a French one, was standing ajar. They quickened their steps. On a night like this, no one in his senses would open a window. There was a light in the room that streamed out in a thin yellow band.

The three men arrived simultaneously at the window—Burnaby was the first man to enter, the constable hard on his heels.

They both stopped dead inside and something like a muffled cry came from the ex-soldier. In another moment Warren was beside them, and saw what they had seen.

Captain Trevelyan lay on the floor, face downwards. His arms sprawled widely. The room was in confusion—drawers of the bureau pulled out, papers lying about the floor. The window beside them was splintered where it had been forced near the lock. Beside Captain Trevelyan was a dark green baize tube about two inches in diameter.

Warren sprang forward. He knelt down by the prostrate figure.

One minute sufficed. He rose to his feet, his face pale.

"He's dead?" asked Burnaby.

The doctor nodded.

Then he turned to Graves.

"It's for you to say what's to be done. I can do nothing except examine the body and perhaps you'd rather I didn't do that until the Inspector comes. I can tell you the cause of death now. Fracture of the base of the skull. And I think I can make a guess at the weapon."

He indicated the green baize tube.

"Trevelyan always had them along the bottom of the door—to keep the draft out," said Burnaby.

His voice was hoarse.

"Yes—a very efficient form of sandbag."

"My God!"

"But this here—" the constable broke in, his wits arriving at the point slowly. "You mean—this here is murder."

The policeman stepped to the table on which stood a telephone.

Major Burnaby approached the doctor.

"Have you any idea," he said, breathing hard, "how long he's been dead?"

"About two hours, I should say, or possibly three. That's a rough estimate."

Burnaby passed his tongue over dry lips.

"Would you say," he asked, "that he might have been killed at five twenty-five?"

The doctor looked at him curiously.

"If I had to give a time definitely, that's just about the time I would suggest."

"Oh! my God," said Burnaby.

Warren stared at him.

The Major felt his way blindly to a chair, collapsed on to it and muttered to himself whilst a kind of staring terror overspread his face.

"*Five and twenty past five*—Oh! my God, then it *was* true after all."

4

Inspector Narracott

IT WAS THE MORNING after the tragedy, and two men were standing in the little study of Hazelmoor.

Inspector Narracott looked round him. A little frown appeared upon his forehead.

"Ye-es," he said thoughtfully. "Ye-es."

Inspector Narrracott was a very efficient officer. He had a quiet persistence, a logical mind and a keen attention to detail which brought him success where many another man might have failed.

He was a tall man with a quiet manner, rather far away gray eyes, and a slow soft Devonshire voice.

Summoned from Exeter to take charge of the case, he had arrived on the first train that morning. The roads had been impassable for cars, even with chains, otherwise he would have arrived the night before. He was standing now in Captain Trevelyan's study having just completed his examination of the room. With him was Sergeant Pollock of the Exhampton police.

"Ye-es," said Inspector Narracott.

A ray of pale wintry sunshine came in through the window. Outside was the snowy landscape. There was a fence about a hundred yards from the window and beyond it the steep ascending slope of the snow-covered hillside.

Inspector Narracott bent once more over the body which had been left for his inspection. An athletic man himself, he recognized the athlete's type, the broad shoulders, narrow flanks, and the good muscular development. The head was small and well set on the shoulders, and the pointed naval beard was carefully trimmed. Captain Trevelyan's age, he had ascertained, was sixty, but he looked not much more than fifty-one or two.

"It's a curious business," said Inspector Narracott.

"Ah!" said Sergeant Pollock.

The other turned on him.

"What is your view of it?"

"Well—" Sergeant Pollock scratched his head. He was a cautious man, unwilling to advance further than necessary.

"Well," he said, "as I see it, sir, I should say that the man came to the window, forced the lock, and started rifling the room. Captain Trevelyan, I suppose, must have been upstairs. Doubtless the burglar thought the house was empty—"

"Where is Captain Trevelyan's bedroom situated?"

"Upstairs, sir. Over this room."

"At the present time of year it is dark at four o'clock. If Captain Trevelyan was up in his bedroom the electric light would have been on, the burglar would have seen it as he approached this window."

"You mean he'd have waited."

"No man in his senses would break into a house with a light in it. If anyone forced this window—he did it because he thought the house was empty."

Sergeant Pollock scratched his head.

"Seems a bit odd, I admit. But there it is."

"We'll let it pass for the moment. Go on."

"Well, suppose the Captain hears a noise downstairs. He comes down to investigate. The burglar hears him coming. He snatches up that bolster arrangement, gets behind the door, and as the Captain enters the room strikes him down from behind."

Inspector Narracott nodded.

"Yes, that's true enough. He was struck down when he was facing the window. But all the same, Pollock, I don't like it."

"No, sir?"

"No, as I say, I don't believe in houses that are broken into at five o'clock in the afternoon."

"We—ell, he may have thought it a good opportunity—"

"It is not a question of opportunity—slipping in because he found a window unlatched. It was deliberate house-breaking—look at the confusion everywhere—what would a burglar go for first? The pantry where the silver is kept."

"That's true enough," admitted the Sergeant.

"And this confusion—this chaos," continued Narracott, "these drawers pulled out and their contents scattered. Pah! It's bunkum."

"Bunkum?"

"Look at the window, Sergeant. *That window was not locked and forced open*! It was merely shut and then splintered from the outside to give the appearance of forcing."

Pollock examined the latch of the window closely, uttering an ejaculation to himself as he did so.

"You are right, sir," he said with respect in his voice. "Who'd have thought of that now!"

"Someone who wishes to throw dust in our eyes—and hasn't succeeded."

Sergeant Pollock was grateful for the "our." In such small ways did Inspector Narracott endear himself to his subordinates.

"Then it wasn't burglary. You mean, sir, it was an inside job."

Inspector Narracott nodded. "Yes," he said. "The only curious thing is, though, that I think the murderer did actually enter by the window. As you and Graves reported, and as I can still see for myself, there are damp patches still visible where the snow melted and was trodden in by the murderer's boots. These damp patches are only in this room. Constable Graves was quite positive that there was nothing of the kind in the hall when he and Dr. Warren passed through it. In this room he noticed them immediately. In that case it seems clear that the murderer was admitted by Captain Trevelyan through the window. Therefore it must have been someone whom Captain Trevelyan knew. You are a local man, Sergeant, can you tell me if Captain Trevelyan was a man who made enemies easily?"

"No, sir, I should say he hadn't an enemy in the world. A bit keen on

money, and a bit of a martinet—wouldn't stand for any slackness or
incivility—but bless my soul he was respected for that."

"No enemies," said Narracott thoughtfully.

"Not here, that is."

"Very true—we don't know what enemies he may have made during
his naval career. It's my experience, Sergeant, that a man who makes
enemies in one place will make them in another, but I agree that we
can't put that possibility entirely aside. We come logically now to the
next motive—the most common motive for every crime—gain.
Captain Trevelyan was, I understand, a rich man?"

"Very warm indeed by all accounts. But close. Not an easy man to
touch for a subscription."

"Ah!" said Narracott thoughtfully.

"Pity it snowed as it did," said the Sergeant. "But for that we'd have
had his footprints as something to go on."

"There was no one else in the house?" asked the Inspector.

"No. For the last five years Captain Trevelyan has only had one
servant—retired naval chap. Up at Sittaford House a woman came in
daily, but this chap, Evans, cooked and looked after his master. About
a month ago he got married—much to the Captain's annoyance. I
believe that's one of the reasons he let Sittaford House to this South
African lady. He wouldn't have any woman living in the house. Evans
lives just round the corner here in Fore Street with his wife, and comes
in daily to do for his master. I've got him here now for you to see. His
statement is that he left here at half past two yesterday afternoon, the
Captain having no further need for him."

"Yes, I shall want to see him. He may be able to tell us
something—useful."

Sergeant Pollock looked at his superior officer curiously. There was
something so odd about his tone.

"You think—" he began.

"I think," said Inspector Narracott deliberately, "that there's a lot
more in this case than meets the eye."

"In what way, sir?"

But the Inspector refused to be drawn.

"You say this man, Evans, is here now?"

"He's waiting in the dining-room."

"Good, I'll see him straight away. What sort of a fellow is he?"

Sergeant Pollock was better at reporting facts than at descriptive
accuracy.

"He's a retired naval chap. Ugly customer in a scrap, I should say."

"Does he drink?"

"Never been the worse for it that I know of."

"What about this wife of his? Not a fancy of the Captain's or anything of that sort?"

"Oh! no, sir, nothing of that kind about Captain Trevelyan. He wasn't that kind at all. He was known as a woman hater, if anything."

"And Evans was supposed to be devoted to his master?"

"That's the general idea, sir, and I think it would be known if he wasn't. Exhampton's a small place."

Inspector Narracott nodded.

"Well," he said, "there's nothing more to be seen here. I'll interview Evans and I'll take a look at the rest of the house and after that we will go over to the Three Crowns and see this Major Burnaby. That remark of his about the time was curious. Twenty-five minutes past five, eh? He must know something he hasn't told, or why should he suggest the time of the crime so accurately."

The two men moved toward the door.

"It's a rum business," said Sergeant Pollock, his eye wandering to the littered floor. "All this burglary fake!"

"It's not that that strikes me as odd," said Narracott, "under the circumstances it was probably the natural thing to do. No—what strikes me as odd is the window."

"The window, sir?"

"Yes. Why should the murderer go to the window? Assuming it was someone Trevelyan knew and admitted without question, why not go to the front door? To get round to this window from the road on a night like last night would have been a difficult and unpleasant proceeding with the snow lying as thick as it does. Yet, there must have been some reason."

"Perhaps," suggested Pollock, "the man didn't want to be seen turning into the house from the road."

"There wouldn't be many people about yesterday afternoon to see him. Nobody who could help it was out of doors. No—there's some other reason. Well, perhaps it will come to light in due course."

5

Evans

THEY FOUND EVANS waiting in the dining-room. He rose respectfully on their entrance.

He was a short thick-set man. He had very long arms and a habit of standing with his hands half clenched. He was clean shaven with small, rather piglike eyes, yet he had a look of cheerfulness and efficiency that redeemed his bulldog appearance.

Inspector Narracott mentally tabulated his impressions.

"Intelligent. Shrewd and practical. Looks rattled."

Then he spoke:

"You're Evans, eh?"

"Yes, sir."

"Christian names?"

"Robert Henry."

"Ah! Now what do you know about this business?"

"Not a thing, sir. It's fair knocked me over. To think of the Capting being done in!"

"When did you last see your master?"

"Two o'clock I should say it was, sir. I cleared away the lunch things and laid the table here as you see for supper. The Capting, he told me as I needn't come back."

"What do you usually do?"

"As a general rule, I come back about seven for a couple of hours. Not always—sometimes the Capting would say as I needn't."

"Then you weren't surprised when he told you that yesterday you wouldn't be wanted again?"

"No, sir. I didn't come back the evening before either—on account of the weather. Very considerate gentleman, the Capting was, as long as you didn't try to shirk things. I knew him and his ways pretty well."

"What exactly did he say?"

"Well, he looked out of the window and he says, 'Not a hope of Burnaby today.' 'Shouldn't wonder,' he says, 'if Sittaford isn't cut off altogether. Don't remember such a winter since I was a boy.' That was his friend Major Burnaby over to Sittaford that he was referring to. Always comes on a Friday, he does, he and the Capting play chess and do acrostics. And on Tuesdays the Capting would go to Major Burnaby's. Very regular in his habits was the Capting. Then he said to

174

me: 'You can go now, Evans, and you needn't come till tomorrow morning.' "

"Apart from his reference to Major Burnaby, he didn't speak of expecting anyone that afternoon?"

"No, sir, not a word."

"There was nothing unusual or different in any way in his manner?"

"No, sir, not that I could see."

"Ah! Now I understand, Evans, that you have lately got married."

"Yes, sir. Mrs. Belling's daughter at the Three Crowns. Matter of two months ago, sir."

"And Captain Trevelyan was not overpleased about it."

A very faint grin appeared for a moment on Evans' face.

"Cut up rough about it, he did, the Capting. My Rebecca is a fine girl, sir, and a very good cook. And I hoped we might have been able to do for the Capting together, but he—he wouldn't hear of it. Said he wouldn't have women servants about his house. In fact, sir, things were rather at a deadlock when this South African lady came along and wanted to take Sittaford House for the winter. The Capting he rented this place, I came in to do for him every day, and I don't mind telling you, sir, that I had been hoping that by the end of the winter the Capting would have come round to the idea; and that me and Rebecca would go back to Sittaford with him. Why, he would never even know she was in the house. She would keep to the kitchen, and she would manage so that he would never meet her on the stairs."

"Have you any idea what lay behind Captain Trevelyan's dislike of women?"

"Nothing to it, sir. Just an 'abit, sir, that's all. I have seen many a gentleman like it before. If you ask me, it's nothing more or less than shyness. Some young lady or other gives them a snub when they are young—and they gets the 'abit."

"Captain Trevelyan was not married?"

"No, indeed, sir."

"What relations had he? Do you know?"

"I believe he had a sister living at Exeter, sir, and I think I have heard him mention a nephew or nephews."

"None of them ever came to see him?"

"No, sir. I think he quarreled with his sister at Exeter."

"Do you know her name?"

"Gardner, I think, sir, but I wouldn't be sure."

"You don't know her address?"

"I'm afraid I don't, sir."

"Well, doubtless we shall come across that in looking through Captain Trevelyan's papers. Now, Evans, what were you yourself doing from four o'clock onwards yesterday afternoon?"

"I was at home, sir."

"Where's home?"

"Just round the corner, sir, 85 Fore Street."

"You didn't go out at all?"

"Not likely, sir. Why, the snow was coming down a fair treat."

"Yes, yes. Is there anyone who can support your statement?"

"Beg pardon, sir?"

"Is there anyone who knows that you were at home during that time?"

"My wife, sir."

"She and you were alone in the house?"

"Yes, sir."

"Well, well, I have no doubt that's all right. That will be all for the present, Evans."

The ex-sailor hesitated. He shifted from one foot to the other.

"Anything I can do here, sir—in the way of tidying up?"

"No—the whole place is to be left exactly as it is for the present."

"I see."

"You had better wait, though, until I have had a look round," said Narracott, "in case there might be any question I want to ask you."

"Very good, sir."

Inspector Narracott transferred his gaze from Evans to the room.

The interview had taken place in the dining-room. On the table an evening meal was set out. A cold tongue, pickles, a Stilton cheese and biscuits, and on a gas ring by the fire a saucepan containing soup. On the sideboard was a tantalus, a soda water siphon, and two bottles of beer. There was also an immense array of silver cups and with them—a rather incongruous item, three very new looking novels.

Inspector Narracott examined one or two of the cups and read the inscriptions on them.

"Bit of a sportsman, Captain Trevelyan," he observed.

"Yes, indeed, sir," said Evans. "Been an athlete all his life, he had."

Inspector Narracott read the titles of the novels.

"Love Turns the Key," "The Merry Men of Lincoln," "Love's Prisoner."

"H'm," he remarked. "The Captain's taste in literature seems somewhat incongruous."

"Oh! that, sir." Evans laughed. "That's not for reading, sir. That's the prizes he won in these Railway Pictures Names Competitions. Ten solutions the Capting sent in under different names, including mine, because he said 85 Fore Street was a likely address to give a prize to! The commoner your name and address the more likely you were to get a prize in the Capting's opinion. And sure enough a prize I got—but not the £2,000, only three new novels—and the kind of novels, in my opinion, that no one would ever pay money for in a shop."

Narracott smiled, then, again mentioning that Evans was to wait, he proceeded on his tour of inspection. There was a large kind of cupboard in one corner of the room. It was almost a small room in itself. Here, packed in unceremoniously, were two pairs of skis, a pair of sculls mounted, ten or twelve hippopotamus tusks, rods and lines and various fishing tackle including a book of flies, a bag of golf clubs, a tennis racket, an elephant's foot stuffed and mounted and a tiger skin. It was clear that, when Captain Trevelyan had let Sittaford House furnished, he had removed his most precious possessions, distrustful of female influence.

"Funny idea—to bring all this with him," said the Inspector. "The house was only let for a few months, wasn't it?"

"That's right, sir."

"Surely these things could have been locked up at Sittaford House?"

For the second time in the course of the interview, Evans grinned.

"That would have been much the easiest way of doing it," he agreed. "Not that there *are* many cupboards at Sittaford House. The architect and the Capting planned it together, and it takes a female to understand the value of cupboard room. Still, as you say, sir, that would have been the common-sense thing to do. Carting them down here was a job—I should say it was a job! But there, the Capting couldn't bear the idea of anyone messing around with his things. And lock things up as you will, he says, a woman will always find a way of getting in. It's curiosity, he says. Better not lock them up at all if you don't want her to handle them, he says. But best of all, take them along, and then you're sure to be on the safe side. So take 'em along we did, and as I say, it was a job, and came expensive too. But there, those things of the Capting's was like his children."

Evans paused out of breath.

Inspector Narracott nodded thoughtfully. There was another point on which he wanted information, and it seemed to him that this was a good moment when the subject had arisen naturally.

"This Mrs. Willett," he said casually. "Was she an old friend or acquaintance of the Captain's?"

"Oh! no, sir, she was quite a stranger to him."

"You are sure of that?" said the Inspector, sharply.

"Well—" the sharpness took the old sailor aback. "The Capting never actually said so—but—Oh! yes, I'm sure of it."

"I ask," explained the Inspector, "because it is a very curious time of year for a let. On the other hand, if this Mrs. Willett was acquainted with Captain Trevelyan and knew the house, she might have written to him and suggested taking it."

Evans shook his head.

"'Twas the agents—Williamsons—that wrote, said they had an offer from a lady."

Inspector Narracott frowned. He found this business of the letting of Sittaford House distinctly odd.

"Captain Trevelyan and Mrs. Willett met, I suppose?" he asked.

"Oh! yes. She came to see the house and he took her over it."

"And you're positive they hadn't met before?"

"Oh! quite, sir."

"Did they—er—" the Inspector paused, as he tried to frame the question naturally. "Did they get on well together? Were they friendly?"

"The lady was." A faint smile crossed Evans' lips. "All over him, as you might say. Admiring the house, and asking him if he'd planned the building of it. Altogether laying it on thick, as you might say."

"And the Captain?"

The smile broadened.

"That sort of gushing lady wasn't likely to cut any ice with him. Polite he was, but nothing more. And declined her invitations."

"Invitations?"

"Yes, to consider the house as his own any time, and drop in, that's how she put it—drop in. You don't drop in to a place when you're living six miles away."

"She seemed anxious to—well—to see something of the Captain?"

Narracott was wondering. Was that the reason for the taking of the house? Was it only a prelude to the making of Captain Trevelyan's acquaintance? Was that the real game? It would probably not have occurred to her that the Captain would have gone as far as Exhampton to live. She might have calculated on his moving into one of the small bungalows, perhaps sharing Major Burnaby's.

Evans' answer was not very helpful.

"She's a very hospitable lady, by all accounts. Someone in to lunch or dinner every day."

Narracott nodded. He could learn no more here. But he determined to seek an interview with this Mrs. Willett at an early date. Her abrupt arrival needed looking into.

"Come on, Pollock, we'll go upstairs now," he said.

They left Evans in the dining-room and proceeded to the upper story.

"All right, do you think?" asked the Sergeant in a low voice, jerking his head over his shoulder in the direction of the closed dining-room door.

"He seems so," said the Inspector. "But one never knows. He's no fool, that fellow, whatever else he is."

"No, he's an intelligent sort of chap."

"His story seems straightforward enough," went on the Inspector. "Perfectly clear and above board. Still, as I say, one never knows."

And with this pronouncement, very typical of his careful and suspicious mind, the Inspector proceeded to search the rooms on the first floor.

There were three bedrooms and a bathroom. Two of the bedrooms were empty and had clearly not been entered for some weeks. The third, Captain Trevelyan's own room, was in exquisite and apple-pie order. Inspector Narracott moved about in it, opening drawers and cupboards. Everything was in its right place. It was the room of a man almost fanatically tidy and neat in his habits. Narracott finished his inspection and glanced into the adjoining bathroom. Here, too, everything was in order. He gave a last glance at the bed, neatly turned down, with folded pajamas laid ready.

Then he shook his head.

"Nothing here," he said.

"No, everything seems in perfect order."

"There are the papers in the desk in the study. You had better go through those, Pollock. I'll tell Evans that he can go. I may call round and see him at his own place later."

"Very good, sir."

"The body can be removed. I shall want to see Warren, by the way. He lives near here, doesn't he?"

"Yes, sir."

"This side of the Three Crowns or the other?"

"The other, sir."

"Then I'll take the Three Crowns first. Carry on, Sergeant."

Pollock went to the dining-room to dismiss Evans. The Inspector passed out of the front door and walked rapidly in the direction of the Three Crowns.

6

At the Three Crowns

INSPECTOR NARRACOTT was not destined to see Major Burnaby until he
had had a protracted interview with Mrs. Belling—licensed proprietor
of the Three Crowns. Mrs. Belling was fat and excitable, and so
voluble that there was nothing to be done but to listen patiently until
such time as the stream of conversation should dry up.

"And such a night as never was," she ended up. "And little did any
of us think what was happening to the poor dear gentleman. Those
nasty tramps—if I've said it once, I've said it a dozen times, I can't
abear those nasty tramps. Do anybody in they would. The Captain had
not so much as a dog to protect him. Can't abear a dog, tramps can't.
Ah, well, you never know what is happening within a stone's throw.

"Yes, Mr. Narracott," she proceeded in answer to his question,
"the Major is having his breakfast now. You will find him in the
coffee-room. And what kind of a night he has passed with no
pajamas or anything, and me a widow woman with nothing to lend
him, I can't say, I am sure. Said it made no matter he did—all upset
and queer he was—and no wonder with his best friend murdered.
Very nice gentlemen the two of them, though the Captain had the
reputation of being close with his money. Ah, well, well, I have
always thought it dangerous to live up to Sittaford, miles away
from anywhere, and here's the Captain struck down in Exhampton
itself. It's always what you don't expect in this life that happens,
isn't it, Mr. Narracott?"

The Inspector said that undoubtedly it was. Then he added:

"Who did you have staying here yesterday, Mrs. Belling? Any
strangers?"

"Now, let me see. There was Mr. Moresby and Mr. Jones—
commercial gentlemen they are, and there was a young gentleman
from London. Nobody else. It stands to reason there wouldn't be this
time of year. Very quiet here in the winter. Oh, and there was another
young gentleman—arrived by the last train. Nosy young fellow I call
him. He isn't up yet."

"The last train?" said the Inspector. "That gets in at ten o'clock, eh?
I don't think we need trouble ourselves about him. What about the
other—the one from London? Did you know him?"

"Never seen him before in my life. Not a commercial gentleman, oh,
no—a cut above that. I can't remember his name for the moment—but

you'll find it in the register. Left on the first train to Exeter this morning, he did. Six ten. Rather curious. What did he want down here anyway, that's what I'd like to know."

"He didn't mention his business?"

"Not a word."

"Did he go out at all?"

"Arrived at lunch time, went out about half past four and came in about twenty past six."

"Where did he go when he went out?"

"I haven't the remotest idea, sir. May have been just for a stroll like. That was before the snow came, but it wasn't what you might call a pleasant day for walking."

"Went out at half past four and returned about twenty past six," said the Inspector thoughtfully. "That's rather odd. He didn't mention Captain Trevelyan?"

Mrs. Belling shook her head decisively.

"No, Mr. Narracott, he didn't mention anybody at all. Kept himself to himself he did. A nice looking young fellow—but worried, I should say."

The Inspector nodded and stepped across to inspect the register.

"James Pearson, London," said the Inspector. "Well—that doesn't tell us much. We'll have to make a few inquiries about Mr. James Pearson."

Then he strode off to the coffee-room in search of Major Burnaby.

The Major was the only occupant of the room. He was drinking some rather muddy looking coffee and the *Times* was propped up in front of him.

"Major Burnaby?"

"That's my name."

"I am Inspector Narracott from Exeter."

"Good morning, Inspector. Any forrarder?"

"Yes, sir. I think we are a little forrarder. I think I can safely say that."

"Glad to hear it," said the Major drily. His attitude was one of resigned disbelief.

"Now there are just one or two points I would like some information on, Major Burnaby," said the Inspector, "and I think you can probably tell me what I want to know."

"Do what I can," said Burnaby.

"Had Captain Trevelyan any enemies to your knowledge?"

"Not an enemy in the world." Burnaby was decisive.

"This man, Evans—do you yourself consider him trustworthy?"

"Should think so. Trevelyan trusted him I know."

"There was no ill feeling about this marriage of his?"

"Not ill feeling, no. Trevelyan was annoyed—didn't like his habits upset. Old bachelor, you know."

"Talking of bachelors, that's another point. Captain Trevelyan was unmarried—do you know if he made a will? And in the event of there being no will, have you any idea who would inherit his estate?"

"Trevelyan made a will," said Burnaby promptly.

"Ah—you know that."

"Yes. Made me executor. Told me so."

"Do you know how he left his money?"

"That I can't say."

"I understand he was very comfortably off?"

"Trevelyan was a rich man," replied Burnaby. "I should say he was much better off than anyone round here suspected."

"What relations had he—do you know?"

"He'd a sister and some nephews and nieces I believe. Never saw much of any of them, but there was no quarrel."

"About this will, do you know where he kept it?"

"It's at Walters & Kirkwood—the solicitors here in Exhampton. They drew it up for him."

"Then, perhaps, Major Burnaby, as you are executor, I wonder if you would come round to Walters & Kirkwood with me now. I should like to have an idea of the contents of that will as soon as possible."

Burnaby looked up alertly.

"What's in the wind?" he said. "What's the will got to do with it?"

Inspector Narracott was not disposed to show his hand too soon.

"The case isn't such plain sailing as we thought," he said. "By the way, there's another question I want to ask you. I understand, Major Burnaby, that you asked Dr. Warren whether death had occurred at five and twenty minutes past five?"

"Well," said the Major gruffly.

"What made you select that exact time, Major?"

"Why shouldn't I?" said Burnaby.

"Well—something must have put it into your head."

There was quite a pause before Major Burnaby replied. Inspector Narracott's interest was aroused. The Major had something which he quite patently wished to conceal. To watch him doing so was almost ludicrous.

"Why shouldn't I say twenty-five past five?" he demanded truculently, "or twenty-five or six—or twenty past four, for that matter?"

"Quite so, sir," said Inspector Narracott soothingly.

He did not wish to antagonize the Major just at this moment. He promised himself that he would get to the bottom of the matter before the day was out.

"There's one thing that strikes me as curious, sir," he went on.

"Yes?"

"This business of the letting of Sittaford House. I don't know what you think about it, but it seems to me a curious thing to have happened."

"If you ask me," said Burnaby, "it's damned odd."

"That's your opinion?"

"It's everyone's opinion."

"In Sittaford?"

"In Sittaford and Exhampton too. The woman must be mad."

"Well, I suppose there's no accounting for tastes," said the Inspector.

"Damned odd taste for a woman of that kind."

"You know the lady?"

"I know her. Why, I was at her house when—"

"When what?" asked Narracott as the Major came to an abrupt halt.

"Nothing," said Burnaby.

Inspector Narracott looked at him keenly. There was something here he would have liked to get at. The Major's obvious confusion and embarrassment did not escape him. He had been on the point of saying—what?

"All in good time," said Narracott to himself. "Now isn't the moment to rub him up the wrong way."

Aloud he said innocently:

"You were at Sittaford House, you say, sir. The lady has been there now—about how long?"

"A couple of months."

The Major was eager to escape the result of his imprudent words. It made him more loquacious than usual.

"A widow lady with her daughter?"

"That's it."

"Does she give any reason for her choice of residence?"

"Well—" the Major rubbed his nose dubiously. "She talks a lot, she's that kind of woman—beauties of nature—out of the world—that sort of thing. But—"

He paused rather helplessly. Inspector Narracott came to his rescue.

"It didn't strike you as natural on her part."

"Well, it's like this. She's a fashionable sort of woman. Dressed up to the nines—daughter's a smart, pretty girl. Natural thing would be for them to be staying at the Ritz or Claridges, or some other big hotel somewhere. You know the sort."

Narracott nodded.

"They don't keep themselves to themselves, do they?" he asked. "You don't think they are—well—hiding?"

Major Burnaby shook his head positively.

"Oh! no, nothing of that kind. They're very sociable—a bit too sociable. I mean, in a little place like Sittaford, you can't have previous engagements, and when invitations are showered on you it's a bit awkward. They're exceedingly kind, hospitable people, but a bit too hospitable for English ideas."

"The Colonial touch," said the Inspector.

"Yes, I suppose so."

"You've no reason to think they were previously acquainted with Captain Trevelyan?"

"Sure they weren't."

"You seem very positive?"

"Joe would have told me."

"And you don't think their motive could have been—well—to scrape acquaintance with the Captain?"

This was clearly a new idea to the Major. He pondered over it for some minutes.

"Well, I never thought of that. They were very gushing to him, certainly. Not that they got any change out of Joe. But no, I think it was just their usual manner. Over friendly, you know, like Colonials are," added the Super Insular soldier.

"I see. Now, as to the house itself. Captain Trevelyan built that, I understand?"

"Yes."

"And nobody else has ever lived in it? I mean, it's not been let before?"

"Never."

"Then it doesn't seem as though it could be anything in the house itself that was the attraction. It's a puzzle. Ten to one it's got nothing to do with the case, but it just struck me as an odd coincidence. This house that Captain Trevelyan took, Hazelmoor, whose property was that?"

"Miss Larpent's. Middle-aged woman, she's gone to a boarding house at Cheltenham for the winter. Does every year. Usually shuts the house up, but lets it if she can, which isn't often."

There seemed nothing promising there. The Inspector shook his head in a discouraged fashion.

"Williamsons were the agents, I understand?" he said.

"Yes."

"Their office is in Exhampton?"

"Next door to Walters & Kirkwood."

"Ah! then, perhaps, if you don't mind, Major, we might just drop in on our way."

"Not at all. You won't find Kirkwood at his office before ten anyway. You know what lawyers are."

"Then, shall we go?"

The Major, who had finished his breakfast some time ago, nodded assent and rose.

7

The Will

AN ALERT LOOKING YOUNG MAN rose to receive them in the office of Messrs. Williamson.

"Good morning, Major Burnaby."

"Morning."

"Terrible business, this," said the young man chattily. "Not been such a thing in Exhampton for years."

He spoke with gusto and the Major winced.

"This is Inspector Narracott," he said.

"Oh! yes," said the young man pleasurably excited.

"I want some information that I think you can give me," said the Inspector. "I understand that you put through this let of Sittaford House."

"To Mrs. Willet? Yes, we did."

"Can you give me full details, please, of how that came about. Did the lady apply personally, or by letter?"

"By letter. She wrote, let me see—" He opened a drawer and turned up a file. "Yes, from the Carlton Hotel, London."

"Did she mention Sittaford House by name?"

"No, she merely said she wanted to rent a house for the winter, it must be right on Dartmoor and have at least eight bedrooms. Being near a railway station or a town was of no consequence."

"Was Sittaford House on your books?"

"No, it was not. But as a matter of fact it was the only house in the neighborhood that at all fulfilled the requirements. The lady mentioned in her letter that she would be willing to go to twelve guineas, and in these circumstances I thought it worth while writing to Captain Trevelyan and asking whether he would consider letting. He replied in the affirmative, and we fixed the thing up."

"Without Mrs. Willett seeing the house?"

"She agreed to take it without seeing it, and signed the agreement. Then she came down here for one day, drove up to Sittaford, saw Captain Trevelyan, arranged with him about plate and linen, etc. and saw over the house."

"She was quite satisfied?"

"She came in and said she was delighted with it."

"And what did you think?" asked Inspector Narracott, eyeing him keenly.

The young man shrugged his shoulders.

"You learn never to be surprised at anything in the house business," he said.

On this note of philosophy they left, the Inspector thanking the young man for his help.

"Not at all, a pleasure, I'm sure."

He accompanied them politely to the door.

The offices of Messrs. Walters & Kirkwood were, as Major Burnaby had said, next door to the estate agents. On reaching there, they were told that Mr. Kirkwood had just arrived and they were shown into his room.

Mr. Kirkwood was an elderly man with a benign expression. He was a native of Exhampton and had succeeded his father and grandfather in the firm.

He rose, put on his mourning face, and shook hands with the Major.

"Good morning, Major Burnaby," he said. "This is a very shocking affair. Very shocking indeed. Poor Trevelyan."

He looked inquiringly at Narracott and Major Burnaby explained his presence in a few succinct words.

"You are in charge of the case, Inspector Narracott?"

"Yes, Mr. Kirkwood. In pursuance of my investigations, I have come to ask you for certain information."

"I shall be happy to give you any information if it is proper for me to do so," said the lawyer.

"It concerns the late Captain Trevelyan's will," said Narracott. "I understand the will is here in your office."

"That is so."

"It was made some time ago?"

"Five or six years ago. I cannot be sure of the exact date at the moment."

"Ah! I am anxious, Mr. Kirkwood, to know the contents of that will as soon as possible. It may have an important bearing on the case."

"Indeed?" said the lawyer. "Indeed! I should not have thought that, but naturally you know your own business best, Inspector. Well—" he glanced across at the other man. "Major Burnaby and myself are joint executors of the will. If he has no objection—"

"None."

"Then I see no reason why I should not accede to your request, Inspector."

Taking up a telephone that stood on his desk he spoke a few words down it. In two or three minutes a clerk entered the room and laid a sealed envelope in front of the lawyer. The clerk left the room, Mr. Kirkwood picked up the envelope, slit it open with a paper knife and drew out a large and important looking document, cleared his throat and began to read—

"I, Joseph Arthur Trevelyan, of Sittaford House, Sittaford, in the County of Devon, declare this to be my last will and testament which I make this thirteenth day of August nineteen hundred and twenty-six.

"(1) I appoint John Edward Burnaby of I The Cottages, Sittaford, and Frederick Kirkwood of Exhampton, to be the executors and trustees of this, my will.

"(2) I give to Robert Henry Evans, who has served me long and faithfully, the sum of £100 (one hundred pounds) free of legacy duty for his own benefit absolutely, provided that he is in my service at the time of my death and not under notice to leave whether given or received.

"(3) I give the said John Edward Burnaby, as a token of our friendship and of my affection and regard for him, all my trophies of sport, including my collection of heads and pelts of big game as well as any challenge cups and prizes awarded to me in any department of sport and any spoils of the chase in my possession.

"(4) I give all my real and personal property, not otherwise disposed of by this, my will, or any codicil hereto, to my Trustees upon Trust that my Trustees shall sell, call in and convert the same into money.

"(5) My Trustees shall out of the moneys to arise out of such sale, calling in and conversion, pay any funeral and testamentary expenses and debts, and the legacies given by this, my will, or any codicil hereto and all death duties and other moneys.

"(6) My Trustees shall hold the residue of such moneys or the investments for the time being, representing the same upon Trust to divide the same into four equal parts or shares.

"(7) Upon such divison as aforesaid my Trustees shall hold one such equal fourth part or share upon Trust to pay the same to my sister Jennifer Gardner for her own use and enjoyment absolutely.

"And my Trustees shall hold the remaining three such equal fourth parts or shares upon Trust to pay one such equal fourth part or share to each of the three children of my deceased sister, Mary Pearson, for the benefit of each such child absolutely.

"In Witness whereof I, the said Joseph Arthur Trevelyan, have hereunto set my hand the day and year first above written.

"Signed by the above named Testator as his last will in the presence of us both present at the same time, who in his presence and at his request and in the presence of each other have hereunto subscribed our names as witness."

Mr. Kirkwood handed the document to the Inspector.

"Witnessed by two of my clerks in this office."

The Inspector ran his eye over the will thoughtfully.

"My deceased sister, Mary Pearson," he said. "Can you tell me anything about Mrs. Pearson, Mr. Kirkwood?"

"Very little. She died about ten years ago, I believe. Her husband, a stockbroker, had predeceased her. As far as I know, she never visited Captain Trevelyan here."

"Pearson," said the Inspector again. Then he added: "One thing more. The amount of Captain Trevelyan's estate is not mentioned. To what sum do you think it will amount?"

"That is difficult to say exactly," said Mr. Kirkwood, enjoying, like all lawyers, making the reply to a simple question difficult. "It is a question of real or personal estate. Besides Sittaford House, Captain Trevelyan owns some property in the neighborhood of Plymouth, and various investments he made from time to time have fluctuated in value."

"I just want an approximate idea," said Inspector Narracott.

"I should not like to commit myself—"

"Just the roughest estimate as a guide. For instance would twenty thousand pounds be out of the way?"

"Twenty thousand pounds. My dear sir! Captain Trevelyan's estate will be worth at least four times as much as that. Eighty or even ninety thousand pounds will be much nearer the mark."

"I told you Trevelyan was a rich man," said Burnaby.

Inspector Narracott rose.

"Thank you very much, Mr. Kirkwood," he said, "for the information you have given me."

"You think you will find it helpful, eh?"

The lawyer very clearly was agog with curiosity, but Inspector Narracott was in no mood to satisfy it at present.

"In a case like this we have to take everything into account," he said, noncommittally. "By the way, have you the names and addresses of this Jennifer Gardner and of the Pearson family?"

"I know nothing of the Pearson family. Mrs. Gardner's address is The Laurels, Waldon Road, Exeter."

The Inspector noted it down in his book.

"That will do to get on with," he said. "You don't know how many children the late Mrs. Pearson left?"

"Three, I fancy. Two girls and a boy—or possibly two boys and a girl—I cannot remember which."

The Inspector nodded and put away his notebook and thanked the lawyer once more and took his departure.

When they had reached the street, he turned suddenly and faced his companion.

"And now, sir," he said, "we'll have the truth about that twenty-five past five business."

Major Burnaby's face reddened with annoyance.

"I have told you already—"

"That won't go down with me. Withholding information, that is what you are doing, Major Burnaby. You must have had some idea in mentioning that specific time to Dr. Warren—and I think I have a very good idea of what that something is."

"Well, if you know about it, why ask me?" growled the Major.

"I take it that you were aware that a certain person had an appointment with Captain Trevelyan somewhere about that time. Now, isn't that so?"

Major Burnaby stared at him in surprise.

"Nothing of the kind," he snarled, "nothing of the kind."

"Be careful, Major Burnaby. What about Mr. James Pearson?"

"James Pearson? James Pearson, who's he? Do you mean one of Trevelyan's nephews?"

"I presume it would be a nephew. He had one called James, hadn't he?"

"Not the least idea. Trevelyan had nephews—I know that. But what their names were, I haven't the vaguest idea."

"The young man in question was at the Three Crowns last night. You probably recognized him there."

"I didn't recognize anybody," growled the Major. "Shouldn't anyway—never saw any of Trevelyan's nephews in my life."

"But you knew that Captain Trevelyan was expecting a nephew to call upon him yesterday afternoon?"

"I did not," roared the Major.

Several people in the street turned round to stare at him.

"Damn it, won't you take plain truth! I knew nothing about any appointment. Trevelyan's nephews may have been in Timbuctoo for all I knew about them."

Inspector Narracott was a little taken aback. The Major's vehement denial bore the mark of truth too plainly for him to be deceived.

"Then why this twenty-five past five business?"

"Oh! well—I suppose I had better tell you," the Major coughed in an embarrassed fashion. "But mind you—the whole thing is damned foolishness! Tommy rot, sir. How any thinking man can believe such nonsense!"

Inspector Narracott looked more and more surprised. Major Burnaby was looking more uncomfortable and ashamed of himself every minute.

"You know what it is, Inspector. You have to join in these things to please a lady. Of course, I never thought there was anything in it."

"In what, Major Burnaby?"

"Table turning."

"*Table turning*?"

Whatever Narracott had expected he had not expected this. The Major proceeded to explain himself. Haltingly, and with many disclaimers to his own belief in the thing, he described the events of the previous afternoon and the message that had purported to come through for himself.

"You mean, Major Burnaby, that the table spelt out the name of Trevelyan and informed you that he was dead—murdered?"

Major Burnaby wiped his forehead.

"Yes, that's what happened. I didn't believe in it—naturally. I didn't believe in it." He looked ashamed. "Well—it was Friday and I thought after all I would make sure and go along and see if everything was all right."

The Inspector reflected on the difficulties of that six mile walk, with the piled up snowdrifts and the prospect of a heavy snow fall, and he realized that deny it as he would Major Burnaby must have been deeply impressed by the spirit message. Narracott turned it over in his mind. A queer thing to happen—a very queer thing to happen. The sort of thing you couldn't explain satisfactorily. There might be something in this spirit business after all. It was the first well authenticated case he had come across.

A very queer business altogether but, as far as he could see, though it explained Major Burnaby's attitude, it had no practical bearing on the case as far as he himself was concerned. He had to deal with the physical world and not the psychic.

It was his job to track down the murderer.

And to do that he required no guidance from the spirit world.

8

Mr. Charles Enderby

GLANCING AT HIS WATCH, the Inspector realized he could just catch the train for Exeter if he hurried off. He was anxious to interview the late Captain Trevelyan's sister as soon as possible and obtain from her the addresses of the other members of the family. So, with a hurried word of farewell to Major Burnaby, he raced off to the station. The Major retraced his steps to the Three Crowns. He had hardly put a foot across the doorstep when he was accosted by a bright young man with a very shiny head and a round, boyish face.

"Major Burnaby?" said the young man.

"Yes."

"Of No. 1 Sittaford Cottages?"

"Yes," said Major Burnaby.

"I represent the *Daily Wire*," said the young man, "and I—"

He got no further. In true military fashion of the old school, the Major exploded.

"Not another word," he roared. "I know you and your kind. No decency. No reticence. Clustering round a murder like vultures round a carcass, but I can tell you, young man, you will get no information from me. Not a word. No story for your damned paper. If you want to know anything, go and ask the police, and have the decency to leave the friends of the dead man alone."

The young man seemed not a whit taken aback. He smiled more encouragingly than ever.

"I say, sir, you know you have got hold of the wrong end of the stick. I know nothing about this murder business."

This was not, strictly speaking, the truth. No one in Exhampton could pretend ignorance of the event that had shaken the quiet moorland town to its core.

"I am empowered on behalf of the *Daily Wire*," went on the young man, "to hand you this check for £5,000 and congratulate you on sending in the only correct solution of our football competition."

Major Burnaby was completely taken aback.

"I have no doubt," continued the young man, "That you have already received our letter yesterday morning informing you of the good news."

"Letter?" said Major Burnaby. "Do you realize, young man, that Sittaford is about ten feet deep in snow? What chance do you think we have had in the last few days of a regular delivery of letters?"

"But doubtless you saw your name announced as winner in the *Daily Wire*, this morning?"

"No," said Major Burnaby. "I haven't glanced at the paper this morning."

"Ah! of course not," said the young man. "This sad business. The murdered man was a friend of yours, I understand."

"My best friend," said the Major.

"Hard lines," said the young man tactfully averting his eyes. Then he drew from his pocket a small folded piece of mauve paper and handed it to Major Burnaby with a bow.

"With the compliments of the *Daily Wire*," he said.

Major Burnaby took it and said the only thing possible under the circumstances.

"Have a drink, Mr.—er—?"

"Enderby, Charles Enderby my name is. I got here last night," he explained. "Made inquiries about getting to Sittaford. We make it a point to hand checks to winners personally. Always publish a little interview. Interests our readers. Well, everyone told me it was out of the question—the snow was falling and it simply couldn't be done, and then with the greatest good luck I find you are actually here, staying at the Three Crowns." He smiled. "No difficulty about identification. Everybody seems to know everybody else in this part of the world."

"What will you have?" said the Major.

"Beer for me," said Enderby.

The Major ordered two beers.

"The whole place seems off its head with this murder," remarked Enderby. "Rather a mysterious business by all accounts."

The Major grunted. He was in something of a quandary. His sentiments towards journalists remained unchanged, but a man who has just handed you a check for £5,000 is in a privileged position. You cannot very well tell him to go to the devil.

"No enemies, had he?" asked the young man.

"No," said the Major.

"But I hear the police don't think it is robbery," went on Enderby.

"How do you know that?" asked the Major.

Mr. Enderby, however, did not reveal the source of his information.

"I hear it was you who actually discovered the body, sir," said the young man.

"Yes."

"It must have been an awful shock."

The conversation proceeded. Major Burnaby was still determined to give no information, but he was no match for the adroitness of Mr. Enderby. The latter made statements with which the Major was forced to agree or disagree thereby providing the information the young man wanted. So pleasant was his manner, however, that the process was really not painful at all and the Major found himself taking quite a liking to the ingenuous young man.

Presently, Mr. Enderby rose and observed that he must go along to the post office.

"If you will just give me a receipt for that check, sir."

The Major went across to the writing table, wrote a receipt and handed it to him.

"Splendid," said the young man and slipped it into his pocket.

"I suppose," said Major Burnaby, "that you are off back to London today?"

"Oh! no," said the young man. "I want to take a few photographs, you know, of your cottage at Sittaford, and of you feeding the pigs, or hoeing up dandelions, or doing anything characteristic that you fancy. You have no idea how our readers appreciate that sort of thing. Then I would like to have a few words from you on 'What I intend to do with the £5,000.' Something snappy. You have no idea how disappointed our readers would be if they didn't get that sort of thing."

"Yes, but look here—it's impossible to get to Sittaford in this weather. The fall of snow was exceptionally heavy. No vehicle has been able to take the road for three days anyway, and it may be another three before the thaw sets in properly."

"I know," said the young man, "it *is* awkward. Well, well, one will just have to resign oneself to kicking up one's heels in Exhampton. They do you pretty well at the Three Crowns. So long, sir, see you later."

He emerged into the main street of Exhampton and made his way to the post office and wired his paper that by the greatest of good luck he would be able to supply them with tasty and exclusive information on the Exhampton Murder Case.

He reflected on his next course of action and decided on interviewing the late Captain Trevelyan's servant, Evans, whose name Major Burnaby had incautiously let slip during their conversation.

A few inquiries brought him to 85 Fore Street. The servant of the murdered man was a person of importance today. Everyone was willing and anxious to point out where he lived.

Enderby beat a smart rat-tat on the door. It was opened by a man so typically an ex-sailor that Enderby had no doubt of his identity.

"Evans, isn't it?" said Mr. Enderby cheerfully. "I have just come along from Major Burnaby."

"Oh!—" Evans hesitated a moment. "Will you come in, sir."

Enderby accepted the invitation. A buxom young woman with dark hair and red cheeks hovered in the background. Enderby judged her as the newly-wed Mrs. Evans.

"Bad thing this about your late master," said Enderby.

"It's shocking, sir, that's what it is."

"Who do you think did it?" demanded Enderby with an ingenuous air of seeking information.

"One of these low down tramps, I suppose," said Evans.

"Oh! no, my dear man. That theory is quite exploded."

"Eh?"

"That's all a put up job. The police saw through that at once."

"Who told you that, sir?"

Enderby's real informant had been the housemaid at the Three Crowns whose sister was the legal spouse of Constable Graves, but he replied:

"Had a tip from headquarters. Yes, the burglary idea was all a put up job."

"Who do they think did it then?" demanded Mrs. Evans coming forward. Her eyes looked frightened and eager.

"Now, Rebecca, don't you take on so," said her husband.

"Cruel stupid the police are," said Mrs. Evans. "Don't mind who they take up as long as they get hold of someone."

She cast a quick glance at Enderby.

"Are you connected with the police, sir?"

"Me? Oh! no. I am from a newspaper, the *Daily Wire*. I came down to see Major Burnaby. He has just won our Free Football Competition for £5,000."

"What?" cried Evans. "Damn it all, then these things are square after all."

"Didn't you think they were?" asked Enderby.

"Well, it's a wicked world, sir." Evans was a little confused, feeling that his exclamation had been wanting in tact. "I have heard there's a lot of trickery concerned. The late Capting used to say that a prize never went to a good address. That's why he used mine time and again."

With a certain naïveté he described the Captain's winning of three new novels.

Enderby encouraged him to talk. He saw a very good story being made out of Evans. The faithful servant—old sea dog touch. He wondered just a little why Mrs. Evans seemed so nervous, he put it down to the suspicious ignorance of her class.

"You find the skunk what done it," said Evans. "Newspapers can do a lot, they say, in hunting down criminals."

"It was a burglar," said Mrs. Evans, "That's what it was."

"Of course, it was a burglar," said Evans, "Why, there's no one in Exhampton would want to harm the Capting."

Enderby rose.

"Well," he said. "I must be going. I will run in now and then and have a little chat if I may. If the Captain won three new novels in a *Daily Wire* Competition, the *Daily Wire* ought to make it a personal matter to hunt down his murderer."

"You can't say fairer than that, sir. No, you can't say fairer than that."

Wishing them a cheery good day, Charles Enderby took his leave.

"I wonder who really did the beggar in?" he murmured to himself. "I don't think our friend Evans. Perhaps it *was* a burglar! Very disappointing, if so. Doesn't seem any women in the case, which is a pity. We've got to have some sensational development soon or the case will fade into insignificance. Just my luck, if so. First time I have ever been on the spot in a matter of this kind. I must make good. Charles, my boy, your chance in life has come. Make the most of it. Our military friend will, I see, soon be eating out of my hand if I remember to be sufficiently respectful and call him 'sir,' often enough. Wonder if he was in the Indian Mutiny. No, of course not, not old enough for that. The South African War, that's it. Ask him about the South African War, that will tame him."

And pondering these good resolutions in his mind Mr. Enderby sauntered back to the Three Crowns.

9

The Laurels

It takes about half an hour from Exhampton to Exeter by train. At five minutes to twelve Inspector Narracott was ringing the front door bell of The Laurels.

The Laurels was a somewhat dilapidated house, badly in need of a new coat of paint. The garden round it was unkempt and weedy and the gate hung askew on its hinges.

"Not too much money about here," thought Inspector Narracott to himself. "Evidently hard up."

He was a very fair-minded man, but inquiries seemed to indicate that there was very little possibility of the Captain's having been done to death by an enemy. On the other hand, four people, as far as he could make out, stood to gain a considerable sum by the old man's death. The movements of each of these four people had got to be inquired into. The entry in the hotel register was suggestive, but after all Pearson was quite a common name. Inspector Narracott was anxious not to come to any decision too rapidly and to keep a perfectly open mind whilst covering the preliminary ground as rapidly as possible.

A somewhat slatternly looking maid answered the bell.

"Good afternoon," said Inspector Narracott. "I want to see Mrs. Gardner, please. It is in connection with the death of her brother, Captain Trevelyan, at Exhampton."

He purposely did not hand his official card to the maid. The mere fact of his being a police officer, as he knew by experience, would render her awkward and tongue-tied.

"She's heard of her brother's death?" asked the Inspector casually as the maid drew back to let him into the hall.

"Yes, got a telegram she did. From the lawyer, Mr. Kirkwood."

"Just so," said Inspector Narracott.

The maid ushered him into the drawing-room—a room which, like the outside of the house, was badly in need of a little money spent upon it, but yet, had with all that an air of charm which the Inspector felt without being able to particularize the why and wherefore of it.

"Must have been a shock to your mistress," he observed.

The girl seemed a little vague about that, he noticed.

"She didn't see much of him," was her answer.

"Shut the door and come here," said Inspector Narracott.

He was anxious to try the effect of a surprise attack.

"Did the telegram say that it was murder?" he asked.

"Murder!"

The girl's eyes opened wide, a mixture of horror and intense enjoyment in them. "Murdered was he?"

"Ah!" said Inspector Narracott, "I thought you hadn't heard that. Mr. Kirkwood didn't want to break the news too abruptly to your mistress, but you see, my dear—what is your name, by the way?"

"Beatrice, sir."

"Well, you see, Beatrice, it will be in the evening papers tonight."

"Well, I never," said Beatrice. "Murdered. 'orrible, isn't it? Did they bash his head in or shoot him or what?"

The Inspector satisfied her passion for detail, then added casually, "I believe there was some idea of your mistress going over to Exhampton yesterday afternoon. But I suppose the weather was too bad for her."

"I never heard anything about it, sir," said Beatrice. "I think you must have made a mistake. The mistress went out in the afternoon to do some shopping and then she went to the Pictures."

"What time did she get in?"

"About six o'clock."

So that let Mrs. Gardner out.

"I don't know much about the family," he went on in a casual tone. "Is Mrs. Gardner a widow?"

"Oh, no, sir, there's master."

"What does he do?"

"He doesn't do anything," said Beatrice staring. "He can't. He's an invalid."

"An invalid, is he? Oh, I'm sorry. I hadn't heard."

"He can't walk. He lies in bed all day. Got a nurse always in the house we have. It isn't every girl what stays on with an 'ospital nurse in the house the whole time. Always wanting trays carried up and pots of tea made."

"Must be very trying," said the Inspector soothingly. "Now, will you go and tell your mistress please, that I am here from Mr. Kirkwood of Exhampton?"

Beatrice withdrew and a few minutes later the door opened and a tall, rather commanding woman came into the room. She had an unusual looking face, broad about the brows, and black hair with a touch of gray at the temples, which she wore combed straight back from her forehead. She looked at the Inspector inquiringly.

"You have come from Mr. Kirkwood at Exhampton?"

"Not exactly, Mrs. Gardner. I put it that way to your maid. Your brother, Captain Trevelyan, was murdered yesterday afternoon and I am Divisional Inspector Narracott in charge of the case."

Whatever else Mrs. Gardner might be she was certainly a woman of iron nerve. Her eyes narrowed and she drew in her breath sharply, then motioning the Inspector to a chair and sitting down herself she said:

"Murdered! How extraordinary! Who in the world would want to murder Joe?"

"That is what I'm anxious to find out, Mrs. Gardner."

"Of course. I hope I shall be able to help you in some way, but I doubt it. My brother and I have seen very little of each other in the last ten years. I know nothing of his friends or of any ties he has formed."

"You'll excuse me, Mrs. Gardner, but had you and your brother quarreled?"

"No—not quarreled. I think estranged would be a better word to describe the position between us. I don't want to go into family details, but my brother rather resented my marriage. Brothers, I think, seldom approve of their sisters' choice, but usually, I fancy, they conceal it better than my brother did. My brother, as perhaps you know, had a large fortune left him by an aunt. Both my sister and myself married poor men. When my husband was invalided out of the army after the war with shell shock, a little financial assistance would have been a wonderful relief—would have enabled me to give him an expensive course of treatment which was otherwise denied to him. I asked my brother for a loan which he refused. That, of course, he was perfectly entitled to do. But since then we have met at very rare intervals, and hardly corresponded at all."

It was a clear succinct statement.

An intriguing personality, this Mrs. Gardner's, the Inspector thought. Somehow, he couldn't quite make her out. She seemed unnaturally calm, unnaturally ready with her recital of facts. He also noticed that, with all her surprise she asked for no details of her brother's death. That struck him as extraordinary.

"I don't know if you want to hear what exactly occurred—at Exhampton," he began.

She frowned.

"Must I hear it? My brother was killed, painlessly—I hope."

"Quite painlessly, I should say."

"Then please spare me any revolting details."

"Unnatural," thought the Inspector, "decidedly unnatural."

As though she had read his mind she used the very word that he had spoken to himself.

"I suppose you think that very unnatural, Inspector, but—I have heard a good many horrors. My husband has told me things when he has had one of his bad turns—" she shivered. "I think you would understand if you knew my circumstances better."

"Oh! quite so, quite so, Mrs. Gardner. What I really came for was to get a few family details from you."

"Yes?"

"Do you know how many relatives living your brother has besides yourself?"

"Of near relations, only the Pearsons. My sister Mary's children."

"And they are?"

"James, Sylvia and Brian."

"James?"

"He is the eldest. He works in an Insurance Office."

"What age is he?"

"Twenty-eight."

"Is he married?"

"No, but he is engaged—to a very nice girl, I believe. I've not yet met her."

"And his address?"

"21 Cromwell Street, S.W.3."

The Inspector noted it down.

"Yes, Mrs. Gardner?"

"Then there's Sylvia. She's married to Martin Dering—you may have read his books. He's a moderately successful author."

"Thank you, and their address?"

"The Nook, Surrey Road, Wimbledon."

"Yes?"

"And the youngest is Brian—but he is out in Australia. I am afraid I don't know his address, but either his brother or sister would know."

"Thank you, Mrs. Gardner. Just as a matter of form, do you mind my asking you how you spent yesterday afternoon?"

She looked surprised.

"Let me see. I did some shopping—yes—then I went to the Pictures. I came home about six and lay down on my bed until dinner, as the Pictures had given me rather a headache."

"Thank you, Mrs. Gardner."

"Is there anything else?"

"No, I don't think I have anything further to ask you. I will now get into communication with your nephew and niece. I don't know if Mr. Kirkwood has informed you of the fact yet, but you and the three young Pearsons are the joint inheritors of Captain Trevelyan's money."

The color came into her face in a slow, rich blush.

"That will be wonderful," she said quietly. "It has been so

difficult—so terribly difficult—always skimping and saving and wishing."

She started up as a man's rather querulous voice came floating down the stairs.

"Jennifer, Jennifer, I want you."

"Excuse me," she said.

As she opened the door the call came again, louder and more imperiously.

"Jennifer, where are you? I want you, Jennifer."

The Inspector had followed her to the door. He stood in the hall looking after her as she ran up the stairs.

"I am coming, dear," she called.

A hospital nurse who was coming down the stairs stood aside to let her pass up.

"Please go to Mr. Gardner, he is getting very excited. You always manage to calm him."

Inspector Narracott stood deliberately in the nurse's way as she reached the bottom of the stairs.

"May I speak to you for a moment?" he said. "My conversation with Mrs. Gardner was interrupted."

The nurse came with alacrity into the drawing-room.

"The news of the murder has upset my patient," she explained, adjusting a well-starched cuff. "That foolish girl, Beatrice, came running up and blurted it all out."

"I am sorry," said the Inspector. "I am afraid that was my fault."

"Oh, of course, you couldn't be expected to know," said the nurse graciously.

"Is Mr. Gardner dangerously ill?" inquired the Inspector.

"It's a sad case," said the nurse. "Of course, in a manner of speaking, there's nothing the matter with him really. He's lost the use of his limbs entirely through nervous shock. There's no visible disability."

"He had no extra strain or shock yesterday afternoon?" inquired the Inspector.

"Not that I know of," the nurse looked somewhat surprised.

"You were with him all the afternoon?"

"I intended to be, but, well—as a matter of fact, Captain Gardner was very anxious for me to change two books for him at the library. He had forgotten to ask his wife before she went out. So, to oblige him I went out with them, and he asked me at the same time to get one or two other little things for him—presents for his wife as a matter of fact. Very nice about it he was, and told me I was to have tea at his expense at Boots. He said nurses never liked missing their tea. His little joke, you know. I didn't get out until past four, and what with the shops being so full just before Christmas, and one thing and another, I didn't get back until after six, but the poor fellow had been quite comfortable. In fact, he told me he had been asleep most of the time."

"Mrs. Gardner was back by then?"

"Yes, I believe she was lying down."

"She's very devoted to her husband, isn't she?"

"She worships him. I really do believe that woman would do anything in the world for him. Quite touching, and very different from some of the cases I have attended. Why, only last month—"

But Inspector Narracott fended off the impending scandal of last month with considerable skill. He glanced at his watch and gave a loud exclamation.

"Goodness gracious," he cried, "I shall miss my train. The station is not far away, is it?"

"St. David's is only three minutes' walk, if it's St. David's you want, or did you mean Queen Street?"

"I must run," said the Inspector, "tell Mrs. Gardner I am sorry not to have seen her to say good-by. Very pleased to have had this little chat with you, nurse."

The nurse bridled ever so slightly.

"Rather a good-looking man," she said to herself as the front door shut after the Inspector. "Really quite good-looking. Such a nice sympathetic manner."

And with a slight sigh she went upstairs to her patient.

10

The Pearson Family

INSPECTOR NARRACOTT'S next move was to report to his superior, Superintendent Maxwell.

The latter listened with interest to the Inspector's narrative.

"It's going to be a big case," he said thoughtfully. "There'll be headlines in the papers over this."

"I agree with you, sir."

"We've got to be careful. We don't want to make any mistake. But I think you're on the right tack. You must get after this James Pearson as soon as possible—find out where he was yesterday afternoon. As you say, it's a common enough name, but there's the Christian name as well. Of course, his signing his own name openly like that shows there wasn't any premeditation about it. He'd hardly have been such a fool otherwise. It looks to me like a quarrel and a sudden blow. If it is the man, he must have heard of his uncle's death that night. And if so, why did he sneak off by the six train in the morning without a word to anyone? No, it looks bad. Always granting that the whole thing's not a coincidence. You must clear that up as quickly as possible."

"That's what I thought, sir. I'd better take the 1:45 to town. Some time or other I want to have a word with this Willett woman who rented the Captain's house. There's something fishy there. But I can't get to Sittaford at present, the roads are impassable with snow. And anyway, she can't have any direct connection with the crime. She and her daughter were actually—well—table turning at the time the crime was committed. And, by the way, rather a queer thing happened—"

The Inspector narrated the story he had heard from Major Burnaby.

"That's a rum go," ejaculated the Superintendent. "Think this old fellow was telling the truth? That's the sort of story that gets cooked up afterwards by those believers in spooks and things of that kind."

"I fancy it's true all right," said Narracott with a grin. "I had a lot of difficulty getting it out of him. *He's* not a believer—just the opposite—old soldier, all damned nonsense attitude."

The Superintendent nodded his comprehension.

"Well, it's odd, but it doesn't get us anywhere," was his conclusion.

"Then I'll take the 1:45 to London."

The other nodded.

On arrival in town Narracott went straight to 21 Cromwell Street. Mr. Pearson, he was told, was at the office. He would be back for certain about seven o'clock.

Narracott nodded carelessly as though the information were of no value to him.

"I'll call back if I can," he said. "It's nothing of importance," and departed quickly without leaving a name.

He decided not to go to the Insurance Office, but to visit Wimbledon instead and have an interview with Mrs. Martin Dering, formerly Miss Sylvia Pearson.

There were no signs of shabbiness about The Nook.

"New and shoddy," was how Inspector Narracott described it to himself.

Mrs. Dering was at home. A rather pert-looking maid dressed in lilac color showed him into a rather overcrowded drawing-room. He gave her his official card to take to her mistress.

Mrs. Dering came to him almost immediately, his card in her hand.

"I suppose you have come about poor Uncle Joseph," was her greeting. "It's shocking—really shocking! I am so dreadfully nervous of burglars myself. I had two extra bolts put on the back door last week, and new patent catches on the windows."

Sylvia Dering, the Inspector knew from Mrs. Gardner, was only twenty-five, but she looked considerably over thirty. She was small and fair and anemic looking, with a worried and harassed expression. Her voice had that faintly complaining note in it which is about the most annoying sound a human voice can contain. Still not allowing the Inspector to speak she went on:

"If there's anything I can do to help you in any way, of course, I shall be only too glad to do so, but one hardly ever saw Uncle Joseph. He wasn't a very nice man—I am sure he couldn't have been. Not the sort of person one could go to in trouble, always carping and criticizing. Not the sort of man who had any knowledge of what literature meant. Success—true success is not always measured in terms of money, Inspector."

At last she paused and the Inspector, to whom those remarks had opened certain fields of conjecture, was given his turn to speak.

"You've heard of the tragedy very quickly, Mrs. Dering."

"Aunt Jennifer wired it to me."

"I see."

"But I suppose it will be in the evening papers. Dreadful, isn't it?"

"I gather you've not seen your uncle of late years."

"I have only seen him twice since my marriage. On the second occasion he was really very rude to Martin. Of course, he was a regular philistine in every way—devoted to sport. No appreciation, as I said just now, of literature."

"Husband applied to him for a loan and got refused," was Inspector Narracott's private comment on the situation.

"Just as a matter of form, Mrs. Dering, will you tell me what your movements were yesterday afternoon?"

"My movements? What a very queer way of putting it, Inspector. I played bridge most of the afternoon and a friend came in and spent the evening with me, as my husband was out."

"Out, was he? Away from home altogether?"

"A literary dinner," explained Mrs. Dering with importance. "He lunched with an American publisher and had this dinner in the evening."

"I see."

That seemed quite fair and above board. He went on.

"Your younger brother is in Australia, I believe, Mrs. Dering?"

"Yes."

"You have his address?"

"Oh, yes, I can find it for you if you wish—rather a peculiar name—I've forgotten it for the minute. Somewhere in New South Wales."

"And now, Mrs. Dering, your elder brother?"

"Jim?"

"Yes. I shall want to get in touch with him."

Mrs. Dering hastened to supply him with the address—the same as that which Mrs. Gardner had already given him.

Then, feeling there was no more to be said on either side, he cut the interview short.

Glancing at his watch, he noted that by the time he had returned to town it would be seven o'clock—a likely time, he hoped, for finding Mr. James Pearson at home.

The same superior looking, middle-aged woman opened the door of No. 21. Yes, Mr. Pearson was at home now. It was on the second floor, if the gentleman would walk up.

She preceded him, tapped at a door, and in a murmured and apologetic voice said: "The gentleman to see you, sir." Then, standing back, allowed the Inspector to enter.

A young man in evening dress was standing in the middle of the room. He was good-looking, indeed handsome, if you took no account of the rather weak mouth and the irresolute slant of the eyes. He had a haggard, worried look and an air of not having had much sleep of late.

He looked inquiringly at the Inspector as the latter advanced.

"I am Detective Inspector Narracott," he began—but got no further.

With a hoarse cry the young man dropped on to a chair, flung his arms out in front of him on the table, bowing his head on them and muttering:

"Oh! my God! It's come."

After a minute or two he lifted his head and said, "Well, why don't you get on with it, man?"

Inspector Narracott looked exceedingly stolid and unintelligent.

"I am investigating the death of your uncle, Captain Joseph Trevelyan. May I ask you, sir, if you have anything to say?"

The young man rose slowly to his feet and said in a low strained voice:

"Are you—arresting me?"

"No, sir, I am not. If I was arresting you I would give you the customary caution. I am simply asking you to account for your movements yesterday afternoon. You may reply to my questions or not as you see fit."

"And if I don't reply to them—it will tell against me. Oh, yes, I know your little ways. You've found out then that I was down there yesterday?"

"You signed your name in the hotel register, Mr. Pearson."

"Oh, I suppose there's no use denying it. I *was* there—why shouldn't I be?"

"Why indeed?" said the Inspector mildly.

"I went down there to see my uncle."

"By appointment?"

"What do you mean, by appointment?"

"Did your uncle know you were coming?"

"I—no—he didn't. It—it was a sudden impulse."

"No reason for it?"

"I—reason? No—no, why should there be? I—I just wanted to see my uncle."

"Quite so, sir. And you did see him?"

There was a pause—a very long pause. Indecision was written on every feature of the young man's face. Inspector Narracott felt a kind of pity as he watched him. Couldn't the boy see that his palpable indecision was as good as an admission of the fact?

At last Jim Pearson drew a deep breath. "I—I suppose I had better make a clean breast of it. Yes—I did see him. I asked at the station how I could get to Sittaford. They told me it was out of the question. The roads were impassable for any vehicle. I said it was urgent."

"Urgent?" murmured the Inspector.

"I—I wanted to see my uncle very much."

"So it seems, sir."

"The porter continued to shake his head and say that it was impossible. I mentioned my uncle's name and at once his face cleared up, and he told me my uncle was actually in Exhampton, and gave me full directions as to how to find the house he had rented."

"This was at what time, sir?"

"About one o'clock, I think. I went to the Inn—the Three Crowns—booked a room and had some lunch there. Then afterwards I—I went out to see my uncle."

"Immediately afterwards?"

"No, not immediately."

"What time was it?"

"Well, I couldn't say for certain."

"Half past three? Four o'clock? Half past four?"

"I—I—" he stammered worse than ever. "I don't think it could have been as late as that."

"Mrs. Belling, the proprietress, said you went out at half past four."

"Did I? I—I think she's wrong. It couldn't have been as late as that."

"What happened next?"

"I found my uncle's house, had a talk with him and came back to the Inn."

"How did you get into your uncle's house?"

"I rang the bell and he opened the door to me himself."

"Wasn't he surprised to see you?"

"Yes—yes—he was rather surprised."

"How long did you remain with him, Mr. Pearson?"

"A quarter of an hour—twenty minutes. But look here, he was perfectly all right when I left him. Perfectly all right. I swear it."

"And what time *did* you leave him?"

The young man lowered his eyes. Again, the hesitation was palpable in his tone. "I don't know exactly."

"I think you do, Mr. Pearson."

The assured tone had its effect. The boy replied in a low tone.

"It was a quarter past five."

"You returned to the Three Crowns at a quarter to six. At most it could only take you seven or eight minutes to walk over from your uncle's house."

"I didn't go straight back. I walked about the town."

"In that icy weather—in the snow!"

"It wasn't actually snowing then. It came on to snow later."

"I see. And what was the nature of your conversation with your uncle?"

"Oh! nothing in particular. I—I just wanted to talk to the old boy, look him up, that sort of thing, you know."

"He's a poor liar," thought Inspector Narracott to himself. "Why, I could manage better than that myself."

Aloud he said:

"Very good, sir. Now, may I ask you why, on hearing of your uncle's murder, you left Exhampton without disclosing your relationship to the murdered man?"

"I was scared," said the young man frankly. "I heard he had been murdered round about the time I left him. Now, dash it all, that's enough to scare anyone, isn't it? I got the wind up and left the place by the first available train. Oh, I dare say I was a fool to do anything of the sort. But you know what it is when you are rattled. And anyone might have been rattled under these circumstances."

"And that's all you have to say, sir?"

"Yes—yes, of course."

"Then, perhaps you'll have no objection, sir, to coming round with me and having this statement taken down in writing, after which you will have it read over to you, and you will sign it."

"Is—is that all?"

"I think it possible, Mr. Pearson, that it may be necessary to detain you until after the inquest."

"Oh! my God," said Jim Pearson. "Can nobody help me?"

At that moment the door opened and a young woman walked into the room.

She was, as the observant Inspector Narracott noted at once, a very exceptional kind of young woman. She was not strikingly beautiful, but she had a face which was arresting and unusual, a face that having once seen you could not forget. There was about her an atmosphere of common sense, *savoir faire*, invincible determination and a most tantalizing fascination.

"Oh! Jim," she exclaimed, "What's happened?"

"It's all over, Emily," said the young man. "They think I murdered my uncle."

"Who thinks so?" demanded Emily.

The young man indicated his visitor by a gesture.

"This is Inspector Narracott," he said, and he added with a dismal attempt at introduction, "Miss Emily Trefusis."

"Oh!" said Emily Trefusis.

She studied Inspector Narracott with keen hazel eyes.

"Jim," she said, "is a frightful idiot. But he doesn't murder people."

The Inspector said nothing.

"I expect," said Emily, turning to Jim, "that you've been saying the most frightfully imprudent things. If you read the papers a little better than you do, Jim, you would know that you must never talk to policemen unless you have a strong solicitor sitting beside you making objections to every word. What's happened? Are you arresting him, Inspector Narracott?"

Inspector Narracott explained technically and clearly exactly what he was doing.

"Emily," cried the young man, "you won't believe I did it? You never will believe it, will you?"

"No, darling," said Emily kindly. "Of course not." And she added in a gentle meditative tone. "You haven't got the guts."

"I don't feel as if I had a friend in the world," groaned Jim.

"Yes, you have," said Emily. "You've got me. Cheer up, Jim, look at the winking diamonds on the third finger of my left hand. Here stands the faithful fiancée. Go with the Inspector and leave everything to me."

Jim Pearson rose, still with a dazed expression on his face. His overcoat was lying over a chair and he put it on. Inspector Narracott handed him a hat which was lying on a bureau near by. They moved towards the door and the Inspector said politely:

"Good evening, Miss Trefusis."

"*Au revoir,* Inspector," said Emily sweetly.

And if he had known Miss Emily Trefusis better he would have known that in these three words lay a challenge.

11

Emily Sets to Work

THE INQUEST ON THE BODY of Captain Trevelyan was held on Monday morning. From the point of view of sensation it was a tame affair, for it was almost immediately adjourned for a week, thus disappointing large numbers of people. Between Saturday and Monday Exhampton had sprung into fame. The knowledge that the dead man's nephew had been detained in connection with the murder made the whole affair spring from a mere paragraph in the back pages of the newspapers to gigantic headlines. On the Monday, reporters had arrived at Exhampton in large numbers. Mr. Charles Enderby had reason once more to congratulate himself on the superior position he had obtained from the purely fortuitous chance of the football competition prize.

It was the journalist's intention to stick to Major Burnaby like a leech. And under the pretext of photographing the latter's cottage, to obtain exclusive information of the inhabitants of Sittaford and their relations with the dead man.

It did not escape Mr. Enderby's notice that at lunch time a small table near the door was occupied by a very attractive girl. Mr. Enderby wondered what she was doing in Exhampton. She was well dressed in a demure and provocative style, and did not appear to be a relation of the deceased, and still less could be labeled as one of the idle curious.

"I wonder how long she's staying?" thought Mr. Enderby. "Rather a pity I am going up to Sittaford this afternoon. Just my luck. Well, you can't have it both ways, I suppose."

But shortly after lunch, Mr. Enderby received an agreeable surprise. He was standing on the steps of the Three Crowns observing the fast melting snow, and enjoying the sluggish rays of wintry sunshine, when he was aware of a voice, an extremely charming voice, addressing him.

"I beg your pardon—but could you tell me—if there is anything to see in Exhampton?"

Charles Enderby rose to the occasion promptly.

"There's a castle, I believe," he said. "Not much to it—but there it is. Perhaps you would allow me to show you the way to it."

"That would be frightfully kind of you," said the girl. "If you are sure you are not too busy—"

Charles Enderby disclaimed immediately the notion of being busy.

They set out together.

"You are Mr. Enderby, aren't you?" said the girl.

"Yes. How did you know?"

"Mrs. Belling pointed you out to me."

"Oh, I see."

"My name is Emily Trefusis. Mr. Enderby—I want you to help me."

"To help you?" said Enderby. "Why, certainly—but—"

"You see, I am engaged to Jim Pearson."

"Oh!" said Mr. Enderby, journalistic possibilities rising before his mind.

"And the police are going to arrest him. I know they are. Mr. Enderby, I *know* that Jim didn't do this thing. I am down here to prove he didn't. But I must have someone to help me. One can't do anything without a man. Men know so much, and are able to get information in so many ways that are simply impossible to women."

"Well—I—yes, I suppose that is true," said Mr. Enderby complacently.

"I was looking at all these journalists this morning," said Emily. "Such a lot of them I thought had such stupid faces. I picked you out as the one really clever one among them."

"Oh! I say. I don't think that's true, you know," said Mr. Enderby still more complacently.

"What I want to propose," said Emily Trefusis, "is a kind of partnership. There would, I think, be advantages on both sides. There are certain things I want to investigate—to find out about. There you in your character of journalist can help me. I want—"

Emily paused. What she really wanted was to engage Mr. Enderby as a kind of private sleuth of her own. To go where she told him, to ask the questions she wanted asked, and in general to be a kind of bond slave. But she was aware of the necessity of couching these proposals in terms at once flattering and agreeable. The whole point was that she was to be the boss, but the matter needed managing tactfully.

"I want," said Emily, "to feel that I can *depend* upon you."

She had a lovely voice, liquid and alluring. As she uttered the last sentence a feeling rose in Mr. Enderby's bosom that this lovely helpless girl could depend upon him to the last ditch.

"It must be ghastly," said Mr. Enderby, and taking her hand he squeezed it with fervor.

"But you know," he went on with a journalistic reaction, "my time is not entirely my own. I mean, I have got to go where I am sent, and all that."

"Yes," said Emily. "I have thought of that, and that you see is where I come in. Surely I am what you call a 'scoop', aren't I? You can do an interview with me every day, you can make me say anything that you think your readers will like. *Jim Pearson's fiancée. Girl who believes passionately in his innocence. Reminiscences of his childhood which she supplies. I* don't really know about his childhood you know," she added, "but that doesn't matter."

"I think," said Mr. Enderby, "that you are marvelous. You really are marvelous."

"And then," said Emily pursuing her advantage, "I have access naturally to Jim's relations. I can get you in there as a friend of mine, where quite possibly you might have the door shut in your face any other way."

"Don't I know that only too well," said Mr. Enderby with feeling, recalling various rebuffs of the past.

A glorious prospect opened out before him. He had been in luck over this affair all round. First the lucky chance of the football competition, and now this.

"It's a deal," he said fervently.

"Good," said Emily becoming brisk and businesslike. "Now, what's the first move?"

"I'm going up to Sittaford this afternoon."

He explained the fortunate circumstance which had put him in such an advantageous position with regard to Major Burnaby. "Because, mind you, he is the kind of old buffer that hates newspaper men like poison. But you can't exactly push a chap in the face who has just handed you £5,000, can you?"

"It would be awkward," said Emily. "Well, if you are going to Sittaford, I am coming with you."

"Splendid," said Mr. Enderby. "I don't know, though, if there's anywhere to stay up there. As far as I know there's only Sittaford House and a few odd cottages belonging to people like Burnaby."

"We shall find something," said Emily. "I always find something."

Mr. Enderby could well believe that. Emily had the kind of personality that soars triumphantly over all obstacles.

They had arrived by now at the ruined castle, but paying no attention to it, they sat down on a piece of wall in the so-called sunshine and Emily proceeded to develop her ideas.

"I am looking at this, Mr. Enderby, in an absolutely unsentimental and business-like way. You've got to take it from me to begin with that Jim didn't do the murder. I'm not saying that simply because I am in love with him, or believe in his beautiful character or anything like that. It's just well—knowledge. You see I have been on my own pretty well since I was sixteen. I have never come into contact with many women and I know very little about them, but I know really a lot about men. And unless a girl can size up a man pretty accurately, and know what she's got to deal with, she will never get on. I have got on. I work as a mannequin at Lucie's, and I can tell you, Mr. Enderby, that to arrive there is a Feat.

"Well, as I was saying, I can size up men pretty accurately. Jim is rather a weak character in many ways. I am not sure," said Emily, forgetting for a moment her rôle of admirer of strong men, "that that's not why I like him. The feeling that I can run him and make something of him. There are quite a lot of—well—even criminal things that I can imagine him doing if pushed to it—but not murder. He simply couldn't pick up a sandbag and hit an old man on the back of the neck with it. He would make a bosh shot and hit him in the wrong place if he did. He is a—he is a *gentle* creature, Mr. Enderby. He doesn't even like killing wasps. He always tries to put them out of a window without hurting them and usually gets stung. However, it's no good my going on like this. You've got to take my word for it and start on the assumption that Jim is innocent."

"Do you think that somebody is deliberately trying to fasten the crime on him?" asked Charles Enderby in his best journalistic manner.

"I don't think so. You see nobody knew about Jim coming down to see his Uncle. Of course, one can't be certain, but I should put that down as just a coincidence and bad luck. What we have to find is someone else with a motive for killing Captain Trevelyan. The police are quite certain that this is not what they call an 'outside job'—I mean, it wasn't a burglar. The broken open window was faked."

"Did the police tell you all this?"

"Practically," said Emily.

"What do you mean by practically?"

"The chambermaid told me, and her sister is married to Constable Graves, so, of course, she knows everything the police think."

"Very well," said Mr. Enderby, "it wasn't an outside job. It was an inside one."

"Exactly," said Emily. "The police—that is Inspector Narracott who, by the way, I should think is an awfully sound man, have started investigating to find who benefits by Captain Trevelyan's death, and with Jim sticking out a mile, so to speak, they won't bother to go on with other investigations much. Well, that's got to be our job."

"What a scoop it would be," said Mr. Enderby, "if you and I discovered the real murderer. The crime expert of the *Daily Wire*—that's the way I should be described. But it's too good to be true," he added despondently. "That sort of thing only happens in books."

"Nonsense," said Emily, "it happens with me."

"You're simply marvelous," said Enderby again.

Emily brought out a little notebook.

"Now let's put things down methodically. Jim himself, his brother and sister, and his Aunt Jennifer benefit equally by Captain Trevelyan's death. Of course Sylvia—that's Jim's sister—wouldn't hurt a fly, but I wouldn't put it past her husband, he's what I call a nasty sort of brute. You know—the artistic nasty kind, has affairs with women—all that sort of thing. Very likely to be in a hole financially. The money they'd come into would actually be Sylvia's, but that wouldn't matter to him. He would soon manage to get it out of her."

"He sounds a most unpleasant person," said Mr. Enderby.

"Oh! yes. Good-looking in a bold sort of way. Women talk about sex with him in corners. Real men hate him."

"Well, that's suspect No. 1," said Mr. Enderby, also writing in a little book. "Investigate his movements on Friday—easily done under the guise of interview with popular novelist connected with the crime. Is that all right?"

"Splendid," said Emily. "Then there's Brian, Jim's younger brother. He's supposed to be in Australia, but he might quite easily have come back. I mean, people do sometimes without saying."

"We could send him a cable."

"We will. I suppose Aunt Jennifer is out of it. From all I've heard she's rather a wonderful person. She's got character. Still, after all, she wasn't very far away, she was only at Exeter. She *might* have come over to see her brother, and he *might* have said something nasty about her husband whom she adores, and she *might* have seen red and snatched up a sandbag and biffed him one."

"Do you really think so?" said Mr. Enderby dubiously.

"No, not really. But one never *knows*. Then, of course, there's the batman. He only gets £100 under the will and he seems all right. But there again, one never knows. His wife is Mrs. Belling's niece. You know Mrs. Belling who keeps the Three Crowns. I think I shall weep on her shoulder when I get back. She looks rather a motherly and romantic soul. I think she would be terribly sorry for me with my young man probably going to prison, and she might let slip something useful. And then, of course, there's Sittaford House. Do you know what struck me as queer?"

"No, what?"

"These people, the Willetts. The ones that took Captain Trevelyan's house furnished in the middle of winter. It's an awfully queer thing to do."

"Yes, it is odd," agreed Mr. Enderby. "There might be something at the bottom of that—something to do with Captain Trevelyan's past life.

"That *séance* business was queer too," he added. "I'm thinking of writing that up for the paper. Get opinions from Sir Oliver Lodge and Sir Arthur Conan Doyle and a few actresses and people about it."

"What *séance* business?"

Mr. Enderby recounted it with gusto. There was nothing connected with the murder that he had not managed somehow or other to hear.

"Bit odd, isn't it?" he finished. "I mean, it makes you think and all that. May be something in these things. First time I've really ever come across anything authentic."

Emily gave a slight shiver. "I hate supernatural things," she said. "Just for once, as you say, it does look as though there was something in it. But how—how gruesome!"

"This *séance* business never seems very practical, does it? If the old boy could get through and say he was dead, why couldn't he say who murdered him? It ought to be all so simple."

"I feel there may be a clue in Sittaford," said Emily thoughtfully.

"Yes, I think we ought to investigate there thoroughly," said Enderby. "I've hired a car and I'm starting there in about half an hour's time. You had better come along with me."

"I will," said Emily. "What about Major Burnaby?"

"He's going to tramp it," said Enderby. "Started immediately after the inquest. If you ask me, he wanted to get out of having my company on the way there. Nobody could like trudging there through all this slush."

"Will the car be able to get up all right?"

"Oh! yes. First day a car has been able to get through though."

"Well," said Emily rising to her feet. "It's about time we went back to the Three Crowns and I will pack my suitcase and do a short weeping act on Mrs. Belling's shoulder."

"Don't you worry," said Mr. Enderby rather fatuously. "You leave everything to me."

"That's just what I mean to do," said Emily with a complete lack of truth. "It's so wonderful to have someone you can really rely on."

Emily Trefusis was really a very accomplished young woman.

12

The Arrest

ON HER RETURN to the Three Crowns, Emily had the good fortune to run right into Mrs. Belling who was standing in the hallway.

"Oh! Mrs. Belling," she exclaimed. "I am leaving this afternoon."

"Yes, Miss. By the four ten train to Exeter, Miss?"

"No, I am going up to Sittaford."

"To Sittaford?"

Mrs Belling's countenance showed the most lively curiosity.

"Yes, and I wanted to ask you if you knew of anywhere there where I could stay."

"You want to stay up there?"

The curiosity was heightened.

"Yes, that is—Oh! Mrs. Belling, is there somewhere I could speak to you privately for a moment?"

With something like alacrity Mrs. Belling led the way to her own private sanctum. A small comfortable room with a large fire burning.

"You won't tell anyone, will you?" began Emily, knowing well that of all openings on earth this one is the most certain to provoke interest and sympathy.

"No, indeed, Miss, that I won't," said Mrs. Belling her dark eyes aglitter with interest.

"You see, Mr. Pearson—you know—"

"The young gentleman that stayed here on Friday? And that the police have arrested?"

"Arrested? Do you mean really arrested?"

"Yes, Miss. Not half an hour ago."

Emily had gone very white.

"You—you're sure of that?"

"Oh! yes, Miss. Our Amy had it from the Sergeant."

"It's too awful!" said Emily. She had, been expecting this but it was none the better for that. "You see, Mrs. Belling, I—I'm engaged to him. And he didn't do it, and, oh dear, it's all too dreadful!"

And here Emily began to cry. She had, earlier in the day, announced her intentions to Charles Enderby of doing so, but what appalled her so was with what ease the tears came. To cry at will is not an easy accomplishment. There was something much too real about these tears. It frightened her. She mustn't really give way. Giving way wasn't the least use to Jim. To be resolute, logical and clear sighted—these were the qualities that were going to count in this game. Sloppy crying had never helped anyone yet.

But it was a relief all the same, to let yourself go. After all she had meant to cry. Crying would be an undeniable passport to Mrs. Belling's sympathy and help. So why not have a good cry while she was about it. A real orgy of weeping in which all her troubles, doubts and unacknowledged fears might find vent and be swept away.

"There, there, my dear, don't ee take on so," said Mrs. Belling.

She put a large motherly arm round Emily's shoulders and patted her consolingly.

"Said from the start I have that he didn't do it. A regular nice young gentleman. A lot of chuckle heads the police are, and so I've said before now. Some thieving tramp is a great deal more likely. Now, don't ee fret, my dear, it'll all come right, you see if it don't."

"I am so dreadfully fond of him," wailed Emily.

Dear Jim, dear, sweet, boyish, helpless, impractical Jim. So utterly to be depended on to do the wrong thing at the wrong moment. What possible chance had he got against that steady, resolute Inspector Narracott?

"We *must* save him," she wailed.

"Of course, we will. Of course, we will," Mrs. Belling consoled her.

Emily dabbed her eyes vigorously, gave one last sniff and gulp, and raising her head demanded fiercely:

"Where can I stay at Sittaford?"

"Up to Sittaford? You're set on going there, my dear?"

"Yes," Emily nodded vigorously.

"Well, now," Mrs. Belling cogitated the matter. "There's only one place for ee to stay. There's not much to Sittaford. There's the big house, Sittaford House, which Captain Trevelyan built, and that's let now to a South African lady. And there's the six cottages he built, and No. 5 of them cottages has got Curtis, what used to be gardener at

Sittaford House, in it, and Mrs. Curtis. She lets rooms in the summer time, the Captain allowing her to do so. There's nowhere else you could stay and that's a fact. There's the blacksmith's and the post office, but Mary Hibbert, she's got six children and her sister-in-law living with her, and the blacksmith's wife she's expecting her eighth, so there won't be so much as a corner there. But, how are you going to get up to Sittaford, Miss? Have you hired a car?"

"I am going to share Mr. Enderby's."

"Ah, and where will he be staying I wonder?"

"I suppose he will have to be put up at Mrs. Curtis's too. Will she have room for both of us?"

"I don't know that that will look quite right for a young lady like you," said Mrs. Belling.

"He's my cousin," said Emily.

On no account, she felt, must a sense of propriety intervene to work against her in Mrs. Belling's mind.

The landlady's brow cleared. "Well, that may be all right then," she allowed grudgingly, "and likely as not if you're not comfortable with Mrs. Curtis they would put you up at the big house."

"I'm sorry I've been such an idiot," said Emily mopping once more at her eyes.

"It's only natural, my dear. And you feel better for it."

"I do," said Emily truthfully. "I feel much better."

"A good cry and a good cup of tea—there's nothing to beat them, and a nice cup of tea you shall have at once, my dear, before you start off on that cold drive."

"Oh, thank you, but I don't think I really want—"

"Never mind what you want, it's what you're going to have," said Mrs. Belling rising with determination and moving towards the door. "And you tell Amelia Curtis from me that she's to look after you and see you take your food proper and see you don't fret."

"You *are* kind," said Emily.

"And what's more I shall keep my eyes and ears open down here," said Mrs. Belling entering with relish into her part of the romance. "There's many a little thing that I hear that never goes to the police. And anything I do hear I'll pass on to you, Miss."

"Will you really?"

"That I will. Don't ee worry, my dear, we'll have your young gentleman out of his trouble in no time."

"I must go and pack," said Emily rising.

"I'll send the tea up to you," said Mrs. Belling.

Emily went upstairs, packed her few belongings into her suitcase, sponged her eyes with cold water and applied a liberal allowance of powder.

"You *have* made yourself look a sight," she apostrophized herself in the glass. She added more powder and a touch of rouge.

"Curious," said Emily, "how much better I feel. It's worth the puffy look."

She rang the bell. The chambermaid (the sympathetic sister-in-law of Constable Graves) came promptly. Emily presented her with a pound note and begged her earnestly to pass on any information she might acquire in roundabout ways from police circles. The girl promised readily.

"Mrs. Curtis's up to Sittaford? I will indeed, Miss. Do anything that I will. We all feel for you, Miss, more than I can say. All the time I keep saying to myself, 'Just fancy if it was you and Fred,' I keep saying. I would be distracted—that I would. The least thing I hears I'll pass it on to you, Miss."

"You angel," said Emily.

"Just like a sixpenny I got at Woolworth's the other day. The Syringa Murders it was called. And do you know what led them to find the real murderer, Miss? Just a bit of common sealing wax. Your gentleman *is* good-looking, Miss, isn't he? Quite unlike his picture in the papers. I'm sure I'll do anything I can, Miss, for you and for him."

Thus the center of romantic attention, Emily left the Three Crowns having duly gulped down the cup of tea prescribed by Mrs. Belling.

"By the way," she said to Enderby as the aged Ford sprang forward, "you are my cousin, don't forget."

"Why?"

"They've got such pure minds in the country," said Emily. "I thought it would be better."

"Splendid. In that case," said Mr. Enderby rising to his opportunities, "I had better call you Emily."

"All right, cousin—what's your name?"

"Charles."

"All right, Charles."

The car went upwards on the Sittaford road.

13
Sittaford

EMILY WAS RATHER FASCINATED by her first view of Sittaford. Turning off the main road about two miles from Exhampton, they went upwards over a rough moorland road until they reached a village that was situated right on the edge of the moor. It consisted of a smithy, and a combined post office and sweet shop. From there they followed a lane and came to a row of newly built small granite bungalows. At the second of these the car stopped and the driver volunteered the information that this was Mrs. Curtis's.

Mrs. Curtis was a small, thin, gray haired woman, energetic and shrewish in disposition. She was all agog with the news of the murder which had only penetrated to Sittaford that morning.

"Yes, of course I can take you in, Miss, and your cousin too, if he can just wait until I shift a few duds. You won't mind having your meals along of us, I don't suppose? Well, who would have believed it! Captain Trevelyan murdered and an inquest and all! Cut off from the world we've been since Friday morning, and this morning when the news came you could have knocked me down with a feather. 'The Captain's dead,' I said to Curtis, 'that *shows* you the wickedness there is in the world nowadays.' But I'm keeping you talking here, Miss. Come away in and the gentleman too. I have got the kettle on and you shall have a cup of tea immediately, for you must be perished by the drive up, though of course, it's warmer today after what it's been. Eight and ten feet the snow has been hereabout."

Drowned in this sea of talk, Emily and Charles Enderby were shown their new quarters. Emily had a small square room, scrupulously clean, looking out and up to the slope of Sittaford Beacon. Charles's room was a small slit facing the front of the house and the lane, containing a bed and a microscopic chest of drawers and washstand.

"The great thing is," he observed after the driver of the car had disposed his suitcase upon the bed, and had been duly paid and thanked, "that we are here. If we don't know all there is to be known about everyone living in Sittaford within the next quarter of an hour, I'll eat my hat."

Ten minutes later, they were sitting downstairs in the comfortable kitchen being introduced to Curtis, a rather gruff looking gray haired old man, and being regaled with strong tea, bread and butter,

Devonshire cream and hard boiled eggs. While they ate and drank they listened. Within half an hour they knew everything there was to be known about the inhabitants of the small community.

First there was Miss Percehouse, who lived in No. 4 The Cottages, a spinster of uncertain years and temper who had come down here to die, according to Mrs. Curtis, six years ago.

"But believe it or not, Miss, the air of Sittaford is that healthy that she picked up from the day she came. Wonderfully pure air for lungs it is.

"Miss Percehouse has a nephew who occasionally comes down to see her," she went on, "and indeed he's staying with her at the present time. Seeing to it that the money doesn't go out of the family, that's what he's doing. Very dull for a young gentleman at this time of year. But there, there's more ways than one of amusing yourself, and his coming has been a providence for the young lady at Sittaford House. Poor young thing, the idea of bringing her to that great barrack of a house in the winter time. Selfish is what some mothers are. A very pretty young lady, too. Mr. Ronald Garfield is up there as often as he can be without neglecting Miss Percehouse."

Charles Enderby and Emily exchanged glances. Charles remembered that Ronald Garfield had been mentioned as one of the party present at the table turning.

"The cottage this side of mine, No. 6," continued Mrs. Curtis, "has only just been took. Gentleman of the name of Duke. That is if you would call him a gentleman. Of course, he may be and he may not. There's no saying, folks aren't so particular nowadays as they used to be. He's been made free of the place in the heartiest manner. A bashful sort of gentleman he is—might be a military gentleman from the look of him, but somehow he hasn't got the manner. Not like Major Burnaby, that you would know as a military gentleman the first time you clapped eyes on him.

"No. 3, that's Mr. Rycroft's, little elderly gentleman. They do say that he used to go after birds to outlandish parts for the British Museum. What they call a naturalist he is. Always out and roaming over the moor when the weather permits. And he has a very fine library of books. His cottage is nearly all bookcases.

"No. 2, is an invalid gentleman's, a Captain Wyatt with an Indian servant. And poor fellow he does feel the cold, he does. The servant I mean, not the Captain. Coming from warm outlandish parts, it's no wonder. The heat they keep up inside the house would frighten you. It's like walking into an oven.

"No. 1 is Major Burnaby's cottage. Lives by himself he does, and I go in to do for him early mornings. He is a very neat gentleman, he is, and very particular. He and Captain Trevelyan were as thick as thieves. Friends of a lifetime they were. And they both have the same kind of outlandish heads stuck up on the walls.

"As for Mrs. Willett and Miss Willett, that's what no one can make out. Plenty of money there. Amos Parker at Exhampton they deal with, and he tells me their weekly book comes to well over eight pounds or nine pounds. You wouldn't believe the eggs that goes into that house! Brought their maid servants from Exeter with them, they did, but they don't like it and want to leave, and I'm sure I don't blame them. Mrs. Willett, she sends them into Exeter twice a week in her car, and what with that and the living being so good, they agreed to stop on, but if you ask me it's a queer business, burying yourself in the country like this, a smart lady like that. Well, well, I suppose I had better be clearing away these tea things."

She drew a deep breath and so did Charles and Emily. The flow of information loosened with so little difficulty had almost overwhelmed them.

Charles ventured to put a question.

"Has Major Burnaby got back yet?" he asked.

Mrs. Curtis paused at once, tray in hand. "Yes, indeed, sir, came tramping in just the same as ever about half an hour before you arrived. 'Why, sir,' I cried to him. 'You've never walked all the way from Exhampton?' And he says in his stern way, 'Why not? If a man has got two legs he doesn't need four wheels. I do it once a week anyway as you know, Mrs. Curtis.' 'Oh, yes, sir,' I says, 'but this is different. What with the shock and the murder and the inquest it's wonderful you've got the strength to do it.' But he only grunted like and walked on. He looks bad though. It's a miracle he ever got through on Friday night. Brave I call it at his age. Tramping off like that and three miles of it in a snowstorm. You may say what you like, but nowadays the young gentlemen aren't a patch on the old ones. That Mr. Ronald Garfield he would never have done it, and it's my opinion, and it's the opinion of Mrs. Hibbert at the post office, and it's the opinion of Mr. Pound, the blacksmith, that Mr. Garfield ought never to have let him go off alone the way he did. He should have gone with him. If Major Burnaby had been lost in a snowdrift, everybody would have blamed Mr. Garfield. And that's a fact."

She disappeared triumphantly into the scullery amid a clatter of tea things.

Mr. Curtis thoughtfully removed an aged pipe from the right side of his mouth to the left side.

"Women," he said, "talk a lot."

He paused and then murmured,

"And half the time they don't know the truth of what they are talking about."

Emily and Charles received this announcement in silence. Seeing that no more was coming, however, Charles murmured approvingly.

"That's very true—yes, very true."

"Ah!" said Mr. Curtis, and relapsed into a pleasant and contemplative silence.

Charles rose, "I think I'll go round and see old Burnaby," he said, "tell him the camera parade will be tomorrow morning."

"I'll come with you," said Emily. "I want to know what he really thinks about Jim and what ideas he has about the crime in general."

"Have you got any rubber boots or anything? It's awfully slushy."

"I bought some Wellingtons in Exhampton," said Emily.

"What a practical girl you are. You think of everything."

"Unfortunately," said Emily, "that's not much help to you in finding out who's done a murder. It might help one to do a murder," she added reflectively.

"Well, don't murder me," said Mr. Enderby.

They went out together. Mrs. Curtis immediately returned.

"They be gone round to the Major's," said Mr. Curtis.

"Ah!" said Mrs. Curtis. "Now, what do you think? Are they sweethearting, or are they not? A lot of harm comes of cousins marrying so they say. Deaf and dumbs and half wits and a lot of other evils. He's sweet on her, that you can see easily enough. As for her, she's a deep one like my Great Aunt Sarah's Belinda, she is. Got a way with her and with the men. I wonder what she's after now? Do you know what I think, Curtis?"

Mr. Curtis grunted.

"This young gentleman that the police are holding on account of the murder, it's my belief that he's the one she's set on. And she's come up here to nose about and see what she can find out. And mark my words," said Mrs. Curtis, rattling china, "if there's anything *to* find out she will find it!"

14

The Willetts

AT THE SAME MOMENT that Charles and Emily started out to visit Major Burnaby, Inspector Narracott was seated in the drawing-room of Sittaford House, trying to formulate an impression of Mrs. Willett.

He had not been able to interview her sooner as the roads had been impassable until this morning. He had hardly known what he had expected to find, but certainly not what he had found. It was Mrs. Willett who had taken charge of the situation, not he.

She had come rushing into the room, thoroughly business-like and efficient. He saw a tall woman, thin faced and keen eyed. She was wearing rather an elaborate knitted silk jumper suit that was just over the border line of unsuitability for country wear. Her stockings were of very expensive gossamer silk, her shoes high heeled patent leather. She wore several valuable rings and rather a large quantity of very good and expensive imitation pearls.

"Inspector Narracott?" said Mrs. Willett. "Naturally, you want to come over the house. What a shocking tragedy! I could hardly believe it. We only heard about it this morning, you know. We were terribly shocked. Sit down, won't you, Inspector? This is my daughter, Violet."

He had hardly noticed the girl who had followed her in, and yet, she was a very pretty girl, tall and fair with big blue eyes.

Mrs. Willett herself took a seat.

"Is there any way in which I can help you, Inspector? I knew very little of poor Captain Trevelyan, but if there is anything you can think of—"

The Inspector said slowly:

"Thank you, madam. Of course, one never knows what may be useful or what may not."

"I quite understand. There may possibly be something in the house that may throw light upon this sad business, but I rather doubt it. Captain Trevelyan removed all his personal belongings. He even feared I should tamper with his fishing rods, poor, dear man."

She laughed a little.

"You were not acquainted with him?"

"Before I took the house, you mean? Oh! no. I've asked him here several times since, but he never came. Terribly shy, poor dear. That was what was the matter with him. I've known dozens of men like it.

They are called women haters and all sorts of silly things, and really all the time it's only shyness. If I could have got at him," said Mrs. Willett with determination, "I'd soon have got over all that nonsense. That sort of man only wants bringing out."

Inspector Narracott began to understand Captain Trevelyan's strongly defensive attitude towards his tenants.

"We both asked him," continued Mrs. Willett. "Didn't we, Violet?"

"Oh! yes, mother."

"A real simple sailor at heart," said Mrs. Willett. "Every woman loves a sailor, Inspector Narracott."

It occurred to Inspector Narracott at this juncture that the interview so far had been run entirely by Mrs. Willett. He was convinced that she was an exceedingly clever woman. She might be as innocent as she appeared. On the other hand she might not.

"The point I am anxious to get information about is this," he said and paused.

"Yes, Inspector?"

"Major Burnaby, as you doubtless know, discovered the body. He was led to do so by an accident that occurred in this house."

"You mean?"

"I mean, the table turning. I beg your pardon—"

He turned sharply.

A faint sound had come from the girl.

"Poor Violet," said her mother. "She was terribly upset—indeed we all were! Most unaccountable. I'm not superstitious, but really it was the most unaccountable thing."

"It did occur then?"

Mrs. Willett opened her eyes very wide.

"Occur? Of course it occurred. At the time I thought it was a joke—a most unfeeling joke and one in very bad taste. I suspected young Ronald Garfield—"

"Oh! no, mother. I'm sure he didn't. He absolutely swore he didn't."

"I'm saying what I thought at the time, Violet. What could one think it but a joke?"

"It was curious," said the Inspector slowly. "You were very upset, Mrs. Willett?"

"We all were. Up to then it had been, oh, just light hearted fooling. You know the sort of thing. Good fun on a winter's evening. And then suddenly—this! I was very angry."

"Angry?"

"Well, naturally. I thought someone was doing it deliberately—for a joke, as I say."

"And now?"

"Now?"

"Yes, what do you think now?"

Mrs. Willett spread her hands out expressively.

"I don't know what to think. It—it's uncanny."

"And you, Miss Willett?"

"I?"

The girl started.

"I—I don't know. I shall never forget it. I *dream* of it. I shall never dare to do table turning again."

"Mr. Rycroft would say it was genuine, I suppose," said her mother. "He believes in all that sort of thing. Really I'm inclined to believe in it myself. What other explanation is there except that it was a genuine message from a spirit?"

The Inspector shook his head. The table turning had been his red herring. His next remark was most casual sounding.

"Don't you find it very bleak here in winter, Mrs. Willett?"

"Oh! we love it. Such a change. We're South Africans, you know."

Her tone was brisk and ordinary.

"Really? What part of South Africa?"

"Oh! the Cape. Violet has never been in England before. She is enchanted with it—finds the snow most romantic. This house is really most comfortable."

"What led you to come to this part of the world?"

There was just gentle curiosity in his voice.

"We've read so many books on Devonshire, and especially on Dartmoor. We were reading one on the boat—all about Widdecombe Fair. I've always had a hankering to see Dartmoor."

"What made you fix on Exhampton? It's not a very well known little town."

"Well—we were reading these books as I told you, and there was a boy on board who talked about Exhampton—he was so enthusiastic about it."

"What was his name?" asked the Inspector. "Did he come from this part of the world?"

"Now, what was his name? Cullen—I think. No—it was Smythe. How stupid of me. I really can't remember. You know how it is on board ship, Inspector, you get to know people so well and plan to meet again—and a week after you've landed, you can't even be sure of their names!"

She laughed.

"But he was such a nice boy—not good-looking, reddish hair, but a delightful smile."

"And on the strength of that you decided to take a house in these parts?" said the Inspector smiling.

"Yes, wasn't it mad of us?"

"Clever," thought Narracott. "Distinctly clever." He began to realize Mrs. Willett's methods. She always carried the war into the enemy's country.

"So you wrote to the house agents and inquired about a house?"

"Yes—and they sent us particulars of Sittaford. It sounded just what we wanted."

"It wouldn't be my taste at this time of year," said the Inspector with a laugh.

"I daresay it wouldn't be ours if we lived in England," said Mrs. Willett brightly.

The Inspector rose.

"How did you know the name of a house agent to write to in Exhampton?" he asked. "That must have presented a difficulty."

There was a pause. The first pause in the conversation. He thought he caught a glimpse of vexation, more, of anger in Mrs. Willett's eyes. He had hit upon something to which she had not thought out the answer. She turned towards her daughter.

"How did we, Violet? I can't remember."

There was a different look in the girl's eyes. She looked frightened.

"Why, of course," said Mrs. Willett. "Delfridges. Their information bureau. It's too wonderful. I always go and inquire there about everything. I asked them the name of the best agent here and they told me."

"Quick," thought the Inspector. "Very quick. But not quite quick enough. I had you there, madam."

He made a cursory examination of the house. There was nothing there. No papers, no locked drawers or cupboards.

Mrs. Willett accompanied him talking brightly. He took his leave, thanking her politely.

As he departed he caught a glimpse of the girl's face over her shoulder. There was no mistaking the expression on her face.

It was fear he saw on her countenance. Fear written there plainly at this moment when she thought herself unobserved.

Mrs. Willett was still talking.

"Alas. We have one grave drawback here. The domestic problem, Inspector. Servants will not stand these country places. All of mine have been threatening to leave us for some time, and the news of the murder seems to have unsettled them utterly. I don't know what I shall do. Perhaps men servants would answer the case. That is what the Registry Office in Exeter advised."

The Inspector answered mechanically. He was not listening to her flow of talk. He was thinking of the expression he had surprised on the girl's face.

Mrs. Willett had been clever—but not quite clever enough.

He went away cogitating on his problem.

If the Willetts had nothing to do with Captain Trevelyan's death, why was Violet Willett afraid?

He fired his last shot. With his foot actually over the threshold of the front door he turned back.

"By the way," he said, "you know young Pearson, don't you?"

There was no doubt of the pause this time. A dead silence of about a second. Then Mrs. Willet spoke:

"Pearson?" she said. "I don't think—"

She was interrupted. A queer sighing breath came from the room behind her and then the sound of a fall. The Inspector was over the threshold and into the room in a flash.

Violet Willett had fainted.

"Poor child," cried Mrs. Willett. "All this strain and shock. That dreadful table turning business and the murder on the top of it. She isn't strong. Thank you so much, Inspector. Yes, on the sofa please. If you would ring the bell. No, I don't think there is anything more you can do. Thank you so much."

The Inspector went down the drive with his lips set in a grim line.

Jim Pearson was engaged he knew, to that extremely charming looking girl he had seen London.

Why then should Violet Willett faint at the mention of his name? What was the connection between Jim Pearson and the Willetts?

He paused indecisively as he emerged from the front gate. Then he took from his pocket a small notebook. In it was entered a list of the inhabitants of the six bungalows built by Captain Trevelyan with a few brief remarks against each name. Inspector Narracott's stubby forefinger paused at the entry against No. 6 The Cottages.

"Yes," he said to himself. "I'd better see him next."

He strode briskly down the lane and beat a firm rat-tat on the knocker of No. 6—the bungalow inhabited by Mr. Duke.

15

Visit to Major Burnaby

LEADING THE WAY up the path to the Major's front door, Mr. Enderby rapped upon it in a cheery fashion. The door was flung open almost immediately and Major Burnaby, red in the face, appeared on the threshold.

"It's you, is it?" he observed with no very great fervor in his voice, and was about to go on in the same strain when he caught sight of Emily and his expression altered.

"This is Miss Trefusis," said Charles with the air of one producing the ace of trumps. "She was very anxious to see you."

"May I come in?" said Emily with her sweetest smile.

"Oh! yes. Certainly. Of course—Oh, yes, of course."

Stumbling in his speech the Major backed into the living-room of his cottage and began pulling forward chairs and pushing aside tables.

Emily, as was her fashion, came straight to the point.

"You see, Major Burnaby, I am engaged to Jim—Jim Pearson, you know. And naturally I am terribly anxious about him."

In the act of pushing a table the Major paused with his mouth open.

"Oh dear," he said, "that's a bad business. My dear young lady, I am more sorry about it than I can say."

"Major Burnaby, tell me honestly. Do you yourself believe he is guilty? Oh, you needn't mind saying if you do. I would a hundred times rather people didn't lie to me."

"No, I do *not* think him guilty," said the Major in a loud assertive voice. He hit a cushion once or twice vigorously, and then sat down facing Emily. "The chap is a nice young chap. Mind you, he might be a bit weak. Don't be offended if I say that he's the kind of young fellow that might easily go wrong if temptation came in his way. But murder—no. And mind you, I know what I am talking about—a lot of subalterns have passed through my hands in my time. It's the fashion to poke fun at retired army officers nowadays, but we know a thing or two all the same, Miss Trefusis."

"I'm sure you do," said Emily. "I'm awfully grateful to you for saying what you've done."

"Have—have a whisky and soda?" said the Major. "I'm afraid there's nothing else," he said apologetically.

"No, thank you, Major Burnaby."

"Some plain soda then?"

"No, thank you," said Emily.

"I ought to be able to produce tea," said the Major with a touch of wistfulness.

"We've had it," said Charles. "At Mrs. Curtis's," he added.

"Major Burnaby," said Emily, "Who do you think did it—have you any idea at all?"

"No. I am damned—er—bothered—if I have," said the Major. "Took it for granted it was some chap that broke in, but now the police say that can't be so. Well, it's their job, and I suppose they know best. They say nobody broke in, so I suppose nobody did break in. But all the same it beats me, Miss Trefusis, Trevelyan hadn't an enemy in the world as far as I know."

"And *you* would know if anybody did," said Emily.

"Yes, I suppose I knew more of Trevelyan than many of his relations did."

"And you can't think of anything—anything that would help, in any way?" asked Emily.

The Major pulled at his short mustache.

"I know what you're thinking. Like in books there ought to be some little incident that I should remember that would be a clue. Well, I'm sorry, but there isn't any such thing. Trevelyan just led an ordinary normal life. Got very few letters and wrote less. There were no female complications in his life, I am sure of that. No, it beats me, Miss Trefusis."

All three were silent.

"What about that servant of his?" asked Charles.

"Been with him for years. Absolutely faithful."

"He had married lately," said Charles.

"Married a perfectly decent respectable girl."

"Major Burnaby," said Emily, "forgive me putting it this way—but didn't you get the wind up rather easily about him?"

The Major rubbed his nose with the embarrassed air that always came over him when the table turning was mentioned.

"Yes, there's no denying it, I did. I knew the whole thing was tommy rot and yet—"

"You felt somehow it wasn't," said Emily helpfully.

The Major nodded.

"That's why I wonder—" said Emily.

The two men looked at her.

"I can't quite put what I mean in the way I want," said Emily. "What I mean is this: You say that you don't believe in all this table turning business—and yet, in spite of the awful weather and what must have seemed to you the absurdity of the whole thing—you felt so uneasy that you had to set out, no matter what the weather conditions, and see for yourself that Captain Trevelyan was all right. Well, don't you think that may have been because—because there was something in the atmosphere.

"I mean," she continued desperately as she saw no trace of comprehension in the Major's face, "that there was something in someone else's mind as well as yours. And that somehow or other you felt it."

"Well, I don't know," said the Major. He rubbed his nose again. "Of course," he added hopefully, "women do take these things seriously."

"Women?" said Emily. "Yes," she murmured softly to herself, "I believe somehow or other that's it."

She turned abruptly to Major Burnaby.

"What are they like, these Willetts?"

"Oh, well," Major Burnaby cast about in his mind, he was clearly no good at personal descriptions. "Well—they are very kind you know—very helpful and all that."

"Why do they want to take a house like Sittaford House at this time of year?"

"I can't imagine," said the Major. "Nobody does," he added.

"Don't you think it's very queer?" persisted Emily.

"Of course it's queer. However, there's no accounting for tastes. That's what the Inspector said."

"That's nonsense," said Emily. "People don't do things without a reason."

"Well, I don't know," said Major Burnaby cautiously. "Some people don't. You wouldn't, Miss Trefusis. But some people—" He sighed and shook his head.

"You are sure they hadn't met Captain Trevelyan before?"

The Major scouted the idea. Trevelyan would have said something to him. No, he was as astonished himself as anyone could be.

"So *he* thought it queer?"

"Of course, I've just told you we all did."

"What was Mrs. Willett's attitude towards Captain Trevelyan?" asked Emily. "Did she try and avoid him?"

A faint chuckle came from the Major.

"No, indeed she didn't. Pestered the life out of him—always asking him to come and see them."

"Oh!" said Emily thoughtfully. She paused and then said, "So she might—just possibly she might have taken Sittaford House just on purpose to get acquainted with Captain Trevelyan."

"Well," the Major seemed to turn it over in his mind. "Yes, I suppose she might have. Rather an expensive way of doing things."

"I don't know," said Emily. "Captain Trevelyan wouldn't have been an easy person to get to know otherwise."

"No, he wouldn't," agreed the late Captain Trevelyan's friend.

"I wonder," said Emily.

"The Inspector thought of that too," said Burnaby.

Emily felt a sudden irritation against Inspector Narracott. Everything that she thought of seemed to have already been thought of by the Inspector. It was galling to a young woman who prided herself on being sharper than other people.

She rose and held out her hand.

"Thank you very much," she said simply.

"I wish I could help you more," said the Major. "I'm rather an obvious sort of person—always have been. If I were a clever chap I might be able to hit upon something that might be a clue. At any rate count on me for anything you want."

"Thank you," said Emily. "I will."

"Good-by, sir," said Enderby. "I shall be along in the morning with my camera you know."

Burnaby grunted.

Emily and Charles retraced their steps to Mrs. Curtis's.

"Come into my room, I want to talk to you," said Emily.

She sat on the one chair and Charles sat on the bed. Emily plucked off her hat and sent it spinning into a corner of the room.

"Now, listen," she said. "I think I've got a kind of starting point. I may be wrong and I may be right, at any rate it's an idea. I think a lot hinges on this table turning business. You've done table turning, haven't you?"

"Oh, yes, now and then. Not serious you know."

"No, of course not. It's the kind of thing one does on a wet afternoon, and everyone accuses everyone else of shoving. Well, if you've played it you know what happens. The table starts spelling out, say, a name, well, it's a name somebody knows. Very often they recognize it at once and hope it isn't going to be that, and all the time unconsciously they are what one calls shoving. I mean sort of recognizing things makes one give an involuntary jerk when the next letter comes and stops the thing. And the less you want to do that sometimes the more it happens."

"Yes, that's true," agreed Mr. Enderby.

"I don't believe for a moment in spirits or anything like that. But supposing that one of those people who were playing knew that

Captain Trevelyan was being murdered at that minute—"

"Oh, I say," protested Charles, "that's awfully far fetched."

"Well, it needn't be quite so crude as that. Yes, I think it must be. We are just taking a hypothesis—that's all. We are asserting that somebody knew that Captain Trevelyan was dead and absolutely couldn't hide their knowledge. The table betrayed them."

"It's awfully ingenious," said Charles, "but I don't believe for a minute it's true."

"We'll assume that it is true," said Emily firmly. "I am sure that in detection of crime you mustn't be afraid to assume things."

"Oh, I'm quite agreeable," said Mr. Enderby. "We'll assume that it is true—anything you like."

"So what we have to do," said Emily, "is to consider very carefully the people who were playing. To begin with there's Major Burnaby and Mr. Rycroft. Well, it seems wildly unlikely that either of them should have an accomplice who was the murderer. Then there is this Mr. Duke. Well, for the moment we know nothing about him. He has only just arrived here lately and of course, he might be a sinister stranger—part of a gang or something. We will put X against his name. And now we come to the Willetts. Charles, there is something awfully mysterious about the Willetts."

"What on earth have they got to gain from Captain Trevelyan's death?"

"Well, on the face of it, nothing. But if my theory is correct there must be a connection somewhere. We've got to find what is the connection."

"Right," said Mr. Enderby. "And supposing it's all a mare's nest?"

"Well, we'll have to start all over again," said Emily.

"Hark!" cried Charles suddenly.

He held up his hand. Then he went over to the window and opened it, and Emily too, heard the sound which had aroused his attention. It was the far off booming of a great bell.

As they stood listening, Mrs. Curtis's voice called excitedly from below.

"Do you hear the bell, Miss—do you hear it?"

Emily opened the door.

"D'you hear it? Plain as plain, isn't it? Well now, to think of that!"

"What is it?" asked Emily.

"It's the bell at Princetown, Miss, near to twelve mile away. It means that a convict's escaped. George, George, where is that man? D'you hear the bell? There's a convict loose."

Her voice died away as she went through the kitchen.

Charles shut the window and sat down on the bed again.

"It's a pity that things happen all wrong," he said dispassionately. "If only this convict had escaped on Friday, why, there would be our murderer nicely accounted for. No farther to look. Hungry man, desperate criminal breaks in. Trevelyan defends his Englishman's castle—and desperate criminal biffs him one. All so simple."

"It would have been," said Emily with a sigh.

"Instead of which," said Charles, "he escapes three days too late. It's—it's hopelessly inartistic."

He shook his head sadly.

16

Mr. Rycroft

EMILY WOKE EARLY the next morning. Being a sensible young woman, she realized there was little possibility of Mr. Enderby's collaboration until the morning was well advanced. So, feeling restless and unable to lie still, she set out for a brisk walk along the lane in the opposite direction from which they had come last night.

She passed the gates of Sittaford House on her right and shortly after that the lane took a sharp turn to the right and ran steeply up hill and came out on the open moor where it degenerated into a grass track and soon petered out altogether. The morning was a fine one, cold and crisp and the view was lovely. Emily ascended to the very top of Sittaford Tor, a pile of gray rock of a fantastic shape. From this height she looked down over an expanse of moorland, unbroken as far as she could see without any habitation or any road. Below her, on the opposite side of the Tor, were gray masses of granite boulders and rocks. After considering the scene for a minute or two she turned to view the prospect to the north from which she had come. Just below her lay Sittaford, clustering on the flank of the hill, the square gray blob of Sittaford House, and the dotted cottages beyond it. In the valley below she could see Exhampton.

"One ought," thought Emily confusedly, "to see things better when you are high up like this. It ought to be like lifting off the top of a doll's house and peering in."

She wished with all her heart that she had met the dead man even if only once. It was so hard to get an idea of people you had never seen. You had to rely on other people's judgment, and Emily had never yet acknowledged that any other person's judgment was superior to her own. Other people's impressions were no good to you. They might be just as true as yours but you couldn't act on them. You couldn't, as it were, use another person's angle of attack.

Meditating vexedly on these questions, Emily sighed impatiently and shifted her position.

She had been so lost in her own thoughts that she had been oblivious to her immediate surroundings. It was with a shock of surprise that she realized that a small elderly gentleman was standing a few feet away from her, his hat held courteously in his hand, while he breathed rather fast.

"Excuse me," he said. "Miss Trefusis, I believe?"

"Yes," said Emily.

"My name is Rycroft. You must forgive me speaking to you, but in this little community of ours the smallest detail is known, and your arrival here yesterday has naturally gone the round. I can assure you that everyone feels a deep sympathy with your position, Miss Trefusis. We are all, one and all, anxious to assist you in any way we can."

"That's very kind of you," said Emily.

"Not at all, not at all," said Mr Rycroft. "Beauty in distress, you will pardon my old-fashioned manner of putting it. But seriously, my dear young lady, do count on me if there is any way in which I can possibly assist you. Beautiful view from up here, is it not?"

"Wonderful," agreed Emily. "The moor is a wonderful place."

"You know that a prisoner must have escaped last night from Princetown."

"Yes. Has he been recaptured?"

"Not yet, I believe. Ah, well, poor fellow, he will no doubt be recaptured soon enough. I believe I am right in saying that no one has escaped successfully from Princetown for the last twenty years."

"Which direction is Princetown?"

Mr. Rycroft stretched out his arm and pointed southwards over the moor.

"It lies over there, about twelve miles as the crow flies over unbroken moorland. It's sixteen miles by road."

Emily gave a faint shiver. The idea of the desperate hunted man impressed her powerfully. Mr. Rycroft was watching her and gave a little nod.

"Yes," he said. "I feel the same myself. It's curious how one's instincts rebel at the thought of a man being hunted down, and yet, these men at Princetown are all dangerous and violent criminals, the kind of men whom probably you and I would do our utmost to put there in the first place."

He gave a little apologetic laugh.

"You must forgive me, Miss Trefusis, I am deeply interested in the study of crime. A fascinating study. Ornithology and criminology are my two subjects." He paused and then went on:

"That's the reason why, if you will allow me to do so, I should like to associate myself with you in this matter. To study a crime at first hand has long been an unrealized dream of mine. Will you place your confidence in me, Miss Trefusis, and allow me to place my experience at your disposal? I have read and studied this subject deeply."

Emily was silent for a minute. She was congratulating herself on the way events were playing into her hand. Here was first-hand knowledge being offered her of life as it had been lived at Sittaford. "Angle of attack," Emily repeated the phrase that had crept into her mind so short a time before. She had had Major Burnaby's angle—matter of fact—simple—direct. Taking cognizance of facts and completely oblivious of subtleties. Now, she was being offered another angle which she suspected might open up a very different field of vision. This little, shriveled, dried-up gentleman had read and studied deeply, was well versed in human nature, had that devouring interested curiosity in life displayed by the man of reflection as opposed to the man of action.

"Please help me," she said simply. "I am so very worried and unhappy."

"You must be, my dear, you must be. Now, as I understand the position, Trevelyan's eldest nephew has been arrested or detained—the evidence against him being of a somewhat simple and obvious nature. I, of course, have an open mind. You must allow me that."

"Of course," said Emily. "Why should you believe in his innocence when you know nothing about him?"

"Most reasonable," said Mr. Rycroft. "Really, Miss Trefusis, you yourself are a most interesting study. By the way, your name—is it Cornish like our poor friend Trevelyan?"

"Yes," said Emily. "My father was Cornish, my mother was Scottish."

"Ah!" said Mr. Rycroft, "very interesting. Now to approach our little problem. On the one hand we assume that young Jim—the name is Jim, is it not? We assume that young Jim had a pressing need of money, that he came down to see his uncle, that he asked for money, that his uncle refused, that in a moment of passion he picked up a sandbag that was lying at the door and that he hit his uncle over the head. The crime was unpremeditated—was in fact a foolish irrational affair most deplorably conducted. Now, all that may be so, on the other hand he may have parted with his uncle in anger and some other person may have stepped in shortly afterwards and committed the crime. That is what you believe—and to put it a little differently, that is what I hope. I do not want your fiancé to have committed the crime, for from my point of view it is so uninteresting that he should have done so. I am therefore backing the other horse. The crime was committed by someone else. We will assume that and go at once to a most important point. Was that someone else aware of the quarrel that had just taken place? Did that quarrel in fact, actually precipitate the murder? You see my point? Someone is meditating doing away with Captain Trevelyan and seizes this opportunity, realizing that suspicion is bound to fall on young Jim."

Emily considered the matter from this angle.

"In that case," she said slowly—

Mr. Rycroft took the words out of her mouth.

"In that case," he said briskly, "the murderer would have to be a person in close association with Captain Trevelyan. He would have to be domiciled in Exhampton. In all probability he would have to be in the house, either during or after the quarrel. And since we are not in a court of law and can bandy about names freely, the name of the servant, Evans, leaps to our minds as a person who could satisfy our conditions. A man who quite possibly might have been in the house. Have overheard the quarrel and seized the opportunity. Our next point is to discover whether Evans benefits in any way from his master's death."

"I believe he gets a small legacy," said Emily.

"That may or may not constitute a sufficient motive. We shall have to discover whether or not Evans had a pressing need of money. We must also consider Mrs. Evans—there is a Mrs. Evans of recent date I understand. If you had studied criminology, Miss Trefusis, you would realize the curious effect caused by inbreeding, especially in country districts. There are at least four young women in Broadmoor, pleasant in manner, but with that curious kink in their dispositions that human life is of little or no account to them. No—we must not leave Mrs. Evans out of account."

"What do you think about this table turning business, Mr. Rycroft?"

"Now, that is very strange. Most strange. I confess, Miss Trefusis, that I am powerfully impressed by it. I am, as perhaps you may have heard, a believer in psychic things. To a certain degree I am a believer in spiritualism. I have already written out a full account and sent it up to the Society of Psychical Research. A well authenticated and amazing case. Five people present, none of whom could have the least idea or suspicion that Captain Trevelyan was murdered."

"You don't think—"

Emily stopped. It was not so easy to suggest her own idea to Mr. Rycroft that one of the five people might have guilty foreknowledge, as he himself had been one of them. Not that she suspected for a moment that there was anything whatever to connect Mr. Rycroft with the tragedy. Still she felt that the suggestion might not be wholly tactful. She pursued her object in a more roundabout manner.

"It all interested me very much, Mr. Rycroft, it is, as you say, an amazing occurrence. You don't think that any of the people present, with the exception of yourself of course, were in any way psychic?"

"My dear young lady, I myself am not psychic. I have no powers in that direction. I am only a very deeply interested observer."

"What about this Mr. Garfield?"

"A nice lad," said Mr. Rycroft, "but not remarkable in any way."

"Well off, I suppose." said Emily.

"Stony broke, I believe," said Mr. Rycroft. "I hope I am using that idiom correctly. He comes down here to dance attendance on an aunt, from whom he has what I call 'expectations.' Miss Percehouse is a very sharp lady and I think she knows what these attentions are worth. But as she has a sardonic form of humor of her own she keeps him dancing."

"I should like to meet her," said Emily.

"Yes, you must certainly meet her. She will no doubt insist on meeting you. Curiosity—alas, my dear Miss Trefusis—curiosity."

"Tell me about the Willetts," said Emily.

"Charming," said Mr. Rycroft, "quite charming. Colonial, of course. No real poise, if you understand me. A little too lavish in their hospitality. Everything a shade on the ornate side. Miss Violet is a charming girl."

"A funny place to come for the winter," said Emily.

"Yes, very odd, is it not? But after all it is only logical. We ourselves living in this country long for the sunshine, hot climates, waving palm trees. People who live in Australia or South Africa are enchanted with the idea of an old-fashioned Christmas with snow and ice."

"I wonder which of them," said Emily to herself, "told him that."

She reflected that it was not necessary to bury yourself in a moorland village in order to obtain an old-fashioned Christmas with snow and ice. Clearly, Mr. Rycroft did not see anything suspicious in the Willetts' choice of a winter resort. But that, she reflected, was perhaps natural in one who was an ornithologist and a criminologist. Sittaford clearly appeared an ideal residence to Mr. Rycroft, and he could not conceive of it as an unsuitable environment to someone else.

They had been slowly descending the slope of the hillside and were now wending their way down the lane.

"Who lives in that cottage?" asked Emily abruptly.

"Captain Wyatt—he is an invalid. Rather unsociable I fear."

"Was he a friend of Captain Trevelyan's?"

"Not an intimate friend in any way. Trevelyan merely made a formal visit to him every now and then. As a matter of fact Wyatt doesn't encourage visitors. A surly man."

Emily was silent. She was reviewing the possibility of how she herself might become a visitor. She had no intention of allowing any angle of attack to remain unexplored.

She suddenly remembered the hitherto unmentioned member of the *séance*.

"What about Mr. Duke?" she asked brightly.

"What about him?"

"Well, who is he?"

"Well," said Mr. Rycroft slowly, "that is what nobody knows."

"How extraordinary," said Emily.

"As a matter of fact," said Mr. Rycroft, "it isn't. You see, Duke is such an entirely unmysterious individual. I should imagine that the only mystery about him was his social origin. Not—not quite, if you understand me. But a very solid good fellow," he hastened to add.

Emily was silent.

"This is my cottage," said Mr. Rycroft pausing, "perhaps you will do me the honor of coming in and inspecting it."

"I should love to," said Emily.

They went up the small path and entered the cottage. The interior was charming. Bookcases lined the walls.

Emily went from one to the other glancing curiously at the titles of the books. One section dealt with occult phenomena, another with modern detective fiction, but by far the greater part of the bookcases was given up to criminology and to the world's famous trials. Books on ornithology held a comparatively small position.

"I think it's all delightful," said Emily. "I must get back now. I expect Mr. Enderby will be up and waiting for me. As a matter of fact I haven't had breakfast yet. We told Mrs. Curtis half past nine, and I see it's ten o'clock. I shall be dreadfully late—that's because you've been so interesting—and so very helpful."

"Anything I can do," burbled Mr. Rycroft as Emily turned a bewitching glance on him. "You can count on me. We are collaborators."

Emily gave him her hand and squeezed his warmly.

"It's so wonderful," she said, using the phrase that in the course of her short life she had found so effectual, "to feel that there's someone on whom one can really rely."

17

Miss Percehouse

EMILY RETURNED to find eggs and bacon, and Charles waiting for her.

Mrs. Curtis was still agog with excitement over the escape of the convict.

"Two years it is since the last one escaped," she said, "and three days it was before they found him. Near to Moretonhampstead he was."

"Do you think he'll come this way?" asked Charles.

Local knowledge vetoed this suggestion.

"They never comes this way, all bare moorland it is, and only small towns when you do come off the moor. He'll make for Plymouth that's the most likely. But they'll catch him long before that."

"You could find a good hiding place among these rocks on the other side of the Tor," said Emily.

"You're right, Miss, and there *is* a hiding place there, the Pixie's Cave they call it. As narrow an opening between two rocks as you could find, but it widens out inside. They say one of King Charles's men hid there once for a fortnight with a serving maid from a farm bringing him food."

"I must take a look at that Pixie's Cave," said Charles.

"You'll be surprised how hard it is to find, sir. Many a picnic party in summer looks for it the whole afternoon and doesn't find it, but if you do find it be sure you leave a pin inside it for luck."

"I wonder," said Charles when breakfast was over and he and Emily had strolled out into the small bit of garden, "if I ought to go off to Princetown? Amazing how things pile up once you have a bit of luck. Here I am—I start with a simple football competition prize, and before I know where I am I run straight into an escaped convict and a murderer. Marvelous!"

"What about this photographing of Major Burnaby's cottage?"

Charles looked up at the sky.

"H'm," he said. "I think I shall say the weather is wrong. I have got to hang on to my *raison d'être* of being in Sittaford as long as possible, and it's coming over misty. Er—I hope you don't mind, I have just posted off an interview with you?"

"Oh! that's all right," said Emily mechanically. "What have you made me say?"

"Oh, the usual sort of things people like to hear," said Mr. Enderby. "Our special representative records his interview with Miss Emily Trefusis, the fiancée of Mr. James Pearson who has been arrested by the police and charged with the murder of Captain Trevelyan—Then my impression of you as a high-spirited, beautiful girl."

"Thank you," said Emily.

"Shingled," went on Charles.

"What do you mean by shingled?"

"You are," said Charles.

"Well, of course I am," said Emily. "But why mention it?"

"Women readers always like to know," said Charles Enderby. "It was a splendid interview. You've no idea what fine womanly touching things you said about standing by your man, no matter if the whole world was against him."

"Did I really say that?" said Emily wincing slightly.

"Do you mind?" said Mr. Enderby anxiously.

"Oh! no," said Emily. "Enjoy yourself, darling." Mr. Enderby looked slightly taken aback.

"It's all right," said Emily. "That's a quotation. I had it on my bib when I was small—my Sunday bib. The week-day one had 'Don't be a glutton' on it."

"Oh! I see. I put in a very good bit about Captain Trevelyan's sea career and just a hint at foreign idols looted and a possibility of a strange priest's revenge—only a hint you know."

"Well, you seem to have done your day's good deed." said Emily.

"What have you been up to? You were up early enough heaven knows."

Emily described her meeting with Mr. Rycroft.

She broke off suddenly and Enderby, glancing over his shoulders and following the direction of her eyes, became aware of a pink, healthy looking young man leaning over the gate and making various apologetic noises to attract attention.

"I say," said the young man, "frightfully sorry to butt in and all that. I mean, it is awfully awkward, but my aunt sent me along."

Emily and Charles both said, "Oh," in an inquiring tone, not being much the wiser for the explanation.

"Yes," said the young man. "To tell the truth my aunt's rather a Tartar. What she says *goes*, if you know what I mean. Of course, I think it's frightfully bad form coming along at a time like this but if you knew my aunt—and if you do as she wants, you will know her in a few minutes—"

"Is your aunt Miss Percehouse?" broke in Emily.

"That's right," said the young man much relieved. "So you know all about her? Old Mother Curtis has been talking I suppose. She can wag a tongue, can't she? Not that she's a bad sort, mind you. Well, the fact is, my aunt said she wanted to see you, and I was to come along and tell you so. Compliments, and all that, and would it be troubling you too much—she was an invalid and quite unable to get out and it would be a great kindness—well, you know the sort of thing. I needn't say it all. It's curiosity really, of course, and if you say you've got a headache, or have got letters to write it will be quite all right and you needn't bother."

"Oh, but I should like to bother," said Emily. "I'll come with you at once. Mr. Enderby has got to go along to see Major Burnaby."

"Have I?" said Enderby in a low voice.

"You have," said Emily firmly.

She dismissed him with a brief nod and joined her new friend in the road.

"I suppose you're Mr. Garfield," she said.

"That's right. I ought to have told you."

"Oh, well," said Emily, "it wasn't very difficult to guess."

"Splendid of you coming along like this," said Mr. Garfield. "Lots of girls would have been awfully offended. But you know what old ladies are."

"You don't live down here, do you Mr. Garfield?"

"You bet your life I don't," said Ronnie Garfield with fervor. "Did you ever see such a god-forsaken spot? Not so much as the Pictures to go to. I wonder someone doesn't commit a murder to—"

He paused appalled by what he had said.

"I say, I *am* sorry. I am the most unlucky devil that ever lived. Always coming out with the wrong thing. I never meant it for a moment."

"I'm sure you didn't," said Emily soothingly.

"Here we are," said Mr. Garfield. He pushed open a gate and Emily passed through and went up the path leading to a small cottage identical with the rest. In the living-room giving on the garden was a couch and on it was lying an elderly lady with a thin wrinkled face and with one of the sharpest and most interrogative noses that Emily had ever seen. She raised herself on an elbow with a little difficulty.

"So you've brought her," she said. "Very kind of you, my dear, to come along to see an old woman. But you know what it is when you are an invalid. You must have a finger in every pie going and if you can't go to the pie, then, the pie has got to come to you. And you needn't think it's all curiosity—it's more than that. Ronnie, go out and paint the garden furniture. In the shed at the end of the garden. Two basket chairs and a bench. You'll find the paint there all ready."

"Right oh, Aunt Caroline."

The obedient nephew disappeared.

"Sit down," said Miss Percehouse.

Emily sat on the chair indicated. Strange to say she had immediately felt conscious of a distinct liking and sympathy for this rather sharp-tongued middle-aged invalid. She felt indeed a kind of kinship with her.

"Here is someone," thought Emily, "who goes straight to the point and means to have her own way and bosses everybody she can. Just like me only I happen to be rather good-looking and she has to do it all by force of character."

"I understand you are the girl who is engaged to Trevelyan's nephew," said Miss Percehouse. "I've heard all about you and now I have seen you I understand exactly what you are up to. And I wish you good luck."

"Thank you," said Emily.

"I hate a slobbering female," said Miss Percehouse. "I like one who gets up and does things."

She looked at Emily sharply.

"I suppose you pity me—lying here never able to get up and walk about?"

"No," said Emily thoughtfully. "I don't know that I do. I suppose that one can, if one has the determination, always get something out of life. If you can't get it in one way you get it in another."

"Quite right," said Miss Percehouse. "You've got to take life from a different angle, that's all."

"Angle of attack," murmured Emily.

"What's that you say?"

As clearly as she was able, Emily outlined the theory that she had evolved that morning and the application of it she had made to the matter in hand.

"Not bad," said Miss Percehouse nodding her head. "Now, my dear—we will get down to business. Not being a born fool, I suppose you've come up to this village to find out what you can about the people here, and to see if what you find out has any bearing on the murder. Well, if there's anything you want to know about the people here, I can tell it to you."

Emily wasted no time. Concise and business-like she came to the point.

"Major Burnaby?" she asked.

"Typical retired army officer, narrow-minded and limited in out-look, jealous disposition. Credulous in money matters. Kind of man who invests in a South Sea Bubble because he can't see a yard in front

of his own nose. Likes to pay his debts promptly and dislikes people
who don't wipe their feet on the mat."

"Mr. Rycroft?" said Emily.

"Queer little man, enormous egoist. Cranky. Likes to think himself a
wonderful fellow. I suppose he has offered to help you solve the case
aright owing to his wonderful knowledge of criminology."

Emily admitted that that was the case.

"Mr. Duke?" she asked.

"Don't know a thing about the man—and yet I ought to. Most
ordinary type. I ought to know—and yet I don't. It's queer. It's like a
name on the tip of your tongue and yet for the life of you, you can't
remember it."

"The Willetts?" asked Emily.

"Ah! the Willetts!" Miss Percehouse hoisted herself up on an elbow
again in some excitement. "What about the Willetts indeed! Now, I'll
tell you something about them, my dear. It may be useful to you, or it
may not. Go over to my writing table there and pull out the little top
drawer—the one to the left—that's right. Bring me the blank envelope
that's there."

Emily brought the envelope as directed.

"I don't say it's important—it probably isn't," said Miss Percehouse. "Everybody tells lies one way or another and Mrs. Willett is
perfectly entitled to do the same as everybody else."

She took the envelope and slipped her hand inside.

"I will tell you all about it. When the Willetts arrived here, with their
smart clothes and their maids and their innovation trunks, she and
Violet came up in Forder's car and the maids and the innovation trunks
came by the station bus. And naturally, the whole thing being an event
as you might say, I was looking out as they passed and I saw a colored
label blow off from one of the trunks and dive down on to one of my
borders. Now, if there is one thing I hate more than another it is a litter
of paper or mess of any kind, so I sent Ronnie out to pick it up, and I
was going to throw it away when it struck me it was a bright, pretty
thing, and I might as well keep it for the scrap-books I make for the
children's hospital. Well, I wouldn't have thought about it again except
for Mrs. Willett deliberately mentioning on two or three occasions that
Violet had never been out of South Africa and that she herself had only
been to South Africa, England, and the Riviera."

"Yes?" said Emily.

"Exactly. Now—look at this."

Miss Percehouse thrust a luggage label into Emily's hand. It bore
the inscription, Mendle's Hotel, Melbourne.

"Australia," said Miss Percehouse, "isn't South Africa—or it wasn't in my young days. I daresay it isn't important but there it is for what it is worth. And I'll tell you another thing, I have heard Mrs. Willett calling to her daughter and she called Coo-ee and that again is more typical of Australia than South Africa. And what I say is, it is queer. Why shouldn't you wish to admit that you come from Australia if you do?"

"It's certainly curious," said Emily. "And it's curious that they should come to live here in winter time as they have."

"That leaps to the eye," said Miss Percehouse. "Have you met them yet?"

"No. I thought of going there this morning. Only I didn't know quite what to say."

"I'll provide you with an excuse," said Miss Percehouse briskly. "Fetch me my fountain pen and some notepaper and an envelope. That's right. Now, let me see." She paused deliberately, then without the least warning raised her voice in a hideous scream.

"Ronnie, Ronnie, Ronnie! Is the boy deaf? Why can't he come when he's called? Ronnie! Ronnie!"

Ronnie arrived at a brisk trot, paint brush in hand.

"Is there anything the matter, Aunt Caroline?"

"What should be the matter? I was calling you, that was all. Did you have any particular cake for tea when you were at the Willetts yesterday?"

"Cake?"

"Cake, sandwiches—anything. How slow you are, boy. What did you have to eat for tea?"

"There was a coffee cake," said Ronnie very much puzzled, "and some *pâté* sandwiches—"

"Coffee cake," said Miss Percehouse. "That'll do." She began to write briskly. "You can go back to your painting, Ronnie. Don't hang about, and don't stand there with your mouth open. You had your adenoids out when you were eight years old, so there is no excuse for it."

She continued to write:

> Dear Mrs. Willett,
> I hear you had the most delicious coffee cake for tea yesterday afternoon. Will you be so very kind as to give me the recipe for it. I know you'll not mind my asking you this—an invalid has so little variety except in her diet. Miss Trefusis has kindly promised to take this note for me as Ronnie is busy this morning. Is not this news about the convict *too* dreadful?
>
> Yours very sincerely,
> Caroline Percehouse.

She put it in an envelope, sealed it down and addressed it.

"There you are, young woman. You will probably find the doorstep littered with reporters. A lot of them passed along the lane in Forder's charabanc. I saw them. But you ask for Mrs. Willett and say you have brought a note from me and you'll sail in. I needn't tell you to keep your eyes open and make the most you can of your visit. You will do that anyway."

"You are kind," said Emily. "You really are."

"I help those who can help themselves," said Miss Percehouse. "By the way, you haven't asked me what I think of Ronnie yet. I presume he is on your list of the village. He is a good lad in his way, but pitifully weak. I am sorry to say he would do almost anything for money. Look at what he stands from me! And he hasn't got the brains to see that I would like him just ten times better if he stood up to me now and again, and told me to go to the devil.

"The only other person in the village is Captain Wyatt. He smokes opium, I believe. And he's easily the worst-tempered man in England. Anything more you want to know?"

"I don't think so," said Emily. "What you have told me seems pretty comprehensive."

18

Emily Visits Sittaford House

As EMILY WALKED BRISKLY along the lane she noticed once more how the character of the morning was changing. The mist was closing up and round.

"What an awful place to live in England is," thought Emily. "If it isn't snowing or raining or blowing it's misty. And if the sun does shine it's so cold that you can't feel your fingers or toes."

She was interrupted in these reflections by a rather hoarse voice speaking rather close to her right ear.

"Excuse me," it said, "but do you happen to have seen a bull terrier?"

Emily started and turned. Leaning over a gate was a tall thin man with a very brown complexion, bloodshot eyes and gray hair. He was propped up with a crutch one side, and was eyeing Emily with enormous interest. She had no difficulty in identifying him as Captain Wyatt, the invalid owner of No. 3 The Cottages.

"No, I haven't," said Emily.

"She's got out," said Captain Wyatt. "An affectionate creature, but an absolute fool. With all these cars and things—"

"I shouldn't think many motors come up this lane," said Emily.

"Charabancs do in the summer time," said Captain Wyatt grimly. "It's the three and sixpenny morning run from Exhampton. Ascent of Sittaford Beacon with a halt halfway up from Exhampton for light refreshments."

"Yes, but this isn't summer time," said Emily.

"All the same a charabanc came along just now. Reporters, I suppose, going to have a look at Sittaford House."

"Did you know Captain Trevelyan well?" asked Emily.

She was of the opinion that the incident of the bull terrier had been a mere subterfuge on Captain Wyatt's part dictated by a very natural curiosity. She was, she was well aware, the principal object of attention in Sittaford at present, and it was only natural that Captain Wyatt should wish to have a look at her as well as everyone else.

"I don't know about well," said Captain Wyatt. "He sold me this cottage."

"Yes," said Emily encouragingly.

"A skinflint, that's what he was," said Captain Wyatt. "The arrangement was that he was to do the place up to suit the purchaser's taste, and just because I had the window sashes in chocolate picked out in lemon, he wanted me to pay half. Said the arrangement was for a uniform color."

"You didn't like him," said Emily.

"I was always having rows with him," said Captain Wyatt. "But I always have rows with everyone," he added as an afterthought. "In a place like this you have to teach people to leave a man alone. Always knocking at the door and dropping in and chattering. I don't mind seeing people when I am in the mood—but it has got to be my mood not theirs. No good Trevelyan giving me his Lord of the Manor airs and dropping in whenever he felt like it. There's not a soul in the place comes near me now," he added with satisfaction.

"Oh!" said Emily.

"That's the best of having a native servant," said Captain Wyatt. "They understand orders. Abdul," he roared.

A tall Indian in a turban came out of the cottage and waited attentively.

"Come in and have something," said Captain Wyatt. "And see my little cottage."

"I'm sorry," said Emily, "but I have to hurry on."

"Oh, no, you haven't," said Captain Wyatt.

"Yes, I have," said Emily. "I've got an appointment."

"Nobody understands the art of living nowadays," said Captain Wyatt. "Catching trains, making appointments, fixing times for everything—all nonsense. Get up with the sun I say, have your meals when you feel like it, and never tie yourself to a time or a date. I could teach people how to live if they would listen to me."

The results of this exalted idea of living were not too hopeful, Emily reflected. Anything more like a battered wreck of a man than Captain Wyatt she had never seen. However, feeling that his curiosity had been sufficiently satisfied for the time being she insisted once more on her appointment and went on her way.

Sittaford House had a solid oak front door, a neat bell pull, an immense wire mat, and a brilliantly polished brass letter box. It represented, as Emily could not fail to see, comfort and decorum. A neat and conventional parlormaid answered the bell.

Emily deduced the journalist evil had been before her as the parlormaid said at once in a distant tone, "Mrs. Willett is not seeing anyone this morning."

"I have brought a note from Miss Percehouse," said Emily.

This clearly altered matters. The parlormaid's face expressed indecision, then she shifted her ground.

"Will you come inside, please."

Emily was ushered into what house agents describe as a "well-appointed hall," and from there into a large drawing-room. A fire was burning brightly and there were traces of feminine occupation in the room. Some glass tulips, an elaborate workbag, a girl's hat, and a Pierrot doll with very long legs were lying about. There were, she noticed, no photographs.

Having taken in all there was to see, Emily was warming her hands in front of the fire when the door opened and a girl about her own age came in. She was a very pretty girl, Emily noticed, smartly and expensively dressed, and she also thought that she had never seen a girl in a greater state of nervous apprehension. Not that this was apparent on the surface however. Miss Willett was making a gallant appearance of being entirely at her ease.

"Good morning," she said advancing and shaking hands. "I'm so sorry mother isn't down, but she's spending the morning in bed."

"Oh, I am so sorry, I'm afraid I have come at an unfortunate time."

"No, of course not. The cook is writing out the recipe for that cake now. We are only too delighted for Miss Percehouse to have it. Are you staying with her?"

Emily reflected with an inward smile that this was perhaps the only house in Sittaford whose members were not exactly aware of who she was and why she was there. Sittaford House had a definite regime of employers and employed. The employed might know about her—the employers clearly did not.

"I am not exactly staying with her," said Emily. "In fact, I'm at Mrs. Curtis's."

"Of course the cottage is terribly small and she has her nephew, Ronnie, with her, hasn't she? I suppose there wouldn't be room for you too. She's a wonderful person, isn't she? So much character, I always think, but I am rather afraid of her really."

"She's a bully, isn't she?" agreed Emily cheerfully. "But it's an awful temptation to be a bully, especially if people won't stand up to you."

Miss Willett sighed.

"I wish I could stand up to people," she said. "We've had the most awful morning absolutely pestered by reporters."

"Oh, of course," said Emily. "This is Captain Trevelyan's house really, isn't it?—the man who was murdered at Exhampton."

She was trying to determine the exact cause of Violet Willett's nervousness. The girl was clearly on the jump. Something was frightening her—and frightening her badly. She mentioned Captain Trevelyan's name bluntly on purpose. The girl didn't noticeably react to it in any way, but then she was probably expecting some such reference.

"Yes, wasn't it dreadful?"

"Do tell me—that's if you don't mind talking about it?"

"No—no—of course not—why should I?"

"There's something very wrong with this girl," thought Emily. "She hardly knows what she's saying. What has made her get the wind up this morning particularly?"

"About that table turning," went on Emily. "I heard about it in a casual sort of way and it seemed to me so frightfully interesting—I mean so absolutely gruesome."

"Girlish thrills," she thought to herself, "that's my line."

"Oh, it was horrid," said Violet. "That evening—I shall never forget it! We thought, of course, that it was somebody just fooling—only it seemed a very nasty kind of joke."

"Yes?"

"I shall never forget when we turned the lights on—everybody looked so queer. Not Mr. Duke and Major Burnaby—they are the stolid kind, they would never like to admit that they were impressed by anything of that kind. But you could see that Major Burnaby was really awfully rattled by it. I think that actually he believed in it more than anybody else. But I thought poor little Mr. Rycroft was going to have a heart attack or something, yet he must be used to that kind of thing because he does a lot of psychic research, and as for Ronnie, Ronnie Garfield you know—he looked as though he had seen a ghost— actually seen one. Even mother was awfully upset—more than I have ever seen her before."

"It must have been most spooky," said Emily. "I wish I had been there to see."

"It was rather horrid really. We all pretended that it was—just fun, you know, but it didn't seem like that. And then Major Burnaby suddenly made up his mind to go over to Exhampton and we all tried to stop him, and said he would be buried in a snowdrift, but he would go. And there we sat, after he had gone, all feeling dreadful and worried. And then, last night—no, yesterday morning—we got the news."

"You think it was Captain Trevelyan's spirit?" said Emily in an awed voice. "Or do you think it was clairvoyance or telepathy?"

"Oh, I don't know. But I shall never, never laugh at these things again."

The parlormaid entered with a folded piece of paper on a salver which she handed to Violet.

The parlormaid withdrew and Violet unfolded the paper, glanced over it and handed it to Emily.

"There you are," she said. "As a matter of fact you are just in time. This murder business has upset the servants. They think it's dangerous to live in this out of the way part. Mother lost her temper with them yesterday evening and has sent them all packing. They are going after lunch. We are going to get two men instead—a house-parlorman and a kind of butler chauffeur. I think it will answer much better."

"Servants are silly, aren't they?" said Emily.

"It isn't even as if Captain Trevelyan had been killed in this house."

"What made you think of coming to live here?" asked Emily, trying to make the question sound artless and girlishly natural.

"Oh, we thought it would be rather fun," said Violet.

"Don't you find it rather dull?"

"Oh, no, I love the country."

But her eyes avoided Emily's. Just for a moment she looked sus- picious and afraid.

She stirred uneasily in her chair and Emily rose rather reluctantly to her feet.

"I must be going now," she said. "Thank you so much, Miss Willett. I do hope your mother will be all right."

"Oh, she's quite well really. It's only the servants—and all the worry."

"Of course."

Adroitly, unperceived by the other, Emily managed to discard her gloves on a small table. Violet Willett accompanied her to the front door and they took leave of each other with a few pleasant remarks.

The parlormaid who had opened the door to Emily had unlocked it, but as Violet Willett closed it behind her retreating guest Emily caught no sound of the key being turned. When she reached the gate therefore, she retraced her steps slowly.

Her visit had more than confirmed the theories she held about Sittaford House. There was something queer going on here. She didn't think Violet Willett was directly implicated—that is unless she was a very clever actress indeed. But there was something wrong, and that something *must* have a connection with the tragedy. There *must* be some link between the Willetts and Captain Trevelyan, and in that link there might lie the clue to the whole mystery.

She came up to the front door, turned the handle very gently and passed across the threshold. The hall was deserted. Emily paused uncertain what to do next. She had her excuse—the gloves left thoughtfully behind in the drawing-room. She stood stock still listening. There was no sound anywhere except a very faint murmur of voices from upstairs. As quietly as possible Emily crept to the foot of the stairs and stood looking up. Then, very gingerly she ascended a step at a time. This was rather more risky. She could hardly pretend that her gloves had walked of their own accord to the first floor, but she had a burning desire to overhear something of the conversation that was going on upstairs. Modern builders never made their doors fit well, in Emily's opinion. You could hear a murmur of voices down here. Therefore, if you reached the door itself you would hear plainly the conversation that was going on inside the room. Another step—one more again . . . Two women's voices—Violet and her mother without doubt.

Suddenly there was a break in the conversation—a sound of footsteps. Emily retreated rapidly.

When Violet Willett opened her mother's door and came down the stairs she was surprised to find her late guest standing in the hall peering about her in a lost dog kind of way.

"My gloves," she explained. "I must have left them. I came back for them."

"I expect they are in here," said Violet.

They went into the drawing-room and there, sure enough, on a little table near where Emily had been sitting lay the missing gloves.

"Oh, thank you," said Emily. "It's so stupid of me. I am always leaving things."

"And you want gloves in this weather," said Violet. "It's so cold." Once again they parted at the hall door, and this time Emily heard the key being turned in the lock.

She went down the drive with plenty to think about for, as that door on the upper landing had opened, she had heard distinctly one sentence spoken in an older woman's fretful and plaintive voice:

"*My God*," the voice had wailed, "*I can't bear it. Will tonight never come?*"

19

Theories

EMILY ARRIVED BACK at the cottage to find her boy friend absent. He had, Mrs. Curtis explained, gone off with several other young gentlemen, but two telegrams had come for the young lady. Emily took them, opened them, and put them in the pocket of her sweater, Mrs Curtis eyeing them hungrily the while.

"Not bad news, I hope?" said Mrs. Curtis.

"Oh, no," said Emily.

"Always gives me a turn a telegram does," said Mrs. Curtis.

"I know," said Emily. "Very disturbing."

At the moment she felt disinclined for anything but solitude. She wanted to sort out and arrange her own ideas. She went up to her own room, and taking pencil and notepaper she set to work on a system of her own. After twenty minutes of this exercise she was interrupted by Mr. Enderby.

"Hullo, hullo, hullo, there you are. Fleet Street has been hard on your tracks all morning but they have just missed you everywhere. Anyway they have had it from me that you are not to be worried. As far as you're concerned, I am the big noise."

He sat down on the chair, Emily was occupying the bed, and chuckled.

"Envy and malice isn't in it!" he said. "I have been handing them out the goods. I know everyone and I am right in it. It's too good to be true. I keep pinching myself and feeling I will wake up in a minute. I say, have you noticed the fog?"

"It won't stop me going to Exeter this afternoon, will it?" said Emily.

"Do you want to go to Exeter?"

"Yes. I have to meet Mr. Dacres there. My solicitor, you know—the one who is undertaking Jim's defence. He wants to see me. And I think I shall pay a visit to Jim's Aunt Jennifer, while I am there. After all, Exeter is only half an hour away."

"Meaning she might have nipped over by train and batted her brother over the head and nobody would have noticed her absence."

"Oh, I know it sounds rather improbable but one has to go into everything. Not that I want it to be Aunt Jennifer—I don't. I would much rather it was Martin Dering. I hate the sort of man who presumes on going to be a brother-in-law and does things in public that you can't smack his face for."

"Is he that kind?"

"Very much that kind. He's an ideal person for a murderer—always getting telegrams from bookmakers and losing money on horses. It's annoying that he's got such a good *alibi*. Mr. Dacres told me about it. A publisher and a literary dinner seems so very unbreakable and respectable."

"A literary dinner," said Enderby. "Friday night. Martin Dering— let me see—Martin Dering—why, yes—I am almost sure of it. Dash it all I am quite sure of it, but I can clinch things by wiring to Carruthers."

"What are you talking about?" said Emily.

"Listen. You know I came down to Exhampton on Friday evening. Well, there was a bit of information I was going to get from a pal of mine, another newspaper man, Carruthers his name is. He was coming round to see me about half past six if he could—before he went on to some literary dinner—he is rather a big bug, Carruthers, and if he couldn't make it he would send me a line to Exhampton. Well, he didn't make it and he did send me a line."

"What *has* all this got to do with it?" said Emily.

"Don't be so impatient, I am coming to the point. The old chap was rather screwed when he wrote it—done himself well at the dinner—after giving me the item I wanted, he went on to waste a good bit of juicy description on me. You know—about the speeches, and what asses so and so, a famous novelist and a famous playwright, were. And he said he had been rottenly placed at the dinner. There was an empty seat on one side of him where Ruby McAlmott, that awful best-seller woman, ought to have sat and an empty place on the other side of him where the sex specialist, Martin Dering, ought to have been, but he moved up near to a poet, who is very well known in Blackheath, and tried to make the best of things. Now, do you see the point?"

"Charles! Darling!" Emily became lyrical with excitement. "How marvelous. Then the brute wasn't at the dinner at all?"

"Exactly."

"You are sure you've remembered the name right?"

"I'm positive. I have torn up the letter, worse luck, but I can always wire to Carruthers to make sure. But I absolutely know that I'm not mistaken."

"There's the publisher still, of course," said Emily. "The one he spent the afternoon with. But I rather think it was a publisher who was just going back to America, and if so, that looks fishy. I mean it looks as though he had selected someone who couldn't be asked without rather a lot of trouble."

"Do you really think we have hit it?" said Charles Enderby.

"Well, it looks like it. I think the best thing to be done is—to go straight to that nice Inspector Narracott and just tell him these new facts. I mean, we can't tackle an American publisher who is on the *Mauretania* or the *Berengaria* or somewhere. That's a job for the police."

"My word if this comes off. What a scoop!" said Mr. Enderby. "If it does, I should think the *Daily Wire* couldn't offer me less than—"

Emily broke in ruthlessly into his dreams of advancement.

"But we mustn't lose our heads," she said, "and throw everything else to the wind. I must go to Exeter. I don't suppose I shall be able to be back here until tomorrow. But I've got a job for you."

"What kind of a job?"

Emily described her visit to the Willetts and the strange sentence she had overheard on leaving.

"We have got absolutely and positively to find out what is going to happen tonight. There's something in the wind."

"What an extraordinary thing!"

"Wasn't it? But of course it may be a coincidence. Or it may not—but you observe that the servants are being cleared out of the way. Something queer is going to happen there tonight, and *you* have to be on the spot to see what it is."

"You mean I have to spend the whole night shivering under a bush in the garden?"

"Well, you don't mind that, do you? Journalists don't mind what they do in a good cause."

"Who told you that?"

"Never mind who told me, I know it. You will do it, won't you?"

"Oh, rather," said Charles. "I am not going to miss anything. If anything queer goes on at Sittaford House tonight, I shall be in it."

Emily then told him about the luggage label.

"It's odd," said Mr. Enderby. "Australia is where the third Pearson is, isn't it?—the youngest one. Not, of course, that that means anything, but still it—well, there might be a connection."

"H'm," said Emily. "I think that's all. Have you anything to report on your side?"

"Well," said Charles, "I've got an idea."

"Yes?"

"The only thing is I don't know how you'll like it."

"What do you mean—how I'll like it?"

"You won't fly out over it, will you?"

"I don't suppose so. I mean I hope I can listen sensibly and quietly to anything."

"Well, the point is," said Charles Enderby eyeing her doubtfully, "don't think I mean to be offensive or anything like that, but you do think that lad of yours is to be depended on for the strict truth?"

"Do you mean," said Emily, "that he did murder him after all? You are quite welcome to that view if you like. I said to you at the beginning that that was the natural view to take, but I said we had to work on the assumption that he didn't."

"I don't mean that," said Enderby. "I am with you in assuming that he didn't do the old boy in. What I mean is, how far is his own story of what happened true? He says that he went there, had a chat with the old fellow, and came away leaving him alive and well."

"Yes."

"Well, it just occurred to me, you don't think it's possible that he went there and actually found the old man dead? I mean, he might have got the wind up and been scared and not liked to say so."

Charles had propounded this theory rather dubiously but he was relieved to find that Emily showed no signs of flying out at him over it. Instead, she frowned and creased her brow in thought.

"I am not going to pretend," she said. "It *is* possible. I hadn't thought of it before. I know Jim wouldn't murder anyone, but he might quite well get rattled and tell a silly lie and then, of course, he would have to stick to it. Yes, it is quite possible."

"The awkward thing is that you can't go and ask him about it now. I mean they wouldn't let you see him alone, would they?"

"I can put Mr. Dacres on to him," said Emily. "You see your solicitor alone, I believe. The worst of Jim is that he is frightfully obstinate, if he has once said a thing he sticks to it."

"That's my story and I'm going to stick to it," said Mr. Enderby comprehendingly.

"Yes. I am glad you mentioned that possibility to me, Charles, it hadn't occurred to me. We have been looking for someone who came in *after* Jim had left—but if it was *before*—"

She paused, lost in thought. Two very different theories stretched out in opposite directions. There was the one suggested by Mr. Rycroft, in which Jim's quarrel with his uncle was the determining point. The other theory, however, took no cognizance of Jim whatsoever. The first thing to do, Emily felt, was to see the doctor who had first examined the body. If it were possible that Captain Trevelyan had been murdered at—say—four o'clock, it might make a considerable difference to the question of alibis. And the other thing to do was to make Mr. Dacres urge most strongly on his client the absolute necessity of speaking the truth on this point.

She rose from the bed.

"Well," she said, "you had better find out how I can get to Exhampton. The man at the smithy has a car of a kind I believe. Will you go and settle with him about it? I'll start immediately after lunch. There's a train at three ten to Exeter. That will give me time to see the doctor first. What's the time now?"

"Half past twelve." said Mr. Enderby, consulting his watch.

"Then we will both go up and fix up about that car," said Emily. "And there's just one other thing I want to do before leaving Sittaford."

"What's that?"

"I am going to pay a call on Mr. Duke. He's the only person in Sittaford I haven't seen. And he was one of the people at the table turning."

"Oh, we'll pass his cottage on the way to the smithy."

Mr. Duke's cottage was the last of the row. Emily and Charles unlatched the gate and walked up the path. And then something rather surprising occurred. For the door opened and a man came out. And that man was Inspector Narracott.

He, too, looked surprised and, Emily fancied, embarrassed.

Emily abandoned her original intention.

"I am so glad to have met you, Inspector Narracott," she said. "There are one or two things I want to talk to you about if I may."

"Delighted, Miss Trefusis." He drew out a watch. "I'm afraid you will have to look sharp, I've a car waiting. I've got to go back to Exhampton almost immediately."

"How extraordinarily fortunate," said Emily, "you might give me a lift, will you, Inspector?"

The Inspector said rather woodenly that he would be very pleased to do so.

"You might go and get my suitcase, Charles," said Emily. "It's packed up and ready."

Charles departed immediately.

"It's a great surprise meeting you here, Miss Trefusis," said Inspector Narracott.

"I said *au revoir*," Emily reminded him.

"I didn't notice it at the time."

"You've not seen the last of me by a long way," said Emily candidly. "You know, Inspector Narracott, you've made a mistake. Jim's not the man you're after."

"Indeed!"

"And what's more," said Emily, "I believe in your heart that you agree with me."

"What makes you think that, Miss Trefusis?"

"What were you doing in Mr. Duke's cottage?" retaliated Emily.

Narracott looked embarrassed and she was quick to follow it up.

"You're doubtful, Inspector—that's what you are—doubtful. You thought you had got the right man and now you are not so sure, and so you are making a few investigations. Well, I have got something to tell you that may help. I'll tell it to you on the way to Exhampton."

Footsteps sounded down the road, and Ronnie Garfield appeared. He had the air of a truant, breathless and guilty.

"I say, Miss Trefusis," he began. "What about a walk this afternoon? While my aunt has a nap, you know."

"Impossible," said Emily. "I'm going away. To Exeter."

"What, not really! For good you mean?"

"Oh, no," said Emily. "I shall be back again tomorrow."

"Oh, that's splendid."

Emily took something from the pocket of her sweater and handed it to him. "Give that to your aunt, will you? It's a recipe for coffee cake, and tell her that she was just in time, the cook is leaving today and so are the other servants. Be sure you tell her, she will be interested."

A faroff scream was borne on the breeze. "Ronnie," it said, "Ronnie, Ronnie."

"There's my aunt," said Ronnie starting nervously. "I had better go."

"I think you had," said Emily. "You've got green paint on your left cheek," she called after him. Ronnie Garfield disappeared through his aunt's gate.

"Here's my boy friend with my suitcase." said Emily. "Come on, Inspector. I'll tell you everthing in the car."

20

Visit to Aunt Jennifer

AT HALF PAST TWO Dr. Warren received a call from Emily. He took an immediate fancy to this business-like and attractive girl. Her questions were blunt and to the point.

"Yes, Miss Trefusis, I see exactly what you mean. You'll understand that contrary to the popular belief in novels it is extremely difficult to fix the time of death accurately. I saw the body at eight o'clock. I can say decidedly that Captain Trevelyan had been dead at least two hours. How much longer than that would be difficult to say. If you were to tell me that he was killed at four o'clock, I should say that it was possible, though my own opinion inclines to a later time. On the other hand he could certainly not have been dead for much longer than that. Four and a half hours would be the outside limit."

"Thank you," said Emily, "that's all that I wanted to know."

She caught the three ten train at the station and drove straight to the hotel where Mr. Dacres was staying.

Their interview was business-like and unemotional. Mr. Dacres had known Emily since she was a small child, and had managed her affairs for her since she came of age.

"You must prepare yourself for a shock, Emily," he said. "Things are much worse for Jim Pearson than we imagined."

"Worse?"

"Yes. It's no good beating about the bush. Certain facts have come to light which are bound to show him up in a most unfavorable light. It is those facts which led the police actually to charge him with the crime. I should not be acting in your interests if I withheld these facts from you."

"Please tell me," said Emily.

Her voice was perfectly calm and composed. Whatever the inward shock she might have felt, she had no intention of making an outward display of her feelings. It was not feelings that were going to help Jim Pearson, it was brains. She must keep all her wits about her.

"There is no doubt that he was in urgent and immediate need of money. I am not going to enter into the ethics of the situation at the moment. Pearson had apparently before now occasionally borrowed money—to use a euphemism—from his firm—I may say without their

256

knowledge. He was fond of speculating in shares, and on one occasion previously, knowing that certain dividends were to be paid into his account in a week's time, he anticipated them by using the firm's money to buy certain shares which he had pretty certain knowledge were bound to go up. The transaction was quite satisfactory, the money was replaced and Pearson really doesn't seem to have had any doubts as to the honesty of the transaction. Apparently he repeated this just over a week ago. This time an unforeseen thing occurred. The books of the firm are examined at certain stated times, but for some reason or other this date was advanced and Pearson was faced with a very unpleasant dilemma. He was quite aware of the constriction that would be put on his action and he was quite unable to raise the sum of money involved. He admits himself that he had tried in various quarters and failed when as a last resource he rushed down to Devonshire to lay the matter before his uncle and persuade him to help him. This Captain Trevelyan absolutely refused to do.

"Now, my dear Emily, we shall be quite unable to prevent these facts from being brought to light. The police have already unearthed the matter. And you see, don't you, that we have here a very pressing and urgent motive for the crime? The moment Captain Trevelyan was dead Pearson could easily have obtained the necessary sum as an advance from Mr. Kirkwood and saved himself from disaster and possibly criminal prosecution."

"Oh, the idiot," said Emily helplessly.

"Quite so," said Mr. Dacres dryly. "It seems to me that our only chance lies in proving that Jim Pearson was quite unaware of the provisions of his uncle's will."

There was a pause while Emily considered the matter. Then she said quietly:

"I'm afraid that's impossible. All three of them knew—Sylvia, Jim and Brian. They often discussed it and laughed and joked about the rich uncle in Devonshire."

"Dear, dear," said Mr. Dacres. "That's unfortunate."

"You don't think him guilty, Mr. Dacres?" asked Emily.

"Curiously enough I do not," replied the lawyer. "In some ways Jim Pearson is a most transparent young man. He hasn't, if you will allow me to say so, Emily, a very high standard of commercial honesty, but I do not believe for one minute that his hand sandbagged his uncle."

"Well, that's a good thing," said Emily. "I wish the police thought the same."

"Quite so. Our own impressions and ideas are of no practical use. The case against him is unfortunately strong. I am not going to disguise from you, my dear child, that the outlook is bad. I should suggest Lorimer, K.C., as the defense. Forlorn hope man they call him," he added cheerfully.

"There is one thing I should like to know," said Emily. "You have, of course, seen Jim?"

"Certainly."

"I want you to tell me honestly if you think he has told the truth in other respects." She outlined to him the idea that Enderby had suggested to her.

The lawyer considered the matter carefully before replying.

"It's my impression," he said, "that he is speaking the truth when he describes his interview with his uncle. But there is little doubt that he has got the wind up badly, and if he went round to the window, entered that way and came across his uncle's dead body—he might just possibly be too scared to admit the fact and have concocted this other story."

"That's what I thought," said Emily. "Next time you see him, Mr. Dacres, will you urge him to speak the truth? It may make the most tremendous difference."

"I will do so. All the same," he said after a moment or two's pause, "I think you are mistaken in this idea. The news of Captain Trevelyan's death was bandied around in Exhampton about eight thirty. At that time the last train had left for Exeter but Jim Pearson got the first train available in the morning—a thoroughly unwise proceeding by the way as it called attention to his movements which without, would not have been aroused if he had left by a train at a more conventional hour. Now if, as you suggest, he discovered his uncle's dead body some time after half past four, I think he would have left Exhampton straight away. There's a train which leaves shortly after six and another at a quarter to eight."

"That's a point," admitted Emily, "I didn't think of that."

"I have questioned him narrowly about his method of entering his uncle's house," went on Mr. Dacres. "He says that Captain Trevelyan made him remove his boots, and leave them on the doorstep. That accounts for no wet marks being discovered in the hall."

"He doesn't speak of having heard any sound—anything at all—that gives him the idea that there might have been someone else in the house?"

"He didn't mention it to me. But I will ask him."

"Thank you," said Emily. "If I write a note can you take it to him?"

"Subject to its being read, of course."

"Oh, it will be a very discreet one."

She crossed to the writing table and scribbled a few words.

Dearest Jim,
 Everything's going to be all right, so cheer up. I am working like fury to find out the truth. What an idiot you've been, darling.

Love from
Emily.

"There," she said.

Mr. Dacres read it but made no comment.

" I have taken pains with my handwriting," said Emily, "so that the prison authorities can read it easily. Now, I must be off."

"You will allow me to offer you a cup of tea."

"No, thank you, Mr. Dacres. I have no time to lose. I am going to see Jim's Aunt Jennifer."

At The Laurels, Emily was informed that Mrs. Gardner was out but would be home shortly.

Emily smiled upon the parlormaid.

"I'll come in and wait then."

"Would you like to see Nurse Davis?"

Emily was always ready to see anybody. "Yes," she said promptly.

A few minutes later Nurse Davis, starched and curious, arrived.

"How do you do," said Emily. "I am Emily Trefusis—a kind of niece of Mrs. Gardner's. That is I am going to be a niece but my fiancé, Jim Pearson, has been arrested as I expect you know."

"Oh, it's been too dreadful," said Nurse Davis. "We saw it all in the papers this morning. What a terrible business. You seem to be bearing up wonderfully, Miss Trefusis—really wonderfully."

There was a faint note of disapproval in the Nurse's voice. Hospital nurses, she implied, were able to bear up owing to their force of character, but lesser mortals were expected to *give way*.

"Well, one mustn't sag at the knees," said Emily. "I hope you don't mind very much. I mean, it must be awkward for you to be associated with a family that has got a murder in it."

"It's very unpleasant, of course," said Nurse Davis unbending at this proof of consideration. "But one's duty to one's patient comes before everything."

"How splendid," said Emily. "It must be wonderful for Aunt Jennifer to feel she has somebody upon whom she can rely."

"Oh, really," said the Nurse simpering, "you are too kind. But, of course, I have had curious experiences before this. Why, at the last case I attended—" Emily listened patiently to a long and scandalous anecdote comprising complicated divorce and paternity questions.

After complimenting Nurse Davis on her tact, discretion and *savoir faire*, Emily slid back to the topic of the Gardners.

"I don't know Aunt Jennifer's husband at all," she said. "I've never met him. He never goes away from home, does he?"

"No, poor fellow."

"What exactly is the matter with him?"

Nurse Davis embarked on the subject with professional gusto.

"So, really he might get well again any minute," Emily murmured thoughtfully.

"He would be terribly weak," said the Nurse.

"Oh, of course. But it makes it seem more hopeful, doesn't it?"

The Nurse shook her head with firm professional despondency.

"I don't suppose there will be any cure in his case."

Emily had copied down in her little notebook the timetable of what she called Aunt Jennifer's *alibi*. She now murmured tentatively:

"How queer it seems to think that Aunt Jennifer was actually at the Pictures when her brother was being killed."

"Very sad, isn't it?" said Nurse Davis. "Of course, she couldn't tell—but it gives one such a shock afterwards."

Emily cast about in her mind to find out what she wanted to know without asking a direct question.

"Didn't she have some queer kind of vision or premonition?" she inquired. "Wasn't it you who met her in the hall when she came in and exclaimed that she looked quite queer?"

"Oh, no," said the Nurse. "It wasn't me. I didn't see her until we were sitting down to dinner together, and she seemed quite her ordinary self then. How very interesting."

"I expect I am mixing it up with something else," said Emily.

"Perhaps it was some other relation," suggested Nurse Davis. "I came in rather late myself. I felt rather guilty about leaving my patient so long, but he himself had urged me to go."

She suddenly looked at her watch.

"Oh, dear. He asked me for another hot water bottle. I must see about it at once. Will you excuse me, Miss Trefusis?"

Emily excused her and going over to the fireplace she put her finger on the bell.

The slipshod maid came with rather a frightened face.

"What's your name?" said Emily.

"Beatrice, Miss."

"Oh, Beatrice, I may not be able to wait to see my aunt—Mrs. Gardner, after all—I wanted to ask her about some shopping she did on Friday. Do you know if she brought a big parcel back with her?"

"No, Miss, I didn't see her come in."

"I thought you said she came in at six o'clock."

"Yes, Miss, she did, I didn't see her come in, but when I went to take some hot water to her room at seven o'clock it gave me a shock to find her lying in the dark on the bed. 'Well, ma'am,' I said to her, 'You gave me quite a shock.' 'I came in quite a long time ago. At six o'clock,' she said. I didn't see a big parcel anywhere," said Beatrice trying her hardest to be helpful.

"It's all very difficult," thought Emily. "One has to invent so many things. I've already invented a premonition and a big parcel, but so far as I can see one has to invent something if one doesn't want to sound suspicious." She smiled sweetly and said:

"That's all right, Beatrice, it doesn't matter."

Beatrice left the room. Emily took a small local timetable out of her handbag and consulted it.

"Leave Exeter, St. David's, three ten," she murmured, "Arrive Exhampton, three forty-two. Time allowed for going to brother's house and murdering him—how beastly and cold-blooded it sounds—and such nonsense too—say half an hour to three quarters. What are the trains back? There's one at four twenty-five and there's one Mr. Dacres mentioned at six ten, that gets in at twenty-three minutes to seven. Yes, it's actually possible either way. It's a pity there's nothing to suspect the Nurse for. She was out all the afternoon and nobody knows where she was. But you can't have a murder without any motive at all. Of course, I don't really believe anybody in this house murdered Captain Trevelyan but in a way it's comforting to know that they could have. Hello—there's the front door."

There was a murmur of voices in the hall and the door opened and Jennifer Gardner came into the room.

"I'm Emily Trefusis," said Emily. "You know—the one who is engaged to Jim Pearson."

"So you are Emily," said Mrs. Gardner shaking hands. "Well, this is a surprise."

Suddenly Emily felt very weak and small. Rather like a little girl in the act of doing something very silly. An extraordinary person, Aunt Jennifer. Character—that was what it was. Aunt Jennifer had about enough character for two and three quarter people instead of one.

"Have you had tea, my dear? No? Then we'll have it here. Just a moment—I must go up and see Robert first."

A strange expression flitted over her face as she mentioned her husband's name. The hard, beautiful voice softened. It was like a light passing over dark ripples of water.

"She does adore him," thought Emily left alone in the drawing-room. "All the same there's something frightening about Aunt

Jennifer. I wonder if Uncle Robert likes being adored quite as much as that."

When Jennifer Gardner returned, she had taken off her hat. Emily admired the smooth sweep of the hair back from her forehead.

"Do you want to talk about things, Emily, or don't you? If you don't I shall quite understand."

"It isn't much good talking about them, is it?"

"We can only hope," said Mrs. Gardner, "that they will find the real murderer quickly. Just press the bell, will you, Emily? I'll send Nurse's tea up to her. I don't want her chattering down here. How I hate hospital nurses."

"Is she a good one?"

"I suppose she is. Robert says she is anyway. I dislike her intensely and always have. But Robert says she's far and away the best nurse we've had."

"She's rather good-looking," said Emily.

"Nonsense. With her ugly beefy hands?"

Emily watched her aunt's long white fingers as they touched the milk jug and the sugar tongs.

Beatrice came, took the cup of tea and a plate of eatables and left the room.

"Robert has been very upset over all this," said Mrs. Gardner. "He works himself into such curious states. I suppose it's all part of his illness really."

"He didn't know Captain Trevelyan well, did he?"

Jennifer Gardner shook her head.

"He neither knew him nor cared about him. To be honest, I, myself can't pretend any great sorrow over his death. He was a cruel grasping man, Emily. He knew the struggle we have had. The poverty! He knew that a loan of money at the right time might have given Robert special treatment that would have made all the difference. Well, retribution has overtaken him."

She spoke in a deep brooding voice.

"What a strange woman she is," thought Emily. "Beautiful and terrible, like something out of a Greek play."

"It may still not be too late," said Mrs. Gardner. "I wrote to the lawyers at Exhampton today, to ask them if I could have a certain sum of money in advance. The treatment I am speaking of is in some respects what they would call a quack remedy, but it has been successful in a large number of cases. Emily—how wonderful it will be if Robert is able to walk again."

Her face was glowing, lit up as though by a lamp.

Emily was tired. She had had a long day, little or nothing to eat, and she was worn out by suppressed emotion. The room kept going away and coming back again.

"Aren't you feeling well, dear?"

"It's all right," gasped Emily, and to her own surprise, annoyance and humiliation burst into tears.

Mrs. Gardner did not attempt to rise and console her, for which Emily was grateful. She just sat silently until Emily's tears should subside. She murmured in a thoughtful voice:

"Poor child. It's very unlucky that Jim Pearson should have been arrested—very unlucky. I wish—something could be done about it."

21

Conversations

LEFT TO HIS OWN DEVICES Charles Enderby did not relax his efforts. To familiarize himself with life as lived in Sittaford village he had only to turn on Mrs. Curtis much as you would turn on the tap of a hydrant. Listening slightly dazed to a stream of anecdote, reminiscence, rumors, surmise and meticulous detail he endeavored valiantly to sift the grain from the chaff. He then mentioned another name and immediately the force of the water was directed in that direction. He heard all about Captain Wyatt, his tropical temper, his rudeness, his quarrels with his neighbors, his occasional amazing graciousness, usually to personable young women. The life he led, his Indian servant, the peculiar times he had his meals and the exact diet that composed them. He heard about Mr. Rycroft's library, his hair tonics, his insistence on strict tidiness and punctuality, his inordinate curiosity over other people's doings, his recent selling of a few old prized personal possessions, his inexplicable fondness for birds, and the prevalent idea that Mrs. Willett was setting her cap at him. He heard about Miss Percehouse and her tongue and the way she bullied her nephew, and of the rumors of the gay life that same nephew led in London. He heard all over again of Major Burnaby's friendship with Captain Trevelyan, their reminiscences of the past and their fondness for chess. He heard everything that was known about the Willetts, including the belief that Miss Violet Willett was leading on Mr. Ronnie Garfield and that she didn't really mean to have him. It was hinted that she made mysterious excursions to the moor and that she had been seen walking there with a young man. And it was doubtless for that reason, so Mrs. Curtis had surmised, that they had come to this desolate spot. Her mother had taken her right away, "to get right over it like." But there—"girls can be far more artful than ladies ever dream of." About Mr. Duke, there was curiously little to hear. He had been there only a short time and his activities seemed to be solely horticultural.

It was half past three and with his head spinning from the effects of Mrs. Curtis's conversation, Mr. Enderby went out for a stroll. His intention was to cultivate the acquaintance of Miss Percehouse's nephew more closely. Prudent reconnaissance in the neighborhood of Miss Percehouse's cottage proved unavailing but by a stroke of good fortune he ran into that young man just as he was emerging disconsolately from the gates of Sittaford House. He had all the appearance of having been sent away with a flea in his ear.

"Hello," said Charles, "I say, isn't that Captain Trevelyan's house?"

"That's right," said Ronnie.

"I was hoping to get a snapshot of it this morning. For my paper, you know," he added. "But this weather is hopeless for photography."

Ronnie accepted this statement in all good faith without reflecting that if photography was only possible on days of brilliant sunshine, the pictures appearing in the daily papers would be few.

"It must be a very interesting job—yours," he said.

"A dog's life," said Charles faithful to the convention of never showing enthusiasm about one's work. He looked over his shoulder at Sittaford House. "Rather a gloomy place I should imagine."

"No end of a difference there since the Willetts moved in," said Ronnie. "I was down here last year about the same time and really you would hardly take it for the same place, and yet, I don't know quite what they have done. Moved the furniture about a bit, I suppose, got cushions and things of that sort about. It's been a godsend to me their being here, I can tell you."

"Can't be a very jolly spot as a rule I suppose," said Charles.

"Jolly? If I lived here a fortnight I should pass out altogether. How my aunt manages to cling on to life in the way she does beats me. You haven't seen her cats, have you? I had to comb one of them this morning and look at the way the brute scratched me." He held out a hand and an arm for inspection.

"Rather rough luck," said Charles.

"I should say it was. I say, are you doing any sleuthing? If so, can I help? Be the Watson to your Sherlock, or anything of that kind?"

"Any clues in Sittaford House?" inquired Charles casually. "I mean did Captain Trevelyan leave any of his things there?"

"I don't think so. My aunt was saying he moved lock, stock and barrel. Took his elephant's trotters and his hippopotamus's toothy pegs and all the sporting rifles and what nots."

"Almost as though he didn't mean to come back," said Charles.

"I say—that's an idea. You don't think it was suicide, do you?"

"A man who can hit himself correctly on the back of the head with a sandbag would be something of an artist in the suicide world," said Charles.

"Yes, I thought there wasn't much in that idea. Looks as if he had had a premonition though," Ronnie's face brightened. "Look here, what about this? Enemies on his track, he knows they're coming, so he clears out and passes the buck, as it were, to the Willetts."

"The Willetts were a bit of a miracle by themselves," said Charles.

"Yes, I can't make it out. Fancy planting yourself down here in the country like this. Violet doesn't seem to mind—actually says she likes it. I don't know what's the matter with her today, I suppose it's the domestic trouble. I can't think why women worry so about servants. If they cut up nasty, just push them out."

"That's just what they have done, isn't it?" said Charles.

"Yes, I know. But they are in a great stew about it all. Mother lying down with screaming hysterics or something and daughter snapping like a turtle. Fairly pushed me out just now."

"They haven't had the police there, have they?"

Ronnie stared.

"The police, no, why would they?"

"Well, I wondered. Seeing Inspector Narracott in Sittaford this morning."

Ronnie dropped his stick with a clatter and stooped to pick it up.

"Who did you say was in Sittaford this morning—Inspector Narracott?"

"Yes."

"Is he—is he the man in charge of the Trevelyan case?"

"That's right."

"What was he doing in Sittaford? Where did you see him?"

"Oh, I suppose he was just nosing about," said Charles, "checking up Captain Trevelyan's past life so to speak."

"You think that's all?"

"I suppose so."

"He doesn't think anyone in Sittaford had anything to do with it?"

"That would be very unlikely, wouldn't it?"

"Oh frightfully. But then you know what the police are—always butting in on the wrong tack. At least that's what it says in detective novels."

"I think they are really rather an intelligent body of men," said Charles. "Of course, the Press does a lot to help them," he added. "But if you really read a case carefully it's amazing the way they track down murderers with practically no evidence to go on."

"Oh—well—it's nice to know that, isn't it? They have certainly got on to this man Pearson pretty quick. It seems a pretty clear case."

"Crystal clear," said Charles. "A good thing it wasn't you or me, eh? Well, I must be sending off a few wires. They don't seem very used to telegrams in this place. If you send more than half a crown's worth at one go they seem to think you are an escaped lunatic."

Charles sent his telegrams, bought a packet of cigarettes, a few doubtful looking bull's eyes and two very aged paper backed novelettes. He then returned to the cottage, threw himself on his bed and slept peacefully, blissfully unaware that he and his affairs, particularly Miss Emily Trefusis, were being discussed in various places all around him.

It is fairly safe to say that there were only three topics of conversation at present in Sittaford. One was the murder, one was the escape of the convict, and the other was Miss Emily Trefusis and her cousin. Indeed, at a certain moment, four separate conversations were going on with her as their main theme.

Conversation No. 1 was at Sittaford House where Violet Willett and her mother had just washed up their own tea things owing to the domestic retreat.

"It was Mrs. Curtis who told me," said Violet.

She still looked pale and wan.

"It's almost a disease the way that woman talks," said her mother.

"I know. It seems the girl is actually stopping there with a cousin or something. She did mention this morning that she was at Mrs. Curtis's, but I thought that that was simply because Miss Percehouse hadn't room for her. And now it seems that she'd never even seen Miss Percehouse till this morning!"

"I dislike that woman intensely," said Mrs. Willett.

"Mrs. Curtis?"

"No, no the Percehouse woman. That kind of woman is dangerous. They live for what they can find out about other people. Sending that girl along here for a recipe for coffee cake! I'd like to have sent her a poisoned cake. That would have stopped her interfering for good and all!"

"I suppose I ought to have realized—" began Violet. But her mother interrupted her.

"How could you, my dear! And anyway what harm is done?"

"Why do you think she came here?"

"I don't suppose she had anything definite in mind. She was just spying out the land. Is Mrs. Curtis sure about her being engaged to Jim Pearson?"

"The girl told Mr. Rycroft so, I believe. Mrs. Curtis said she suspected it from the first."

"Well, then the whole thing's natural enough. She's just looking about aimlessly for something that might help."

"You didn't see her, mother," said Violet. "She isn't aimless."

"I wish I had seen her," said Mrs. Willett. "But my nerves were all to pieces this morning. Reaction, I suppose, after that interview with the police inspector yesterday."

"You were wonderful, mother. If only I hadn't been such an utter fool—to go and *faint*. Oh! I'm ashamed of myself for giving the whole show away. And there were you perfectly calm and collected—not turning a hair."

"I'm in pretty good training," said Mrs. Willett in a hard dry voice. "If you'd been through what I've been through—but there, I hope you never will, my child. I trust and believe that you've got a happy, peaceful life ahead of you."

Violet shook her head.

"I'm afraid—I'm afraid—"

"Nonsense—and as for saying you gave the show away by fainting yesterday—nothing of the kind. Don't worry."

"But that Inspector—he's bound to think—"

"That it was the mention of Jim Pearson made you faint? Yes—he'll think that all right. He's no fool, that Inspector Narracott. But what if he does? He'll suspect a connection—and he'll look for it—*and he won't find it*."

"You think not?"

"Of course not! How can he? Trust me, Violet dear. That's cast-iron certainty and, in a way, perhaps that faint of yours was a lucky happening. We'll think so, anyway."

Conversation No. 2 was in Major Burnaby's cottage. It was a somewhat one-sided one, the brunt of it being borne by Mrs. Curtis, who had been poised for departure for the last half hour, having dropped in to collect Major Burnaby's laundry.

"Like my Great Aunt Sarah's Belinda, that's what I said to Curtis this morning," said Mrs. Curtis triumphantly. "A deep one—and one that can twist all the men round her little finger."

A great grunt from Major Burnaby.

"Engaged to one young man and carrying on with another," said Mrs. Curtis. "That's my Great Aunt Sarah's Belinda all over. And not for the fun of it, mark you. It's not just flightiness—she's a deep one. And now young Mr. Garfield—she'll have him roped in before you can say knife. Never have I seen a young gentleman look more like a sheep than he did this morning—and that's a sure sign."

She paused for breath.

"Well, well," said Major Burnaby. "Don't let me keep you, Mrs. Curtis."

"Curtis will be wanting his tea and that's a fact," said Mrs. Curtis without moving. "I was never one to stand about gossiping. Get on with your job—that's what I say. And talking about jobs, what do you say, sir, to a good turn out."

"No!" said Major Burnaby with force.

"It's a month since it's been done."

"No. I like to know where to lay my hand on everything. After one of these turn outs nothing's ever put back in its place."

Mrs. Curtis sighed. She was an impassioned cleaner and turner out.

"It's Captain Wyatt as could do with a spring cleaning," she observed. "That nasty native of his—what does he know about cleaning, I should like to know? Nasty black fellow."

"Nothing better than a native servant," said Major Burnaby. "They know their job and they don't talk."

Any hint the last sentence might have contained was lost upon Mrs. Curtis. Her mind had reverted to a former topic.

"Two telegrams she got—two arriving in half an hour. Gave me quite a turn it did. But she read them as cool as anything. And then she told me she was going to Exeter and wouldn't be back till tomorrow."

"Did she take her young man with her?" inquired the Major with a gleam of hope.

"No, he's still here. A pleasant spoken young gentleman. He and she'd make a nice pair."

Grunt from Major Burnaby.

"Well," said Mrs. Curtis. "I'll be getting along."

The Major hardly dared breathe for fear he might distract her from her purpose. But this time Mrs. Curtis was as good as her word. The door closed behind her.

With a sigh of relief the Major drew forth a pipe and began to peruse a prospectus of a certain mine which was couched in terms so blatantly optimistic that it would have aroused suspicion in any heart but that of a widow or a retired soldier.

"Twelve per cent," murmured Major Burnaby. "That sounds pretty good . . . ."

Next door Captain Wyatt was laying down the law to Mr. Rycroft.

"Fellows like you," he said, "don't know anything of the world. You've never lived. You've never roughed it."

Mr. Rycroft said nothing. It was so difficult not to say the wrong thing to Captain Wyatt that it was usually safer not to reply at all.

The Captain leaned over the side of his invalid chair.

"Where's that bitch got to? Nice looking girl," he added.

The association of ideas in his mind was quite natural. It was less so to Mr. Rycroft who looked at him in a scandalized fashion.

"What's she doing here? That's what I want to know," demanded Captain Wyatt. "Abdul!"

"Sahib?"

"Where's Bully? Has she got out again?"

"She in kitchen, Sahib."

"Well, don't feed her." He sank back in his chair again and proceeded on his second tack. "What does she want here? Who's she going to talk to in a place like this? All you old fogies will bore her stiff. I had a word with her this morning. Expect she was surprised to find a man like me in a place like this."

He twisted his mustache.

"She's James Pearson's fiancée," said Mr. Rycroft. "You know—the man who has been arrested for Trevelyan's murder."

Wyatt dropped a glass of whiskey he was just raising to his lips with a crash upon the floor. He immediately roared for Abdul and cursed him in no measured terms for not placing a table at a convenient angle to his chair. He then resumed the conversation.

"So that's who she is. Too good for a counter jumper like that. A girl like that wants a real man."

"Young Pearson is very good looking," said Mr. Rycroft.

"Good looking—good looking—a girl doesn't want a barber's block. What does that sort of young man who works in an office every day know of life? What experience has he had of reality?"

"Perhaps the experience of being tried for murder will be sufficient reality to last him for some time," said Mr. Rycroft drily.

"Police sure he did it, eh?"

"They must be fairly sure or they wouldn't have arrested him."

"Country bumpkins," said Captain Wyatt contemptuously.

"Not quite," said Mr. Rycroft. "Inspector Narracott struck me this morning as an able and efficient man."

"Where did you see him this morning?"

"He called at my house."

"He didn't call at mine," said Captain Wyatt in an injured fashion.

"Well, you weren't a close friend of Trevelyan's or anything like that."

"I don't know what you mean. Trevelyan was a skinflint and I told him so to his face. He couldn't come bossing it over me. I didn't kowtow to him like the rest of the people here. Always dropping in—dropping in—too much dropping in. If I don't choose to see anyone for a week, or a month, or a year, that's my business."

"You haven't seen anyone for a week now, have you?" said Mr. Rycroft.

"No, and why should I?" The irate invalid banged the table. Mr. Rycroft was aware, as usual, of having said the wrong thing. "Why the bloody hell should I? Tell me that?"

Mr. Rycroft was prudently silent. The Captain's wrath subsided.

"All the same," he growled, "if the police want to know about Trevelyan I'm the man they should have come to. I've knocked about the world, and I've got judgment. I can size a man up for what he's worth. What's the good of going to a lot of dodderers and old women. What they want is a *man's* judgment."

He banged the table again.

"Well," said Mr. Rycroft, "I suppose they think they know themselves what they are after."

"They inquired about me," said Captain Wyatt. "They would naturally."

"Well—er—I don't quite remember," said Mr. Rycroft cautiously.

"Why can't you remember? You're not in your dotage yet."

"I expect I was—er—rattled," said Mr. Rycroft soothingly.

"Rattled, were you? Afraid of the police? I'm not afraid of the police. Let 'em come here. That's what I say. I'll show them. Do you know I shot a cat at a hundred yards the other night?"

"Did you?" said Mr. Rycroft.

The Captain's habit of letting off a revolver at real or imaginary cats was a sore trial to his neighbors.

"Well, I'm tired," said Captain Wyatt suddenly. "Have another drink before you go?"

Rightly interpreting his hint, Mr. Rycroft rose to his feet. Captain Wyatt continued to urge a drink upon him.

"You'd be twice the man if you drank a bit more. A man who can't enjoy a drink isn't a man at all."

But Mr. Rycroft continued to decline the offer. He had already consumed one whiskey and soda of most unusual strength.

"What tea do you drink?" asked Wyatt. "I don't know anything about tea. Told Abdul to get some. Thought that girl might like to come in to tea one day. Darned pretty girl. Must do something for her. She must be bored to death in a place like this with no one to talk to."

"There's a young man with her," said Mr. Rycroft.

"The young men of the present day make me sick," said Captain Wyatt. "What's the good of them?"

This being a difficult query to answer suitably, Mr. Rycroft did not attempt it, he took his departure.

The bull terrier bitch accompanied him to the gate and caused him acute alarm.

In No. 4 The Cottages, Miss Percehouse was speaking to her nephew, Ronald.

"If you like to moon about after a girl who doesn't want you, that is your affair, Ronald," she was saying. "Better stick to the Willett girl. You may have a chance there, though I think it is extremely unlikely."

"Oh, I say," protested Ronnie.

"The other thing I have to say is, that if there was a police officer in Sittaford I should have been informed of it. Who knows, I might have been able to give him valuable information."

"I didn't know about it myself till after he had gone."

"That is so like you, Ronnie. Absolutely typical."

"Sorry, Aunt Caroline."

"And when you are painting the garden furniture, there is no need to paint your face as well. It doesn't improve it and it wastes the paint."

"Sorry, Aunt Caroline."

"And now," said Miss Percehouse closing her eyes, "don't argue with me any more. I'm tired."

Ronnie shuffled his feet and looked uncomfortable.

"Well?" said Miss Percehouse sharply.

"Oh! nothing—only—"

"Yes?"

"Well, I was wondering if you'd mind if I blew in to Exeter to-morrow?"

"Why?"

"Well, I want to meet a fellow there."

"What kind of a fellow?"

"Oh! Just a fellow."

"If a young man wishes to tell lies, he should do so well," said Miss Percehouse.

"Oh! I say—but—"

"Don't apologize."

"It's all right then? I can go?"

"I don't know what you mean by saying, 'I can go?' as though you were a small child. You are over twenty-one."

"Yes, but what I mean is, I don't want—"

Miss Percehouse closed her eyes again.

"I have asked you once before not to argue. I am tired and wish to rest. If the 'fellow' you are meeting in Exeter wears skirts and is called Emily Trefusis, more fool you—that is all I have to say."

"But look here—"

"I am tired, Ronald. That's enough."

22

Nocturnal Adventures of Charles

CHARLES WAS NOT LOOKING FORWARD with any relish to the prospect of his night's vigil. He privately considered that it was likely to be a wild goose chase. Emily, he considered, was possessed of a too vivid imagination.

He was convinced that she had read into the few words she had overheard a meaning that had its origin in her own brain. Probably sheer weariness had induced Mrs. Willett to yearn for night to come.

Charles looked out of his window and shivered. It was a piercingly cold night, raw and foggy—the last night one would wish to spend in the open hanging about and waiting for something, very nebulous in nature, to happen.

Still he dared not yield to his intense desire to remain comfortably indoors. He recalled the liquid melodiousness of Emily's voice as she said, "It's wonderful to have someone you can really rely on."

She relied on him, Charles, and she should not rely in vain. What? Fail that beautiful, helpless girl? Never.

Besides, he reflected as he donned all the spare underclothes he possessed before encasing himself in two pullovers and his overcoat, things were likely to be deucedly unpleasant if Emily on her return found out that he had not carried out his promise.

She would probably say the most unpleasant things. No, he couldn't risk it. But as for anything happening—

And anyway, when and how was it going to happen? He couldn't be everywhere at once. Probably whatever was going to happen would happen inside Sittaford House and he would never know a thing about it.

"Just like a girl," he grumbled to himself, "waltzing off to Exeter and leaving me to do the dirty work."

And then he remembered once more the liquid tones of Emily's voice as she expressed her reliance on him, and he felt ashamed of his outburst.

He completed his toilet, rather after the model of Tweedledee, and effected a surreptitious exit from the cottage.

The night was even colder and more unpleasant than he had thought. Did Emily realize all he was about to suffer on her behalf? He hoped so.

His hand went tenderly to a pocket and caressed a hidden flask concealed in a near pocket.

"The boy's best friend," he murmured. "It *would* be a night like this of course."

With suitable precautions he introduced himself into the grounds of Sittaford House. The Willetts kept no dog so there was no fear of alarm from that quarter. A light in the gardener's cottage showed that it was inhabited. Sittaford House itself was in darkness save for one lighted window on the first floor.

"Those two women are alone in the house," thought Charles. "I shouldn't care for that myself. A bit creepy!"

He supposed Emily had really overheard that sentence, "*Will tonight never come?*" What did it really mean?

"I wonder," he thought to himself, "if they mean to do a flit? Well, whatever happens, little Charles is going to be here to see it."

He circled the house at a discreet distance. Owing to the foggy nature of the night he had no fears of being observed. Everything as far as he could see appeared to be as usual. A cautious visiting of the out-buildings showed them to be locked.

"I hope something does happen," said Charles as the hours passed. He took a prudent sip from his flask. "I've never known anything like this cold. 'What did you do in the Great War, Daddy,' can't have been any worse than this."

He glanced at his watch and was surprised to find that it was still only twenty minutes to twelve. He had been convinced that it must be nearly dawn.

An unexpected sound made him prick up his ears excitedly. It was the sound of a bolt being very gently drawn back in its socket, and it came from the direction of the house. Charles made a noiseless sprint from bush to bush. Yes, he had been quite right, the small side door was slowly opening. A dark figure stood on the threshold. It was peering anxiously out into the night.

"Mrs. or Miss Willett," said Charles to himself. "The fair Violet, I think."

After waiting a minute or two, the figure stepped out on the path and closed the door noiselessly behind her and started to walk away from the house in the opposite direction to the front drive. The path in question led up behind Sittaford House, passing through a small plantation of trees and so out on to the open moor.

The path wound quite near the bushes where Charles was concealed, so near that Charles was able to recognize the woman as she passed. He had been quite right, it was Violet Willett. She was wearing a long dark coat and had a beret on her head.

She went on up and as quietly as possible Charles followed her. He had no fears of being seen, but he was alive to the danger of being overheard. He was particularly anxious not to alarm the girl. Owing to his care in this respect she outdistanced him. For a moment or two he was afraid lest he should lose her, but as he in his turn wound his way anxiously through the plantation of trees he saw her standing a little way ahead of him. Here the low wall which surrounded the estate was broken by a gate. Violet Willett was standing by this gate, leaning over it peering out into the night.

Charles crept up as near as he dared and waited. The time passed. The girl had a small pocket torch with her and once she switched it on for a moment or two, directing it, Charles thought, to see the time by the wrist watch she was wearing, then she leant over the gate again in the same attitude of expectant interest. Suddenly, Charles heard a low whistle twice repeated.

He saw the girl start to sudden attention. She leant farther over the gate and from her lips came the same signal—a low whistle twice repeated.

Then with startling suddenness a man's figure loomed out of the night. A low exclamation came from the girl. She moved back a pace or two, the gate swung inward and the man joined her. She spoke to him in a low hurried voice. Unable to catch what they said, Charles moved forward somewhat imprudently. A twig snapped beneath his feet. The man swung round instantly.

"What's that?" he said.

He caught sight of Charles's retreating figure.

"Hie, you stop! What are you doing here?"

With a bound he sprang after Charles. Charles turned and tackled him adroitly. The next moment they were rolling over and over together locked in a tight embrace.

The tussle was a short one. Charles's assailant was by far the heavier and stronger of the two. He rose to his feet jerking his captive with him.

"Switch on that light, Violet," he said, "let's have a look at this fellow."

The girl, who had been standing terrified a few paces away, came forward and switched on the torch obediently.

"It must be the man who is staying in the village," she said. "A journalist."

"A journalist, eh?" exclaimed the other. "I don't like the breed. What are you doing, you skunk, nosing round private grounds at this time of night?"

The torch wavered in Violet's hand. For the first time Charles was given a full view of his antagonist. For a few minutes he had entertained the wild idea that the visitor might have been the escaped convict. One look at the other dispelled any such fancy. This was a young man not more than twenty-four or -five years of age. Tall, good-looking and determined, with none of the hunted criminal about him.

"Now then," he said sharply, "What's your name?"

"My name is Charles Enderby," said Charles. "You haven't told me yours," he continued.

"Confound your cheek!"

A sudden flash of inspiration came to Charles. An inspired guess had saved him more than once. It was a long shot but he believed that he was right.

"I think, however," he said quietly, "that I can guess it."

"Eh?"

The other was clearly taken aback.

"I think," said Charles, "that I have the pleasure of addressing Mr. Brian Pearson from Australia. Is that so?"

There was a silence—rather a long silence. Charles had a feeling that the tables were turned.

"How the devil you knew that I can't think," said the other at last, "but you're right. My name *is* Brian Pearson."

"In that case," said Charles, "supposing we adjourn to the house and talk things over!"

23

At Hazelmoor

MAJOR BURNABY was doing his accounts or—to use a more Dickens-like phrase, he was looking into his affairs. The Major was an extremely methodical man. In a calf-bound book he kept a record of shares bought, shares sold and the accompanying loss or profit—usually a loss, for in common with most retired army men the Major was attracted by a high rate of interest rather than a modest percentage coupled with safety.

"These oil wells looked all right," he was muttering. "Seems as though there ought to have been a fortune in it. Almost as bad as that diamond mine! Canadian land, that ought to be sound now."

His cogitations were interrupted as the head of Mr. Ronald Garfield appeared at the open window.

"Hello," said Ronnie cheerfully, "I hope I'm not butting in?"

"If you are coming in go round to the front door," said Major Burnaby. "Mind the rock plants. I believe you are standing on them at the moment."

Ronnie retreated with an apology and presently presented himself at the front door.

"Wipe your feet on the mat, if you don't mind," cried the Major.

He found young men extremely trying. Indeed, the only young man towards whom he had felt any kindliness for a long time was the journalist, Charles Enderby.

"A nice young chap," the Major had said to himself. "And very interested, too, in what I have told him about the Boer War."

Towards Ronnie Garfield the Major felt no such kindliness. Practically everything that the unfortunate Ronnie said or did managed to rub the Major up the wrong way. Still, hospitality is hospitality.

"Have a drink?" said the Major loyal to that tradition.

"No thanks. As a matter of fact I just dropped in to see if we couldn't get together. I wanted to go to Exhampton today and I hear Elmer is booked to take you in."

Burnaby nodded.

"Got to go over Trevelyan's things," he explained. "The police have done with the place now."

"Well, you see," said Ronnie rather awkwardly, "I particularly wanted to go into Exhampton today. I thought if we could get together and share and share alike as it were. Eh? What about it?"

"Certainly," said the Major. "I am agreeable. Do you a lot more good to walk," he added. "Exercise. None of you young chaps nowadays take any exercise. A brisk six miles there and a brisk six miles back would do you all the good in the world. If it weren't that I needed the car to bring some of Trevelyan's things back here, I should be walking myself. Getting soft—that's the curse of the present day."

"Oh, well," said Ronnie, "I don't believe in being strenuous myself. But I'm glad we've settled that all right. Elmer said you were starting at eleven o'clock. Is that right?"

"That's it."

"Good. I'll be there."

Ronnie was not quite so good as his word, his idea of being on the spot was to be ten minutes late and he found Major Burnaby fuming and fretting and not at all inclined to be placated by a careless apology.

"What a fuss old buffers make," thought Ronnie to himself. "They have no idea what a curse they are to everybody with their punctuality, and everything done on the dot of the minute, and their cursed exercise and keeping fit."

His mind played agreeably for a few minutes with the idea of a marriage between Major Burnaby and his aunt. Which, he wondered, would get the better of it? He thought his aunt every time. Rather amusing to think of her clapping her hands and uttering piercing cries to summon the Major to her side.

Banishing these reflections from his mind he proceeded to enter into cheerful conversation.

"Sittaford has become a pretty gay spot—what? Miss Trefusis and this chap Enderby and the lad from Australia—by the way when did he blow in? There he was as large as life this morning and nobody knew where he had come from. It's been worrying my aunt blue in the face."

"He is staying with the Willetts," said Major Burnaby tartly.

"Yes, but where did he blow in from? Even the Willetts haven't got a private aerodrome. You know, I think there's something deuced mysterious about this lad Pearson. He's got what I call a nasty gleam in his eye—a very nasty glint. It's my impression that he's the chap who did in poor old Trevelyan."

The Major made no reply.

"The way I look at it is this," continued Ronnie, "fellows that go off to the Colonies are usually bad hats. Their relations don't like them and push them out there for that reason. Very well then—there you are. The bad hat comes back, short of money, visits wealthy uncle in the neighborhood of Christmas time, wealthy relative won't cough up to impecunious nephew—and impecunious nephew bats him one. That's what I call a theory."

"You should mention it to the police," said Major Burnaby.

"I thought you might do that," said Mr. Garfield. "You're Narracott's little pal, aren't you? By the way he hasn't been nosing about Sittaford again, has he?"

"Not that I know about."

"Not meeting you at the house today, is he?"

"No."

The shortness of the Major's answers seemed to strike Ronnie at last.

"Well," he said vaguely, "that's that," and relapsed into a thoughtful silence.

At Exhampton the car drew up outside the Three Crowns. Ronnie alighted and after arranging with the Major that they would rendezvous there at half past four for the return journey, he strode off in the direction of such shops as Exhampton offered.

The Major went first to see Mr. Kirkwood. After a brief conversation with him, he took the keys and started off for Hazelmoor.

He had told Evans to meet him there at twelve o'clock and he found the faithful retainer waiting on the doorstep. With a rather grim face, Major Burnaby inserted the key into the front door and passed into the empty house, Evans at his heels. He had not been in it since the night of the tragedy, and in spite of his iron determination to show no weakness, he gave a slight shiver as he passed the drawing-room.

Evans and the Major worked together in sympathy and silence. When either of them made a brief remark it was duly appreciated and understood by the other.

"Unpleasant job this, but it has to be done," said Major Burnaby and Evans, sorting out socks into neat piles, and counting pajamas, responded.

"It seems rather unnatural like, but as you say, sir, it's got to be done."

Evans was deft and efficient at his work. Everything was neatly sorted and arranged and classified in heaps. At one o'clock they repaired to the Three Crowns for a short mid-day meal. When they returned to the house the Major suddenly caught Evans by the arm as the latter closed the front door behind him.

"Hush," he said. "Do you hear that footstep overhead? It's—it's in Joe's bedroom."

"My Gawd, sir. So it is."

A kind of superstitious terror held them both for a minute and then breaking loose from it, and with an angry squaring of the shoulders the Major strode to the foot of the stairs and shouted in a stentorian voice:

"Who's that? Come out of there I say."

To his intense surprise and annoyance and yet, be it confessed, to his slight relief, Ronnie Garfield appeared at the top of the stairs. He looked embarrassed and sheepish.

"Hello," he said. "I have been looking for you."

"What do you mean, looking for me?"

"Well, I wanted to tell you that I shan't be ready at half past four. I've got to go into Exeter. So don't wait for me. I'll have to get a car up from Exhampton."

"How did you get into this house?" asked the Major.

"The door was open," exclaimed Ronnie. "Naturally I thought you were here."

The Major turned to Evans sharply.

"Didn't you lock it when you came out?"

"No, sir, I hadn't got the key."

"Stupid of me," muttered the Major.

"You don't mind, do you?" said Ronnie. "I couldn't see anyone downstairs so I went upstairs and had a look round."

"Of course, it doesn't matter," snapped the Major. "You startled me, that's all."

"Well," said Ronnie airily. "I shall be pushing along now. So long."

The Major grunted. Ronnie came down the stairs.

"I say," he said boyishly, "do you mind telling me er—er—where it happened?"

The Major jerked a thumb in the directon of the drawing-room.

"Oh, may I look inside?"

"If you like," growled the Major.

Ronnie opened the drawing-room door. He was absent a few minutes and then returned.

The Major had gone up the stairs but Evans was in the hall. He had the air of a bulldog on guard, his small deepset eyes watched Ronnie with a somewhat malicious scrutiny.

"I say," said Ronnie. "I thought you could never wash out blood stains. I thought, however much you washed them, they always came back. Oh, of course—the old fellow was sandbagged, wasn't he? Stupid of me. It was one of these, wasn't it?" He took up a long narrow bolster that lay against one of the other doors. He weighed it thoughtfully and balanced it in his hand. "Nice little toy, eh?" He made a few tentative swings with it in the air.

Evans was silent.

"Well," said Ronnie realizing that the silence was not a wholly appreciative one, "I'd better be getting along. I'm afraid I've been a bit tactless, eh?" He jerked his head towards the upper story. "I forgot about them being such pals and all that. Two of a kind, weren't they? Well, I'm really going now. Sorry if I've said all the wrong things."

He walked across the hall and out through the front door. Evans stayed impassively in the hall, and only when he had heard the latch of the gate close behind Mr. Garfield did he mount the stairs and rejoin Major Burnaby. Without any word or comment he resumed where he had left off, going straight across the room and kneeling down in front of the boot cupboard.

At half past three their task was finished. One trunk of clothes and underclothes was allotted to Evans, and another was strapped up ready to be sent to the Seamen's Orphanage. Papers and bills were packed into an attaché case and Evans was given instructions to see a local firm of removers about the storage of the various sporting trophies and heads, as there was no room for them in Major Burnaby's cottage. Since Hazelmoor was only rented furnished no other question arose.

When all this was settled Evans cleared his throat nervously once or twice and then said:

"Beg pardon, sir, but—I'll be wanting a job to look after a gentleman, same as I did to look after the Capting."

"Yes, yes, you can tell anyone to apply to me for a recommendation. That will be quite all right."

"Begging your pardon, sir, that wasn't quite what I meant. Rebecca and me, sir, we've talked it over and we was wondering if, sir—if maybe you would give us a trial?"

"Oh! but—well—I look after myself as you know. That old what's her name comes in and cleans for me once a day and cooks a few things. That's—er—about all I can afford."

"It isn't the money that matters so much, sir," said Evans quickly. "You see, sir, I was very fond of the Capting and—well, if I could do for you, sir, the same as I did for him, well, it would be almost like the same thing, if you know what I mean."

The Major cleared his throat and averted his eyes.

"Very decent of you, pon my word. I'll—I'll think about it." And escaping with alacrity he almost bolted down the road. Evans stood looking after him an understanding smile upon his face.

"Like as two peas, him and the Capting," he murmured.

And then a puzzled expression came over his face.

"Where can they have got to?" he murmured. "It's a bit queer that. I must ask Rebecca what she thinks."

24

Inspector Narracott
Discusses the Case

"I AM NOT ENTIRELY HAPPY about it, sir," said Inspector Narracott.

The Chief Constable looked at him inquiringly.

"No," said Inspector Narracott. "I'm not nearly as happy about it as I was."

"You don't think we've got the right man?"

"I'm not satisfied. You see, to start with, everything pointed the one way but now—it's different."

"The evidence against Pearson remains the same."

"Yes, but there's a good deal of further evidence come to light, sir. There's the other Pearson—Brian. Feeling that we had no further to look I accepted the statement that he was in Australia. Now, it turns out that he was in England all the time. It seems he arrived back in England two months ago—traveled on the same boat as these Willetts apparently. Looks as though he had got sweet on the girl on the voyage. Anyway, for whatever reason he didn't communicate with any of his family. Neither his sister nor his brother had any idea he was in England. On Thursday of last week he left the Ormsby Hotel in Russell Square and drove to Paddington, from there until Tuesday night, when Enderby ran across him, he refuses to account for his movements in any way."

"You pointed out to him the gravity of such a course of action?"

"Said he didn't give a damn. He had had nothing to do with the murder and it was up to us to prove he had. The way he had employed his time was his own business and none of ours, and he declined definitely to state where he had been and what he had been doing."

"Most extraordinary," said the Chief Constable.

"Yes, sir. It's an extraordinary case. You see, there's no use getting away from the facts, this man's far more the type than the other. There's something incongruous about James Pearson hitting an old man on the head with a sandbag—but in a manner of speaking it might be all in the day's work to Brian Pearson. He's a hot-tempered,

281

highhanded young man—and he profits to exactly the same extent remember.

"Yes—he came over with Mr. Enderby this morning, very bright and breezy, quite square and above-board, that was his attitude. But it won't wash, sir, it won't wash."

"H'm—you mean—"

"It isn't borne out by the facts. Why didn't he come forward before? His uncle's death was in all the papers Saturday. His brother was arrested Monday. And he doesn't give a sign of life. And he wouldn't have, either, if that journalist hadn't run across him in the garden of Sittaford House at midnight last night."

"What was he doing there? Enderby, I mean?"

"You know what journalists are," said Narracott, "always nosing round. They're uncanny."

"They are a darned nuisance very often," said the Chief Constable. "Though they have their uses too."

"I fancy it was the young lady put him up to it," said Narracott.

"The young lady?"

"Miss Emily Trefusis."

"How did she know anything about it?"

"She was up at Sittaford nosing around. And she's what you'd call a sharp young lady. There's not much gets past her."

"What was Brian Pearson's own account of his movements?"

"Said he came to Sittaford House to see his young lady, Miss Willett, that is. She came out of the house to meet him when everyone was asleep because she didn't want her mother to know about it. That's their story."

Inspector Narracott's voice expressed distinct disbelief.

"It's my belief, sir, that if Enderby hadn't run him to earth, he never would have come forward. He'd have gone back to Australia and claimed his inheritance from there."

A faint smile crossed the Chief Constable's lips.

"How he must have cursed these pestilential prying journalists," he murmured.

"There's something else come to light," continued the Inspector. "There are three Pearsons, you remember, and Sylvia Pearson is married to Martin Dering, the novelist. He told me that he lunched and spent the afternoon with an American publisher and went to a literary dinner in the evening, but it now seems that he wasn't at that dinner at all."

"Who says so?"

"Enderby again."

"I think I must meet Enderby," said the Chief Constable. "He appears to be one of the live wires of this investigation. No doubt about it the *Daily Wire* does have some bright young men on their staff."

"Well, of course, that may mean little or nothing," continued the Inspector. "Captain Trevelyan was killed before six o'clock, so where Dering spent his evening is really of no consequence—but why should he have deliberately lied about it? I don't like it, sir."

"No," agreed the Chief Constable. "It seems a little unnecessary."

"It makes one think that the whole thing may be false. It's a far-fetched supposition, I suppose, but Dering *might* have left Paddington by the twelve ten train—arrived at Exhampton some time after five, have killed the old man, got the six ten train and been back home again before midnight. At any rate it's got to be looked into, sir. We've got to investigate his financial position, see if he was desperately hard up. Any money his wife came into he would have the handling of—you've only got to look at her to know that. We've got to make perfectly sure that the afternoon *alibi* holds water."

"The whole thing is extraordinary," commented the Chief Constable. "But I still think the evidence against Pearson is pretty conclusive. I see that you don't agree with me—you've a feeling you've got hold of the wrong man."

"The evidence is all right," admitted Inspector Narracott, "circumstantial and all that, and any jury ought to convict on it. Still, what you say is true enough—I don't see him as a murderer."

"And his young lady is very active in the case," said the Chief Constable.

"Miss Trefusis, yes, she's a one and no mistake. A real fine young lady. And absolutely determined to get him off. She's got hold of that journalist, Enderby, and she's working him for all she's worth. She's a great deal too good for Mr. James Pearson. Beyond his good looks I wouldn't say there was much to him in the way of character."

"But if she's a managing young woman that's what she likes," said the Chief Constable.

"Ah well," said Inspector Narracott, "there's no accounting for tastes. Well, you agree, sir, that I had better take up this *alibi* of Dering's without any more delay."

"Yes, get on to it at once. What about the fourth interested party in the will? There's a fourth, isn't there?"

"Yes, the sister. That's perfectly all right. I have made inquiries there. She was at home at six o'clock all right, sir. I'll get right on with the Dering business."

It was about five hours later that Inspector Narracott found himself once more in the small sitting-room of The Nook. This time Mr. Dering was at home. He couldn't be disturbed as he was writing, the maid had said at first, but the Inspector had produced an official card and bade her take it to her master without delay. Whilst waiting he strode up and down the room. His mind was working actively. Every now and then he picked up a small object from a table, looked at it almost unseeingly, and then replaced it. The cigarette box of Australian fiddleback—a present from Brian Pearson possibly. He picked up a rather battered old book. 'Pride and Prejudice.' He opened the cover and saw scrawled on the fly-leaf in rather faded ink the name, Martha Rycroft. Somehow, the name of Rycroft seemed familiar, but he could not for the moment remember why. He was interrupted as the door opened and Martin Dering came into the room.

The novelist was a man of middle height with thick rather heavy chestnut hair. He was good-looking in a somewhat heavy fashion, with lips that were rather full and red.

Inspector Narracott was not prepossessed by his appearance.

"Good morning, Mr. Dering. Sorry to trouble you all here again."

"Oh, it doesn't matter, Inspector, but really I can't tell you any more than you've been told already."

"We were led to understand that your brother-in-law, Mr. Brian Pearson, was in Australia. Now, we find that he has been in England for the last two months. I might have been given an inkling of that I think. Your wife distinctly told me that he was in New South Wales."

"Brian in England!" Dering seemed genuinely astonished. "I can assure you, Inspector, that I had no knowledge of the fact—nor, I'm sure, had my wife."

"He has not communicated with you in any way?"

"No, indeed, I know for a fact that Sylvia has twice written him letters to Australia during that time."

"Oh, well, in that case I apologize, sir. But naturally I thought he would have communicated with his relations and I was a bit sore with you for holding out on me."

"Well, as I tell you we knew nothing. Have a cigarette, Inspector? By the way, I see you've recaptured your escaped convict."

"Yes, got him late Tuesday night. Rather bad luck for him the mist coming down. He walked right round in a circle. Did about twenty miles to find himself about half a mile from Princetown at the end of it."

"Extraordinary how everyone goes round in circles in a fog. Good thing he didn't escape on the Friday. I suppose he would have had this murder put down to him as a certainty."

"He's a dangerous man. Freemantle Freddy, they used to call him. Robbery with violence, assault—led the most extraordinary double life. Half the time he passed as an educated, respectable wealthy man. I am not at all sure myself that Broadmoor wasn't the place for him. A kind of criminal mania used to come over him from time to time. He would disappear and consort with the lowest characters."

"I suppose many people don't escape from Princetown?"

"It's well-nigh impossible, sir. But this particular escape was extraordinarily well planned and carried out. We haven't nearly got to the bottom of it yet."

"Well," Dering rose and glanced at his watch, "if there's nothing more, Inspector—I'm afraid I am rather a busy man—"

"Oh, but there *is* something more, Mr. Dering. I want to know why you told me that you were at a literary dinner at the Cecil Hotel on Friday night?"

"I—I don't understand you, Inspector."

"I think you do, sir. You weren't at that dinner, Mr. Dering."

Martin Dering hesitated. His eyes ran uncertainly from the Inspector's face, up to the ceiling, then to the door, and then to his feet.

The Inspector waited calm and stolid.

"Well," said Martin Dering at last, "supposing I wasn't. What the hell has that got to do with you? What have my movements, five hours after my uncle was murdered, got to do with you or anyone else?"

"You made a certain statement to us, Mr. Dering, and I want that statement verified. Part of it has already proved to be untrue. I've got to check up on the other half. You say you lunched and spent the afternoon with a friend."

"Yes—my American publisher."

"His name?"

"Rosenkraun, Edgar Rosenkraun."

"Ah, and his address?"

"He's left England. He left last Saturday."

"For New York?"

"Yes."

"Then he'll be on the sea at the present moment. What boat is he on?"

"I—I really can't remember."

"You know the line? Was it a Cunard or White Star?"

"I—I really don't remember."

"Ah well," said the Inspector, "we'll cable his firm in New York. They'll know."

"It was the *Gargantua*," said Dering sullenly.

"Thank you, Mr. Dering, I thought you could remember if you tried. Now, your statement is that you lunched with Mr. Rosenkraun and that you spent the afternoon with him. At what time did you leave him?"

"About five o'clock I should say."

"And then?"

"I decline to state. It's no business of yours. That's all you want surely."

Inspector Narracott nodded thoughtfully. If Rosenkraun confirmed Dering's statement then any case against Dering must fall to the ground. Whatever his mysterious activities had been that evening could not affect the case.

"What are you going to do?" demanded Dering uneasily.

"Wireless Mr. Rosenkraun on board the *Gargantua*."

"Damn it all," cried Dering, "you'll involve me in all sorts of publicity. Look here—"

He went across to his desk, scribbled a few words on a bit of paper, then took it to the Inspector.

"I suppose you've got to do what you're doing," he said ungraciously, "but at least you might do it in my way. It's not fair to run a chap in for a lot of trouble."

On the sheet of paper was written:

Rosenkraun S.S. "Gargantua." Please confirm my statement I was with you lunch-time until five o'clock Friday 14th. Martin Dering.

"Have the reply sent straight to you—I don't mind. But don't have it sent to Scotland Yard or a Police Station. You don't know what these Americans are like. Any hint of me being mixed up in a police case and this new contract that I've been discussing will go to the winds. Keep it a private matter, Inspector."

"I've no objection to that, Mr. Dering. All I want is the truth. I'll send this reply paid, the reply to be sent to my private address in Exeter."

"Thank you, you are a good chap. It's not such easy going earning your living by literature, Inspector. You'll see the answer will be all right. I did tell you a lie about the dinner, but as a matter of fact I had told my wife that that was where I had been, and I thought I might as well stick to the same story to you. Otherwise I would have let myself in for a lot of trouble."

"If Mr. Rosenkraun confirms your statement, Mr. Dering, you will have nothing else to fear."

"An unpleasant character," the Inspector thought, as he left the house. "But he seems pretty certain that this American publisher will confirm the truth of his story."

A sudden remembrance came to the Inspector, as he hopped into the train which would take him back to Devon.

"Rycroft," he said, "of course—that's the name of the old gentleman who lives in one of the cottages at Sittaford. A curious coincidence."

25

At Deller's Café

Emily Trefusis and Charles Enderby were seated at a small table in Deller's Café in Exeter. It was half past three and at that hour there was comparative peace and quiet. A few people were having a quiet cup of tea, but the restaurant on the whole was deserted.

"Well," said Charles, "what do you think of him?"

Emily frowned.

"It's difficult," she said.

After his interview with the police, Brian Pearson had lunched with them. He had been extremely polite to Emily, rather too polite in her opinion.

To that astute girl it seemed a shade unnatural. Here was a young man conducting a clandestine love affair and an officious stranger butts in.

Brian Pearson had taken it like a lamb, had fallen in with Charles's suggestion of having a car and driving over to see the police.

Why this attitude of meek acquiescence? It seemed to Emily entirely untypical of the natural Brian Pearson as she read his character.

"I'll see you in hell first!" would, she felt sure have been far more his attitude.

This lamb-like demeanor was suspicious. She tried to convey something of her feelings to Enderby.

"I get you," said Enderby. "Our Brian has got something to conceal, therefore he can't be his natural high-handed self."

"That's it exactly."

"Do you think he might possibly have killed old Trevelyan?"

"Brian," said Emily thoughtfully, "is—well, a person to be reckoned with. He is rather unscrupulous, I should think, and if he wanted anything, I don't think he would let ordinary conventional standards stand in his way. He's not plain tame English."

"Putting all personal considerations on one side, he's a more likely starter than Jim?" said Enderby.

Emily nodded.

"Much more likely. He would carry a thing through well—because he would never lose his nerve."

"Honestly, Emily, do you think he did it?"

"I—I don't know. He fulfils the conditions—the only person who does."

"What do you mean by fulfils the conditions?"

"Well (1) *Motive*." She ticked off the items on her fingers. "The same motive. Twenty thousand pounds. (2) *Opportunity*. Nobody knows where he was on Friday afternoon, and if he was anywhere that he could say—well—surely he would say it? So we assume that he was actually in the neighborhood of Hazelmoor on Friday."

"They haven't found anyone who saw him in Exhampton," Charles pointed out, "and he's a fairly noticeable person."

Emily shook her head scornfully.

"He wasn't in Exhampton. Don't you see, Charles, if he committed the murder, he planned it before-hand. It's only poor innocent Jim who came down like a mug and stayed there. There's Lydford and Chagford or perhaps Exeter. He might have walked over from Lydford—that's a main road and the snow wouldn't have been impassable. It would have been pretty good going."

"I suppose we ought to make inquiries all round."

"The police are doing that," said Emily, "and they'll do it a lot better than we shall. All public things are much better done by the police. It's private and personal things like listening to Mrs. Curtis and picking up a hint from Miss Percehouse and watching the Willetts—that's where we score."

"Or don't, as the case may be," said Charles.

"To go back to Brian Pearson fulfilling the conditions," said Emily. "We've done two, motive and opportunity, and there's the third—the one that in a way I think is the most important of all."

"What's that?"

"Well, I have felt from the beginning that we couldn't ignore that queer business of the table turning. I have tried to look at it as logically and clearsightedly as possible. There are just three solutions of it. (1) That it was supernatural. Well, of course, that may be so, but personally I am ruling it out. (2) That it was deliberate—someone did it on purpose, but as one can't arrive at any conceivable reason, we can rule that out also. (3) Accidental. Someone gave himself away without meaning to do so—indeed quite against his will. An unconscious piece of self-revelation. If so, someone among those six people either knew definitely that Captain Trevelyan was going to be killed at a certain time that afternoon, or that someone was having an interview with him from which violence might result. None of those six people could have been the actual murderer, but one of them must have been in collusion with the murderer. There's no link between Major Burnaby and anybody else, or Mr. Rycroft and anybody else, or Ronald Garfield and anyone else, but when we come to the Willetts it's different. There's a link between Violet Willett and Brian Pearson. Those two are on very intimate terms and that girl was all on the jump after the murder."

"You think she knew?" said Charles.

"She or her mother—one or other of them."

"There's one person you haven't mentioned," said Charles. "Mr. Duke."

"I know," said Emily. "It's queer. He's the one person we know absolutely nothing about. I've tried to see him twice and failed. There seems no connection between him and Captain Trevelyan, or between him and any of Captain Trevelyan's relations, there's absolutely nothing to connect him with the case in any way, and yet—"

"Well?" said Charles Enderby as Emily paused.

"And yet we met Inspector Narracott coming out of his cottage. What does Inspector Narracott know about him that we don't? I wish I knew."

"You think—"

"Supposing Duke is a suspicious character and the police know it. Supposing Captain Trevelyan had found out something about Duke. He was particular about his tenants, remember, and supposing he was going to tell the police what he knew. And Duke arranges with an accomplice to have him killed. Oh, I know it all sounds dreadfully melodramatic put like that, and yet, after all, something of the kind might be possible."

"It's an idea certainly," said Charles slowly.

They were both silent, each one deep in thought.

Suddenly Emily said:

"Do you know that queer feeling you get when somebody is looking at you. I feel now as though someone's eyes were burning the back of my neck. Is it all fancy or is there really someone staring at me now?"

Charles moved his chair an inch or two and looked around the café in a casual manner.

"There's a woman at a table in the window," he reported. "Tall, dark and handsome. She's staring at you."

"Young?"

"No, not very young. Hello!"

"What is it?"

"Ronnie Garfield. He has just come in and he's shaking hands with her and he's sitting down at her table. I think she's saying something about us."

Emily opened her handbag. Rather ostentatiously she powdered her nose, adjusting the small pocket mirror to a convenient angle.

"It's Aunt Jennifer," she said softly. "They are getting up."

"They are going," said Charles. "Do you want to speak to her?"

"No," said Emily. "I think it's better for me to pretend that I haven't seen her."

"After all," said Charles, "why shouldn't Aunt Jennifer know Ronnie Garfield and ask him to tea?"

"Why should she?" said Emily.

"Why shouldn't she?"

"Oh, for goodness sake, Charles, don't let's go on and on like this, *should—shouldn't—should—shouldn't.* Of course it's all nonsense, and it doesn't mean anything! But we *were* just saying that nobody else at the *séance* had any relation with the family, and not five minutes later we see Ronnie Garfield having tea with Captain Trevelyan's sister."

"It shows," said Charles, "that you never know."

"It shows," said Emily, "that you are always having to begin again."

"In more ways than one," said Charles.

Emily looked at him.

"What do you mean?"

"Nothing at present," said Charles.

He put his hand over hers. She did not draw it away.

"We've got to put this through," said Charles. "Afterwards—"

"Afterwards?" said Emily softly.

"I'd do anything for you, Emily," said Charles. "Simply anything—"

"Would you?" said Emily. "That's rather nice of you, Charles dear."

26

Robert Gardner

IT WAS JUST TWENTY MINUTES LATER when Emily rang the front door bell of The Laurels. It had been a sudden impulse. She smiled beamingly on Beatrice when the latter opened the door to her.

"It's me again," said Emily. "Mrs. Gardner's out, I know, but can I see Mr. Gardner?"

Such a request was clearly unusual. Beatrice seemed doubtful.

"Well, I don't know. I'll go up and see, shall I?"

"Yes, do," said Emily.

Beatrice went upstairs leaving Emily alone in the hall. She returned in a few minutes to ask the young lady to please step this way.

Robert Gardner was lying on a couch by the window in a big room on the first floor. He was a big man, blue eyed and fair haired. He looked, Emily thought, as Tristran ought to look in the third act of *Tristran and Isolde* and as no Wagnerian tenor has ever looked yet.

"Hello," he said. "You are the criminal's spouse to be, aren't you?"

"That's right, Uncle Robert," said Emily. "I suppose I *do* call you Uncle Robert, don't I?" she asked.

"If Jennifer will allow it. What's it like having a young man languishing in prison?"

A cruel man Emily decided. A man who would take a malicious joy in giving you sharp digs in painful places. But she was a match for him. She said smilingly:

"Very thrilling."

"Not so thrilling for Master Jim, eh?"

"Oh, well," said Emily, "it's an experience, isn't it?"

"Teach him life can't be all beer and skittles," said Robert Gardner maliciously. "Too young to fight in the Great War, wasn't he? Able to live soft and take it easily. Well, well. . . . He got it in the neck from another source."

He looked at her curiously.

"What did you want to come and see me for, eh?"

There was a tinge of something like suspicion in his voice.

"If you are going to marry into a family it's just as well to see all your relations-in-law beforehand."

"Know the worst before it's too late. So you really think you are going to marry young Jim, eh?"

"Why not?"

"In spite of this murder charge?"

"In spite of this murder charge."

"Well," said Robert Gardner, "I have never seen anybody less cast down. Anyone would think you were enjoying yourself."

"I am. Tracking down a murderer is frightfully thrilling."

"Eh?"

"I said tracking down a murderer is frightfully thrilling," said Emily.

Robert Gardner stared at her then he threw himself back on his pillows.

"I am tired," he said in a fretful voice. "I can't talk any more. Nurse, where's Nurse? Nurse, I'm tired."

Nurse Davis had come swiftly at his call from an adjoining room.

"Mr. Gardner gets tired very easily. I think you had better go now if you don't mind, Miss Trefusis."

Emily rose to her feet. She nodded brightly and said:

"Good-by, Uncle Robert. Perhaps I'll come back some day."

"What do you mean?"

"Au revoir," said Emily.

She was going out of the front door when she stopped.

"Oh!" she said to Beatrice. "I have left my gloves."

"I will get them, Miss."

"Oh, no," said Emily. "I'll do it." She ran lightly up the stairs and entered without knocking.

"Oh," said Emily. "I beg your pardon. I am so sorry. It was my gloves." She took them up ostentatiously and smiling sweetly at the two occupants of the room who were sitting hand in hand ran down the stairs and out of the house.

"This glove leaving is a terrific scheme," said Emily to herself. "This is the second time it's come off. Poor Aunt Jennifer, does she know, I wonder? Probably not. I must hurry or I'll keep Charles waiting."

Enderby was waiting in Elmer's Ford at the agreed rendezvous.

"Any luck?" he asked as he tucked the rug round her.

"In a way, yes. I'm not sure."

Enderby looked at her inquiringly.

"No," said Emily in answer to his glance. "I'm not going to tell you about it. You see, it may have nothing whatever to do with it—and if so, it wouldn't be fair."

Enderby sighed.

"I call that hard," he observed.

"I'm sorry," said Emily firmly. "But there it is."

"Have it your own way," said Charles coldly.

They drove on in silence—an offended silence on Charles's part—an oblivious one on Emily's.

They were nearly at Exhampton when she broke the silence by a totally unexpected remark.

"Charles," she said, "are you a bridge player?"

"Yes, I am. Why?"

"I was thinking. You know what they tell you to do when you're assessing the value of your hand? If you're defending—count the winners—but if you're attacking count the losers. Now, we're attacking in this business of ours—but perhaps we have been doing it the wrong way."

"How do you mean?"

"Well, we've been counting the winners, haven't we? I mean going over the people who *could* have killed Captain Trevelyan, however improbable it seems. And that's perhaps why we've got so terribly muddled."

"I haven't got muddled," said Charles.

"Well, I have then. I'm so muddled I can't think at all. Let's look at it the other way round. Let's count the losers—the people who can't possibly have killed Captain Trevelyan."

"Well, let's see—" Enderby reflected. "To begin with there's the Willetts and Burnaby and Rycroft and Ronnie—Oh! and Duke."

"Yes," agreed Emily. "We know none of them can have killed him. Because at the time he was killed they were all at Sittaford House and they all saw each other and they can't all be lying. Yes, they're all out of it."

"As a matter of fact everyone in Sittaford is out of it," said Enderby. "Even Elmer," he lowered his voice in deference to the possibility of the driver hearing him. "Because the road to Sittaford was impassable for cars on Friday."

"He could have walked," said Emily in an equally low voice. "If Major Burnaby could have got there that evening Elmer could have started at lunch time—got to Exhampton at five, murdered him, and walked back again."

Enderby shook his head.

"I don't think he could have walked back again. Remember the snow started to fall about half past six. Anyway, you're not accusing Elmer, are you?"

"No," said Emily, "though, of course, he might be a homicidal maniac."

"Hush," said Charles. "You'll hurt his feelings if he hears you."

"At any rate," said Emily, "you can't say definitely that he couldn't have murdered Captain Trevelyan."

"Almost," said Charles. "He couldn't walk to Exhampton and back without all Sittaford knowing about it and saying it was queer."

"It certainly is a place where everyone knows everything," agreed Emily.

"Exactly," said Charles, "and that's why I say that everyone in Sittaford is out of it. The only ones that weren't at the Willetts—Miss Percehouse and Captain Wyatt are invalids. They couldn't go plowing through snowstorms. And dear old Curtis and Mrs. C. If any of them did it, they must have gone comfortably to Exhampton for the week-end and come back when it was all over."

Emily laughed.

"You couldn't be absent from Sittaford for the week-end without its being noticed, certainly," she said.

"Curtis would notice the silence if Mrs. C. was," said Enderby.

"Of course," said Emily, "the person it ought to be is Abdul. It would be in a book. He'd be a Lascar really, and Captain Trevelyan would have thrown his favorite brother overboard in a mutiny—something like that."

"I decline to believe," said Charles, "that that wretched depressed looking native ever murdered anybody."

"I know," he said suddenly.

"What?" said Emily eagerly.

"The blacksmith's wife. The one who's expecting her eighth. The intrepid woman despite her condition walked all the way to Sittaford and batted him one with the sandbag."

"And why, pray?"

"Because, of course, although the blacksmith was the father of the preceding seven, Captain Trevelyan was the father of her coming che-ild."

"Charles," said Emily. "Don't be indelicate.

"And anyway," she added, "it would be the blacksmith who did it, not her. A really good case there. Think how that brawny arm could wield a sandbag! And his wife would never notice his absence with seven children to look after. She wouldn't have time to notice a mere man."

"This is degenerating into mere idiocy," said Charles.

"It is rather," agreed Emily. "Counting losers hasn't been a great success."

"What about you?" said Charles.

"Me?"

"Where you when the crime was committed?"

"How extraordinary! I never thought of that. I was in London, of course. But I don't know that I could prove it. I was alone in my flat."

"There you are," said Charles. "Motive and everything. Your young man coming into twenty thousand pounds. What more do you want?"

"You are clever, Charles," said Emily. "I can see that really I'm a most suspicious character. I never thought of it before."

27

Narracott Acts

Two MORNINGS LATER Emily was seated in Inspector Narracott's office. She had come over from Sittaford that morning.

Inspector Narracott looked at her appraisingly. He admired Emily's pluck, her courageous determination not to give in and her resolute cheerfulness. She was a fighter and Inspector Narracott admired fighters. It was his private opinion that she was a great deal too good for Jim Pearson, even if that young man was innocent of the murder.

"It's generally understood in books," he said, "that the police are intent on having a victim and don't in the least care if that victim is innocent or not as long as they have enough evidence to convict him. That's not the truth, Miss Trefusis, it's only the guilty man we want."

"Do you honestly believe Jim to be guilty, Inspector Narracott?"

"I can't give you an official answer to that, Miss Trefusis. But I'll tell you this—that we are examining not only the evidence against him but the evidence against other people very carefully."

"You mean against his brother—Brian?"

"A very unsatisfactory gentleman, Mr. Brian Pearson. Refused to answer questions or to give any information about himself, but I think—" Inspector Narracott's slow Devonshire smile widened, "I think I can make a pretty good guess at some of his activities. If I am right I shall know in another half hour. Then there's the lady's husband, Mr. Dering."

"You've seen him?" asked Emily curiously.

Inspector Narracott looked at her vivid face, and felt tempted to relax official caution. Leaning back in his chair he recounted his interview with Mr. Dering, then from a file at his elbow he took out a copy of the wireless message he had dispatched to Mr. Rosenkraun. "That's what I sent," he said. "And here's the reply."

Emily read it.

Narracott 2 Drysdale Road Exeter. Certainly confirm Mr. Dering's statement. He was in my company all Friday afternoon. Rosenkraun.

"Oh!—bother," said Emily, selecting a milder word than that she had meant to use knowing that the police force was old-fashioned and easily shocked.

"Ye-es," said Inspector Narracott reflectively. "It's annoying, isn't it?"

And his slow Devonshire smile broke out again.

"But I am a suspicious man, Miss Trefusis. Mr. Dering's reasons sounded very plausible—but I thought it a pity to play into his hands too completely. So I sent another wireless message."

Again he handed her two pieces of paper. The first ran:

> *Information wanted re murder of Captain Trevelyan. Do you support Martin Dering's statement of alibi for Friday afternoon. Divisional Inspector Narracott Exeter.*

The return message showed agitation and a reckless disregard for expense.

> *Had no idea it was criminal case did not see Martin Dering Friday agreed support his statement as one friend to another believed his wife was having him watched for divorce proceedings.*

"Oh," said Emily. "Oh!—you *are* clever, Inspector."

The Inspector evidently thought that he *had* been rather clever. His smile was gentle and contented.

"How men do stick together," went on Emily looking over the telegrams. "Poor Sylvia. In some ways I really think that men are beasts. That's why," she added, "it's so nice when one finds a man on whom one can really rely."

And she smiled admiringly at the Inspector.

"Now, all this is very confidential, Miss Trefusis," the Inspector warned her. "I have gone further than I should in letting you know about this."

"I think it's adorable of you," said Emily. "I shall never, *never* forget it."

"Well, mind," the Inspector warned her. "Not a word to *anybody*."

"You mean that I am not to tell Charles—Mr. Enderby."

"Journalists will be journalists," said Inspector Narracott. "However well you have got him tamed, Miss Trefusis—well, news is news, isn't it?"

"I won't tell him then," said Emily. "I think I've got him muzzled all right, but as you say newspaper men will be newspaper men."

"Never part with information unnecessarily. That's my rule," said Inspector Narracott.

A faint twinkle appeared in Emily's eyes, her unspoken thought being that Inspector Narracott had infringed this rule rather badly during the last half hour.

A sudden recollection came into her mind, not of course that it probably mattered now. Everything seemed to be pointing in a totally different direction. But still it would be nice to know.

"Inspector Narracott?" she said suddenly. "Who is Mr. Duke?"

"Mr. Duke?"

She thought the Inspector was rather taken aback by her question.

"You remember," said Emily, "we met you coming out of his cottage in Sittaford."

"Ah, yes, yes, I remember. To tell you the truth, Miss Trefusis, I thought I would like to have an independent account of that table turning business. Major Burnaby is not a first-rate hand at description."

"And yet," said Emily thoughtfully, "if I had been you, I should have gone to somebody like Mr. Rycroft for it. Why Mr. Duke?"

There was a silence and then the Inspector said:

"Just a matter of opinion."

"I wonder. I wonder if the police know something about Mr. Duke."

Inspector Narracott didn't answer. He had got his eyes fixed very steadily on the blotting paper.

"The man who leads a blameless life!" said Emily, "that seems to describe Mr. Duke awfully accurately, but perhaps he hasn't always led a blameless life? Perhaps the police know that?"

She saw a faint quiver on Inspector Narracott's face as he tried to conceal a smile.

"You like guessing, don't you, Miss Trefusis?" he said amiably.

"When people don't tell you things you have to guess!" retaliated Emily.

"If a man, as you say, is leading a blameless life," Inspector Narracott said, "and if it would be an annoyance and an inconvenience for him to have his past life raked up, well, the police are capable of keeping their own counsel. We have no wish to give a man away."

"I see," said Emily, "but all the same—you went to see him, didn't you? That looks as though you thought, to begin with at any rate, that he might have had a hand in it. I wish—I wish I knew who Mr. Duke really was? And what particular branch of criminology he indulged in in the past?"

She looked appealingly at Inspector Narracott but the latter preserved a wooden face, and realizing that on this point she could not hope to move him, Emily sighed and took her departure.

When she had gone the Inspector sat staring at the blotting pad, a trace of a smile still lingering on his lips. Then he rang the bell and one of his underlings entered.

"Well?" demanded Inspector Narracott.

"Quite right, sir. But it wasn't the Duchy at Princetown, it was the hotel at Two Bridges."

"Ah!" The Inspector took the papers the other handed to him.

"Well," he said. "That settles that all right. Have you followed up the other young chap's movements on Friday?"

"He certainly arrived at Exhampton by the last train, but I haven't found out yet what time he left London. Inquiries are being made."

Narracott nodded.

"Here is the entry from Somerset House, sir."

Narracott unfolded it. It was the record of a marriage in 1894 between William Martin Dering and Martha Elizabeth Rycroft.

"Ah!" said the Inspector, "anything else?"

"Yes, sir. Mr. Brian Pearson sailed from Australia on a Blue Funnel Boat, the *Phidias*. She touched at Cape Town but no passengers of the name of Willett were aboard. No mother and daughter at all from South Africa. There was a Mrs. and Miss Evans and a Mrs. and Miss Johnson from Melbourne—the latter answer the description of the Willetts."

"H'm," said the Inspector—"Johnson. Probably neither Johnson nor Willett is the right name. I think I've got them taped out all right. Anything more?"

There was nothing else it seemed.

"Well," said Narracott, "I think we have got enough to go on with."

28

Boots

"BUT, MY DEAR YOUNG LADY," said Mr. Kirkwood, "what can you possibly expect to find at Hazelmoor? All Captain Trevelyan's effects have been removed. The police have made a thorough search of the house. I quite understand your position and your anxiety that Mr. Pearson shall be—er—cleared if possible. But what can you do?"

"I don't expect to find anything," Emily replied, "or to notice anything that the police have overlooked. I can't explain to you, Mr. Kirkwood, I want—I want to get the *atmosphere* of the place. Please let me have the key. There's no harm in it."

"Certainly there's no harm in it," said Mr. Kirkwood with dignity.

"Then, please be kind," said Emily.

So Mr. Kirkwood was kind and handed over the key with an indulgent smile. He did his best to come with her which catastrophe was only averted by great tact and firmness on Emily's part.

That morning Emily had received a letter. It was couched in the following terms:

> "Dear Miss Trefusis,"—wrote Mrs. Belling, "You said as how you would like to hear if anything at all should happen that was in any way out of the common even if not important, and, as this is peculiar, though not in any way important, I thought it my duty Miss to let you know at once, hoping this will catch you by the last post tonight or by the first post tomorrow. My niece she come round and said it wasn't of any importance but peculiar which I agreed with her. The police said, and it was generally thought that nothing was taken from Captain Trevelyan's house and nothing was in a manner of speaking nothing that is of any value, but something there is missing though not noticed at the time being unimportant. But it seems Miss that a pair of the Captain's boots is missing which Evans noticed when he went over the things with Major Burnaby. Though I don't suppose it is of any importance Miss I thought you would like to know. It was a pair of boots Miss the thick kind you rubs oil into and which the Captain would have worn if he had gone out in the snow but as he didn't go out in the snow it doesn't seem to make sense. But missing they are and who took them nobody knows and though I well know it's of no importance I felt it my duty to write and hoping this finds you as it leaves me at present and hoping you are not worrying too much about the young gentleman I remain Miss Yours truly—Mrs. J. Belling."

Emily had read and reread this letter. She had discussed it with Charles.

"Boot," said Charles thoughtfully. "It doesn't seem to make sense."

"It must mean something," Emily pointed out. "I mean—why should a pair of boots be missing?"

"You don't think Evans is inventing?"

"Why should he? And after all if people do invent, they invent something sensible. Not a silly pointless thing like this."

"Boots suggests something to do with footprints," said Charles thoughtfully.

"I know. But footprints don't seem to enter into this case at all. Perhaps if it hadn't come on to snow again—"

"Yes, perhaps, but even then."

"Could he have given them to some tramp," suggested Charles, "and then the tramp did him in."

"I suppose that's possible," said Emily, "but it doesn't sound very like Captain Trevelyan. He might perhaps have found a man some work to do or given him a shilling, but he wouldn't have pressed his best winter boots on him."

"Well, I give it up," said Charles.

"I'm not going to give it up," said Emily. "By hook or by crook I'm going to get to the bottom of it."

Accordingly she came to Exhampton and went first to the Three Crowns where Mrs. Belling received her with great enthusiasm.

"And your young gentleman still in prison, Miss! Well, it's a cruel shame and none of us don't believe it was him at least I would like to hear them say so when I am about. So you got my letter? You'd like to see Evans? Well, he lives right round the corner, 85 Fore Street it is. I wish I could come with you, but I can't leave the place, but you can't mistake it."

Emily did not mistake it. Evans himself was out, but Mrs. Evans received her and invited her in. Emily sat down and induced Mrs. Evans to do so also and plunged straight into the matter on hand.

"I've come to talk about what your husband told Mrs. Belling. I mean about a pair of Captain Trevelyan's boots being missing."

"It's an odd thing, to be sure," said the girl.

"Your husband is quite certain about it?"

"Oh, yes. Wore these boots most of the time in winter, the Captain did. Big ones they were, and he wore a couple of pairs of socks inside them."

Emily nodded.

"They can't have gone to be mended or anything like that?" she suggested.

"Not without Evans knowing, they couldn't," said his wife boastfully.

"No, I suppose not."

"It's queer like," said Mrs. Evans, "but I don't suppose it had anything to do with the murder, do you, Miss?"

"It doesn't seem likely," agreed Emily.

"Have they found out anything new, Miss?" The girl's voice was eager.

"Yes, one or two things—nothing very important."

"Seeing as that the Inspector from Exeter was here again today, I thought as though they might."

"Inspector Narracott?"

"Yes, that's the one, Miss."

"Did he come by my train?"

"No, he came by car. He went to the Three Crowns first and asked about the young gentleman's luggage."

"What young gentleman's luggage?"

"The gentleman you go about with, Miss."

Emily stared.

"They asked Tom," went on the girl. "I was passing by just after and he told me about it. He's a one for noticing is Tom. He remembered there were two labels on the young gentleman's luggage, one to Exeter and one to Exhampton."

A sudden smile illuminated Emily's face as she pictured the crime being committed by Charles in order to provide a scoop for himself. One could, she decided, write a gruesome little story on that theme. But she admired Inspector Narracott's thoroughness in checking every detail to do with anyone, however remote their connection with the crime. He must have left Exeter almost immediately after his interview with her. A fast car would easily beat the train and in any case she had lunched in Exeter.

"Where did the Inspector go afterwards?" she asked.

"To Sittaford, Miss. Tom heard him tell the driver."

"To Sittaford House?"

Brian Pearson was, she knew, still staying at Sittaford House with the Willetts.

"No, Miss, to Mr. Duke's."

Duke again. Emily felt irritated and baffled. Always Duke—the unknown factor. She ought, she felt, to be able to deduce him from the evidence but he seemed to have produced the same effect on everyone—a normal, ordinary, pleasant man.

"I've got to see him," said Emily to herself. "I'll go straight there as soon as I get back to Sittaford."

Then she had thanked Mrs. Evans, gone on to Mr. Kirkwood's and obtained the key and was now standing in the hall of Hazelmoor and wondering how and what she had expected to feel there.

She mounted the stairs slowly and went into the first room at the top of the stairs. This was quite clearly Captain Trevelyan's bedroom. It had, as Mr. Kirkwood had said, been emptied of personal effects. Blankets were folded in a neat pile, the drawers were empty, there was not so much as a hanger left in the cupboard. The boot cupboard showed a row of bare shelves.

Emily sighed and then turned and went downstairs. Here was the sitting-room where the dead man had lain, the snow blowing in from the open window.

She tried to visualize the scene. Whose hand had struck Captain Trevelyan down, and why? Had he been killed at five and twenty past five as everyone believed—or had Jim really lost his nerve and lied? Had he failed to make anyone hear at the front door and gone round to the window, looked in and seen his dead uncle's body and dashed away in an agony of fear? If only she knew. According to Mr. Dacres, Jim stuck to his story. Yes—but Jim might have lost his nerve. She couldn't be sure.

Had there been, as Mr. Rycroft had suggested, someone else in the house—someone who had overheard the quarrel and seized his chance?

If so—did that throw any light on the boot problem? Had someone been upstairs—perhaps in Captain Trevelyan's bedroom? Emily passed through the hall again. She took a quick look into the dining room, there were a couple of trunks there neatly strapped and labeled. The sideboard was bare. The silver cups were at Major Burnaby's bungalow.

She noticed, however, that the prize of three new novels, an account of which Charles had had from Evans and had reported with amusing embellishments to her, had been forgotten and lay dejectedly on a chair.

She looked round the room and shook her head. There was nothing here.

She went up the stairs again and once more entered the bedroom.

She *must* know why these boots were missing! Until she could concoct some theory reasonably satisfactory to her herself which would account for their disappearance, she felt powerless to put them out of her mind. They were soaring to ridiculous proportions, dwarfing everything else to do with the case. Was there *nothing* to help her?

She took each drawer out and felt behind it. In detective stories there was always an obliging scrap of paper. But evidently in real life one could not expect such fortunate accidents, or else Inspector Narracott and his men had been wonderfully thorough. She felt for loose boards, she felt round the edge of the carpet with her fingers. She investigated the spring mattress. What she expected to find in all these places she hardly knew but she went on looking with dogged perseverance.

And then, as she straightened her back and stood upright, her eye was caught by the one incongruous touch in this room of apple pie order, a little pile of soot in the grate.

Emily looked at it with the fascinated gaze of a bird for a snake. She drew nearer eyeing it. It was no logical deduction, no reasoning of cause and effect, it was simply that the sight of soot as such, suggested a certain possibility. Emily rolled up her sleeves and thrust both arms up the chimney.

A moment later she was staring with incredulous delight at a parcel wrapped loosely in newspaper. One shake detached the newspaper and there, before her, were the missing pair of boots.

"But why?" said Emily. "Here they are. But why? Why? Why? Why?"

She stared at them. She turned them over. She examined them outside and inside and the same question beat monotonously in her brain. Why?

Granted that someone had removed Captain Trevelyan's boots and hidden them up the chimney. Why had they done so?

"Oh!" cried Emily desperately, "I shall go mad!"

She put the boots carefully in the middle of the floor and drawing up a chair opposite them she sat down. And then deliberately she set herself to think out things from the beginning, going over every detail that she knew herself or had learned by hearsay from other people. She considered every actor in the drama and outside the drama.

And suddenly, a queer nebulous idea began to take shape—an idea suggested by that pair of innocent boots that stood there dumbly on the floor.

"But if so," said Emily—"if so—"

She picked up the boots in her hand and hurried downstairs. She pushed open the dining-room door and went to the cupboard in the corner. Here was Captain Trevelyan's motley array of sporting trophies and sporting outfits, all the things he had not trusted within reach of the female tenants. The skis, the sculls, the elephant's foot, the tusks, the fishing rods—everything still waiting for Messrs. Young and Peabody to pack them expertly for store.

Emily bent down boots in hand.

In a minute or two she stood upright, flushed, incredulous.

"So that was it," said Emily. "So that was it."

She sank into a chair. There was still much that she did not understand.

After some minutes she rose to her feet. She spoke aloud.

"I know who killed Captain Trevelyan," she said. "But I don't know why. I still can't think why. But I mustn't lose time."

She hurried out of Hazelmoor. To find a car to drive her to Sittaford was the work of a few minutes. She ordered it to take her to Mr. Duke's bungalow. Here she paid the man and then walked up the path as the car drove away.

She lifted the knocker and gave a loud rat-tat.

After a moment or two's interval the door was opened by a big burly man with a rather impassive face.

For the first time, Emily met Mr. Duke face to face.

"Mr. Duke?" she asked.

"Yes."

"I am Miss Trefusis. May I come in, please?"

There was a momentary hesitation. Then he stood aside to let her pass. Emily walked into the living-room. He closed the front door and followed her.

"I want to see Inspector Narracott," said Emily. "Is he here?"

Again there was a pause. Mr. Duke seemed uncertain how to answer. At last he appeared to make up his mind. He smiled—a rather curious smile.

"Inspector Narracott is here," he said. "What do you want to see him about?"

Emily took the parcel she was carrying and unwrapped it. She took out a pair of boots and placed them on the table in front of him.

"I want," she said, "to see him about those boots."

29

The Second Séance

"HULLO, HULLO, HULLO," said Ronnie Garfield.

Mr. Rycroft slowly ascending the steep slope of the lane from the post office, paused, till Ronnie overtook him.

"Been to the local Harrods, eh?" said Ronnie. "Old Mother Hibbert."

"No," said Mr. Rycroft. "I have been for a short walk along past the forge. Very delightful weather today."

Ronnie looked up at the blue sky.

"Yes, a bit of a difference from last week. By the way, you're going to the Willetts, I suppose?"

"I am. You also?"

"Yes. Our bright spot in Sittaford—the Willetts. Mustn't let yourself get downhearted, that's their motto. Carry on as usual. My aunt says it is unfeeling of them to ask people to tea so soon after the funeral and all that, but that's all bunkum. She just says that because she's feeling rattled about the Emperor of Peru."

"The Emperor of Peru?" said Mr. Rycroft surprised.

"One of the blinking cats. It's turned out to be an Empress instead and Aunt Caroline's naturally annoyed about it. She doesn't like these sex problems—so, as I say, she got her feelings off her chest by making catty remarks about the Willetts. Why shouldn't they ask people to tea? Trevelyan wasn't a relation, or anything like that."

"Very true," said Mr. Rycroft turning his head and examining a bird which flew past and in which he thought he recognized a rare species.

"How annoying," he murmured. "I haven't got my glasses with me."

"Eh! I say, talking of Trevelyan, do you think Mrs. Willett can have known the old boy better than she says?"

"Why do you ask that?"

"Because of the change in her. Have you ever seen anything like it? She's aged about twenty years in the last week. You must have noticed it."

"Yes," said Mr. Rycroft. "I have noticed it."

"Well, there you are. Trevelyan's death must have been the most frightful shock to her in some way or other. Queer if she turned out to be the old man's long lost wife whom he deserted in his youth and didn't recognize."

"I hardly think that likely, Mr. Garfield."

"Bit too much of a Movie stunt, eh? All the same very odd things happen. I've read some really amazing things in the *Daily Wire*— things you wouldn't credit if a newspaper didn't print them."

"Are they any more to be credited on that account?" inquired Mr. Rycroft acidly.

"You have got a down on young Enderby, haven't you?" said Ronnie.

"I dislike ill-bred nosing into affairs that do not concern you," said Mr. Rycroft.

"Yes, but then they do concern him," Ronnie persisted. "I mean nosing about is the poor chap's job. He seems to have tamed old Burnaby all right. Funny, the old boy can hardly bear the sight of me. I'm like a red rag to a bull to him."

Mr. Rycroft did not reply.

"By Jove," said Ronnie again glancing up at the sky. "Do you realize it's Friday? Just a week ago today at about this time we were trudging up to the Willetts just as we are now. But a bit of a change in the weather."

"A week ago," said Mr. Rycroft. "It seems infinitely longer."

"More like a bally year, doesn't it? Hullo, Abdul."

They were passing Captain Wyatt's gate over which the melancholy Indian was leaning.

"Good afternoon, Abdul," said Mr. Rycroft. "How's your master?"

The native shook his head.

"Master bad today, Sahib. Not see anyone. Not see anyone for long time."

"You know," said Ronnie as they passed on, "that chap could murder Wyatt quite easily and no one would know. He could go on for weeks shaking his head and saying the master wouldn't see anyone and no one would think it the least odd."

Mr. Rycroft admitted the truth of the statement.

"But there would still be the problem of the disposal of the body," he pointed out.

"Yes, that's always the snag, isn't it? Inconvenient thing, a human body."

They passed Major Burnaby's cottage. The Major was in his garden looking sternly at a weed which was growing where no weed should be.

"Good afternoon, Major," said Mr. Rycroft. "Are you also coming to Sittaford House?"

Burnaby rubbed his nose.

"Don't think so. They sent a note asking me. But—well—I don't feel like it. Expect you'll understand."

Mr. Rycroft bowed his head in token of understanding.

"All the same," he said, "I wish you'd come. I've got a reason."

"A reason. What sort of a reason?"

Mr. Rycroft hesitated. It was clear that the presence of Ronnie Garfield constrained him. But Ronnie, completely oblivious of the fact, stood his ground listening with ingenuous interest.

"I'd like to try an experiment," he said at last slowly.

"What sort of experiment?" demanded Burnaby.

Mr. Rycroft hesitated.

"I'd rather not tell you before-hand. But if you come, I'll ask you to back me up in anything I suggest."

Burnaby's curiosity was aroused.

"All right," he said. "I'll come. You can count on me. Where's my hat?"

He rejoined them in a minute, hat on head and all three turned in at the gates of Sittaford House.

"Hear you are expecting company, Rycroft," said Burnaby conversationally.

A shade of vexation passed over the older man's face.

"Who told you that?"

"That chattering magpie of a woman, Mrs. Curtis. She's clean and she's honest, but her tongue never stops, and she pays no attention to whether you listen or whether you don't."

"It's quite true," admitted Mr. Rycroft. "I am expecting my niece, Mrs. Dering, and her husband, tomorrow."

They had arrived at the front door by now, and on pressing the bell it was opened to them by Brian Pearson.

As they removed their overcoats in the hall, Mr. Rycroft observed the tall broad-shouldered young man with an interested eye.

"Fine specimen," he thought. "Very fine specimen. Strong temper. Curious angle of the jaw. Might be a nasty customer to tackle in certain circumstances. What you might call a dangerous young man."

A queer feeling of unreality stole over Major Burnaby as he entered the drawing-room, and Mrs. Willett rose to greet him.

"Splendid of you to turn out."

The same words as last week. The same blazing fire on the hearth. He fancied, but was not sure, the same gowns on the two women.

It did give one a queer feeling. As though it were last week again—as though Joe Trevelyan hadn't died—as though nothing had happened or were changed. Stop, that was wrong. The Willett woman had changed. A wreck, that was the only way of describing her. No longer the prosperous determined woman of the world, but a broken nervy creature making an obvious and pathetic effort to appear as usual.

"But I'm hanged if I can see what Joe's death meant to her," thought the Major.

For the hundredth time he registered the impression that there was something deuced odd about the Willetts.

As usual, he awoke to the realization that he was being silent and that someone was speaking to him.

"Our last little gathering, I am afraid," Mrs. Willett was saying.

"What's that?" Ronnie Garfield looked up suddenly.

"Yes." Mrs. Willett shook her head with a would-be smile. "We have got to forego the rest of the winter in Sittaford. Personally, of course, I love it—the snow and the tors and the wildness of it all. But the domestic problem! The domestic problem is too difficult—it defeats me!"

"I thought you were going to get a chauffeur butler and a handy man," said Major Burnaby.

A sudden shiver shook Mrs. Willett's frame.

"No," she said, "I—I have had to give up that idea."

"Dear, dear," said Mr. Rycroft. "This is a great blow to us all. Very sad indeed. We will sink back into our little rut after you have gone. When do you go, by the way?"

"On Monday, I expect," said Mrs. Willett. "Unless I can get away tomorrow. It's so very awkward with no servants. Of course, I must arrange things with Mr. Kirkwood. I took the house for four months."

"You are going to London?" inquired Mr. Rycroft.

"Yes, probably, to start with anyway. Then I expect we shall go abroad to the Riviera."

"A great loss," said Mr. Rycroft bowing gallantly.

Mrs. Willett gave a queer aimless little titter.

"Too kind of you, Mr. Rycroft. Well, shall we have tea?"

Tea was laid ready. Mrs. Willett poured out. Ronnie and Brian handed things. A queer kind of embarrassment lay over the party.

"What about you?" said Burnaby abruptly to Brian Pearson. "You off too?"

"To London, yes. Naturally I shan't go abroad till this business is over."

"This business?"

"I mean until my brother is cleared of this ridiculous charge."

He flung the words at them defiantly in such a challenging manner that nobody knew quite what to say. Major Burnaby relieved the situation.

"Never have believed he did it. Not for a moment." he said.

"*None* of us think so," said Violet, flinging him a grateful glance.

The tinkle of a bell broke the ensuing pause.

"That's Mr. Duke," said Mrs. Willett. "Let him in, Brian."

Young Pearson had gone to the window.

"It's not Duke," he said. "It's that damned journalist."

"Oh! dear," said Mrs. Willett. "Well, I suppose we must let him in all the same."

Brian nodded and reappeared in a few minutes with Charles Enderby.

Enderby entered with his usual ingenuous air of beaming satisfaction. The idea that he might not be welcome did not seem to occur to him.

"Hullo, Mrs. Willett. How are you? Thought I'd just drop in and see how things were. I wondered where everyone in Sittaford had got to. Now I see."

"Have some tea, Mr. Enderby?"

"Awfully kind of you. I will. I see Emily isn't here. I suppose she's with your aunt, Mr. Garfield."

"Not that I know of," said Ronnie staring. "I thought she'd gone to Exhampton."

"Ah! but she's back from there. How do I know? A little bird told me. The Curtis bird, to be accurate. Saw the car pass the post office and go up the lane and come back empty. She is not in No. 5 and she's not in Sittaford House. Puzzle—where is she? Failing Miss

Percehouse, she must be sipping tea with that determined lady killer, Captain Wyatt."

"She may have gone up Sittaford Beacon to see the sunset," suggested Mr. Rycroft.

"Don't think so," said Burnaby. "Should have seen her pass. I've been in the garden for the last hour."

"Well, I don't think it's a very vital problem," said Charles cheerfully. "I mean I don't think she's been kidnapped or murdered or anything."

"That's a pity from the point of view of your paper, isn't it?" sneered Brian.

"Even for copy, I wouldn't sacrifice Emily," said Charles. "Emily," he added thoughtfully, "is unique."

"Very charming," said Mr. Rycroft. "Very charming. We are—er—collaborators, she and I."

"Has everyone finished?" said Mrs. Willett. "What about some bridge?"

"Er—one moment," said Mr. Rycroft.

He cleared his throat importantly. Everyone looked at him.

"Mrs. Willett, I am, as you know, deeply interested in psychic phenomena. A week ago today, in this very room, we had an amazing, indeed an awe inspiring experience."

There was a faint sound from Violet Willett. He turned to her.

"I know, my dear Miss Willett, I know. The experience upset you, it was upsetting. I do not deny it. Now, ever since the crime the police force have been seeking the murderer of Captain Trevelyan. They have made an arrest. But some of us, at least, in this room, do not believe that Mr. James Pearson is the guilty party. What I propose is this, that we repeat the experiment of last Friday, though approaching it this time in a rather different spirit."

"No," cried Violet.

"Oh! I say," said Ronnie. "That's a bit too thick. I'm not going to join in anyway."

Mr. Rycroft took no notice of him.

"Mrs. Willett, what do you say?"

She hesitated.

"Frankly, Mr. Rycroft, I do not like the idea. I don't like it at all. That miserable business last week made a most disagreeable impression on me. It will take me a long time to forget it."

"What are you getting at exactly?" asked Enderby interestedly. "Do you propose that the spirits should tell us the name of Captain Trevelyan's murderer? That seems a pretty tall order."

"It was a pretty tall order, as you call it, when last week a message came through saying that Captain Trevelyan was dead."

"That's true," agreed Enderby. "But—well—you know this idea of yours might have consequences you haven't considered."

"Such as?"

"Supposing a name was mentioned? Could you be sure that someone present did not deliberately—"

He paused and Ronnie Garfield tendered the word.

"Shove. That's what he means. Supposing somebody goes and shoves."

"This is a serious experiment, sir," said Mr. Rycroft warmly. "Nobody would do such a thing."

"I don't know," said Ronnie dubiously. "I wouldn't put it past them. I don't mean myself. I swear I wouldn't, but suppose everyone turns on me and says I have. Jolly awkward, you know."

"Mrs. Willett, I am in earnest," the little old gentleman disregarded Ronnie. "I beg of you, let us make the experiment."

She wavered.

"I don't like it. I really don't. I—" She looked round her uneasily, as though for a way of escape. "Major Burnaby, you were Captain Trevelyan's friend. What do you say?"

The Major's eyes met those of Mr. Rycroft. This, he understood, was the contingency which the latter had foreshadowed.

"Why not?" he said gruffly.

It had all the decision of a casting vote.

Ronnie went into the adjoining room and brought the small table which had been used before. He set it in the middle of the floor and chairs were drawn up round it. No one spoke. The experiment was clearly not popular.

"That is correct, I think," said Mr. Rycroft. "We are about to repeat the experiment of last Friday under precisely similar conditions."

"Not precisely similar," objected Mrs. Willett. "Mr. Duke is missing."

"True," said Mr. Rycroft. "A pity he is not here. A great pity. Well—er—we must consider him as replaced by Mr. Pearson."

"Don't take part in it, Brian. I beg of you. Please don't," cried Violet.

"What does it matter. It's all nonsense anyway."

"That is quite the wrong spirit," said Mr. Rycroft severely.

Brian Pearson did not reply but took his place beside Violet.

"Mr. Enderby," began Mr. Rycroft, but Charles interrupted him.

"I was not in on this. I'm a journalist and you mistrust me. I'll take notes in shorthand of any phenomena—that's the word isn't it?—that occur."

Matters were settled like that. The other six took their places round the table. Charles turned off the lights and sat down on the fender.

"One minute," he said. "What's the time?" He peered at his wrist watch in the firelight.

"That's odd," he said.

"What's odd?"

"It's just twenty-five minutes past five. . . ."

Violet uttered a little cry.

Mr. Rycroft said severely:

"Silence."

The minutes passed. A very different atmosphere this to the one a week ago. There was no muffled laughter, no whispered comments—only silence, broken at last by a slight crack from the table.

Mr. Rycroft's voice rose.

"Is there anyone there?"

Another faint crack—somehow an eerie sound in that darkened room.

"Is there anyone there?"

Not a crack this time but a deafening tremendous rap.

Violet screamed and Mrs. Willett gave a cry.

Brian Pearson's voice rose reassuringly.

"It's all right. That's a knock at the front door. I'll go and open it."

He strode from the room.

Still nobody spoke.

Suddenly the door flew open, the lights were switched on.

In the doorway stood Inspector Narracott. Behind him were Emily Trefusis and Mr. Duke.

Narracott took a step into the room and spoke.

"John Burnaby, I charge you with the murder of Joseph Trevelyan on Friday the 14th instant, and I hereby warn you that anything you may say will be taken down and may be used in evidence."

30

Emily Explains

IT WAS A CROWD OF PEOPLE almost too surprised for words that crowded round Emily Trefusis.

Inspector Narracott had led his prisoner from the room.

Charles Enderby found his voice first.

"For heaven's sake, cough it up, Emily," he said. "I want to get to the telegraph office. Every moment's vital."

"It was Major Burnaby who killed Captain Trevelyan."

"Well, I saw Narracott arrest him. And I suppose Narracott's sane—hasn't gone off his nut suddenly. But how *can* Burnaby have killed Trevelyan? I mean how is it humanly possible? If Trevelyan was killed at five and twenty past five—"

"He wasn't. He was killed at about a quarter to six."

"Well, but even then—"

"I know. You'd never guess unless you just happened to think of it. *Skis*—that's the explanation—*skis.*"

"Skis?" repeated everyone.

Emily nodded.

"Yes. He deliberately engineered that table turning. It wasn't accident and done unconsciously as we thought, Charles. It was the second alternative that we rejected—done on purpose. He saw it was going to snow before very long. That would make it perfectly safe and wipe out all tracks. He created the impression that Captain Trevelyan was dead—got everyone all worked up. Then he pretended to be very upset and insisted on starting off for Exhampton.

"He went home, buckled on his skis (they were kept in a shed in the garden with a lot of other tackle) and started. He was an expert on skis. It's all down hill to Exhampton—a wonderful run. It would only take about ten minutes.

"He arrived at the window and rapped. Captain Trevelyan let him in, all unsuspecting. Then, when Captain Trevelyan's back was turned he seized his opportunity, picked up that sandbag thing and—and killed him. Ugh! It makes me sick to think of it."

She shuddered.

"It was all quite easy. He had plenty of time. He must have wiped and cleaned the skis and then put them into the cupboard in the dining-room, pushed in among all the other things. Then, I suppose he

312

forced the window and pulled out all the drawers and things—to make it look as though someone had broken in.

"Then just before eight o'clock, all he had to do was to go out, make a detour on to the road higher up and come puffing and panting into Exhampton as though he'd walked all the way from Sittaford. So long as no one suspected about the skis, he'd be perfectly safe. The doctor couldn't fail to say that Captain Trevelyan had been dead at least two hours. And, as I say, so long as no one thought of skis, Major Burnaby would have a perfect alibi."

"But they were friends—Burnaby and Trevelyan," said Mr. Rycroft. "Old friends—they've always been friends. It's incredible."

"I know," said Emily. "That's what I thought. I couldn't see *why*. I puzzled and I puzzled and at last I had to come to Inspector Narracott and Mr. Duke."

She paused and looked at the impassive Mr. Duke.

"May I tell them?" she said.

Mr. Duke smiled.

"If you like, Miss Trefusis."

"Anyway—no, perhaps you'd rather I didn't. I went to them, and we got the thing clear. Do you remember telling me, Charles, that Evans mentioned that Captain Trevelyan used to send in solutions of competitions in his name? He thought Sittaford House was too grand an address. Well—that's what he did in that Football Competition that you gave Major Burnaby five thousand pounds for. It was Captain Trevelyan's solution really, and he sent it in in Burnaby's name. No. 1, The Cottages, Sittaford, sounded much better, he thought. Well, you see what happened? On Friday morning Major Burnaby got the letter saying he'd won five thousand pounds (and by the way, that ought to have made us suspicious. He told you he never got the letter—that nothing had come through on Friday owing to the weather. That was a lie. Friday morning was the last day things did come through). Where was I? Oh!—Major Burnaby getting the letter. He wanted that five thousand—wanted it badly. He'd been investing in some rotten shares or other and had lost a terrible lot of money.

"The idea must have come into his head quite suddenly, I should think. Perhaps when he realized it was going to snow that evening. *If Trevelyan were dead*—he could keep that money and no one would ever know."

"Amazing," murmured Mr. Rycroft. "Quite amazing. I never dreamed—But my dear young lady, how did you learn all this? What put you on the right track?"

For answer, Emily explained Mrs. Belling's letter, and told how she had discovered the boots in the chimney.

"It was looking at them that put it into my mind. They were ski boots, you see, and it made me think of skis. And suddenly I wondered if perhaps—I rushed downstairs to the cupboard, and sure enough there were *two* pairs of skis there. One pair was longer than the other. And the boots fitted the long pair—*but they didn't fit the other*. The toe clip things were adjusted for a much smaller pair of boots. The shorter pair of skis belonged to a different person."

"He ought to have hidden the skis somewhere else," said Mr. Rycroft with artistic disapproval.

"No—no," said Emily. "Where else could he hide them? It was a very good place really. In a day or two the whole collection would have been stored, and in the meantime it wasn't likely that the police would bother whether Captain Trevelyan had had one or two pairs of skis."

"But why did he hide the boots?"

"I suppose," said Emily, "that he was afraid the police might do exactly what I did— The sight of ski boots might have suggested skis to them. So he stuffed them up the chimney. And that's really, of course, where he made his mistake, because Evans noticed that they'd gone and I got to know of it."

"Did he deliberately mean to fasten the crime on Jim?" demanded Brian Pearson angrily.

"Oh! no. That was just Jim's usual idiotic luck. He *was* an idiot, poor lamb."

"He's all right now," said Charles. "You needn't worry about him. Have you told me everything, Emily, because if so, I want to rush to the telegraph office. You'll excuse me everybody."

He dashed out of the room.

"The live wire," said Emily.

Mr. Duke spoke in his deep voice.

"You've been rather a live wire yourself, Miss Trefusis."

"You have," said Ronnie admiringly.

"Oh! dear," said Emily suddenly and dropped limply on a chair.

"What you need is a pick-me-up," said Ronnie. "A cocktail, eh?"

Emily shook her head.

"A little brandy," suggested Mr. Rycroft solicitously.

"A cup of tea," suggested Violet.

"I'd like a spot of face powder," said Emily wistfully. "I've left my powder puff in the car. And I know I'm simply shining with excitement."

Violet led her upstairs in search of this sedative to the nerves.

"That's better," said Emily dabbing her nose firmly. "What a nice kind. I feel much better now. Have you got any lipstick? I feel almost human."

"You've been wonderful," said Violet. "So brave."

"Not really," said Emily. "Underneath this camouflage I've been as wobbly as a jelly, with a sort of sick feeling in my middle."

"I know," said Violet. "I've felt much the same myself. I have been so terrified this last few days—about Brian, you know. They couldn't hang him for murdering Captain Trevelyan, of course, but if once he had said where he was during that time, they would soon have ferreted out that it was he who engineered father's escape."

"What's that?" said Emily pausing in her facial repairs.

"Father was the convict who escaped. That's why we came here. Mother and I. Poor father, he's always—been queer at times. Then he does these dreadful things. We met Brian on the way over from Australia, and he and I—well—he and I—"

"I see," said Emily helpfully. "Of course you did."

"I told him everything and between us we concocted a plan. Brian was wonderful. We had got plenty of money fortunately, and Brian made all the plans. It's awfully hard to get away from Princetown, you know, but Brian engineered it. Really it was a kind of miracle. The arrangement was that after father got away he was to go straight across country here and hide in the Pixie's Cave and then later he and Brian were to be our two men servants. You see with our arriving so long before-hand we imagined we would be quite free from suspicion. It was Brian who told us about this place, and suggested us offering a big rent to Captain Trevelyan."

"I'm awfully sorry," said Emily—"I mean that it all went wrong."

"It's broken mother up completely," said Violet. "I think Brian's wonderful. It isn't everybody who would want to marry a convict's daughter. But I don't think it's really father's fault, he had an awful kick on the head from a horse about fifteen years ago, and since then he has been a bit queer. Brian says if he had a good counsel he would have got off. But don't let's talk about me any more."

"Can't anything be done?"

Violet shook her head.

"He's very ill—the exposure, you know. That awful cold. It's pneumonia. I can't help feeling that if he dies—well—it may be the best for him really. It sounds dreadful to say so, but you know what I mean."

"Poor Violet," said Emily. "It *is* a rotten shame."

The girl shook her head.

"I've got Brian," she said. "And you've got—"

She stopped embarrassed.

"Ye-es," said Emily thoughtfully. "That's just it."

31

The Lucky Man

TEN MINUTES LATER Emily was hurrying down the lane. Captain Wyatt, leaning over his gate, tried to arrest her progress.

"Hie," he said, "Miss Trefusis. What's all this I hear?"

"It's all true," said Emily hurrying on.

"Yes, but look here. Come in—have a glass of wine or a cup of tea. There's plenty of time. No need to hurry. That's the worst of you civilized people."

"We're awful, I know," said Emily and sped on.

She burst in on Miss Percehouse with the explosive force of a bomb.

"I've come to tell you all about it," said Emily.

And straight away she poured forth the complete story. It was punctuated by various ejaculations of "Bless us," "You don't say so?" "Well, I declare," from Miss Percehouse.

When Emily had finished her narrative, Miss Percehouse raised herself on her elbow and wagged a finger portentously.

"What did I say?" she demanded. "I told you Burnaby was a jealous man. Friends indeed! For more than twenty years Trevelyan has done everything a bit better than Burnaby. He skied better, and he climbed better and he shot better and he did Cross Word Puzzles better. Burnaby wasn't a big enough man to stand it. Trevelyan was rich and he was poor.

"It's been going on a long time. I can tell you it's a difficult thing to go on really liking a man who can do everything just a little better than you can. Burnaby was a narrow-minded, small-natured man. He let it get on his nerves."

"I expect you're right," said Emily. "Well, I had to come and tell you. It seemed so unfair you should be out of everything. By the way, did you know that your nephew knew my Aunt Jennifer? They were having tea together at Deller's on Wednesday."

"She's his godmother," said Miss Percehouse. "So that's the 'fellow' he wanted to see in Exeter. Borrowing money, if I know Ronnie. I'll speak to him."

"I forbid you to bite anyone on a joyful day like this," said Emily. "Good-by. I must fly. I've got a lot to do."

"What have you got to do, young woman? I should say you'd done your bit."

"Not quite. I must go up to London and see Jim's Insurance Company people and persuade them not to prosecute him over that little matter of the borrowed money."

"H'm," said Miss Percehouse.

"It's all right," said Emily. "Jim will keep straight enough in future. He's had his lesson."

"Perhaps. And you think you'll be able to persuade them?"

"Yes," said Emily firmly.

"Well," said Miss Percehouse. "Perhaps you will. And after that?"

"After that," said Emily. "I've finished. I'll have done all I can for Jim."

"Then suppose we say—what next?" said Miss Percehouse.

"You mean?"

"What next? Or if you want it put clearer: *Which of them?*"

"Oh!" said Emily.

"Exactly. That's what I want to know. Which of them is to be the unfortunate man?"

Emily laughed. Bending over she kissed the old lady.

"Don't pretend to be an idiot," she said. "You know perfectly well which it is."

Miss Percehouse chuckled.

Emily ran lightly out of the house and down to the gate just as Charles came racing up the lane.

He caught her by both hands.

"Emily darling!"

"Charles! Isn't everything marvelous?"

"I shall kiss you," said Mr. Enderby and did.

"I'm a made man, Emily," he said. "Now, look here, darling, what about it?"

"What about what?"

"Well—I mean—well, of course, it wouldn't have been playing the game with poor old Pearson in prison and all the rest of it. But he's cleared now and—well, he has got to take his medicine just like anybody else."

"What *are* you talking about?" said Emily.

"You know well enough I am crazy about you," said Mr. Enderby, "and you like me. Pearson was just a mistake. What I mean is—well—you and I, we are made for each other. All this time, we have known it, both of us, haven't we? Do you like a Registry Office or a Church, or what?"

"If you are referring to marriage," said Emily, "there's nothing doing."

"What—but I say—"

"No," said Emily.

"But—Emily—"

"If you will have it," said Emily. "I love Jim. Passionately!"

Charles stared at her in speechless bewilderment.

"You can't!"

"I can! And I do! And I always have! And I always shall!"

"You—you made me think—"

"I said," said Emily demurely, "that it was wonderful to have someone one could rely on."

"Yes, but I thought—"

"I can't help what you thought."

"You *are* an unscrupulous devil, Emily."

"I know, Charles darling. I know. I'm everything you like to call me. But never mind. Think how great you are going to be. You've got your scoop! Exclusive news for the *Daily Wire*. You're a made man. What's a woman anyway? Less than the dust. No really strong man needs a woman. She only hampers him by clinging to him like the ivy. Every great man is one who is independent of women. A career— there's nothing so fine, so absolutely satisfying to a man, as a great career. You are a strong man, Charles, one who can stand alone—"

"Will you stop talking, Emily? It's like a talk to Young Men on the Wireless! You've broken my heart. You don't know how lovely you looked as you came into that room with Narracott. Just like something triumphant and avenging off an arch."

A footstep crunched on the lane, and Mr. Duke appeared.

"Oh! there you are, Mr. Duke," said Emily. "Charles, I want to tell you. This is Ex-Chief Inspector Duke of Scotland Yard."

"What?" cried Charles recognizing the famous name. "Not *the* Inspector Duke?"

"Yes," said Emily. "When he retired, he came here to live, and being nice and modest he didn't want his renown to get about. I see now why Inspector Narracott twinkled so when I wanted him to tell me what kind of crimes Mr. Duke had committed."

Mr. Duke laughed.

Charles wavered. There was a short tussle between the lover and the journalist. The journalist won.

"I'm delighted to meet you, Inspector," he said. "Now, I wonder if we could persuade you to do us a short article, say eight hundred words, on the Trevelyan Case."

Emily stepped quickly up the lane and into Mrs. Curtis's cottage.

She ran up to her bedroom and pulled out her suitcase. Mrs. Curtis had followed her up.

"You're not going, Miss?"

"I am. I've got a lot to do—London, and my young man."

Mrs. Curtis drew nearer.

"Just tell me, Miss, which of 'em is it?"

Emily was throwing clothes haphazard into the suitcase.

"The one in prison, of course. There's never been any other."

"Ah! You don't think, Miss, that maybe you're making a mistake. You're sure the other young gentleman is worth as much as this one?"

"Oh! no," said Emily. "He isn't. This one will get on." She glanced out of the window where Charles was still holding Ex-Chief Inspector Duke in earnest parley. "He's the kind of young man who's simply born to get on—but I don't know what would happen to the other one if I weren't there to look after him. Look where he would be now if it weren't for me!"

"And you can't say more than that, Miss," said Mrs. Curtis.

She retreated downstairs to where her lawful spouse was sitting and staring into vacancy.

"The living image of my Great Aunt Sarah's Belinda she is," said Mrs. Curtis. "Threw herself away she did on that miserable George Plunket down at the Three Cows. Mortgaged and all it was. And in two years she had the mortgage paid off and the place a going concern."

"Ah!" said Mr. Curtis and shifted his pipe slightly.

"He was a handsome fellow, George Plunket," said Mrs. Curtis reminiscently.

"Ah!" said Mr. Curtis.

"But after he married Belinda he never so much as looked at another woman."

"Ah!" said Mr. Curtis.

"She never gave him the chance," said Mrs. Curtis.

"Ah!" said Mr. Curtis.

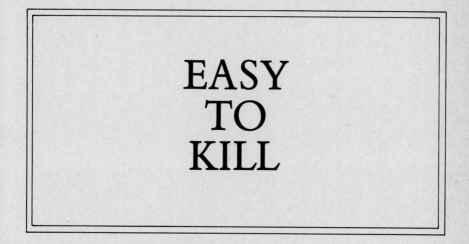

EASY
TO
KILL

Cast of Characters

LUKE FITZWILLIAM—Just retired from a police career in Asia, he ran smack into multiple murders before he'd been back in England a day.

LAVINIA FULLERTON—Ostensibly she was a woolly-minded old lamb, but the wolf feared she knew too much.

BRIDGET CONWAY—A devilishly clever beauty who'd decided to marry her boss because the salary was higher.

LORD EASTERFIELD—Bridget's fiancé, a pot-bellied, moralistic newspaper magnate who believed what he read in his own papers.

ALFRED WAKE—The vicar of Wychwood under Ashe, he gossiped of many deaths and obscure feuds and weird witchcraft.

MR. ABBOT—The village lawyer—too genial, too florid, too hot-tempered and, perhaps, too indiscreet with his lady friends.

HONORIA WAYNFLETE—Another elderly but sharp-witted spinster who suspected more than she mentioned about the strange accidents in Wychwood.

MR. ELLSWORTHY—The arty and disreputable keeper of an antique shop whose odd tastes included strange midnight rites in the Witches' Meadow.

MAJOR HORTON—A retired military man. His wife's death had released him and his beloved dogs from unrelenting henpecking.

DOCTOR GEOFFREY THOMAS—An affable young chap who remarked how surprisingly easy it was to get away with murder.

ROSE HUMBLEBY—Lovely, timid daughter of Doctor Thomas' late senior partner, whose death cleared the way for Rose to become Mrs. Thomas.

MRS. HUMBLEBY—Rose's mother. Her husband's recent death had unsettled her so much that she saw wickedness in the most improbable places.

SIR WILLIAM OSSINGTON—Of Scotland Yard. Because of their long friendship, Billy Bones reluctantly listened to Luke's yarn of eight unsuspected murders.

SUPERINTENDENT BATTLE—The Yard's stolid-faced top deputy. Despite his calm, reassuring manner, not a detail escaped his shrewd eye.

I

ENGLAND! ENGLAND AFTER many years!

How was he going to like it? Luke Fitzwilliam asked himself that question as he walked down the gangplank to the dock. It was present at the back of his mind all through the wait in the customs shed. It came suddenly to the fore when he was finally seated in the boat train. Here he was, honorably retired on a pension, with some small private means of his own, a gentleman of leisure, come home to England. What was he going to do with himself? With an effort, Luke Fitzwilliam averted his eyes from the landscape outside the railway-carriage window and settled down to a perusal of the papers he had just bought. The *Times,* the *Daily Clarion* and *Punch.*

He started with the *Daily Clarion.* The *Clarion* was given over entirely to Epsom. He had drawn a horse in the club sweep and he looked now to see what the *Clarion's* racing correspondent thought of its chances. He found it dismissed contemptuously in a sentence:

Of the others, Jujube the II, Mark's Mile, Santony and Jerry Boy are hardly likely to qualify for a place. A likely outsider is—

But Luke paid no attention to the likely outsider. His eye had shifted to the betting. Jujube the II was listed at a modest 40 to 1. He glanced at his watch. A quarter to four. "Well," he thought, "it's over now." And he wished he'd had a bet on Clarigold, who was the second favorite.

Then he opened the *Times* and became absorbed in more serious matters. A full half hour afterward the train slowed down and finally stopped. Luke looked out of the window. They were in a large empty-looking station with many platforms. He caught sight of a bookstall some way up the platform with a placard DERBY RESULT. Luke opened the door, jumped out, and ran toward the bookstall. A

325

moment later he was staring with a broad grin at a few smudged lines in the stop press.

DERBY RESULT

JUJUBE THE II
MAZEPPA
CLARIGOLD

Luke grinned broadly. A hundred pounds to blow! Good old Jujube the II, so scornfully dismissed by all the tipsters. He folded the paper, still grinning to himself, and turned back—to face emptiness. In the excitement of Jujube the II's victory, his train had slipped out of the station unnoticed by him. "When the devil did that train go out?" he demanded of a gloomy-looking porter.

"What train? There hasn't been no train since the 3:14."

"There was a train here just now. I got out of it. The boat express."

"The boat express don't stop anywhere till London."

"But it did," Luke assured him. "I got out of it."

Faced by facts, the porter changed his ground. "You didn't ought to have done," he said reproachfully. "It don't stop here."

"But it did."

"That was signal, that was. Signal against it. It didn't what you'd call 'stop.' You didn't ought to have got out."

"We'll admit that," said Luke. "The wrong is done, past all recall. What I'm trying to get at is, what do you, a man experienced in the services of the railway company, advise me to do?"

"Reckon," said the porter, "you'd best go on by the 4:25."

"If the 4:25 goes to London," said Luke, "the 4:25 is the train for me."

Reassured on that point, Luke strolled up and down the platform. A large board informed him that he was at FENNY CLAYTON JUNCTION FOR WYCHWOOD UNDER ASHE, and presently a train consisting of one carriage pushed backward by an antiquated little engine came slowly puffing in and deposited itself in a modest way.

At last, with immense importance, the London train came in. Luke scrutinized each compartment. The first, a smoker, contained a gentleman of military aspects smoking a cigar. He passed on to the next one, which contained a tired-looking, genteel young woman, possibly a nursery governess, and an active-looking small boy of about three. Luke passed on quickly. The next door was open and the carriage contained one passenger, an elderly lady. She reminded Luke slightly of one of his aunts, his Aunt Mildred, who had courageously allowed him to keep a grass snake when he was ten years old. Aunt Mildred had been decidedly a good aunt as aunts go. Luke entered the carriage and sat down.

After some five minutes of intense activity on the part of milk vans, luggage trucks and other excitements, the train moved slowly out of the station. Luke unfolded his paper and turned to such items of news as might interest a man who had already read his morning paper. He did not hope to read it for long. Being a man of many aunts, he was fairly certain that the nice old lady in the corner did not propose to travel in silence to London. He was right—a window that needed adjusting, a dropped umbrella, and the old lady was telling him what a good train this was. "Only an hour and ten minutes. That's very good, you know, very good indeed. Much better than the morning one. That takes an hour and forty minutes." She went on: "Of course, nearly everyone goes by the morning one. I mean when it is the cheap way it's silly to go up in the afternoon. I meant to go up this morning, but Wonky Pooh was missing—that's my cat, a Persian; such a beauty, only he's had a painful ear lately—and of course I couldn't leave home till he was found!"

Luke murmured, "Of course not," and let his eyes drop ostentatiously to his paper. But it was of no avail. The flood went on:

"So I just made the best of a bad job and took the afternoon train instead, and, of course, it's a blessing in one way, because it's not so crowded—not that that matters when one is traveling first class. Of course, I don't usually do that, but really I was so upset because, you see, I'm going up on very important business, and I wanted to think out exactly what I was going to say—just quietly, you know." Luke repressed a smile. "So I thought, just for once, the expense was quite permissible. Of course," she went on quickly, with a swift glance at Luke's bronzed face, "I know soldiers on leave have to travel first class, I mean, being officers, it's expected of them."

Luke sustained the inquisitive glance of a pair of bright twinkling eyes. He capitulated at once. It would come to it, he knew, in the end. "I'm not a soldier," he said.

"Oh, I'm so sorry. I didn't mean—I just thought—you were so brown—perhaps home from the East on leave."

"I'm home from the East," said Luke, "but not on leave." He stalled off further researches with a bald statement, "I'm a policeman."

"In the police? Now, really, that's very interesting. A dear friend of mine, her boy has just joined the Palestinian police."

"Mayang Straits," said Luke, taking another short cut.

"Oh, dear; very interesting. Really, it's quite a coincidence—I mean that you should be traveling in this carriage. Because, you see, this business I'm going up to town about—well, actually it is to Scotland Yard I'm going."

"Really?" said Luke.

The old lady continued happily, "Yes, I meant to go up this morning, and then, as I told you, I was so worried about Wonky Pooh. But you don't think it will be too late, do you? I mean there aren't any special office hours at Scotland Yard."

"I don't think they close down at four or anything like that," said Luke.

"No, of course, they couldn't, could they? I mean somebody might want to report a serious crime at any minute, mightn't they?"

"Exactly," said Luke.

For a moment the old lady relapsed into silence. She looked worried. "I always think it's better to go to the fountain-head," she said at last. "John Reed is quite a nice fellow—that's our constable in Wychwood—a very civil-spoken, pleasant man, but I don't feel, you know, that he would be quite the person to deal with anything serious. He's quite used to dealing with people who've drunk too much, or with exceeding the speed limit, or lighting-up time, or people who haven't taken out a dog license, and perhaps with burglary even. But I don't think—I'm quite sure—he isn't the person to deal with murder!"

Luke's eyebrows rose. "Murder?"

The old lady nodded vigorously. "Yes, murder. You're surprised, I can see. I was, myself, at first. I really couldn't believe it. I thought I must be imagining things."

"Are you quite sure you weren't?" Luke asked gently.

"Oh, no." She shook her head positively. "I might have been the first time, but not the second, or the third, or the fourth. After that, one knows."

Luke said, "Do you mean there have been—er—several murders?"

The quiet, gentle voice replied, "A good many, I'm afraid." She went on, "That's why I thought it would be best to go straight to Scotland Yard and tell them about it. Don't you think that's the best thing to do?"

Luke looked at her thoughtfully, then he said, "Why, yes, I think you're quite right."

He thought to himself: "They'll know how to deal with her. Probably get half a dozen old ladies a week coming in burbling about the amount of murders committed in their nice quiet country villages. There may be a special department for dealing with the old dears."

He was roused from these meditations by the thin gentle voice continuing, "You know, I remember reading once—I think it was the Abercrombie case. Of course he'd poisoned quite a lot of people before any suspicion was aroused . . . .What was I saying? Oh, yes, somebody said that there was a look—a special look that he gave anyone, and then, very shortly afterwards, that person would be taken ill. I didn't really believe that when I read about it, but it's true."

"What's true?"

"The look on a person's face." Luke stared at her. She was trembling a little and her nice pink cheeks had lost some of their color. "I saw it first with Amy Gibbs—and she died. And then it was Carter. And Tommy Pierce. But now, yesterday, it was Doctor Humbleby—and he's such a good man—a really good man. Carter, of course, drank, and Tommy Pierce was a dreadfully cheeky, impertinent little boy, and bullied the tiny boys, twisting their arms and pinching them. I didn't feel quite so badly about them, but Doctor Humbleby's different. He must be saved. And the terrible thing is that if I went to him and told him about it, he wouldn't believe me! He'd only laugh! And John Reed wouldn't believe me either. But at Scotland Yard it will be different. Because, naturally, they're used to crime there!"

She glanced out of the window. "Oh, dear, we shall be in in a minute." She fussed a little, opening and shutting her bag, collecting her umbrella. "It's been such a relief talking to you. Most kind of you, I'm sure. So glad you think I'm doing the right thing."

Luke said kindly, "I'm sure they'll give you good advice at Scotland Yard."

"I really am most grateful." She fumbled in her bag. "My card—oh dear, I only have one. I must keep that for Scotland Yard."

"Of course, of course."

"But my name is Fullerton."

"Miss Fullerton," said Luke, smiling. "My name is Luke Fitzwilliam." As the train drew into the platform, he added, "Can I get you a taxi?"

"Oh, no, thank you." Miss Fullerton seemed quite shocked at the idea. "I shall take the tube. That will take me to Trafalgar Square, and I shall walk down Whitehall."

"Well, good luck," said Luke.

Miss Fullerton shook him warmly by the hand. "So kind," she murmured again. "You know, just at first I thought you didn't believe me."

Luke had the grace to blush. "Well," he said. "So many murders! Rather hard to do a lot of murders and get away with it, eh?"

Miss Fullerton shook her head. She said earnestly, "No, no, my dear boy, that's where you're wrong. It's very easy to kill, so long as no one suspects you. And, you see, the person in question is just the last person anyone would suspect."

"Well, anyway, good luck," said Luke.

Miss Fullerton was swallowed up in the crowd. He himself went off in search of his luggage, thinking as he did so: "Just a little bit batty? No, I don't think so. A vivid imagination, that's all. Hope they let her down lightly. Rather an old dear."

2

JIMMY LORRIMER was one of Luke's oldest friends. As a matter of course, Luke stayed with Jimmy as soon as he got to London. It was with Jimmy that he sailed forth on the evening of his arrival in search of amusement. It was Jimmy's coffee that he drank with an aching head the morning after, and it was Jimmy's voice that went unanswered while he read, twice over, a small, insignificant paragraph in the morning paper. "Sorry, Jimmy," he said, coming to himself with a start.

"What were you absorbed in—the political situation?"

Luke grinned. "No fear. No, it's rather queer. Old pussy I traveled up with in the train yesterday got run over."

"Probably trusted to a Belisha Beacon," said Jimmy. "How do you know it's her?"

"Of course, it mayn't be. But it's the same name—Fullerton. She was knocked down and killed by a car as she was crossing Whitehall. The car didn't stop."

"Whoever was driving that car will pay for it. Bring in manslaughter as likely as not. I tell you I'm scared stiff of driving a car nowadays."

"What have you got at present in the way of a car?"

"Ford V-8. I tell you, my boy—"

The conversation became severely mechanical.

It was over a week later that Luke, carelessly scanning the front page of the *Times*, gave a sudden startled exclamation: "Well, I'm damned!"

Jimmy Lorrimer looked up. "What's the matter?"

Luke raised his head and looked at his friend. His expression was so peculiar that Jimmy was quite taken aback. "What's up, Luke? You look as though you'd seen a ghost."

For a minute or two, the other did not reply. He dropped the paper, strode to the window and back again. Jimmy watched him with increasing surprise. Luke dropped into a chair and leaned forward. "Jimmy, old son, do you remember my mentioning an old lady I traveled up to town with the day I arrived in England?"

"The one you said reminded you of your Aunt Mildred? And then she got run over by a car?"

"That's the one. Listen, Jimmy. The old girl came out with a long rigmarole of how she was going up to Scotland Yard to tell them about a lot of murders. There was a murderer loose in her village, that's what it amounted to, and he'd been doing some pretty rapid execution."

"You didn't tell me she was batty," said Jimmy.

"I didn't think she was off her head. She was quite circumstantial; mentioned one or two victims by name, and then explained that what had really rattled her was the fact that she knew who the next victim was going to be."

"Yes?" said Jimmy encouragingly.

"The point is that the man's name was Humbleby—Doctor Humbleby. My old lady said Doctor Humbleby would be the next, and she was distressed because he was 'such a good man.' "

"Well?" said Jimmy.

"Well, look at this." Luke passed over the paper, his finger pressed against an entry in the column of deaths. *Humbleby—On June 12, suddenly, at his residence Sandgate, Wychwood under Ashe, John Ward Humbleby, M.D., beloved husband of Jessie Rose Humbleby. Funeral Friday. No flowers, by request.*

"You see, Jimmy? That's the name and the place, and he's a doctor. What do you make of it?"

Jimmy took a moment or two to answer. His voice was serious when he said, at last, rather uncertainly, "I suppose it's just a damned odd coincidence."

Luke wheeled round suddenly. "Suppose that every word that dear bleating old sheep said was true! Suppose that that fantastic story was just the plain literal truth!"

"Oh, come now, old boy! That would be a bit thick. Things like that don't happen."

"How do you know? They may happen a good deal oftener than you suppose."

"There speaks the police wallah! Can't you forget you're a policeman, now that you've retired into private life?"

"Once a policeman, always a policeman, I suppose," said Luke.

"Now look here, Jimmy. The case stands like this. I was told a story—an improbable but not an impossible story. One piece of evidence—the death of Doctor Humbleby—supports that story. And there's one other significant fact. Miss Fullerton was going to Scotland Yard with this improbable story of hers. But she didn't get there. She was run over and killed by a car that didn't stop."

Jimmy objected, "You don't know that she didn't get there. She might have been killed after her visit, not before."

"She might have been, yes; but I don't think she was."

"That's pure supposition. It boils down to this: You believe in this—this melodrama."

Luke shook his head sharply. "No. I don't say that. All I say is, there's a case for investigation."

"In other words, you are going to Scotland Yard?"

"No, it hasn't come to that yet—not nearly. As you say, this man Humbleby's death may be merely a coincidence."

"Then what, may I ask, is the idea?"

"The idea is to go down to this place and look into the matter."

"So that's the idea, is it?"

"Don't you agree that that is the only sensible way to set about it?"

Jimmy stared at him, then he said, "Are you serious about this business, Luke?"

"Absolutely."

"Suppose the whole thing's a mare's nest?"

"That would be the best thing that could happen."

"Yes, of course." Jimmy frowned. "But you don't think it is, do you?"

"My dear fellow, I'm keeping an open mind."

Jimmy was silent for a minute or two. Then he said, "Got any plan? I mean, you'll have to have some reason for suddenly arriving in this place."

"Yes, I suppose I shall."

"No 'suppose' about it. Do you realize what a small English country town is like? Anyone new sticks out a mile!"

"I shall have to adopt a disguise," said Luke, with a sudden grin. "What do you suggest? Artist? Hardly; I can't draw, let alone paint."

Jimmy said, "Wait a sec. Give me that paper again." Taking it, he gave it a cursory glance and announced triumphantly, "I thought so! Luke, old boy, to put it in a nutshell, I'll fix you O.K. Everything's as easy as winking."

Luke wheeled round. "What?"

Jimmy was continuing with modest pride, "I thought something struck a chord! Wychwood under Ashe. Of course! The very place!"

"Have you, by any chance, a pal who knows the coroner there?"

"Not this time. Better than that, my boy. Nature, as you know, has endowed me plentifully with aunts and cousins; my father having been one of a family of thirteen. Now listen to this: I have a cousin in Wychwood under Ashe."

"Jimmy, you're a blinking marvel."

"It is pretty good, isn't it?" said Jimmy modestly.

"Tell me about him."

"It's a her. Her name's Bridget Conway. For the last two years she's been secretary to Lord Easterfield."

"The man who owns those nasty little weekly papers?"

"That's right. Rather a nasty little man too. Pompous! He was born in Wychwood under Ashe, and being the kind of snob who rams his birth and breeding down your throat and glories in being self-made, he has returned to his home village, bought up the only big house in the neighborhood—it belonged to Bridget's family originally, by the way—and is busy making the place into a model estate."

"And your cousin is his secretary?"

"She was," said Jimmy darkly. "Now she's gone one better! She's engaged to him!"

"Oh!" said Luke, rather taken aback.

"He's a catch, of course," said Jimmy. "Rolling in money. Bridget took rather a toss over some fellow. It pretty well knocked the romance out of her. I dare say this will pan out very well. She'll probably be kind but firm with him and he'll eat out of her hand."

"And where do I come in?"

Jimmy replied promptly, "You go down there to stay. You'd better be another cousin. Bridget's got so many that one more or less won't matter. I'll fix that up with her all right. She and I have always been pals. Now, for your reason for going there—witchcraft, my boy!"

"Witchcraft?"

"Folklore, local superstitions—all that sort of thing. Wychwood under Ashe has got rather a reputation that way. One of the last places where they had a witches' Sabbath; witches were still burnt there in the last century, all sorts of traditions. You're writing a book, see? Correlating the customs of the Mayang Straits and old English folklore—points of resemblance, and so on. You know the sort of stuff. Go round with a notebook and interview the oldest inhabitant about local superstitions and customs. They're quite used to that sort of thing down there, and if you're staying at Ashe Manor, it vouches for you."

"What about Lord Easterfield?"

"He'll be all right. He's quite uneducated and completely credulous—actually believes things he reads in his own papers.

Anyway, Bridget will fix him. Bridget's all right. I'll answer for her."

Luke drew a deep breath. "Jimmy, old scout, it looks as though the thing was going to be easy. You're a wonder. If you can really fix me up with your cousin—"

"That will be absolutely O.K. Leave it to me."

"I'm no end grateful to you."

Jimmy said, "All I ask is, if you're hunting down a homicidal murderer, let me be in at the death." He added sharply, "What is it?"

Luke said slowly, "Just something I remembered my old lady saying to me. I'd said to her that it was a bit thick to do a lot of murders and get away with it, and she answered that I was wrong—that it was very easy to kill." He stopped, and then said slowly, "I wonder if that's true, Jimmy? I wonder if it is—"

"What?"

"—easy to kill."

3

THE JUNE SUN was shining when Luke came over the hill and down into the little country town of Wychwood under Ashe. It lay innocently and peacefully in the sunlight; mainly composed of a long straggling street that ran along under the overhanging brow of Ashe Ridge. It seemed singularly remote, strangely untouched. Luke thought: *I'm probably mad. The whole thing's fantastic.*

He drove gently down the twisting road, and so entered the main street. Wychwood, as has been said, consisted mainly of its one principal street. There were shops, small Georgian houses, prim and aristocratic, with whitened steps and polished knockers; there were picturesque cottages with flower gardens. There was an inn, the Bells and Motley, standing a little back from the street. There was a village green and a duck pond, and presiding over them a dignified Georgian house which Luke thought at first must be his destination, Ashe Manor. But on coming nearer he saw that there was a large painted board announcing that it was the Museum and Library. Farther on there was an anachronism, a large white modern building, austere and irrelevant to the cheerful haphazardness of the rest of the place. It was, Luke gathered, a local Institute and Lad's Club. It was at this point that he stopped and asked the way to his destination.

He was told that Ashe Manor was about half a mile farther on; he would see the gates on his right. Luke continued his course. He found the gates easily; they were of new and elaborate wrought iron. He drove in, caught a gleam of red brick through the trees, and turned a corner of the drive to be stupefied by the appalling and incongruous castellated mass that greeted his eyes.

While he was contemplating the nightmare, the sun went in. He became suddenly conscious of the overlying menace of Ashe Ridge. There was a sudden sharp gust of wind, blowing back the leaves of the trees, and at that moment a girl came round the corner of the castellated mansion. Her black hair was blown up off her head by the sudden gust, and Luke was reminded of a picture he had once seen—Nevinson's Witch. The long, pale, delicate face, the black hair flying up to the stars. He could see this girl on a broomstick flying up to the moon. She came straight toward him. "You must be Luke Fitzwilliam. I'm Bridget Conway."

He took the hand she held out. He could see her now as she was—not in a sudden moment of fantasy. Tall, slender, a long delicate face with slightly hollow cheekbones, ironic black brows, black eyes and hair. She was like a delicate etching, he thought—poignant and beautiful. He said, "How d'you do? I must apologize for wishing myself on you like this. Jimmy would have it that you wouldn't mind."

"Oh, we don't. We're delighted." She smiled, a sudden curving smile that brought the corners of her mouth halfway up her cheeks. "Jimmy and I always stand in together. And if you're writing a book on folklore, this is a splendid place. All sorts of legends and picturesque spots."

"Splendid," said Luke.

They went together toward the house. Luke stole another glance at it. He discerned now traces of a sober Queen Anne dwelling overlaid and smothered by the florid magnificence. He remembered that Jimmy had mentioned the house as having originally belonged to Bridget's family. That, he thought, grimly, was in its unadorned days. Inside, Bridget Conway led the way to a room with book shelves and comfortable chairs where a tea table stood near the window with two people sitting by it. She said, "Gordon, this is Luke, a sort of cousin of mine."

Lord Easterfield was a small man with a semibald head. His face was round and ingenuous, with a pouting mouth and boiled gooseberry eyes. He was dressed in careless-looking country clothes. They were unkind to his figure, which ran mostly to stomach. He greeted Luke with affability, "Glad to see you—very glad. Just come back from the East, I hear. Interesting place. Writing a book, so Bridget tells me.

They say too many books are written nowadays. I say 'no,' always room for a good one."

Bridget said, "My aunt, Mrs. Anstruther," and Luke shook hands with a middle-aged woman with a rather foolish mouth.

Mrs. Anstruther, as Luke soon learned, was devoted, body and soul, to gardening. After acknowledging the introduction, she said now, "I believe those new rock roses would do perfectly in this climate," and proceeded to immerse herself in catalogues.

Throwing his squat little figure back in his chair, Lord Easterfield sipped his tea and studied Luke appraisingly.

"So you write books," he murmured. Feeling slightly nervous, Luke was about to enter on explanations, when he perceived that Lord Easterfield was not really seeking for information. "I've often thought," said His Lordship complacently, "that I'd like to write a book myself. Trouble is, I haven't got the time. I'm a very busy man."

"Of course. You must be."

"You wouldn't believe what I've got on my shoulders," said Lord Easterfield. "I take a personal interest in each one of my publications. I consider that I'm responsible for molding the public mind. Next week millions of people will be thinking and feeling just exactly what I've intended to make them feel and think. That's a very solemn thought. That means responsibility. Well, I don't mind responsibility. I'm not afraid of it. I can do with responsibility."

Lord Easterfield swelled out his chest, attempted to draw in his stomach, and glared amiably at Luke. Bridget Conway said lightly, "You're a great man, Gordon. Have some more tea."

Lord Easterfield replied simply, "I am a great man. No, I won't have any more tea." Then, descending from his own Olympian heights to the level of more ordinary mortals, he inquired kindly of his guest: "Know anybody round this part of the world?"

Luke shook his head. Then, on an impulse, and feeling that the sooner he began to get down to his job the better, he added: "At least, there's a man here that I promised to look up—friend of mine. Man called Humbleby. He's a doctor."

"Oh!" Lord Easterfield struggled upright in his chair. "Doctor Humbleby? Pity."

"What's a pity?"

"Died about a week ago," said Lord Easterfield.

"Oh, dear," said Luke. "I'm sorry about that."

"Don't think you'd have cared for him," said Lord Easterfield. "Opinionated, pestilential, muddle-headed old fool."

"Which means," put in Bridget, "that he disagreed with Gordon."

"Question of our water supply," said Lord Easterfield. "I may tell you, Mr. Fitzwilliam, that I'm a public-spirited man. I've got the welfare of this town at heart. I was born here. Yes, born in this very town."

Exhaustive details of Lord Easterfield's career were produced for Luke's benefit, and the former wound up triumphantly: "Do you know what stands where my father's shop used to be? A fine building, built and endowed by me—Institute, Boy's Club, everything tiptop and up to date. Employed the best architect in the country! I must say he's made a bare plain job of it—looks like a workhouse or a prison to me—but they say it's all right, so I suppose it must be."

"Cheer up," said Bridget. "You had your own way over this house."

Lord Easterfield chuckled appreciatively. "Yes, they tried to put it over on me here! When one architect wouldn't do what I wanted, I sacked him and got another. The fellow I got in the end understood my ideas pretty well."

"He pandered to your worst flights of imagination," said Bridget.

"She'd have liked the place left as it was," said Lord Easterfield. He patted her arm. "No use living in the past, my dear. I always had a fancy for a castle, and now I've got one!"

"Well," said Luke, a little at a loss for words, "it's a great thing to know what you want."

"And I usually get it too," said the other, chuckling.

"You nearly didn't get your way about the water scheme," Bridget reminded him.

"Oh, that!" said Lord Easterfield. "Humbleby was a fool. These elderly men are inclined to be pigheaded. They won't listen to reason."

"Doctor Humbleby was rather an outspoken man, wasn't he?" Luke ventured. "He made a good many enemies that way, I should imagine."

"N-no, I don't know that I should say that," demurred Lord Easterfield, rubbing his nose. "Eh, Bridget?"

"He was very popular with everyone, I always thought," said Bridget. "I only saw him when he came about my ankle that time, but I thought he was a dear."

"Yes, he was popular enough, on the whole," admitted Lord Easterfield. "Though I know one or two people who had it in for him. Lots of little feuds and cliques in a place like this," he said.

"Yes, I suppose so," said Luke. He hesitated, uncertain of his next step. "What sort of people live here mostly?" he queried.

It was rather a weak question, but he got an instant response. "Relicts, mostly," said Bridget. "Clergymen's daughters and sisters and wives. Doctors' dittos. About six women to every man."

"But there are some men?" hazarded Luke.

"Oh, yes, there's Mr. Abbot, the solicitor, and young Doctor Thomas, Doctor Humbleby's partner, and Mr. Wake, the rector, and—Who else is there, Gordon? Oh! Mr. Ellsworthy, who keeps the antique shop. And Major Horton and his bulldogs."

"There's somebody else I believe my friends mentioned as living down here," said Luke. "They said she was a nice old pussy, but talked a lot. What was the name, now? I've got it. Fullerton."

Lord Easterfield said, with a hoarse chuckle, "Really, you've no luck! She's dead too. Got run over the other day in London. Killed outright."

"You seem to have a lot of deaths here," said Luke lightly.

Lord Easterfield bridled immediately. "Not at all. One of the healthiest places in England. Can't count accidents. They may happen to anyone."

But Bridget Conway said thoughtfully, "As a matter of fact, Gordon, there have been a lot of deaths in the last year. They're always having funerals."

"Nonsense, my dear."

Luke said, "Was Doctor Humbleby's death an accident too?"

Lord Easterfield shook his head. "Oh, no," he said. "Humbleby died of acute septicemia. Just like a doctor. Scratched his finger with a rusty nail or something, paid no attention to it, and it turned septic. He was dead in three days."

"Doctors are rather like that," said Bridget. "And of course they're very liable to infection, I suppose, if they don't take care. It was sad though. His wife was broken-hearted."

"No good of rebelling against the will of Providence," said Lord Easterfield easily.

But was it the will of Providence? Luke asked himself later as he changed into his dinner jacket. Septicemia? Perhaps. A very sudden death though. And there echoed through his head Bridget Conway's lightly spoken words: "—there have been a lot of deaths in the last year."

LUKE HAD THOUGHT out his plan of campaign with some care, and prepared to put it into action without more ado when he came down to breakfast the following morning. The gardening aunt was not in evidence, but Lord Easterfield was eating kidneys and drinking coffee, and Bridget Conway had finished her meal and was standing at the window looking out. After good-mornings had been exchanged and Luke had sat down with a plentifully heaped plate of eggs and bacon, he began.

"I must get to work," he said. "Difficult thing is to induce people to talk. You know what I mean; not people like you and—er—Bridget." He remembered just in time not to say "Miss Conway." "You'd tell me anything you knew. But the trouble is, you wouldn't know the things I want to know—that is, the local superstitions. You'd hardly believe the amount of superstition that still lingers in out-of-the-way parts of the world. Why, there's a village in Devonshire. The rector had to remove some old granite menhirs that stood by the church, because the people persisted in marching round them in some old ritual every time there was a death. Extraordinary how old heathen rites persist."

Here followed almost verbatim a page of a work that Luke had read up for the occasion. "Deaths are the most hopeful line," he ended. "Burial rites and customs always survive longer than any others. Besides, for some reason or other, village people always like talking about deaths."

"They enjoy funerals," agreed Bridget from the window.

"I thought I'd make that my starting point," went on Luke. "If I can get a list of recent demises in the parish, track down the relatives and get into conversation, I've no doubt I shall soon get a hint of what I'm after. Who had I better get the data from—the parson?"

"Mr. Wake would probably be very interested," said Bridget. "He's quite an old dear and a bit of an antiquary. He could give you a lot of stuff, I expect."

Luke had a momentary qualm during which he hoped that the clergyman might not be so efficient an antiquary as to expose his own pretensions. Aloud, he said heartily, "Good. You've no idea, I suppose, of likely people who've died during the last year."

Bridget murmured, "Let me see. Carter, of course. He was the landlord of the Seven Stars, that nasty little pub down by the river."

"A drunken ruffian," said Lord Easterfield. "One of these socialistic, abusive brutes. A good riddance."

"And Mrs. Rose, the laundress," went on Bridget. "And little Tommy Pierce; he was a nasty little boy, if you like. Oh, of course, and that girl Amy What's-Her-Name?" Her voice changed slightly as she uttered the last name.

"Amy?" said Luke.

"Amy Gibbs. She was housemaid here, and then she went to Miss Waynflete. There was an inquest on her."

"Why?"

"Fool of a girl mixed up some bottles in the dark," said Lord Easterfield.

"She took what she thought was cough mixture, and it was hat paint," explained Bridget.

Luke raised his eyebrows. "Somewhat of a tragedy."

Bridget said, "There was some idea of her having done it on purpose. Some row with a young man." She spoke slowly, almost reluctantly. There was a pause. Luke felt instinctively the presence of some unspoken feeling weighing down the atmosphere.

He thought, "Amy Gibbs? Yes, that was one of the names old Miss Fullerton mentioned." She had also mentioned a small boy—Tommy someone—of whom she had evidently held a low opinion—this, it seemed, was shared by Bridget. And, yes, he was almost sure; the name Carter had been spoken too. Rising, he said lightly, "Talking like this makes me feel rather ghoulish—as though I dabbled only in graveyards. Marriage customs are interesting, too, but rather more difficult to introduce into conversation unconcernedly."

"I should imagine that was likely," said Bridget, with a faint twitch of the lips.

"Ill-wishing or overlooking—there's another interesting subject," went on Luke, with a would-be show of enthusiasm. "You often get that in these Old World places. Know of any gossip of that kind here?"

Lord Easterfield slowly shook his head.

Bridget Conway said, "We shouldn't be likely to hear of things like that."

Luke took it up almost before she finished speaking: "No doubt about it, I've got to move in lower social spheres to get what I want. I'll be off to the vicarage first and see what I can get there. After there perhaps a visit to the—Seven Stars, did you say? And what about the small boy of unpleasant habits? Did he leave any sorrowing relatives?"

"Mrs. Pierce keeps a tobacco and paper shop in High Street."

"That," said Luke, "is nothing less than providential. Well, I'll be on my way."

With a swift, graceful movement, Bridget moved from the window. "I think," she said, "I'll come with you, if you don't mind."

"Of course not." He said it as heartily as possible, but he wondered if she had noticed that, just for a moment, he had been taken aback. It would have been easier for him to handle an elderly antiquarian clergyman without an alert, discerning intelligence by his side. "Oh, well," he thought to himself. "It's up to me to do my stuff convincingly."

Bridget said, "Will you just wait, Luke, whilst I change my shoes?"

Luke, the Christian name, uttered so easily, gave him a queer warm feeling. And yet what else could she have called him? Since she had agreed to Jimmy's scheme of cousinship, she could hardly call him Mr. Fitzwilliam. He thought, suddenly and uneasily, "What does she think of it all? What does she think?" He had thought of her—if he had thought of her at all—as a little blond secretary person, astute enough to have captured a rich man's fancy. Instead she had force, brains, a cool clear intelligence, and he had no idea what she was thinking of him. He thought: "She's not an easy person to deceive."

"I'm ready now." She had joined him so silently that he had not heard her approach. She wore no hat, and there was no net on her hair. As they stepped out from the house, the wind, sweeping round the corner of the castellated monstrosity, caught her long black hair and whipped it into a sudden frenzy round her face.

Looking back at the battlements behind him, he said irritably, "What an abomination! Couldn't anyone stop him?"

Bridget answered, "An Englishman's house is his castle—literally so in Gordon's case! He adores it."

Conscious that the remark was in bad taste, yet unable to control his tongue, he said: "It's your old home, isn't it? Do you 'adore' to see it the way it is now?"

She looked at him then—a steady, slightly amused look, it was. "I hate to destroy the dramatic picture you are building up," she murmured. "But actually I left here when I was two and a half, so you see the old-home motive doesn't apply. I can't even remember this place."

"You're right," said Luke. "Forgive the lapse into film language."

She laughed. "Truth," she said, "is seldom romantic." And there was a sudden bitter scorn in her voice that startled him. He flushed a deep red under his tan, then realized suddenly that the bitterness had not been aimed at him. It was her own scorn and her own bitterness. Luke was wisely silent. But he wondered a good deal about Bridget Conway.

Five minutes brought them to the church and to the vicarage that adjoined it. They found the vicar in his study. Alfred Wake was a small stooping old man with very mild blue eyes and an absent-minded but courteous air. He seemed pleased, but a little surprised by the visit.

"Mr. Fitzwilliam is staying with us at Ashe Manor," said Bridget, "and he wants to consult you about a book he is writing."

Mr. Wake turned his mild, inquiring eyes toward the younger man, and Luke plunged into explanations. He was nervous—doubly so. Nervous, in the first place, because this man had no doubt a far deeper knowledge of folklore and superstitious rites and customs than one could acquire by merely hurriedly cramming from a haphazard collection of books. Secondly, he was nervous because Bridget Conway was standing by, listening.

Luke was relieved to find that Mr. Wake's special interest was Roman remains. He confessed gently that he knew very little of medieval folklore and witchcraft. He mentioned the existence of certain items in the history of Wychwood, offered to take Luke to the particular ledge of hill where it was said the witches' Sabbaths had been held, but expressed himself regretful that he could add no special information of his own.

Inwardly much relieved, Luke expressed himself as somewhat disappointed, and then plunged into inquiries as to deathbed superstitions.

Mr. Wake shook his head gently. "I am afraid I should be the last person to know about those. My parishioners would be careful to keep anything unorthodox from my ears."

"That's so, of course."

"But I've no doubt, all the same, there is a lot of superstition still rife. These village communities are very backward."

Luke plunged boldly. "I've been asking Miss Conway for a list of all the recent deaths she could remember. I thought I might get at something that way. I suppose you could supply me with a list, so that I could pick out the likelies."

"Yes, yes; that could be managed. Giles, our sexton, a good fellow, but sadly deaf, could help you there. Let me see now. There have been a good many—a good many—a treacherous spring and a hard winter behind it—and then a good many accidents. Quite a cycle of bad luck there seems to have been."

"Sometimes," said Luke, "a cycle of bad luck is attributed to the presence of a particular person."

"Yes, yes. The old story of Jonah. But I do not think there have been any strangers here—nobody that is to say, outstanding in any way—and I've certainly never heard any rumor of such a feeling, but then again, as I said, perhaps I shouldn't. Now, let me see. Quite recently we have had Doctor Humbleby and poor Lavinia Fullerton. A fine man, Doctor Humbleby."

Bridget put in, "Mr. Fitzwilliam knows friends of his."

"Do you indeed? Very sad. His loss will be much felt. A man with many friends."

"But surely a man with some enemies, too," said Luke. "I'm only going by what I've heard my friends say," he went on hastily.

Mr. Wake sighed. "A man who spoke his mind, and a man who wasn't always very tactful, shall we say?" He shook his head. "It does get people's backs up. But he was greatly beloved among the poorer classes."

Luke said carelessly, "You know, I always feel that one of the most unpalatable facts to be faced in life is the fact that every death that occurs means a gain to someone—I don't mean only financially."

The vicar nodded thoughtfully. "I see your meaning, yes. We read in an obituary notice that a man is regretted by everybody, but that can only be true very rarely, I fear. In Doctor Humbleby's case, there is no denying that his partner, Doctor Thomas, will find his position very much improved by Doctor Humbleby's death."

"How is that?"

"Thomas, I believe, is a very capable fellow—certainly Humbleby always said so—but he didn't get on here very well. He was, I think, overshadowed by Humbleby, who was a man of very definite magnetism. Thomas appeared rather colorless in contrast. He didn't impress his patients at all. I think he worried over it, too, and that made him worse—more nervous and tongue-tied. As a matter of fact, I've noticed an astonishing difference already. More aplomb, more personality. I think he feels a new confidence in himself. He and Humbleby didn't always agree, I believe. Thomas was all for newer methods of treatment and Humbleby preferred to stick to the old ways. There were clashes between them more than once—over that as well as over a matter nearer home. But there, I mustn't gossip."

Bridget said softly and clearly, "But I think Mr. Fitzwilliam would like you to gossip."

Luke shot her a quick, disturbed look.

Mr. Wake shook his head doubtfully and then went on, smiling a little in deprecation: "I am afraid one learns to take too much interest in one's neighbors' affairs. Rose Humbleby is a very pretty girl. One doesn't wonder that Geoffrey Thomas lost his heart. And of course Humbleby's point of view was quite understandable, too—the girl is young, and buried away here, she hadn't much chance of seeing other men."

"He objected?" said Luke.

"Very definitely. Said they were far too young. And of course young people resent being told that. There was a very definite coldness between the two men. But I must say that I'm sure Doctor Thomas was deeply distressed at his partner's unexpected death."

"Septicemia, Lord Easterfield told me."

"Yes, just a little scratch that got infected. Doctors run grave risks in the course of their profession, Mr. Fitzwilliam."

"They do indeed," said Luke.

Mr. Wake gave a sudden start. "But I have wandered a long way from what we were talking about," he said. "A gossiping old man, I am afraid. We were speaking of the survival of pagan death customs and of recent deaths. There was Lavinia Fullerton—one of our most kindly church helpers. Then there was that poor girl, Amy Gibbs; you might discover something in your line there, Mr. Fitzwilliam. There was just a suspicion, you know, that it might have been suicide, and there are certain rather eerie rites in connection with that type of death. There is an aunt—not, I fear, a very estimable woman, and not very much attached to her niece, but a great talker."

"Valuable," said Luke.

"Then there was Tommy Pierce; he was in the choir at one time—a beautiful treble—quite angelic, but not a very angelic boy otherwise, I am afraid. We had to get rid of him in the end; he made the other boys behave badly too. Poor lad, I'm afraid he was not very much liked anywhere. He was dismissed from the post office, where we got him a job as telegraph boy. He was in Mr. Abbot's office for a while, but there again he was dismissed very soon—interfered with some confidential papers, I believe. Then, of course, he was at Ashe Manor for a time—wasn't he, Miss Conway?—as a garden boy, and Lord Easterfield had to discharge him for gross impertinence. I was so sorry for his mother—a very decent hardworking soul. Miss Waynflete very kindly got him some odd window-cleaning work. Lord Easterfield objected at first, then suddenly he gave in; actually, it was sad that he did so."

"Why?"

"Because the boy was killed that way. He was cleaning the top windows of the library—the old hall, you know—and tried some silly fooling—dancing on the window ledge or something of that sort—lost his balance, or else became dizzy, and fell. A nasty business! He never recovered consciousness and died a few hours after they got him to the hospital."

"Did anyone else see him fall?" asked Luke with interest.

"No. He was on the garden side, not the front of the house. They estimate he lay there for about half an hour before anyone found him."

"Who did find him?"

"Miss Fullerton. You remember, the lady I mentioned just now who was unfortunately killed in a street accident the other day. Poor soul, she was terribly upset. A nasty experience! She had obtained permission to take a cutting of some plants and found the boy there, lying where he had fallen."

"It must have been a very unpleasant shock," said Luke thoughtfully. "A greater shock," he thought to himself, "than you know."

"He was a disgusting bully," said Bridget. "You know he was, Mr. Wake. Always tormenting cats and stray puppies and pinching other little boys."

"I know—I know." Mr. Wake shook his head sadly. "But you know, my dear Miss Conway, sometimes cruelty is not so much innate as due to the fact that imagination is slow in ripening. That is why, if you conceive of a grown man with the mentality of a child, you realize that the cunning and brutality of a lunatic may be quite unrealized by the man himself. A lack of growth somewhere, that, I am convinced, is at the root of much of the cruelty and stupid brutality in the world today. One must put away childish things—" He shook his head and spread out his hands.

Bridget said, in a voice suddenly hoarse, "Yes, you're right. I know what you mean. A man who is a child is the most frightening thing in the world."

Luke Fitzwilliam wondered very much who the person Bridget was thinking of might be.

5

MR. WAKE murmured a few more names to himself.

"Let me see now. Poor Mrs. Rose, and old Bell, and that child of the Elkins', and Harry Carter. They're not all my people, you understand. Mrs. Rose and Carter were dissenters. And that cold spell in March took off poor old Ben Stanbury at last—ninety-two he was."

"Amy Gibbs died in April," said Bridget.

"Yes, poor girl; a sad mistake to happen."

Luke looked up to find Bridget watching him. She lowered her eyes quickly. He thought, with some annoyance: "There's something here that I haven't got on to. Something to do with this girl, Amy Gibbs." When they had taken leave of the vicar and were outside again, he said: "Just who and what was Amy Gibbs?"

Bridget took a minute or two to answer. Then she said—and Luke noticed the slight constraint in her voice—"Amy was one of the most inefficient housemaids I have ever known."

"That's why she got the sack?"

"No. She stayed out after hours, playing about with some young man. Gordon has very moral and old-fashioned views. Sin, in his view, does not take place until after eleven o'clock, but then it is rampant. So he gave the girl notice and she was impertinent about it!"

Luke asked, "She's the one who swallowed off hat paint in mistake for cough mixture?"

"Yes."

"Rather a stupid thing to do," Luke hazarded.

"Very stupid."

"Was she stupid?"

"No, she was quite a sharp girl."

Luke stole a look at her. He was puzzled. Her replies were given in an even tone, without emphasis or even much interest. But behind what she said there was, he felt convinced, something not put into words.

At that moment Bridget stopped to speak to a tall man who swept off his hat and greeted her with breezy heartiness. Bridget, after a word or two, introduced Luke, "This is my cousin, Mr. Fitzwilliam, who is staying at the Manor. He's down here to write a book. This is Mr. Abbot."

Luke looked at Mr. Abbot with some interest. This was the solicitor who had employed Tommy Pierce. Mr. Abbot was not at all the conventional type of lawyer, he was neither thin, spare, nor tight-lipped. He was a big florid man, dressed in tweeds, with a hearty manner and a jovial effusiveness. There were little creases at the corners of his eyes, and the eyes themselves were more shrewd than one appreciated in a first casual glance. "Writing a book, eh? Novel?"

"Folklore," said Bridget.

"You've come to the right place for that," said the lawyer. "Wonderfully interesting part of the world here."

"So I've been led to understand," said Luke. "I dare say you could help me a bit. You must come across curious old deeds or know of some interesting surviving customs."

"Well, I don't know about that. Maybe—maybe."

"No haunted houses?"

"No, I don't know of anything of that kind."

"There's the child superstition, of course," said Luke. "Death of a boy child—a violent death, that is—the boy always walks. Not a girl child—interesting that."

"Very," said Mr. Abbot. "I never heard that before."

Since Luke had just invented it, that was hardly surprising. "Seems there's a boy here—Tommy something—was in your office at one time. I've reason to believe they think that he's walking."

Mr. Abbot's red face turned slightly purple. "Tommy Pierce? A good-for-nothing, prying, meddlesome jackanapes. Who's seen him? What's this story?"

"These things are difficult to pin down," said Luke. "People won't come out into the open with a statement. It's just in the air, so to speak."

"Yes, yes, I suppose so."

Luke changed the subject adroitly. "The real person to get hold of is the local doctor. They hear a lot in the poorer cases they attend. All sorts of superstitions and charms—probably love philters and all the rest of it."

"You must get on to Thomas. Good fellow, Thomas, thoroughly up-to-date man. Not like poor old Humbleby."

"Bit of a reactionary, wasn't he?"

"Absolutely pigheaded; a diehard of the worst description."

"You had a real row over the water scheme, didn't you?" asked Bridget.

Again a rich ruddy glow suffused Abbot's face. "Humbleby stood dead in the way of progress," he said sharply. "He held out against the scheme! He was pretty rude, too, in what he said. Didn't mince his words. Some of the things he said to me were positively actionable."

Bridget murmured, "But lawyers never go to law, do they? They know better."

Abbot laughed immoderately. His anger subsided as quickly as it had risen. "Pretty good, Miss Bridget! And you're not far wrong. We who are in it know too much about the law, ha-ha. Well, I must be getting along. Give me a call if you think I can help you in any way, Mr.— er—"

"Fitzwilliam," said Luke. "Thanks, I will."

As they walked on, Bridget said, "If you want to hear more about Amy Gibbs, I can take you to someone who could help you."

"Who is that?"

"A Miss Waynflete. Amy went there after she left the Manor. She was there when she died."

"Oh, I see." He was a little taken aback. "Well, thank you very much."

"She lives just here."

They were crossing the village green. Inclining her head in the direction of the big Georgian house that Luke had noticed the day before, Bridget said: "That's Wych Hall. It's a library now."

Adjoining the Hall was a little house that looked rather like a doll's house in proportion. Its steps were dazzlingly white, its knocker shone and its window curtains showed white and prim. Bridget pushed open the gate and advanced to the steps. As she did so, the front door opened and an elderly woman came out. She was, Luke thought, completely the country spinster. Her thin form was neatly dressed in a tweed coat and skirt, and she wore a gray silk blouse with a cairngorm brooch. Her hat, a conscientious felt, sat squarely upon her well-shaped head. Her face was pleasant and her eyes, through their pince-nez, decidedly intelligent.

"Good morning, Miss Waynflete," said Bridget. "This is Mr. Fitzwilliam." Luke bowed. "He's writing a book—about deaths and village customs and general gruesomeness."

"Oh, dear," said Miss Waynflete. "How very interesting." And she beamed encouragingly upon him.

He was reminded of Miss Fullerton.

"I thought," said Bridget—and again he noted that curious flat tone in her voice—"that you might tell him something about Amy."

"Oh," said Miss Waynflete. "About Amy? Yes. About Amy Gibbs." He was conscious of a new factor in her expression. She seemed to be thoughtfully summing him up. Then, as though coming to a decision, she drew back into the hall. "Do come in," she said. "I can go out later. No, no"—in answer to a protest from Luke—"I had really nothing important to do. Just a little unimportant shopping." The small drawing room was exquisitely neat and smelled faintly of burnt lavender. Miss Waynflete offered her guests chairs, and then said apologetically, "I'm afraid I don't smoke myself, so I have no cigarettes, but do please smoke if you like." Luke refused, but Bridget promptly lighted a cigarette.

Sitting bolt upright in a chair with carved arms, Miss Waynflete studied her guest for a moment or two, and then, dropping her eyes as though satisfied, she said: "You want to know about that poor girl, Amy? The whole thing was very sad and caused me a great deal of distress. Such a tragic mistake."

"Wasn't there some question of—suicide?" asked Luke.

Miss Waynflete shook her head. "No, no, that I cannot believe for a moment. Amy was not at all that type."

"What type was she?" asked Luke bluntly. "I'd like to hear your account of her."

Miss Waynflete said, "Well, of course, she wasn't at all a good servant. But nowadays, really, one is thankful to get anybody. She was very slipshod over her work and always wanting to go out. Well, of course, she was young and girls are like that nowadays. They don't seem to realize that their time is their employer's."

Luke looked properly sympathetic and Miss Waynflete proceeded to develop her theme. "She was fond of admiration," went on Miss Waynflete, "and was inclined to think a lot of herself. Mr. Ellsworthy—he keeps the new antique shop, but he is actually a gentleman—he dabbles a little in water colors and he had done one or two sketches of the girl's head—and I think you know, that that rather gave her ideas. She was rather inclined to quarrel with the young man she was engaged to—Jim Harvey. He's a mechanic at the garage and very fond of her." Miss Waynflete paused and then went on, "I shall never forget that dreadful night. Amy had been out of sorts; a nasty cough and one thing and another—those silly, cheap silk stockings they will wear, and shoes with paper soles, practically, of course, they catch chills—and she'd been to the doctor that afternoon."

Luke asked quickly, "Doctor Humbleby or Doctor Thomas?"

"Doctor Thomas. And he gave her a bottle of cough mixture that she brought back with her. Something quite harmless—a stock mixture, I believe. She went to bed early, and it must have been about one in the morning when the noise began—an awful kind of choking scream. I got up and went to her door, but it was locked on the inside. I called to her, but couldn't get any answer. Cook was with me, and we were both terribly upset. And then we went to the front door and, luckily, there was Reed—our constable—just passing on his beat, and we called to him. He went round the back of the house and managed to climb up on the outhouse roof, and as her window was open, he got in quite easily that way and unlocked the door. Poor girl, it was terrible. They couldn't do anything for her, and she died in hospital a few hours later."

"And it was—what?—hat paint?"

"Yes. Oxalic-acid poisoning is what they called it. The bottle was about the same size as the coughlinctus one. The latter was on her washstand and the hat paint was by her bed. She must have picked up the wrong bottle and put it by her in the dark, ready to take if she felt badly. That was the theory at the inquest."

Miss Waynflete stopped. Her intelligent goat's eyes looked at him, and he was aware that some particular significance lay behind them. He had the feeling that she was leaving some part of the story untold, and a stronger feeling that, for some reason, she wanted him to be aware of the fact.

There was a silence—a long and rather difficult silence. Luke felt like an actor who does not know his cue. He said rather weakly, "And you don't think it was suicide?"

Miss Waynflete said promptly, "Certainly not. If the girl had decided to make away with herself, she would have bought something, probably. This was an old bottle of stuff that she must have had for years. And anyway, as I've told you, she wasn't that kind of girl."

"So you think—what?" said Luke bluntly.

Miss Waynflete said, "I think it was very unfortunate." She closed her lips and looked at him earnestly.

Just when Luke was feeling that he must try desperately to say something anticipated, a diversion occurred. There was a scratching at the door and a plaintive mew. Miss Waynflete sprang up and went to open the door, whereupon a magnificent orange Persian walked in. He paused, looked disapprovingly at the visitor, and sprang up on the arm of Miss Waynflete's chair. Miss Waynflete addressed him in a cooing voice. "Why, Wonky Pooh! Where's my Wonky Pooh been all the morning?"

The name struck a chord of memory. Where had he heard something about a Persian cat called Wonky Pooh? He said, "That's a very handsome cat. Have you had him long?"

Miss Waynflete shook her head. "Oh, no, he belonged to an old friend of mine, Miss Fullerton. She was run over by one of these horrid motorcars, and, of course, I couldn't have let Wonky Pooh go to strangers. Lavinia would have been most upset. She simply worshipped him—and he is very beautiful, isn't he?"

Luke admired the cat gravely. Miss Waynflete said, "Be careful of his ears. They've been rather painful lately."

Luke stroked the animal warily. Bridget rose to her feet. She said, "We must be going."

Miss Waynflete shook hands with Luke. "Perhaps," she said, "I shall see you again before long."

Luke said cheerfully, "I hope so, I'm sure." He thought she looked puzzled and a little disappointed. Her gaze shifted to Bridget—a rapid look with a hint of interrogation in it. Luke felt that there was some understanding between the two women from which he was excluded. It annoyed him, but he promised himself to get to the bottom of it before long. Miss Waynflete came out with them. Luke stood a minute on the top of the steps, looking with approval on the untouched primness of the village green and the duck pond. "Marvelously unspoilt, this place," he said.

Miss Waynflete's face lit up. "Yes, indeed," she said eagerly. "Really, it is still just as I remember it as a child. We lived in the Hall, you know. But when it came to my brother, he did not care to live in it—indeed, could not afford to do so—and it was put up for sale. A builder had made an offer and was, I believe, going to 'develop the land'—I think that was the phrase. Fortunately, Lord Easterfield stepped in and acquired the property and saved it. He turned the house into a library and museum, really it is practically untouched. I act as librarian twice a week there—unpaid, of course—and I can't tell you what a pleasure it is to be in the old place and know that it will not be vandalized. And really it is a perfect setting; you must visit our little museum one day, Mr. Fitzwilliam. There are some quite interesting local exhibits."

"I certainly shall make a point of doing so, Miss Waynflete."

"Lord Easterfield has been a great benefactor to Wychwood," said Miss Waynflete. "It grieves me that there are people who are sadly ungrateful."

Her lips pressed themselves together. Luke discreetly asked no questions. He said good-by again.

When they were outside the gate, Bridget said, "Do you want to pursue further researches, or shall we go home by way of the river? It's a pleasant walk."

Luke answered promptly. He had no mind for further investigations, with Bridget Conway standing by listening. He said, "Go around by the river, by all means."

They walked along the High Street. One of the last houses had a sign decorated in old gold lettering with the word ANTIQUES on it. Luke paused and peered through one of the windows into the cool depths. "Rather a nice slipware dish there," he remarked. "Do for an aunt of mine. Wonder how much they want for it?"

"Shall we go in and see?"

"Do you mind? I like pottering about antique shops. Sometimes one picks up a good bargain."

"I doubt if you will here," said Bridget dryly. "Ellsworthy knows the value of his stuff pretty accurately, I should say."

The door was open. In the hall were chairs and settees and dressers with china and pewter in them. Two rooms full of goods opened at either side. Luke went into the room on the left and picked up the slipware dish. At the same moment a dim figure came forward from the back of the room, where he had been sitting at a Queen Anne walnut desk. "Ah, dear Miss Conway, what a pleasure to see you."

"Good morning, Mr. Ellsworthy."

Mr. Ellsworthy was a thin young man dressed in russet brown. He had a long pale face and long black hair. Luke was introduced, and Mr. Ellsworthy immediately transferred his attention to him. "Genuine old English slipware. Lovely, isn't it? I have some good pieces, but I hate to sell them. It's always been my dream to live in the country and have a little shop. Marvelous place, Wychwood; it has atmosphere, if you know what I mean."

"The artistic temperament," murmured Bridget.

Ellsworthy turned on her with a flash of long white hands. "Not that terrible phrase, Miss Conway. I'm a tradesman, that's all, just a tradesman."

"But you're really an artist, aren't you?" said Luke. "I mean, you do water colors, don't you? Miss Waynflete told us that you had made several sketches of a girl—Amy Gibbs."

"Oh, Amy," said Mr. Ellsworthy. He took a step backward and set a beer mug rocking. He steadied it carefully. He said, "Did I? Oh, yes, I suppose I did." His poise seemed somewhat shaken.

"She was a pretty girl," said Bridget.

Mr. Ellsworthy had recovered his aplomb. "Oh, do you think so?" he asked. "Very commonplace, I always thought.... If you're interested in slipware," he went on, to Luke, "I've got a couple of slipware birds."

Luke displayed a faint interest in the birds and then asked the price of the dish. Ellsworthy named a figure. "Thanks," said Luke. "But I don't think I'll deprive you of it, after all."

"I'm always relieved, you know," said Ellsworthy, "when I don't make a sale. Foolish of me, isn't it? Look here, I'll let you have it for a guinea less. You care for the stuff. I can see that; it makes all the difference. And after all, this is a shop."

"No, thanks," said Luke. Mr. Ellsworthy accompanied them out to the door. "Queer chap—Mr. Ellsworthy," he remarked, when he and Bridget were out of earshot.

"I believe he dabbles in black magic. Not quite Black Masses, but that sort of thing," Bridget said. "The reputation of this place helps."

Luke said, rather awkwardly, "Good Lord, I suppose he's the kind of chap I really need. I ought to have talked to him on the subject."

"Do you think so?" said Bridget. "He knows a lot about it."

Luke said, rather uneasily, "I'll look him up some other day."

Bridget did not answer. They were out of the town now. She turned aside to follow a footpath, and presently they came to the river. There they passed a small man with a stiff mustache and protuberant eyes. He had three bulldogs with him to whom he was shouting hoarsely in turn: "Nero, come here, sir! ... Nelly, leave it! Drop it, I tell you! ... Augustus—Augustus, I say—" He broke off to raise his hat to Bridget, stared at Luke with what was evidently a devouring curiosity, and passed on, resuming his hoarse expostulations.

"Major Horton and his bulldogs?" quoted Luke.

"Quite right."

"Haven't we seen practically everyone of note in Wychwood this morning?"

"Practically."

"I feel rather obtrusive," said Luke. "I suppose a stranger in an English village is bound to stick out a mile," he added ruefully, remembering Jimmy Lorrimer's remarks.

"Major Horton never disguises his curiosity very well," said Bridget. "He did stare rather."

"He's the sort of man you could tell was a major anywhere," said Luke rather viciously.

Bridget said abruptly, "Shall we sit on the bank a bit? We've got lots of time."

They sat on a fallen tree that made a convenient seat. Bridget went on, "Yes, Major Horton is very military; has an orderly-room manner. You'd hardly believe he was the most henpecked man in existence a year ago."

"What, that fellow?"

"Yes. He had the most disagreeable woman for a wife that I've ever known. She had the money, too, and never scrupled to underline the fact in public."

"Poor brute—Horton, I mean."

"He behaved very nicely to her—always the officer and gentleman. Personally, I wonder he didn't take a hatchet to her."

"She wasn't popular, I gather."

"Everybody disliked her. She snubbed Gordon and patronized me, and made herself generally unpleasant wherever she went."

"But I gather a merciful Providence removed her?"

"Yes, about a year ago. Acute gastritis. She gave her husband, Doctor Thomas, and two nurses absolute hell, but she died all right. The bulldogs brightened up at once."

"Intelligent brutes."

There was a silence. Bridget was idly picking at the long grass. Luke frowned at the opposite bank unseeingly. Once again the dreamlike quality of his mission obsessed him. How much was fact, how much imagination? Wasn't it bad for one to go about studying every fresh person you met as a potential murderer? Something degrading about that point of view.

"Damn it all," thought Luke. "I've been a policeman too long."

He was brought out of his abstraction with a shock. Bridget's cold clear voice was speaking. "Mr. Fitzwilliam," she said, "just exactly why have you come down here?"

6

LUKE HAD BEEN just in the act of applying a match to a cigarette. The unexpectedness of her remark momentarily paralyzed his hand. He remained quite motionless for a second or two; the match burned down and scorched his finger. "Damn!" said Luke, as he dropped the match and shook his hand vigorously. "I beg your pardon. You gave me rather a nasty jolt." He smiled ruefully.

"Did I?"

"Yes." He sighed. "Oh well, I suppose anyone of real intelligence was bound to see through me. That story of my writing a book on folklore didn't take you in for a moment, I suppose?"

"Not after I'd once seen you."

"Not sufficient brains to write a book? Don't spare my feelings. I'd rather know."

"You might write a book, but not that kind of book—old superstitions, delving into the past—not that sort of thing! You're not the kind of man to whom the past means much—perhaps not even the future—only just the present."

"H'm. I see." He made a wry face. "Damn it all, you've made me nervous ever since I got here! You looked so confoundedly intelligent."

"I'm sorry," said Bridget dryly. "What did you expect?"

"Well, I really hadn't thought about it."

But she went on calmly, "A fluffy little person with just enough brains to realize her opportunities and marry her boss?" Luke made a confused noise. She turned a cool, amused glance on him. "I quite understand. It's all right. I'm not annoyed."

Luke chose effrontery. "Well, perhaps, it was something faintly approaching that. But I didn't think much about it."

She said slowly, "No, you wouldn't. You don't cross your fences till you get to them." She paused a minute, then said: "Why are you down here, Mr. Fitzwilliam?"

They had returned full circle to the original question. Luke had been aware that it must be so. In the last few seconds he had been trying to make up his mind. He looked up now and met her eyes—shrewd, inquiring eyes that met his with a calm steady gaze. There was a gravity in them which he had not quite expected to find there. "It would be better, I think," he said meditatively, "not to tell you any more lies."

"Much better."

"But the truth's awkward. Look here, have you yourself formed any opinions? I mean has anything occurred to you about my being here?"

354

She nodded slowly and thoughtfully. "What was your idea? Will you tell me? I fancy it may help somehow."

Bridget said quietly, "I had an idea that you came down here in connection with the death of that girl, Amy Gibbs."

"That's it then! That's what I saw—what I felt—whenever her name cropped up! I knew there was something. So you thought I came down about that?"

"Didn't you?"

"In a way, yes."

He was silent, frowning. The girl beside him sat equally silent, not moving. She said nothing to disturb his train of thought.

He made up his mind. "I've come down here on a wild-goose chase—on a fantastical and probably quite absurd and melodramatic supposition. Amy Gibbs is part of that whole business. I'm interested to find out exactly how she died."

"Yes, I thought so."

"But dash it all, why did you think so? What is there about her death that—well, aroused your interest?"

Bridget said, "I've thought all along that there was something wrong about it. That's why I took you to see Miss Waynflete."

"Why?"

"Because she thinks so too."

"Oh." Luke thought back rapidly. He understood now the underlying suggestions of that intelligent spinster's manner. "She thinks as you do—that there's something odd about it?" Bridget nodded. "Why, exactly?"

"Hat paint, to begin with."

"What do you mean—hat paint?"

"Well, about twenty years ago people did paint hats—one season you had a pink straw; next season, a bottle of hat paint and it became dark blue; then, perhaps, another bottle and a black hat! But not nowadays. Hats are cheap—tawdry stuff, to be thrown away when out of fashion."

"Even girls of the class of Amy Gibbs?"

"I'd be more likely to paint a hat than she would. Thrift's gone out. And there's another thing. It was red hat paint."

"Well?"

"And Amy Gibbs had red hair—carrots!"

"You mean it doesn't go together?"

Bridget nodded. "You wouldn't wear a scarlet hat with carroty hair. It's the sort of thing a man wouldn't realize, but—"

Luke interrupted her with heavy significance. "No, a man wouldn't realize that. It fits in—it all fits in."

Bridget said, "Jimmy has got some odd friends at Scotland Yard. You're not—"

Luke said quickly, "I'm not an official detective, and I'm not a well-known private investigator with rooms in Baker Street, and so on. I'm exactly what Jimmy told you I was—a retired policeman from the East. I'm horning in on this business because of an odd thing that happened in the train to London." He gave a brief synopsis of his conversation with Miss Fullerton and the subsequent events which had brought about his presence in Wychwood. "So, you see," he ended, "it's fantastic! I'm looking for a certain man—a secret killer—a man here in Wychwood, probably well known and respected. If Miss Fullerton's right and you're right and Miss What's-Her-Name is right, that man killed Amy Gibbs."

Bridget said, "I see."

"It could have been done from outside, I suppose?"

"Yes, I think so," said Bridget slowly. "Reed, the constable, climbed up to her window by means of an outhouse. The window was open. It was a bit of a scramble, but a reasonably active man would find no real difficulty."

"And having done that, he did what?"

"Substituted a bottle of hat paint for the cough linctus."

"Hoping she'd do exactly what she did do—wake up, drink it off, and that everyone would say she'd made a mistake or committed suicide?"

"Yes."

"There was no suspicion of what they call in books 'foul play,' at the inquest?"

"No."

"Men again, I suppose. The hat-paint point wasn't raised?"

"No."

"But it occurred to you?"

"Yes."

"And to Miss Waynflete? Have you discussed it together?"

Bridget smiled faintly. "Oh, no; not in the sense you mean. I mean we haven't said anything right out. I don't really know how far the old pussy has gone in her own mind. I'd say she'd been just worried to start with, and gradually getting more so. She's quite intelligent, you know, went to Girton, or wanted to, and was advanced when she was young. She's not got quite the woolly mind of most of the people down here."

"Miss Fullerton had rather a woolly mind, I should imagine," said Luke. "That's why I never dreamed there was anything in her story, to begin with."

"She was pretty shrewd, I always thought," said Bridget. "Most of these rambling old dears are as sharp as nails in some ways. You said she mentioned other names?"

Luke nodded. "Yes. A small boy—that was Tommy Pierce. I remembered the name as soon as I heard it. And I'm pretty sure that the man Carter came in too."

"Carter, Tommy Pierce, Amy Gibbs, Doctor Humbleby," said Bridget thoughtfully. "As you say, it's almost too fantastic to be true. Who on earth would want to kill those people? They were all so different!"

Luke asked, "Any idea as to why anyone should want to do away with Amy Gibbs?"

Bridget shook her head. "I can't imagine."

"What about the man Carter? How did he die, by the way?"

"Fell into the river and was drowned. He was on his way home, it was a misty night and he was quite drunk. There's a footbridge with a rail on only one side. It was taken for granted that he missed his footing."

"But someone could quite easily have given him a shove?"

"Oh, yes."

"And somebody else could quite easily have given nasty little Tommy a push when he was window-cleaning?"

"Again, yes."

"So it boils down to the fact that it's really quite easy to remove three human beings without anyone suspecting."

"Miss Fullerton suspected," Bridget pointed out.

Luke said: "I suppose it's no good my asking you if you've a hunch of any kind? There's no particular individual in Wychwood who gives you a creepy feeling down the spine, or who has strange pale eyes or a queer, maniacal giggle?"

Bridget said, "You think this man is definitely mad?"

"Oh, I should say so. A lunatic all right, but a cunning one. My Miss Fullerton spoke of the look in his eyes when he was measuring up his next victim. From the way she spoke, I got the impression—it's only an impression, mark you—that the man she was speaking of was at least her social equal. Of course, I may be wrong."

"You're probably quite right! Those nuances of conversation can't be put down in black and white, but they're the sort of things one doesn't really make mistakes about."

"You know," said Luke, "it's a great relief to have you knowing all about it."

"It will probably cramp your style less, I agree. And I can probably help you."

"Your help will be invaluable. You really mean to see it through?"

"Of course."

Luke said, with a sudden slight embarrassment, "What about Lord Easterfield? Do you think—"

"Naturally, we won't tell Gordon anything about it," said Bridget.

"You mean, he wouldn't believe it?"

"Oh, he'd believe it! Gordon could believe anything! He'd probably be simply thrilled and insist on having half a dozen of his bright young men down to beat up the neighborhood! He'd simply adore it!"

"That does rather rule it out," agreed Luke.

"Yes, we can't allow him to have his simple pleasures, I'm afraid."

Luke looked at her. He seemed about to say something, then changed his mind. He looked, instead, at his watch.

"Yes," said Bridget, "we ought to be getting home." She got up. There was a sudden constraint between them, as though Luke's unspoken words hovered uncomfortably in the air. They walked home in silence.

7

LUKE SAT IN his bedroom. At lunchtime he had sustained an interrogation by Mrs. Anstruther as to what flowers he'd had in his garden in the Mayang Straits. He had then been told what flowers would have done well there. He had also listened to further Talks to Young Men on the Subject of Myself by Lord Easterfield. Now he was mercifully alone.

He took a sheet of paper and wrote down a series of names. It ran as follows:

Doctor Thomas

Mr. Abbot

Major Horton

Mr. Ellsworthy

Mr. Wake

Amy's young man

The butcher, the baker, the candlestick maker, etc.

He then took another sheet of paper and headed it VICTIMS. Under this heading he wrote:

Amy Gibbs	Poisoned
Tommy Pierce	Pushed out of window
Harry Carter	Shoved off footbridge (drunk? drugged?)
Doctor Humbleby	Blood poisoning
Miss Fullerton	Run down by car

He added:
  Mrs Rose?
  Old Ben?
And after a pause:
  Mrs. Horton?
  He considered his lists, smoked awhile, then took up his pencil once more.

Doctor Thomas. Possible case against him:

Definite motive in the case of Doctor Humbleby. Manner of latter's death suitable—namely, scientific poisoning by germs. Amy Gibbs visited him on afternoon of the day she died. Anything between them? Blackmail?

Tommy Pierce? No connection known. Did Tommy know of connection between him and Amy Gibbs?

Henry Carter? No connection known.

Was Doctor Thomas absent from Wychwood on the day Miss Fullerton went to London?

Luke sighed and started a fresh heading.

Mr. Abbot. Possible case against him:

Feel a lawyer is definitely a suspicious person. Possibly prejudice. His personality, florid, genial, etc., would be definitely suspicious in a book—always suspect bluff genial men. Objection: This is not a book but real life.

Motive for murder of Doctor Humbleby:

Definite antagonism existed between them. H. defies Abbot. Sufficient motive for a deranged brain. Antagonism could have been easily noted by Miss Fullerton.

Tommy Pierce? Latter snooped among Abbot's papers. Did he find out something he shouldn't have known?

Henry Carter? No definite connection.

Amy Gibbs? No connection known. Hat paint quite suitable to Abbot's mentality—an old-fashioned mind.

Was Abbot away from the village the day Miss Fullerton was killed?

Major Horton.

No connection known with Amy Gibbs, Tommy Pierce or Carter.

What about Mrs. Horton? Death sounds as though it might be

arsenical poisoning. If so, other murders might be result of that—blackmail? N.B.: Thomas was doctor in attendance. Suspicious for Thomas again.

Mr. Ellsworthy.

Nasty bit of goods—dabbles in black magic. Might be temperament of a blood-lust killer. Connection with Amy Gibbs. Any connection with Tommy Pierce? Carter? Nothing known. Humbleby? Might have tumbled to Ellsworthy's mental condition.

Miss Fullerton? Was Ellsworthy away from Wychwood when Miss Fullerton was killed?

Mr. Wake.

Very unlikely. Possibly religious mania? A mission to kill? Saintly old clergymen likely starters in books, but (as before) this is real life.

NOTE: Carter, Tommy, Amy, all definitely unpleasant characters. Better removed by divine decree?

Amy's young man.

Probably every reason to kill Amy, but seems unlikely on general grounds.

The etceteras?

Don't fancy them.

He read through what he had written. Then he shook his head. He murmured softly, ". . . which is absurd! How nicely Euclid put things." He tore up the lists and burnt them. He said to himself, "This job isn't going to be exactly easy."

8

DOCTOR THOMAS LEANED back in his chair and passed a long delicate hand over his thick fair hair. He was a young man whose appearance was deceptive. Immature as he might look, though, the diagnosis he had just pronounced on Luke's rheumatic knee agreed almost precisely with that delivered by an eminent Harley Street specialist only a week earlier.

"Thanks," said Luke. "Well, I'm relieved you think that electrical treatment will do the trick. I don't want to turn into a cripple at my age."

Doctor Thomas smiled boyishly. "Oh, I don't think there's any danger of that, Mr. Fitzwilliam."

"Well, you've relieved my mind," said Luke. "I was thinking of going to some specialist chap, but I'm sure there's no need now."

Doctor Thomas smiled again. "Go if it makes your mind easier. After all, it's always a good thing to have an expert's opinion."

Luke said quickly, "Men get the wind up pretty badly in these ways. I expect you find that? I often think a doctor must feel himself a medicine man—a kind of magician to most of his patients."

"The element of faith enters in very largely."

"I know. 'The doctor says so' is a remark always uttered with something like reverence."

Doctor Thomas raised his shoulders. "If one's patients only knew," he murmured humorously. Then he said, "You're writing a book on magic, aren't you, Mr. Fitzwilliam?"

"Now, how did you know that?" exclaimed Luke, perhaps with somewhat overdone surprise.

Doctor Thomas looked amused. "Oh, my dear sir, news gets about very rapidly in a place like this. We have so little to talk about."

"It probably gets exaggerated too. You'll be hearing I'm raising the local spirits and emulating the witch of Endor."

"Rather odd you should say that."

"Why?"

"Well, the rumor has been going round that you had raised the ghost of Tommy Pierce."

"Pierce? Pierce? Is that the small boy who fell out of a window?"

"Yes."

"Now, I wonder how—Of course. I made some remark to the solicitor—what's his name?—Abbot."

"Yes, the story originated with Abbot."

361

"Don't say I've converted a hard-headed solicitor to a belief in ghosts?"

"You believe in ghosts yourself, then?"

"Your tone suggests that you do not, doctor. No. I wouldn't say I actually 'believe in ghosts'—to put it crudely. But I have known curious phenomena in the case of sudden or violent death. But I'm more interested in the various superstitions pertaining to violent deaths—that a murdered man, for instance, can't rest in his grave. And the interesting belief that the blood of a murdered man flows if his murderer touches him. I wonder how that arose."

"Very curious," said Thomas. "But I don't suppose many people remember that nowadays."

"More than you would think. Of course, I don't suppose you have many murders down here, so it's hard to judge."

Luke had smiled as he spoke, his eyes resting with seeming carelessness on the other's face. But Doctor Thomas seemed quite unperturbed and smiled in return.

"No, I don't think we've had a murder here for—oh, very many years—certainly not in my time."

"No, this is a peaceful spot. Not conducive to foul play. Unless somebody pushed little Tommy What's-His-Name out of the window."

Luke laughed. Again Doctor Thomas' smile came in answer—a natural smile full of boyish amusement. "A lot of people would have been willing to wring that child's neck," he said, "but I don't think they actually got to the point of throwing him out of windows."

"He seems to have been a thoroughly nasty child; the removal of him might have been conceived as a public duty."

"It's a pity one can't apply that theory fairly often."

"I've always thought a few wholesale murders would be beneficial to the community," said Luke. "I haven't the respect for human life that the normal Englishman has. Any man who is a stumbling block on the way of progress ought to be eliminated—that's how I see it."

Running his hand through his short fair hair, Doctor Thomas said, "Yes, but who is to be the judge of a man's fitness or unfitness?"

"You'd have to have a scientific man as judge," said Luke. "Someone with an unbiased but highly specialized mind—a doctor, for instance. Come to that, I think you'd be a pretty good judge yourself, doctor."

"Of unfitness to live?"

"Yes."

Doctor Thomas shook his head. "My job is to make the unfit fit. Most of the time it's an uphill job, I'll admit."

"Now, just for the sake of argument," said Luke. "Take a man like the late Henry Carter—"

Doctor Thomas said sharply, "Carter? You mean the landlord of the Seven Stars?"

"Yes, that's the man. I never knew him myself, but my cousin, Miss Conway, was talking about him. He seems to have been a really thoroughgoing scoundrel."

"Well," said the other, "he drank, of course, ill-treated his wife, bullied his daughter. He was quarrelsome and abusive, and had had a row with most people in the place."

"In fact, the world is a better place without him?"

"One might be inclined to say so, I agree."

"In fact, if somebody had given him a push and sent him into the river instead of his kindly electing to fall in of his own accord, that person would have been acting in the public interest?"

Doctor Thomas said dryly, "These methods that you advocate—did you put them into practice in the—Mayang Straits, I think you said?"

Luke laughed. "Oh, no, with me it's theory, not practice."

"No, I do not think you are the stuff of which murderers are made."

"Tell me—it interests me—have you ever come across a man you believed might be a murderer?"

Doctor Thomas said sharply, "Really, what an extraordinary question!"

"Is it? After all, a doctor must come across so many queer characters. He would be better able to detect, for instance, the signs of homicidal mania in an early stage, before it's noticeable."

Thomas said rather irritably, "You have the general layman's idea of a homicidal maniac—a man who runs amok with a knife, a man more or less foaming at the mouth. Let me tell you, a homicidal lunatic may be the most difficult thing on this earth to spot. To all seeming, he may be exactly like everyone else—a man, perhaps, who is easily frightened, who may tell you, perhaps, that he has enemies. No more than that. A quiet inoffensive fellow."

"Is that really so?"

"Of course it's so. A homicidal lunatic often kills, as he thinks, in self-defense. But, of course, a lot of killers are ordinary sane fellows like you and me."

"Doctor, you alarm me! Fancy if you should discover later that I have five or six quiet little killings to my credit."

Doctor Thomas smiled. "I don't think it's very likely, Mr. Fitzwilliam."

"Don't you? I'll return the compliment. I don't believe you've got five or six murders to your credit either."

Doctor Thomas said cheerfully, "You're not counting my professional failures."

Both men laughed. Luke got up and said good-by. "I'm afraid I've taken up a lot of your time," he said apologetically.

"Oh, I'm not busy. Wychwood is a pretty healthy place. It's a pleasure to have a talk with someone from the outside world."

"I was wondering—" said Luke and stopped.

"Yes?"

"Miss Conway told me, when she sent me to you, what a very— well, what a first-class man you were. I wondered if you didn't feel rather buried down here? Not much opportunity for talent."

"Oh, general practice is a good beginning. It's valuable experience."

"But you won't be content to stay in a rut all your life. Your late partner, Doctor Humbleby, was an unambitious fellow, so I've heard—quite content with his practice here. He'd been here for a good many years, I believe.

"Practically a lifetime."

"He was sound but old-fashioned, so I hear."

Doctor Thomas said, "At times he was difficult. Very suspicious of modern innovations, but a good example of the old school of physicians."

"Left a very pretty daughter, I'm told," said Luke in jocular fashion.

He had the pleasure of seeing Doctor Thomas' pale pink countenance go a deep scarlet. "Oh—er—yes," he said.

Luke gazed at him kindly. He was pleased at the prospect of erasing Doctor Thomas from his list of suspected persons. The latter recovered his normal hue and said abruptly, "Talking about crime just now, I can lend you rather a good book, as you are interested in the subject. Translation from the German. Kreuzhammer on *Inferiority and Crime*."

"Thank you," said Luke.

Doctor Thomas ran his finger along a shelf and drew out the book in question. "Here you are. Some of the theories are rather startling, and of course they are only theories, but they are interesting. The early life of Menzheld, for instance, the Frankfort butcher, as they called him, and the chapter on Anna Helm, the little nursemaid killer, are really extremely interesting."

"She killed about a dozen of her charges before the authorities tumbled to it, I believe," said Luke.

Doctor Thomas nodded. "Yes. She had a most sympathetic personality—devoted to children, and apparently quite genuinely heartbroken at each death. The psychology is amazing."

"Amazing how these people get away with it."

He was on the doorstep now. Doctor Thomas had come out with him. "Not amazing, really," said Doctor Thomas. "It's quite easy, you know."

"What is?"

"To get away with it." He was smiling again—a charming, boyish smile. "If you're careful. One just has to be careful, that's all. But a clever man is extremely careful not to make a slip. That's all there is to it." He smiled again and went into the house.

Luke stood staring up the steps. There had been something condescending in the doctor's smile. Throughout their conversation, Luke had been conscious of himself as a man of full maturity and of Doctor Thomas as a youthful and ingenuous young man. Just for the moment he felt the roles reversed. The doctor's smile had been that of a grownup amused by the cleverness of a child.

9

IN THE LITTLE shop in the High Street, Luke had bought a tin of cigarettes and today's copy of *Good Cheer*, the enterprising little weekly which provided Lord Easterfield with a good portion of his substantial income. Turning to the football competition, Luke, with a groan, gave forth the information that he had just failed to win a hundred and twenty pounds. Mrs. Pierce was roused at once to sympathy and explained similar disappointments on the part of her husband. Friendly relations thus established, Luke found no difficulty in prolonging the conversation.

"A great interest in football, Mr. Pierce takes," said Mr. Pierce's spouse. "Turns to it first of all in the news, he does. And, as I say, many a disappointment he's had, but there, everybody can't win, that's what I say, and what I say is you can't go against luck."

Luke concurred heartily in these sentiments, and proceeded to advance by an easy transition to a further profound statement that troubles never come singly.

"Ah, no, indeed, sir; that I do know." Mrs. Pierce sighed. "And when a woman has a husband and eight children—six living, and buried two, that is—well, she knows what trouble is, as you may say."

"I suppose she does. Oh, undoubtedly," said Luke. "You've—er buried two, you say?"

"One no longer than a month ago," said Mrs. Pierce, with a kind of melancholy enjoyment.

"Dear me, very sad."

"It wasn't only sad, sir. It was a shock, that's what it was—a shock! I came all over queer, I did, when they broke it to me. Never having expected anything of that kind to happen to Tommy, as you might say, for when a boy's trouble to you, it doesn't come natural to think of him being took. Now my Emma Jane, a sweet little mite she was. 'You'll never rear her.' That's what they said. 'She's too good to live.' And it was true, sir. The Lord knows his own."

Luke acknowledged the sentiment and strove to return from the subject of the saintly Emma Jane to that of the less saintly Tommy. "Your boy died quite recently?" he asked. "An accident?"

"An accident it was, sir. Cleaning the windows of the old hall, which is now the library, and he must have lost his balance and fell—from the top windows, that was."

Mrs. Pierce expatiated at some length on all the details of the accident.

"Wasn't there some story," said Luke carelessly, "of his having been seen dancing on the window sill?" Mrs. Pierce said that boys would be boys, but no doubt it did give the Major a turn, him being a fussy gentleman.

"Major Horton?"

"Yes, sir, the gentleman with the bulldogs. After the accident happened, he chanced to mention having seen our Tommy acting very rashlike—and, of course, it does show that if something sudden had startled him, he would have fallen easy enough. High spirits, sir, that was Tommy's trouble. A sore trial he's been to me in many ways," she finished, "but there it was just high spirits—nothing but high spirits, such as any lad might have. There wasn't no real harm in him, as you might say."

"No, no, I'm sure there wasn't but sometimes, you know, Mrs. Pierce, people—sober middle-aged people—find it hard to remember they've ever been young themselves."

Mrs. Pierce sighed. "Very true those words are, sir. I can't help but hope that some gentlemen I could name, but won't, will have taken it to heart, the way they were hard upon the lad just on account of his high spirits."

"Played a few tricks upon his employers, did he?" asked Luke, with an indulgent smile.

Mrs. Pierce responded immediately, "It was just his fun, sir, that was all. Tommy was always good at imitations. Make us hold our sides with laughing, the way he'd pretend to be that Mr. Ellsworthy at the curio shop, or old Mr. Hobbs, the churchwarden, and he was imitating his lordship up at the Manor, and the two undergardeners laughing, when up came his lordship quiet like and gave Tommy the sack on the spot; and, naturally, that was only to be expected and quite right, and his lordship didn't bear malice afterwards, and helped Tommy to get another job."

"But other people weren't so magnanimous, eh?" said Luke.

"That they were not, sir. Naming no names. And you'd never think it, with Mr. Abbot so pleasant in his manner and always a kind word or a joke."

"Tommy got into trouble with him?"

Mrs. Pierce said, "It's not, I'm sure, that the boy meant any harm. And after all, if papers are private and not meant to be looked at, they shouldn't be laid out on a table—that's what I say."

"Oh, quite," said Luke. "Private papers in a lawyer's office ought to be kept in the safe."

"That's right, sir. That's what I think, and Mr. Pierce, he agrees with me. It's not even as though Tommy had read much of it."

"What was it—a will?" asked Luke. He judged—probably rightly—that a question as to what the document in question had been might make Mrs. Pierce halt. But this direct question brought an instant response.

"Oh, no, sir; nothing of that kind. Nothing really important. Just a private letter it was—from a lady—and Tommy didn't even see who the lady was. All such a fuss about nothing—that's what I say."

"Mr. Abbot must be the sort of man who takes offense very easily," said Luke.

"Well, it does seem so, doesn't it, sir? Although, as I say, he's always such a pleasant gentleman to speak to—always a joke or a cheery word. But it's true that I have heard he was a difficult man to get up against, and him and Doctor Humbleby was daggers drawn, as the saying is, just before the poor gentleman died. And not a pleasant thought for Mr. Abbot afterwards. For, once there's a death, one doesn't like to think there's been harsh words spoken and no chance of taking them back."

Luke shook his head solemnly and murmured, "Very true—very true." He went on, "A bit of a coincidence, that. Hard words with Doctor Humbleby, and Doctor Humbleby died; harsh treatment of your Tommy, and the boy dies. I should think that a double experience like that would tend to make Mr. Abbot careful of his tongue in future."

"Harry Carter, too, down at the Seven Stars," said Mrs. Pierce. "Very sharp words passed between them only a week before Carter went and drowned himself, but one can't blame Mr. Abbot for that. The abuse was all on Carter's side. Went up to Mr. Abbot's house, he did, being in liquor at the time, and shouting out the foulest language at the top of his voice. Poor Mrs. Carter, she had a deal to put up with, and, it must be owned, Carter's death was a merciful release as far as she was concerned."

"He left a daughter, too, didn't he?"

"Ah," said Mrs. Pierce, "I'm never one to gossip." This was unexpected, but promising. Luke pricked up his ears and waited. "I don't say there was anything in it but talk. Lucy Carter's a fine-looking young woman in her way, and if it hadn't been for the difference in station, I dare say no notice would have been taken. But talk there has been, and you can't deny it; especially after Carter went right up to his house, shouting and swearing."

Luke gathered the implications of this somewhat confused speech. "Mr. Abbot looks as though he'd appreciate a good-looking girl," he said.

"It's often the way with gentlemen,"said Mrs. Pierce. "They don't mean anything by it—just a word or two in passing—but the gentry's the gentry and it gets noticed in consequence. It's only to be expected in a quiet place like this."

"It's a very charming place," said Luke. "So unspoilt."

"That's what artists always say, but I think we're a bit behind the times, myself. Why, there's been no building here to speak of. Over at Ashevale, for instance, they've got a lovely lot of new houses, some of them with green roofs and stained glass in the windows."

Luke shuddered slightly. "You've got a grand new Institute here," he said.

"They say it's a very fine building," said Mrs. Pierce, without great enthusiasm. "Of course, his lordship's done a lot for the place. He means well; we all know that."

"But you don't think his efforts are quite successful?" said Luke, amused.

"Well, of course, sir, he isn't really gentry—not like Miss Waynflete, for instance, and Miss Conway. Why, Lord Easterfield's father kept a boot shop only a few doors from here. My mother remembers Gordon Ragg serving in the shop—remembers it as well as anything. Of course, he's his lordship now and he's a rich man, but it's never the same, is it, sir?"

"Evidently not," said Luke.

"You'll excuse me mentioning it, sir," said Mrs. Pierce. "And of course I know you're staying at the Manor and writing a book. But you're a cousin of Miss Bridget's, I know, and that's quite a different thing. Very pleased we shall be to have her back as mistress of Ashe Manor."

"Rather," said Luke. "I'm sure you will." He paid for his cigarettes and paper with sudden abruptness. He thought to himself: "The personal element. One must keep that out of it. Hell, I'm here to track down a criminal. What does it matter who that black-haired witch marries or doesn't marry? She doesn't come into this."

He walked slowly along the street. With an effort, he thrust Bridget into the back of his mind. "Now then," he said to himself. "Abbot. The case against Abbot. I've linked him up with three of the victims. He had a row with Humbleby, a row with Carter and a row with Tommy Pierce, and all three died. What about the girl, Amy Gibbs? What was the private letter that infernal boy saw? Did he know who it was from? Or didn't he? He mayn't have said so to his mother. But suppose he did. Suppose Abbot thought it necessary to shut his mouth. It could be. That's all one can say about it. It could be. Not good enough."

Luke quickened his pace, looking about him with sudden exasperation. "This damned village—it's getting on my nerves. So smiling and peaceful, so innocent, and all the time this crazy streak of murder running through it. Or am I the crazy one? Was Lavinia Fullerton crazy? After all, the whole thing could be coincidence—yes, Humbleby's death and all." He glanced back down the length of the High Street, and he was assailed by a strong feeling of unreality. He said to himself, "These things don't happen." Then he lifted his eyes to the long frowning line of Ashe Ridge, and at once the unreality passed. Ashe Ridge was real; it knew strange things—witchcraft and cruelty and forgotten blood lusts and evil rites.

He started. Two figures were walking along the side of the ridge. He recognized them easily—Bridget and Ellsworthy. The young man was gesticulating with those curious unpleasant hands of his. His head was bent to Bridget's. They looked like two figures out of a dream. One felt that their feet made no sound as they sprang cat-like from tuft to tuft. He saw her black hair stream out behind her, blown by the wind. Again that queer magic of hers held him. "Bewitched, that's what I am—bewitched," he said to himself.

He stood quite still; a queer numbed feeling spreading over him. He thought to himself ruefully, "Who's to break the spell? There's no one."

10

A SOFT SOUND behind him made him turn sharply. A girl was standing there, a remarkably pretty girl, with brown hair curling round her ears and rather timid-looking dark blue eyes. She flushed a little with embarrassment before she spoke. "Mr. Fitzwilliam, isn't it?" she said.

"Yes. I—"

"I'm Rose Humbleby. Bridget told me that—that you knew some people who knew my father."

Luke had the grace to flush slightly under his tan. "It was a long time ago," he said rather lamely. "They—er—knew him as a young man—before he was married."

"Oh, I see." Rose Humbleby looked a little crestfallen. But she went on, "You're writing a book, aren't you?"

"Yes. I'm making notes for one, that is. About local superstitions. All that sort of thing."

"I see. It sounds frightfully interesting."

Luke smiled at her. He thought, "Our Doctor Thomas is in luck."

"There are people," he said, "who can make the most exciting subject unbearably boring. I'm afraid I'm one of them."

Rose Humbleby smiled back. Then she said, "Do you believe in—in superstitions and all that?"

"That's a difficult question. It doesn't follow, you know. One can be interested in things one doesn't believe in."

"Yes, I suppose so." The girl sounded doubtful.

"Are you superstitious?"

"N-no, I don't think so. But I do think things come in—in waves."

"Waves?"

"Waves of bad luck and good luck. I mean, I feel as though lately all Wychwood was under a spell of—of misfortune. Father dying, and Miss Fullerton being run over, and that little boy who fell out of the window. I—I began to feel as though I hated this place—as though I must get away."

Her breath came rather faster. Luke looked at her thoughtfully. "So you feel like that?"

"Oh, I know it's silly. I suppose really it was poor daddy dying so unexpectedly—it was so horribly sudden." She shivered. "And then Miss Fullerton. She said—" The girl paused.

"What did she say? She was a delightful old lady, I thought—very like a rather special aunt of mine."

370

"Oh, did you know her?" Rose's face lit up. "I was very fond of her and she was devoted to daddy. But I've sometimes wondered if she was what the Scotch call 'fey.' "

"Why?"

"Because—it's so odd—she seemed quite afraid that something was going to happen to daddy. She almost warned me. Especially about accidents. And then that day, just before she went up to town, she was so odd in her manner—absolutely in a dither. I really do think, Mr. Fitzwilliam, that she was one of those people who have second sight. I think she knew that something was going to happen to her. And she must have known that something was going to happen to daddy too. It's—it's rather frightening, that sort of thing!" She moved a step nearer to him.

"There are times when one can foresee the future," said Luke. "It isn't always supernatural, though."

"No, I suppose it's quite natural, really—just a faculty that most people lack. All the same it worries me."

"You mustn't worry," said Luke gently. "Remember, it's all behind you now. It's no good going back over the past. It's the future one has to live for."

"I know. But there's more, you see." Rose hesitated. "There was something—to do with your cousin."

"My cousin? Bridget?"

"Yes. Miss Fullerton was worried about her in the same way. She was always asking me questions. I think she was afraid for her too."

Luke turned, sharply scanning the hillside. He had an unreasoning sense of fear for Bridget. Fancy—all fancy! Ellsworthy was only a harmless dilettante who played at shopkeeping. As though reading his thoughts, Rose said, "Do you like Mr. Ellsworthy?"

"Emphatically no."

"Geoffrey—Doctor Thomas, you know—doesn't like him either."

"And you?"

"Oh, no; I think he's dreadful." She drew a little nearer. "There's a lot of talk about him. I was told that he had some queer ceremony in the Witches' Meadow—a lot of his friends came down from London—frightfully queer-looking people. And Tommy Pierce was a kind of acolyte."

"Tommy Pierce?" said Luke sharply.

"Yes. He had a surplice and a red cassock."

"When was this?"

"Oh, some time ago. I think it was in March."

"Tommy Pierce seems to have been mixed up in everything that ever took place in this village."

Rose said, "He was frightfully inquisitive. He always had to know whatever was going on."

"He probably knew a bit too much in the end," said Luke grimly.

Rose accepted the words at their face value. "He was rather an odious little boy. He liked cutting up wasps and he teased dogs."

"The kind of boy whose decease is hardly to be regretted."

"No, I suppose not. It was terrible for his mother, though."

"I gather she has six blessings left to console her. She's got a good tongue, that woman."

"She does talk a lot, doesn't she?"

"After buying a few cigarettes from her, I feel I know the full history of everyone in the place."

Rose said ruefully, "That's the worst of a place like this. Everybody knows everything about everybody else."

"Oh, no," said Luke.

She looked at him inquiringly.

Luke said, with significance, "No one human being knows the full truth about another human being. Not even one's nearest and dearest."

"Not even—" She stopped. "Oh, I suppose you're right, but I wish you wouldn't say frightening things like that, Mr. Fitzwilliam."

"Does it frighten you?"

Slowly, she nodded her head. Then she turned abruptly. "I must be going now. If—if you have nothing better to do—I mean if you could—do come and see us. Mother would—would like to see you because of your knowing friends of daddy's so long ago." She walked slowly away down the road. Her head was bent a little, as though some weight of care or perplexity bowed it down.

Luke stood looking after her. A sudden wave of solicitude swept over him. He felt a longing to shield and protect this girl. From what? Asking himself the question, he shook his head with a momentary impatience at himself. It was true that Rose Humbleby had recently lost her father, but she had a mother, and she was engaged to be married to a decidedly attractive young man who was fully adequate to anything in the protection line. Then why should he, Luke Fitzwilliam, be assailed by this protection complex?

"All the same," he said to himself, as he strolled on toward the looming mass of Ashe Ridge, "I like that girl. She's much too good for Thomas—a cool, superior devil like that." A memory of the doctor's last smile on the doorstep recurred to him. Decidedly smug, it had been! Complacent!

The sound of footsteps a little way ahead roused Luke from his slightly irritable meditations. He looked up to see young Mr. Ellsworthy coming down the path from the hillside. His eyes were on the ground and he was smiling to himself. His expression struck Luke disagreeably. Ellsworthy was not so much walking as prancing—like a man who keeps time to some devilish little jig running in his brain. His smile was a strange secret contortion of the lips; it had a gleeful slyness that was definitely unpleasant. Luke had stopped and Ellsworthy was nearly abreast of him when he at last looked up. His eyes, malicious and dancing, met the other man's for just a minute before recognition came. Then—or so it seemed to Luke—a complete change came over the man. Where, a minute before, there had been the suggestion of a dancing satyr, there was now a somewhat priggish young man. "Oh, Mr. Fitzwilliam, good morning."

"Good morning," said Luke. "Have you been admiring the beauties of Nature?"

Mr. Ellsworthy's long pale hands flew up in a reproving gesture. "Oh, no, no. I abhor Nature. But I do enjoy life, Mr. Fitzwilliam."

"So do I," said Luke.

"*Mens sana in corpore sano*," said Mr. Ellsworthy. His tone was delicately ironic. "I'm sure that's so true of you."

"There are worse things," said Luke.

"My dear fellow! Sanity is the one unbelievable bore. One must be mad, slightly twisted—then one sees life from a new and entrancing angle."

"The leper's squint," suggested Luke.

"Oh, very good, very good; quite witty! But there's something in it, you know. An interesting angle of vision. But I mustn't detain you. You're having exercise. One must have exercise—the public-school spirit!"

"As you say," said Luke, and, with a curt nod, walked on. He thought, "I'm getting too darned imaginative. The fellow's just an ass, that's all." But some indefinable uneasiness drove his feet on faster. That queer, sly triumphant smile that Ellsworthy had had on his face—was that just imagination on his, Luke's part? And his subsequent impression that it had been wiped off, as though by a sponge, the moment the other man caught sight of Luke coming toward him—what of that? And with quickening uneasiness he thought, "Bridget? Is she all right? They came up here together and he came back alone."

He hurried on. The sun had come out while he was talking to Rose Humbleby. Now it had gone in again. The sky was dull and menacing, and wind came in sudden erratic little puffs. It was as though he had stepped out of normal everyday life into that queer half world of enchantment, the consciousness of which had enveloped him ever since he came to Wychwood. He turned a corner and came out on the flat ledge of green grass that had been pointed out to him from below, and which went, he knew, by the name of Witches' Meadow. It was here, so tradition had it, that the witches had held revelry on Walpurgis Night and Halloween. And then a quick wave of relief swept over him. Bridget was here. She sat with her back against a rock on the hillside. She was sitting bent over, her head in her hands. He walked quickly over to her. Lovely spring turf, strangely green and fresh. He said, "Bridget?"

Slowly she raised her face from her hands. Her face troubled him. She looked as though she were returning from some far-off world, as though she had difficulty in adjusting herself to the world of now and here.

Luke said, rather inadequately, "I say, you're—you're all right, aren't you?"

It was a minute or two before she answered—as though she still had not quite come back from that far-off world that had held her. Luke felt that his words had to travel a long way before they reached her. Then she said, "Of course I'm all right. Why shouldn't I be?" And now her voice was sharp and almost hostile.

Luke grinned. "I'm hanged if I know. I got the wind-up about you suddenly."

"Why?"

"Mainly, I think, because of the melodramatic atmosphere in which I'm living at present. It makes me see things out of all proportion. If I lose sight of you for an hour or two, I naturally assume that the next thing will be to find your gory corpse in a ditch. It would be, in a play or a book."

"Heroines are never killed," said Bridget.

"No, but—" Luke stopped just in time.

"What were you going to say?"

"Nothing."

Thank goodness, he had just stopped himself in time. One couldn't very well say to an attractive young woman, "But you're not the heroine."

Bridget went on, "They are abducted, imprisoned, left to die of sewer gas or be drowned in cellars; they are always in danger, but they don't ever die."

"Nor even fade away," said Luke. He went on, "So this is the Witches' Meadow?"

"Yes."

He looked down at her. "You only need a broom-stick," he said kindly.

"Thank you. Mr. Ellsworthy said much the same."

"I met him just now," said Luke.

"Did you talk to him at all?"

"Yes, I think he tried to annoy me."

"Did he succeed?"

"His methods were rather childish." He paused, and then went on abruptly, "He's an odd sort of fellow. One minute you think he's just a mess, and then suddenly one wonders if there isn't a bit more to it than that."

Bridget looked up at him. "You've felt that too?"

"You agree, then?"

"Yes." Luke waited. Bridget said, "There's something—odd about him. I've been wondering, you know. I lay awake last night racking my brains. About the whole business. It seemed to me that if there was a—a killer about, I ought to know who it was. I mean, living down here, and all that. I thought and thought, and it came to this—if there is a killer, he must definitely be mad."

Thinking of what Doctor Thomas had said, Luke asked: "You don't think that a murderer can be as sane as you or I?"

"Not this kind of murderer. As I see it, this murderer must be crazy. And that, you see, brought me straight to Ellsworthy. Of all the people down here, he's the only one who is definitely queer. He is queer, you can't get away from it!"

Luke said doubtfully, "There are a good many of his sort— dilettantes, poseurs—usually quite harmless."

"Yes. But I think there might be a little more than that. He's got such nasty hands."

"You noticed that? Funny, I did too!"

"They're not just white, they're green."

"They do give one that effect. All the same, you can't convict a man of being a murderer because of the color of his flesh."

"Oh, quite. What we want is evidence."

"Evidence," growled Luke. "Just the one thing that's absolutely lacking. The man's been too careful. A careful murderer! A careful lunatic!"

"I've been trying to help," said Bridget.

"With Ellsworthy, you mean?"

"Yes. I thought I could probably tackle him better than you could. I've made a beginning."

"Tell me."

"Well, it seems that he has a kind of little coterie—a band of nasty friends. They come down here from time to time and celebrate."

"Do you mean what are called nameless orgies?"

"I don't know about nameless but certainly orgies. Actually, it all sounds very silly and childish."

"I suppose they worship the devil and do obscene dances."

"Something of the kind. Apparently they get a kick out of it."

"I can contribute something to this," said Luke. "Tommy Pierce took part in one of their ceremonies. He was an acolyte. He had a red cassock."

"So he knew about it?"

"Yes. And that might explain his death."

"You mean he talked about it?"

"Yes—or he may have tried a spot of quiet blackmail."

Bridget said thoughtfully, "I know it's all fantastic, but it doesn't seem quite so fantastic when applied to Ellsworthy as it does to anyone else."

"No, I agree. The thing becomes just conceivable instead of being ludicrously unreal."

"We've got a connection with two of the victims," said Bridget. "Tommy Pierce and Amy Gibbs."

"Where do the publican and Humbleby come in?"

"At the moment, they don't."

"Not the publican. But I can imagine a motive for Humbleby's removal. He was a doctor and he may have tumbled to Ellsworthy's abnormal state."

"Yes, that's possible."

Then Bridget laughed. "I did my stuff pretty well this morning. My psychic possibilities are grand, it seems, and when I told how one of my great-great-grandmothers had a near escape of being burnt for witchcraft, my stock went soaring up. I rather think that I shall be invited to take part in the orgies at the next meeting of the Satanic Games, whenever that may be."

Luke said, "Bridget, for God's sake, be careful." She looked at him, surprised. He got up. "I met Humbleby's daughter just now. We were talking about Miss Fullerton. And the Humbleby girl said that Miss Fullerton had been worried about you."

Bridget, in the act of rising, stopped as though frozen into immobility. "What's that? Miss Fullerton worried—about me?"

"That's what Rose Humbleby said."

"Rose Humbleby said that?"

"Yes."

"What more did she say?"

"Nothing more."

"Are you sure?"

"Quite sure."

There was a pause, then Bridget said, "I see."

"Miss Fullerton was worried about Humbleby, and he died. Now I hear she was worried about you—"

Bridget laughed. She stood up and shook her head, so that her long black hair flew out round her head. "Don't worry," she said. "The devil looks after his own."

11

LUKE LEANED BACK in his chair on the other side of the bank manager's table. "Well, that seems very satisfactory," he said. "I'm afraid I've been taking up a lot of your time."

Mr. Jones waved a deprecating hand. His small, dark, plump face wore a happy expression. "No, indeed, Mr. Fitzwilliam. This is a quiet spot, you know. We are always glad to see a stranger."

"It's a fascinating part of the world," said Luke. "Full of super-stitions."

Mr. Jones sighed and said it took a long time for education to eradicate superstition. Luke remarked that he thought education was too highly rated nowadays, and Mr. Jones was slightly shocked by the statement.

"Lord Easterfield," he said, "has been a handsome benefactor here. He realizes the disadvantages under which he himself suffered as a boy, and is determined that the youth of today shall be better equipped."

"Early disadvantages haven't prevented him from making a large fortune," said Luke.

"No, he must have had ability—great ability."

"Or luck," said Luke.

Mr. Jones looked rather shocked. "Luck is the one thing that counts," said Luke. "Take a murderer, for example. Why does the successful murderer get away with it? Is it ability? Or is it sheer luck?" Mr. Jones admitted that it was probably luck. Luke continued, "Take a fellow like this man Carter, the landlord of one of your pubs. The fellow was probably drunk six nights out of seven, yet one night he goes and pitches himself off the footbridge into the river. Luck again."

"Good luck for some people," said the bank manager.

"You mean?"

"For his wife and daughter."

"Oh, yes, of course."

A clerk knocked and entered, bearing papers. Luke gave two specimen signatures and was given a checkbook. He rose. "Well, I'm glad that's all fixed up. Had a bit of luck over the Derby this year. Did you?"

Mr. Jones said smilingly that he was not a betting man. He added that Mrs. Jones held very strong views on the subject of horse racing.

"Then I suppose you didn't go to the Derby?"

"No, indeed."

"Anybody go to it from here?"

"Major Horton did. He's quite a keen racing man. And Mr. Abbot usually takes the day off. He didn't back the winner, though."

"I don't suppose many people did," said Luke, and departed after the exchange of farewells.

He lit a cigarette as he emerged from the bank. Apart from the theory of the least likely person, he saw no reason for retaining Mr. Jones on his list of suspects. The bank manager had shown no interesting reactions to Luke's test questions. It seemed quite impossible to visualize him as a murderer. Moreover, he had not been absent on Derby Day. Incidentally, Luke's visit had not been wasted; he had received two small items of information. Both Major Horton and Mr. Abbot, the solicitor, had been away from Wychwood on Derby Day. Either of them, therefore, could have been in London at the time when Miss Fullerton was run down by a car.

Although Luke did not now suspect Doctor Thomas, he felt he would be more satisfied if he knew for a fact that the latter had been at Wychwood, engaged in his professional duties, on that particular day. He made a mental note to verify that point. Then there was Ellsworthy. Had Ellsworthy been in Wychwood on Derby Day? If he had, the presumption that he was the killer was correspondingly weakened. Although, Luke noted, it was possible that Miss Fullerton's death had been neither more nor less than the accident that it was supposed to be. But he rejected that theory. Her death was too opportune.

Luke got into his own car, which was standing by the curb, and drove it to Pipewell's Garage, situated at the far end of the High Street. There were various small matters in the car's running that he wanted to discuss. A good-looking young mechanic with a freckled face listened intelligently. The two men lifted the hood and became absorbed in a technical discussion.

A voice called, "Jim, come here a minute." The freckle-faced mechanic obeyed. Jim Harvey. That was right. Jim Harvey, Amy

Gibbs' young man. He returned presently, apologizing, and the conversation became technical once more. Luke agreed to leave the car there. As he was about to leave, he inquired casually, "Do any good on the Derby this year?"

"No, sir. Backed Clarigold."

"Can't be many people who backed Jujube the II?"

"No, indeed, sir. I don't believe any of the papers even tipped it as an outside chance."

Luke shook his head. "Racing's an uncertain game. Ever seen the Derby run?"

"No, sir, wish I had. Asked for a day off this year. There was a cheap ticket up to town and down to Epsom, but the boss wouldn't hear of it. We were short-handed, as a matter of fact, and had a lot of work in that day."

Luke nodded and took his departure. Jim Harvey was crossed off his list. That pleasant-faced boy was not a secret killer, and it was not he who had run down Lavinia Fullerton.

He strolled home by way of the riverbank. Here, as once before, he encountered Major Horton and his dogs. The Major was still in the same condition of apoplectic shouting: "Augustus! . . . Nelly! Nelly, I say! . . . Nero, Nero, Nero!" Again the protuberant eyes stared at Luke. But this time there was more to follow. Major Horton said, "Excuse me. Mr. Fitzwilliam, isn't it?"

"Yes."

"Horton here—Major Horton. Believe I'm going to meet you tomorrow up at the Manor. Tennis party. Miss Conway very kindly asked me. Cousin of yours, isn't she?"

"Yes."

"Thought so. Soon spot a new face down here, you know." Here a diversion occurred, the two bulldogs advancing upon a nondescript white mongrel. "Augustus! . . . Nero! Come here, sir! Come here, I say!" When Augustus and Nero had finally reluctantly obeyed the command, Major Horton returned to the conversation. Luke was patting Nelly, who was gazing up at him sentimentally. "Nice bitch, that, isn't she?" said the Major. "I like bulldogs. I've always had 'em. Prefer 'em to any other breed. My place is just near here; come in and have a drink."

Luke accepted and the two men walked together while Major Horton held forth on the subject of dogs and the inferiority of all other breeds to that which he himself preferred. Luke heard of the prizes Nelly had won, of the infamous conduct of a judge in awarding Augustus merely a Highly Commended, and of the triumphs of Nero in the show ring.

By then they had turned in at the Major's gate. He opened the front door, which was not locked, and the two men passed into the house. Leading the way into a small, slightly doggy-smelling room lined with bookshelves, Major Horton busied himself with the drinks. Luke looked round him. There were photographs of dogs, copies of the *Field and Country Life,* and a couple of well-worn armchairs. Silver cups were arranged round the bookcases. There was one oil painting over the mantelpiece. "My wife," said the Major, looking up from the siphon and noting the direction of Luke's glance. "Remarkable woman. A lot of character in her face, don't you think?"

"Yes, indeed," said Luke, looking at the late Mrs. Horton. She was represented in a pink satin dress and was holding a bunch of lilies of the valley. Her brown hair was parted in the middle and her lips were pressed grimly together. Her eyes, of a cold gray, looked out ill-temperedly at the beholder.

"A remarkable woman," said the Major, handing a glass to Luke. "She died over a year ago. I haven't been the same man since."

"No?" said Luke, a little at a loss to know what to say.

"Sit down," said the Major, waving a hand toward one of the leather chairs. He himself took the other one and, sipping his whisky and soda, he went on: "No, I haven't been the same man since."

"You must miss her," said Luke awkwardly.

Major Horton shook his head darkly. "Fellow needs a wife to keep him up to scratch," he said. "Otherwise he gets slack—yes, slack. He lets himself go."

"But surely—"

"My boy, I know what I'm talking about. Mind you, I'm not saying marriage doesn't come hard on a fellow at first. It does. Fellow says to himself, 'Damn it all,' he says, 'I can't call my soul my own!' But he gets broken in. It's all discipline."

Luke thought that Major Horton's married life must have been more like a military campaign than an idyll of domestic bliss. "Women," soliloquized the Major, "are a rum lot. It seems sometimes that there's no pleasing them. But, by Jove, they keep a man up to the mark." Luke preserved a respectful silence. "You married?" inquired the Major.

"No."

"Ah, well, you'll come to it. And mind you, my boy, there's nothing like it."

"It's always cheering," said Luke, "to hear someone speak well of the marriage state. Especially in these days of easy divorce."

"Pah!" said the Major. "Young people make me sick. No stamina, no endurance. They can't stand anything. No fortitude!" Luke itched to ask why such exceptional fortitude should be needed, but he controlled himself. "Mind you," said the Major. "Lydia was a woman in a thousand—in a thousand! Everyone here respected and looked up to her."

"Yes?"

"She wouldn't stand any nonsense. She'd got a way of fixing a person with her eye, and the person wilted—just wilted. Some of these half-baked girls who call themselves servants nowadays. They think you'll put up with any insolence. Lydia soon showed them! Do you know, we had fifteen cooks and house-parlormaids in one year. Fifteen!" Luke felt that this was hardly a tribute to Mrs. Horton's domestic management, but since it seemed to strike his host differently, he merely murmured some vague remark. "Turned 'em out neck and crop, she did, if they didn't suit."

"Was it always that way about?" asked Luke.

"Well, of course, a lot of them walked out on us. A good riddance— that's what Lydia used to say!"

"A fine spirit," said Luke. "But wasn't it sometimes rather awkward?"

"Oh, I didn't mind turning to and putting my hand to things," said Horton. "I'm a pretty fair cook and I can lay a fire with anyone. I've never cared for washing up, but of course it's got to be done; you can't get away from that."

Luke agreed that you couldn't. He asked whether Mrs. Horton had been good at domestic work. "I'm not the sort of fellow to let his wife wait on him," said Major Horton. "And anyway, Lydia was far too delicate to do any housework."

"She wasn't strong, then?"

Major Horton shook his head. "She had wonderful spirit. She wouldn't give in. But what that woman suffered! And no sympathy from the doctors either. Doctors are callous brutes. They only understand downright physical pain. Anything out of the ordinary is beyond most of them. Humbleby, for instance; everyone seemed to think he was a good doctor."

"You don't agree?"

"The man was an absolute ignoramus. Knew nothing of modern discoveries. Doubt if he'd ever heard of a neurosis! He understands measles and mumps and broken bones, all right, I suppose. But nothing else. Had a row with him in the end. He didn't understand Lydia's case at all. I gave it to him straight from the shoulder and he didn't like it. Got huffed and backed right out. Said I could send for any other doctor I chose. After that, we had Thomas."

"You liked him better?"

"Altogether a much cleverer man. If anyone could have pulled her through her last illness, Thomas would have done it. As a matter of fact, she was getting better, but she had a sudden relapse."

"Was it painful?"

"H'm, yes. Gastritis. Acute pain, sickness, all the rest of it. How that poor woman suffered! She was a martyr, if there ever was one. And a couple of hospital nurses in the house who were about as sympathetic as a brace of grandfather clocks. 'The patient this' and 'the patient that.' " The Major shook his head and drained his glass. "Can't stand hospital nurses! So smug. Lydia insisted they were poisoning her. That wasn't true, of course—a regular sick fancy; lots of people have it, so Thomas said—but there was this much truth behind it—those women disliked her. That's the worst of women—always down on their own sex."

"I suppose," said Luke, feeling that he was putting it awkwardly, but not seeing how to put it better, "that Mrs. Horton had a lot of devoted friends in Wychwood?"

"People were very kind," said the Major, somewhat grudgingly. "Easterfield sent down grapes and peaches from his hothouses. And the old tabbies used to come and sit with her. Honoria Waynflete and Lavinia Fullerton."

"Miss Fullerton came often, did she?"

"Yes. Regular old maid, but a kind creature! Very worried about Lydia, she was. Used to inquire into the diet and the medicines. All kindly meant, you know, but what I call a lot of fuss." Luke nodded comprehendingly. "Can't stand fuss," said the Major. "Too many women in this place. Difficult to get a decent game of golf."

"What about the young fellow at the antique shop?" said Luke.

The Major snorted. "He doesn't play golf."

"Has he been in Wychwood long?"

"About two years. Nasty sort of fellow. Hate those long-haired, purring chaps. Funnily enough, Lydia liked him. You can't trust women's judgment about men. They cotton to some amazing bounders. She even insisted on taking some patent quack nostrum of his. Stuff in a purple glass jar with signs of the Zodiac all over it! Supposed to be certain herbs picked at the full of the moon. Lot of tomfoolery, but women swallow that stuff—swallow it literally, too—ha-ha!"

Luke said, feeling that he was changing the subject rather abruptly, but correctly judging that Major Horton would not be aware of the fact, "What sort of a fellow is Abbot, the local solicitor? Pretty sound on the law? I've got to have some legal advice about something and I thought I might go to him."

"They say he's pretty shrewd," acknowledged Major Horton. "I don't know. Matter of fact, I've had a row with him. Not seen him since he came out here to make Lydia's will for her just before she died. In my opinion, the man's a cad. But of course," he added, "that doesn't affect his ability as a lawyer."

"No, of course not," said Luke. "He seems a quarrelsome sort of man, though. Seems to have fallen out with a good many people, from what I hear."

"Trouble with him is that he's so confoundedly touchy," said Major Horton. "Seems to think he's God Almighty and that anyone who disagrees with him is committing *lèse-majesté*. Heard of his row with Humbleby?"

"They had a row, did they?"

"First-class row. Mind you, that doesn't surprise me. Humbleby was an opinionated ass. Still, there it is."

"His death was very sad."

"Humbleby's? Yes, I suppose it was. Lack of ordinary care. Blood poisoning's a damned dangerous thing. Always put iodine on a cut, I do! Simple precaution. Humbleby, who's a doctor, doesn't do anything of the sort. It just shows." Luke was not quite sure what it showed, but he let that pass. Glancing at his watch, he got up. Major Horton said, "Getting on for lunchtime? So it is. Well, glad to have had a chat with you. Does me good to see a man who's been about a bit. We must have a yarn some other time. Where was your show? Mayang Straits? Never been there. Hear you're writing a book. Superstitions and all that."

"Yes, I—"

But Major Horton swept on, "I can tell you several very interesting things. When I was in India, my boy—"

Luke escaped some ten minutes later, after enduring the usual histories of fakirs, rope and mango tricks, dear to the retired Anglo-Indian. As he stepped out into the open air and heard the Major's voice bellowing to Nero behind him, he marveled at the miracle of married life. Major Horton seemed genuinely to regret a wife who, by all accounts, not excluding his own, must have been nearly allied to a man-eating tiger. Or was it, Luke asked himself the question suddenly—was it an exceedingly clever bluff?

12

THE AFTERNOON OF the tennis party was, fortunately, fine. Lord Easterfield was in his most genial mood, acting the part of the host with a good deal of enjoyment. He referred frequently to his humble origin. The players were eight in all—Lord Easterfield, Bridget, Luke, Rose Humbleby, Mr. Abbot, Doctor Thomas, Major Horton and Hetty Jones, a giggling young woman who was the daughter of the bank manager.

In the second set of the afternoon, Luke found himself partnering Bridget against Lord Easterfield and Rose Humbleby. Rose was a good player with a strong forehand drive, and played in county matches. She atoned for Lord Easterfield's failures, and Bridget and Luke, who were neither of them particularly strong, made quite an even match of it. They were three games all, and then Luke found a streak of erratic brilliance and he and Bridget forged ahead to 5-3. It was then he observed that Lord Easterfield was losing his temper. He argued over a line ball, declared a serve to be a fault, in spite of Rose's disclaimer, and displayed all the attributes of a peevish child. It was set point, but Bridget sent an easy shot into the net and immediately after served a double fault. Deuce. The next ball was returned down the middle line, and as he prepared to take it, he and his partner collided. Then Bridget served another double fault and the game was lost. Bridget apologized, "Sorry; I've gone to pieces."

It seemed true enough. Bridget's shots were wild and she seemed to be unable to do anything right. The set ended with Lord Easterfield and his partner victorious with the score of 8-6. There was a momentary discussion as to the composition of the next set. In the end, Rose played again, with Mr. Abbot as her partner, against Doctor Thomas and Miss Jones.

Lord Easterfield sat down, wiping his forehead and smiling complacently, his good humor quite restored. He began to talk to Major Horton on the subject of a series of articles on "Fitness for Britain" which one of his papers was starting. Luke said to Bridget, "Show me the kitchen garden."

"Why the kitchen garden?"

"I have a feeling for cabbages."

"Won't green peas do?"

"Green peas would be admirable."

They walked away from the tennis court and came to the walled kitchen garden. It was empty of gardeners this Saturday afternoon and looked lazy and peaceful in the sunshine. "Here are your peas," said Bridget.

Luke paid no attention to the object of the visit. He said, "Why did you give them the set?"

Bridget's eyebrows went up a fraction. "I'm sorry. I went to bits. My tennis is erratic."

"Not so erratic as that! Those double faults of yours wouldn't deceive a child! And those wild shots—each of them half a mile out!"

Bridget said calmly, "That's because I'm such a rotten tennis player. If I were a bit better I could, perhaps, have made it a bit more plausible! But as it is, if I try to make a ball go just out, it's always just on the line and all the good work still to do."

"Oh, you admit it then."

"Obvious, my dear Watson."

"And the reason?"

"Equally obvious, I should have thought. Gordon doesn't like losing."

"And what about me? Supposing I like to win?"

"I'm afraid, my dear Luke, that that isn't equally important."

"Would you like to make your meaning just a little clearer still?"

"Certainly, if you like. One mustn't quarrel with one's bread and butter. Gordon is my bread and butter. You are not."

Luke drew a deep breath. Then he exploded, "What do you mean by marrying that absurd little man? Why are you doing it?"

"Because as his secretary I get six pounds a week, and as his wife I shall get a hundred thousand settled on me, a jewel case full of pearls and diamonds, a handsome allowance, and various perquisites of the married state."

"But for somewhat different duties!"

Bridget said coldly, "Must we have this melodramatic attitude towards every single thing in life? If you are contemplating a pretty picture of Gordon as an uxorious lover, you can wash it right out. Gordon, as you should have realized, is a small boy who has not quite grown up. What he needs is a mother, not a wife. Unfortunately, his mother died when he was four years old. What he wants is someone at hand to whom he can brag, someone who will reassure him about himself and who is prepared to listen indefinitely to Lord Easterfield on the subject of himself."

"You've got a bitter tongue, haven't you?"

Bridget retorted sharply, "I don't tell myself fairy stories, if that's what you mean! I'm a young woman with a certain amount of intelligence, very moderate looks, and no money. I intend to earn an honest living. My job as Gordon's wife will be practically indistinguishable from my job as Gordon's secretary. After a year, I doubt if he'll remember to kiss me good night. The only difference is in the salary." They looked at each other. Both of them were pale with anger. Bridget said jeeringly, "Go on. You're rather old-fashioned, aren't you, Mr. Fitzwilliam? Hadn't you better trot out the old clichés—say that I'm selling myself for money—that's always a good one, I think!"

Luke said, "You're a cold-blooded little devil!"

"That's better than being a hot-blooded little fool!"

"Is it?"

"Yes. I know."

Luke sneered. "What do you know?"

"I know what it is to care about a man! Did you ever meet Johnnie Cornish? I was engaged to him for three years. He was adorable. I cared like hell about him—cared so much that it hurt! Well, he threw me over and married a nice plump widow with a North Country accent and three chins, and an income of thirty thousand a year! That sort of thing rather cures one of romance, don't you think?"

Luke turned away with a sudden groan. He said, "It might."

"It did."

There was a pause. The silence lay heavy between them. Bridget broke it at last. She said, but with a slight uncertainty in her tone, "I hope you realize that you had no earthly right to speak to me as you did. You're staying in Gordon's house and it's damned bad taste."

Luke had recovered his composure. "Isn't that rather a cliché too?" he inquired politely.

Bridget flushed. "It's true, anyway."

"It isn't. I had every right."

"Nonsense!"

Luke looked at her. His face had a queer pallor, like a man who is suffering physical pain. He said, "I have a right. I've the right of caring for you—what did you say just now?—of caring so much that it hurts!"

She drew back a step. She said, "You—"

"Yes, funny, isn't it? The sort of thing that ought to give you a hearty laugh! I came down here to do a job of work and you came round the corner of that house and—how can I say it?—put a spell on me! That's what it feels like. You mentioned fairy stories just now. I'm caught up in a fairy story! You've bewitched me. I've a feeling that if you pointed your finger at me and said, 'Turn into a frog,' I'd go hopping away with my eyes popping out of my head." He took a step nearer to her. "I love you like hell, Bridget Conway. And, loving you like hell, you can't expect me to enjoy seeing you get married to a pot-bellied, pompous little peer who loses his temper when he doesn't win at tennis."

"What do you suggest I should do?"

"I suggest that you should marry me instead. But doubtless that suggestion will give rise to a lot of merry laughter."

"The laughter is positively uproarious."

"Exactly. Well, now we know where we are. Shall we return to the tennis court? Perhaps this time you will find me a partner who can play to win."

"Really," said Bridget sweetly. "I believe you mind losing just as much as Gordon does."

Luke caught her suddenly by the shoulders. "You've got a devilish tongue, haven't you, Bridget?"

"I'm afraid you don't like me very much, Luke, however great your passion for me."

"I don't think I like you at all."

Bridget said, watching him, "You meant to get married and settle down when you came home, didn't you?"

"Yes."

"But not to someone like me?"

"I never thought of anyone in the least like you."

"No, you wouldn't. I know your type. I know it exactly."

"You are so clever, dear Bridget."

"A really nice girl, thoroughly English, fond of the country and good with dogs. You probably visualized her in a tweed skirt, stirring a log fire with the tip of her shoe."

"The picture sounds most attractive."

"I'm sure it does. Shall we return to the tennis court? You can play with Rose Humbleby. She's so good that you're practically certain to win."

"Being old-fashioned, I must allow you to have the last word."

Again there was a pause. Then Luke took his hands slowly from her shoulders. They both stood uncertain, as though something still unsaid lingered between them.

Then Bridget turned abruptly and led the way back. The next set was just ending. Rose protested against playing again. "I've played two sets running."

Bridget, however, insisted. "I'm feeling tired. I don't want to play. You and Mr. Fitzwilliam take on Miss Jones and Major Horton."

But Rose continued to protest, and in the end a men's four was arranged. Afterward came tea.

Lord Easterfield conversed with Doctor Thomas, describing at length and with great self-importance a visit he had recently paid to the Wellerman Kreitz Research Laboratories. "I wanted to understand the trend of the latest scientific discoveries for myself," he explained earnestly. "I'm responsible for what my papers print. I feel that very keenly. This is a scientific age. Science must be made easily assimilable by the masses."

"A little science might possibly be a dangerous thing," said Doctor Thomas, with a slight shrug of his shoulders.

"Science in the home—that's what we have to aim at," said Lord Easterfield. "Science-minded—"

"Test-tube conscious," said Bridget gravely.

"I was impressed," said Lord Easterfield. "Wellerman took me round himself, of course. I begged him to leave me to an underling, but he insisted."

"Naturally," said Luke.

Lord Easterfield looked gratified. "And he explained everything most clearly—the cultures, the serum, the whole principle of the thing. He agreed to contribute the first article in the series himself."

Mrs. Anstruther murmured, "They use guinea pigs, I believe. So cruel—though, of course, not so bad as dogs, or even cats."

"Fellows who use dogs ought to be shot," said Major Horton hoarsely.

"I really believe, Horton," said Mr. Abbot, "that you value canine life above human life."

"Every time!" said the Major. "Dogs can't turn round on you like human beings can. Never get a nasty word from a dog."

"Only a nasty tooth stuck into your leg," said Mr. Abbot. "What about that, eh, Horton?"

"Dogs are a good judge of character," said Major Horton.

"One of your brutes nearly pinned me by the leg last week. What do you say to that, Horton?"

"Same as I said just now!"

Bridget interposed tactfully, "What about some more tennis?"

A couple more sets were played. Then, as Rose Humbleby said good-by, Luke appeared beside her. "I'll see you home," he said. "And carry the tennis racket. You haven't got a car, have you?"

"No, but it's no distance."

"I'd like a walk." He said no more, merely taking her racket and shoes from her. They walked down the drive without speaking. Then Rose mentioned one or two trivial matters. Luke answered rather shortly, but the girl did not seem to notice.

As they turned into the gate of her house, Luke's face cleared. "I'm feeling better now," he said.

"Were you feeling badly before?"

"Nice of you to pretend you didn't notice it. You've exorcised the brute's sulky temper, though. Funny, I feel as though I'd come out of a dark cloud into the sun."

"So you have. There was a cloud over the sun when we left the Manor, and now it's passed over."

"So it has, literally as well as figuratively. Well, well, the world's a good place, after all."

"Of course it is."

"Miss Humbleby, may I be impertinent?"

"I'm sure you couldn't be."

"Oh, don't be too sure of that. I wanted to say that I think Doctor Thomas is a very lucky man." Rose blushed and smiled. "So it is true. You and he are engaged?"

Rose nodded. "Only, just now we're not announcing it officially. You see, daddy was against it, and it seems—well, unkind to—to blazon it abroad the moment he's dead."

"Your father disapproved?"

Rose bent her head slowly and reluctantly. "Yes, I'm afraid what it really amounted to was that daddy didn't—well, didn't really like Geoffrey."

"They were antagonistic to each other?"

"It seemed like that sometimes. Of course, daddy was rather a prejudiced old dear."

"And I suppose he was very fond of you and didn't like the thought of losing you?" Rose assented, but still with a shade of reservation in her manner. "It went deeper than that?" asked Luke. "He definitely didn't want Thomas as a husband for you?"

"No. You see, daddy and Geoffrey are so very unlike and in some ways they clashed. Geoffrey was really very patient and good about it, but knowing daddy didn't like him made him even more reserved and shy in his manner, so that daddy really never got to know him any better."

"Prejudices are very hard to combat," said Luke.

"It was so completely unreasonable!"

"Your father didn't advance any reasons?"

"Oh, no. He couldn't! Naturally, I mean, there wasn't anything he could say against Geoffrey except that he didn't like him."

> *"I do not love thee, Doctor Fell;*
> *The reason why I cannot tell."*

"Exactly."

"No tangible thing to get hold of? I mean, your Geoffrey doesn't drink or back horses?"

"Oh, no. I don't believe Geoffrey even knows what won the Derby."

"That's funny," said Luke. "You know, I could swear I saw your Doctor Thomas at Epsom on Derby Day."

For a moment he was anxious lest he might already have mentioned that he only arrived in England on that day. But Rose responded at once, quite unsuspiciously.

"You thought you saw Geoffrey at the Derby? Oh, no. He couldn't get away, for one thing. He was over at Ashewold nearly all that day at a difficult confinement case."

"What a memory you've got!"

Rose laughed. "I remember that because he told me they called the baby Jujube as a nickname!" Luke nodded abstractedly. "Anyway," said Rose, "Geoffrey never goes to race meetings. He'd be bored to death." She added, in a different tone, "Won't you come in? I think mother would like to see you."

"If you're sure of that?"

Rose led the way into a room where twilight hung rather sadly. A woman was sitting in an armchair in a curiously huddled-up position. "Mother, this is Mr. Fitzwilliam." Mrs. Humbleby gave a start and shook hands. Rose went quietly out of the room.

"I'm glad to see you, Mr. Fitzwilliam. Some friends of yours knew my husband many years ago, so Rose tells me."

"Yes, Mrs. Humbleby." He rather hated repeating the lie to the widowed woman, but there was no way out of it.

Mrs. Humbleby said, "I wish you could have met him. He was a fine man and a great doctor. He cured many people who had been given up as hopeless, just by the strength of his personality."

Luke said gently, "I've heard a lot about him since I've been here. I know how much people thought of him."

He could not see Mrs. Humbleby's face very distinctly. Her voice was rather monotonous, but its very lack of feeling seemed to emphasize the fact that actually feeling was in her, strenuously held back. She said, rather unexpectedly, "The world is a very wicked place, Mr. Fitzwilliam. Do you know that?"

Luke was a little surprised. "Yes, perhaps that may be."

She insisted, "No, but you do know it? It's important, that. There's a lot of wickedness about. One must be prepared—to fight it! John was. He knew. He was on the side of the right!"

Luke said gently, "I'm sure he was."

"He knew the wickedness there was in this place," said Mrs. Humbleby.

"He knew—" She burst suddenly into tears.

Luke murmured, "I'm so sorry," and stopped.

She controlled herself as suddenly as she had lost control. "You must forgive me," she said. She held out her hand and he took it. "Do come and see us while you are here," she said. "It would be so good for Rose. She likes you so much."

"I like her. I think your daughter is the nicest girl I've met for a long time, Mrs. Humbleby."

"She's very good to me."

"Doctor Thomas is a very lucky man."

"Yes." Mrs. Humbleby dropped his hand. Her voice had gone flat again. "I don't know. It's all so difficult."

Luke left her standing in the half gloom, her fingers nervously twisting and untwisting themselves. As he walked home, his mind went over various aspects of the conversation. Doctor Thomas had been absent from Wychwood for a good part of Derby Day. He had been absent in a car. Wychwood was thirty-five miles from London. Supposedly he had been attending a confinement case. Was there more than his word? The point, he supposed, could be verified. His mind went on to Mrs. Humbleby. What had she meant by her insistence on that phrase: "There's a lot of wickedness about." Was she just nervous and overwrought by the shock of her husband's death? Or was there something more to it than that? Did she, perhaps, know something? Something that Dr. Humbleby had known before he died? "I've got to go on with this," said Luke to himself. "I've got to go on."

Resolutely, he averted his mind from the passage of arms that had taken place between him and Bridget.

13

ON THE FOLLOWING morning, Luke came to a decision. He had, he felt, proceeded as far as he could with indirect inquiries. It was inevitable that sooner or later he would be forced into the open. He felt that the time had come to drop the book-writing camouflage and reveal that he had come to Wychwood with a definite aim in view. In pursuance of this plan of campaign, he decided to call upon Honoria Waynflete. He believed that she had told him what she knew. He wanted to induce her to tell him what she might have guessed. He had a shrewd idea that Miss Waynflete's guesses might be fairly near the truth.

Miss Waynflete received him in a matter-of-fact manner, showing no surprise at his call. As she sat down near him, her prim hands folded and her intelligent eyes—so like an amiable goat's—fixed on his face, he found little difficulty in coming to the object of his visit. He said, "I dare say you have guessed, Miss Waynflete, that the reason for my coming here is not merely to write a book on local customs?" Miss Waynflete inclined her head and continued to listen.

"I am down here to inquire into the circumstances of the death of that poor girl, Amy Gibbs."

Miss Waynflete said, "You mean you have been sent down by the police?"

"Oh, no, I'm not a plain-clothes dick." He added, with a slightly humorous inflection, "I'm afraid I'm that well-known character in fiction, the private investigator."

"I see. Then it was Bridget Conway who brought you down here?" Luke hesitated a moment. Then he decided to let it go at that. Without going into the whole Fullerton story, it was difficult to account for his presence.

Miss Waynflete was continuing, a note of gentle admiration in her voice: "Bridget is so practical, so efficient! I'm afraid if it had been left to me, I should have distrusted my own judgment. I mean that if you are not absolutely sure of a thing, it is so difficult to commit yourself to a definite course of action."

"But you are sure, aren't you?"

Miss Waynflete said gravely, "No, indeed, Mr. Fitzwilliam. It is not a thing one can be sure about. I mean, it might all be imagination. Living alone, with no one to consult or to talk to, one might easily become melodramatic, and imagine things which had no foundation in fact."

Luke assented readily to this statement, recognizing its inherent truth, but he added gently, "But you are sure in your own mind?"

Even here Miss Waynflete showed a little reluctance. "We are not talking at cross purposes, I hope?" she demurred.

Luke smiled. "You would like me to put it in plain words? Very well. You do think that Amy Gibbs was murdered?"

Honoria Waynflete flinched a little at the crudity of the language. She said, "I don't feel at all happy about her death. Not at all happy. The whole thing is profoundly unsatisfactory, in my opinion."

Luke said patiently, "But you don't think her death was a natural one?"

"No."

"You don't believe it was an accident?"

"It seems to me most improbable. There are so many—"

Luke cut her short, "You don't think it was suicide?"

"Emphatically not."

"Then," said Luke gently, "you do think that it was murder?"

Miss Waynflete hesitated, gulped, and bravely took the plunge. "Yes," she said, "I do!"

"Good. Now we can get on with things."

"But I have really no evidence on which to base that belief," Miss Waynflete explained anxiously. "It is entirely an idea."

"Quite so. This is a private conversation. We are merely speaking about what we think and suspect. We suspect Amy Gibbs was murdered. Who do we think murdered her?"

Miss Waynflete shook her head. She was looking very troubled. Luke said, watching her, "Who had reason to murder her?"

Miss Waynflete said slowly, "She had had a quarrel, I believe, with her young man at the garage, Jim Harvey—a most steady, superior young man. I know one reads in the papers of young men attacking their sweethearts, and dreadful things like that, but I really can't believe that Jim would do such a thing." Luke nodded. Miss Waynflete went on, "Besides, I can't believe that he would do it that way. Climb up to her window and substitute a bottle of poison for the other one with the cough mixture. I mean, that doesn't seem—"

Luke came to the rescue as she hesitated. "It's not the act of an angry lover? I agree. In my opinion, we can wash Jim Harvey right out. Amy was killed—we're agreeing she was killed—by someone who wanted to get her out of the way and who planned the crime carefully, so that it should appear to be an accident. Now, have you any idea—any hunch—shall we put it like that?—who that person could be?"

Miss Waynflete said, "No—really—no, I haven't the least idea!"

"Sure?"

"N-no; no indeed."

Luke looked at her thoughtfully. The denial, he felt, had not rung quite true. He went on, "You know of no motive?"

"No motive whatever." That was more emphatic.

"Had she been in many places in Wychwood?"

"She was with the Hortons for a year before going to Lord Easterfield."

Luke summed up rapidly, "It's like this, then: Somebody wanted that girl out of the way. From the given facts, we assume that, first, it was a man, and a man of moderately old-fashioned outlook—as shown by the hat-paint touch—and secondly, that it must have been a reasonably athletic man, since it is clear he must have climbed up over the outhouse to the girl's window. You agree on those points?"

"Absolutely," said Miss Waynflete.

"Do you mind if I go round and have a try myself?"

"Not at all. I think that is a very good idea."

She led him out by a side door and round to the back yard. Luke managed to reach the outhouse roof without much trouble. From there he could easily raise the sash of the girl's window and with a slight effort hoist himself into the room. A few minutes later he rejoined Miss Waynflete on the path below, wiping his hands on his handkerchief. "Actually it's easier than it looks," he said. "You want a certain amount of muscle, that's all. There were no signs on the sill or outside?"

Miss Waynflete shook her head. "I don't think so. Of course, the constable climbed up this way."

"So that if there were any traces, they would be taken to be his. How the police force assists the criminal! Well, that's that!"

Miss Waynflete led the way back to the house.

"Was Amy Gibbs a heavy sleeper?" he asked.

Miss Waynflete replied acidly, "It was extremely difficult to get her up in the morning. Sometimes I would knock again and again, and call out to her before she answered. But then, you know, Mr. Fitzwilliam, there's a saying there are 'none so deaf as those who will not hear.'"

"That's true," acknowledged Luke. "Well, now, Miss Waynflete, we come to the question of motive. Starting with the most obvious one, do you think there was anything between that fellow Ellsworthy and the girl?" He added hastily, "This is just your opinion I'm asking. Only that."

"If it's a matter of opinion, I would say yes."

Luke nodded. "In your opinion, would the girl Amy have stuck at a spot of blackmail?"

"Again as a matter of opinion, I should say that that was quite possible."

"Do you happen to know if she had much money in her possession at the time of her death?"

Miss Waynflete reflected. "I don't think so. If she had had any unusual amount, I think I should have heard about it."

"And she hadn't launched into any unusual extravagance before she died?"

"I don't think so."

"That rather militates against the blackmail theory. The victim usually pays once before he decides to proceed to extremes. There's another theory. The girl might know something."

"What kind of thing?"

"She might have knowledge that was dangerous to someone here in

Wychwood. We'll take a strictly hypothetical case. She'd been in service in a good many houses here. Supposing she came to know of something that would damage, say, someone like Mr. Abbot professionally."

"Mr. Abbot?"

Luke said quickly, "Or possibly some negligence or unprofessional conduct on the part of Doctor Thomas."

Miss Waynflete began, "But surely—" and then stopped.

Luke went on, "Amy Gibbs was housemaid, you said, in the Hortons' house at the time when Mrs. Horton died."

There was a moment's pause, then Miss Waynflete said, "Will you tell me, Mr. Fitzwilliam, why you bring the Hortons into this? Mrs. Horton died over a year ago."

"Yes, and the girl Amy was there at the time."

"I see. What have the Hortons to do with it?"

"I don't know. I just wondered. Mrs. Horton died of acute gastritis, didn't she?"

"Yes."

"Was her death at all unexpected?"

Miss Waynflete said slowly, "It was to me. You see, she had been getting much better—seemed well on the road to recovery—and then she had a sudden relapse and died."

"Was Doctor Thomas surprised?"

"I don't know. I believe he was."

"And the nurses—what did they say?"

"In my experience," said Miss Waynflete, "hospital nurses are never surprised at any case taking a turn for the worse. It is recovery that surprises them."

"But her death surprised you?" Luke persisted.

"Yes. I had been with her only the day before, and she had seemed very much better, talked and seemed quite cheerful."

"What did she think about her own illness?"

"She complained that the nurses were poisoning her. She had had one nurse sent away, but she said these two were just as bad."

"I suppose you didn't pay much attention to that?"

"Well, no, I thought it was all part of the illness. And she was a very suspicious woman and—it may be unkind to say so, but she liked to make herself important. No doctor ever understood her case, and it was never anything simple; it must either be some very obscure disease or else somebody was 'trying to get her out of the way.'"

Luke tried to make his voice casual. "She didn't suspect her husband of trying to do her in?"

"Oh, no, that idea never occurred to her!" Miss Waynflete paused a minute, then she asked quietly, "Is that what you think?"

Luke said slowly, "Husbands have done that before and got away with it. Mrs. Horton, from all accounts, was a woman any man might have longed to be rid of. And I understand that he came into a good deal of money on her death."

"Yes, he did."

"What do you think, Miss Waynflete?"

"You want my opinion?"

"Yes, just your opinion."

Miss Waynflete said, quietly and deliberately, "In my opinion, Major Horton was quite devoted to his wife and would never have dreamed of doing such a thing."

Luke looked at her and received the mild amber glance in reply. It did not waver.

"Well," he said, "I expect you're right. You'd probably know if it was the other way round."

Miss Waynflete permitted herself a smile. "We women are good observers, you think?"

"Absolutely first class. Would Miss Fullerton have agreed with you, do you think?"

"I don't think I ever heard Lavinia express an opinion."

"What did she think about Amy Gibbs?"

Miss Waynflete frowned a little, as though thinking. "It's difficult to say. Lavinia had a very curious idea."

"What idea?"

"She thought that there was something odd going on here in Wychwood."

"She thought, for instance, that somebody pushed Tommy Pierce out of that window?"

Miss Waynflete stared at him in astonishment. "How did you know that, Mr. Fitzwilliam?"

"She told me so. Not in those words, but she gave me the general idea."

Miss Waynflete leaned forward, pink with excitement. "When was this, Mr. Fitzwilliam?"

Luke said quietly, "The day she was killed. We traveled together to London."

"What did she tell you exactly?"

"She told me that there had been too many deaths in Wychwood. She mentioned Amy Gibbs, and Tommy Pierce, and that man, Carter. She also said that Doctor Humbleby would be the next to go."

Miss Waynflete nodded slowly. "Did she tell you who was responsible?"

"A man with a certain look in his eyes," said Luke grimly. "A look you couldn't mistake, according to her. She'd seen that look in his eye when he was talking to Humbleby. That's why she said Humbleby would be the next to go."

"And he was," whispered Miss Waynflete. "Oh, dear! Oh, dear!" She leaned back. Her eyes had a stricken look in them.

"Who was the man?" said Luke. "Come now, Miss Waynflete; you know—you must know!"

"I don't. She didn't tell me."

"But you can guess," said Luke keenly. "You've a very shrewd idea of who was in her mind." Reluctantly, Miss Waynflete bowed her head. "Then tell me."

But Miss Waynflete shook her head energetically. "No, indeed. You're asking me to do something that is highly improper! You're asking me to guess at what may—only may, mind you—have been in the mind of a friend who is now dead. I couldn't make an accusation of that kind!"

"It wouldn't be an accusation, only an opinion."

But Miss Waynflete was unexpectedly firm. "I've nothing to go on—nothing whatever," she said. "Lavinia never actually said anything to me. I may think she had a certain idea, but, you see, I might be entirely wrong. And then I should have misled you, and perhaps serious consequences might ensue. It would be very wicked and unfair of me to mention a name. And I may be quite, quite wrong! In fact, I probably am wrong!" And Miss Waynflete set her lips firmly and glared at Luke with a grim determination.

Luke knew how to accept defeat when he met it. He realized that Miss Waynflete's sense of rectitude and something else more nebulous that he could not quite place were both against him. He accepted defeat with a good grace and rose to say good-by. He had every intention of returning to the charge later, but he allowed no hint of that to escape into his manner. "You must do as you think right, of course," he said. "Thank you for the help you have given me."

Miss Waynflete seemed to become a little less sure of herself as she accompanied him to the door. "I hope you don't think—" she began; then changed the form of the sentence. "If there is anything else I can do to help you, please, please, let me know."

"I will. You won't repeat this conversation, will you?"

"Of course not. I shan't say a word to anybody." Luke hoped that that was true. "Give my love to Bridget," said Miss Waynflete. "She's such a handsome girl, isn't she? And clever too. I—I hope she will be happy." And, as Luke looked a question, she added, "Married to Lord Easterfield, I mean. Such a great difference in age."

"Yes, there is."

Miss Waynflete sighed, "You know that I was engaged to him once," she said unexpectedly.

Luke stared in astonishment. She was nodding her head and smiling rather sadly. "A long time ago. He was such a promising boy. I had helped him, you know, to educate himself. And I was so proud of his—his spirit and the way he was determined to succeed." She sighed again. "My people, of course, were scandalized. Class distinctions in those days were very strong." She added, after a minute or two, "I've always followed his career with great interest. My people, I think, were wrong." Then, with a smile, she nodded a farewell and went back into the house.

Luke tried to collect his thoughts. He had placed Miss Waynflete as definitely "old." He realized now that she was probably still under sixty. Lord Easterfield must be well over fifty. She might, perhaps, be a year or two older than he, no more. And he was going to marry Bridget. Bridget, who was twenty-eight, Bridget, who was young and alive. "Oh, damn," said Luke. "Don't let me go on thinking of it. The job. Get on with the job."

14

MRS. CHURCH, Amy Gibbs' aunt, was definitely an unpleasant woman. Her sharp nose, shifty eyes and her voluble tongue all alike filled Luke with nausea. He adopted a curt manner with her and found it unexpectedly successful. "What you've got to do," he told her, "is to answer my questions to the best of your ability. If you hold back anything or tamper with the truth, the consequences may be extremely serious to you."

"Yes, sir. I see. I'm sure I'm only too willing to tell you anything I can. I've never been mixed up with the police—"

"And you don't want to be," finished Luke. "Well, if you do as I've told you, there won't be any question of that. I want to know all about your late niece—who her friends were, what money she had, anything she said that might be out of the way. We'll start with her friends. Who were they?"

Mrs. Church leered at him slyly out of the corner of an unpleasant eye. "You'll be meaning gentlemen, sir?"

"Had she any girlfriends?"

"Well, hardly—not to speak of, sir. Of course, there was girls she'd been in service with, but Amy didn't keep up with them much. You see—"

"She preferred the sterner sex. Go on. Tell me about that."

"It was Jim Harvey down at the garage she was actually going with, sir. And a nice steady young fellow he was. 'You couldn't do better,' I've said to her many a time."

Luke cut in, "And the others?"

Again he got the sly look. "I expect you're thinking of the gentleman who keeps the curiosity shop? I didn't like it myself, and I tell you that straight, sir! I've always been respectable and I don't hold with carryings on! But with what girls are nowadays, it's no use speaking to them. They go their own way. And often they live to regret it."

"Did Amy live to regret it?" asked Luke bluntly.

"No, sir, that I do not think."

"She went to consult Doctor Thomas on the day of her death. That wasn't the reason?"

"No, sir, I'm nearly sure it wasn't. Oh, I'd take my oath on it! Amy had been feeling ill and out of sorts, but it was just a bad cough and cold she had. It wasn't anything of the kind you suggest; I'm sure it wasn't, sir."

"I'll take your word for that. How far had matters gone between her and Ellsworthy?"

Mrs. Church leered. "I couldn't exactly say, sir. Amy wasn't one for confiding in me."

Luke said curtly, "But they'd gone pretty far?"

Mrs. Church said smoothly, "The gentleman hasn't got at all a good reputation here, sir. All sorts of goings on. And friends down from town and many queer happenings. Up in the Witches' Meadow in the middle of the night."

"Did Amy go?"

"She did go once, sir, I believe. Stayed out all night, and his lordship found out about it—she was at the Manor then—and spoke to her pretty sharp, and she sauced him back and he gave her notice for it, which was only to be expected."

"Did she ever talk to you much about what went on in the places she was in?"

Mrs. Church shook her head. "Not very much, sir. More interested in her own doings, she was."

"She was with Major and Mrs. Horton for a while, wasn't she?"

"Nearly a year, sir."

"Why did she leave?"

"Just to better herself. There was a place going at the Manor and, of course, the wages was better there."

Luke nodded. "She was with the Hortons at the time of Mrs. Horton's death?" he asked.

"Yes, sir. She grumbled a lot about that—with two hospital nurses in the house, and all that extra work nurses make and the trays and one thing and another."

"She wasn't with Mr. Abbot, the lawyer, at all?"

"No, sir. Mr. Abbot has a man and wife do for him. Amy did go to see him once at his office, but I don't know why."

Luke stored away that small fact as possibly relevant. Since Mrs. Church, however, clearly knew nothing more about it, he did not pursue the subject. "Any other gentlemen in the town who were friends of hers?"

"Nothing that I'd care to repeat."

"Come now, Mrs. Church. I want the truth, remember."

"It wasn't a gentleman, sir; very far from it. Demeaning herself, that's what it was, and so I told her."

"Do you mind speaking more plainly, Mrs. Church?"

"You'll have heard of the Seven Stars, sir? Not a good-class house, and the landlord, Harry Carter, a low-class fellow and half seas over most of the time."

"Amy was a friend of his?"

"She went for a walk with him once or twice. I don't believe there was more in it than that. I don't indeed, sir."

Luke nodded thoughtfully and changed the subject. "Did you know a small boy, Tommy Pierce?"

"What? Mrs. Pierce's son? Of course I did. Always up to mischief."

"He ever see much of Amy?"

"Oh, no, sir. Amy would soon send him off with a flea in his ear if he tried any of his tricks on her."

"Was she happy in her place with Miss Waynflete?"

"She found it a bit dull, sir, and the pay wasn't high. But of course, after she'd been dismissed the way she was from Ashe Manor, it wasn't so easy to get another good place."

"She could have gone away, I suppose?"

"To London, you mean?"

"Or some other part of the country?"

Mrs. Church shook her head. She said slowly, "Amy didn't want to leave Wychwood; not as things were."

"How do you mean, 'as things were'?"

"What with Jim and the gentleman at the curio shop." Luke nodded thoughtfully. Mrs. Church went on, "Miss Waynflete is a very nice lady, but very particular about brass and silver and everything being dusted and the mattresses turned. Amy wouldn't have put up with the fussing if she hadn't been enjoying herself in other ways."

"I can imagine that," said Luke dryly. He turned things over in his mind. He could see no further questions to ask. He was fairly certain that he had extracted all that Mrs. Church knew. He decided on one last tentative attack: "I dare say you can guess the reason for all these questions. The circumstances of Amy's death were rather mysterious. We're not entirely satisfied as to its being an accident. If not, you realize what it must have been."

Mrs. Church said, with a certain ghoulish relief, "Foul play!"

"Quite so. Now, supposing your niece did meet with foul play, who do you think is likely to be responsible for her death?"

Mrs. Church wiped her hands on her apron. "There'd be a reward, as likely as not, for setting the police on the right track?" she inquired meaningly.

"There might be," said Luke.

"I wouldn't like to say anything definite"—Mrs. Church passed a hungry tongue over her thin lips—"but the gentleman at the curio shop is a queer one. You'll remember the Castor case, sir, and that poor girl. And there've been five or six other poor girls served the same way later. Maybe this Mr. Ellsworthy is one of that kind?"

"That's your suggestion, is it?"

"Well, it might be that way, sir, mightn't it?"

Luke admitted that it might. Then he said, "Was Ellsworthy away from here on the afternoon of Derby Day? That's a very important point."

Mrs. Church stared. "Derby Day?"

"Yes, a fortnight ago last Wednesday."

She shook her head. "Really, I couldn't say as to that. He usually was away on Wednesdays; went up to town as often as not. It's early closing Wednesday, you see."

"Oh," said Luke, "early closing."

He took his leave of Mrs. Church, disregarding her insinuations that her time had been valuable and that she was therefore entitled to monetary compensation. He found himself disliking Mrs. Church intensely. Nevertheless, the conversation he had had with her, though not strikingly illuminative in any way, had provided several suggestive small points.

HE WENT OVER things carefully in his mind. Yes, it still boiled down to those four people—Thomas, Abbot, Horton and Ellsworthy. The attitude of Miss Waynflete seemed, to him, to prove that. Her distress and reluctance to mention a name. Surely that meant—that must mean—that the person in question was someone of standing in Wychwood, someone whom a chance insinuation might definitely injure. It tallied, too, with Miss Fullerton's determination to take her suspicions to headquarters. The local police would ridicule her theory. It was not a case of the butcher, the baker, the candlestick maker. It was not a case of a mere garage mechanic. The person in question was one against whom an accusation of murder was a fantastic and, moreover, a serious matter. There were four possible candidates. It was up to him to go carefully once more into the case against each one and make up his own mind.

First to examine the reluctance of Miss Waynflete. She was a conscientious and scrupulous person. She believed that she knew the man whom Miss Fullerton had suspected, but it was, as she had pointed out, only a belief on her part. It was possible that she was mistaken. Who was the person in Miss Waynflete's mind? Miss Waynflete was distressed lest an accusation by her might injure an innocent man. Therefore, the object of her suspicions must be a man of high standing, generally liked and respected by the community. Therefore, Luke argued, that automatically barred out Ellsworthy. He was practically a stranger to Wychwood; his local reputation was bad, not good. Luke did not believe that, if Ellsworthy was the person in Miss Waynflete's mind, she would have had any objection to mentioning him. Therefore, as far as Miss Waynflete was concerned, wash out Ellsworthy.

Now, as to the others. Luke believed that he could also eliminate Major Horton. Miss Waynflete had rebutted with some warmth the suggestion that Horton might have poisoned his wife. If she had suspected him of later crimes, she would hardly have been so positive about his innocence of the death of Mrs. Horton.

That left Doctor Thomas and Mr. Abbot. Both of them fulfilled the necessary requirements. They were men of high professional standing, against whom no word of scandal had ever been uttered. They were, on the whole, both popular and well liked, and were known as men of integrity and rectitude.

Luke proceeded to another aspect of the matter. Could he, himself, eliminate Ellsworthy and Horton? Immediately he shook his head. It was not so simple. Miss Fullerton had known—really known—who the man was. That was proved, in the first case, by her own death, and, in the second case, by the death of Doctor Humbleby. But Miss Fullerton had never actually mentioned a name to Honoria Waynflete. Therefore, though Miss Waynflete thought she knew, she might quite easily be wrong. We often know what other people are thinking, but sometimes we find out that we did not know, after all, and have, in fact, made an egregious mistake.

Therefore, the four candidates were still in the field. Miss Fullerton was dead and could give no further assistance. It was up to Luke to do what he had done before, on the day after he came to Wychwood—weigh up the evidence and consider the probabilities.

He began with Ellsworthy. On the face of it, Ellsworthy was the likeliest starter.

"Let's take it this way," said Luke to himself. "Suspect everyone in turn. Ellsworthy, for instance. Let's say he's the killer. For the moment, let's take it quite definitely that I know that. Now we'll take the possible victims in chronological order. First, Mrs. Horton. Difficult to see what motive Ellsworthy could have had for doing away with Mrs. Horton. But there was a means. Horton spoke of some quack nostrum that she got from him and took. Some poison like arsenic could have been given that way. The question is: Why?

"Now the others. Amy Gibbs. Why did Ellsworthy kill Amy Gibbs? The obvious reason—she was being a nuisance. Threatened an action for breach of promise, perhaps? Or had she assisted at a midnight orgy? Did she threaten to talk? Lord Easterfield has a good deal of influence in Wychwood, and Lord Easterfield, according to Bridget, is a very moral man. He might have taken up the matter against Ellsworthy if the latter had been up to anything particularly objectionable. So, exit Amy. Not, I think, a sadistic murder. The method employed is against that.

"Who's next? Carter? Why Carter? Unlikely he would know about midnight orgies—or did Amy tell him? Was the pretty daughter mixed up in it? Did Ellsworthy start making love to her? Must have a look at Lucy Carter. Perhaps he was just abusive to Ellsworthy, and Ellsworthy resented it. If he'd already committed one or two murders, he would be getting sufficiently callous to contemplate a killing for a very slight reason.

"Now Tommy Pierce. Why did Ellsworthy kill Tommy Pierce? Easy. Tommy had assisted at a midnight ritual of some kind. Tommy threatened to talk about it. Perhaps Tommy was talking about it. Shut Tommy's mouth.

"Doctor Humbleby. Why did Ellsworthy kill Doctor Humbleby? That's the easiest of the lot. Humbleby was a doctor, and he'd noticed that Ellsworthy's mental balance was none too good. Probably was getting ready to do something about it. So Humbleby was doomed. There's a stumbling block there in the method. How did Ellsworthy insure that Humbleby should die of blood poisoning? Or did Humbleby die of something else? Was the poisoned finger a coincidence?

"Last of all, Miss Fullerton. Wednesday's early closing. Ellsworthy might have gone up to town that day. Has he a car, I wonder? Never seen him in one, but that proves nothing. He knew she'd suspected him, and he was going to take no chances of Scotland Yard believing her story. Perhaps they already knew something about him then?

"That's the case against Ellsworthy! Now, what is there for him? Well, for one thing, he's certainly not the man Miss Waynflete thought Miss Fullerton meant. For another, he doesn't fit—quite—with my own vague impression. When she was talking, I got a picture of a man—and it wasn't a man like Ellsworthy. The impression she gave me was of a very ordinary man—outwardly, that is—the kind of man nobody would suspect. Ellsworthy is the kind of man you would suspect. No, I got more the impression of a man like—Doctor Thomas.

"Thomas, now. What about Thomas? I wiped him clean off the list after I'd had a chat with him. Nice, unassuming fellow. But the whole point of this murderer—unless I've got the whole thing wrong—is that he would be a nice, unassuming fellow. The last person you'd think ever would be a murderer! Which, of course, is exactly what one feels about Thomas.

"Now then, let's go through it again. Why did Doctor Thomas kill Amy Gibbs? Really, it seems most unlikely that he did. But she did go to see him that day, and he did give her that bottle of cough mixture. Suppose that was really oxalic acid. That would be very simple and clever. Who was called in, I wonder, when she was found poisoned—Humbleby or Thomas? If it was Thomas, he might just come along with an old bottle of hat paint in his pocket, put it down unobtrusively on the table, and take off both bottles to be analyzed, as bold as brass. Something like that. It could be done if you were cool enough.

"Tommy Pierce? Again I can't see a likely motive. That's the difficulty with our Doctor Thomas—motive. There's not even a crazy motive. Same with Carter. Why should Doctor Thomas want to dispose of Carter? One can only assume that Amy, Tommy and the publican all knew something about Doctor Thomas that it was unhealthy to know. Ah, supposing, now, that that something was the death of Mrs. Horton. Doctor Thomas attended her. And she died of a rather unexpected relapse. He could have managed that easily enough. And Amy Gibbs, remember, was in the house at the time. She might have seen or heard something. That would account for her. Tommy Pierce, we have it on good authority, was a particularly inquisitive small boy. He may have got wise to something. Can't fit Carter in. Unless Amy Gibbs told him something. He may have repeated it in his cups and Thomas may have decided to silence him too. All this, of course, is pure conjecture. But what else can one do?

"Now Humbleby. Ah, at last we come to a perfectly plausible murder. Adequate motive and ideal means. If Doctor Thomas couldn't give his partner blood poisoning, no one could. He could reinfect the wound every time he dressed it. I wish the earlier killings were a little more plausible.

"Miss Fullerton? She's more difficult, but there is one definite fact. Doctor Thomas was not in Wychwood for at least a good part of the day. He gave out that he was attending a confinement. That may be. But the fact remains that he was away from Wychwood in a car. Is there anything else? Yes, just one thing. The look he gave me when I went away from the house the other day. Superior, condescending, the smile of a man who'd just led me up the garden path and knew it."

Luke sighed, shook his head and went on with his reasoning. "Abbot? He's the right kind of man too. Normal, well-to-do, respected, last sort of man, and so on. He's conceited, too, and confident. Murderers usually are. They've got overweening conceit. Always think they'll get away with it. Amy Gibbs paid him a visit once. Why? What did she want to see him for? To get legal advice? Why? Or was it a personal matter? There's the mention of 'a letter from a lady' that Tommy saw. Was that letter from Amy Gibbs? Or was it a letter written by Mrs. Horton—a letter, perhaps, that Amy Gibbs had got hold of? What other lady could there be writing to Mr. Abbot on a matter so private that he loses control when the office boy inadvertently sees it? What else can we think of re Amy Gibbs? The hat paint? Yes, right kind of old-fashioned touch—men like Abbot are usually well behind the times where women are concerned. The Old World style of philanderer. Tommy Pierce? Obvious, on account of the letter—really it must have been a very damning letter. Carter? Well, there was trouble about Carter's daughter. Abbot wasn't going to have a scandal—a low-down ruffianly half-wit like Carter dare to threaten him. He who had got away with two clever killings! Away with Mr. Carter! Dark night and a well-directed push. Really, this killing business is almost too easy.

"Have I got the Abbot mentality? I think so. Nasty look in an old lady's eye. She's thinking things about him. Then, row with Humbleby. Old Humbleby daring to set himself against Abbot, the clever solicitor and murderer. 'The old fool—he little knows what's in store for him! He's for it! Daring to browbeat me!'

"And then—what? Turning to catch Lavinia Fullerton's eyes. And his own eyes falter, show a consciousness of guilt. He who was boasting of being unsuspected has definitely aroused suspicion. Miss Fullerton knows his secret. She knows what he has done. Yes, but she can't have proof. But suppose she goes about looking for it. Suppose she talks. Suppose—He's quite a shrewd judge of character. He guesses what she will finally do. If she goes, with this tale of hers, to Scotland Yard, they may believe her; they may start making inquiries. Something pretty desperate has got to be done. Has Abbot got a car or did he hire one in London? Anyway, he was away from here on Derby Day."

Again Luke paused. He was so entering into the spirit of the thing that he found it hard to make a transition from one suspect to another. He had to wait a minute before he could force himself into the mood where he could visualize Major Horton as a successful murderer.

"Horton murdered his wife. Let's start with that. He had ample provocation and he gained considerably by her death. In order to carry it off successfully, he had to make a good show of devotion. He'd had to keep that up. Sometimes, shall we say, he overdoes it a bit?

"Very good, one murder successfully accomplished. Who's the next? Amy Gibbs. Yes, perfectly credible. Amy was in the house. She may have seen something—the Major administering a soothing cup of beef tea or gruel. She mayn't have realized the point of what she saw till some time later. The hat-paint trick is the sort of thing that would occur to the Major quite naturally—a very masculine man with little knowledge of women's fripperies. Amy Gibbs all serene and accounted for.

"The drunken Carter? Same suggestion as before—Amy told him something. Another straightforward murder.

"Now Tommy Pierce. We've got to fall back on his inquisitive nature. I suppose the letter in Abbot's office couldn't have been a complaint from Mrs. Horton that her husband was trying to poison her? That's only a wild suggestion, but it might be so. Anyway, the Major becomes alive to the fact that Tommy is a menace, so Tommy joins Amy and Carter. All quite simple and straightforward and according to Cocker. Easy to kill? My God, yes!

"But now we come to something rather difficult. Humbleby! Motive? Very obscure. Humbleby was attending Mrs. Horton originally. Did he get puzzled by the illness, and did Horton influence his wife to change to the younger, more unsuspicious doctor? But if so, what made Humbleby a danger so long after? Difficult, that. The manner of his death too. A poisoned finger. Doesn't connect up with the Major.

"Miss Fullerton? That's perfectly possible. He has a car. I saw it. And he was away from Wychwood that day, supposedly gone to the Derby. It might be, yes. Is Horton a cold-blooded killer? Is he? Is he? I wish I knew."

Luke stared ahead of him. His brow was puckered with thought. "It's one of them. I don't think it's Ellsworthy, but it might be. He's the most obvious one. Thomas is wildly unlikely—if it weren't for the manner of Humbleby's death. That blood poisoning definitely points to a medical murderer. It could be Abbot; there's not so much evidence against him as against the others, but I can see him in the part, somehow. Yes, he fits as the others don't. And it could be Horton. Bullied by his wife for years, feeling his insignificance—yes, it could be. But Miss Waynflete doesn't think it is, and she's no fool—and she knows the place and the people in it.

"Which one does she suspect, Abbot or Thomas? It must be one of these two. If I tackled her outright—'which of them is it?'—I'd get it out of her then, perhaps. But even then she might be wrong. There's no way of proving her right—like Miss Fullerton proved herself. More evidence—that's what I want. If there were to be one more case—just one more—then I'd know."

He stopped himself with a start. "What I'm asking for is another murder," he said under his breath.

16

IN THE BAR of the Seven Stars, Luke drank his pint and felt somewhat embarrassed. The stare of half a dozen bucolic pairs of eyes followed his least movement, and conversation had come to a standstill upon his entrance. Luke essayed a few comments of general interest, such as the crops, the state of the weather, and football coupons, but to none did he get any response. He was reduced to gallantry. The fine-looking girl behind the counter, with her black hair and red cheeks, he rightly judged to be Miss Lucy Carter. His advances were received in a pleasant spirit. Miss Carter duly giggled and said, "Go on with you!

I'm sure you don't think nothing of the kind! . . .That's telling!"—and
other such rejoinders. But the performance was clearly mechanical.

Luke, seeing no advantage to be gained by remaining, finished his
beer and departed. He walked along the path to where the river was
spanned by a footbridge. He was standing looking at this when a
quavering voice behind him said: "That's it mister; that's where old
Harry went over." Luke turned to see one of his late fellow
drinkers—one who had been particularly unresponsive to the topic of
crops, weather and coupons. He was now clearly about to enjoy
himself as a guide to the macabre. "Went over into the mud, he did,"
said the ancient laborer. "Right into the mud, and stuck in it head
downward."

"Perhaps someone pushed him over," said Luke, making the
suggestion in a casual fashion.

"They might of," the rustic agreed. "But I don't know who'd go for
to do that," he added.

"He might have made a few enemies. He was fairly abusive when he
was drunk, wasn't he?"

"His language was a treat to hear. Didn't mince his words, Harry
didn't. But no one would go for to push a man what's drunk."

Luke did not combat this statement. It was evidently regarded as
wildly unsporting for advantage to be taken of a man's state of
intoxication. The rustic had sounded quite shocked at the idea.
"Well," he said vaguely, "it was a sad business."

"None so sad for his missus," said the old man. "Reckon her and
Lucy haven't no call to be sad about it."

"There may be other people who are glad to have him out of the
way."

The old man was vague about that. "Maybe," he said. "But he
didn't mean no harm, Harry didn't." On this epitaph for the late Mr.
Carter, they parted.

Luke bent his steps toward the old Hall. The library transacted its
business in the two front rooms. Luke passed on to the back through a
door which was labeled MUSEUM. There he moved from case to case,
studying the not-very-inspiring exhibits. Some Roman pottery and
coins. Some South Sea curiosities, a Malay headdress. Various Indian
gods "presented by Major Horton," together with a large and
malevolent-looking Buddha and a case of doubtful-looking Egyptian
beads.

Luke wandered out again into the hall. There was no one about. He
went quietly up the stairs. There was a room with magazines and
papers there, and a room filled with non-fiction books. Luke went a
story higher. Here were rooms filled with what he designated himself

as junk. Stuffed birds, removed from the museum owing to the moths having attacked them, stacks of torn magazines and a room whose shelves were covered with out-of-date works of fiction and children's books.

Luke approached the window. Here it must have been that Tommy Pierce had sat, possibly whistling and occasionally rubbing a pane of glass vigorously when he heard anyone coming. Somebody had come in. Tommy had shown his zeal, sitting half out of the window and polishing with zest. And then that somebody had come up to him and, while talking, had given a sudden sharp push.

Luke turned away. He walked down the stairs and stood a minute or two in the hall. Nobody had noticed him come in. Nobody had seen him go upstairs. "Anyone might have done it," said Luke. "Easiest thing in the world." He heard footsteps coming from the direction of the library proper. Since he was an innocent man, with no objection to being seen, he could remain where he was. If he had not wanted to be seen, how easy just to step back inside the door of the museum room.

Miss Waynflete came out from the library, a little pile of books under her arm. She was pulling on her gloves. She looked happy and busy. When she saw him, her face lit up and she exclaimed: "Oh, Mr. Fitzwilliam, have you been looking at the museum? I'm afraid there isn't very much there, really. Lord Easterfield is talking of getting us some really interesting exhibits."

"Really?"

"Yes, something modern, you know, and up to date. Like they have at the Science Museum in London. He suggests a model aeroplane and a locomotive and some chemical things too."

"That would, perhaps, brighten things up."

"Yes, I don't think a museum should deal solely with the past, do you?"

"Perhaps not."

"Then some food exhibits, too—calories and vitamins—all that sort of thing. Lord Easterfield is so keen on the Greater Fitness Campaign."

"So he was saying the other night."

"It's the thing at present, isn't it? Lord Easterfield was telling me how he'd been to the Wellerman Laboratories and seen such a lot of germs and cultures and bacteria; it quite made me shiver. And he told me all about mosquitoes and sleeping sickness, and something about a liver fluke that, I'm afraid, was a little too difficult for me."

"It was probably too difficult for Lord Easterfield," said Luke cheerfully. "I'll bet he got it all wrong. You've got a much clearer brain than he has, Miss Waynflete."

Miss Waynflete said sedately, "That's very nice of you, Mr. Fitz-william, but I'm afraid women are never quite such deep thinkers as men."

Luke repressed a desire to criticize adversely Lord Easterfield's processes of thought. Instead he said, "I did look into the museum, but afterwards I went up to have a look at the top windows."

"You mean where Tommy—" Miss Waynflete shivered. "It's really very horrible."

"Yes, it's not a nice thought. I've spent about an hour with Mrs. Church—Amy's aunt—not a nice woman."

"Not at all."

"I had to take rather a strong line with her," said Luke. "I fancy she thinks I'm a kind of super policeman."

He stopped as he noted a sudden change of expression on Miss Waynflete's face. "Oh, Mr. Fitzwilliam, do you think that was wise?"

Luke said, "I don't really know. I think it was inevitable. The book story was wearing thin. I can't get much farther on that. I had to ask the kind of questions that were directly to the point."

Miss Waynflete shook her head, the troubled expression still on her face. "In a place like this, you see, everything gets round so fast."

"You mean that everybody will say, 'There goes the tec,' as I walk down the street? I don't think that really matters now. In fact, I may get more that way."

"I wasn't thinking of that." Miss Waynflete sounded a little breath-less. "What I meant was that he'll know. He'll realize that you're on his track."

Luke said slowly, "I suppose he will."

Miss Waynflete said, "But don't you see that's horribly dangerous? Horribly!"

"You mean"—Luke grasped her point at last—"you mean that the killer will have a crack at me?"

"Yes."

"Funny," said Luke. "I never thought of that! I believe you're right, though. Well, that might be the best thing that could happen."

Miss Waynflete said earnestly, "I don't think you realize that he's—he's a very clever man. He's cautious too. And remember, he's got a great deal of experience—perhaps more than we know."

"Yes," said Luke thoughtfully, "that's probably true."

Miss Waynflete exclaimed, "Oh, I don't like it! Really, I feel quite alarmed!"

Luke said gently, "You needn't worry. I shall be very much on my guard, I can assure you. You see, I've narrowed the possibilities down pretty closely. I've an idea, at any rate, who the killer might be." She looked up sharply. Luke came a step nearer. He lowered his voice to a whisper, "Miss Waynflete, if I were to ask you which of two men you considered most likely—Doctor Thomas or Mr. Abbot—what would you say?"

"Oh!" said Miss Waynflete. Her hand flew to her breast. She stepped back. Her eyes met Luke's in an expression that puzzled him. They showed impatience and something closely allied to it that he could not quite place. She said, "I can't say anything."

She turned away abruptly, with a curious sound—half a sigh, half a sob. Luke resigned himself. "Are you going home?" he asked.

"No, I was going to take these books to Mrs. Humbleby. That lies on your way back to the Manor. We might go part of the way together."

"That will be very nice," said Luke.

They went down the steps, turned to the left, skirting the village green. Luke looked back at the stately lines of the house they had left. "It must have been a lovely house in your father's day," he said.

Miss Waynflete sighed. "Yes, we were all very happy there. I am so thankful it hasn't been pulled down. So many of the old houses are going."

"I know. It's sad."

"And really the new ones aren't nearly so well built."

"I doubt if they will stand the test of time as well."

"But of course," said Miss Waynflete, "the new ones are convenient—so labor-saving, and not such big drafty passages to scrub."

Luke assented. When they arrived at the gate of Doctor Humbleby's house, Miss Waynflete hesitated and said: "Such a beautiful evening. I think, if you don't mind, I will come a little farther. I am enjoying the air."

Somewhat surprised, Luke expressed pleasure politely. It was hardly what he would have described as a beautiful evening. There was a strong wind blowing, turning back the leaves viciously on the trees. A storm, he thought, might come at any minute. Miss Waynflete, however, clutching her hat with one hand, walked by his side with every appearance of enjoyment, talking, as she went, in little gasps.

It was a somewhat lonely lane they were taking, since from Doctor Humbleby's house the shortest way to Ashe Manor was not by the main road but by a side lane which led to one of the back gates of the manor house. This gate was not of the same ornate ironwork, but had two handsome gate pillars surmounted by two vast pink pineapples. Why pineapples, Luke had been unable to discover. But he gathered that to Lord Easterfield pineapples spelt distinction and good taste. As they approached the gate, the sound of voices raised in anger came to them. A moment later they came in sight of Lord Easterfield confronting a young man in chauffeur's uniform. "You're fired!" Lord Easterfield was shouting. "D'you hear? You're fired!"

"If you'd overlook it, m'lord, just this once."

"No, I won't overlook it! Taking my car out! My car! And what's more, you've been drinking! . . . Yes, you have; don't deny it! I've made it clear there are three things I won't have on my estate—one's drunkenness, another's immorality and the last's impertinence!"

Though the man was not actually drunk, he had had enough to loosen his tongue. His manner changed. "You won't have this and you won't have that, you old buzzard! Your estate! Think we don't all know your father kept a boot shop down here? Makes us laugh ourselves sick, it does, seeing you strutting about as cock of the walk! Who are you, I'd like to know? You're no better than I am, that's what you are!"

Lord Easterfield turned purple. "How dare you speak to me like that? How dare you?"

The young man took a threatening step forward. "If you wasn't such a miserable pot-bellied little swine, I'd give you a sock on the jaw—yes, I would."

Lord Easterfield hastily retreated a step, tripped over a root and went down in a sitting position. Luke had come up. "Get out of here," he said roughly to the chauffeur.

The latter regained sanity. He looked frightened. "I'm sorry, sir. I don't know what came over me, I'm sure."

"A couple of glasses too much, I should say," said Luke. He assisted Lord Easterfield to his feet.

"I'm sorry, m'lord," stammered the man.

"You'll be sorry for this, Rivers," said Lord Easterfield. His voice trembled with intense feeling. The man hesitated a minute, then shambled away slowly. Lord Easterfield exploded, "Colossal impertinence! To me! Speaking to me like that! Something very serious will happen to that man! No respect, no proper sense of his station in life. When I think of what I do for these people—good wages, every comfort, a pension when they retire. The ingratitude—the base ingratitude!"

He choked with excitement, then perceived Miss Waynflete, who was standing silently by. "Is that you, Honoria? I'm deeply distressed that you should have witnessed such a disgraceful scene. That man's language—"

"I'm afraid he wasn't quite himself, Lord Easterfield," said Miss Waynflete primly.

"He was drunk, that's what he was—drunk!"

"Just a bit lit up," said Luke.

"Do you know what he did?" Lord Easterfield looked from one to the other of them. "Took out my car—my car! Thought I shouldn't be back so soon. Bridget drove me over to Lyne in the two-seater. And this fellow had the impertinence to take a girl—Lucy Carter, I believe—out in my car!"

Miss Waynflete said gently, "A most improper thing to do."

Lord Easterfield seemed a little comforted. "Yes, wasn't it?"

"But I'm sure he'll regret it."

"I shall see that he does."

"You've dismissed him," Miss Waynflete pointed out.

Lord Easterfield shook his head. "He'll come to a bad end, that fellow." He threw back his shoulders. "Come up to the house, Honoria, and have a glass of sherry."

"Thank you, Lord Easterfield, but I must go to Mrs. Humbleby with these books . . . . Good night, Mr. Fitzwilliam. You'll be quite all right now." She gave him a smiling nod and walked briskly away. It was so much the attitude of a nurse who delivers a child at a party that Luke caught his breath as a sudden idea struck him. Was it possible that Miss Waynflete had accompanied him solely in order to protect him? The idea seemed ludicrous, but—

Lord Easterfield's voice interrupted his meditations, "Very capable woman, Honoria Waynflete."

"Very, I should think."

Lord Easterfield began to walk toward the house. He moved rather stiffly and his hand went to his posterior and rubbed it gingerly. Suddenly he chuckled. "I was engaged to Honoria once, years ago. She was a nice-looking girl—not so skinny as she is today. Seems funny to think of now. Her people were the nobs of this place."

"Yes?"

Lord Easterfield ruminated. "Old Colonel Waynflete bossed the show. One had to come out and touch one's cap pretty sharp. One of the old school he was, and proud as Lucifer." He chuckled again. "The fat was in the fire all right when Honoria announced she was going to marry me! Called herself a radical, she did. Very earnest. Was all for abolishing class distinctions. She was a serious kind of girl."

"So her family broke up the romance?"

Lord Easterfield rubbed his nose. "Well, not exactly. Matter of fact, we had a bit of a row over something. Blinking bird she had—one of those beastly twittering canaries; always hated them—bad business—wrung its neck. Well, no good dwelling on all that now.

Let's forget it." He shook his shoulders like a man who throws off an unpleasant memory. Then he said, rather jerkily, "Don't think she's ever forgiven me. Well, perhaps it's only natural."

"I think she's forgiven you, all right," said Luke.

Lord Easterfield brightened up. "Do you? Glad of that. You know, I respect Honoria. Capable woman and a lady! That still counts, even in these days. She runs that library business very well." He looked up and his voice changed. "Hullo," he said. "Here comes Bridget."

17

LUKE FELT A tightening of his muscles as Bridget approached. He had had no word alone with her since the day of the tennis party. By mutual consent, they had avoided each other. He stole a glance at her now. She looked provokingly calm, cool, and indifferent. She said lightly, "I was beginning to wonder what on earth had become of you, Gordon."

Lord Easterfield grunted. "Had a bit of a dust-up! That fellow, Rivers, had the impertinence to take the Rolls out this afternoon."

"Lèse-majesté," said Bridget.

"It's no good making a joke out of it, Bridget. The thing's serious. He took a girl out."

"I don't suppose it would have given him any pleasure to go solemnly for a drive by himself."

Lord Easterfield drew himself up. "On my estate I'll have decent moral behavior."

"It isn't actually immoral to take a girl joy riding."

"It is when it's my car."

"That, of course, is worse than immorality! It practically amounts to blasphemy. But you can't cut out the sex stuff altogether, Gordon. The moon is at the full and it's actually Midsummer Eve."

"Is it, by Jove?" said Luke.

Bridget threw him a glance. "That seems to interest you?"

"It does."

Bridget turned back to Lord Easterfield. "Three extraordinary people have arrived at the Bells and Motley. Item one, a man with shorts, spectacles and a lovely plum-colored silk shirt! Item two, a female with no eyebrows, dressed in a peplum, a pound of assorted sham Egyptian beads, and sandals. Item three, a fat man in a lavender suit and co-respondent shoes. I suspect them of being friends of our Mr. Ellsworthy. Says the gossip writer: 'Someone has whispered that there will be gay doings in the Witches' Meadow to-night.'"

Lord Easterfield turned purple and said, "I won't have it!"

"You can't help it, darling. The Witches' Meadow is public property."

"I won't have this irreligious mumbo jumbo going on down here! I'll expose it in *Scandals.*" He paused, then said, "Remind me to make a note about that and get Siddely on to it. I must go up to town to-morrow."

"Lord Easterfield's campaign against witchcraft," said Bridget flippantly. "Medieval superstitions still rife in quiet country village."

Lord Easterfield stared at her with a puzzled frown, then he turned and went into the house.

Luke said pleasantly, "You must do your stuff better than that, Bridget."

"What do you mean?"

"It would be a pity if you lost your job. That hundred thousand isn't yours yet. Nor are the diamonds and pearls. I should wait until after the marriage ceremony to exercise your sarcastic gifts, if I were you."

Her glance met his coolly. "You are so thoughtful, dear Luke. It's kind of you to take my future so much to heart."

"Kindness and consideration have always been my strong points."

"I hadn't noticed it."

"No? You surprise me."

Bridget twitched the leaf off a creeper. She said, "What have you been doing today?"

"The usual spot of sleuthing."

"Any results?"

"Yes and no, as the politicians say. By the way, have you got any tools in the house?"

"I expect so. What kind of tools?"

"Oh, any handy little gadgets. Perhaps I could inspect same." Ten minutes later Luke had made his selection from a cupboard shelf. "That little lot will do nicely," he said, slapping the pocket in which he had stowed them away.

"Are you thinking of doing a spot of forcing and entering?"

"Maybe."

"You're very uncommunicative on the subject."

"Well, after all, the situation bristles with difficulties. I'm in the hell of a position. After our little dust-up on Saturday, I suppose I ought to clear out of here."

"To behave as a perfect gentleman, you should."

"But since I'm convinced that I am pretty hot on the trail of a homicidal maniac, I'm more or less forced to remain. If you could think of any convincing reason for me to leave here and take up my quarters at the Bells and Motley, for goodness' sake trot it out."

Bridget shook her head. "That's not feasible—you being a cousin and all that. Besides, the inn is full of Mr. Ellsworthy's friends. They only run to three guest rooms."

"So I am forced to remain, painful as it must be for you."

Bridget smiled sweetly at him. "Not at all. I can always do with a few scalps to dangle."

"That," said Luke appreciatively, "was a particularly dirty crack. What I admire about you, Bridget, is that you have practically no instincts of kindliness. Well, well. The rejected lover will now go and change for dinner."

The evening passed uneventfully. Luke won Lord Easterfield's approval even more deeply than before by the apparent absorbed interest with which he listened to the other's nightly discourse. When they came into the drawing room, Bridget said, "You men have been a long time."

Luke replied, "Lord Easterfield was being so interesting that the time passed like a flash. He was telling me how he founded his first newspaper."

Mrs. Anstruther said, "These new little fruiting trees in pots are perfectly marvelous, I believe. You ought to try them along the terrace, Gordon." The conversation then proceeded on normal lines.

Luke retired early. He did not, however, go to bed. He had other plans. It was just striking twelve when he descended the stairs noiselessly in tennis shoes, passed through the library and let himself out by a window. The wind was still blowing in violent gusts interspersed with brief lulls. Clouds scudded across the sky, obliterating the moon, so that darkness alternated with bright moonlight. Luke made his way by a circuitous route to Mr. Ellsworthy's establishment. He saw his way clear to doing a little investigation. He was fairly certain that Mr. Ellsworthy and his friends would be out together on this particular date. Midsummer Eve, Luke thought, was sure to be marked by some ceremony or other. Whilst this was in progress, it would be a good opportunity to search Mr. Ellsworthy's house.

He climbed a couple of walls, got round to the back of the house, took the assorted tools from his pocket and selected a likely implement. He found a scullery window amenable to his efforts. A few minutes later he had slipped back the catch, raised the sash and hoisted himself over. He had a torch in his pocket. He used it sparingly—a brief flash just to show him his way and to avoid running into things.

In a quarter of an hour he had satisfied himself that the house was empty. The owner was out and abroad on his own affairs. Luke smiled with satisfaction and settled down to his task. He made a minute and thorough search of every available nook and corner. In a locked drawer, below two or three innocuous water-color sketches, he came upon some artistic efforts which caused him to lift his eyebrows and whistle. Mr. Ellsworthy's correspondence was unilluminating, but some of his books—those tucked away at the back of a cupboard— repaid attention. Besides these, Luke accumulated three meager but suggestive scraps of information. The first was a pencil scrawl in a little notebook: "Settle with Tommy Pierce"—the date being a couple of days before the boy's death. The second was a crayon sketch of Amy Gibbs with a furious red cross right across the face. The third was a bottle of cough mixture. None of these things was in any way conclusive, but taken together they might be considered as encouraging.

Luke was just restoring some final order, replacing things in their place, when he suddenly stiffened and switched off his torch. He had heard the key inserted in the lock of a side door. He stepped across to the door of the room he was in and applied an eye to a crack. He hoped Ellsworthy—if it was he—would go straight upstairs.

The side door opened and Ellsworthy stepped in, switching on a hall light as he did so. As he passed along the hall, Luke saw his face and caught his breath. It was unrecognizable. The eyes were alight with a strange mad exultation, but what caused Luke to catch his breath was the sight of Ellsworthy's hands. They were stained a deep brownish red, the color of dried blood. He disappeared up the stairs. A moment later the light in the hall was extinguished.

Luke waited a little longer, then very cautiously he crept out into the hall, made his way to the scullery and left by the window. He looked up at the house, but it was dark and silent. He drew a deep breath. "The fellow's mad all right!" he said. "I wonder what he's been up to? I'll swear that was blood on his hands!"

He made a detour round the village and returned to Ashe Manor by a roundabout route. It was as he was turning into the side lane that a sudden rustle of leaves wrapped in a dark cloak came out from the shadow of a tree. It looked so eerie that Luke felt his heart miss a beat. Then he recognized the long pale face under the hood. "Bridget? How you startled me!"

She said sharply, "Where have you been? I saw you go out."

"And you followed me?"

"No. You'd gone too far. I've been waiting till you came back."

"That was a silly thing to do," Luke grumbled.

She repeated her question impatiently, "Where have you been?"

Luke said gaily, "Raiding our Mr. Ellsworthy."

Bridget caught her breath. "Did you—find anything?"

"I don't know. I know a bit more about the swine's tastes, and all that—and there are three things that might be suggestive." She listened attentively as he recounted the result of his search. "It's very slight evidence, though," he ended. "But, Bridget, just as I was leaving, Ellsworthy came back. And I tell you this—the man's as mad as a hatter!"

"You really think so?"

"I saw his face! It was—unspeakable! God knows what he'd been up to! He was in a delirium of mad excitement. And his hands were stained, I'll swear, with blood."

Bridget shivered. "Horrible," she murmured.

Luke said irritably, "You shouldn't have come out by yourself, Bridget. It was absolute madness. Somebody might have knocked you on the head."

She laughed shakily. "The same applies to you, my dear."

"I can look after myself."

"I'm pretty good at taking care of myself, too. Hard-boiled, I should think you'd call me."

A sharp gust of wind came. Luke said suddenly, "Take off that hood thing."

"Why?"

With an unexpected movement, he snatched at her cloak and whipped it away. The wind caught her hair and blew it out straight up from her head. She stared at him, her breath coming fast. Luke said, "You certainly are incomplete without a broomstick, Bridget. That's how I saw you first." He stared a minute longer, and said, "You're a cruel devil." With a sharp impatient sigh, he tossed the cloak back to her. "There; put it on. Let's go home."

"Wait."

"Why?"

She came up to him. She spoke in a low, rather breathless voice, "Because I've got something to say to you. That's partly why I waited for you here, outside the Manor. I want to say it to you now, before we go inside into Gordon's property."

"Well?"

She gave a short, rather bitter laugh. "Oh, it's quite simple. You win, Luke. That's all."

He said sharply, "What do you mean?"

"I mean that I've given up the idea of being Lady Easterfield."

He took a step nearer. "Is that true?" he demanded.

"Yes, Luke."

"You'll marry me?"

"Yes."

"Why, I wonder."

"I don't know. You say such beastly things to me, and I seem to like it."

He took her in his arms and kissed her. He said, "It's a mad world."

"Are you happy, Luke?"

"Not particularly."

"Do you think you'll ever be happy with me?"

"I don't know. I'll risk it."

"Yes, that's what I feel."

He slipped his arm through hers. "We're rather queer about all this, my sweet. Come along. Perhaps we shall be more normal in the morning."

"Yes. It's rather frightening the way things happen to one." She looked down and tugged him to a standstill. "Luke—Luke, what's that?"

The moon had come out from the clouds. Luke looked down to where Bridget's shoe trembled by a huddled mass. With a startled exclamation, he dragged his arm free and knelt down. He looked from the shapeless heap to the gatepost above. The pineapple was gone. He stood up at last. Bridget was standing, her hands pressed together on her mouth. He said, "It's the chauffeur—Rivers. He's dead."

"That beastly stone thing—it's been loose for some time. I suppose it blew down on him."

Luke shook his head. "The wind wouldn't do a thing like that. Oh, that's what it's meant to look like, that is what it's meant to be—another accident! But it's a fake. It's the killer again."

"No; no, Luke!"

"I tell you it is. Do you know what I felt on the back of his head, in with the stickiness and mess—grains of sand. There's no sand about here. I tell you, Bridget, somebody stood here and slugged him as he came through the gate back to his cottage. Then they laid him down and rolled that pineapple thing down on top of him."

Bridget said faintly, "Luke, there's blood—on your hands!"

Luke said grimly, "There was blood on someone else's hands. Do you know what I was thinking this afternoon? That if there were to be one more crime, we'd surely know. And we do know! Ellsworthy! He was out tonight, and he came in with blood on his hands, capering and prancing and mad—drunk with the homicidal maniac's exultation."

Looking down, Bridget shivered and said in a low voice, "Poor Rivers."

Luke said pityingly, "Yes, poor fellow. It's damnable bad luck. But this will be the last, Bridget! Now we know, we'll get him!"

He saw her sway, and in two steps he had caught her in his arms. She said, in a small childlike voice, "Luke, I'm frightened."

He said, "It's all over, darling. It's all over."

She murmured, "Be kind to me, please. I've been hurt so much."

He said, "We've hurt each other. We won't do that any more."

18

DOCTOR THOMAS stared across his consulting-room desk at Luke. "Remarkable," he said. "Remarkable! You are really serious, Mr. Fitzwilliam?"

"Absolutely. I am convinced that Ellsworthy is a dangerous maniac."

"I have not paid special attention to the man. I should say, though, that he is possibly an abnormal type."

"I'd go a good deal farther than that," said Luke grimly.

"You seriously believe that this man, Rivers, was murdered?"

"I do. You noticed the grains of sand in the wound?"

Doctor Thomas nodded. "I looked out for them after your statement. I am bound to say that you were correct."

"That makes it clear, does it not, that the accident was faked and that the man was killed by a blow from a sandbag, or at any rate was stunned by one?"

"Not necessarily."

"What do you mean?"

Doctor Thomas leaned back and joined his finger tips together. "Supposing that this man Rivers had been lying out in a sand pit during the day—there are several about in this part of the world. That might account for grains of sand in the hair."

"Man, I tell you he was murdered!"

"You may tell me so," said Doctor Thomas dryly; "but that doesn't make it a fact."

Luke controlled his exasperation. "I suppose you don't believe a word of what I'm telling you."

Doctor Thomas smiled, a kindly superior smile. "You must admit, Mr. Fitzwilliam, that it's rather a wild story. You assert that this man

Ellsworthy has killed a servant girl, a small boy, a drunken publican, my own partner, and finally this man Rivers."

"You don't believe it?"

Doctor Thomas shrugged his shoulders. "I have some knowledge of Humbleby's case. It seems to me quite out of the question that Ellsworthy could have caused his death, and I really cannot see that you have any evidence at all that he did so."

"I don't know how he managed it," confessed Luke, "but it all hangs together with Miss Fullerton's story."

"There again you assert that Ellsworthy followed her up to London and ran her down in a car. Again you haven't a shadow of proof that happened! It's all—well, romancing!"

Luke said sharply, "Now that I know where I am, it will be my business to get proofs. I'm going up to London tomorrow to see an old pal of mine. I saw in the paper two days ago that he's been made assistant commissioner. He knows me and he'll listen to what I have to say. One thing I'm sure of. He'll order a thorough investigation of the whole business."

Doctor Thomas stroked his chin thoughtfully. "Well, no doubt that should be very satisfactory. If it turns out that you're mistaken—"

Luke interrupted him, "You definitely don't believe a word of all this?"

"In wholesale murder?" Doctor Thomas raised his eyebrows. "Quite frankly, Mr. Fitzwilliam, I don't. The thing is too fantastic."

"Fantastic, perhaps, but it hangs together. You've got to admit it hangs together. Once you accept Miss Fullerton's story as true."

Doctor Thomas was shaking his head. A slight smile came to his lips.

"If you knew some of these old maids as well as I do—" he murmured.

Luke rose, trying to control his annoyance. "At any rate, you're well named," he said. "A doubting Thomas if there ever was one!"

Thomas replied good-humoredly, "Give me a few proofs, my dear fellow. That's all I ask. Not just a long melodramatic rigmarole based on what an old lady fancied she saw."

"What old ladies fancy they see is very often right. My Aunt Mildred was positively uncanny! Have you got any aunts yourself, Thomas?"

"Well—er—no."

"A mistake!" said Luke. "Every man should have aunts. They illustrate the triumph of guesswork over logic. It is reserved for aunts to know that Mr. A is a rogue because he looks like a dishonest butler they once had. Other people say, reasonably enough, that a respectable man like Mr. A couldn't be a crook. The old ladies are right every time." Doctor Thomas smiled his superior smile again. Luke said, his exasperation mounting once more, "Don't you realize that I'm a policeman myself? I'm not the complete amateur."

Doctor Thomas smiled and murmured, "In the Mayang Straits."

"Crime is crime even in the Mayang Straits."

"Of course—of course."

Luke left Doctor Thomas' surgery in a state of suppressed irritation. He joined Bridget, who said, "Well, how did you get on?"

"He didn't believe me," said Luke. "Which, when you come to think of it, is hardly surprising. It's a wild story with no proofs. Doctor Thomas is emphatically not the sort of man who believes six impossible things before breakfast."

"Will anybody believe you?"

"Probably not, but when I get hold of old Billy Bones tomorrow, the wheels will start turning. They'll check up on our long-haired friend, Ellsworthy, and in the end they're bound to get somewhere."

Bridget said thoughtfully, "We're coming out into the open very much, aren't we?"

"We've got to. We can't—we simply can't afford any more murders."

Bridget shivered. "Do be careful, Luke."

"I'm being careful, all right. Don't walk near gates with pineapples on them, avoid the lonely woods at nightfall, watch out for your food and drink. I know all the ropes."

"It's horrible feeling you're a marked man."

"So long as you're not a marked woman, my sweet."

"Perhaps I am."

"I don't think so. But I don't intend to take risks. I'm watching over you like an old-fashioned guardian angel."

"Is it any good saying anything to the police here?"

Luke considered. "No, I don't think it is. Better go straight to Scotland Yard."

Bridget murmured, "That's what Miss Fullerton thought."

"Yes, but I shall be watching out for trouble."

Bridget said, "I know what I'm going to do tomorrow. I shall march Gordon down to that brute's shop and make him buy things."

"Thereby insuring that our Mr. Ellsworthy is not lying in ambush for me on the steps of Whitehall?"

"That's the idea."

Luke said, with some slight embarrassment, "About Easterfield."

Bridget said quickly, "Let's leave it till you come back tomorrow. Then we'll have it out."

"Will he be very cut up, do you think?"

"Well"—Bridget considered the question—"he'll be annoyed."

"Annoyed? Ye gods! Isn't that putting it a bit mildly?"

"No. Because, you see, Gordon doesn't like being annoyed. It upsets him."

Luke said soberly, "I feel rather uncomfortable about it all."

That feeling was uppermost in his mind when he prepared that evening to listen for the twentieth time to Lord Easterfield on the subject of Lord Easterfield. It was, he admitted, a cad's trick to stay in a man's house and steal his fiancée. He still felt, however, that a pot-bellied, pompous, strutting little nincompoop like Lord Easterfield ought never to have aspired to Bridget at all. But his conscience so far chastened him that he listened with an extra dose of fervent attention and, in consequence, made a thoroughly favorable impression on his host. Lord Easterfield was in high good humor this evening. The death of his erstwhile chauffeur seemed to have exhilarated rather than depressed him. "Told you that fellow would come to a bad end," he crowed, holding up a glass of port to the light and squinting through it. "Didn't I tell you so yesterday evening?"

"You did, indeed, sir."

"And, you see, I was right! It's amazing how often I'm right!"

"That must be splendid for you," said Luke.

"I've had a wonderful life—yes, a wonderful life! My path's been smoothed clear before me. I've always had great faith and trust in Providence. That's the secret, Fitzwilliam—that's the secret."

"Yes?"

"I'm a religious man. I believe in good and evil and eternal justice. There is such a thing as divine justice, Fitzwilliam; not a doubt of it!"

"I believe in justice too," said Luke.

Lord Easterfield, as usual, was not interested in the beliefs of other people. "Do right by your Creator, and your Creator will do right by you! I've always been an upright man. I've subscribed to charity, and I've made my money honestly. I'm not beholden to any man! I stand alone. You remember in the Bible how the patriarchs became prosperous, herds and flocks were added to them, and their enemies were smitten down."

Luke stifled a yawn and said, "Quite, quite."

"It's remarkable—absolutely remarkable," said Lord Easterfield. "The way that a righteous man's enemies are struck down! Look at yesterday. That fellow abuses me; even goes so far as to try to raise his hand against me. And what happens? Where is he today?" He paused rhetorically, and then answered himself in an impressive voice, "Dead! Struck down by divine wrath!"

Opening his eyes a little, Luke said, "Rather an excessive punishment, perhaps, for a few hasty words uttered after a glass too much."

Lord Easterfield shook his head. "It's always like that! Retribution comes swiftly and terribly. And there's a good authentic authority for it. Remember the children that mocked Elisha—how the bears came out and devoured them. That's the way things happen, Fitzwilliam."

"I always thought that was rather unnecessarily vindictive."

"No, no. You're looking at it the wrong way. Elisha was a great and holy man. No one could be suffered to mock at him and live. I understand that because of my own case." Luke looked puzzled. Lord Easterfield lowered his voice, "I could hardly believe it at first. But it happened every time! My enemies and detractors were cast down and exterminated."

"Exterminated?"

Lord Easterfield nodded gently and sipped his port.

"Time after time. One case quite like Elisha—a little boy. I came upon him in the gardens here—he was employed by me then. Do you know what he was doing? He was giving an imitation of me—of me! Mocking me! Strutting up and down, with an audience to watch him. Making fun of me on my own ground! D'you know what happened to him? Not ten days later he fell out of an upper window and was killed!

"Then there was that ruffian Carter—a drunkard and a man of evil tongue. He came here and abused me. What happened to him? A week later he was dead—drowned in the mud. There had been a servant girl too. She lifted her voice and called me names. Her punishment soon came. She drank poison by mistake. I could tell you heaps more. Humbleby dared to oppose me over the water scheme. He died of blood poisoning. Oh, it's been going on for years. Mrs. Horton, for instance, was abominably rude to me, and it wasn't long before she passed away." He paused and, leaning forward, passed the port decanter round to Luke. "Yes," he said, "they all died. Amazing, isn't it?"

Luke stared at him. A monstrous, an incredible suspicion leaped into his mind. With new eyes he stared at the small fat man who sat at the head of the table, who was gently nodding his head and whose light protuberant eyes met Luke's with a smiling insouciance.

A rush of disconnected memories flashed rapidly through Luke's brain. Major Horton saying, "Lord Easterfield was very kind. Sent down grapes and peaches from his hothouse." It was Lord Easterfield who so graciously allowed Tommy Pierce to be employed on window cleaning at the library. Lord Easterfield holding forth on his visit to the

Wellerman Kreitz Laboratories, with its serums and germ cultures, just a short time before Doctor Humbleby's death. Everything pointing plainly in one direction, and he, fool that he had been, never even suspecting.

Lord Easterfield was still smiling. A quiet happy smile. He nodded his head gently at Luke. "They all die," said Lord Easterfield.

19

SIR WILLIAM OSSINGTON, known to the cronies of earlier days as Billy Bones, stared incredulously at his friend. "Didn't you have enough crime out in Mayang?" he asked plaintively. "Have you got to come home and do our work for us here?"

"Crime in Mayang isn't on a wholesale basis," said Luke. "What I'm up against now is a man who's done a round half dozen murders at least—and got away with it without a breath of suspicion."

Sir William sighed. "It does happen. What's his speciality—wives?"

"No, he's not that kind. He doesn't actually think he's God yet, but he soon will."

"Mad?"

"Oh, unquestionably, I should say."

"Ah, but he probably isn't legally mad. There's a difference, you know."

"I should say he knows the nature and consequence of his acts," said Luke.

"Exactly," said Billy Bones.

"Well, don't let's quibble about legal technicalities. We're not nearly at that stage yet. Perhaps we never shall be. What I want from you, old boy, is a few facts. There was a street accident took place on Derby Day between five and six o'clock in the afternoon. Old lady run over in Whitehall and the car didn't stop. Her name was Lavinia Fullerton. I want you to dig up all the facts you can about that."

Sir William sighed. "I can soon get hold of that for you. Twenty minutes ought to do it."

He was as good as his word. In less than that time Luke was talking to the police officer in charge of the matter. "Yes, sir, I remember the details. I've got most of them written down here." He indicated the sheet that Luke was studying. "An inquest was held, Mr. Satcherverell was the coroner. Censure of the driver of the car."

"Did you ever get him?"

"No, sir."

"What make of car was it?"

"It seems pretty certain it was a Rolls—big car driven by a chauffeur. All witnesses unanimous on that point. Most people know a Rolls by sight."

"You didn't get the number?"

"No, unfortunately, nobody thought to look at it. There was a note of a Number FZX 4498, but it was the wrong number. A woman spotted it and mentioned it to another woman, who gave it to me. I don't know whether the second woman got it wrong, but anyway it was no good."

Luke asked sharply, "How did you know it was no good?"

The young officer smiled. "FZX 4498 is the number of Lord Easterfield's car. That car was standing outside Boomington House at the time in question and the chauffeur was having tea. He had a perfect alibi, no question of his being concerned, and the car never left the building till 6:30, when his lordship came out."

"I see," said Luke.

"It's always the way, sir," the man sighed. "Half the witnesses have disappeared before a constable can get there and take down particulars." Sir William nodded. "We assumed it was probably a number not unlike that—FZX 4498—a number beginning probably with two fours. We did our best, but could not trace any car. We investigated several likely numbers, but they could all give satisfactory accounts of themselves."

Sir William looked at Luke questioningly. Luke shook his head. Sir William said, "Thanks, Bonner; that will do." When the man had gone out, Billy Bones looked inquiringly at his friend. "What's it all about, Fitz?"

Luke sighed. "It all tallies. Lavinia Fullerton was coming up to blow the gaff—to tell the clever people at Scotland Yard all about the wicked murderer. I don't know whether you'd have listened to her—probably not."

"We might," said Sir William. "Things do come through to us that way. Just hearsay and gossip. We don't neglect that sort of thing, I assure you."

"That's what the murderer thought. He wasn't going to risk it. He eliminated Lavinia Fullerton, and although one woman was sharp enough to spot his number, no one believed her."

Billy Bones sprang upright in his chair. "You don't mean—"

"Yes, I do. I'll bet you anything you like it was Easterfield who ran her down. I don't know how he managed it. The chauffeur was away at tea. Somehow or other, I suppose, he sneaked the car away, putting on a chauffeur's coat and cap. But he did it, Billy!"

"Impossible!"

"Not at all. Lord Easterfield has committed at least seven murders to my certain knowledge, and probably a lot more."

"Impossible," said Sir William.

"My dear fellow, he practically boasted to me of it last night!"

"He's mad, then?"

"He's mad, all right, but he's a cunning devil. You'll have to go warily. Don't let him know we suspect him."

Billy Bones murmured, "Incredible."

Luke said, "But true!" He laid a hand on his friend's shoulder. "Look here, Billy old son; we must get right down to this. Here are the facts."

The two men talked long and earnestly.

On the following day, Luke returned to Wychwood. He drove down early in the morning. He could have returned the night before, but he felt a marked distaste for sleeping under Lord Easterfield's roof or accepting his hospitality under the circumstances. On his way through Wychwood, he drew up his car at Miss Waynflete's house. The maid who opened the door stared at him in astonishment, but showed him into the little dining room where Miss Waynflete was sitting at breakfast. She rose to receive him in some surprise.

He did not waste time. "I must apologize for breaking in on you at this hour." He looked round. The maid had left the room, shutting the door. "I'm going to ask you a question, Miss Waynflete. It's rather a personal one, but I think you will forgive me for asking it."

"Please ask me anything you like. I am quite sure your reason for doing so will be a good one."

"Thank you." He paused. "I want to know exactly why you broke off your engagement to Lord Easterfield all those years ago."

She had not expected that. The color rose in her cheeks and one hand went to her breast. "Has he told you anything?"

Luke replied, "He told me there was something about a bird—a bird whose neck was wrung."

"He said that?" Her voice was wondering. "He admitted it? That's extraordinary!"

"Will you tell me, please?"

"Yes, I will tell you. But I beg that you will never speak of the matter to him—to Gordon. It is all past—all over and finished with. I don't want it—raked up." She looked at him appealingly.

Luke nodded. "It is only for my personal satisfaction," he said. "I shall not repeat what you tell me."

"Thank you." She had recovered her composure. Her voice was quite steady as she went on. "It was like this: I had a little canary. I was very fond of it, and, perhaps, rather silly about it—girls were, then. They were rather—well, coy about their pets. It must have been irritating to a man—I do realize that."

"Yes," said Luke, as she paused.

"Gordon was jealous of the bird. He said one day, quite ill-temperedly, 'I believe you prefer that bird to me.' And I, in the rather silly way girls went on in those days laughed, and held it up on my finger, saying something like: 'Of course I love you, dicky bird, better than a great silly boy! Of course I do!' Then—oh, it was frightening—Gordon snatched the bird from me and wrung its neck. It was such a shock. I shall never forget it!" Her face had gone very pale.

"And so you broke off the engagement?" said Luke.

"Yes. I couldn't feel the same afterwards. You see, Mr. Fitzwilliam"—she hesitated—"it wasn't just the action—that might have been done in a fit of jealousy and temper—it was the awful feeling I had that he'd enjoyed doing it. It was that that frightened me!"

"Even long ago," murmured Luke. "Even in those days."

She laid a hand on his arm. "Mr. Fitzwilliam—"

He met the frightened appeal in her eyes with a grave, steady look. "It is Lord Easterfield who has committed all those murders," he said. "You've known that all along, haven't you?"

She shook her head with vigor. "Not known it! If I had known it, then—then, of course I would have spoken out. No, it was just a fear."

"And yet you never gave me a hint?"

She clasped her hands in a sudden anguish. "How could I? How could I? I was fond of him once."

"Yes," said Luke gently. "I see."

She turned away, fumbled in her bag, and a small lace-edged handkerchief was pressed for a moment to her eyes. Then she turned back again, dry-eyed, dignified and composed. "I am so glad," she said, "that Bridget has broken off her engagement. She is going to marry you instead, is she not?"

"Yes."

"That will be much more suitable," said Miss Waynflete rather primly. Luke was unable to help smiling a little. But Miss Waynflete's face grew grave and anxious. She leaned forward and once more laid a hand on his arm. "But be very careful," she said. "Both of you must be very careful."

"You mean—with Lord Easterfield?"

"Yes. It would be better not to tell him."

Luke frowned. "I don't think either of us would like the idea of that."

"Oh, what does that matter? You don't seem to realize that he's mad—mad. He won't stand for it—not for a moment! If anything happens to her—"

"Nothing shall happen to her!"

"Yes, I know, but do realize that you're not a match for him! He's so dreadfully cunning! Take her away at once; it's the only hope. Make her go abroad! You'd better both go abroad!"

Luke said slowly, "It might be as well if she went. I shall stay."

"I was afraid you would say that. But at any rate, get her away. At once, mind!"

Luke nodded slowly. "I think," he said, "that you're right."

"I know I'm right! Get her away—before it's too late."

20

BRIDGET HEARD LUKE drive up. She came out on the steps to meet him. She said, without preamble, "I've told him."

"What?" Luke was taken aback.

His dismay was so patent that Bridget noticed it. "Luke, what is it? You seem quite upset."

He said slowly, "I thought we agreed to wait until I came back."

"I know, but I thought it was better to get it over. He was making plans—for our marriage, our honeymoon—all that! I simply had to tell him!" She added—a touch of reproach in her voice—"It was the only decent thing to do."

He acknowledged it. "From your point of view, yes. Oh, yes, I see that."

"From every point of view, I should have thought!"

Luke said slowly, "There are times when one can't afford decency."

"Luke, what do you mean?"

He made an impatient gesture. "I can't tell you now and here. How did Easterfield take it?"

Bridget said slowly, "Extraordinarily well. Really, extraordinarily well. I felt ashamed. I believe, Luke, that I've underestimated Gordon, just because he's rather pompous and occasionally futile. I believe really he's rather—well, a great little man."

Luke nodded. "Yes, possibly, he is a great man—in ways we haven't suspected. Look here, Bridget; you must get out of here as soon as possible."

"Naturally, I shall pack up my things and leave today. You might drive me up to town. I suppose we can't both go and stay at the Bells and Motley—that is, if the Ellsworthy contingent has left?"

Luke shook his head. "No, you'd better go back to London. I'll explain presently. In the meantime, I suppose I'd better see Easterfield."

"I suppose it's the thing to do. It's all rather beastly, isn't it? I feel such a rotten little gold digger."

Luke smiled at her. "It was a fair enough bargain. You'd have played straight with him. Anyway, it's no use lamenting over things that are past and done with. I'll go in and see Easterfield now."

He found Lord Easterfield striding up and down the drawing room. He was outwardly calm; there was even a slight smile on his lips. But Luke noticed that a pulse in his temple was beating furiously. He wheeled round as Luke entered. "Oh, there you are, Fitzwilliam."

Luke said, "It's no good my saying I'm sorry for what I've done. That would be hypocritical. I admit that from your point of view I've behaved badly and I've very little to say in defense. These things happen."

Lord Easterfield resumed his pacing. "Quite—quite!" He waved a hand.

Luke went on, "Bridget and I have treated you shamefully. But there it is! We care for each other, and there's nothing to be done about it, except to tell you the truth and clear out."

Lord Easterfield stopped. He looked at Luke with his pale protuberant eyes. "No," he said, "there's nothing you can do about it." There was a very curious tone in his voice. He stood looking at Luke, gently shaking his head, as though in commiseration.

Luke said sharply, "What do you mean?"

"There's nothing you can do," said Lord Easterfield. "It's too late."

Luke took a step nearer him. "Tell me what you mean."

Lord Easterfield said, unexpectedly, "Ask Honoria Waynflete. She'll understand. She knows what happens. She spoke to me about it once."

"What does she understand?"

Lord Easterfield said, "Evil doesn't go unpunished. There must be justice. I'm sorry, because I'm fond of Bridget. In a way, I'm sorry for you both."

Luke said, "Are you threatening us?"

Lord Easterfield seemed genuinely shocked. "No, no, my dear fellow. I've no feeling in the matter. When I did Bridget the honor to choose her as my wife, she accepted certain responsibilities. Now, she repudiates them, but there's no going back in this life. If you break laws, you pay the penalty."

Luke clenched both hands. He said, "You mean that something is going to happen to Bridget? Now, understand me, Easterfield; nothing is going to happen to Bridget, nor to me! If you attempt anything of that kind, it's the finish. You'd better be careful! I know a good deal about you!"

"It's nothing to do with me," said Lord Easterfield. "I'm only the instrument of a higher Power. What that Power decrees, happens."

"I see you believe that," said Luke.

"Because it's the truth! Anyone who goes against me pays the penalty. You and Bridget will be no exception."

Luke said, "That's where you're wrong. However long a run of luck may be, it breaks in the end. Yours is very near breaking now."

Lord Easterfield said gently, "My dear young man, you don't know who it is you're talking to. Nothing can touch me!"

"Can't it? We'll see. You'd better watch your step, Easterfield."

A little ripple of movement passed over the other. His voice had changed when he spoke. "I've been very patient," said Lord Easterfield. "Don't strain my patience too far. Get out of here."

"I'm going," said Luke, "as quick as I can. Remember that I've warned you."

He turned on his heel and went quickly out of the room. He ran upstairs. He found Bridget in her room, superintending the packing of her clothes by a housemaid. "Ready soon?"

"In ten minutes."

Her eyes asked a question which the presence of the maid prevented her from putting into words. Luke gave a short nod. He went to his own room and flung his things hurriedly into his suitcases. He returned ten minutes later to find Bridget ready for departure. "Shall we go now?"

"I'm ready."

As they descended the staircase, they met the butler ascending. "Miss Waynflete has called to see you, miss."

"Miss Waynflete? Where is she?"

"In the drawing room with his lordship."

Bridget went straight to the drawing room, Luke close behind her. Lord Easterfield was standing by the window talking to Miss Waynflete. He had a knife in his hand—a long slender blade. "Perfect workmanship," he was saying. "One of my young men brought it back to me from Morocco, where he'd been special correspondent. It's Moorish, of course, a Riff knife." He drew a finger lovingly along the blade. "What an edge!"

Miss Waynflete said sharply, "Put it away, Gordon, for goodness' sake!"

He smiled and laid it down among a collection of other weapons on the table. "I like the feel of it," he said softly.

Miss Waynflete had lost some of her usual poise. She looked white and nervous. "Ah, there you are, Bridget, my dear," she said.

Lord Easterfield chuckled. "Yes, there's Bridget. Make the most of her, Honoria. She won't be with us long."

Miss Waynflete said sharply, "What d'you mean?"

"Mean? I mean she's going to London. That's right, isn't it? That's all I meant."

He looked round at them all. "I've got a bit of news for you, Honoria," he said. "Bridget isn't going to marry me, after all. She prefers Fitzwilliam here! A queer thing, life. Well, I'll leave you to have your talk." He went out of the room, his hands jingling the coins in his pockets.

"Oh dear!" said Miss Waynflete. "Oh, dear!"

The deep distress in her voice was so noticeable that Bridget looked slightly surprised. She said uncomfortably, "I'm sorry. I really am frightfully sorry."

Miss Waynflete said, "He's angry—he's frightfully angry. Oh, dear, this is terrible! What are we going to do?"

Bridget stared. "Do? What do you mean?"

Miss Waynflete said, including them both in her reproachful glance, "You should never have told him!"

Bridget said, "Nonsense. What else could we do?"

"You shouldn't have told him now. You should have waited till you'd got right away."

Bridget said shortly, "That's a matter of opinion. I think myself it's better to get unpleasant things over as quickly as possible."

"Oh, my dear, if it were only a question of that—" She stopped. Then her eyes asked a question of Luke.

Luke shook his head. His lips formed the words, "Not yet."

Miss Waynflete murmured, "I see."

Bridget said, with some slight exasperation, "Did you want to see me about something in particular, Miss Waynflete?"

"Well, yes. As a matter of fact, I came to suggest that you should come and pay me a little visit. I thought—er—you might find it uncomfortable to remain on here, and that you might want a few days to—er—well, mature your plans."

"Thank you, Miss Waynflete; that was very kind of you."

"You see, you'd be quite safe with me and—"

Bridget interrupted, "Safe?"

Miss Waynflete, a little flustered, said hurriedly, "Comfortable—that's what I mean—quite comfortable with me. I mean, not nearly so luxurious as here, naturally, but the hot water is hot and my little maid, Emily, really cooks quite nicely."

"Oh, I'm sure everything would be lovely, Miss Waynflete," said Bridget mechanically.

"But, of course, if you are going up to town, that is much better."

Bridget said slowly, "It's a little awkward. My aunt went off early to a flower show today. I haven't had a chance yet to tell her what has happened. I shall leave a note for her, telling her I've gone up to the flat."

"You're going to your aunt's flat in London?"

"Yes. There's no one there. But I can go out for meals."

"You'll be alone in the flat? Oh, dear, I shouldn't do that. Not stay there alone."

"Nobody will eat me," said Bridget impatiently. "Besides, my aunt will come up tomorrow."

Miss Waynflete shook her head in a worried manner.

Luke said, "Better go to a hotel."

Bridget wheeled round on him. "Why? What's the matter with you all? Why are you treating me as though I were an imbecile child?"

"No, no, dear," protested Miss Waynflete. "We just want you to be careful, that's all!"

"But why? Why? What's it all about?"

"Look here, Bridget," said Luke. "I want to have a talk with you. But I can't talk here. Come with me now in the car and we'll go somewhere quiet." He looked at Miss Waynflete. "May we come to your house in about an hour's time? There are several things I want to say to you."

"Please do. I will wait for you there."

Luke put his hand on Bridget's arm. He gave a nod of thanks to Miss Waynflete. He said, "We'll pick up the luggage later. Come on." He led her out of the room and along the hall to the front door. He opened the door of the car. Bridget got in. Luke started the engine and drove rapidly down the drive. He gave a sigh of relief as they emerged from the iron gates. "Thank God I've got you out of there safely," he said.

"Have you gone quite mad, Luke? Why all this 'hush-hush, I can't tell you what I mean now' business?"

Luke said grimly, "Well, there are difficulties, you know, in explaining that a man's a murderer, when you're actually under his roof."

21

BRIDGET SAT FOR a minute motionless beside him. She said, "Gordon?" Luke nodded. "Gordon? Gordon a murderer? Gordon the murderer? I never heard anything so ridiculous in all my life!"

"That's how it strikes you?"

"Yes, indeed. Why, Gordon wouldn't hurt a fly."

Luke said grimly, "That may be true. I don't know. But he certainly killed a canary bird, and I'm pretty certain he's killed a large number of human beings as well."

"My dear Luke, I simply can't believe it!"

"I know," said Luke. "It does sound quite incredible. Why, he never even entered my head as a possible suspect until the night before last."

Bridget protested, "But I know all about Gordon! I know what he's like! He's really a sweet little man—pompous, yes, but rather pathetic, really."

Luke shook his head. "You've got to readjust your ideas about him, Bridget."

"It's no good, Luke; I simply can't believe it! What put such an absurd idea into your head? Why, two days ago you were quite positive it was Ellsworthy."

Luke winced slightly. "I know. I know. You probably think that tomorrow I shall suspect Thomas, and the day after I shall be convinced that it's Horton I'm after. I'm not really so unbalanced as that. I admit the idea's completely startling when it first comes to you, but if you look into it a bit closer, you'll see that it all fits in remarkably well. No wonder Miss Fullerton didn't dare to go to the local authorities. She knew they'd laugh at her! Scotland Yard was her only hope."

"But what possible motive could Gordon have for all this killing business? Oh, it's all so silly!"

"I know. But don't you realize that Gordon Easterfield has a very exalted opinion of himself?"

Bridget said, "He pretends to be very wonderful and very important. That's just inferiority complex, poor lamb!"

"Possibly that's at the root of the trouble. I don't know. But think, Bridget—just think a minute. Remember all the phrases you've used laughingly yourself about him—*Lèse-majesté*, and so on. Don't you realize that the man's ego is swollen out of all proportion? And it's allied with religion. My dear girl, the man's as mad as a hatter!"

434

Bridget thought for a minute. She said at last, "I still can't believe it. What evidence have you got, Luke?"

"Well, there are his own words. He told me, quite plainly and distinctly, the night before last, that anyone who opposed him in any way always died."

"Go on."

"I can't quite explain to you what I mean, but it was the way he said it. Quite calm and complacent and—how shall I put it?—quite used to the idea! He just sat there smiling to himself. It was uncanny and rather horrible, Bridget!"

"Go on."

"Well, then he went on to give me a list of people who'd passed out because they'd incurred his sovereign displeasure! And, listen to this, Bridget: the people he mentioned were Mrs. Horton, Amy Gibbs, Tommy Pierce, Harry Carter, Humbleby and that chauffeur fellow, Rivers."

Bridget was shaken at last. She went very pale. "He mentioned those actual people?"

"Those actual people! Now, do you believe?"

"Oh, I suppose I must. What were his reasons?"

"Horribly trivial. That's what made it so frightening. Mrs. Horton had snubbed him, Tommy Pierce had done imitations of him and made the gardeners laugh, Harry Carter had abused him, Amy Gibbs had been grossly impertinent, Humbleby had dared to oppose him publicly, Rivers threatened him before me and Miss Waynflete."

Bridget put her hands to her eyes. "Horrible. Quite horrible," she murmured.

"I know. Then there's some other outside evidence. The car that ran down Miss Fullerton in London was a Rolls and its number was the number of Lord Easterfield's car."

"That definitely clinches it," said Bridget slowly.

"Yes. The police thought the woman who gave them that number must have made a mistake. Mistake indeed!"

"I can understand that," said Bridget. "When it comes to a rich powerful man like Lord Easterfield, naturally, his story is the one to be believed."

"Yes. One appreciates Miss Fullerton's difficulty."

Bridget said thoughtfully, "Once or twice she said rather queer things to me. As though she were warning me against something. I didn't understand in the least at the time. I see now!"

"It all fits in," said Luke. "That's the way of it. At first one says—as you said—'Impossible!' and then, once one accepts the idea, everything fits in. The grapes he sent to Mrs. Horton—and she thought the nurses were poisoning her! And that visit of his to the Wellerman Kreitz Research Laboratories—Somehow or other, he must have got hold of some culture of germs and infected Humbleby."

"I don't see how he managed that."

"I don't either, but the connection is there. One can't get away from that."

"No. As you say, it fits. And of course he could do things that other people couldn't. I mean he would be so completely above suspicion."

"I think Miss Waynflete suspected. She mentioned that visit to the laboratories. Brought it into conversation quite casually, but I believe she hoped I'd act upon it."

"She knew, then, all along?"

"She had a very strong suspicion. I think she was handicapped by having once been in love with him."

Bridget nodded. "Yes, that accounts for several things. Gordon told me they had once been engaged."

"She wanted, you see, not to believe it was him. But she became more and more sure that it was. She tried to give me hints, but she couldn't bear to do anything outright against him. Women are odd creatures. I think, in a way, she still cares about him."

"Even after he jilted her?"

"She jilted him. It was rather an ugly story. I'll tell you." He recounted the short, violent episode.

Bridget stared at him. "Gordon did that?"

"Yes. Even in those days, you see, he can't have been normal."

Bridget shivered and murmured, "All those years ago—all those years—"

Luke said, "He may have got rid of a lot more people than we shall ever know about. It's just the rapid succession of deaths lately that drew attention to him. As though he'd got reckless with success."

Bridget nodded. She was silent for a minute or two, thinking, then she said abruptly, "What exactly did Miss Fullerton say to you in the train that day? How did she begin?"

Luke cast his mind back. "Told me she was going to Scotland Yard; mentioned the village constable; said he was a nice fellow, but not up to dealing with murder."

"That was the first mention of the word?"

"Yes."

"Go on."

"Then she said, 'You're surprised, I can see. I was myself at first. I really couldn't believe it. I thought I must be imagining things.'"

"And then?"

"I asked her if she was sure she wasn't—imagining things, I mean—and she said, quite placidly, 'Oh, no. I might have been the first time, but not the second, or the third, or the fourth. After that, one knows.'"

"Marvelous," commented Bridget. "Go on."

"So of course I humored her; said I was sure she was doing the right thing. I was an unbelieving Thomas if there ever was one."

"I know. So easy to be wise after the event. I'd have felt just the same—nice and superior to the poor old dame. How did the conversation go on?"

"Let me see. Oh, she mentioned the Abercrombie case—you know, the Welsh poisoner. Said she hadn't really believed that there had been a look—a special look—that he gave his victims. But that she believed it now, because she had seen it herself."

"What words did she use exactly?"

Luke thought, creasing his brow, "She said, still in that nice ladylike voice: 'Of course, I didn't really believe that when I read about it, but it's true.' And I said, 'What's true?' And she said, 'The look on a person's face.' And, by Jove, Bridget, the way she said that, absolutely got me! Her quiet voice and the look on her face—like someone who had really seen something almost too horrible to speak about!"

"Go on, Luke. Tell me everything."

"And then she enumerated the victims—Amy Gibbs and Carter and Tommy Pierce, and said that Tommy was a horrid boy and Carter drank. And then she said, 'But now—yesterday—it was Doctor Humbleby—and he's such a good man—a really good man.' And she said if she went to Humbleby and told him, he wouldn't believe her; he'd only laugh!"

Bridget gave a deep sigh. "I see," she said. "I see."

Luke looked at her. "What is it, Bridget? What are you thinking of?"

"Something Mrs. Humbleby once said. I wondered—No, never mind, go on. What was it she said to you right at the end?"

Luke repeated the words soberly. They had made an impression on him and he was not likely to forget them. "I'd said it was difficult to get away with a lot of murders, and she answered, 'No, no, my dear boy, that's where you're wrong. It's very easy to kill, so long as no one suspects you. And, you see, the person in question is just the last person anyone would suspect.'" He was silent.

Bridget said, with a shiver, "Easy to kill? Horribly easy—that's true enough! No wonder those words stuck in your mind, Luke. They'll stick in mine—all my life! A man like Gordon Easterfield—Oh, of course it's easy!"

"It's not so easy to bring it home to him," said Luke.

"Don't you think so? I've an idea I can help there."

"Bridget, I forbid you—"

"You can't. One can't just sit back and play safe. I'm in this, Luke. It may be dangerous—yes, I'll admit that—but I've got to play my part."

"Bridget—"

"I'm in this, Luke! I shall accept Miss Waynflete's invitation and stay down here."

"My darling, I implore you—"

"It's dangerous for both of us. I know that. But we're in it, Luke—we're in it together!"

22

THE CALM INTERIOR of Miss Waynflete's house was almost an anti-climax after that tense moment in the car. Miss Waynflete received Bridget's acceptance of her invitation a little doubtfully; hastening, however, to reiterate her offer of hospitality by way of showing that her doubts were due to quite another cause than unwillingness to receive the girl. Luke said, "I really think it will be the best thing, since you are so kind, Miss Waynflete. I am staying at the Bells and Motley. I'd rather have Bridget under my eye than up in town. After all, remember what happened there before."

Miss Waynflete said, "You mean Lavinia Fullerton?"

"Yes. You would have said, wouldn't you, that anyone would be quite safe in the middle of a crowded city."

"You mean," said Miss Waynflete, "that anyone's safety depends principally on the fact that nobody wishes to kill them?"

"Exactly. We have come to depend upon what has been called the good will of civilization."

Miss Waynflete nodded her head thoughtfully.

Bridget said, "How long have you known that—that Gordon was the killer, Miss Waynflete?"

Miss Waynflete sighed. "That is a difficult question to answer, my dear. I suppose that I have been quite sure in my inmost heart, for some time. But I did my best not to recognize that belief. You see, I didn't want to believe it, and so I pretended to myself that it was a wicked and monstrous idea on my part."

Luke said bluntly, "Have you never been afraid for yourself?"

Miss Waynflete considered. "You mean that if Gordon had suspected that I knew, he would have found some means of getting rid of me?"

"Yes."

Miss Waynflete said gently, "I have, of course, been alive to that possibility. I tried to be careful of myself. But I do not think that Gordon would have considered me a real menace."

"Why?"

Miss Waynflete flushed a little. "I don't think that Gordon would ever believe that I would do anything to—to bring him into danger."

Luke said abruptly, "You went as far, didn't you, as to warn him?"

"Yes. That is, I did hint to him that it was odd that anyone who displeased him should shortly meet with an accident."

Bridget demanded, "And what did he say?"

A worried expression passed over Miss Waynflete's face. "He didn't react at all in the way I meant. He seemed—really it's most extraordinary!—he seemed pleased. He said, 'So, you've noticed that?' He quite—quite preened himself, if I may use that expression."

"He's mad, of course," said Luke.

Miss Waynflete agreed eagerly, "Yes, indeed; there isn't any other explanation possible. He's not responsible for his acts." She laid a hand on Luke's arm. "They—they won't hang him, will they, Mr. Fitzwilliam?"

"No, no. Send him to Broadmoor, I expect."

Miss Waynflete sighed and leaned back. "I'm so glad." Her eyes rested on Bridget, who was frowning down at the carpet.

Luke said, "But we're a long way from all that, still. I've notified the powers that be, and I can say this much: They're prepared to take the matter seriously. But you must realize that we've got remarkably little evidence to go upon."

"We'll get evidence," said Bridget.

Miss Waynflete looked up at her. There was some quality in her expression that reminded Luke of someone or something that he had seen not long ago. He tried to pin down the elusive memory, but failed. Miss Waynflete said doubtfully, "You are confident, my dear. Well, perhaps you are right."

Luke said, "I'll go along with the car, Bridget, and fetch your things from the Manor."

Bridget said immediately, "I'll come too."

"I'd rather you didn't."

"Yes, but I'd rather come."

Luke said irritably, "Don't do the mother-and-child act with me, Bridget! I refuse to be protected by you."

Miss Waynflete murmured, "I really think, Bridget, that it will be quite all right—in the car, and in daylight."

Bridget gave a slightly shamefaced laugh. "I'm being rather an idiot. This business gets on one's nerves."

Luke said, "Miss Waynflete protected me home the other night. . . . Come now, Miss Waynflete, admit it! You did, didn't you?"

She admitted it, smiling. "You see, Mr. Fitzwilliam, you were so completely unsuspicious. And if Gordon Easterfield had really grasped the fact that you were down here to look into this business, and for no other reason—well, it wasn't very safe. And that's a very lonely lane. Anything might have happened!"

"Well, I'm alive to the danger now all right," said Luke grimly. "I shan't be caught napping, I can assure you."

Miss Waynflete said anxiously, "Remember, he is very cunning. And much cleverer than you would ever imagine. Really, a most ingenious mind."

"I'm forewarned."

"Men have courage—one knows that," said Miss Waynflete—"but they are more easily deceived than women."

"That's true," said Bridget.

Luke said, "Seriously, Miss Waynflete, do you really think that I am in any danger? Do you think, in film parlance, that Lord Easterfield is really out to get me?"

Miss Waynflete hesitated. "I think," she said, "that the principal danger is to Bridget. It is her rejection of him that is the supreme insult. I think that after he has dealt with Bridget, he will turn his attention to you. But I think that undoubtedly he will try for her first."

Luke groaned, "I wish to goodness you'd go abroad—now—at once, Bridget."

Bridget's lips set themselves together. "I'm not going."

Miss Waynflete sighed. "You are a brave creature, Bridget. I admire you."

"You'd do the same in my place."

"Well, perhaps."

Bridget said, her voice dropping to a full rich note, "Luke and I are in this together."

She went out with him to the door. Luke said, "I'll give you a ring from the Bells and Motley when I'm safely out of the lion's den."

"Yes, do."

"My sweet, don't let's get all het up! Even the most accomplished murderers have to have a little time to mature their plans. I should say we're quite all right for a day or two. Superintendent Battle is coming down from London today. From then on, Easterfield will be under observation."

"In fact, everything is O.K. and we can cut out the melodrama."

Luke said gravely, laying a hand on her shoulder, "Bridget, my sweet, you will oblige me by not doing anything rash."

"Same to you, darling Luke."

He squeezed her shoulder, jumped into the car and drove off. Bridget returned to the sitting room. Miss Waynflete was fussing a little in a gentle spinsterish manner. "My dear, your room's not quite ready yet. Emily is seeing to it. Do you know what I'm going to do? I'm going to get you a nice cup of tea. It's just what you need after all these upsetting incidents."

"It's frightfully kind of you, Miss Waynflete, but I really don't want any."

Bridget disliked tea intensely. It usually gave her indigestion. Miss Waynflete, however, had decided that tea was what her young guest needed. She bustled out of the room and reappeared about five minutes later, her face beaming, carrying a tray on which stood two dainty Dresden cups full of a fragrant steaming beverage.

"Real Lapsang souchong," said Miss Waynflete proudly. Bridget, who disliked China tea even more than Indian, gave a wan smile.

At that moment, Emily, a small clumsy-looking girl with pronounced adenoids, appeared in the doorway and said, "If you blease, biss, did you bean the frilled billow cases?"

Miss Waynflete hurriedly left the room, and Bridget took advantage of the respite to pour her tea out of the window, narrowly escaping scalding Wonky Pooh, who was on the flower bed below.

Wonky Pooh accepted her apologies, sprang up on the window sill and proceeded to wind himself in and out over Bridget's shoulders, purring in an affected manner.

"Handsome!" said Bridget, drawing a hand down his back. Wonky Pooh arched his tail and purred with redoubled vigor. "Nice pussy," said Bridget, tickling his ears.

Miss Waynflete returned at that minute. "Dear me," she exclaimed. "Wonky Pooh has quite taken to you, hasn't he? He's so standoffish as a rule! Mind his ear, my dear. He's had a bad ear lately and it's still very painful." The injunction came too late. Bridget's hand had tweaked the painful ear. Wonky Pooh spat at her and retired, a mass of orange offended dignity. "Oh dear, has he scratched you?" cried Miss Waynflete.

"Nothing much," said Bridget, sucking a diagonal scratch on the back of her hand.

"Shall I put some iodine on?"

"Oh, no, it's quite all right. Don't let's fuss."

Miss Waynflete seemed a little disappointed. Feeling that she had been ungracious, Bridget said hastily, "I wonder how long Luke will be?"

"Now don't worry, my dear. I'm sure Mr. Fitzwilliam is well able to look after himself."

"Oh, Luke's tough all right!"

At that moment the telephone rang. Bridget hurried to it. Luke's voice spoke. "Hullo? That you, Bridget? I'm at the Bells and Motley. Can you wait for your traps till after lunch? Because Battle has arrived here—you know who I mean."

"The superintendent man from Scotland Yard?"

"Yes. And he wants to have a talk with me right away."

"That's all right by me. Bring my things round after lunch and tell me what he says about it all."

"Right. So long, my sweet."

Bridget replaced the receiver and retailed the conversation to Miss Waynflete. Then she yawned. A feeling of fatigue had succeeded her excitement. Miss Waynflete noticed it. "You're tired, my dear! You'd better lie down. No, perhaps that would be a bad thing just before lunch. I was just going to take some old clothes to a woman in a cottage not very far away—quite a pretty walk over the fields. Perhaps you'd care to come with me? We'll just have time before lunch."

Bridget agreed willingly. They went out the back way. Miss Waynflete wore a straw hat and, to Bridget's amusement, had put on gloves. "We might be going to Bond Street," she thought to herself.

Miss Waynflete chatted pleasantly of various small village matters as they walked. They went across two fields, crossed a rough lane and then took a path leading through a ragged copse. The day was hot and Bridget found the shade of the trees pleasant. Miss Waynflete suggested that they should sit down and rest a minute. "It's really rather oppressively warm today, don't you think? I fancy there must be thunder about."

Bridget acquiesced somewhat sleepily. She lay back against the bank, her eyes half closed, some lines of poetry wandering through her brain:

> O why do you walk through the fields in gloves,
> O fat white woman whom nobody loves?

But that wasn't quite right! Miss Waynflete wasn't fat. She amended the words to fit the case:

O why do you walk through the fields in gloves,
O lean gray woman whom nobody loves?

Miss Waynflete broke in upon her thoughts, "You're very sleepy, dear, aren't you?"

The words were said in a gentle everyday tone, but something in them jerked Bridget's eyes suddenly open.

Miss Waynflete was leaning forward toward her. Her eyes were eager, her tongue passed gently over her lips. She repeated her question: "You're very sleepy, aren't you?"

This time there was no mistaking the definite significance of the tone. A flash passed through Bridget's brain—a lightning flash of comprehension, succeeded by one of contempt at her own density. She had suspected the truth, but it had been no more than a dim suspicion. She had meant, working quietly and secretly, to make sure. But not for one moment had she realized that anything was to be attempted against herself. She had, she thought, concealed her suspicions entirely. Nor would she have dreamed that anything would be contemplated so soon. Fool—seven times fool! And she thought suddenly: "The tea—there was something in the tea. She doesn't know I never drank it. Now's my chance. I must pretend. What stuff was it, I wonder? Poison? Or just sleeping stuff? She expects me to be sleepy—that's evident."

She let her eyelids droop again. In what she hoped was a natural drowsy voice, she said: "I do—frightfully. How funny! I don't know when I've felt so sleepy."

Miss Waynflete nodded softly. Bridget watched the older woman narrowly through her almost-closed eyes. She thought: "I'm a match for her anyway. My muscles are pretty tough; she's a skinny frail old pussy. But I've got to make her talk—that's it, make her talk."

Miss Waynflete was smiling. It was not a nice smile. It was sly and not very human. Bridget thought: "She's like a goat. How like a goat she is! A goat's always been an evil symbol. I see why now. I was right—I was right in that fantastic idea of mine. Hell has no fury like a woman scorned. That was the start of it; it's all there."

She murmured, and this time her voice held a definite note of apprehension: "I don't know what's the matter with me. I feel so queer—so very queer."

Miss Waynflete gave a swift glance round her. The spot was entirely desolate. It was too far from the village for a shout to be heard. There were no houses or cottages near. She began to fumble with the parcel she carried—the parcel that was supposed to contain old clothes. Apparently, it did. The paper came apart, revealing a soft woolly garment. And still those gloved hands fumbled and fumbled.

O why do you walk through the fields in gloves?

Yes, why? Why gloves? Of course! Of course! The whole thing so beautifully planned!

The wrapping fell aside. Carefully, Miss Waynflete extracted the knife, holding it very carefully, so as not to obliterate the fingerprints which were already on it—where the short podgy fingers of Lord Easterfield had held it earlier that day in the drawing room at Ashe Manor. The Moorish knife with the sharp blade.

Bridget felt slightly sick. She must play for time—yes, and she must make the woman talk—this lean gray woman whom nobody loved. It ought not to be difficult—not really. Because she must want to talk, oh, so badly—and the only person she could ever talk to was someone like Bridget—someone who was going to be silenced forever. Bridget said, in a faint thick voice, "What's that knife?"

And then Miss Waynflete laughed. It was a horrible laugh, soft and musical and ladylike and quite inhuman. She said, "It's for you, Bridget. For you! I've hated you, you know, for a very long time."

Bridget said, "Because I was going to marry Gordon Easterfield?"

Miss Waynflete nodded. "You're clever. You're quite clever! This, you see, will be the crowning proof against him. You'll be found here, with your throat cut—and his knife, and his fingerprints on the knife! Clever, the way I asked to see it this morning! And then I slipped it into my bag, wrapped in a handkerchief, whilst you were upstairs. So easy! But the whole thing has been easy. I would hardly have believed it."

Bridget said—still in the thick muffled voice of a person heavily drugged, "That's because you're so devilishly clever."

Miss Waynflete laughed her ladylike little laugh again. She said, with a horrible kind of pride, "Yes, I always had brains, even as a girl. But they wouldn't let me do anything. I had to stay at home, doing nothing. And then Gordon—just a common bootmaker's son, but he had ambition. I knew—I knew he would rise in the world. And then he jilted me—jilted me! All because of that ridiculous business with the bird." Her hands made a queer gesture, as though she were twisting something. Again a wave of sickness passed over Bridget.

"Gordon Ragg daring to jilt me, Colonel Waynflete's daughter! I swore I'd pay him out for that! I used to think about it night after night. And then we got poorer and poorer. The house had to be sold. He bought it! He came along, patronizing me, offering me a job in my own old home. How I hated him then! But I never showed my feelings. We were taught that as girls—a most valuable training. That, I always think, is where breeding tells."

She was silent a minute. Bridget watched her, hardly daring to breathe, lest she should stem the flow of words.

Miss Waynflete went on softly, "All the time I was thinking and thinking. First of all, I just thought of killing him. That's when I began to read up criminology—quietly, you know—in the library. And really I found my reading came in most useful more than once later. The door of Amy's room, for instance, turning the key in the lock from the outside with pincers after I'd changed the bottles by her bed. How she snored, that girl. Quite disgusting, it was!" She paused. "Let me see, where was I?"

That gift which Bridget had cultivated, which had charmed Lord Easterfield—the gift of the perfect listener—stood her in good stead now. Honoria Waynflete might be a homicidal maniac, but she was also something much more common than that. She was a human being who wanted to talk about herself. And with that class of human being Bridget was well fitted to cope. She said, and her voice had exactly the right invitation in it, "You meant at first to kill him."

"Yes, but that didn't satisfy me—much too ordinary. It had to be something better than just killing. And then I got this idea. It just came to me. He should suffer for committing a lot of crimes of which he was quite innocent. He should be a murderer! He should be hanged for my crimes. Or else they'd say he was mad and he would be shut up all his life. That might be even better." She giggled now. A horrible little giggle. Her eyes were light and staring, with queer, elongated pupils.

"As I told you, I read a lot of books on crime. I chose my victims carefully; there was not to be too much suspicion at first. You see"—her voice deepened—"I enjoyed the killing. That disagreeable woman, Lydia Horton—she'd patronized me—once she referred to me as an 'old maid.' I was glad when Gordon quarreled with her. Two birds with one stone, I thought. Such fun, sitting by her bedside and slipping the arsenic in her tea, and then going out and telling the nurse how Mrs. Horton had complained of the bitter taste of Lord Easterfield's grapes! The stupid woman never repeated that, which was such a pity.

"And then the others! As soon as I heard that Gordon had a grievance against anyone, it was so easy to arrange for an accident! And he was such a fool—such an incredible fool! I made him believe that there was something very special about him! That anyone who went against him suffered. He believed it quite easily. Poor dear Gordon, he'd believe anything. So gullible!"

Bridget thought of herself saying to Luke scornfully, "Gordon! He could believe anything!" Easy? How easy! Poor pompous, credulous little Gordon. But she must learn more. Easy? This was easy too. She'd done it as a secretary for years. Quietly encouraged her employers to talk about themselves. And this woman wanted badly to talk, to boast about her own cleverness. Bridget murmured, "But how did you manage it all? I don't see how you could."

"Oh, it was quite easy. It just needed organization! When Amy was discharged from the Manor, I engaged her at once. I think the hat-paint idea was quite clever—and the door being locked on the inside made me quite safe. But of course I was always safe, because I never had any motive, and you can't suspect anyone of murder if there isn't a motive. Carter was quite easy, too; he was lurching about in the fog, and I caught up with him on the foot-bridge and gave him a quick push. I'm really very strong, you know."

She paused and the soft horrible little giggle came again. "The whole thing was such fun! I shall never forget Tommy's face when I pushed him off the window sill that day. He hadn't had the least idea." She leaned toward Bridget confidentially. "People are really very stupid, you know. I'd never realized that before."

Bridget said very softly, "But then, you're unusually clever."

"Yes, yes; perhaps you're right."

Bridget said, "Doctor Humbleby—that must have been more difficult?"

"Yes, it was really amazing how that succeeded. It might not have worked, of course. But Gordon had been talking to everybody of his visit to the Wellerman Kreitz Laboratories, and I thought if I could manage it so that people remembered that visit and connected it afterwards—And Wonky Pooh's ear was really very nasty, a lot of discharge. I managed to run the point of my scissors into the doctor's hand, and then I was so distressed and insisted on putting on a dressing and bandaging it up. He didn't know the dressing had been infected first from Wonky Pooh's ear. Of course it mightn't have worked; it was just a long shot. I was delighted when it did—especially as Wonky Pooh had been Lavinia's cat."

Her face darkened. "Lavinia Fullerton! She guessed. It was she who found Tommy that day. And then, when Gordon and old Doctor Humbleby had that row, she caught me looking at Humbleby. I was off my guard. I was just wondering exactly how I'd do it. And she knew! I turned round to find her watching me and—I gave myself away. I saw that she knew. She couldn't prove anything, of course; I knew that. But I was afraid, all the same, someone might believe her. I was afraid they might believe her at Scotland Yard. I felt sure that was where she was going that day. I was in the same train and I followed her.

"The whole thing was so easy. She was on an island crossing

Whitehall. I was close behind her. She never saw me. A big car came along and I shoved with all my might. I'm very strong! She went right down in front of it. I told the woman next to me I'd seen the number of the car and gave her the number of Gordon's Rolls. I hoped she'd repeat it to the police. It was lucky the car didn't stop. Some chauffeur joyriding without his master's knowledge, I suspect. Yes, I was lucky there. I'm always lucky. That scene the other day with Rivers, and Luke Fitzwilliam as witness. I've had such fun with him, leading him along! Odd how difficult it was to make him suspect Gordon. But after Rivers' death he would be sure to do so. He must! And now—well, this will just finish the whole thing nicely."

She got up and came toward Bridget. She said softly: "Gordon jilted me! He was going to marry you. All my life I've been disappointed. I've had nothing—nothing at all . . ."

O lean gray woman whom nobody loves—

She was bending over her, smiling, with mad light eyes. The knife gleamed.

With all her youth and strength, Bridget sprang. Like a tiger cat, she flung herself full force on the other woman, knocking her back, seizing her right wrist.

Taken by surprise, Honoria Waynflete fell back before the onslaught. But then, after a moment's inertia, she began to fight. In strength there was no comparison between them. Bridget was young and healthy, with muscles toughened by games. Honoria Waynflete was a slender-built, fragile creature. But there was one factor on which Bridget had not reckoned. Honoria Waynflete was mad. Her strength was the strength of the insane. She fought like a devil, and her insane strength was stronger than the sane muscled strength of Bridget. They swayed to and fro, and still Bridget strove to wrest the knife away from her, and still Honoria Waynflete hung on to it.

And then, little by little, the mad woman's strength began to prevail. Bridget cried out now, "Luke! Help! Help!" But she had no hope of help coming. She and Honoria Waynflete were alone. Alone in a dead world. With a supreme effort, she wrenched the other's wrist back, and at last she heard the knife fall. The next minute Honoria Waynflete's two hands had fastened round her neck in a maniac's grasp, squeezing the life out of her. She gave one last choked cry.

23

LUKE WAS FAVORABLY impressed by the appearance of Superintendent Battle. He was a solid comfortable-looking man with a broad red face and a large handsome mustache. He did not exactly express brilliance at a first glance, but a second glance was apt to make an observant person thoughtful, for Superintendent Battle's eye was unusually shrewd. Luke did not make the mistake of underestimating him. He had met men of Battle's type before. He knew that they could be trusted, and that they invariably got results. He could not have wished for a better man to be put in charge of the case. When they were alone together, Luke said, "You're rather a big noise to be sent down on a case like this."

Superintendent Battle smiled. "It may turn out to be a serious business, Mr. Fitzwilliam. When a man like Lord Easterfield is concerned, we don't want to have any mistakes."

"I appreciate that. Are you alone?"

"Oh, no. Got a detective sergeant with me. He's at the other pub, the Seven Stars, and his job is to keep an eye on his lordship."

"I see."

Battle asked, "In your opinion, Mr. Fitzwilliam, there's no doubt whatever? You're pretty sure of your man?"

"On the facts, I don't see that any alternative theory is possible. Do you want me to give you the facts?"

"I've had them, thank you, from Sir William."

"Well, what do you think? I suppose it seems to you wildly unlikely that a man in Lord Easterfield's position should be a homicidal criminal?"

"Very few things seem unlikely to me," said Superintendent Battle. "Nothing's impossible in crime. That's what I've always said. If you were to tell me that a dear old maiden lady, or an archbishop, or a schoolgirl, was a dangerous criminal, I wouldn't say no. I'd look into the matter."

"If you've heard the main facts of the case from Sir William, I'll just tell you what happened this morning," said Luke.

He ran over briefly the main lines of his scene with Lord Easterfield. Superintendent Battle listened with a good deal of interest.

He said, "You say he was fingering a knife. Did he make a special point of that knife, Mr. Fitzwilliam? Was he threatening with it?"

"Not openly. He tested the edge in rather a nasty way—a kind of esthetic pleasure about that that I didn't care about. Miss Waynflete felt the same, I believe."

"That's the lady you spoke about—the one who's known Lord Easterfield all her life, and was once engaged to marry him?"

"That's right."

Superintendent Battle said, "I think you can make your mind easy about the young lady, Mr Fitzwilliam. I'll have someone put on to keep a sharp watch on her. With that, and with Jackson tailing his lordship, there ought to be no danger of anything happening."

"You relieve my mind a good deal," said Luke.

The superintendent nodded sympathetically. "It's a nasty position for you, Mr. Fitzwilliam. Worrying about Miss Conway. Mind you, I don't expect this will be an easy case. Lord Easterfield must be a pretty shrewd man. He will probably lie low for a good long while. That is, unless he's got to the last stage."

"What do you call the last stage?"

"A kind of swollen egoism where a criminal thinks he simply can't be found out. He's too clever and everybody else is too stupid. Then, of course, we get him."

Luke nodded. He rose. "Well," he said, "I wish you luck. Let me help in any way I can."

"Certainly."

"There's nothing that you can suggest?"

Battle turned the question over in his mind. "I don't think so. Not at the moment. I just want to get the general hang of things in the place. Perhaps I could have another word with you in the evening?"

"Rather."

"I shall know better where we are then."

Luke felt vaguely comforted and soothed. Many people had had that feeling after an interview with Superintendent Battle. He glanced at his watch. Should he go round and see Bridget before lunch? Better not, he thought. Miss Waynflete might feel that she had to ask him to stay for the meal and it might disorganize her housekeeping. Middle-aged ladies, Luke knew from experience with aunts, were liable to be fussed over problems of housekeeping. He wondered if Miss Waynflete was an aunt? Probably.

He had strolled out to the door of the inn. A figure in black hurrying down the street stopped suddenly when she saw him. "Mr. Fitzwilliam."

"Mrs. Humbleby." He came forward and shook hands.

She said, "I thought you had left."

"No, only changed my quarters. I'm staying here now."

"And Bridget? I heard she had left Ashe Manor."

"Yes, she has."

Mrs. Humbleby sighed. "I am so glad—so very glad she has gone right away from Wychwood."

"Oh, she's still here. As a matter of fact, she's staying with Miss Waynflete."

Mrs. Humbleby moved back a step. Her face, Luke noted with surprise, looked extraordinarily distressed. "Staying with Honoria Waynflete? Oh, but why?"

"Miss Waynflete very kindly asked her to stay for a few days."

Mrs. Humbleby gave a little shiver. She came close to Luke and laid a hand on his arm.

"Mr. Fitzwilliam, I know I have no right to say anything—anything at all. I have had a lot of sorrow and grief lately and, perhaps, it makes me fanciful. These feelings of mine may be only sick fancies."

Luke said gently, "What feelings?"

"This conviction I have of—of evil!" She looked timidly at Luke. Seeing that he merely bowed his head gravely and did not appear to question her statement, she went on, "So much wickedness—that is the thought that is always with me—wickedness here in Wychwood. And that woman is at the bottom of it all. I am sure of it."

Luke was mystified. "What woman?"

Mrs. Humbleby said, "Honoria Waynflete is, I am sure, a very wicked woman! Oh, I see you don't believe me! No one believed Lavinia Fullerton either. But we both felt it. She, I think, knew more than I did. Remember, Mr. Fitzwilliam, if a woman is not happy, she is capable of terrible things."

Luke said gently, "That may be, yes."

Mrs. Humbleby said quickly, "You don't believe me? Well, why should you? But I can't forget the day when John came home with his hand bound up from her house, though he pooh-poohed it and said it was only a scratch." She turned. "Good-by. Please forget what I have just said. I—I don't feel quite myself these days."

Luke watched her go. He wondered why Mrs. Humbleby called Honoria Waynflete a wicked woman. Had Doctor Humbleby and Honoria Waynflete been friends, and was the doctor's wife jealous? What had she said? "No one believed Lavinia Fullerton either." Then Lavinia Fullerton must have confided some of her suspicions to Mrs. Humbleby. With a rush, the memory of the railway carriage came back, and the worried face of a nice old lady. He heard again an earnest voice saying: "The look on a person's face." And the way her own face had changed, as though she were seeing something very clearly in her mind. Just for a moment, he thought, her face had been quite different;

the lips drawn back from the teeth and a queer almost gloating look in her eyes.

He suddenly thought: "But I've seen someone look just like that—that same expression. Quite lately. When? This morning. Of course. Miss Waynflete when she was looking at Bridget in the drawing room at the Manor." And quite suddenly another memory assailed him. One of many years ago. His Aunt Mildred saying: "She looked, you know, my dear, quite half-witted." And just for a minute her own sane, comfortable face had borne an imbecile, mindless expression. Lavinia Fullerton had been speaking of the look she had seen on a man's—no, a person's—face. Was it possible that, just for a second, her vivid imagination had reproduced the look that she saw—the look of a murderer looking at his next victim?

Half unaware of what he was doing, Luke quickened his pace toward Miss Waynflete's house. A voice in his brain was saying over and over again: "Not a man—she never mentioned a man. You assumed it was a man because you were thinking of a man, but she never said so. Oh, God, am I quite mad? It isn't possible, what I'm thinking. Surely it isn't possible; it wouldn't make sense. But I must get to Bridget. I must know she's all right. Those eyes—those queer amber eyes. Oh, I'm mad. I must be mad. Easterfield's the criminal. He must be. He practically said so." And still, like a nightmare, he saw Miss Fullerton's face in its momentary impersonation of something horrible and not quite sane.

The stunted little maid opened the door to him. A little startled by his vehemence, she said, "The lady's gone out. Miss Waynflete told me so. I'll see if Miss Waynflete's in." He pushed past her, went into the drawing room. Emily ran upstairs. She came down breathless. "The mistress is out too."

Luke took her by the shoulder. "Which way? Where did they go?"

She gaped at him. "They must have gone out by the back. I'd have seen them if they'd gone out front ways, because the kitchen looks out there."

She followed him as he raced out through the door into the tiny garden and out beyond. There was a man clipping a hedge. Luke went up to him and asked a question, striving to keep his voice normal.

The man said slowly, "Two ladies? Yes. Some while since. I was having my dinner under the hedge. Reckon they didn't notice me."

"Which way did they go?"

He strove desperately to make his voice normal. Yet the other's eyes opened a little wider as he replied slowly: "Across them fields. Over that way. I don't know where after that."

Luke thanked him and began to run. His strong feeling of urgency was deepened. He must catch up with them—he must! He might be quite mad. In all probability, they were just taking an amicable stroll, but something in him clamored for haste. More haste!

He crossed the two fields, stood hesitating in a country lane. Which way now? And then he heard the call—faint, far away, but ummistakable: "Luke! Help!" And again, "Luke!" Unerringly he plunged into the wood and ran in the direction from which the cry had come. There were more sounds now—scuffling, panting, a low gurgling cry. He came through the trees in time to tear a mad woman's hands from her victim's throat, to hold her, struggling, foaming, cursing, till at last she gave a convulsive shudder and turned rigid in his grasp.

24

"BUT I DON'T understand," said Lord Easterfield. "I don't understand." He strove to maintain his dignity, but beneath the pompous exterior a rather pitiable bewilderment was evident. He could hardly credit the extraordinary things that were being told him.

"It's like this, Lord Easterfield," said Battle patiently. "To begin with, there is a touch of insanity in the family. We've found that out now. Often the way with these old families. I should say she had a predisposition that way. And then she was an ambitious lady, and she was thwarted. First her career and then her love affair." He coughed. "I understand it was you who jilted her."

Lord Easterfield said stiffly, "I don't like the term 'jilt.'"

Superintendent Battle amended the phrase, "It was you who terminated the engagement?"

"Well, yes."

"Tell us why, Gordon," said Bridget.

Lord Easterfield got rather red. He said, "Oh, very well, if I must. Honoria had a canary. She was very fond of it. It used to take sugar from her lips. One day it pecked her violently instead. She was angry and picked it up and—wrung its neck! I—I couldn't feel the same after that. I told her I thought we'd both made a mistake."

Battle nodded. He said, "That was the beginning of it. As she told Miss Conway, she turned her thoughts and her undoubted mental ability to one aim and purpose."

Lord Easterfield said incredulously, "To get me convicted as a murderer? I can't believe it."

Bridget said, "It's true, Gordon. You know, you were surprised yourself at the extraordinary way that everybody who annoyed you was instantly struck down."

"There was a reason for that."

"Honoria Waynflete was the reason," said Bridget. "Do get it into your head, Gordon, that it wasn't Providence that pushed Tommy Pierce out of the window, and all the rest of them. It was Honoria."

Lord Easterfield shook his head. "It all seems to me quite incredible!" he said.

Battle said, "You say you got a telephone message this morning?"

"Yes, about twelve o'clock. I was asked to go to the Shaw Wood at once, as you, Bridget, had something to say to me. I was not to come by car, but to walk."

Battle nodded. "Exactly. That would have been the finish. Miss Conway would have been found with her throat cut, and beside her your knife with your fingerprints on it! And you yourself would have been seen in the vicinity at the time! You wouldn't have had a leg to stand on. Any jury in the world would have convicted you."

"Me?" said Lord Easterfield, startled and distressed. "Anyone would have believed a thing like that of me?"

Bridget said gently, "I didn't, Gordon. I never believed it."

Lord Easterfield looked at her coldly, then he said stiffly, "In view of my character and my standing in the country, I do not believe that anyone for one moment would have believed such a monstrous charge." He went out with dignity and closed the door behind him.

Luke said, "He'll never realize that he was really in danger." Then he said, "Go on, Bridget. Tell me how you came to suspect the Waynflete woman."

Bridget explained. "It was when you were telling me that Gordon was the killer. I couldn't believe it! You see, I knew him so well. I'd been his secretary for two years. I knew him in and out. I knew that he was pompous and petty and competely self-absorbed, but I knew, too, that he was a kindly person and almost absurdly tenderhearted. It worried him even to kill a wasp. That story about his killing Miss Waynflete's canary—it was all wrong. He just couldn't have done it. He'd told me once that he had jilted her. Now you insisted that it was the other way about. Well, that might be so! His pride might not have allowed him to admit that she had thrown him over. But not the canary story! That simply wasn't Gordon! He didn't even shoot, because seeing things killed made him feel sick.

"So I simply knew that that part of the story was untrue. But if so, Miss Waynflete must have lied. And it was really, when you came to think of it, a very extraordinary lie. And I wondered suddenly if she'd told any more lies. She was a very proud woman—one could see that. To be thrown over must have hurt her pride horribly. It would probably make her feel very angry and revengeful against Lord Easterfield—especially, I felt, if he turned up again later, all rich and prosperous and successful. I thought, 'Yes, she'd probably enjoy helping to fix a crime upon him.' And then a curious sort of whirling feeling came in my brain, and I thought: 'But suppose everything she says is a lie,' and I suddenly saw how easily a woman like that could make a fool of a man. And I thought: 'It's fantastic, but suppose it was she who killed all these people and fed Gordon up with the idea that it was a kind of divine retribution.' It would be quite easy for her to make him believe that. As I told you once, Gordon would believe anything! And I thought: 'Could she have done all those murders?' And I saw that she could! She could give a shove to a drunken man, push a boy out of a window, and Amy Gibbs had died in her house. Mrs. Horton too—she used to go and sit with her when she was ill. Doctor Humbleby was more difficult. I didn't know then that Wonky Pooh had a nasty septic ear. Miss Fullerton's death was even more difficult, because I couldn't imagine Miss Waynflete dressed up as a chauffeur, driving a Rolls.

"And then, suddenly, I saw that that was the easiest of the lot! It was the old shove from behind—easily done in a crowd. The car didn't stop, and she saw a fresh opportunity and told another woman she had seen the number of the car, and gave the number of Lord Easterfield's Rolls.

"Of course, all this only came very confusedly through my head. But if Gordon definitely hadn't done the murders—and I knew, yes, knew that he hadn't—well, who did? And the answer seemed quite clear. Someone who hates Gordon! Who hates Gordon? Honoria Waynflete of course.

"And then I remembered that Miss Fullerton had definitely spoken of a man as the killer. That knocked out all my beautiful theory, because, unless Miss Fullerton was right, she wouldn't have been killed. So I got you to repeat exactly Miss Fullerton's words, and I soon discovered that she hadn't actually said 'man' once. Then I felt that I was definitely on the right track! I decided to accept Miss Waynflete's invitation to stay with her, and I resolved to try to ferret out the truth."

"Without saying a word to me?" said Luke angrily.

"But, my sweet, you were so sure—and I wasn't sure a bit! It was all vague and doubtful. But I never dreamed that I was in any danger. I thought I'd have plenty of time."

She shivered. "Oh, Luke, it was horrible! Her eyes—and that dreadful polite, inhuman laugh!"

Luke said, with a slight shiver, "I shan't forget how I only got there just in time." He turned to Battle. "What's she like now?"

"Gone right over the edge," said Battle. "They do, you know. They can't face the shock of not having been so clever as they thought they were."

Luke said ruefully, "Well, I'm not much of a policeman! I never suspected Honoria Waynflete once. You'd have done better, Battle."

"Maybe, sir, maybe not. You'll remember my saying that nothing's impossible in crime. I mentioned a maiden lady, I believe."

"You also mentioned an archbishop and a schoolgirl! Am I to understand that you consider all these people as potential criminals?"

Battle's smile broadened to a grin. "Anyone may be a criminal, sir; that's what I meant.'

"Except Gordon," said Bridget. "Luke, let's go and find him."

They found Lord Easterfield in his study, busily making notes. "Gordon," said Bridget in a small meek voice. "Please, now that you know everything, will you forgive us?"

Lord Easterfield looked at her graciously. "Certainly, my dear, certainly. I realize the truth. I was a busy man. I neglected you. The truth of the matter is, as Kipling so wisely puts it, 'He travels the fastest who travels alone.' My path in life is a lonely one." He squared his shoulders. "I carry a big responsibility. I must carry it alone. For me there can be no companionship, no easing of the burden. I must go through life alone, till I drop by the wayside."

Bridget said, "Dear Gordon! You really are sweet!"

Lord Easterfield frowned. "It is not a question of being sweet. Let us forget all this nonsense. I am a busy man."

"I know you are."

"I am arranging for a series of articles to start at once. Crimes committed by women through the ages."

Bridget gazed at him with admiration. "Gordon, I think that's a wonderful idea."

Lord Easterfield puffed out his chest. "So please leave me now. I must not be disturbed. I have a lot of work to get through."

Luke and Bridget tiptoed from the room. "But he really is sweet," said Bridget.

"Bridget, I believe you were really fond of that man."

"Do you know, Luke, I believe I was."

Luke looked out of the window. "I'll be glad to get away from Wychwood. I don't like this place. There's a lot of wickedness here, as Mrs. Humbleby would say. I don't like the way Ashe Ridge broods over the village."

"Talking of Ashe Ridge, what about Ellsworthy?"

Luke laughed a little shamefacedly. "That blood on his hands?"

"Yes."

"They'd sacrificed a white cock, apparently."

"How perfectly disgusting!"

"I think something unpleasant is going to happen to our Mr. Ellsworthy. Battle is planning a little surprise."

Bridget said, "And poor Major Horton never even attempted to kill his wife, and Mr. Abbot, I suppose, just had a compromising letter from a lady, and Doctor Thomas is just a nice unassuming young doctor."

"He's a superior ass."

"You say that because you're jealous of his marrying Rose Humbleby."

"She's much too good for him."

"I always have felt you liked that girl better than me."

"Darling, aren't you being rather absurd?"

"No, not really." She was silent a minute, and then said, "Luke, do you like me now?"

He made a movement toward her, but she warded him off. "I said 'like,' Luke; not 'love.'"

"Oh, I see. Yes, I do. I like you, Bridget, as well as loving you."

Bridget said, "I like you, Luke." They smiled at each other a little timidly, like children who have made friends at a party. Bridget said, "Liking is more important than loving. It lasts. I want what is between us to last, Luke. I don't want us just to love each other and marry and get tired of each other, and then want to marry someone else."

"Oh, my dear love, I know. You want reality. So do I. What's between us will last forever, because it's founded on reality."

"Is that true, Luke?"

"It's true, my sweet. That's why, I think, I was afraid of loving you."

"I was afraid of loving you too."

"Are you afraid now?"

"No."

He said, "We've been close to death for a long time. Now that's over! Now we'll begin to live."

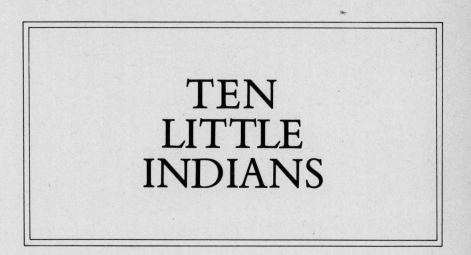

TEN
LITTLE
INDIANS

Cast of Characters

MR. JUSTICE WARGRAVE—The reptilian old man, known in the press and the courts as a "hanging judge," had the blood of countless prisoners on his hands. How many of them were innocent?

VERA CLAYTHORNE—An ex-governess with a Coroner's Inquest in her past, she had been completely absolved of all guilt, she explained—even the boy's mother hadn't blamed her.

CAPTAIN PHILIP LOMBARD—A soldier-of-fortune, his past didn't bear close examination, either. He was the only one who thought it necessary to carry a gun to Indian Island.

EMILY BRENT—A sixty-five-year-old spinster whose troubled dreams and rambling diary were the only indications of a disturbed—and perhaps dangerous—mind.

GENERAL MACARTHUR—His life, as far as he was concerned, had ended in the trenches in the Great War. "I'll never leave Indian Island alive," he said to anyone who would listen.

DR. ARMSTRONG—At first the physician was a convenient dispenser of sedatives and diagnostician of causes of death, but later the others remembered that he was the only one who had easy access to poison.

ANTHONY MARSTON—Like a young, bronzed god, he came careening into their lives as if he would live forever. His stunning strength proved pitifully inadequate against that of his unknown adversary.

MR. BLORE—The blunt, bearlike ex-C.I.D. man tried to pass himself off as an African colonial, but when the game was up he amused himself by suspecting everyone else's motives.

FRED NARRACOTT—The Devonshire boatman, like Charon ferrying the Styx, motored the doomed group to Indian Island. He felt it a queer business indeed—they seemed such a dull, ill-assorted lot.

MR. AND MRS. ROGERS—The stammering butler and white, bloodless cook for the strange gathering on Indian Island had been the perfect servants, as the others learned when circumstances forced them to fend for themselves.

SIR THOMAS LEGGE—The Assistant Commissioner at Scotland Yard was presented with a round number of corpses, a handful of diaries and a coroner's careful report. Yet he was forced to conclude there had been no murderer!

INSPECTOR MAINE—Also of Scotland Yard, he had painstakingly and accurately compiled the corpus delicti. And, in the end, he agreed with his superior—the case of murder on Indian Island was incredible.

1

IN THE CORNER of a first-class smoking carriage, Mr. Justice Wargrave, lately retired from the bench, puffed at a cigar and ran an interested eye through the political news in the *Times*. He laid the paper down and glanced out of the window. They were running now through Somerset. He glanced at his watch—another two hours to go.

He went over in his mind all that had appeared in the papers about Indian Island. There had been its original purchase by an American millionaire who was crazy about yachting—and an account of the luxurious modern house he had built on this little island off the Devon coast. The unfortunate fact that the new third wife of the American millionaire was a bad sailor had led to the subsequent putting up of the house and island for sale. Various glowing advertisements of it had appeared in the papers. Then came the first bald statement that it had been bought—by a Mr. Owen. After that the rumors of the gossip writers had started. Indian Island had really been bought by Miss Gabrielle Turl, the Hollywood film star! She wanted to spend some months there free from all publicity! *Busy Bee* had hinted delicately that it was to be an abode for Royalty??! *Mr. Merryweather* had had it whispered to him that it had been bought for a honeymoon—Young Lord L——had surrendered to Cupid at last! *Jonas* knew for a *fact* that it had been purchased by the Admiralty with a view to carrying out some very hush-hush experiments! Definitely, Indian Island was news!

From his pocket Mr. Justice Wargrave drew out a letter. The handwriting was practically illegible but words here and there stood out with unexpected clarity. *Dearest Lawrence . . . such years since I heard anything of you . . . must come to Indian Island . . . the most enchanting place . . . so much to talk over . . . old days . . . communion with Nature . . . bask in sunshine . . . 12:40 from Paddington . . . meet you at*

Oakbridge . . . and his correspondent signed herself with a flourish his *ever Constance Culmington.*

Mr. Justice Wargrave cast back in his mind to remember when exactly he had last seen Lady Constance Culmington. It must be seven—no, eight years ago. She had then been going to Italy to bask in the sun and be at one with Nature and the *contadini.* Later, he had heard, she had proceeded to Syria where she proposed to bask in yet stronger sun and live at one with Nature and the Bedouin.

Constance Culmington, he reflected to himself, was exactly the sort of woman who *would* buy an island and surround herself with mystery! Nodding his head in gentle approval of his logic, Mr. Justice Wargrave allowed his head to nod. . . . He slept. . . .

ii

Vera Claythorne, in a third-class carriage with five other travelers in it, leaned her head back and shut her eyes. How hot it was traveling by train today! It would be nice to get to the sea! Really a great piece of luck getting this job. When you wanted a holiday post it nearly always meant looking after a swarm of children—secretarial holiday posts were much more difficult to get. Even the agency hadn't held out much hope.

And then the letter had come.

> I have received your name from the Skilled Women's Agency together with their recommendation. I understand they know you personally. I shall be glad to pay you the salary you ask and shall expect you to take up your duties on August 8th. The train is the 12:40 from Paddington and you will be met at Oakbridge station. I enclose five pound notes for expenses.
>
> Yours truly,
> Una Nancy Owen

And at the top was the stamped address INDIAN ISLAND, STICKLE-HAVEN, DEVON. . . .

Indian Island! Why, there had been nothing else in the papers lately! All sorts of hints and interesting rumors. Though probably that was mostly untrue. But the house had certainly been built by a millionaire and was said to be absolutely the last word in luxury.

Vera Claythorne, tired by a recent strenuous term at school, thought to herself: Being a games mistress in a third-class school isn't much of a catch. . . . If only I could get a job at some *decent* school. And then, with a cold feeling round her heart, she thought: But I'm lucky to have even this. After all, people don't like a Coroner's Inquest, even if the Coroner *did* acquit me of all blame!

He had even complimented her on her presence of mind and courage, she remembered. For an inquest it couldn't have gone better. And Mrs. Hamilton had been kindness itself to her. Only Hugo *(but she wouldn't think of Hugo!).*

Suddenly, in spite of the heat in the carriage she shivered and wished she wasn't going to the sea. A picture rose clearly before her mind. *Cyril's head, bobbing up and down, swimming to the rock....* Up and down—up and down.... And herself, swimming in easy, practiced strokes after him—cleaving her way through the water but knowing, only too surely, that she wouldn't be in time....

The sea—its deep, warm blue—mornings spent lying out on the sands—Hugo—Hugo who had said he loved her.... She must *not* think of Hugo....

She opened her eyes and frowned across at the man opposite her. A tall man with a brown face, light eyes set rather close together and an arrogant, almost cruel mouth. She thought to herself: I bet he's been to some interesting parts of the world and seen some interesting things....

iii

Philip Lombard, summing up the girl opposite in a mere flash of his quick-moving eyes, thought to himself: Quite attractive—a bit schoolmistressy perhaps.... A cool customer, he should imagine—and one who could hold her own—in love or war. He'd rather like to take her on....

He frowned. No, cut out all that kind of stuff. This was business. He'd got to keep his mind on the job.

What exactly was up? he wondered. Morris had been damned mysterious. "Take it or leave it, Captain Lombard."

He had said thoughtfully, "A hundred guineas, eh?"

He had said it in a casual way as though a hundred guineas were nothing to him. *A hundred guineas,* when he was literally down to his last square meal! He had fancied, though, that Morris had not been deceived—that was the damnable part about Morris, you couldn't deceive him about money—he *knew!*

He had said in the same casual tone, "And you can't give me any further information?"

Mr. Isaac Morris had shaken his little bald head very positively. "No, Captain Lombard, the matter rests there. It is understood by my client that your reputation is that of a good man in a tight place. I am empowered to hand you one hundred guineas in return for which you will travel to Sticklehaven, Devon. The nearest station is Oakbridge. You will be met there and motored to Sticklehaven where a motor launch will convey you to Indian Island. There you will hold yourself at the disposal of my client."

Lombard had said abruptly, "For how long?"

"Not longer than a week at most."

Fingering his small mustache, Captain Lombard said, "You understand I can't undertake anything—illegal?"

He had darted a very sharp glance at the other as he had spoken. There had been a very faint smile on the thick lips of Mr. Morris as he answered gravely, "If anything illegal is proposed, you will, of course, be at perfect liberty to withdraw."

Damn the smooth little brute, he had smiled! It was as though he knew very well that in Lombard's past actions legality had not always been a *sine qua non.* . . .

Lombard's own lips parted in a grin. By Jove, he'd sailed pretty near the wind once or twice! But he'd always got away with it! There wasn't much he drew the line at really. . . . No, there wasn't much he'd draw the line at. He fancied that he was going to enjoy himself at Indian Island. . . .

iv

In a non-smoking carriage Miss Emily Brent sat very upright as was her custom. She was sixty-five and she did not approve of lounging. Her father, a Colonel of the old school, had been particular about deportment. The present generation was shamelessly lax—in their carriage, *and in every other way.* . . .

Enveloped in an aura of righteousness and unyielding principles, Miss Brent sat in her crowded third-class carriage and triumphed over its discomfort and its heat. Everyone made such a fuss over things nowadays! They wanted injections before they had teeth pulled—they took drugs if they couldn't sleep—they wanted easy chairs and cushions and the girls allowed their figures to slop about anyhow and lay about half-naked on the beaches in summer. Miss Brent's lips set closely. She would like to make an example of certain people.

She remembered last year's summer holiday. This year, however, it would be quite different. Indian Island. . . . Mentally she reread the letter which she had already read so many times.

Dear Miss Brent,

I do hope you remember me? We were together at Bellhaven Guest House in August some years ago, and we seemed to have so much in common.

I am starting a guest house of my own on an island off the coast of Devon. I think there is really an opening for a place where there is good plain cooking and a nice old-fashioned type of person. None of this nudity and gramophones half the night. I shall be very glad if you could see your way to spending your summer holiday on Indian Island—quite free—as my guest. Would early in August suit you? Perhaps the 8th.

Yours sincerely,
U.N.——

What was the name? The signature was rather difficult to read. Emily Brent thought impatiently: So many people write their signatures quite illegibly.

She let her mind run back over the people at Bellhaven. She had been there two summers running. There had been that nice middle-aged woman—Mrs.—Mrs.—now what *was* her name?—her father had been a Canon. And there had been a Miss Olton—Ormen—No, surely it was *Oliver*! Yes—Oliver.

Indian Island! There had been things in the paper about Indian Island—something about a film star—or was it an American millionaire? Of course often those places went very cheap—islands didn't suit everybody. They thought the idea was romantic but when they came to live there they realized the disadvantages and were only too glad to sell.

Emily Brent thought to herself: I shall be getting a free holiday at any rate. With her income so much reduced and so many dividends not being paid, that was indeed something to take into consideration. If only she could remember a little more about Mrs.—or was it Miss—Oliver?

V

General Macarthur looked out of the carriage window. The train was just coming into Exeter where he had to change. Damnable, these slow branch-line trains! This place, Indian Island, was really no distance at all as the crow flies.

He hadn't got it clear who this fellow Owen was. A friend of Spoof Leggard's, apparently—and of Johnny Dyer's.

—One or two of your old cronies are coming—would like to have a talk over old times.

Well, he'd enjoy a chat about old times. He'd had a fancy lately that fellows were rather fighting shy of him. All owing to that damned rumor! By God, it was pretty hard—nearly thirty years ago now! Armitage had talked, he supposed. Damned young pup! What did *he* know about it? Oh, well, no good brooding about these things! One fancied things sometimes—fancied a fellow was looking at you queerly.

This Indian Island now, he'd be interested to see it. A lot of gossip flying about. Looked as though there might be something in the rumor that the Admiralty or the War Office or the Air Force had got hold of it. . . .

Young Elmer Robson, the American millionaire, had actually built the place. Spent thousands on it, so it was said. Every mortal luxury. . . .

Exeter! And an hour to wait! And he didn't want to wait. He wanted to get on. . . .

vi

Dr. Armstrong was driving his Morris across Salisbury Plain. He was very tired. . . . Success had its penalties. There had been a time when he had sat in his consulting room in Harley Street, correctly appareled, surrounded with the most up-to-date appliances and the most luxurious furnishings, and waited—waited through the empty days for his venture to succeed or fail. . . .

Well, it had succeeded! He'd been lucky! Lucky *and* skillful, of course. He was a good man at his job—but that wasn't enough for success. You had to have luck as well. And he'd had it! An accurate diagnosis, a couple of grateful women patients—women with money and position—and word had got about. "You ought to try Armstrong—*quite* a young man—but *so* clever—Pam had been to all sorts of people for *years* and he put his finger on the trouble at once!" The ball had started rolling.

And now Dr. Armstrong had definitely arrived. His days were full. He had little leisure. And so, on this August morning, he was glad that he was leaving London and going to be for some days on an island off the Devon coast. Not that it was exactly a holiday. The letter he had received had been rather vague in its terms, but there was nothing vague about the accompanying check. A whacking fee. These Owens must be rolling in money. Some little difficulty, it seemed, a husband who was worried about his wife's health and wanted a report on it without her being alarmed. She wouldn't hear of seeing a doctor. Her nerves—

Nerves! The doctor's eyebrows went up. These women and their nerves! Well, it was good for business, after all. Half the women who consulted him had nothing the matter with them but boredom, but they wouldn't thank you for telling them so! And one could usually find something.

"A slightly uncommon condition of the—some long word—nothing at all serious—but it just needs putting right. A simple treatment."

Well, medicine was mostly faith-healing when it came to it. And he had a good manner—he could inspire hope and belief.

Lucky that he'd managed to pull himself together in time after that business ten—no, fifteen years ago. It had been a near thing, that! He'd been going to pieces. The shock had pulled him together. He'd cut out drink altogether. By Jove, it had been a near thing though. . . .

With a devastating, ear-splitting blast on the horn, an enormous Super Sports Dalmain car rushed past him at eighty miles an hour. Dr. Armstrong nearly went into the hedge. One of these young fools who tore around the country. He hated them! That had been a near shave, too. Damned young fool!

vii

Tony Marston, roaring down into Mere, thought to himself: The amount of cars crawling about the roads is frightful. Always something blocking your way. *And* they will drive in the middle of the road! Pretty hopeless driving in England, anyway. . . . Not like France where you really *could* let out. . . .

Should he stop here for a drink, or push on? Heaps of time! Only another hundred miles and a bit to go. He'd have a gin and ginger beer. Fizzing hot day!

This island place ought to be rather good fun—if the weather lasted. Who *were* these Owens, he wondered? Rich and stinking, probably. Badger was rather good at nosing people like that out. Of course, he *had* to, poor old chap, with no money of his own. . . .

Hope they'd do one well in drinks. Never knew with these fellows who'd made their money and weren't born to it. Pity that story about Gabrielle Turl having bought Indian Island wasn't true. He'd like to have been in with that film-star crowd. Oh, well, he supposed there'd be a few girls there. . . .

Coming out of the hotel, he stretched himself, yawned, looked up at the blue sky and climbed into the Dalmain. Several young women looked at him admiringly—his six feet of well-proportioned body, his crisp hair, tanned face, and intensely blue eyes.

He let in the clutch with a roar and leapt up the narrow street. Old men and errand boys jumped for safety. The latter looked after the car admiringly.

Anthony Marston proceeded on his triumphal progress.

viii

Mr. Blore was in the slow train from Plymouth. There was only one other person in his carriage, an elderly seafaring gentleman with a bleary eye. At the present moment he had dropped off to sleep. Mr. Blore was writing carefully in a little notebook.

"That's the lot," he muttered to himself. "Emily Brent, Vera Claythorne, Dr. Armstrong, Anthony Marston, old Justice Wargrave, Philip Lombard, General Macarthur, C.M.G., D.S.O. Manservant and wife: Mr. and Mrs. Rogers."

He closed the notebook and put it back in his pocket. He glanced over at the corner and the slumbering man. "Had one over the eight," diagnosed Mr. Blore accurately.

He went over things carefully and conscientiously in his mind. "Job ought to be easy enough," he ruminated. "Don't see how I can slip up on it. Hope I look all right."

He stood up and scrutinized himself anxiously in the glass. The face reflected there was of a slightly military cast with a mustache. There was very little expression in it. The eyes were gray and set rather close together. "Might be a major," said Mr. Blore. "No, I forgot. There's that old military gent. He'd spot me at once. South Africa," said Mr. Blore, "that's my line! None of these people have anything to do with South Africa, and I've just been reading that travel folder so I can talk about it all right."

Fortunately there were all sorts and types of colonials. As a man of means from South Africa, Mr. Blore felt that he could enter into any society unchallenged.

Indian Island. He remembered Indian Island as a boy. . . . Smelly sort of rock covered with gulls—stood about a mile from the coast. It had got its name from its resemblance to a man's head—an American Indian profile.

Funny idea to go and build a house on it! Awful in bad weather! But millionaires were full of whims!

The old man in the corner woke up and said, "You can't never tell at sea—never!"

Mr. Blore said soothingly, "That's right. You can't."

The old man hiccuped twice and said plaintively, "There's a squall coming."

Mr. Blore said, "No, no, mate, it's a lovely day."

The old man said angrily, "There's a squall ahead I can *smell* it."

"Maybe you're right," said Mr. Blore pacifically.

The train stopped at a station and the old fellow rose unsteadily. "Thish where I get out." He fumbled with the window. Mr. Blore helped him.

The old man stood in the doorway. He raised a solemn hand and blinked his bleary eyes. "Watch and pray," he said. "Watch and pray. The day of judgment is at hand."

He collapsed through the doorway onto the platform. From a recumbent position he looked up at Mr. Blore and said with immense dignity, "I'm talking to *you*, young man. The day of judgment is very close at hand."

Subsiding into his seat Mr. Blore thought to himself: He's nearer the day of judgment than I am!

But there, as it happens, he was wrong. . . .

2

OUTSIDE OAKBRIDGE STATION a little group of people stood in momentary uncertainty. Behind them stood porters with suitcases. One of these called "Jim!" The driver of one of the taxis stepped forward. "You'm for Indian Island, maybe?" he asked in a soft Devon voice. Four voices gave assent—and then immediately afterwards gave quick surreptitious glances at each other.

The driver said, addressing his remarks to Mr. Justice Wargrave as the senior member of the party: "There are two taxis here, sir. One of them must wait till the slow train from Exeter gets in—a matter of five minutes—there's one gentleman coming by that. Perhaps one of you wouldn't mind waiting? You'd be more comfortable that way."

Vera Claythorne, her own secretarial position clear in her mind, spoke at once. "I'll wait," she said, "if you will go on." She looked at the other three; her glance and voice had that slight suggestion of command in them that comes from having occupied a position of authority. She might have been directing which tennis sets the girls were to play in.

Miss Brent said stiffly, "Thank you," bent her head and entered one of the taxis, the door of which the driver was holding open. Mr. Justice Wargrave followed her.

Captain Lombard said, "I'll wait with Miss—"

"Claythorne," said Vera.

"My name is Lombard, Philip Lombard."

The porters were piling luggage on the taxi. Inside, Mr. Justice Wargrave said with due legal caution, "Beautiful weather we are having."

Miss Brent said, "Yes, indeed."

A very distinguished old gentleman, she thought to herself. Quite unlike the usual type of man in seaside guest houses. Evidently Mrs. or Miss Oliver had good connections. . . .

Mr. Justice Wargrave inquired, "Do you know this part of the world well?"

"I have been to Cornwall and to Torquay, but this is my first visit to this part of Devon."

The judge said, "I also am unacquainted with this part of the world."

The taxi drove off. The driver of the second taxi said, "Like to sit inside while you're waiting?"

Vera said decisively, "Not at all."

Captain Lombard smiled. He said, "That sunny wall looks more attractive. Unless you'd rather go inside the station?"

"No, indeed. It's so delightful to get out of that stuffy train."

He answered, "Yes, traveling by train *is* rather trying in this weather."

Vera said conventionally, "I do hope it lasts—the weather, I mean. Our English summers are so treacherous."

With a slight lack of originality Lombard asked, "Do you know this part of the world well?"

"No, I've never been here before." She added quickly, conscientiously determined to make her position clear at once, "I haven't even seen my employer yet."

"Your employer?"

"Yes, I'm Mrs. Owen's secretary."

"Oh, I see." Just imperceptibly his manner changed. It was slightly more assured—easier in tone. He said, "Isn't that rather unusual?"

Vera laughed. "Oh, no, I don't think so. Her own secretary was suddenly taken ill and she wired to an agency for a substitute and they sent me."

"So that was it. And suppose you don't like the post when you've got there?"

Vera laughed again. "Oh, it's only temporary—a holiday post. I've got a permanent job at a girls' school. As a matter of fact, I'm frightfully thrilled at the prospect of seeing Indian Island. There's been such a lot about it in the papers. Is it really very fascinating?"

Lombard said, "I don't know. I haven't seen it."

"Oh, really? The Owens are frightfully keen on it, I suppose. What are they like? Do tell me."

Lombard thought: Awkward, this—am I supposed to have met them or not? He said quickly, "There's a wasp crawling up your arm. No—keep quite still." He made a convincing pounce. "There. It's gone!"

"Oh, thank you. There are a lot of wasps about this summer."

"Yes, I suppose it's the heat. Who are we waiting for, do you know?"

"I haven't the least idea."

The loud, drawn-out scream of an approaching train was heard. Lombard said, "That will be the train now."

ii

It was a tall, soldierly old man who appeared at the exit from the platform. His gray hair was clipped close and he had a neatly trimmed white mustache. His porter, staggering slightly under the weight of the solid leather suitcase, indicated Vera and Lombard.

Vera came forward in a competent manner. She said, "I am Mrs. Owen's secretary. There is a car here waiting." She added, "This is Mr. Lombard."

The faded blue eyes, shrewd in spite of their age, sized up Lombard. For a moment a judgment showed in them—had there been anyone to read it.

Good-looking fellow. Something just a little wrong about him....

The three of them got into the waiting taxi. They drove through the sleepy streets of little Oakbridge and continued about a mile on the main Plymouth road. Then they plunged into a maze of cross-country lanes, steep, green and narrow.

General Macarthur said, "Don't know this part of Devon at all. My little place is in East Devon—just on the borderline of Dorset."

Vera said, "It really is lovely here. The hills and the red earth and everything so green and luscious looking."

Philip Lombard said critically, "It's a bit shut in. . . . I like open country myself. Where you can see what's coming. . . ."

General Macarthur said to him, "You've seen a bit of the world, I fancy?"

Lombard shrugged his shoulders disparagingly. "I've knocked about here and there, sir."

He thought to himself: He'll ask me now if I was old enough to be in the War. These old boys always do.

But General Macarthur did not mention the War.

iii

They came up over a steep hill and down a zigzag track to Stickle-haven—a mere cluster of cottages with a fishing boat or two drawn up on the beach. Illuminated by the setting sun, they had their first glimpse of Indian Island jutting up out of the sea to the south.

Vera said, surprised, "It's a long way out."

She had pictured it differently, close to shore, crowned with a beautiful white house. But there was no house visible, only the boldly silhouetted rock with its faint resemblance to a giant Indian's head. There was something sinister about it. She shivered faintly.

Outside a little inn, the Seven Stars, three people were sitting. There was the hunched elderly figure of the judge, the upright form of Miss Brent, and a third man—a big, bluff man who came forward and introduced himself. "Thought we might as well wait for you," he said. "Make one trip of it. Allow me to introduce myself. Name's Davis. Natal, South Africa's my natal spot, ha, ha!" He laughed.

Mr. Justice Wargrave looked at him with active malevolence. He seemed to be wishing that he could order the court to be cleared. Miss Emily Brent was clearly not sure if she liked Colonials.

"Anyone care for a little nip before we embark?" asked Mr. Davis hospitably.

Nobody assenting to his proposition, Mr. Davis turned and held up a finger. "Mustn't delay, then. Our good host and hostess will be expecting us," he said. He might have noticed that a curious constraint came over the other members of the party. It was as though the mention of their host and hostess had a curiously paralyzing effect upon the guests.

In response to Davis' beckoning finger, a man detached himself from a nearby wall against which he was leaning and came up to them. His rolling gait proclaimed him a man of the sea. He had a weather-beaten face and dark eyes with a slightly evasive expression. He spoke in a soft Devon voice. "Will you be ready to be starting for the island, ladies and gentlemen? The boat's waiting. There's two gentlemen coming by car, but Mr. Owen's orders was not to wait for them as they might arrive at any time."

The party got up. Their guide led them along a small stone jetty. Alongside it a motor boat was lying. Emily Brent said, "That's a very small boat."

The boat's owner said persuasively, "She's a fine boat, that, ma'am. You could go to Plymouth in her as easy as winking."

Mr. Justice Wargrave said sharply, "There are a good many of us."

"She'd take double the number, sir."

Philip Lombard said in his pleasant, easy voice, "It's quite all right. Glorious weather—no swell."

Rather doubtfully, Miss Brent permitted herself to be helped into the boat. The others followed suit. There was as yet no fraternizing among the party. It was as though each member of it was puzzled by the other members.

They were just about to cast loose when their guide paused, boat hook in hand. Down the steep track into the village a car was coming. A car so fantastically powerful, so superlatively beautiful that it had all the nature of an apparition. At the wheel sat a young man, his hair blown back by the wind. In the blaze of the evening light he looked, not a man, but a young god, a Hero God out of some Northern Saga. He touched the horn and a great roar of sound echoed from the rocks of the bay. It was a fantastic moment. In it, Anthony Marston seemed to be something more than mortal. Afterwards, more than one of those present remembered that moment.

iv

Fred Narracott sat by the engine thinking to himself that this was a queer lot. Not at all his idea of what Mr. Owen's guests were likely to be. He'd expected something altogether more classy. Togged-up women and gentlemen in yachting costume and all very rich and important looking.

Not at all like Mr. Elmer Robson's parties. A faint grin came to Fred Narracott's lips as he remembered the millionaire's guests. That had been a party if you like—and the drink they'd got through!

This Mr. Owen must be a very different sort of gentleman. Funny it was, thought Fred, that he'd never yet set eyes on Owen—or his

Missus either. Never been down here yet, he hadn't. Everything ordered and paid for by that Mr. Morris. Instructions always very clear and payment prompt, but it was odd, all the same. The papers said there was some mystery about Owen. Mr. Narracott agreed with them.

Perhaps, after all, it *was* Miss Gabrielle Turl who had bought the island. But that theory departed from him as he surveyed his passengers. Not this lot—none of them looked likely to have anything to do with a film star.

He summed them up dispassionately. One old maid—the sour kind—he knew them well enough. She was a tartar, he could bet. Old military gentleman—real Army by the look of him. Nice-looking young lady—but the ordinary kind, not glamorous—no Hollywood touch about her. That bluff, cheery gent—*he* wasn't a real gentleman. Retired tradesman, that's what he is, thought Fred Narracott. The other gentleman, the lean, hungry-looking gentleman with the quick eyes, he was a queer one, he was. Just possible *he* might have something to do with the pictures.

No, there was only one satisfactory passenger in the boat. The last gentleman, the one who had arrived in the car (and what a car! A car such as had never been seen in Sticklehaven before. Must have cost hundreds and hundreds, a car like that). He was the right kind. Born to money, he was. If the party had been all like him, he'd understand it. . . .

Queer business when you came to think of it—the whole thing was queer—very queer. . . .

v

The boat churned its way round the rock. Now at last the house came into view. The south side of the island was quite different. It shelved gently down to the sea. The house was there facing south—low and square and modern-looking with rounded windows letting in all the light. An exciting house—a house that lived up to expectation!

Fred Narracott shut off the engine; they nosed their way gently into a little natural inlet between rocks.

Philip Lombard said sharply, "Must be difficult to land here in dirty weather."

Fred Narracott said cheerfully, "Can't land on Indian Island when there's a southeasterly. Sometimes 'tis cut off for a week or more."

Vera Claythorne thought: The catering must be very difficult. That's the worst of an island. All the domestic problems are so worrying.

The boat grated against the rocks. Fred Narracott jumped out and he and Lombard helped the others to alight. Narracott made the boat fast to a ring in the rock. Then he led the way up steps cut in the rock.

General Macarthur said, "Ha, delightful spot!" But he felt uneasy. Damned odd sort of place.

As the party ascended the steps, and came out on a terrace above, their spirits revived. In the open doorway of the house a correct butler was awaiting them, and something about his gravity reassured them. And then the house itself was really most attractive, the view from the terrace magnificent. . . .

The butler came forward, bowing slightly. He was a tall, lank man, gray-haired and very respectable. He said, "Will you come this way, please?"

In the wide hall drinks stood ready. Rows of bottles. Anthony Marston's spirits cheered up a little. He'd just been thinking this was a rum kind of show. None of *his* lot! What could old Badger have been thinking about to let him in for this? However the drinks were all right. Plenty of ice, too.

What was it the butler chap was saying? Mr. Owen—unfortunately delayed—unable to get here till tomorrow. Instructions—everything they wanted—if they would like to go to their rooms? Dinner would be at 8 o'clock.

vi

Vera had followed Mrs. Rogers upstairs. The woman had thrown open a door at the end of a passage and Vera had walked into a delightful bedroom with a big window that opened wide upon the sea and another looking east. She uttered a quick exclamation of pleasure.

Mrs. Rogers was saying, "I hope you've got everything you want, miss?"

Vera looked round. Her luggage had been brought up and had been unpacked. At one side of the room a door stood open into a pale-blue tiled bathroom. She said quickly, "Yes, everything, I think."

"You'll ring the bell if you want anything, miss?"

Mrs. Rogers had a flat, monotonous voice. Vera looked at her curiously. What a white, bloodless ghost of a woman! Very respectable looking, with her hair dragged back from her face and her black dress. Queer light eyes that shifted the whole time from place to place.

Vera thought: She looks frightened of her own shadow. Yes, that was it—frightened! She looked like a woman who walked in mortal fear. . . . A little shiver passed down Vera's back. What on earth was the woman afraid of? She said pleasantly, "I'm Mrs. Owen's new secretary. I expect you know that."

Mrs. Rogers said, "No, miss, I don't know anything. Just a list of the ladies and gentlemen and what rooms they were to have."

Vera said, "Mrs Owen didn't mention me?"

Mrs. Rogers' eyelashes flickered. "I haven't seen Mrs. Owen—not yet. We only came here two days ago."

Extraordinary people, these Owens, thought Vera. Aloud she said, "What staff is there here?"

"Just me and Rogers, miss."

Vera frowned. Eight people in the house—ten with the host and hostess—and only one married couple to do for them.

Mrs. Rogers said, "I'm a good cook and Rogers is handy about the house. I didn't know, of course, that there was to be such a large party."

Vera said, "But you can manage?"

"Oh, yes, miss, I can manage. If there's to be large parties often perhaps Mrs. Owen could get extra help in."

Vera said, "I expect so."

Mrs. Rogers turned to go. Her feet moved noiselessly over the ground. She drifted from the room like a shadow.

Vera went over to the window and sat down on the window seat. She was faintly disturbed. Everything—somehow—was a little queer. The absence of the Owens, the pale, ghostlike Mrs. Rogers. And the guests! Yes, the guests were queer too. An oddly assorted party. Vera thought: I wish I'd seen the Owens. . . . I wish I knew what they were like.

She got up and walked restlessly about the room. A perfect bedroom decorated throughout in the modern style. Offwhite rugs on the gleaming parquet floor—faintly tinted walls—a long mirror surrounded by lights. A mantelpiece bare of ornaments save for an enormous block of white marble shaped like a bear, a piece of modern sculpture in which was inset a clock. Over it, in a gleaming chromium frame, was a big square of parchment—a poem.

She stood in front of the fireplace and read it. It was the old nursery rhyme that she remembered from her childhood days.

Ten little Indian boys went out to dine;
One choked his little self and then there were nine.

Nine little Indian boys sat up very late;
One overslept himself and then there were eight.

Eight little Indian boys traveling in Devon;
One said he'd stay there and then there were seven.

Seven little Indian boys chopping up sticks;
One chopped himself in halves and then there were six.

Six little Indian boys playing with a hive;
A bumblebee stung one and then there were five.

Five little Indian boys going in for law;
One got in Chancery and then there were four.

Four little Indian boys going out to sea;
A red herring swallowed one and then there were three.

Three little Indian boys walking in the Zoo;
A big bear hugged one and then there were two.

Two little Indian boys sitting in the sun;
One got frizzled up and then there was one.

One little Indian boy left all alone;
He went and hanged himself and then there were none.

Vera smiled. Of course! This was Indian Island! She went and sat again by the window looking out to sea. How big the sea was! From here there was no land to be seen anywhere—just a vast expanse of blue water rippling in the evening sun.

The sea. . . . So peaceful today—sometimes so cruel—The sea that dragged you down to its depths. Drowned. . . . Found drowned. . . . Drowned at sea. . . . Drowned—drowned—drowned. . . . No, she wouldn't remember. . . . She would *not* think of it! All that was over.

vii

Dr. Armstrong came to Indian Island just as the sun was sinking into the sea. On the way across he had chatted to the boatman—a local man. He was anxious to find out a little about these people who owned Indian Island, but the man Narracott seemed curiously ill informed, or perhaps unwilling to talk. So Dr. Armstrong chatted instead of the weather and of fishing.

He was tired after his long motor drive. His eyeballs ached. Driving west you were driving against the sun. Yes, he was very tired. The sea and perfect peace—that was what he needed. He would like, really, to take a long holiday. But he couldn't afford to do that. He could afford it financially, of course, but he couldn't afford to drop out. You were soon forgotten nowadays. No, now that he had arrived, he must keep his nose to the grindstone. He thought: All the same, this evening, I'll imagine to myself that I'm not going back—that I've done with London and Harley Street and all the rest of it.

There was something magical about an island—the mere word suggested fantasy. You lost touch with the world—an island was a world of its own. A world, perhaps, from which you might never return. He thought: I'm leaving my ordinary life behind me.

And, smiling to himself, he began to make plans, fantastic plans for the future. He was still smiling when he walked up the rock-cut steps.

In a chair on the terrace an old gentleman was sitting and the sight of him was vaguely familiar to Dr. Armstrong. Where had he seen that froglike face, that tortoiselike neck that hunched-up attitude—yes, and those pale, shrewd little eyes? Of course—old Wargrave. He'd given evidence once before him. Always looked half-asleep, but was shrewd as could be when it came to a point of law. Had great power with a jury—it was said he could make their minds up for them any day of the week. He'd got one or two unlikely convictions out of them. A hanging judge, some people said.

Funny place to meet him . . . here—out of the world.

viii

Mr. Justice Wargrave thought to himself: Armstrong? Remember him in the witness box. Very correct and cautious. All doctors are damned fools. Harley Street ones are the worst of the lot. And his mind dwelt malevolently on a recent interview he had had with a suave personage in that very street.

Aloud he grunted, "Drinks are in the hall."

Dr. Armstrong said, "I must go and pay my respects to my host and hostess."

Mr. Justice Wargrave closed his eyes again, looking decidedly reptilian, and said, "You can't do that."

Dr. Armstrong was startled. "Why not?"

The judge said, "No host and hostess. Very curious state of affairs. Don't understand this place."

Dr. Armstrong stared at him for a minute. When he thought the old gentleman had actually gone to sleep, Wargrave said suddenly, "D'you know Constance Culmington?"

"Er—no, I'm afraid I don't."

"It's of no consequence," said the judge. "Very vague woman—and practically unreadable handwriting. I was just wondering if I'd come to the wrong house."

Dr. Armstrong shook his head and went on up to the house.

Mr. Justice Wargrave reflected on the subject of Constance Culmington. Undependable like all women.

His mind went on to the two women in the house, the tight-lipped old maid and the girl. He didn't care for the girl, cold-blooded young hussy. No, three women, if you counted the Rogers woman. Odd creature, she looked scared to death. Respectable pair and knew their job.

Rogers coming out on the terrace that minute, the judge asked him, "Is Lady Constance Culmington expected, do you know?"

Rogers stared at him. "No, sir, not to my knowledge."

The judge's eyebrows rose. But he only grunted. He thought: Indian Island, eh? There's a nigger in the woodpile.

ix

Anthony Marston was in his bath. He luxuriated in the steaming water. His limbs had felt cramped after his long drive. Very few thoughts passed through his head. Anthony was a creature of sensation—and of action. He thought to himself: Must go through with it, I suppose, and thereafter dismissed everything from his mind.

Warm steaming water—tired limbs—presently a shave—a cocktail—dinner.... And after—?

x

Mr. Blore was tying his tie. He wasn't very good at this sort of thing. Did he look all right? He supposed so. Nobody had been exactly cordial to him.... Funny the way they all eyed each other—as though they *knew*.... Well, it was up to him.

He didn't mean to bungle his job. He glanced up at the framed nursery rhyme over the mantelpiece. Neat touch, having that there!

He thought: Remember this island when I was a kid. Never thought I'd be doing this sort of a job in a house here. Good thing, perhaps, that one can't foresee the future....

xi

General Macarthur was frowning to himself.

Damn it all, the whole thing was deuced odd! Not at all what he'd been led to expect. . . . For two pins he'd make an excuse and get away. . . . Throw up the whole business. . . . But the motor boat had gone back to the mainland. He'd have to stay.

That fellow Lombard now, he was a queer chap.

Not straight. He'd swear the man wasn't straight.

xii

As the gong sounded, Philip Lombard came out of his room and walked to the head of the stairs. He moved like a panther, smoothly and noiselessly. There was something of the panther about him altogether. A beast of prey—pleasant to the eye.

He was smiling to himself. A week—eh?

He was going to enjoy that week.

xiii

In her bedroom, Emily Brent, dressed in black silk ready for dinner, was reading her Bible. Her lips moved as she followed the words:

"The heathen are sunk down in the pit that they made: in the net which they hid is their own foot taken. The Lord is known by the judgment which he executeth: the wicked is snared in the work of his own hands. The wicked shall be turned into hell."

Her tight lips closed. She shut the Bible.

Rising, she pinned a cairngorm brooch at her neck, and went down to dinner.

3

DINNER WAS DRAWING to a close. The food had been good, the wine perfect. Rogers waited well.

Everyone was in better spirits. They had begun to talk to each other with more freedom and intimacy. Mr. Justice Wargrave, mellowed by the excellent port, was being amusing in a caustic fashion; Dr. Armstrong and Tony Marston were listening to him. Miss Brent chatted to General Macarthur; they had discovered some mutual friends. Vera Claythorne was asking Mr. Davis intelligent questions about South Africa. Mr. Davis was quite fluent on the subject. Lombard listened to the conversation. Once or twice he looked up quickly, and his eyes narrowed. Now and then his eyes played round the table, studying the others.

Anthony Marston said suddenly, "Quaint, these things, aren't they?"

In the center of the round table, on a circular glass stand, were some little china figures. "Indians," said Tony. "Indian Island. I suppose that's the idea."

Vera leaned forward. "I wonder. How many are there? Ten?"

"Yes—ten there are."

Vera cried, "What fun! They're the ten little Indian boys of the nursery rhyme, I suppose. In my bedroom the rhyme is framed and hung up over the mantelpiece."

Lombard said, "In my room, too."

"And mine."

"And mine."

Everybody joined the chorus. Vera said, "It's an amusing idea, isn't it?"

Mr. Justice Wargrave grunted, "Remarkably childish," and helped himself to port.

Emily Brent looked at Vera Claythorne. Vera Claythorne looked at Miss Brent. The two women rose. In the drawing room, the French windows were open onto the terrace and the sound of the sea murmuring against the rocks came up to them. Emily Brent said, "Pleasant sound."

Vera said sharply, "I hate it."

Miss Brent's eyes looked at her in surprise. Vera flushed. She said, more composedly, "I don't think this place would be very agreeable in a storm."

Emily Brent agreed. "I've no doubt the house is shut up in winter," she said. "You'd never get servants to stay here for one thing."

Vera murmured, "It must be difficult to get servants anyway."

Emily Brent said, "Mrs. Oliver has been lucky to get these two. The woman's a good cook."

Vera thought: Funny how elderly people always get names wrong. She said, "Yes, I think Mrs. Owen has been very lucky indeed."

Emily Brent had brought a small piece of embroidery out of her bag.

Now, as she was about to thread her needle, she paused. She said sharply, "Owen? Did you say Owen?"

"Yes."

Emily Brent said sharply, "I've never met anyone called Owen in my life."

Vera stared. "But surely—" She did not finish her sentence. The door opened and the men joined them. Rogers followed them into the room with the coffee tray.

The judge came and sat down by Emily Brent. Armstrong came up to Vera. Tony Marston strolled to the open window. Blore studied with naïve surprise a statuette in brass—wondering perhaps if its bizzarre angularities were really supposed to be the female figure. General Macarthur stood with his back to the mantelpiece. He pulled at his little white mustache. That had been a damned good dinner! His spirits were rising. Lombard turned over the pages of *Punch* that lay with other papers on a table by the wall.

Rogers went round with the coffee tray. The coffee was good—really black and very hot.

The whole party had dined well. They were satisfied with themselves and with life. The hands of the clock pointed to twenty minutes past nine. There was a silence—a comfortable, replete silence. Into that silence came The Voice. Without warning, inhuman, penetrating . . .

"Ladies and gentlemen! Silence, please!"

Everyone was startled. They looked round—at each other, at the walls. Who was speaking?

The Voice went on—a high clear voice.

> You are charged with the following indictments:
> Edward George Armstrong, that you did upon the 14th day of March, 1925, cause the death of Louisa Mary Clees.
> Emily Caroline Brent, that upon the 5th of November, 1931, you were responsible for the death of Beatrice Taylor.
> William Henry Blore, that you brought about the death of James Stephen Landor on October 10th, 1928.
> Vera Elizabeth Claythorne, that on the 11th day of August, 1935, you killed Cyril Ogilvie Hamilton.
> Philip Lombard, that upon a date in February, 1932, you were guilty of the death of twenty-one men, members of an East African tribe.
> John Gordon Macarthur, that on the 4th of January, 1917, you deliberately sent your wife's lover, Arthur Richmond, to his death.

Anthony James Marston, that upon the 14th day of November last, you were guilty of the murder of John and Lucy Combes.

Thomas Rogers and Ethel Rogers, that on the 6th of May, 1929, you brought about the death of Jennifer Brady.

Lawrence John Wargrave, that upon the 10th day of June, 1930, you were guilty of the murder of Edward Seton.

Prisoners at the bar, have you anything to say in your defense?

ii

The Voice had stopped. There was a moment's petrified silence and then a resounding crash! Rogers had dropped the coffee tray! At that same moment, from somewhere outside the room there came a scream and the sound of a thud.

Lombard was the first to move. He leapt to the door and flung it open. Outside, lying in a huddled mass, was Mrs. Rogers. Lombard called, "Marston."

Anthony sprang to help him. Between them, they lifted up the woman and carried her into the drawing room. Dr. Armstrong came across quickly. He helped them to lift her onto the sofa and bent over her. He said quickly, "It's nothing. She's fainted, that's all. She'll be round in a minute."

Lombard said to Rogers, "Get some brandy."

Rogers, his face white, his hands shaking, murmured, "Yes, sir," and slipped quickly out of the room.

Vera cried out, *"Who was that speaking?* Where was he? It sounded—it sounded—"

General Macarthur spluttered out, "What's going on here? What kind of a practical joke was that?" His hand was shaking. His shoulders sagged. He looked suddenly ten years older.

Blore was mopping his face with a handkerchief. Only Mr. Justice Wargrave and Miss Brent seemed comparatively unmoved. Emily Brent sat upright, her head held high. In both cheeks was a spot of hard color. The judge sat in his habitual pose, his head sunk down into his neck. With one hand he gently scratched his ear. Only his eyes were active, darting round and round the room, puzzled, alert with intelligence.

Again it was Lombard who acted. Armstrong being busy with the collapsed woman, Lombard was free once more to take the initiative. He said, "That voice? It sounded as though it were in the room."

Vera cried, "*Who was it*? Who was it? It wasn't one of us."

Like the judge, Lombard's eyes wandered slowly round the room. They rested a minute on the open window, then he shook his head decisively. Suddenly his eyes lighted up. He moved forward swiftly to where a door near the fireplace led into an adjoining room.

With a swift gesture, he caught the handle and flung the door open. He passed through and immediately uttered an exclamation of satisfaction. He said, "Ah, here we are."

The others crowded after him. Only Miss Brent remained alone sitting erect in her chair.

Inside the second room a table had been brought up close to the wall which adjoined the drawing room. On the table was a gramophone—an old-fashioned type with a large trumpet attached. The mouth of the trumpet was against the wall, and Lombard, pushing it aside, indicated where two or three small holes had been unobtrusively bored through the wall. Adjusting the gramophone he replaced the needle on the record and immediately they heard again: "*You are charged with the following indictments—*"

Vera cried, "Turn it off! Turn it off! It's horrible!" Lombard obeyed.

Dr. Armstrong said, with a sigh of relief, "A disgraceful and heartless practical joke, I suppose."

The small, clear voice of Mr. Justice Wargrave murmured, "So you think it's a joke, do you?"

The doctor stared at him. "What else could it be?"

The hand of the judge gently stroked his upper lip. He said, "At the moment I'm not prepared to give an opinion."

Anthony Marston broke in. He said, "Look here, there's one thing you've forgotten. Who the devil turned the thing on and set it going?"

Wargrave murmured, "Yes, I think we must inquire into that." He led the way back into the drawing room. The others followed.

Rogers had just come in with a glass of brandy. Miss Brent was bending over the moaning form of Mrs. Rogers. Adroitly Rogers slipped between the two women. "Allow me, madam, I'll speak to her. Ethel—Ethel—it's all right. All right, do you hear? Pull yourself together."

Mrs. Rogers' breath came in quick gasps. Her eyes, staring frightened eyes, went round and round the ring of faces. There was urgency in Rogers' tone. "Pull yourself together, Ethel."

Dr. Armstrong spoke to her soothingly. "You'll be all right now, Mrs. Rogers. Just a nasty turn."

She said, "Did I faint, sir?"

"Yes."

"It was The Voice—that awful voice—*like a judgment*—" Her face turned green again, her eyelids fluttered.

Dr. Armstrong said sharply, "Where's that brandy?"

Rogers had put it down on a little table. Someone handed it to the doctor and he bent over the gasping woman with it. "Drink this, Mrs. Rogers."

She drank, choking a little and gasping. The spirit did her good. The color returned to her face. She said, "I'm all right now. It just—gave me a turn."

Rogers said quickly, "Of course it did. It gave me a turn too. Fair made me drop that tray. Wicked lies, it was! I'd like to know—"

He was interrupted. It was only a cough—a dry little cough but it had the effect of stopping him in full cry. He stared at Mr. Justice Wargrave and the latter coughed again. Then he said, "Who put that record on the gramophone? Was it you, Rogers?"

Rogers cried, "I didn't know what it was. Before God, I didn't know what it was, sir. If I had I'd never have done it."

The judge said dryly, "That is probably true. But I think you'd better explain, Rogers."

The butler wiped his face with a handkerchief. He said earnestly, "I was just obeying orders, sir, that's all."

"Whose orders?"

"Mr. Owen's."

Mr. Justice Wargrave said, "Let me get this quite clear. Mr. Owen's orders were—what exactly?"

Rogers said, "I was to put a record on the gramophone. I'd find the record in the drawer and my wife was to start the gramophone when I'd gone into the drawing room with the coffee tray."

The judge murmured, "A very remarkable story."

Rogers cried, "It's the truth, sir. I swear to God it's the truth. I didn't know what it was—not for a moment. It had a name on it—I thought it was just a piece of music."

Wargrave looked at Lombard. "Was there a title on it?"

Lombard nodded. He grinned suddenly, showing his white, pointed teeth. He said, "Quite right, sir. It was entitled 'Swan Song.'"

iii

General Macarthur broke out suddenly. He exclaimed, "The whole thing is preposterous—preposterous! Slinging accusations about like this! Something must be done about it. This fellow Owen, whoever he is—"

Emily Brent interrupted. She said sharply, "That's just it, who is he?"

The judge interposed. He spoke with the authority that a lifetime in the courts had given him. He said, "That is exactly what we must go into very carefully. I should suggest that you get your wife to bed first of all, Rogers. Then come back here."

"Yes, sir."

Dr. Armstrong said, "I'll give you a hand, Rogers."

Leaning on the two men, Mrs. Rogers tottered out of the room. When they had gone Tony Marston said, "Don't know about you, sir, but I could do with a drink."

Lombard said, "I agree."

Tony said, "I'll go and forage."

He went out of the room. He returned a second or two later. "Found them all waiting on a tray outside ready to be brought in."

He set down his burden carefully. The next minute or two was spent in dispensing drinks. General Macarthur had a stiff whisky and so did the judge. Everyone felt the need of a stimulant. Only Emily Brent demanded and obtained a glass of water.

Dr. Armstrong re-entered the room. "She's all right,"he said. "I've given her a sedative to take. What's that, a drink? I could do with one."

Several of the men refilled their glasses. A moment or two later Rogers re-entered the room. Mr. Justice Wargrave took charge of the proceedings. The room became an impromptu court of law. The judge said, "Now then, Rogers, we must get to the bottom of this. Who is this Mr. Owen?"

Rogers stared. "He owns this place, sir."

"I am aware of that fact. What I want you to tell me is what you yourself know about the man."

Rogers shook his head. "I can't say, sir. You see, I've never seen him."

There was a faint stir in the room. General Macarthur said, "You've never seen him? What d'yer mean?"

"We've only been here just under a week, sir, my wife and I. We were engaged by letter, through an agency. The Regina Agency in Plymouth."

Blore nodded. "Old established firm," he volunteered.

Wargrave said, "Have you got that letter?"

"The letter engaging us? No, sir. I didn't keep it."

"Go on with your story. You were engaged, as you say, by letter."

"Yes, sir. We were to arrive on a certain day. We did. Everything was in order here. Plenty of food in stock and everything very nice. Just needed dusting and that."

"What next?"

"Nothing, sir. We got orders—by letter again—to prepare the rooms for a house party and then yesterday by the afternoon post I got another letter from Mr. Owen. It said he and Mrs. Owen were detained and to do the best we could and it gave the instructions about dinner and coffee and putting on the gramophone record."

The judge said sharply, "Surely you've got *that* letter?"

"Yes, sir, I've got it here."

He produced it from a pocket. The judge took it. "H'm," he said. "Headed Ritz Hotel and typewritten."

With a quick movement Blore was beside him. He said, "If you'll just let me have a look." He twitched it out of the other's hand, and ran his eye over it. He murmured, "Coronation machine. Quite new—no defects. Ensign paper—the most widely used make. You won't get anything out of that. Might be fingerprints, but I doubt it."

Wargrave stared at him with sudden attention. Anthony Marston was standing beside Blore looking over his shoulder. He said, "Got some fancy Christian names, hasn't he? Ulick Norman Owen. Quite a mouthful."

The old judge said with a slight start, "I am obliged to you, Mr. Marston. You have drawn my attention to a curious and suggestive point." He looked round at the others, and thrusting his neck forward like an angry tortoise, he said, "I think the time has come for us all to pool our information. It would be well, I think, for everybody to come forward with all the information they have regarding the owner of this house." He paused and then went on. "We are all his guests. I think it would be profitable if each one of us were to explain exactly how that came about."

There was a moment's pause and then Emily Brent spoke with decision. "There's something very peculiar about all this," she said. "I received a letter with a signature that was not very easy to read. It purported to be from a woman I had met at a certain summer resort two or three years ago. I took the name to be either Ogden or Oliver. I am acquainted with a Mrs. Oliver and also with a Miss Ogden. I am quite certain that I have never met, or become friendly with, anyone of the name of Owen."

Mr. Justice Wargrave said, "You have that letter, Miss Brent?"

"Yes, I will fetch it for you."

She went away and returned a minute later with the letter. The judge read it. He said, "I begin to understand. . . . Miss Claythorne?"

Vera explained the circumstances of her secretarial engagement. The judge said, "Marston?"

Anthony said, "Got a wire. From a pal of mine. Badger Berkeley. Surprised me at the time because I had an idea the old horse had gone to Norway. Told me to roll up here."

Again Wargrave nodded. He said, "Dr. Armstrong?"

"I was called in professionally."

"I see. You had no previous acquaintanceship with the family?"

"No. A colleague of mine was mentioned in the letter."

The judge said, "To give verisimilitude. . . . Yes, and that colleague, I presume, was momentarily out of touch with you?"

"Well—er—yes."

Lombard, who had been staring at Blore, said suddenly, "Look here, I've just thought of something—"

The judge lifted a hand. "In a minute—"

"But I—"

"We will take one thing at a time, Mr. Lombard. We are at present inquiring into the causes which have resulted in our being assembled here tonight. General Macarthur?"

Pulling at his mustache, the General muttered, "Got a letter—from this fellow Owen—mentioned some old pals of mine who were to be here—hoped I'd excuse informal invitation. Haven't kept the letter, I'm afraid."

Wargrave said, "Mr. Lombard?"

Lombard's brain had been active. Was he to come out in the open, or not? He made up his mind. "Same sort of thing," he said. "Invitation, mention of mutual friends—I fell for it, all right. I've torn up the letter."

Mr. Justice Wargrave turned his attention to Mr. Blore. His forefinger stroked his upper lip and his voice was dangerously polite. He said, "Just now we had a somewhat disturbing experience. An apparently disembodied voice spoke to us all by name, uttering certain precise accusations against us. We will deal with those accusations presently. At the moment I am interested in a minor point. Amongst the names recited was that of William Henry Blore. But as far as we know there is no one named Blore amongst us. The name of Davis was *not* mentioned. What have you to say about that, Mr. Davis?"

Blore said sulkily, "Cat's out of the bag, it seems. I suppose I'd better admit that my name isn't Davis."

"You are William Henry Blore?"

"That's right."

"I will add something," said Lombard. "Not only are you here under a false name, Mr. Blore, but in addition I've noticed this evening that you're a first-class liar. You claim to have come from Natal, South Africa. I know South Africa and Natal and I'm prepared to swear that you've never set foot in South Africa in your life."

All eyes were turned on Blore. Angry, suspicious eyes. Anthony Marston moved a step nearer to him. His fists clenched themselves. "Now then, you swine," he said. "Any explanation?"

Blore flung back his head and set his square jaw. "You gentlemen have got me wrong," he said. "I've got my credentials and you can see them. I'm an ex-C.I.D. man. I run a detective agency in Plymouth. I was put on this job."

Mr. Justice Wargrave asked, "By whom?"

"This man Owen. Enclosed a handsome money order for expenses and instructed me as to what he wanted done. I was to join the house party, posing as a guest. I was given all your names. I was to watch you all."

"Any reason given?"

Blore said bitterly, "Mrs. Owen's jewels. Mrs. Owen, my foot! I don't believe there's any such person."

Again the forefinger of the judge stroked his lip, this time appreciatively.

"Your conclusions are, I think, justified," he said. "Ulick Norman Owen! In Miss Brent's letter, though the signature of the surname is a mere scrawl the Christian names are reasonably clear—Una Nancy—in either case, you notice, the same initials. Ulick Norman Owen—Una Nancy Owen—each time, that is to say, U.N. Owen. Or by a slight stretch of fancy, UNKNOWN!"

Vera cried, "But this is fantastic—mad!"

The judge nodded gently. He said, "Oh, yes. I've no doubt in my own mind that we have been invited here by a madman—probably a dangerous homicidal lunatic."

4

THERE WAS A moment's silence—a silence of dismay and bewilderment. Then the judge's small, clear voice took up the thread once more. "We will now proceed to the next stage of our inquiry. First, however, I will just add my own credentials to the list."

He took a letter from his pocket and tossed it onto the table. "This purports to be from an old friend of mine, Lady Constance Culmington. I have not seen her for some years. She went to the East. It is exactly the kind of vague, incoherent letter she would write, urging me to join her here and referring to her host and hostess in the vaguest of terms. The same technique, you will observe. I only mention it because it agrees with the other evidence—from all of which emerges one interesting point. *Whoever it was who enticed us here, that person knows or has taken the trouble to find out a good deal about us all.* He, whoever he may be, is aware of my friendship for Lady Constance—and is familiar with her epistolary style. He knows something about Dr. Armstrong's colleagues and their present whereabouts. He knows the nickname of Mr. Marston's friend and the kind of telegrams he sends. He knows exactly where Miss Brent was two years ago for her holiday and the kind of people she met there. He knows all about General Macarthur's old cronies." He paused. Then he said, "*He knows, you see, a good deal.* And out of his knowledge concerning us, he has made certain definite accusations."

Immediately a babel broke out. General Macarthur shouted, "A pack of damn lies! Slander!"

Vera cried out, "It's iniquitous!" Her breath came fast. "Wicked!"

Rogers said hoarsely, "A lie—a wicked lie ... we never did— neither of us. ..."

Anthony Marston growled, "Don't know what the damned fool was getting at!"

The upraised hand of Mr. Justice Wargrave calmed the tumult. He said, picking his words with care, "I wish to say this. Our unknown friend accuses me of the murder of one Edward Seton. I remember Seton perfectly well. He came up before me for trial in June of the year 1930. He was charged with the murder of an elderly woman. He was very ably defended and made a good impression on the jury in the witness box. Nevertheless, on the evidence, he was certainly guilty. I summed up accordingly, and the jury brought in a verdict of Guilty. In passing sentence of death I concurred with the verdict. An appeal was lodged on the grounds of misdirection. The appeal was rejected and the man was duly executed. I wish to say before you all that my conscience is perfectly clear on the matter. I did my duty and nothing more. I passed sentence on a rightly convicted murderer."

Armstrong was remembering now. The Seton case! The verdict had come as a great surprise. He had met Matthews, K.C., on one of the days of the trial dining at a restaurant. Matthews had been confident. "Not a doubt of the verdict. Acquittal practically certain." And then afterwards he had heard comments: Judge was dead against him. Turned the jury right round and they brought him in guilty. Quite legal, though. Old Wargrave knows his law. It was almost as though he had a private down on the fellow. All these memories rushed through the doctor's mind. Before he could consider the wisdom of the question he had asked impulsively, "Did you know Seton at all? I mean previous to the case."

The hooded reptilian eyes met his. In a clear, cold voice the judge said, "I knew nothing of Seton previous to the case."

Armstrong said to himself,"The fellow's lying—I know he's lying."

ii

Vera Claythorne spoke in a trembling voice. She said, "I'd like to tell you. About that child—Cyril Hamilton. I was nursery governess to him. He was forbidden to swim out far. One day, when my attention was distracted, he started off. I swam after him. . . . I couldn't get there in time. . . . It was awful. . . . But it wasn't my fault. At the inquest the Coroner exonerated me. And his mother—she was so kind. If even she didn't blame me, why should—why should this awful thing be said? It's not fair—not fair. . . ." She broke down,weeping bitterly.

General Macarthur patted her shoulder. He said, "There, there, my dear. Of course it's not true. Fellow's a madman. A madman! Got a bee in his bonnet! Got hold of the wrong end of the stick all round."

He stood erect, squaring his shoulders. He barked out, "Best really to leave this sort of thing unanswered. However, feel I ought to say—no truth—no truth whatever in what he said about—er—young Arthur Richmond. Richmond was one of my officers. I sent him on a reconnaissance. He was killed. Natural course of events in war time. Wish to say resent very much—slur on my wife. Best woman in the world. Absolutely—Caesar's wife!"

General Macarthur sat down. His shaking hand pulled at his mustache. The effort to speak had cost him a good deal.

Lombard spoke. His eyes were amused. He said, "About those natives—"

Marston said, "What about them?"

Philip Lombard grinned. "Story's quite true! I left 'em! Matter of self-preservation. We were lost in the bush. I and a couple of other fellows took what food there was and cleared out."

General Macarthur said sternly, "You abandoned your men—left them to starve?"

Lombard said, "Not quite the act of a *pukka sahib,* I'm afraid. But self-preservation's a man's first duty. And natives don't mind dying, you know. They don't feel about it as Europeans do."

Vera lifted her face from her hands. She said, staring at him, "You left them—to *die*?"

Lombard answered, "I left them to die." His amused eyes looked into her horrified ones.

Anthony Marston said in a slow puzzled voice, "I've just been thinking—John and Lucy Combes. Must have been a couple of kids I ran over near Cambridge. Beastly bad luck."

Mr Justice Wargrave said acidly, "For them, or for you?"

Anthony said, "Well, I was thinking—for me—but of course, you're right, sir, it was damned bad luck on them. Of course it was a pure accident. They rushed out of some cottage or other. I had my license endorsed for a year. Beastly nuisance."

Dr. Armstrong said warmly, "This speeding's all wrong—all wrong! Young men like you are a danger to the community."

Anthony shrugged his shoulders. He said "Speed's come to stay. English roads are hopeless, of course. Can't get up a decent pace on them." He looked round vaguely for his glass, picked it up off a table and went over to the side table and helped himself to another whisky and soda. He said over his shoulder, "Well, anyway, it wasn't my fault. Just an accident!"

iii

The manservant, Rogers, had been moistening his lips and twisting his hands. He said now in a low, deferential voice, "If I might just say a word, sir."

Lombard said, "Go ahead, Rogers."

Rogers cleared his throat and passed his tongue once more over his dry lips. "There was a mention, sir, of me and Mrs. Rogers. And of Miss Brady. There isn't a word of truth in it, sir. My wife and I were with Miss Brady till she died. She was always in poor health, sir, always from the time we came to her. There was a storm, sir, that night—the night she was taken bad. The telephone was out of order. We couldn't get the doctor to her. I went for him, sir, on foot. But he got there too late. We'd done everything possible for her, sir. Devoted to her, we were. Anyone will tell you the same. There was never a word said against us. Not a word."

Lombard looked thoughtfully at the man's twitching face, his dry lips, the fright in his eyes. He remembered the crash of the falling coffee tray. He thought, but did not say, "Oh, yeah?"

Blore spoke—spoke in his hearty, bullying, official manner. He said, "Came into a little something at her death, though? Eh?"

Rogers drew himself up. He said stiffly, "Miss Brady left us a legacy in recognition of our faithful services. And why not, I'd like to know?"

Lombard said, "What about yourself, Mr Blore?"

"What about me?"

"Your name was included in the list."

Blore went purple. "Landor, you mean? That was the bank robbery—London and Commercial."

Mr. Justice Wargrave stirred. He said, "I remember. It didn't come before me, but I remember the case. Landor was convicted on your evidence. You were the police officer in charge of the case?"

Blore said, "I was."

"Landor got penal servitude for life and died in Dartmoor a year later. He was a delicate man."

Blore said, "He was a crook. It was he who knocked out the night watchman. The case was quite clear against him."

Wargrave said slowly, "You were complimented, I think, on your able handling of the case."

Blore said sulkily, "I got my promotion." He added in a thick voice, "I was only doing my duty."

Lombard laughed—a sudden, ringing laugh. He said, "What a duty-loving, law-abiding lot we all seem to be! Myself excepted. What about you, doctor—and your little professional mistake? Illegal operation, was it?"

Emily Brent glanced at him in sharp distaste and drew herself away a little.

Dr Armstrong, very much master of himself, shook his head good-humoredly. "I'm at a loss to understand the matter," he said. "The name meant nothing to me when it was spoken. What was it—Clees? Close? I really can't remember having a patient of that name, or being connected with a death in any way. The thing's a complete mystery to me. Of course, it's a long time ago. It might possibly be one of my operation cases in hospital. They come too late, so many of these people. Then, when the patient dies, they always consider it's the surgeon's fault." He sighed, shaking his head.

He thought: Drunk—that's what it was—drunk . . . And I operated! Nerves all to pieces—hands shaking. I killed her, all right. Poor devil—elderly woman—simple job if I'd been sober. Lucky for me there's loyalty in our profession. The Sister knew, of course—but she held her tongue. God, it gave me a shock! Pulled me up. But who could have known about it—after all these years?

iv

There was a silence in the room. Everybody was looking, covertly or openly, at Emily Brent. It was a minute or two before she became aware of the expectation. Her eyebrows rose on her narrow forehead.

She said, "Are you waiting for me to say something? I have nothing to say."

The judge said, "Nothing, Miss Brent?"

"Nothing." Her lips closed tightly.

The judge stroked his face. He said mildly, "You reserve your defense?"

Miss Brent said coldly, "There is no question of defense. I have always acted in accordance with the dictates of my conscience. I have nothing with which to reproach myself."

There was an unsatisfied feeling in the air. But Emily Brent was not one to be swayed by public opinion. She sat unyielding.

The judge cleared his throat once or twice. Then he said, "Our inquiry rests there. Now, Rogers, who else is there on this island besides ourselves and you and your wife?"

"Nobody, sir. Nobody at all."

"You're sure of that?"

"Quite sure, sir."

Wargrave said, "I am not yet clear as to the purpose of our Unknown host in getting us to assemble here. But in my opinion this person, whoever he may be, is not sane in the accepted sense of the word. He may be dangerous. In my opinion it would be well for us to leave this place as soon as possible. I suggest that we leave tonight."

Rogers said, "I beg your pardon, sir, but there's no boat on the island."

"No boat at all?"

"No, sir."

"How do you communicate with the mainland?"

"Fred Narracott, he comes over every morning, sir. He brings the bread and the milk and the post, and takes the orders."

Mr. Justice Wargrave said, "Then in my opinion it would be well if we all left tomorrow morning as soon as Narracott's boat arrives."

There was a chorus of agreement with only one dissentient voice. It was Anthony Marston who disagreed with the majority. "A bit unsporting, what?" he said. "Ought to ferret out the mystery before we go. Whole thing's like a detective story. Positively thrilling."

The judge said acidly, "At my time of life, I have no desire for 'thrills,' as you call them."

Anthony said with a grin, "The legal life's narrowing! I'm all for crime! Here's to it." He picked up his drink and drank it off at a gulp. Too quickly, perhaps. He choked—choked badly. His face contorted, turned purple. He gasped for breath—then slid down off his chair, the glass falling from his hand.

5

It was so sudden and so unexpected that it took everyone's breath away. They remained stupidly staring at the crumpled figure on the ground. Then Dr. Armstrong jumped up and went over to him, kneeling beside him. When he raised his head his eyes were bewildered. He said in a low, awestruck whisper, "My God! he's dead."

They didn't take it in. Not at once. Dead? *Dead*? That young Norse God in the prime of his health and strength. Struck down all in a moment. Healthy young men didn't die like that, choking over a whisky and soda. . . . No, they couldn't take it in.

Dr. Armstrong was peering into the dead man's face. He sniffed at the blue, twisted lips. Then he picked up the glass from which Anthony Marston had been drinking.

General Macarthur said, "Dead? D'you mean the fellow just choked and—and died?"

The physician said, "You can call it choking, if you like. He died of asphyxiation right enough."

He was sniffing now at the glass. He dipped a finger into the dregs and very cautiously just touched the finger with the tip of his tongue. His expression altered.

General Macarthur said, "Never knew a man could die like that—just of a choking fit!"

Emily Brent said in a clear voice, "In the midst of life we are in death."

Dr. Armstrong stood up. He said brusquely, "No, a man doesn't die of a mere choking fit. Marston's death wasn't what we call a natural death."

Vera said almost in a whisper, "Was there—something—in the whisky?"

Armstrong nodded. "Yes. Can't say exactly. Everything points to one of the cyanides. No distinctive smell of prussic acid, probably potassium cyanide. It acts pretty well instantaneously."

The judge said sharply, "It was in his glass?"

"Yes."

The doctor strode to the table where the drinks were. He removed the stopper from the whisky and smelt and tasted it. Then he tasted the soda water. He shook his head. "They're both all right."

Lombard said, "You mean—he must have put the stuff in his glass *himself*?"

Armstrong nodded with a curiously dissatisfied expression. He said, "Seems like it."

Blore said, "Suicide, eh? That's a queer go."

Vera said slowly, "You'd never think that *he* would kill himself. He was so alive. He was—oh—enjoying himself! When he came down the hill in his car this evening he looked—he looked—oh, I can't *explain!*"

But they knew what she meant. Anthony Marston, in the height of his youth and manhood, had seemed like a being who was immortal. And now, crumpled and broken, he lay on the floor. Dr. Armstrong said, "Is there any possibility other than suicide?"

Slowly everyone shook his head. There could be no other explanation. The drinks themselves were untampered with. They had all seen Anthony Marston go across and help himself. It followed therefore that any cyanide in the drink must have been put there by Anthony Marston himself. And yet—why should Anthony Marston commit suicide?

Blore said thoughtfully, "You know, doctor, it doesn't seem right to me. I shouldn't have said Mr. Marston was a suicidal type of gentleman."

Armstrong answered, "I agree."

ii

They had left it like that. What else was there to say? Together Armstrong and Lombard had carried the inert body of Anthony Marston to his bedroom and had laid him there covered over with a sheet.

When they came downstairs again, the others were standing in a group, shivering a little, though the night was not cold. Emily Brent said, "We'd better go to bed. It's late."

It was past twelve o'clock. The suggestion was a wise one—yet everyone hesitated. It was as though they clung to each other's company for reassurance. The judge said, "Yes, we must get some sleep."

Rogers said, "I haven't cleared yet—in the dining room."

Lombard said curtly, "Do it in the morning."

Armstrong said to him, "Is your wife all right?"

"I'll go and see, sir."

He returned a minute or two later. "Sleeping beautiful, she is."

"Good," said the doctor. "Don't disturb her."

"No, sir. I'll just put things straight in the dining room and make sure everything's locked up right, and then I'll turn in." He went across the hall into the dining room.

The others went upstairs, a slow, unwilling procession.

If this had been an old house, with creaking wood, and dark shadows, and heavily paneled walls, there might have been an eerie feeling. But this house was the essence of modernity. There were no dark corners—no possible sliding panels—it was flooded with electric light—everything was new and bright and shining. There was nothing hidden in this house, nothing concealed. It had no atmosphere about it. Somehow, that was the most frightening thing of all. . . .

They exchanged good nights on the upper landing. Each of them went into his or her own room, and each of them automatically, almost without conscious thought, locked the door. . . .

iii

In his pleasant, softly tinted room, Mr. Justice Wargrave removed his garments and prepared himself for bed. He was thinking about Edward Seton. He remembered Seton very well. His fair hair, his blue eyes, his habit of looking you straight in the face with a pleasant air of straightforwardness. That was what had made so good an impression on the jury.

Llewellyn, for the Crown, had bungled it a bit. He had been overvehement, had tried to prove too much. Matthews, on the other hand, for the Defense, had been good. His points had told. His cross-examinations had been deadly. His handling of his client in the witness box had been masterly.

And Seton had come through the ordeal of cross-examination well. He had not got excited or overvehement. The jury had been impressed. It had seemed to Matthews, perhaps, as though everything had been over bar the shouting.

The judge wound up his watch carefully and placed it by the bed. He remembered exactly how he had felt sitting there—listening, making notes, appreciating everything, tabulating every scrap of evidence that told against the prisoner. He'd enjoyed that case! Matthews' final speech had been first class. Llewellyn, coming after it, had failed to remove the good impression that the defending counsel had made. And then had come his own summing up. . . .

Carefully, Mr. Justice Wargrave removed his false teeth and dropped them into a glass of water. The shrunken lips fell in. It was a cruel mouth now, cruel and predatory. Hooding his eyes, the judge smiled to himself. He'd cooked Seton's goose all right!

With a slightly rheumatic grunt, he climbed into bed and turned out the electric light.

iv

Downstairs in the dining room, Rogers stood puzzled. He was staring at the china figures in the center of the table. He muttered to himself, "That's a rum go! I could have sworn there were ten of them."

v

General Macarthur tossed from side to side. Sleep would not come to him. In the darkness he kept seeing Arthur Richmond's face. He'd liked Arthur—he'd been damned fond of Arthur. He'd been pleased that Leslie liked him too.

Leslie was so capricious. Lots of good fellows that Leslie would turn up her nose at and pronounce dull. "Dull!" Just like that. But she hadn't found Arthur Richmond dull. They'd got on well together from the beginning. They'd talked of plays and music and pictures together. She'd teased him, made fun of him, ragged him. And he, Macarthur, had been delighted at the thought that Leslie took quite a motherly interest in the boy.

Motherly indeed! Damn fool not to remember that Richmond was twenty-eight to Leslie's twenty-nine. He'd loved Leslie. He could see her now. Her heart-shaped face, and her dancing, deep-gray eyes, and the brown curling mass of her hair. He'd loved Leslie and he'd believed in her absolutely.

Out there in France, in the middle of all the hell of it, he'd sat thinking of her, taken her picture out of the breast pocket of his tunic. And then—he'd found out!

It had come about exactly in the way things happened in books. The letter in the wrong envelope. She'd been writing to them both and she'd put her letter to Richmond in the envelope addressed to her husband. Even now, all these years after, he could feel the shock of it—the pain. . . .God, it had hurt!

And the business had been going on some time. The letter made that clear. Weekends! Richmond's last leave . . . Leslie—Leslie and Arthur!

God damn the fellow! Damn his smiling face, his brisk "Yes, sir." Liar and hypocrite! Stealer of another man's wife!

It had gathered slowly—that cold, murderous rage. He'd managed to carry on as usual—to show nothing. He'd tried to make his manner to Richmond just the same. Had he succeeded? He thought so. Richmond hadn't suspected. Inequalities of temper were easily accounted for out there, where men's nerves were continually snapping under the strain. Only young Armitage had looked at him curiously once or twice. Quite a young chap, but he'd had perceptions, that boy. Armitage, perhaps, had guessed—when the time came.

He'd sent Richmond deliberately to death. Only a miracle could have brought him through unhurt. That miracle didn't happen. Yes, he'd sent Richmond to his death and he wasn't sorry. It had been easy enough. Mistakes were being made all the time, officers being sent to death needlessly. All was confusion, panic. People might say afterwards, "Old Macarthur lost his nerve a bit, made some colossal blunders, sacrificed some of his best men." They couldn't say more.

But young Armitage was different. He'd looked at his commanding officer very oddly. He'd known, perhaps, that Richmond was being deliberately sent to death. (And after the war was over—had Armitage talked?)

Leslie hadn't known. Leslie had wept for her lover (he supposed) but her weeping was over by the time he'd come back to England. He'd never told her that he'd found her out. They'd gone on together—only, somehow, she hadn't seemed very real any more. And then, three or four years later, she'd got double pneumonia and died. That had been a long time ago. Fifteen years—sixteen years?

And he'd left the Army and come to live in Devon—bought the sort of little place he'd always meant to have. Nice neighbors—pleasant part of the world. There was a bit of shooting and fishing. He'd gone to church on Sundays. (But not the day that the lesson was read about David putting Uriah in the forefront of the battle. Somehow he couldn't face that. Gave him an uncomfortable feeling.)

Everybody had been very friendly. At first, that is. Later, he'd had an uneasy feeling that people were talking about him behind his back. They eyed him differently, somehow. As though they'd heard something—some lying rumor . . . (Armitage? Supposing Armitage had talked?)

He'd avoided people after that—withdrawn into himself. Unpleasant to feel that people were discussing you.

And all so long ago. So—so purposeless now. Leslie had faded into the distance and Arthur Richmond, too. Nothing of what had happened seemed to matter any more. It made life lonely, though. He'd taken to shunning his old Army friends. (If Armitage had talked, they'd know about it.)

And now—this evening—a hidden voice had blared out that old hidden story. Had he dealt with it all right? Kept a stiff upper lip? Betrayed the right amount of feeling—indignation, disgust—but no guilt, no discomfiture? Difficult to tell. Surely nobody could have taken the accusation seriously. There had been a pack of other nonsense, just as farfetched. That charming girl—the voice had accused her of drowning a child! Idiotic! Some madman throwing crazy accusations about! Emily Brent, too—actually a niece of old Tom Brent of the Regiment. It had accused her of murder! Anyone could see with half an eye that the woman was as pious as could be—the kind that was hand and glove with parsons.

Damned curious business, the whole thing! Crazy, nothing less. Ever since they had got here—when was that? Why, damn it, it was only this afternoon! Seemed a good bit longer than that. He thought: I wonder when we shall get away again. Tomorrow, of course, when the motorboat came from the mainland.

Funny, just this minute he didn't want much to get away from the island. . . . To go back to the mainland, back to his little house, back to all the troubles and worries. Through the open window he could hear the waves breaking on the rocks—a little louder now than earlier in the evening. Wind was getting up, too. He thought: Peaceful sound. Peaceful place. . . . He thought: Best of an island is once you get there—you can't go any further . . . you've come to the end of things. . . . *He knew suddenly, that he didn't want to leave the island.*

vi

Vera Claythorne lay in bed, wide awake, staring up at the ceiling. The light beside her was on. She was frightened of the dark. She was thinking: Hugo . . . Hugo . . . Why do I feel you're so near to me tonight? . . . .Somewhere quite close . . . Where is he really? I don't know. I never shall know. He just went away—right away—out of my life.

It was no good trying not to think of Hugo. He was close to her. She *had* to think of him—to remember . . . Cornwall . . . The black rocks, the smooth yellow sand. Mrs. Hamilton, stout, good humored. Cyril, whining a little always, pulling at her hand. "*I want to swim out to the rock, Miss Claythorne. Why can't I swim out to the rock?*" Looking up—meeting Hugo's eyes watching her.

The evenings after Cyril was in bed . . . "*Come out for a stroll, Miss Claythorne." "I think perhaps I will.". . .* The decorous stroll down to the beach. The moonlight—the soft Atlantic air. And then, Hugo's arms around her.

"*I love you. I love you. You know I love you, Vera?*"

Yes, she knew. (Or thought she knew.)

"*I can't ask you to marry me. I've not got a penny. It's all I can do to keep myself. Queer, you know, once, for three months, I had the chance of being a rich man to look forward to. Cyril wasn't born until three months, after Maurice died. If he'd been a girl . . ."*

If the child had been a girl, Hugo would have come into everything. He'd been disappointed, he admitted. *"I hadn't built on it, of course. But it was a bit of a knock. Oh, well, luck's luck! Cyril's a nice kid. I'm awfully fond of him."* And he was fond of him, too. Always ready to play games or amuse his small nephew. No rancor in Hugo's nature.

Cyril wasn't really strong. A puny child—no stamina. The kind of child, perhaps, who wouldn't live to grow up . . .

And then—?

"Miss Claythorne, why can't I swim to the rock?" Irritating whiny repetition.

"It's too far, Cyril."

"But, Miss Claythorne . . ."

Vera got up. She went to the dressing table and swallowed three aspirins. She thought: I wish I had some proper sleeping stuff.

She thought: If *I* were doing away with myself I'd take an overdose of veronal—something like that—not cyanide! She shuddered as she remembered Anthony Marston's convulsed purple face.

As she passed the mantelpiece, she looked up at the framed doggerel:

> *Ten little Indian boys went out to dine;*
> *One choked his little self and then there were nine.*

She thought to herself: It's horrible—just like us this evening. . . .

Why had Anthony Marston wanted to die? *She* didn't want to die. She couldn't imagine wanting to die. . . . Death was for—the other people. . . .

6

DR. ARMSTRONG was dreaming. . . . It was very hot in the operating room. . . . Surely they'd got the temperature too high? The sweat was rolling down his face. His hands were clammy. Difficult to hold the scalpel firmly. . . . How beautifully sharp it was. . . . Easy to do a murder with a knife like that. And of course he *was* doing a murder. . . .

The woman's body looked different. It had been a large, unwieldy body. This was a spare, meager body. And the face was hidden. Who was it that he had to kill? He couldn't remember. But he *must* know! Should he ask Sister? Sister was watching him. No, he couldn't ask her. She was suspicious, he could see that.

But who was it on the operating table? They shouldn't have covered up the face like that. . . . If he could only see the face . . . Ah! that was better. A young probationer was pulling off the handkerchief.

Emily Brent, of course. It was Emily Brent that he had to kill. How malicious her eyes were! Her lips were moving. What was she saying? "*In the midst of life we are in death. . . .*"

She was laughing now. No, nurse, don't put the handkerchief back. I've got to see. I've got to give the anesthetic. Where's the ether? I must have brought the ether with me. What have you done with the ether, Sister? Château Neuf du Pape? Yes, that will do quite as well. Take the handkerchief away, nurse.

Of course! I knew it all the time! *It's Anthony Marston!* His face is purple and convulsed. But he's not dead—he's laughing. I tell you he's laughing! He's shaking the operating table. Look out, man, look out. Nurse, steady it—steady—it—

With a start Dr. Armstrong woke up. It was morning. Sunlight was pouring into the room. And someone was leaning over him—shaking him. It was Rogers. Rogers, with a white face, saying, "Doctor—doctor!"

Dr. Armstrong woke up completely. He sat up in bed. He said sharply, "What is it?"

"It's the wife, doctor. *I can't get her to wake.* My God! I can't get her to wake. And—and she don't look right to me."

Dr. Armstrong was quick and efficient. He wrapped himself in his dressing gown and followed Rogers.

He bent over the bed where the woman was lying peacefully on her side. He lifted the cold hand, raised the eyelid. It was some few minutes before he straightened himself and turned from the bed.

Rogers whispered, "Is—she—is she—?" He passed a tongue over dry lips.

Armstrong nodded. "Yes, she's gone."

His eyes rested thoughtfully on the man before him. Then they went to the table by the bed, to the washstand, then back to the sleeping woman.

Rogers said, "Was it—was it—'er 'eart, doctor?"

Dr. Armstrong was a minute or two before replying. Then he said, "What was her health like normally?"

Rogers said, "She was a bit rheumaticky."

"Any doctor been attending her recently?"

"Doctor?" Rogers stared. "Not been to a doctor for years—neither of us."

"You'd no reason to believe she suffered from heart trouble?"

"No, doctor. I never knew of anything."

Armstrong said, "Did she sleep well?"

Now Rogers' eyes evaded his. The man's hands came together and turned and twisted uneasily. He muttered, "She didn't sleep extra well—no."

The doctor said sharply, "Did she take things to make her sleep?"

Rogers stared at him, surprised. "Take things? To make her sleep? Not that I knew of. I'm sure she didn't."

Armstrong went over to the washstand. There were a certain number of bottles on it. Hair lotion, lavender water, cascara, glycerin of cucumber for the hands, a mouthwash, tooth paste and some Elliman's. Rogers helped by pulling out the drawers of the dressing table. From there they moved on to the chest of drawers. But there was no sign of sleeping draughts or tablets. Rogers said, "She didn't have nothing last night, sir, except what you gave her. . . . "

ii

When the gong sounded for breakfast at nine o'clock it found everyone up and awaiting the summons. General Macarthur and the judge had been pacing the terrace outside, exchanging desultory comments on the political situation. Vera Claythorne and Philip Lombard had been up to the summit of the island behind the house. There they had discovered William Henry Blore, standing staring at the mainland. He said, "No sign of that motorboat yet. I've been watching for it."

Vera said, smiling, "Devon's a sleepy county. Things are usually late."

Philip Lombard was looking the other way, out to sea. He said abruptly, "What d'you think of the weather?"

Glancing up at the sky, Blore remarked, "Looks all right to me."

Lombard pursed up his mouth into a whistle. He said, "It will come on to blow before the day's out."

Blore said, "Squally—eh?"

From below them came the boom of a gong. Philip Lombard said,"Breakfast? Well, I could do with some."

As they went down the steep slope Blore said to Lombard in a ruminating voice, "You know, it beats me—why that young fellow wanted to do himself in! I've been worrying about it all night."

Vera was a little ahead. Lombard hung back slightly. He said, "Got any alternative theory?"

"I'd want some proof. Motive, to begin with. Well off I should say he was."

Emily Brent came out of the drawing-room window to meet them. She said sharply, "Is the boat coming?"

"Not yet," said Vera.

They went in to breakfast. There was a vast dish of eggs and bacon on the sideboard and tea and coffee. Rogers held the door open for them to pass in, then shut it from the outside.

Emily Brent said, "That man looks ill this morning."

Dr. Armstrong, who was standing by the window, cleared his throat. He said, "You must excuse any—er—shortcomings this morning. Rogers has had to do the best he can for breakfast single-handed. Mrs. Rogers has—er—not been able to carry on this morning."

Emily Brent said sharply, "What's the matter with the woman?"

Dr. Armstrong said easily, "Let us start our breakfast. The eggs will be cold. Afterwards, there are several matters I want to discuss with you all."

They took the hint. Plates were filled, coffee and tea were poured. The meal began. Discussion of the island was, by mutual consent, tabooed. They spoke instead in a desultory fashion of current events. The news from abroad, events in the world of sport, the latest reappearance of the Loch Ness monster.

Then, when plates were cleared, Dr. Armstrong moved back his chair a little, cleared his throat importantly and spoke. He said, "I thought it better to wait until you had had your breakfast before telling you of a sad piece of news. Mrs. Rogers died in her sleep."

There were startled and shocked ejaculations. Vera exclaimed, "How awful! Two deaths on this island since we arrived!"

Mr Justice Wargrave, his eyes narrowed, said in his small, precise, clear voice, "H'm—very remarkable—what was the cause of death?"

Armstrong shrugged his shoulders. "Impossible to say offhand."

"There must be an autopsy?"

"I certainly couldn't give a certificate. I have no knowledge whatsoever of the woman's state of health."

Vera said, "She was a very nervous-looking creature. And she had a shock last night. It might have been heart failure, I suppose?"

Dr. Armstrong said dryly, "Her heart certainly failed to beat—but what caused it to fail is the question."

One word fell from Emily Brent. It fell hard and clear into the listening group. "Conscience!" she said.

Armstrong turned to her. "What exactly do you mean by that, Miss Brent?"

Emily Brent, her lips tight and hard, said, "You all heard. She was accused, together with her husband, of having deliberately murdered her former employer—an old lady."

"And you think?"

Emily Brent said, "I think that that accusation was true. You all saw her last night. She broke down completely and fainted. The shock of having her wickedness brought home to her was too much for her. She literally died of fear."

Dr. Armstrong shook his head doubtfully. "It is a possible theory," he said. "One cannot adopt it without more exact knowledge of her state of health. If there was cardiac weakness—"

Emily Brent said quietly, "Call it, if you prefer, an Act of God."

Everyone looked shocked. Mr. Blore said uneasily, "That's carrying things a bit far, Miss Brent."

She looked at them with shining eyes. Her chin went up. She said, "You regard it as impossible that a sinner should be struck down by the wrath of God! I do not!"

The judge stroked his chin. He murmured in a slightly ironic voice, "My dear lady, in my experience of ill-doing, Providence leaves the work of conviction and chastisement to us mortals—and the process is often fraught with difficulties. There are no short cuts."

Emily Brent shrugged her shoulders. Blore said sharply, "What did she have to eat and drink last night after she went up to bed?"

Armstrong said, "Nothing."

"She didn't take anything? A cup of tea? A drink of water? I'll bet you she had a cup of tea. That sort always does."

"Rogers assures me she had nothing whatsoever."

"Ah," said Blore. "But he *might* say so!" His tone was so significant that the doctor looked at him sharply.

Philip Lombard said, "So that's your idea?"

Blore said aggressively, "Well, why not? We all heard that accusation last night. May be sheer moonshine—just plain lunacy! On the other hand, it may not. Allow for the moment that it's true. Rogers and his missus polished off that old lady. Well, where does that get you? They've been feeling quite safe and happy about it—"

Vera interrupted. In a low voice she said, "No, I don't think Mrs. Rogers ever felt safe."

Blore looked slightly annoyed at the interruption. "Just like a woman," his glance said. He resumed, "That's as may be. Anyway there's no active danger to them as far as they know. Then, last night, some unknown lunatic spills the beans. What happens? The woman cracks—she goes to pieces. Notice how her husband hung over her as she was coming round. Not all husbandly solicitude! Not on your life! He was like a cat on hot bricks. Scared out of his life as to what she might say.

"And there's the position for you! They've done a murder and got away with it. But if the whole thing's going to be raked up, what's going to happen? Ten to one, the woman will give the show away. She hasn't got the nerve to stand up and brazen it out. She's a living danger to her husband, that's what she is. He's all right. *He*'ll lie with a straight face till kingdom comes—but he can't be sure of *her*! And if *she* goes to pieces, his neck's in danger! So he slips something into a cup of tea and makes sure that her mouth is shut permanently."

Armstrong said slowly, "There was no empty cup by her bedside—there was nothing there at all. I looked."

Blore snorted. "Of course there wouldn't be! First thing he'd do when she'd drunk it would be to take that cup and saucer away and wash it up carefully."

There was a pause. Then General Macarthur said doubtfully, "It may be so. But I should hardly think it possible that a man would do that—to his wife."

Blore gave a short laugh. He said, "When a man's neck's in danger, he doesn't stop to think too much about sentiment."

There was a pause. Before anyone could speak, the door opened and Rogers came in. He said, looking from one to the other, "Is there anything more I can get you? I'm sorry there was so little toast, but we've run right out of bread. The new bread hasn't come over from the mainland yet."

Mr. Justice Wargrave stirred a little in his chair. He asked, "What time does the motorboat usually come over?"

"Between seven and eight, sir. Sometimes it's a bit after eight. Don't know what Fred Narracott can be doing this morning. If he's ill he'd send his brother."

Philip Lombard said, "What's the time now?"

"Ten minutes to ten, sir."

Lombard's eyebrows rose. He nodded slowly to himself. Rogers waited a minute or two. General Macarthur spoke suddenly and explosively. "Sorry to hear about your wife, Rogers. Doctor's just been telling us."

Rogers inclined his head. "Yes, sir. Thank you, sir." He took up the empty bacon dish and went out. Again there was a silence.

iii

On the terrace outside Philip Lombard said, "About this motor-boat—"

Blore looked at him. Blore nodded his head. He said, "I know what you're thinking, Mr. Lombard. I've asked myself the same question.

Motorboat ought to have been here nigh on two hours ago. It hasn't come. Why?"

"Found the answer?" asked Lombard.

"*It's not an accident*—that's what I say. It's part and parcel of the whole business. It's all bound up together."

Philip Lombard said, "It won't come, you think?"

A voice spoke behind him—a testy, impatient voice. "The motorboat's not coming," he said.

Blore turned his square shoulder slightly and viewed the last speaker thoughtfully. "You think not too, General?"

General Macarthur said sharply, "Of course it won't come. We're counting on the motorboat to take us off the island. That's the meaning of the whole business. *We're not going to leave the island....* None of us will ever leave.... It's the end, you see—the end of everything...." He hesitated, then he said in a low, strange voice, "That's peace—real peace. To come to the end—not to have to go on.... Yes, peace...."

He turned abruptly and walked away. Along the terrace, then down the slope towards the sea—obliquely—to the end of the island where loose rocks went out into the water. He walked a little unsteadily, like a man who was only half-awake.

Blore said, "There goes another one who's balmy! Looks as though it'll end with the whole lot going that way."

Philip Lombard said, "I don't fancy *you* will, Blore."

The ex-Inspector laughed. "It would take a lot to send me off my head." He added dryly, "And I don't think you'll be going that way either, Mr. Lombard."

Philip Lombard said, "I feel quite sane at the minute, thank you."

iv

Dr. Armstrong came out onto the terrace. He stood there hesitating. To his left were Blore and Lombard. To his right was Wargrave, slowly pacing up and down, his head bent down. Armstrong, after a moment of indecision, turned towards the latter. But at that moment Rogers came quickly out of the house. "Could I have a word with you, sir, please?"

Armstrong turned. He was startled at what he saw.

Rogers' face was working. Its color was grayish green. His hands shook. It was such a contrast to his restraint of a few minutes ago that Armstrong was quite taken aback. "Please, sir, if I could have a word with you. Inside, sir."

The doctor turned back and re-entered the house with the frenzied butler. He said, "What's the matter, man? Pull yourself together."

"In here, sir, come in here." He opened the dining-room door. The doctor passed in. Rogers followed him and shut the door behind him.

"Well," said Armstrong, "what is it?"

The muscles of Rogers' throat were working. He was swallowing. He jerked out, "There's things going on, sir, that I don't understand."

Armstrong said sharply, "Things? What things?"

"You'll think I'm crazy, sir. You'll say it isn't anything. But it's got to be explained, sir. It's got to be explained. Because it doesn't make any sense."

"Well, man, tell me what it is. Don't go on talking in riddles."

Rogers swallowed again. He said, "It's those little figures, sir. In the middle of the table. The little china figures. Ten of them, there were. I'll swear to that, ten of them."

Armstrong said, "Yes, ten. We counted them last night at dinner."

Rogers came nearer. "That's just it, sir. Last night, when I was clearing up, there wasn't but nine, sir. I noticed it and thought it queer. But that's all I thought. And now, sir, this morning. I didn't notice when I laid the breakfast. I was upset and all that. But now, sir, when I came to clear away. See for yourself if you don't believe me. *There's only eight, sir!* Only eight! It doesn't make sense, does it? *Only eight . . .*"

7

AFTER BREAKFAST, EMILY BRENT had suggested to Vera Claythorne that they should walk up to the summit again and watch for the boat. Vera had acquiesced.

The wind had freshened. Small white crests were appearing on the sea. There were no fishing boats out—and no sign of the motorboat. The actual village of Sticklehaven could not be seen, only the hill above it, a jutting-out cliff of red rock concealed the actual little bay.

Emily Brent said, "The man who brought us out yesterday seemed a dependable sort of person. It is really very odd that he should be so late this morning."

Vera did not answer. She was fighting down a rising feeling of panic. She said to herself angrily, "You must keep cool. This isn't like you. You've always had excellent nerves." Aloud she said after a minute or two, "I wish he would come. I—I want to get away."

Emily Brent said dryly, "I've no doubt we all do."

Vera said, "It's all so extraordinary. . . . There seems no—no meaning in it all."

The elderly woman beside her said briskly, "I'm very annoyed with myself for being to easily taken in. Really that letter is absurd when one comes to examine it. But I had no doubts at the time—none at all."

Vera murmured mechanically, "I suppose not."

"One takes things for granted too much," said Emily Brent.

Vera drew a deep shuddering breath. She said, "Do you really think—what you said at breakfast?"

"Be a little more precise, my dear. To what in particular are you referring?"

Vera said in a low voice, "Do you really think that Rogers and his wife did away with that old lady?"

Emily Brent gazed thoughtfully out to sea. Then she said, "Personally, I am quite sure of it. What do you think?"

"I don't know what to think."

Emily Brent said, "Everything goes to support the idea. The way the woman fainted. And the man dropped the coffee tray, remember. Then the way he spoke about it—it didn't ring true. Oh, yes, I'm afraid they did it."

Vera said, "The way she looked—scared of her own shadow! I've never seen a woman look so frightened. . . . She must have been always haunted by it. . . ."

Miss Brent murmured, "I remember a text that hung in my nursery as a child. 'Be sure thy sin will find thee out.' It's very true, that. 'Be sure thy sin will find thee out.'"

Vera scrambled to her feet. She said, "But, Miss Brent—Miss Brent—in that case—"

"Yes, my dear?"

"The others? What about the others?"

"I don't quite understand you."

"All the other accusations—they—*they* weren't true? But if it's true about the Rogerses—" She stopped, unable to make her chaotic thought clear.

Emily Brent's brow, which had been frowning perplexedly, cleared. She said, "Ah, I understand you now. Well, there is that Mr. Lombard. He admits to having abandoned twenty men to their deaths."

Vera said, "They were only natives. . . ."

Emily Brent said sharply, "Black or white, they are our brothers."

Vera thought: Our black brothers—our black brothers. Oh, I'm going to laugh. I'm hysterical. I'm not myself. . . .

Emily Brent continued thoughtfully, "Of course, some of the other accusations were very farfetched and ridiculous. Against the judge, for instance, who was only doing his duty in his public capacity. And the ex-Scotland Yard man. My own case, too." She paused and then went on, "Naturally, considering the circumstances, I was not going to say anything last night. It was not a fit subject to discuss before gentlemen."

"No?"

Vera listened with interest. Miss Brent continued serenely, "Beatrice Taylor was in service with me. *Not a nice girl*—as I found out too late. I was very much deceived in her. She had nice manners and was very clean and willing. I was very pleased with her. Of course all that was the sheerest hypocrisy! She was a loose girl with no morals. Disgusting! It was some time before I found out that she was what they call 'in trouble.'" She paused, her delicate nose wrinkling itself in distaste. "It was a great shock to me. Her parents were decent folk, too, who had brought her up very strictly. I'm glad to say they did not condone her behavior."

Vera said, staring at Miss Brent, "What happened?"

"Naturally I did not keep her an hour under my roof. No one shall ever say that I condoned immorality."

Vera said in a lower voice, "What happened—to her?"

Miss Brent said, "The abandoned creature, not content with having one sin on her conscience, committed a still graver sin. She took her own life."

Vera whispered, horror struck, "She killed herself?"

"Yes, she threw herself into the river."

Vera shivered. She stared at the calm, delicate profile of Miss Brent. She said, "What did you feel like when you knew she'd done that? Weren't you sorry? Didn't you blame yourself?"

Emily Brent drew herself up. "I? I had nothing with which to reproach myself."

Vera said, "But if your—hardness—drove her to it."

Emily Brent said sharply, "Her own action—her own sin—that was what drove her to it. If she had behaved like a decent modest young woman none of this would have happened."

She turned her face to Vera. There was no self-reproach, no uneasiness in those eyes. They were hard and self-righteous. Emily Brent sat on the summit of Indian Island, encased in her own armor of virtue. The little elderly spinster was no longer slightly ridiculous to Vera. Suddenly—she was terrible.

ii

Dr. Armstrong came out of the dining room and once more came out on the terrace. The judge was sitting in a chair now, gazing placidly out to sea. Lombard and Blore were over to the left, smoking but not talking. As before, the doctor hesitated for a moment. His eyes rested speculatively on Mr. Justice Wargrave. He wanted to consult with someone. He was conscious of the judge's acute, logical brain. But nevertheless he wavered. Mr. Justice Wargrave might have a good brain but he was an elderly man. At this juncture, Armstrong felt what was needed was a man of action. He made up his mind. "Lombard, can I speak to you for a minute?"

Philip started. "Of course."

The two men left the terrace. They strolled down the slope towards the water. When they were out of earshot, Armstrong said, "I want a consultation."

Lombard's eyebrows went up. He said, "My dear fellow, I've no medical knowledge."

"No, no, I mean as to the general situation."

"Oh, that's different."

Armstrong said, "Frankly, what do you think of the position?"

Lombard reflected a minute. Then he said, "It's rather suggestive, isn't it?"

"What are your ideas on the subject of that woman? Do you accept Blore's theory?"

Philip puffed smoke into the air. He said, "It's perfectly feasible— taken alone."

"Exactly."

Armstrong's tone sounded relieved. Philip Lombard was no fool. The latter went on, "That is, accepting the premise that Mr. and Mrs. Rogers have successfully got away with murder in their time. And I don't see why they shouldn't. What do you think they did exactly? Poisoned the old lady?"

Armstrong said slowly, "It might be simpler than that. I asked Rogers this morning what this Miss Brady had suffered from. His answer was enlightening. I don't need to go into medical details, but in a certain form of cardiac trouble, amyl nitrite is used. When an attack comes on an ampoule of amyl nitrite is broken and it is inhaled. If amyl nitrite were withheld—well, the consequences might easily be fatal."

Philip Lombard said thoughtfully, "As simple as that. It must have been—rather tempting."

The doctor nodded. "Yes, no positive action. No arsenic to obtain and administer—nothing definite—just—negation! And Rogers hurried through the night to fetch a doctor and they both felt confident that no one could ever know.''

"And, even if anyone knew, nothing could ever be proved against them,'' added Philip Lombard. He frowned suddenly. "Of course— that explains a good deal.''

Armstrong said, puzzled, "I beg your pardon.''

Lombard said, "I mean—it explains Indian Island. There are crimes that cannot be brought home to their perpetrators. Instance, the Rogerses'. Another instance, old Wargrave, who committed his murder strictly within the law.''

Armstrong said sharply, "You believe that story?''

Philip Lombard smiled. "Oh, yes, I believe it. Wargrave murdered Edward Seton all right, murdered him as surely as if he'd stuck a stiletto through him! But he was clever enough to do it from the judge's seat in wig and gown. So in the ordinary way you can't bring his little crime home to him.''

A sudden flash passed like lightning through Armstrong's mind. *Murder in Hospital. Murder on the Operating Table. Safe—yes, safe as houses*! Philip Lombard was saying, "Hence—Mr. Owen— hence—Indian Island!''

Armstrong drew a deep breath. "Now we're getting down to it. What's the real purpose of getting us all here?''

Philip Lombard said, "What do *you* think?''

Armstrong said abruptly, "Let's go back a minute to this woman's death. What are the possible theories? Rogers killed her because he was afraid she would give the show away. Second possibility, she lost her nerve and took an easy way out herself.''

Philip Lombard said, "Suicide, eh?''

"What do you say to that?''

Lombard said, "It could have been—yes—*if it hadn't been for Marston's death.* Two suicides within twelve hours is a little *too* much to swallow! And if you tell me that Anthony Marston, a young bull with no nerves and precious little brains, got the wind up over having mowed down a couple of kids and deliberately put himself out of the way—well, the idea's laughable! And anyway, how did he get hold of the stuff? From all I've ever heard, potassium cyanide isn't the kind of stuff you take about with you in your waistcoat pocket. But that's your line of country.''

Armstrong said, "Nobody in their senses carries potassium cyanide. It might be done by someone who was going to take a wasps' nest.''

"The ardent gardener or landowner, in fact? Again, not Anthony Marston. It strikes me that cyanide is going to need a bit of explaining. Either Anthony Marston meant to do away with himself before he came here, and therefore came prepared—or else—''

Armstrong prompted him. "Or else?"

Philip Lombard grinned. "Why make me say it? When it's on the tip of your own tongue. *Anthony Marston was murdered, of course.*"

iii

Dr. Armstrong drew a deep breath. "And Mrs. Rogers?"

Lombard said slowly, "I could believe in Anthony's suicide (with difficulty) if it weren't for Mrs. Rogers. I could believe in Mrs. Rogers' suicide (easily) if it weren't for Anthony Marston. I can believe that Rogers put his wife out of the way—if it were not for the unexplained death of Anthony Marston. But what we need is a theory to explain two deaths following rapidly on each other."

Armstrong said, "I can perhaps give you some help towards that theory." And he repeated the facts that Rogers had given him about the disappearance of the two little china figures.

Lombard said, "Yes, little china Indian figures . . . There were certainly ten last night at dinner. And now there are eight, you say?"

Dr. Armstrong recited:

> *"Ten little Indian boys going out to dine;*
> *One went and choked himself and then there were nine.*
>
> *"Nine little Indian boys sat up very late;*
> *One overslept himself and then there were eight."*

The two men looked at each other. Philip Lombard grinned and flung away his cigarette. "Fits too damned well to be a coincidence! Anthony Marston dies of asphyxiation or choking last night after dinner, and Mother Rogers oversleeps herself with a vengeance."

"And therefore?" said Armstrong.

Lombard took him up. "And therefore another kind of puzzle. The nigger in the woodpile! X! Mr. Owen! U. N. Owen. One Unknown Lunatic at Large!"

"Ah!" Armstrong breathed a sight of relief. "You agree. But you see what it involves? Rogers swore that there was no one but ourselves and him and his wife on the island."

"Rogers is wrong! Or possibly Rogers is lying!"

Armstrong shook his head. "I don't think he's lying. The man's scared. He's scared nearly out of his senses."

Philip Lombard nodded. He said, "No motorboat this morning. That fits in. Mr. Owen's little arrangements again to the fore. Indian Island is to be isolated until Mr. Owen has finished his job."

Armstrong had gone pale. He said, "You realize—the man must be a raving maniac!"

Philip Lombard said, and there was a new ring in his voice, "There's one thing Mr. Owen didn't realize."

"What's that?"

"This island's more or less a bare rock. We shall make short work of searching it. We'll soon ferret out U. N. Owen, Esq."

Dr. Armstrong said warningly, "He'll be dangerous."

Philip Lombard laughed. "Dangerous? Who's afraid of the big bad wolf? *I*'ll be dangerous when I get hold of him!"

He paused and said, "We'd better rope in Blore to help us. He'll be a good man in a pinch. Better not tell the women. As for the others, the General's gaga, I think, and old Wargrave's forte is masterly inactivity. The three of us can attend to this job."

8

BLORE WAS EASILY roped in. He expressed immediate agreement with their arguments. "What you've said about those china figures, sir, makes all the difference. That's crazy, that is! There's only one thing. You don't think this Owen's idea might be to do the job by proxy, as it were?"

"Explain yourself, man."

"Well, I mean like this. After the racket last night this young Mr. Marston gets the wind up and poisons himself. And Rogers, *he* gets the wind up too and bumps off his wife! All according to U.N.O's plan."

Armstrong shook his head. He stressed the point about the cyanide. Blore agreed. "Yes, I'd forgotten that. Not a natural thing to be carrying about with you. But how did it get into his drink, sir?"

Lombard said, "I've been thinking about that. Marston had several drinks that night. Between the time he had his last one and the time he finished the one before it, there was quite a gap. During that time his glass was lying about on some table or other. I think, though I can't be sure, it was on the little table near the window. The window was open. Somebody could have slipped a dose of the cyanide into the glass."

Blore said unbelievingly, "Without our all seeing him, sir?"

Lombard said dryly, "We were all—rather concerned elsewhere."

Armstrong said slowly, "That's true. We'd all been attacked. We were walking about, moving about the room. Arguing, indignant, intent on our own business. I think it *could* have been done. . . ."

Blore shrugged his shoulders. "Fact is, it must have been done! Now then, gentlemen, let's make a start. Nobody's got a revolver, by any chance? I suppose that's too much to hope for."

Lombard said, "I've got one." He patted his pocket.

Blore's eyes opened very wide. He said in an overcasual tone: "Always carry that about with you, sir?"

Lombard said, "Usually. I've been in some tight places, you know."

"Oh," said Blore and added, "Well, you've probably never been in a tighter place than you are today! If there's a lunatic hiding on this island, he's probably got a young arsenal on him—to say nothing of a knife or dagger or two."

Armstrong coughed. "You may be wrong there, Blore. Many homicidal lunatics are very quiet, unassuming people. Delightful fellows."

Blore said, "I don't feel this one is going to be of that kind, Dr. Armstrong."

ii

The three men started on their tour of the island. It proved unexpectedly simple. On the northwest side, towards the coast, the cliffs fell sheer to the sea below, their surface unbroken. On the rest of the island there were no trees and very little cover. The three men worked carefully and methodically, beating up and down from the highest point to the water's edge, narrowly scanning the least irregularity in the rock which might point to the entrance to a cave. But there were no caves.

They came at last, skirting the water's edge, to where General Macarthur sat looking out to sea. It was very peaceful here with the lap of the waves breaking over the rocks. The old man sat very upright, his eyes fixed on the horizon. He paid no attention to the approach of the searchers. His oblivion of them made one at least faintly uncomfortable.

Blore thought to himself, 'Tisn't natural—looks as though he'd gone into a trance or something. He cleared his throat and said in a would-be conversational tone, "Nice peaceful spot you've found for yourself, sir."

The General frowned. He cast a quick look over his shoulder. He said, "There is so little time—so little time. I really must insist that no one disturbs me."

Blore said genially, "We won't disturb you. We're just making a tour of the island, so to speak. Just wondered, you know, if someone might be hiding on it."

The General frowned and said, "You don't understand—you don't understand at all. Please go away."

Blore retreated. He said, as he joined the other two, "He's crazy. . . . It's no good talking to him."

Lombard asked with some curiosity, "What did he say?"

Blore shrugged his shoulders. "Something about there being no time and that he didn't want to be disturbed."

Dr. Armstrong frowned. He murmured, "I wonder now. . . ."

iii

The search of the island was practically completed. The three men stood on the highest point looking over towards the mainland. There were no boats out. The wind was freshening. Lombard said, "No fishing boats out. There's a storm coming. Damned nuisance you can't see the village from here. We could signal or do something."

Blore said, "We might light a bonfire tonight."

Lombard said frowning, "The devil of it is that's all probably been provided for."

"In what way, sir?"

"How do I know? Practical joke, perhaps. We're to be marooned here, no attention is to be paid to signals, etc. Possibly the village has been told there's a wager on. Some damn fool story anyway."

Blore said dubiously, "Think they'd swallow that?"

Lombard said drily, "It's easier of belief than the truth! If the village were told that the island was to be isolated until Mr. Unknown Owen had quietly murdered all his guests—do you think they'd believe that?"

Dr. Armstrong said, "There are moments when I can't believe it myself. And yet—"

Philip Lombard, his lips curling back from his teeth, said, "*And yet*—that's just it! You've said it, doctor!"

Blore was gazing down into the water. He said, "Nobody could have clambered down here, I suppose?"

Armstrong shook his head. "I doubt it. It's pretty sheer. And where could he hide?"

Blore said, "There might be a hole in the cliff. If we had a boat now, we could row round the island."

Lombard said, "If we had a boat, we'd all be halfway to the mainland by now!"

"True enough, sir."

Lombard said suddenly, "We can make sure of this cliff. There's only one place where there *could* be a recess—just a little to the right below here. If you fellows can get hold of a rope, you can let me down to make sure."

Blore said, "Might as well *be* sure. Though it seems absurd—on the face of it! I'll see if I can get hold of something." He started off briskly down to the house.

Lombard stared up at the sky. The clouds were beginning to mass themselves together. The wind was increasing. He shot a sideways look at Armstrong. He said, "You're very silent, doctor. What are you thinking?"

Armstrong said slowly, "I was wondering exactly how mad old Macarthur was. . . ."

iv

Vera had been restless all the morning. She had avoided Emily Brent with a kind of shuddering aversion. Miss Brent herself had taken a chair just round the corner of the house so as to be out of the wind. She sat there knitting. Every time Vera thought of her she seemed to see a pale drowned face with seaweed entangled in the hair. . . . A face that had once been pretty—impudently pretty perhaps—and which was now beyond the reach of pity or terror. And Emily Brent, placid and righteous, sat knitting.

On the main terrace, Mr. Justice Wargrave sat huddled in a porter's chair. His head was poked down well into his neck. When Vera looked at him, she saw a man standing in the dock—a young man with fair hair and blue eyes and a bewildered, frightened face. Edward Seton. And in imagination she saw the judge's old hands put the black cap on his head and begin to pronounce sentence. . . .

After a while Vera strolled slowly down to the sea. She walked along towards the extreme end of the island where an old man sat staring out to the horizon. General Macarthur stirred at her approach. His head turned—there was a queer mixture of questioning and apprehension in his look. It startled her. He stared intently at her for a minute or two. She thought to herself: How queer. It's almost as though he *knew*. . . .

He said, "Oh! it's you! You've come. . . ."

Vera sat down beside him. She said, "Do you like sitting here looking out to sea?"

He nodded his head gently. "Yes," he said. "It's pleasant. It's a good place, I think, to wait."

"To wait?" said Vera sharply. "What are you waiting for?"

He said gently, "The end. But I think you know that, don't you? It's true, isn't it? We're all waiting for the end."

She said unsteadily, "What do you mean?"

General Macarthur said gravely, "*None of us are going to leave the island.* That's the plan. You know it, of course, perfectly. What, perhaps, you can't understand is the relief!"

Vera said wonderingly, "The relief?"

He said, "Yes. Of course, you're very young . . . you haven't got to that yet. But it does come! The blessed relief when you know that you've done with it all—that you haven't got to carry the burden any longer. You'll feel that too some day . . . ."

Vera said hoarsely, "I don't understand you." Her fingers worked spasmodically. She felt suddenly afraid of this quiet old soldier. . . .

He said musingly, "You see, I loved Leslie. I loved her very much. . . ."

Vera said questioningly, "Was Leslie your wife?"

"Yes, my wife . . . . I loved her—and I was very proud of her. She was so pretty—and so gay." He was silent for a minute or two, then he said, "Yes, I loved Leslie. That's why I did it."

Vera said, "You mean—" and paused.

General Macarthur nodded his head gently. "It's not much good denying it now—not when we're all going to die. *I sent Richmond to his death.* I suppose, in a way, it was murder. Curious. *Murder*—and I've always been such a law-abiding man! But it didn't seem like that at the time. I had no regrets. 'Serves him damned well right!'—that's what I thought. But afterwards—"

In a hard voice, Vera said, "Well, afterwards?"

He shook his head vaguely. He looked puzzled and a little distressed. "I don't know. I—don't know. It was all different, you see. I don't know if Leslie ever guessed . . . I don't think so. But you see, I didn't know about her any more. She'd gone far away where I couldn't reach her. And then she died—and I was alone. . . . "

Vera said, "Alone—alone—" and the echo of her voice came back to her from the rocks.

General Macarthur said, "You'll be glad, too, when the end comes."

Vera got up. She said sharply, "I don't know what you mean!"

He said, "I *know*, my child, I *know*. . . ."

"You don't. You don't understand at all. . . ."

General Macarthur looked out to sea again. He seemed unconscious of her presence behind him. He said very gently and softly, "Leslie . . . ?"

V

When Blore returned from the house with a rope coiled over his arm, he found Armstrong where he had left him staring down into the depths. Blore said breathlessly, "Where's Mr. Lombard?"

Armstrong said carelessly, "Gone to test some theory or other. He'll be back in a minute. Look here, Blore, I'm worried."

"I should say we were all worried."

The doctor waved an impatient hand. "Of course—of course. I don't mean it that way. I'm thinking of old Macarthur."

"What about him, sir?"

Dr. Armstrong said grimly, "What we're looking for is a madman. *What price Macarthur?*"

Blore said incredulously, "You mean he's homicidal?"

Armstrong said doubtfully, "I shouldn't have said so. Not for a minute. But of course I'm not a specialist in mental diseases. I haven't really had any conversation with him—I haven't studied him from that point of view."

Blore said doubtfully, "Gaga, yes! But I wouldn't have said—"

Armstrong cut in with a slight effort as of a man who pulls himself together. "You're probably right! Damn it all, there *must* be someone hiding on the island! Ah! here comes Lombard."

They fastened the rope carefully. Lombard said, "I'll help myself all I can. Keep a lookout for a sudden strain on the rope."

After a minute or two, while they stood together watching Lombard's progress, Blore said, "Climbs like a cat, doesn't he?" There was something odd in his voice.

Dr. Armstrong said, "I should think he must have done some mountaineering in his time."

"Maybe."

There was a silence and the ex-Inspector said, "Funny sort of cove altogether. D'you know what I think?"

"What?"

"He's a wrong 'un!"

Armstrong said doubtfully, "In what way?"

Blore grunted. Then he said, "I don't know—exactly. But I wouldn't trust him a yard."

Dr. Armstrong said, "I suppose he's led an adventurous life."

Blore said, "I bet some of his adventures have had to be kept pretty dark." He paused and then went on, "Did you happen to bring a revolver along with you, Doctor?"

Armstrong stared. "Me? Good Lord, no. Why should I?"

Blore said, "*Why did Mr. Lombard?*"

Armstrong said doubtfully, "I suppose—habit."

Blore snorted.

A sudden pull came on the rope. For some moments they had their hands full. Presently, when the strain relaxed, Blore said, "There are habits *and* habits! Mr. Lombard takes a revolver to out-of-the-way places, right enough, *and* a primus and a sleeping bag and a supply of bug powder, no doubt! But habit wouldn't make him bring the whole outfit down here! It's only in books people carry revolvers around as a matter of course."

Dr. Armstrong shook his head perplexedly. They leaned over and watched Lombard's progress. His search was thorough and they could see at once that it was futile. Presently he came up over the edge of the cliff. He wiped the perspiration from his forehead. "Well," he said. "We're up against it. It's the house or nowhere."

vi

The house was easily searched. They went through the few outbuildings first and then turned their attention to the building itself. Mrs. Rogers' yard measure found in the kitchen dresser assisted them. But there were no hidden spaces left unaccounted for. Everything was plain and straightforward, a modern structure devoid of concealments. They went through the ground floor first. As they mounted to the bedroom floor, they saw through the landing window Rogers carrying out a tray of cocktails to the terrace. Philip Lombard said lightly, "Wonderful animal, the good servant. Carries on with an impassive countenance."

Armstrong said appreciatively, "Rogers is a first-class butler, I'll say that for him!"

Blore said, "His wife was a pretty good cook, too. That dinner—last night—"

They turned in to the first bedroom. Five minutes later they faced each other on the landing. No one hiding—no possible hiding place. Blore said, "There's a little stair here."

Dr. Armstrong said, "It leads up to the servants' room."

Blore said, "There must be a place under the roof—for cisterns, water tank, etc. It's the best chance—and the only one!"

And it was then, as they stood there, that they heard the sound from above. A soft, furtive footfall overhead.

They all heard it. Armstrong grasped Blore's arm. Lombard held up an admonitory finger. "Quiet—listen."

It came again—someone moving softly, furtively, overhead.

Armstrong whispered, "He's actually in the bedroom itself. The room where Mrs. Roger's body is."

Blore whispered back, "Of course! Best hiding place he could have chosen! Nobody likely to go there. Now then—quiet as you can."

They crept stealthily upstairs. On the little landing outside the door of the bedroom they paused again. Yes, someone was in the room. There was a faint creak from within. Blore whispered, "Now."

He flung open the door and rushed in, the other two close behind him. Then all three stopped dead. Rogers was in the room, his hands full of garments.

vii

Blore recovered himself first. He said, "Sorry—er—Rogers. Heard someone moving about in here, and thought—well—" He stopped.

Rogers said, "I'm sorry, gentlemen. I was just moving my things. I take it there will be no objection if I take one of the vacant guest chambers on the floor below? The smallest room."

It was to Armstrong that he spoke, and Armstrong replied, "Of course. Of course. Get on with it." He avoided looking at the sheeted figure lying on the bed.

Rogers said, "Thank you, sir."

He went out of the room with his arm full of belongings and went down the stairs to the floor below. Armstrong moved over to the bed and, lifting the sheet, looked down on the peaceful face of the dead woman. There was no fear there now. Just emptiness. Armstrong said, "Wish I'd got my stuff here. I'd like to know what drug it was." Then he turned to the other two. "Let's get finished. I feel it in my bones we're not going to find anything."

Blore was wrestling with the bolts of a low manhole. He said, "That chap moves damned quietly. A minute or two ago we saw him in the garden. None of us heard him come upstairs."

Lombard said, "I suppose that's why we assumed it must be a stranger moving about up here."

Blore disappeared into a cavernous darkness. Lombard pulled a torch from his pocket and followed. Five minutes later three men stood on an upper landing and looked at each other. They were dirty and festooned with cobwebs and their faces were grim. There was no one on the island but their eight selves.

9

Lombard said slowly, "So we've been wrong—wrong all along! Built up a nightmare of superstition and fantasy all because of the coincidence of two deaths!"

Armstrong said gravely, "And yet, you know, the argument holds. Hang it all, I'm a doctor, I know something about suicides. Anthony Marston wasn't a suicidal type."

Lombard said doubtfully, "It couldn't, I suppose, have been an accident?"

Blore snorted, unconvinced. "Damned queer sort of accident," he grunted.

There was a pause, then Blore said, "About the woman—" and stopped.

"Mrs. Rogers?"

"Yes. It's possible, isn't it, that that might have been an accident?"

Philip Lombard said, "An accident? In what way?"

Blore looked slightly embarrassed. His red-brick face grew a little deeper in hue. He said, almost blurting out the words, "Look here, doctor, you did give her some dope, you know."

Armstrong stared at him. "Dope? What do you mean?"

"Last night. You said yourself you'd give her something to make her sleep."

"Oh, that, yes. A harmless sedative."

"What was it exactly?"

"I gave her a mild dose of trional. A perfectly harmless preparation."

Blore grew redder still. He said, "Look here—not to mince matters—you didn't give her an overdose, did you?"

Dr. Armstrong said angrily, "I don't know what you mean."

Blore said, "It's possible, isn't it, that you may have made a mistake? These things do happen once in a while."

Armstrong said sharply, "I did nothing of the sort. The suggestion is ridiculous." He stopped and added in a cold, biting tone, "Or do you suggest that I gave her an overdose on purpose?"

Philip Lombard said quickly, "Look here, you two, got to keep our heads. Don't let's start slinging accusations about."

Blore said sullenly, "I only suggested the doctor had made a mistake."

Dr. Armstrong smiled with an effort. He said, showing his teeth in a somewhat mirthless smile, "Doctors can't afford to make mistakes of that kind, my friend."

Blore said deliberately, "It wouldn't be the first you've made—if that gramophone record is to be believed!"

Armstrong went white. Philip Lombard said quickly and angrily to Blore, "What's the sense of making yourself offensive? We're all in the same boat. We've got to pull together. What about your own pretty little spot of perjury?"

Blore took a step forward, his hands clenched. He said in a thick voice, "Perjury be damned! That's a foul lie! You may try and shut me up, Mr. Lombard, but there's things I want to know—and one of them is about *you!*"

Lombard's eyebrows rose. "About me?"

"Yes. I want to know why you brought a revolver down here on a pleasant social visit."

Lombard said, "You do, do you?"

"Yes, I do, Mr. Lombard."

Lombard said unexpectedly, "You know, Blore, you're not nearly such a fool as you look."

"That's as may be. What about that revolver?"

Lombard smiled. "I brought it because I expected to run into a spot of trouble."

Blore said suspiciously, "You didn't tell us that last night." Lombard shook his head.

"You were holding out on us?" Blore persisted.

"In a way, yes," said Lombard.

"Well, come on, out with it."

Lombard said slowly, "I allowed you all to think that I was asked here in the same way as most of the others. That's not quite true. As a matter of fact I was approached by a mysterious Johnny—Morris his name was. He offered me a hundred guineas to come down here and keep my eyes open—said I'd got a reputation for being a good man in a tight place."

"Well?" Blore prompted impatiently.

Lombard said with a grin, "That's all."

Dr. Armstrong said, "But surely he told you more than that?"

"Oh, no, he didn't. Just shut up like a clam. I could take it or leave it—those were his words. I was hard up. I took it."

Blore looked unconvinced. He said, "Why didn't you tell us all this last night?"

"My dear man—" Lombard shrugged eloquent shoulders. "How was I to know that last night wasn't exactly the eventuality I was here to cope with? I lay low and told a noncommittal story."

Dr. Armstrong said shrewdly, "But now—you think differently?"

Lombard's face changed. It darkened and hardened. He said, "Yes. I believe now that I'm in the same boat as the rest of you. That hundred guineas was just Mr. Owen's little bit of cheese to get me into the trap along with the rest of you." He said slowly, "*For we are in a trap*—I'll take my oath on that! Mrs. Rogers' death! Tony Marston's! The disappearing Indian boys on the dinner table! Oh, yes, Mr. Owen's hand is plainly to be seen—*but where the devil is Mr. Owen himself?*"

Downstairs the gong pealed a solemn call to lunch.

ii

Rogers was standing by the dining-room door. As the three men descended the stairs he moved a step or two forward. He said in a low, anxious voice, "I hope lunch will be satisfactory. There is cold ham and cold tongue, and I've boiled some potatoes. And there's cheese and biscuits and some tinned fruits."

Lombard said, "Sounds all right. Stores are holding out, then?"

"There is plenty of food, sir—of a tinned variety. The larder is very well stocked. A necessity, that, I should say, sir, on an island where one may be cut off from the mainland for a considerable period."

Lombard nodded. Rogers murmured as he followed the three men into the dining room: "It worries me that Fred Narracott hasn't been over today. It's peculiarly unfortunate, as you might say."

"Yes," said Lombard, "peculiarly unfortunate describes it very well."

Miss Brent came into the room. She had just dropped a ball of wool and was carefully rewinding the end of it. As she took her seat at table she remarked, "The weather is changing. The wind is quite strong and there are white horses on the sea."

Mr. Justice Wargrave came in. He walked with a slow measured tread. He darted quick looks from under his bushy eyebrows at the other occupants of the dining room. He said, "You have had an active morning." There was a faint malicious pleasure in his voice.

Vera Claythorne hurried in. She was a little out of breath. She said quickly, "I hope you didn't wait for me. Am I late?"

Emily Brent said, "You're not the last. The General isn't here yet."

They sat round the table. Rogers addressed Miss Brent, "Will you begin, madam, or will you wait?"

Vera said, "General Macarthur is sitting right down by the sea. I don't expect he would hear the gong there and anyway"—she hesitated—"he's a little vague today, I think."

Rogers said quickly, "I will go down and inform him luncheon is ready."

Dr. Armstrong jumped up. "I'll go," he said. "You others start lunch."

He left the room. Behind him he heard Rogers' voice. "Will you take cold tongue or cold ham, madam?"

iii

The five people sitting round the table seemed to find conversation difficult. Outside sudden gusts of wind came up and died away. Vera shivered a little and said, "There is a storm coming."

Blore made a contribution to the discourse. He said conversationally, "There was an old fellow in the train from Plymouth yesterday. *He* kept saying a storm was coming. Wonderful how they know weather, these old salts."

Rogers went round the table collecting the meat plates. Suddenly, with the plates held in his hands, he stopped. He said in an odd, scared voice, "There's somebody running. . . ."

They could all hear it—running feet along the terrace. In that minute, they knew—knew without being told. . . . As by common accord, they all rose to their feet. They stood looking towards the door. Dr. Armstrong appeared, his breath coming fast. He said, "General Macarthur—"

"Dead!" The word burst from Vera explosively.

Armstrong said, "Yes, he's dead. . . ." There was a pause—a long pause. Seven people looked at each other and could find no words to say.

iv

The storm broke just as the old man's body was borne in through the door. The others were standing in the hall. There was a sudden hiss and roar as the rain came down.

As Blore and Armstrong passed up the stairs with their burden, Vera Claythorne turned suddenly and went into the deserted dining room. It was as they had left it. The sweet course stood ready on the sideboard untasted. Vera went up to the table. She was there a minute or two later when Rogers came softly into the room. He started when he saw her. Then his eyes asked a question. He said, "Oh, miss, I—I just came to see . . ."

In a loud, harsh voice that surprised herself Vera said, "You're quite right, Rogers. Look for yourself. *There are only seven.* . . ."

v

General Macarthur had been laid on his bed. After making a last examination Armstrong left the room and came downstairs. He found the others assembled in the drawing room. Miss Brent was knitting. Vera Claythorne was standing by the window looking out at the hissing rain. Blore was sitting squarely in a chair, his hands on his knees. Lombard was walking restlessly up and down. At the far end of the room Mr. Justice Wargrave was sitting in a grandfather chair. His eyes were half-closed. They opened as the doctor came into the room. He said in a clear, penetrating voice, "Well, doctor?"

Armstrong was very pale. He said, "No question of heart failure or anything like that. Macarthur was hit with a life preserver or some such thing on the back of the head."

A little murmur went round, but the clear voice of the judge was raised once more. "Did you find the actual weapon used?"

"No."

"Nevertheless you are sure of your facts?"

"I am quite sure."

Mr. Justice Wargrave said quietly, "We know now exactly where we are."

There was no doubt now who was in charge of the situation. This morning Wargrave had sat huddled in his chair on the terrace refraining from any overt activity. Now he assumed command with the ease born of a long habit of authority. He definitely presided over the court. Clearing his throat, he once more spoke. "This morning, gentlemen, whilst I was sitting on the terrace, I was an observer of your activities. There could be little doubt of your purpose. You were searching the island for an unknown murderer?"

"Quite right, sir," said Philip Lombard.

The judge went on. "You had come, doubtless, to the same conclusion that I had—namely that the deaths of Anthony Marston and Mrs. Rogers were neither accidental nor were they suicides. No doubt you also reached a certain conclusion as to the purpose of Mr. Owen in enticing us to this island?"

Blore said hoarsely, "He's a madman! A loony."

The judge coughed. "That almost certainly. But it hardly affects the issue. Our main preoccupation is this—to save our lives."

Armstrong said in a trembling voice, "There's no one on the island, I tell you. *No one!*"

The judge stroked his jaw. He said gently, "In the sense you mean, no. I came to that conclusion early this morning. I could have told you that your search would be fruitless. Nevertheless I am strongly of the opinion that 'Mr. Owen' (to give him the name he himself has adopted) *is* on the island. Very much so. Given the scheme in question which is neither more nor less than the execution of justice upon certain individuals for offenses which the law cannot touch, *there is only one way in which that scheme could be accomplished.* Mr. Owen could only come to the island in one way. It is perfectly clear. *Mr. Owen is one of us. . . .*"

vi

"Oh, no, no, no . . ." It was Vera who burst out—almost in a moan.

The judge turned a keen eye on her. He said, "My dear young lady, this is no time for refusing to look facts in the face. We are all in grave danger. One of us is U. N. Owen. And we do not know which of us. Of the ten people who came to this island three are definitely cleared. Anthony Marston, Mrs. Rogers, and General Macarthur have gone beyond suspicion. There are seven of us left. Of those seven, one is, if I may so express myself, a bogus little Indian boy." He paused and looked round. "Do I take it that you all agree?"

Armstrong said, "It's fantastic—but I suppose you're right."

Blore said, "Not a doubt of it. And if you ask me, I've a very good idea—"

A quick gesture of Mr. Justice Wargrave's hand stopped him. The judge said quietly, "We will come to that presently. At the moment all I wish to establish is that we are in agreement on the facts."

Emily Brent, still knitting, said, "Your argument seems logical. I agree that one of us is possessed by a devil."

Vera murmured, "I can't believe it. . . . I can't. . . ."

Wargrave said, "Lombard?"

"I agree, sir, absolutely."

The judge nodded his head in a satisfied manner. He said, "Now let us examine the evidence. To begin with, is there any reason for suspecting one particular person? Mr. Blore, you have, I think, something to say."

Blore was breathing hard. He said, "Lombard's got a revolver. He didn't tell the truth—last night. He admits it."

Philip Lombard smiled scornfully. He said, "I suppose I'd better explain again." He did so, telling the story briefly and succinctly.

Blore said sharply, "What's to prove it? There's nothing to corroborate your story."

The judge coughed. "Unfortunately," he said, "we are all in that position. There is only our own word to go upon." He leaned forward.

"You have none of you yet grasped what a very peculiar situation this is. To my mind there is only one course of procedure to adopt. Is there anyone whom we can definitely eliminate from suspicion on the evidence which is in our possession?"

Dr. Armstrong said quickly, "I am a well-known professional man. The mere idea that I can be suspected of—"

Again a gesture of the judge's hand arrested a speaker before he finished his speech. Mr. Justice Wargrave said in his small, clear voice: "I, too, am a well-known person! But, my dear sir, that proves less than nothing! Doctors have gone mad before now. Judges have gone mad. So," he added, looking at Blore, "have policemen!"

Lombard said, "At any rate, I suppose you'll leave the women out of it."

The judge's eyebrows rose. He said in the famous "acid" tone that Counsel knew so well, "Do I understand you to assert that women are not subject to homicidal mania?"

Lombard said irritably, "Of course not. But all the same, it hardly seems possible—"

He stopped. Mr. Justice Wargrave, still in the same thin, sour voice, addressed Armstrong. "I take it, Dr. Armstrong, that a woman would have been physically capable of striking the blow that killed poor Macarthur?"

The doctor said calmly, "Perfectly capable—given a suitable instrument, such as a rubber truncheon or cosh."

"It would require no undue exertion of force?"

"Not at all."

Mr. Justice Wargrave wriggled his tortoiselike neck. He said, "The other two deaths have resulted from the administration of drugs. That, no one will dispute, is easily compassed by a person of the smallest physical strength."

Vera cried angrily, "I think you're mad!"

His eyes turned slowly till they rested on her. It was the dispassionate stare of a man well used to weighing humanity in the balance. She thought: He's just seeing me as a—as a specimen. And—the thought came to her with real surprise—he doesn't like me much!

In measured tones the judge was saying, "My dear young lady, do try and restrain your feelings. I am not accusing you." He bowed to Miss Brent. "I hope, Miss Brent, that you are not offended by my insistence that *all* of us are equally under suspicion?"

Emily Brent was knitting. She did not look up. In a cold voice she said, "The idea that I should be accused of taking a fellow creature's life—not to speak of the lives of *three* fellow creatures—is, of course, quite absurd to anyone who knows anything of my character. But I quite appreciate the fact that we are all strangers to one another and that in those circumstances nobody can be exonerated without the fullest proof. There is, as I have said, a devil amongst us."

The judge said, "Then we are agreed. There can be no elimination on the ground of character or position alone."

Lombard said, "What about Rogers?"

The judge looked at him unblinkingly. "What about him?"

Lombard said, "Well, to my mind, Rogers seems pretty well ruled out."

Mr. Justice Wargrave said, "Indeed, and on what grounds?"

Lombard said, "He hasn't got the brains, for one thing. And for another, his wife was one of the victims."

The judge's heavy eyebrows rose once more. He said, "In my time, young man, several people have come before me accused of the murders of their wives—and have been found guilty."

"Oh! I agree. Wife murder is perfectly possible—almost natural, let's say! But not this particular kind! I can believe in Rogers killing his wife because he was scared of her breaking down and giving him away, or because he'd taken a dislike to her, or because he wanted to link up with some nice little bit rather less long in the tooth. But I can't see him as the lunatic Mr. Owen dealing out crazy justice and starting on his own wife for a crime they both committed."

Mr. Justice Wargrave said, "You are assuming hearsay to be evidence. We do not know that Rogers and his wife conspired to murder their employer. That may have been a false statement, made so that Rogers should appear to be in the same position as ourselves. Mrs. Rogers' terror last night may have been due to the fact that she realized her husband was mentally unhinged."

Lombard said, "Well, have it your own way. U. N. Owen is one of us. No exceptions allowed. We all qualify."

Mr. Justice Wargrave said, "My point is that there can be no exceptions allowed on the score of *character, position,* or *probability.* What we must now examine is the possibility of eliminating one or more persons on the *facts.* To put it simply, is there among us one or more persons who could not possibly have administered either cyanide to Anthony Marston, or an overdose of sleeping draught to Mrs. Rogers, and who had no opportunity of striking the blow that killed General Macarthur?"

Blore's rather heavy face lit up. He leant forward. "Now you're talking, sir!" he said. "That's the stuff! Let's go into it. As regards young Marston I don't think there's anything to be done. It's already been suggested that someone from outside slipped something into the dregs of his glass before he refilled it for the last time. A person actually in the room could have done that even more easily. I can't remember if Rogers was in the room, but any of the rest of us could certainly have done it."

He paused, then went on. "Now take the woman Rogers. The people who stand out there are her husband and the doctor. Either of them could have done it as easy as winking—"

Armstrong sprang to his feet. He was trembling. "I protest—This is absolutely uncalled for! I swear that the dose I gave the woman was perfectly—"

"Dr. Armstrong." The small, sour voice was compelling. The doctor stopped with a jerk in the middle of his sentence. The small, cold voice went on. "Your indignation is very natural. Nevertheless you must admit that the facts have got to be faced. Either you or Rogers *could* have administered a fatal dose with the greatest ease. Let us now consider the position of the other people present. What chance had I, had Inspector Blore, had Miss Brent, had Miss Claythorne, had Mr. Lombard of administering poison? Can any one of us be completely and entirely eliminated?" He paused. "I think not."

Vera said angrily, "I was nowhere near the woman! All of you can swear to that."

Mr. Justice Wargrave waited a minute, then he said, "As far as my memory serves me the facts were these—will anyone please correct me if I make a misstatement? Mrs. Rogers was lifted onto the sofa by Anthony Marston and Mr. Lombard and Dr. Armstrong went to her. He sent Rogers for brandy. There was then a question raised as to where the voice we had just heard had come from. We all went into the next room with the exception of Miss Brent, who remained in this room—alone with the unconscious woman."

A spot of color came into Emily Brent's cheeks. She stopped knitting. She said, "This is outrageous!"

The remorseless small voice went on. "When we returned to this room, you, Miss Brent, were bending over the woman on the sofa."

Emily Brent said, "Is common humanity a criminal offense?"

Mr. Justice Wargrave said, "I am only establishing facts. Rogers then entered the room with the brandy which, of course, he could quite well have doctored before entering the room. The brandy was administered to the woman and shortly afterwards her husband and Dr. Armstrong assisted her up to bed where Dr. Armstrong gave her a sedative."

Blore said, "That's what happened. Absolutely. And that lets out the judge, Mr. Lombard, myself and Miss Claythorne."

His voice was loud and jubilant. Mr. Justice Wargrave, bringing a cold eye to bear upon him, murmured, "Ah, but does it? We must take into account *every possible eventuality*."

Blore stared. He said, "I don't get you."

Mr. Justice Wargrave said, "Upstairs in her room, Mrs. Rogers is lying in bed. The sedative that the doctor has given her begins to take effect. She is vaguely sleepy and acquiescent. Supposing that at that moment there is a tap on the door and someone enters bringing her, shall we say, a tablet, or a draught, with the message that 'the doctor says you're to take this.' Do you imagine for one minute that she would not have swallowed it obediently without thinking twice about it?"

There was silence. Blore shifted his feet and frowned. Philip Lombard said, "I don't believe in that story for a minute. Besides, none of us left this room for hours afterwards. There was Marston's death and all the rest of it."

The judge said, "Someone could have left his or her bedroom— later."

Lombard objected, "But then Rogers would have been up there."

Dr. Armstrong stirred. "No," he said. "Rogers went downstairs to clear up in the dining room and pantry. Anyone could have gone up to the woman's bedroom then without being seen."

Emily Brent said, "Surely, doctor, the woman would have been fast asleep by then under the influence of the drug you had administered?"

"In all likelihood, yes. But it is not a certainty. Until you have prescribed for a patient more than once you cannot tell their reaction to different drugs. There is, sometimes, a considerable period before a sedative takes effect. It depends on the personal idiosyncrasy of the patient towards that particular drug."

Lombard said, "Of course you *would* say that, doctor. Suits your book—eh?"

Again Armstrong's face darkened with anger. But again that passionless, cold little voice stopped the words on his lips. "No good result can come from recrimination. Facts are what we have to deal with. It is established, I think, that there is a possibility of such a thing as I have outlined occurring. I agree that its probability value is not high; though there again, it depends on who that person might have been. The appearance of Miss Brent or of Miss Claythorne on such an errand would have occasioned no surprise in the patient's mind. I agree that the appearance of myself, or of Mr. Blore, or of Mr. Lombard could have been, to say the least of it, unusual, but I still think the visit would have been received without the awakening of any real suspicion."

Blore said, "And that gets us—*where*?"

vii

Mr. Justice Wargrave, stroking his lip and looking quite passionless and inhuman, said, "We have now dealt with the second killing, and have established the fact that no one of us can be completely exonerated from suspicion." He paused and went on. "We come now to the death of General Macarthur. That took place this morning. I will ask anyone who considers that he or she has an alibi to state it in so many words. I myself will state at once that I have no valid alibi. I spent the morning sitting on the terrace and meditating on the singular position in which we all find ourselves. I sat on that chair on the terrace for the whole morning until the gong went, but there were, I should imagine, several periods during the morning when I was quite unobserved and during which it would have been possible for me to walk down to the sea, kill the General, and return to my chair. There is only my word for the fact that I never left the terrace. In the circumstances that is not enough. There must be *proof*."

Blore said, "I was with Mr. Lombard and Dr. Armstrong all the morning. They'll bear me out."

Dr. Armstrong said, "You went to the house for a rope."

Blore said, "Of course I did. Went straight there and straight back. You know I did."

Armstrong said, "You were a long time. . . ."

Blore turned crimson. He said, "What the hell do you mean by that, Dr. Armstrong?"

Armstrong repeated, "I only said you were a long time."

"Had to find it, didn't I? Can't lay your hands on a coil of rope all in a minute."

Mr. Justice Wargrave said, "During Inspector Blore's absence, were you two gentlemen together?"

Armstrong said hotly, "Certainly. That is, Lombard went off for a few minutes. I remained where I was."

Lombard said with a smile, "I wanted to test the possibilities of heliographing to the mainland. Wanted to find the best spot. I was only absent a minute or two."

Armstrong nodded. He said, "That's right. Not long enough to do a murder, I assure you."

The judge said, "Did either of you two glance at your watches?"

"Well, no."

Philip Lombard said, "I wasn't wearing one."

The judge said evenly, "A minute or two is a vague expression." He turned his head to the upright figure with her knitting on her lap. "Miss Brent?"

Emily Brent said, "I took a walk with Miss Claythorne up to the top of the island. Afterwards I sat on the terrace in the sun."

The judge said, "I don't think I noticed you there."

"No, I was round the corner of the house to the east. It was out of the wind there."

"And you sat there till lunch time?"

"Yes."

"Miss Claythorne?"

Vera answered readily and clearly. "I was with Miss Brent early this morning. After that I wandered about a bit. Then I went down and talked to General Macarthur."

Mr. Justice Wargrave interrupted. He said, "What time was that?"

Vera for the first time was vague. She said, "I don't know. About an hour before lunch, I think—or it might have been less."

Blore asked, "Was it after we'd spoken to him or before?"

Vera said, "I don't know. He—he was very queer." She shivered.

"In what way was he queer?" the judge wanted to know.

Vera said in a low voice, "He said we were all going to die—he said he was waiting for the end. He—he frightened me. . . ."

The judge nodded. He said, "What did you do next?"

"I went back to the house. Then, just before lunch, I went out again and up behind the house. I've been terribly restless all day."

Mr. Justice Wargrave stroked his chin. He said, "There remains Rogers. Though I doubt if his evidence will add anything to our sum of knowledge."

Rogers, summoned before the court, had very little to tell. He had been busy all the morning about household duties and with the preparation of lunch. He had taken cocktails onto the terrace before lunch and had then gone up to remove his things from the attic to another room. He had not looked out of the window during the morning and had seen nothing that could have any bearing upon the death of General Macarthur. He would swear definitely that there had been eight china figures upon the dining table when he laid the table for lunch.

At the conclusion of Rogers' evidence there was a pause. Mr. Justice Wargrave cleared his throat. Lombard murmured to Vera Claythorne, "The summing up will now take place!"

The judge said, "We have inquired into the circumstances of these three deaths to the best of our ability. Whilst probability in some cases is against certain people being implicated, yet we cannot say definitely that any one person can be considered as cleared of all complicity. I reiterate my positive belief that of the seven persons assembled in this room one is a dangerous and probably insane criminal. There is no evidence before us as to who that person is. All we can do at the present juncture is to consider what measures we can take for communicating with the mainland for help, and in the event of help being delayed (as is only too possible given the state of the weather) what measures we must adopt to ensure our safety.

"I would ask you all to consider this carefully and to give me any suggestions that may occur to you. In the meantime I warn everybody to be upon his or her guard. So far the murderer has had an easy task, since his victims have been unsuspicious. From now on, it is our task to suspect each and every one amongst us. Forewarned is forearmed. Take no risks and be alert to danger. That is all."

Philip Lombard murmured beneath his breath, "The court will now adjourn. . . ."

10

"Do you believe it?" Vera asked. She and Philip Lombard sat on the window sill of the living room. Outside the rain poured down and the wind howled in great shuddering gusts against the window panes. Philip Lombard cocked his head slightly on one side before answering. Then he said, "You mean, do I believe that old Wargrave is right when he says it's one of us?"

"Yes."

Philip Lombard said slowly, "It's difficult to say. Logically, you know, he's right, and yet—"

Vera took the words out of his mouth. "And yet it seems so incredible!"

Philip Lombard made a grimace. "The whole thing's incredible! But after Macarthur's death there's no more doubt as to one thing. There's no question now of accidents or suicides. It's definitely murder. Three murders up to date."

Vera shivered. She said, "It's like some awful dream. I keep feeling that things like this *can't* happen!"

He said with understanding, "I know. Presently a tap will come on the door, and early-morning tea will be brought in."

Vera said, "Oh, how I wish that could happen!"

Philip Lombard said gravely, "Yes, but it won't! We're all in the dream! And we've got to be pretty much upon our guard from now on."

Vera said, lowering her voice, "If—if it *is* one of them—which do you think it is?"

Philip Lombard grinned suddenly. He said, "I take it you are excepting our two selves? Well, that's all right. I know very well that I'm not the murderer, and I don't fancy that there's anything insane about you, Vera. You strike me as being one of the sanest and most level-headed girls I've come across. I'd stake my reputation on your sanity."

With a slightly wry smile, Vera said, "Thank you."

He said, "Come now, Miss Vera Claythorne, aren't you going to return the compliment?"

Vera hesitated a minute, then she said, "You've admitted, you know, that you don't hold human life particularly sacred, but all the same I can't see you as—as the man who dictated that gramophone record."

Lombard said, "Quite right. If I were to commit one or more murders it would be solely for what I could get out of them. This mass clearance isn't my line of country. Good, then we'll eliminate ourselves and concentrate on our five fellow prisoners. Which of them is U. N. Owen? Well, at a guess, and with absolutely nothing to go upon, I'd plump for Wargrave!"

"Oh!" Vera sounded surprised. She thought a minute or two and then said, "Why?"

"Hard to say exactly. But to begin with, he's an old man and he's been presiding over courts of law for years. That is to say, he's played God Almighty for a good many months every year. That must go to a man's head eventually. He gets to see himself as all-powerful, as holding the power of life and death—and it's possible that his brain might snap and he might want to go one step farther and be Executioner and Judge Extraordinary."

Vera said slowly, "Yes, I suppose that's *possible*. . . ."

Lombard said, "Who do you plump for?"

Without any hesitation Vera answered, "Dr. Armstrong."

Lombard gave a low whistle. "The doctor, eh? You know, I should have put him last of all."

Vera shook her head. "Oh, no! Two of the deaths have been poison. That rather points to a doctor. And then you can't get over the fact that the only thing we are certain Mrs. Rogers had was the sleeping draught that *he* gave her."

Lombard admitted, "Yes, that's true."

Vera persisted, "If a doctor went mad, it would be a long time before anyone suspected. And doctors overwork and have a lot of strain."

Philip Lombard said, "Yes, but I doubt if he could have killed

Macarthur. He wouldn't have had time during that brief interval when I left him—not, that is, unless he fairly hared down there and back again, and I doubt if he's in good enough training to do that and show no signs of it."

Vera said, "He didn't do it then. He had an opportunity later."

"When?"

"When he went down to call the General to lunch."

Philip whistled again very softly. He said, "So you think he did it then? Pretty cool thing to do."

Vera said impatiently, "What risk was there? He's the only person here with medical knowledge. He can swear the body's been dead at least an hour and who's to contradict him?"

Philip looked at her thoughtfully. "You know," he said, "that's a clever idea of yours. I wonder—"

ii

"Who is it, Mr. Blore? That's what I want to know. Who is it?" Rogers' face was working. His hands were clenched tightly round the polishing leather that he had just then been using.

Ex-Inspector Blore said, "Eh, my lad, that's the question!"

"One of us, 'is lordship said. Which one? That's what I want to know. Who's the fiend in 'uman form?"

"That, " said Blore, "is what we all would like to know."

Rogers said shrewdly, "But you've got an idea, Mr. Blore. You've got an idea, 'aven't you?"

"I may have an idea," said Blore slowly. "But that's a long way from being sure. I may be wrong. All I can say is that if I'm right the person in question is a very cool customer—a very cool customer indeed."

Rogers wiped the perspiration from his forehead. He said hoarsely, "It's like a bad dream, that's what it is."

Blore said, looking at him curiously, "Got any ideas yourself, Rogers?"

The butler shook his head. He said hoarsely, "I don't know. I don't know at all. And that's what's frightening the life out of me. To have no idea. . . ."

iii

Dr. Armstrong said violently, "We must get out of here—we must—we must! At all costs!"

Mr. Justice Wargrave looked thoughtfully out of the smoking-room window. He played with the cord of his eyeglasses. He said, "I do not, of course, profess to be a weather prophet. But I should say that it is very unlikely that a boat could reach us—even if they knew of our plight—under twenty-four hours—and even then only if the wind drops."

Dr. Armstrong dropped his head in his hands and groaned. He said, "And in the meantime we may all be murdered in our beds?"

"I hope not," said Mr. Justice Wargrave. "I intend to take every possible precaution against such a thing happening."

It flashed across Dr. Armstrong's mind that an old man like the judge was far more tenacious of life than a younger man would be. He had often marveled at that fact in his professional career. Here was he, junior to the judge by perhaps twenty years, and yet with a vastly inferior sense of self-preservation.

Mr. Justice Wargrave was thinking: Murdered in our beds! These doctors are all the same—they think in clichés. A thoroughly commonplace mind.

The doctor said, "There have been three victims already, remember."

"Certainly. But you must remember that they were unprepared for the attack. We are forewarned."

Dr. Armstrong said bitterly, "What can we do? Sooner or later—"

"I think," said Mr. Justice Wargrave, "that there are several things we can do."

Armstrong said, "We've no idea, even, who it can be—"

The judge stroked his chin and murmured, "Oh, you know, I wouldn't quite say that."

Armstrong stared at him. "Do you mean you *know*?"

Mr. Justice Wargrave said cautiously, "As regards actual evidence, such as is necessary in court, I admit that I have none. But it appears to me, reviewing the whole business, that one particular person is sufficiently clearly indicated. Yes, I think so."

Armstrong stared at him. He said, "I don't understand."

iv

Miss Brent was upstairs in her bedroom. She took up her Bible and went to sit by the window. She opened it. Then, after a minute's hesitation, she set it aside and went over to the dressing table. From a drawer in it she took out a small black-covered notebook. She opened it and began writing.

> A terrible thing has happened. General Macarthur is dead. (His cousin married Elsie MacPherson.) There is no doubt but that he was murdered. After luncheon the judge made us a most interesting speech. He is convinced that the murderer is one of us. That means that one of us is possessed by a devil. I had already suspected that. Which of us is it? They are all asking themselves that. I alone know . . . .

She sat for some time without moving. Her eyes grew vague and filmy. The pencil straggled drunkenly in her fingers. In shaking loose capitals she wrote: THE MURDERER'S NAME IS BEATRICE TAYLOR. . . . Her eyes closed. Suddenly, with a start, she awoke. She looked down at the notebook. With an angry exclamation she scored through the vague, unevenly scrawled characters of the last sentence. She said in a low voice: "Did *I* write that? Did I? *I must be going mad. . . .*"

v

The storm increased. The wind howled against the side of the house. Everyone was in the living room. They sat listlessly huddled together. And, surreptitiously, they watched each other. When Rogers brought in the tea tray, they all jumped. He said: "Shall I draw the curtains? It would make it more cheerful-like."

Receiving an assent to this, the curtains were drawn and the lamps turned on. The room grew more cheerful. A little of the shadow lifted. Surely, by tomorrow, the storm would be over and someone would come—a boat would arrive. . . .

Vera Claythorne said, "Will you pour out tea, Miss Brent?"

The elder woman replied, "No, you do it, dear. That teapot is so heavy. And I have lost two skeins of my gray knitting wool. So annoying." Vera moved to the tea table. There was a cheerful rattle and clink of china. Normality returned.

Tea! Blessed ordinary everyday afternoon tea! Philip Lombard made a cheery remark. Blore responded. Dr. Armstrong told a humorous story. Mr. Justice Wargrave, who ordinarily hated tea, sipped approvingly.

Into this relaxed atmosphere came Rogers. And Rogers was upset. He said nervously and at random, "Excuse me, sir, but does anyone know what's become of the bathroom curtain?"

Lombard's head went up with a jerk. "The bathroom curtain? What the devil do you mean, Rogers?"

"It's gone, sir, clean vanished. I was going round drawing all the curtains and the one in the lav—bathroom wasn't there any longer."

Mr. Justice Wargrave asked, "Was it there this morning?"

"Oh, yes, sir."

Blore said, "What kind of a curtain was it?"

"Scarlet oilsilk, sir. It went with the scarlet tiles."

Lombard said, "And it's gone?"

"Gone, sir."

They stared at each other. Blore said heavily, "Well—after all—what of it? It's mad—but so's everything else. Anyway, it doesn't matter. You can't kill anybody with an oilsilk curtain. Forget about it."

Rogers said, "Yes, sir, thank you, sir." He went out, shutting the door behind him.

Inside the room, the pall of fear had fallen anew. Again, surreptitiously, they watched each other.

vi

Dinner came, was eaten, and cleared away. A simple meal, mostly out of tins. Afterwards, in the living room, the strain was almost too great to be borne. At nine o'clock, Emily Brent rose to her feet. She said, "I'm going to bed."

Vera said, "I'll go to bed too."

The two women went up the stairs and Lombard and Blore came with them. Standing at the top of the stairs, the two men watched the women go into their respective rooms and shut the doors. They heard the sound of two bolts being shot and the turning of two keys. Blore said with a grin, "No need to tell 'em to lock their doors!"

Lombard said, "Well, *they*'re all right for the night, at any rate!"

He went down again and the other followed him.

vii

The four men went to bed an hour later. They went up together. Rogers, from the dining room where he was setting the table for breakfast, saw them go up. He heard them pause on the landing above. Then the judge's voice spoke. "I need hardly advise you, gentlemen, to lock your doors."

Blore said, "And, what's more, put a chair under the handle. There are ways of turning locks from the outside."

Lombard murmured, "My dear Blore, the trouble with you is you know too much!"

The judge said gravely, "Good night, gentlemen. May we all meet safely in the morning!"

Rogers came out of the dining room and slipped halfway up the stairs. He saw four figures pass through four doors and heard the turning of four locks and the shooting of four bolts. He nodded his head. "That's all right," he muttered.

He went back into the dining room. Yes, everything was ready for the morning. His eye lingered on the center plaque of looking glass and the seven little china figures. A sudden grin transformed his face. He murmured, "I'll see no one plays tricks tonight, at any rate."

Crossing the room he locked the door to the pantry. Then, going through the other door to the hall he pulled the door to, locked it and slipped the key into his pocket. Then, extinguishing the lights, he hurried up the stairs and into his new bedroom.

There was only one possible hiding place in it, the tall wardrobe, and he looked into that immediately. Then, locking and bolting the door, he prepared for bed. He said to himself, "No more Indian tricks tonight. I've seen to that. . . . "

11

PHILIP LOMBARD had the habit of waking at daybreak. He did so on this particular morning. He raised himself on an elbow and listened. The wind had somewhat abated but was still blowing. He could hear no sound of rain . . . . At eight o'clock the wind was blowing more strongly, but Lombard did not hear it. He was asleep again.

At nine-thirty he was sitting on the edge of his bed looking at his watch. He put it to his ear. Then his lips drew back from his teeth in that curious wolflike smile characteristic of the man. He said very softly, "I think the time has come to do something about this."

At twenty-five minutes to ten he was tapping on the closed door of Blore's room. The latter opened it cautiously. His hair was tousled and his eyes were still dim with sleep. Philip Lombard said affably, "Sleeping the clock round? Well, shows you've got an easy conscience."

Blore said shortly, "What's the matter?"

Lombard answered, "Anybody called you—or brought you any tea? Do you know what time it is?"

Blore looked over his shoulder at a small traveling clock by his bedside. He said, "Twenty-five to ten. Wouldn't have believed I could have slept like that. Where's Rogers?"

Philip Lombard said, "It's a case of echo answers where."

"What d'you mean?" asked the other sharply.

Lombard said, "I mean that Rogers is missing. He isn't in his room or anywhere else. And there's no kettle on and the kitchen fire isn't even lit."

Blore swore under his breath. He said, "Where the devil can he be? Out on the island somewhere? Wait till I get some clothes on. See if the others know anything."

Philip Lombard nodded. He moved along the line of closed doors. He found Armstrong up and nearly dressed. Mr. Justice Wargrave, like Blore, had to be roused from sleep. Vera Claythorne was dressed. Emily Brent's room was empty.

The little party moved through the house. Rogers' room, as Philip Lombard had already ascertained, was untenanted. The bed had been slept in, and his razor and sponge and soap were wet. Lombard said, "He got up, all right."

Vera said in a low voice which she tried to make firm and assured, "You don't think he's—hiding somewhere—waiting for us?"

Lombard said, "My dear girl, I'm prepared to think anything of anyone! My advice is that we keep together until we find him."

Armstrong said, "He must be out on the island somewhere."

Blore, who had joined them, dressed but still unshaved, said, "Where's Miss Brent got to—that's another mystery?"

But as they arrived in the hall, Emily Brent came in through the front door. She had on a mackintosh. She said, "The sea is as high as ever. I shouldn't think any boat could put out today."

Blore said, "Have you been wandering about the island alone, Miss Brent? Don't you realize that that's an exceedingly foolish thing to do?"

Emily Brent said, "I assure you, Mr. Blore, that I kept an extremely sharp lookout."

Blore grunted. He said, "Seen anything of Rogers?"

Miss Brent's eyebrows rose. "Rogers? No, I haven't seen him this morning. Why?"

Mr. Justice Wargrave, shaved, dressed and with his false teeth in position, came down the stairs. He moved to the open dining-room door. He said, "Ha, laid the table for breakfast, I see."

Lombard said, "He might have done that last night."

They all moved inside the room, looking at the neatly set plates and cutlery. At the row of cups on the sideboard. At the felt mats placed ready for the coffee urn. It was Vera who saw it first. She caught the judge's arm and the grip of her athletic fingers made the old gentleman wince. She cried out, "The Indians! Look!"

There were only six china figures in the middle of the table.

ii

They found him shortly afterwards. He was in the little wash house across the yard. He had been chopping sticks in preparation for lighting the kitchen fire. The small chopper was still in his hand. A bigger chopper, a heavy affair, was leaning against the door—the metal of it stained a dull brown. It corresponded only too well with the deep wound in the back of Rogers' head. . . .

iii

"Perfectly clear," said Armstrong. "The murderer must have crept up behind him, swung the chopper once and brought it down on his head as he was bending over."

Blore was busy on the handle of the chopper and the flour sifter from the kitchen. Mr. Justice Wargrave asked, "Would it have needed great force, doctor?"

Armstrong said gravely, "A woman could have done it if that's what you mean." He gave a quick glance round. Vera Claythorne and Emily Brent had retired to the kitchen. "The girl could have done it easily—she's an athletic type. In appearance Miss Brent is fragile looking, but that type of woman has often a lot of wiry strength. And you must remember that anyone who's mentally unhinged has a good deal of unsuspected strength."

The judge nodded thoughtfully. Blore rose from his knees with a sigh. He said, "No fingerprints. Handle was wiped afterwards."

A sound of laughter was heard—they turned sharply. Vera Clay-thorne was standing in the yard. She cried out in a high, shrill voice, shaken with wild bursts of laughter, "Do they keep bees on this island? Tell me that. Where do we go for honey? Ha! ha!"

They stared at her uncomprehendingly. It was as though the sane, well-balanced girl had gone mad before their eyes. She went on in that high, unnatural voice, "Don't stare like that! As though you thought I was mad. It's sane enough what I'm asking. Bees, hives, bees! Oh, don't you understand? Haven't you read that idiotic rhyme? It's up in all your bedrooms—put there for you to study! We might have come here straightaway if we'd had sense. *Seven little Indian boys chopping up sticks.* And the next verse. I know the whole thing by heart, I tell you! *Six little Indian boys playing with a hive.* And that's why I'm asking—do they keep bees on this island?—isn't it funny?—isn't it damned funny. . . ?"

She began laughing wildly again. Dr. Armstrong strode forward. He raised his hand and struck her a flat blow on the cheek. She gasped, hiccuped—and swallowed. She stood motionless a minute, then she said, "Thank you . . . I'm all right now." Her voice was once more calm and controlled—the voice of the efficient games mistress.

She turned and went across the yard into the kitchen saying, "Miss Brent and I are getting you breakfast. Can you—bring some sticks to light the fire?" The marks of the doctor's hand stood out red on her cheek.

As she went into the kitchen Blore said, "Well, you dealt with that all right, doctor."

Armstrong said apologetically, "Had to! We can't cope with hysteria on the top of everything else."

Philip Lombard said, "She's not a hysterical type."

Armstrong agreed. "Oh, no. Good healthy sensible girl. Just the sudden shock. It might happen to anybody."

Rogers had chopped a certain amount of firewood before he had been killed. They gathered it up and took it into the kitchen. Vera and Emily Brent were busy. Miss Brent was raking out the stove. Vera was cutting the rind off the bacon. Emily Brent said, "Thank you. We'll be as quick as we can—say half an hour to three-quarters. The kettle's got to boil."

iv

Ex-Inspector Blore said in a low, hoarse voice to Philip Lombard, "Know what I'm thinking?"

Philip Lombard said, "As you're just about to tell me, it's not worth the trouble of guessing."

Ex-Inspector Blore was an earnest man. A light touch was incomprehensible to him. He went on heavily, "There was a case in America. Old gentleman and his wife—both killed with an ax. Middle of the morning. Nobody in the house but the daughter and the maid. Maid, it was proved, couldn't have done it. Daughter was a respectable middle-aged spinster. Seemed incredible. So incredible that they acquitted her. But they never found any other explanation." He paused. "I thought of that when I saw the ax—and then when I went into the kitchen and saw her there so neat and calm. Hadn't turned a hair! That girl, coming all over hysterical—well, that's natural—the sort of thing you'd expect—don't you think so?"

Philip Lombard said laconically, "It might be."

Blore went on. "But the other! So neat and prim—wrapped up in that apron—Mrs. Rogers' apron, I suppose—saying, 'Breakfast will be ready in half an hour or so.' If you ask me, that woman's as mad as a hatter! Lots of elderly spinsters go that way—I don't mean go in for homicide on the grand scale, but go queer in their heads. Unfortunately it's taken her this way. Religious mania—thinks she's God's instrument, something of that kind! She sits in her room, you know, reading her Bible."

Philip Lombard sighed and said, "That's hardly proof positive of an unbalanced mentality, Blore."

But Blore went on, ploddingly, perseveringly: "And then she was out—in her mackintosh, said she'd been down to look at the sea."

The other shook his head. He said, "Rogers was killed as he was chopping firewood—that is to say first thing when he got up. The Brent wouldn't have needed to wander about outside for hours afterwards. If you ask me, the murderer of Rogers would take jolly good care to be rolled up in bed snoring."

Blore said, "You're missing the point, Mr. Lombard. If the woman was innocent she'd be too dead scared to go wandering about by herself. She'd only do that *if she knew that she had nothing to fear.* That's to say *if she herself is the criminal.*"

Philip Lombard said, "That's a good point. . . . Yes, I hadn't thought of that." He added with a faint grin, "Glad you don't still suspect me."

Blore said rather shamefacedly, "I did start by thinking of you—that revolver—and the queer story you told—or didn't tell. But I've realized now that that was really a bit too obvious." He paused and said, "Hope you feel the same about me."

Philip said thoughtfully, "I may be wrong, of course, but I can't feel that you've got enough imagination for this job. All I can say is, if you're the criminal, you're a damned fine actor and I take my hat off to you." He lowered his voice. "Just between ourselves, Blore, and taking into account that we'll probably both be a couple of stiffs before another day is out, you did indulge in that spot of perjury, I suppose?"

Blore shifted uneasily from one foot to the other. He said at last, "Doesn't seem to make much odds now. Oh, well, here goes. Landor was innocent right enough. The gang had got me squared and between us we got him put away for a stretch. Mind you, I wouldn't admit this—"

"If there were any witnesses," finished Lombard with a grin. "It's just between you and me. Well, I hope you made a tidy bit out of it."

"Didn't make what I should have done. Mean crowd, the Purcell gang. I got my promotion, though."

"And Landor got penal servitude and died in prison."

"I couldn't know he was going to die, could I?" demanded Blore.

"No, that was your bad luck."

"Mine? His, you mean."

"Yours, too. Because, as a result of it, it looks as though your own life is going to be cut unpleasantly short."

"Me?" Blore stared at him. "Do you think I'm going to go the way of Rogers and the rest of them? Not me! I'm watching out for myself pretty carefully, I can tell you."

Lombard said, "Oh, well—I'm not a betting man. And anyway if you were dead I wouldn't get paid."

"Look here, Mr. Lombard, what do you mean?"

Philip Lombard showed his teeth. He said, "I mean, my dear Blore, that in my opinion you haven't got a chance!"

"What?"

"Your lack of imagination is going to make you absolutely a sitting target. A criminal of the imagination of U.N. Owen can make rings round you any time he—or she—wants to."

Blore's face went crimson. He demanded angrily, "And what about you?"

Philip Lombard's face went hard and dangerous. He said, "I've a pretty good imagination of my own. I've been in tight places before now and got out of them! I think—I won't say more than that but I *think* I'll get out of this one."

V

The eggs were in the frying pan. Vera, at the stove, thought to herself: Why did I make a hysterical fool of myself? That was a mistake. Keep calm, my girl, keep calm. After all, she'd always prided herself on her level-headedness!

"Miss Claythorne was wonderful—kept her head—started off swimming after Cyril at once."

Why think of that now? All that was over—over.... Cyril had disappeared long before she got near the rock. She had felt the current take her, sweeping her out to sea. She had let herself go with it—swimming quietly, floating—till the boat arrived at last.... They had praised her courage and her *sang-froid.... But not Hugo. Hugo had just—looked at her....* God, how it hurt, even now, to think of Hugo.... *Where was he? What was he doing? Was he engaged—married?*

Emily Brent said sharply, "Vera, that bacon is burning."

"Oh, sorry, Miss Brent, so it is. How stupid of me."

Emily Brent lifted out the last egg from the sizzling fat. Vera, putting fresh pieces of bacon in the frying pan, said curiously, "You're wonderfully calm, Miss Brent."

Emily Brent said, pressing her lips together, "I was brought up to keep my head and never to make a fuss."

Vera thought mechanically: Repressed as a child ... That accounts for a lot.... She said, "Aren't you afraid?" She paused and then added, "Or don't you mind dying?"

Dying! It was as though a sharp little gimlet had run into the solid congealed mass of Emily Brent's brain. Dying? But *she* wasn't going to die! The others would die—yes—but not she, Emily Brent. This girl didn't understand! Emily wasn't afraid, naturally—none of the Brents were afraid. All her people were Service people. They faced death unflinchingly. They led upright lives just as she, Emily Brent, had led an upright life.... She had never done anything to be ashamed of.... And so, naturally, *she* wasn't going to die....

"The Lord is mindful of His own." "Thou shalt not be afraid for the terror by night; nor for the arrow that flieth by day...." It was daylight now—there was no terror. *"We shall none of us leave this island."* Who had said that? General Macarthur, of course, whose cousin had married Elsie MacPherson. He hadn't seemed to *care*. He had seemed—actually—to *welcome* the idea! Wicked! Almost impious to feel that way. Some people thought so little of death that they actually took their own lives. *Beatrice Taylor....* Last night she had dreamed of Beatrice—dreamt that she was outside pressing her face against the

window and moaning, asking to be let in. But Emily Brent hadn't wanted to let her in. Because, if she did, something terrible would happen . . . .

Emily came to herself with a start. That girl was looking at her very strangely. She said in a brisk voice, "Everything's ready, isn't it? We'll take the breakfast in."

vi

Breakfast was a curious meal. Everyone was very polite. . . . "May I get you some more coffee, Miss Brent?". . . "Miss Claythorne, a slice of ham?". . . "Another piece of bacon?". . . Six people, all outwardly self-possessed and normal.

And within? Thoughts that ran round in a circle like squirrels in a cage. . . . *"What next? What next? Who? Which?. . ."* *"Would it work? I wonder. It's worth trying. If there's time. My God, if there's time. . . ."* *"Religious mania, that's the ticket. . . . Looking at her, though, you can hardly believe it. . . . Suppose I'm wrong. . . ."* *"It's crazy—everything's crazy. I'm going crazy. Wool disappearing—red silk curtains—it doesn't make sense. I can't get the hang of it. . . ."* *"The damned fool, he believed every word I said to him. It was easy. . . . I must be careful, though, very careful."* *"Six of those little china figures . . . only six—how many will there be by tonight?. . ."*

"Who'll have the last egg?"

"Marmalade?"

"Thanks, can I give you some ham?"

Six people, behaving normally at breakfast. . . .

12

THE MEAL WAS OVER. Mr. Justice Wargrave cleared his throat. He said in a small, authoritative voice, "It would be advisable, I think, if we met to discuss the situation. Shall we say in half an hour's time in the drawing room?"

Everyone made a sound suggestive of agreement. Vera began to pile plates together. She said, "I'll clear away and wash up."

Philip Lombard said, "We'll bring the stuff out to the pantry for you."

"Thanks."

Emily Brent, rising to her feet, sat down again. She said, "Oh, dear."

The judge said, "Anything the matter, Miss Brent?"

Emily said apologetically, "I'm sorry. I'd like to help Miss Claythorne, but I don't know how it is. I feel just a little giddy."

"Giddy, eh?" Dr. Armstrong came towards her. "Quite natural. Delayed shock. I can give you something to—"

"No!" The word burst from her lips like an exploding shell. It took everyone aback. Dr. Armstrong flushed a deep red.

There was no mistaking the fear and suspicion in her face. He said stiffly, "Just as you please, Miss Brent."

She said, "I don't wish to take anything—anything at all. I will just sit here quietly till the giddiness passes off."

They finished clearing away the breakfast things. Blore said, "I'm a domestic sort of man. I'll give you a hand, Miss Claythorne."

Vera said, "Thank you."

Emily Brent was left alone sitting in the dining room. For a while she heard a faint murmur of voices from the pantry. The giddiness was passing. She felt drowsy now, as though she could easily go to sleep. There was a buzzing in her ears—or was it a real buzzing in the room? She thought: It's like a bee—a bumblebee.

Presently she saw the bee. It was crawling up the window pane. Vera Claythorne had talked about bees this morning.

Bees and honey . . . She liked honey. Honey in the comb, and strain it yourself through a muslin bag. Drip, drip, drip . . .

There was somebody in the room . . . somebody all wet and dripping . . . *Beatrice Taylor came from the river. . . .* She had only to turn her head and she would see her.

But she couldn't turn her head. . . .

If she were to call out . . . But she couldn't call out. . . . There was no one else in the house. She was all alone. . . . She heard footsteps—soft, dragging footsteps coming up behind her. The stumbling footsteps of the drowned girl. . . . There was a wet, dank smell in her nostrils. . . . On the window pane the bee was buzzing—buzzing. . . . And then she felt the prick. The bee sting on the side of her neck. . . .

ii

In the drawing room they were waiting for Emily Brent. Vera Claythorne said, "Shall I go and fetch her?"

Blore said quickly, "Just a minute."

Vera sat down again. Everyone looked inquiringly at Blore. He said, "Look here, everybody, my opinion's this: we needn't look farther for the author of these deaths than the dining room at this minute. I'd take my oath that woman's the one we're after!"

Armstrong said, "And the motive?"

"Religious mania. What do you say, doctor?"

Armstrong said, "It's perfectly possible. I've nothing to say against it. But of course we've no proof."

Vera said, "She was very odd in the kitchen when we were getting breakfast. Her eyes—" She shivered.

Lombard said, "You can't judge her by that. We're all a bit off our heads by now!"

Blore said, "There's another thing. She's the only one who wouldn't give an explanation after that gramophone record. Why? Because she hadn't any to give."

Vera stirred in her chair. She said, "That's not quite true. She told me—afterwards."

Wargrave said, "What did she tell you, Miss Claythorne?"

Vera repeated the story of Beatrice Taylor. Mr. Justice Wargrave observed, "A perfectly straightforward story. I personally should have no difficulty in accepting it. Tell me, Miss Claythorne, did she appear to be troubled by a sense of guilt or a feeling of remorse for her attitude in the matter?"

"None whatever," said Vera. "She was completely unmoved."

Blore said, "Hearts as hard as flints, these righteous spinsters! Envy, mostly!"

Mr. Justice Wargrave said, "It is now five minutes to eleven. I think we should summon Miss Brent to join our conclave."

Blore said, "Aren't you going to take any action?"

The judge said, "I fail to see what action we can take. Our suspicions are, at the moment, only suspicions. I will, however, ask Dr. Armstrong to observe Miss Brent's demeanor very carefully. Let us now go into the dining room."

They found Emily Brent sitting in the chair in which they had left her. From behind they saw nothing amiss, except that she did not seem to hear their entrance into the room.

And then they saw her face—suffused with blood, with blue lips and starting eyes. Blore said, "My God, she's dead!"

iii

The small, quiet voice of Mr. Justice Wargrave said, "One more of us acquitted—too late!"

Armstrong was bent over the dead woman. He sniffed the lips, shook his head, peered into the eyelids. Lombard said impatiently, "How did she die, doctor? She was all right when we left her here!"

Armstrong's attention was riveted on a mark on the right side of the neck. He said, "That's the mark of a hypodermic syringe."

There was a buzzing sound from the window. Vera cried, "Look—a bee—*a bumblebee*. Remember what I said this morning!"

Armstrong said grimly, "It wasn't that bee that stung her! A human hand held the syringe."

The judge asked, "What poison was injected?"

Armstrong answered, "At a guess, one of the cyanides. Probably potassium cyanide, same as Anthony Marston. She must have died almost immediately by asphyxiation."

Vera cried, "But that *bee*? It can't be *coincidence*!"

Lombard said grimly, "Oh, no, it isn't coincidence! It's our murderer's touch of local color! He's a playful beast. Likes to stick to his damnable nursery jingle as closely as possible!" For the first time his voice was uneven, almost shrill. It was as though even his nerves, seasoned by a long career of hazards and dangerous undertakings, had given out at last. He said violently, "It's mad!—absolutely mad— we're all mad!"

The judge said calmly, "We have still, I hope, our reasoning powers. *Did anyone bring a hypodermic syringe to this house?*"

Dr. Armstrong, straightening himself, said in a voice that was not too well assured, "Yes, I did."

Four pairs of eyes fastened on him. He braced himself against the deep, hostile suspicion of those eyes. He said, "Always travel with one. Most doctors do."

Mr. Justice Wargrave said calmly, "Quite so. Will you tell us, doctor, where that syringe is now?"

"In the suitcase in my room."

Wargrave said, "We might, perhaps, verify that fact."

The five of them went upstairs, a silent procession. The contents of the suitcase were turned out on the floor. The hypodermic syringe was not there.

iv

Armstrong said violently, "Somebody must have taken it!"

There was silence in the room. Armstrong stood with his back to the window. Four pairs of eyes were on him, black with suspicion and accusation. He looked from Wargrave to Vera and repeated helplessly—weakly, "I tell you someone must have taken it."

Blore was looking at Lombard, who returned his gaze. The judge said, "There are five of us here in this room. *One of us is a murderer.* The position is fraught with grave danger. Everything must be done in order to safeguard the four of us who are innocent. I will now ask you, Dr. Armstrong, what drugs you have in your possession?"

Armstrong replied, "I have a small medicine case here. You can examine it. You will find some sleeping stuff—trional and sulphonal tablets—a packet of bromide, bicarbonate of soda, aspirin. Nothing else. I have no cyanide in my possession."

The judge said, "I have myself, some sleeping tablets—sulphonal, I think they are. I presume they would be lethal if a sufficiently large dose were given. You, Mr. Lombard, have in your possession a revolver."

Philip Lombard said sharply, "What if I have?"

"Only this. I propose that the doctor's supply of drugs, my own sulphonal tablets, your revolver and anything else of the nature of drugs or firearms should be collected together and placed in a safe place. That after this is done, we should each of us submit to a search—both of our persons and of our effects."

Lombard said, "I'm damned if I'll give up my revolver!"

Wargrave said sharply, "Mr. Lombard, you are a very strongly built and powerful young man, but ex-Inspector Blore is also a man of powerful physique. I do not know what the outcome of a struggle between you would be but I can tell you this. On Blore's side, assisting him to the best of our ability, will be myself, Dr. Armstrong and Miss Claythorne. You will appreciate, therefore, that the odds against you if you choose to resist will be somewhat heavy."

Lombard threw his head back. His teeth showed in what was almost a snarl. "Oh, very well, then. Since you've got it all taped out."

Mr. Justice Wargrave nodded his head. "You are a sensible young man. Where is this revolver of yours?"

"In the drawer of the table by my bed."

"Good."

"I'll fetch it."

"I think it would be desirable if we went with you."

Philip said with a smile that was still nearer a snarl, "Suspicious devil, aren't you?"

They went along the corridor to Lombard's room. Philip strode across to the bed table and jerked open the drawer. Then he recoiled with an oath. The drawer of the bed table was empty.

v

"Satisfied?" asked Lombard. He had stripped to the skin and he and his room had been meticulously searched by the other three men. Vera Claythorne was outside in the corridor. The search proceeded methodically. In turn, Armstrong, the judge and Blore submitted to the same test.

The four men emerged from Blore's room and approached Vera. It was the judge who spoke. "I hope you will understand, Miss Claythorne, that we can make no exceptions. That revolver must be found. You have, I presume, a bathing dress with you?"

Vera nodded.

"Then I will ask you to go into your room and put it on and then come out to us here."

Vera went into her room and shut the door. She reappeared in under a minute dressed in a tight-fitting silk ruched bathing dress.

Wargrave nodded approval. "Thank you, Miss Claythorne. Now if you will remain here, we will search your room."

Vera waited patiently in the corridor until they emerged. Then she went in, dressed, and came out to where they were waiting. The judge said, "We are now assured of one thing. There are no lethal weapons or drugs in the possession of any of us five. That is one point to the good. We will now place the drugs in a safe place. There is, I think, a silver chest, is there not, in the pantry?"

Blore said, "That's all very well, but who's to have the key? You, I suppose."

Mr. Justice Wargrave made no reply. He went down to the pantry and the others followed him. There was a small case there designed for the purpose of holding silver and plate. By the judge's directions, the various drugs were placed in this and it was locked. Then, still on Wargrave's instructions, the chest was lifted into the plate cupboard and this in turn was locked. The judge then gave the key of the chest to Philip Lombard and the key of the cupboard to Blore. He said, "You two are the strongest physically. It would be difficult for either of you to get the key from the other. It would be impossible for any of us three to do so. To break open the cupboard—or the plate chest—would be a noisy and cumbrous proceeding and one which could hardly be carried out without attention being attracted to what was going on."

He paused, then went on, "We are still faced by one very grave problem. *What has become of Mr. Lombard's revolver?*"

Blore said, "Seems to me its owner is the most likely person to know that."

A white dint showed in Philip Lombard's nostrils. He said, "You damned pig-headed fool! I tell you it's been stolen from me!"

Wargrave asked, "When did you see it last?"

"Last night. It was in the drawer when I went to bed—ready in case anything happened."

The judge nodded. He said, "It must have been taken this morning during the confusion of searching for Rogers or after his dead body was discovered."

Vera said, "It must be hidden somewhere about the house. We must look for it."

Mr. Justice Wargrave's finger was stroking his chin. He said, "I doubt if our search will result in anything. Our murderer has had plenty of time to devise a hiding place. I do not fancy we shall find that revolver easily."

Blore said forcefully, "I don't know where the revolver is, but I'll bet I know where something else is—that hypodermic syringe. Follow me."

He opened the front door and led the way round the house. A little distance away from the dining-room window he found the syringe. Beside it was a smashed china figure—a sixth broken Indian boy. Blore said in a satisfied voice, "Only place it could be. After he'd killed her, he opened the window and threw out the syringe and picked up the china figure from the table and followed on with that."

There were no prints on the syringe. It had been carefully wiped. Vera said in a determined voice, "Now let us look for the revolver."

Mr. Justice Wargrave said: "By all means. But in doing so let us be careful to keep together. Remember, if we separate, the murderer gets his chance."

They searched the house carefully from attic to cellar, but without result. The revolver was still missing.

13

"ONE OF *us* . . . *One of us* . . . *One of us* . . .*" Three words, endlessly repeated, dinning themselves hour after hour into receptive brains. Five people—five frightened people. Five people who watched each other, who now hardly troubled to hide their state of nervous tension. There was little pretense now—no formal veneer of conversation. They were five enemies linked together by a mutual instinct of self-preservation.

And all of them, suddenly, looked less like human beings. They were reverting to more bestial types. Like a wary old tortoise, Mr. Justice Wargrave sat hunched up, his body motionless, his eyes keen and alert. Ex-Inspector Blore looked coarser and clumsier in build. His walk was that of a slow, padding animal. His eyes were bloodshot. There was a look of mingled ferocity and stupidity about him. He was like a beast at bay ready to charge its pursuers. Philip Lombard's senses seemed heightened, rather than diminished. His ears reacted to the slightest sound. His step was lighter and quicker, his body was lithe and graceful. And he smiled often, his lips curling back from his long, white teeth.

Vera Claythorne was very quiet. She sat most of the time huddled in a chair. Her eyes stared ahead of her into space. She looked dazed. She was like a bird that has dashed its head against glass and that has been picked up by a human hand. It crouches there, terrified, unable to move, hoping to save itself by its immobility.

Armstrong was in a pitiable condition of nerves. He twitched and his hands shook. He lighted cigarette after cigarette and stubbed them out almost immediately. The forced inaction of their position seemed to gall him more than the others. Every now and then he broke out into a torrent of nervous speech. "We—we shouldn't just sit here doing nothing! There must be *something*—surely, surely, there is *something* that we can do? If we lit a bonfire—"

Blore said heavily, "In this weather?"

The rain was pouring down again. The wind came in fitful gusts. The depressing sound of the pattering rain nearly drove them mad. By tacit consent, they had adopted a plan of campaign. They all sat in the big drawing room. Only one person left the room at a time. The other four waited till the fifth returned.

Lombard said, "It's only a question of time. The weather will clear. Then we can do something—signal—light fires—make a raft—something!"

Armstrong said with a sudden cackle of laughter, "A question of *time*? We can't afford time! We shall all be dead. . . ."

Mr. Justice Wargrave said, and his small, clear voice was heavy with passionate determination, "Not if we are careful. *We must be very careful.* . . ."

The midday meal had been duly eaten—but there had been no conventional formality about it. All five of them had gone to the kitchen. In the larder they had found a great store of tinned foods. They had opened a tin of tongue and two tins of fruit. They had eaten standing round the kitchen table. Then, herding close together, they had returned to the drawingroom—to sit there—sit—watching each other. . . .

And by now the thoughts that ran through their brains were abnormal, feverish, diseased. . . . "It's Armstrong. . . . I saw him looking at me sideways just then . . . his eyes are mad . . . quite mad. . . . Perhaps he isn't a doctor at all. . . . That's it, of course! . . . He's a lunatic, escaped from some doctor's house—pretending to be a doctor. . . . It's true . . . shall I tell them? . . . Shall I scream out? . . . No, it won't do to put him on his guard. . . . Besides, he can seem so sane. . . . What time is it? . . . Only a quarter past three! . . . Oh, God, I shall go mad myself. . . . *Yes, it's Armstrong.* . . . He's watching me now. . . ."

"They won't get *me*! I can take care of myself. . . . I've been in tight places before. . . . Where the hell is that revolver? . . . Who took it? . . . Who's got it? . . . Nobody's got it—we know that. We were all searched. Nobody *can* have it. . . . *But someone knows where it is.* . . ."

"They're going mad . . . they'll all go mad. . . . Afraid of death . . . we're all afraid of death. . . . *I*'m afraid of death. . . . Yes, but that doesn't stop death coming. . . . '*The hearse is at the door, sir.*' Where did I read that? The girl . . . I'll watch the girl. Yes, I'll watch the girl. . . ."

"Twenty to four . . . only twenty to four . . . perhaps the clock has stopped. . . . I don't understand—no, I don't understand. . . . This sort of thing can't happen . . . *it is happening.* . . . Why don't we wake up? Wake up—Judgment Day—no, not that! If I could only think. . . . My head—something's happening in my head—it's going to burst—it's going to split. . . . This sort of thing can't happen. . . . What's the time? Oh, God! it's only a quarter to four."

"I must keep my head. . . . I must keep my head. . . . If only I keep my head. . . . It's all perfectly clear—all worked out. But nobody must suspect. It may do the trick. It must! Which one? That's the question—which one? I think—yes, I rather think—yes—*him*."

When the clock struck five they all jumped. Vera said, "Does anyone—want tea?"

There was a moment's silence. Blore said, "I'd like a cup."

Vera rose. She said, "I'll go and make it. You can all stay here."

Mr. Justice Wargrave said gently, "I think, my dear young lady, we would all prefer to come and watch you make it."

Vera stared, then gave a short rather hysterical laugh. She said, "Of course! You would!"

Five people went into the kitchen. Tea was made and drunk by Vera and Blore. The other three had whisky—opening a fresh bottle and using a siphon from a nailed-up case. The judge murmured with a reptilian smile, "We must be very careful. . . ."

They went back again to the drawing room. Although it was summer the room was dark. Lombard switched on the lights but they did not come on. He said, "Of course! The engine's not been run today since Rogers hasn't been there to see to it." He hesitated and said, "We could go out and get it going, I suppose."

Mr. Justice Wargrave said, "There are packets of candles in the larder, I saw them, better use those."

Lombard went out. The other four sat watching each other. He came back with a box of candles and a pile of saucers. Five candles were lit and placed about the room. The time was a quarter to six.

ii

At twenty past six, Vera felt that to sit there longer was unbearable. She would go to her room and bathe her aching head and temples in cold water. She got up and went towards the door. Then she remembered and came back and got a candle out of the box. She lighted it, let a little wax pour into a saucer and stuck the candle firmly to it. Then she went out of the room, shutting the door behind her and leaving the four men inside. She went up the stairs and along the passage to her room. As she opened her door, she suddenly halted and stood stock still. Her nostrils quivered. The sea. . . . The smell of the sea at St. Tredennick. . . .

That was it. She could not be mistaken. Of course one smelt the sea on an island anyway, but this was different. It was the smell there had been on the beach that day—with the tide out and the rocks covered with seaweed drying in the sun. . . . "*Can I swim out to the island, Miss Claythorne?*" "*Why can't I swim out to the island? . . .*" Horrid whiny spoilt little brat! If it weren't for him, Hugo would be rich . . . able to marry the girl he loved. . . .

Hugo . . . Surely—surely—Hugo was beside her? No, waiting for her in the room . . .

She took a step forward. The draught from the window caught the

flame of the candle. It flickered and went out. . . . In the dark she was
suddenly afraid. . . . "Don't be a fool," Vera Claythorne urged herself.
"It's all right. The others are downstairs. All four of them. There's no
one in the room. There can't be. You're imagining things, my girl."

But that smell—that smell of the beach at St. Tredennick . . . That
wasn't imagined. *It was true.* . . .

And there *was* someone in the room. . . . She had heard something—surely she had heard something. . . . And then, as she stood
there, listening—a cold, clammy hand touched her throat—a wet hand,
smelling of the sea. . . .

iii

Vera screamed. She screamed and screamed—screams of the
utmost terror—wild, desperate cries for help. She did not hear the
sounds from below, of a chair being overturned, of a door opening, of
men's feet running up the stairs. She was conscious only of supreme
terror. Then, restoring her sanity, lights flickered in the
doorway—candles—men hurrying into the room.

"What the devil?" "What's happened?" "Good God, what is it?"

She shuddered, took a step forward, collapsed on the floor. She was
only half-aware of someone bending over her, of someone forcing her
head down between her knees.

Then at a sudden exclamation, a quick "My God, look at that!" her
senses returned. She opened her eyes and raised her head. She saw
what it was the men with the candles were looking at. A broad ribbon
of wet seaweed was hanging down from the ceiling. It was that which in
the darkness had swayed against her throat. It was that which she had
taken for a clammy hand, a drowned hand come back from the dead to
squeeze the life out of her!

She began to laugh hysterically. She said, "It was seaweed—only
seaweed—and that's what the smell was. . . ."

And then the faintness came over her once more—waves upon
waves of sickness. Again someone took her head and forced it between
her knees.

Eons of time seemed to pass. They were offering her something to
drink—pressing the glass against her lips. She smelt brandy. She was
just about to gulp the spirit gratefully down when, suddenly, a warning
note—like an alarm bell—sounded in her brain. She sat up, pushing the
glass away. She said sharply, "Where did this come from?"

Blore's voice answered. He stared a minute before speaking. He
said, "I got it from downstairs."

Vera cried, "I won't drink it. . . ."

There was a moment's silence, then Lombard laughed. He said with appreciation, "Good for you, Vera! You've got your wits about you—even if you have been scared half out of your life. I'll get a fresh bottle that hasn't been opened." He went swiftly out.

Vera said uncertainly, "I'm all right now. I'll have some water."

Armstrong supported her as she struggled to her feet. She went over to the basin, swaying and clutching at him for support. She let the cold tap run and then filled the glass.

Blore said resentfully, "That brandy's all right."

Armstrong said, "How do you know?"

Blore said angrily, "I didn't put anything in it. That's what you're getting at, I suppose."

Armstrong said, "I'm not saying you did. You might have done it, or someone might have tampered with the bottle for just this emergency."

Lombard came swiftly back into the room. He had a new bottle of brandy in his hands and a corkscrew. He thrust the sealed bottle under Vera's nose. "There you are, my girl. Absolutely no deception." He peeled off the tin foil and drew the cork. "Lucky there's a good supply of spirits in the house. Thoughtful of U.N. Owen."

Vera shuddered violently. Armstrong held the glass while Philip poured the brandy into it. He said, "You'd better drink this, Miss Claythorne. You've had a nasty shock."

Vera drank a little of the spirit. The color came back to her face. Philip Lombard said with a laugh, "Well, here's one murder that hasn't gone according to plan!"

Vera said almost in a whisper, "You think—that was what was meant?"

Lombard nodded. "Expected you to pass out through fright! Some people would have, wouldn't they, doctor?"

Armstrong did not commit himself. He said doubtfully, "H'm, impossible to say. Young, healthy subject—no cardiac weakness. Unlikely. On the other hand—" He picked up the glass of brandy that Blore had brought. He dipped a finger in it, tasted it gingerly. His expression did not alter. He said dubiously, "H'm, tastes all right."

Blore stepped forward angrily. He said, "If you're saying that I tampered with that, I'll knock your ruddy block off."

Vera, her wits revived by the brandy, made a diversion by saying, "Where's the judge?"

The three men looked at each other. "*That's odd.* . . . Thought he came up with us." Blore said, "*So did I.* . . . What about it, doctor? You came up the stairs behind me."

Armstrong said, "I thought he was following me. . . . Of course, he'd be bound to go slower than we did. He's an old man."

They looked at each other again. Lombard said, "It's damned odd. . . ."

Blore cried, "We must look for him."

He started for the door. The others followed him, Vera last. As they went down the stairs Armstrong said over his shoulder: "Of course he *may* have stayed in the living room. . . ."

They crossed the hall. Armstrong called out loudly, "Wargrave, Wargrave, where are you?"

There was no answer. A deadly silence filled the house apart from the gentle patter of the rain. Then, in the entrance to the drawing room door, Armstrong stopped dead. The others crowded up and looked over his shoulder. Somebody cried out.

Mr. Justice Wargrave was sitting in his high-backed chair at the end of the room. Two candles burnt on either side of him. But what shocked and startled the onlookers was the fact that he sat there robed in scarlet with a judge's wig upon his head. . . .

Dr. Armstrong motioned to the others to keep back. He himself walked across to the silent, staring figure, reeling a little as he walked like a drunken man. He bent forward, peering into the still face. Then, with a swift movement, he raised the wig. It fell to the floor, revealing the high bald forehead with in the very middle a round stained mark from which something had trickled. . . .

Dr. Armstrong raised the limp hand and felt for the pulse. Then he turned to the others. He said—and his voice was expressionless, dead, far away, "*He's been shot. . . .*"

Blore said, "God—*the revolver!*"

The doctor said, still in the same lifeless voice, "Got him through the head. Instantaneous."

Vera stooped to the wig. She said, and her voice shook with horror, "*Miss Brent's missing gray wool. . . .*"

Blore said, "And the scarlet curtain that was missing from the bathroom. . . ."

Vera whispered, "So this is what they wanted them for. . . ."

Suddenly Philip Lombard laughed—a high, unnatural laugh. "*Five little Indian boys going in for law; one got in Chancery and then there were four.* That's the end of Mr. Bloody Justice Wargrave. No more pronouncing sentence for him! No more putting on the black cap! Here's the last time *he'*ll ever sit in court! No more summing up and sending innocent men to death. How Edward Seton would laugh if he were here! God, how he'd laugh!"

His outburst shocked and startled the others. Vera cried, "Only this morning you said *he* was the one!"

Philip Lombard's face changed—sobered. He said in a low voice, "I know I did. . . . Well, I was wrong. Here's one more of us who's been proved innocent—*too late!*"

14

THEY HAD CARRIED Mr. Justice Wargrave up to his room and laid him on the bed. Then they had come down again and had stood in the hall looking at each other. Blore said heavily, "What do we do now?"

Lombard said briskly, "Have something to eat. We've got to eat, you know."

Once again they went into the kitchen. Again they opened a tin of tongue. They ate mechanically, almost without tasting. Vera said, "I shall never eat tongue again."

They finished the meal. They sat round the kitchen table staring at each other. Blore said, "Only four of us now. . . . *Who'll be the next?*"

Armstrong stared. He said, almost mechanically, "We must be very careful—" and stopped.

Blore nodded. "That's what *he* said. . . . And now he's dead!"

Armstrong said, "How did it happen, I wonder?"

Lombard swore. He said, "A damned clever double cross! That stuff was planted in Miss Claythorne's room and it worked just as it was intended to. Everyone dashed up there thinking *she's* been murdered. And so—in the confusion—someone—caught the old boy off his guard."

Blore said, "Why didn't anyone hear the shot?"

Lombard shook his head. "Miss Claythorne was screaming, the wind was howling, we were running about and calling out. No, it wouldn't be heard." He paused. "But that trick's not going to work again. He'll have to try something else next time."

Blore said, "He probably will." There was an unpleasant tone in his voice. The two men eyed each other.

Armstrong said, "Four of us, and we don't know which. . . ."

Blore said, "*I* know. . . ."

Vera said, "I haven't the least doubt. . . ."

Armstrong said slowly, "I suppose I do know really. . . ."

Philip Lombard said, "I think I've got a pretty good idea now. . . ."
Again they all looked at each other.

Vera staggered to her feet. She said, "I feel awful. I must go to bed. . . . I'm dead beat."

Lombard said, "Might as well. No good sitting watching each other."

Blore said, "*I've* no objection. . . . "

The doctor murmured, "The best thing to do—although I doubt if any of us will sleep."

They moved to the door. Blore said, "I wonder where that revolver is now? . . ."

ii

They went up the stairs.

The next move was a little like a scene in a farce. Each one of the four stood with a hand on his or her bedroom door handle. Then, as though at a signal, each one stepped into the room and pulled the door shut. There were sounds of bolts and locks, of the moving of furniture. Four frightened people were barricaded in until morning.

iii

Philip Lombard drew a breath of relief as he turned from adjusting a chair under the door handle. He strolled across to the dressing table. By the light of the flickering candle he studied his face curiously. He said softly to himself, "Yes, this business has got you rattled all right."

His sudden wolflike smile flashed out. He undressed quickly. He went over to the bed, placing his wristwatch on the table by the bed. Then he opened the drawer of the table. He stood there, staring down at the revolver that was inside it. . . .

iv

Vera Claythorne lay in bed. The candle still burned beside her. As yet she could not summon the courage to put it out. She was afraid of the dark. . . .

She told herself again and again: *You're all right until morning. Nothing happened last night. Nothing will happen tonight. Nothing can happen. You're locked and bolted in. No one can come near you.* . . . And she thought suddenly: Of course! I can stay here! Stay here locked in! Food doesn't really matter! I can stay here—safely till help comes! Even if it's a day—or two days. . . .

Stay here. Yes, but could she stay here? Hour after hour—with no one to speak to, with nothing to do but *think.* . . .

She'd begin to think of Cornwall—of Hugo—of—of what she'd said to Cyril. Horrid whiny little boy, always pestering her. . . . "*Miss* Claythorne, why can't I swim out to the rock? I can. I know I can."

Was it her voice that had answered? "*Of course you can, Cyril, really. I know that.*"

"Can I go then, Miss Claythorne?"

"Well, you see, Cyril, your mother gets so nervous about you. I'll tell you what. Tomorrow you can swim out to the rock. I'll talk to your mother on the beach and distract her attention. And then, when she looks for you, there you'll be standing on the rock waving to her! It *will* be a surprise!"

"Oh, good egg, Miss Claythorne! That will be a lark!"

She'd said it now. Tomorrow! Hugo was going to Newquay. When he came back—it would be all over. . . .

Yes, but supposing it wasn't? Supposing it went wrong? Cyril might be rescued in time. And then—then he'd say, "*Miss Claythorne said I could.*" Well, what of it? One must take *some* risk! If the worst happened she'd brazen it out. "*How can you tell such a wicked lie, Cyril? Of course I never said any such thing!*" They'd believe her all right. Cyril often told stories. He was an untruthful child. Cyril would know, of course. But that didn't matter. . . . And anyway nothing *would* go wrong. She'd pretend to swim out after him. But she'd arrive too late. . . . Nobody would ever suspect. . . .

Had Hugo suspected? Was that why he had looked at her in that queer far-off way. . . ? Had Hugo *known*? Was that why he had gone off after the inquest so hurriedly?

He hadn't answered the one letter she had written to him. . . .

Hugo. . . .

Vera turned restlessly in bed. No, no, she mustn't think of Hugo. It hurt too much! That was all over, over and done with. . . . Hugo must be forgotten. . . . Why, this evening, had she suddenly felt that Hugo was in the room with her?

She stared up at the ceiling, stared at the big black hook in the middle of the room. She'd never noticed that hook before. The seaweed had hung from that. . . .

She shivered as she remembered that cold, clammy touch on her neck. . . . She didn't like that hook on the ceiling. It drew your eyes, fascinated you . . . a big black hook. . . .

V

Ex-Inspector Blore sat on the side of his bed. His small eyes, red-rimmed and bloodshot, were alert in the solid mass of his face. He was like a wild boar waiting to charge. He felt no inclination to sleep. The menace was coming very near now. . . . Six out of ten! For all his sagacity, for all his caution and astuteness, the old judge had gone the way of the rest.

Blore snorted with a kind of savage satisfaction. What was it the old geezer had said? "We must be very careful. . . ."

Self-righteous smug old hypocrite. Sitting up in court feeling like God Almighty. He'd got his all right. . . . No more being careful for him.

And now there were four of them. The girl, Lombard, Armstrong and himself. Very soon another of them would go. . . . But it wouldn't be William Henry Blore. He'd see to that all right.

(But the revolver. . . . What about the revolver? That was the disturbing factor—the revolver!)

Blore sat on his bed, his brow furrowed, his little eyes creased and puckered while he pondered the problem of the revolver. . . . In the silence he could hear the clocks strike downstairs. Midnight. He relaxed a little now—even went so far as to lie down on his bed. But he did not undress.

He lay there, thinking. Going over the whole business from the beginning, methodically, painstakingly, as he had been wont to do in his police officer days. It was thoroughness that paid in the end.

The candle was burning down. Looking to see if the matches were within easy reach of his hand, he blew it out. Strangely enough, he found the darkness disquieting. It was as though a thousand age-old fears awoke and struggled for supremacy in his brain. Faces floated in the air—the judge's face crowned with that mockery of gray wool—the cold dead face of Mrs. Rogers—the convulsed purple face of Anthony Marston. . . . Another face—pale, spectacled, with a small, straw-colored mustache . . . a face he had seen sometime or other—but when? Not on the island. No, much longer ago than that. Funny, that he couldn't put a name to it. . . . Silly sort of face really—fellow looked a bit of a mug.

Of course! It came to him with a real shock. Landor!

Odd to think he'd completely forgotten what Landor looked like. Only yesterday he'd been trying to recall the fellow's face, and hadn't been able to. And now here it was, every feature clear and distinct, as though he had seen it only yesterday. . . .

Landor had had a wife—a thin slip of a woman with a worried face. There'd been a kid too, a girl about fourteen. For the first time, he wondered what had become of them. . . .

(The revolver. What had become of the revolver? That was much more important. . . .) The more he thought about it the more puzzled he was. . . . He didn't understand this revolver business. . . . Somebody in the house had got that revolver. . . .

Downstairs a clock struck one. Blore's thoughts were cut short. He sat up on the bed, suddenly alert. For he had heard a sound—a very faint sound—somewhere outside his bedroom door. *There was someone moving about in the darkened house.* The perspiration broke out on his forehead. Who was it, moving secretly and silently along the corridors? Someone who was up to no good, he'd bet that!

Noiselessly, in spite of his heavy build, he dropped off the bed and with two strides was standing by the door listening. But the sound did not come again. Nevertheless Blore was convinced that he was not mistaken. He had heard a footfall just outside his door. The hair rose slightly on his scalp. He knew fear again. . . .

Someone creeping about stealthily in the night. . . . He listened—but the sound was not repeated.

And now a new temptation assailed him. He wanted, desperately, to go out and investigate. If he could only see who it was prowling about in the darkness. But to open his door would be the action of a fool. Very likely that was exactly what the other was waiting for. He might even have meant Blore to hear what he had heard, counting on him coming out to investigate.

Blore stood rigid—listening. He could hear sounds everywhere now, cracks, rustles, mysterious whispers—but his dogged, realistic brain knew them for what they were—the creations of his own heated imagination. And then suddenly he heard something that was *not* imagination. Footsteps, very soft, very cautious, but plainly audible to a man listening with all his ears as Blore was listening. They came softly along the corridor (both Lombard's and Armstrong's rooms were further from the stair head than his). They passed his door without hesitating or faltering.

And as they did so, Blore made up his mind. He meant to see who it was! The footsteps had definitely passed his door going to the stairs. Where was the man going? When Blore acted, he acted quickly, surprisingly so for a man who looked so heavy and slow. He tiptoed back to the bed, slipped matches into his pocket, detached the plug of the electric lamp by his bed, and picked it up winding the flex round it. It was a chromium affair with a heavy ebonite base—a useful weapon.

He sprinted noiselessly across the room, removed the chair from under the door handle and with precaution unlocked and unbolted the door. He stepped out into the corridor. There was a faint sound in the hall below. Blore ran noiselessly in his stockinged feet to the head of the stairs. At that moment he realized why it was he had heard all these sounds so clearly. The wind had died down completely and the sky must have cleared. There was faint moonlight coming in through the landing window and it illuminated the hall below. Blore had an instantaneous glimpse of a figure just passing out through the front door.

In the act of running down the stairs in pursuit, he paused. Once again, he had nearly made a fool of himself! This was a trap, perhaps, to lure him out of the house!

But what the other man didn't realize was that he had made a mistake, had delivered himself neatly into Blore's hands. For, of the three tenanted rooms upstairs, *one must now be empty*. All that had to be done was to ascertain *which*! Blore went swiftly back along the corridor. He paused first at Dr. Armstrong's door and tapped. There was no answer. He waited a minute, then went on to Philip Lombard's room. Here the answer came at once. "Who's there?"

"It's Blore. I don't think Armstrong is in his room. Wait a minute." He went on to the door at the end of the corridor. Here he tapped again. "Miss Claythorne. Miss Claythorne."

Vera's voice, startled, answered him. "Who is it? What's the matter?"

"It's all right, Miss Claythorne. Wait a minute. I'll come back."

He raced back to Lombard's room. The door opened as he did so. Lombard stood there. He held a candle in his left hand. He had pulled on his trousers over his pajamas. His right hand rested in the pocket of his pajama jacket. He said sharply, "What the hell's all this?"

Blore explained rapidly. Lombard's eyes lit up. "*Armstrong—eh*? So *he's* our pigeon!" He moved along to Armstrong's door. "Sorry, Blore, but I don't take anything on trust."

He rapped sharply on the panel. "Armstrong—Armstrong."

There was no answer. Lombard dropped to his knees and peered through the keyhole. He inserted his little finger gingerly into the lock. He said, "Key's not in the door on the inside."

Blore said, "That means he locked it on the outside and took it with him."

Philip nodded, "Ordinary precaution to take. *We'll get him, Blore*. . . . This time, *we'll get him*! Half a second."

He raced along to Vera's room. "Vera."

"Yes."

"We're hunting Armstrong. He's out of his room. Whatever you do, *don't open your door*. Understand?"

"Yes, I understand."

"If Armstrong comes along and says that I've been killed, or Blore's been killed, *pay no attention*. See? Only open your door if *both Blore and I* speak to you. Got that?"

Vera said, "Yes. I'm not a complete fool."

Lombard said, "Good."

He joined Blore. He said, "And now—after him! The hunt's up!"

Blore said, "We'd better be careful. He's got a revolver, remember."

Philip Lombard, racing down the stairs, chuckled. He said, "That's where you're wrong." He undid the front door, remarking, "Latch pushed back—so that he could get in again easily." He went on, "I've got that revolver!" He took it half out of his pocket as he spoke. "Found it put back in my drawer tonight."

Blore stopped dead on the doorstep. His face changed. Philip Lombard saw it. He said impatiently, "Don't be a damned fool, Blore! I'm not going to shoot you! Go back and barricade yourself in if you like! I'm off after Armstrong."

He started off into the moonlight. Blore, after a minute's hesitation, followed him. He thought to himself: I suppose I'm asking for it. But after all—After all he had tackled criminals armed with revolvers before now. Whatever else he lacked, Blore did not lack courage. Show him the danger and he would tackle it pluckily. He was not afraid of danger in the open, only of danger undefined and tinged with the supernatural.

vi

Vera, left to await results, got up and dressed. She glanced over once or twice at the door. It was a good solid door. It was both bolted and locked and had an oak chair wedged under the handle. It could not be broken open by force. Certainly not by Dr. Armstrong. He was not a physically powerful man. If she were Armstrong intent on murder, it was cunning that she would employ, not force.

She amused herself by reflecting on the means he might employ. He might, as Philip had suggested, announce that one of the other two men was dead. Or he might possibly pretend to be mortally wounded himself, might drag himself groaning to her door.

There were other possibilities. He might inform her that the house was on fire. More, he might actually set the house on fire. . . . Yes, that would be a possibility. Lure the other two men out of the house, then, having previously laid a trail of petrol, he might set light to it. And she, like an idiot, would remain barricaded in her room until it was too late.

She crossed over to the window. Not too bad. At a pinch one could escape that way. It would mean a drop—but there was a handy flowerbed.

She sat down and, picking up her diary, began to write in it in a clear, flowing hand. One must pass the time.

Suddenly she stiffened to attention. She had heard a sound. It was, she thought, a sound like breaking glass. And it came from somewhere downstairs. She listened hard, but the sound was not repeated.

She heard, or thought she heard, stealthy sounds of footsteps, the creak of stairs, the rustle of garments—but there was nothing definite, and she concluded, as Blore had done earlier, that such sounds had their origin in her own imagination.

But presently she heard sounds of a more concrete nature. People moving about downstairs—the murmur of voices. Then the very decided sound of someone mounting the stairs—doors opening and shutting—feet going up to the attic overhead. More noises from there. Finally the steps came along the passage. Lombard's voice said, "Vera? You all right?"

"Yes. What's happened?"

Blore's voice said, "Will you let us in?"

Vera went to the door. She removed the chair, unlocked the door and slid back the bolt. She opened the door. The two men were breathing hard; their feet and the bottom of their trousers were soaking wet.

She said again, "What's happened?"

Lombard said, "*Armstrong's disappeared. . . .*"

vii

Vera cried, "What?"

Lombard said, "Vanished clean off the island."

Blore concurred, "Vanished—that's the word! Like some damned conjuring trick."

Vera said impatiently, "Nonsense! He's hiding somewhere!"

Blore said, "No, he isn't! I tell you, there's nowhere to hide on this island. It's as bare as your hand! There's moonlight outside. As clear as day it is. *And he's not to be found.*"

Vera said, "He doubled back into the house."

Blore said, "We thought of that. We've searched the house too. You must have heard us. *He's not here*, I tell you. He's gone—clean vanished, vamoosed. . . ."

Vera said incredulously, "I don't believe it."

Lombard said, "It's true, my dear." He paused and then said, "There's one other fact. A pane in the dining-room window has been smashed—*and there are only three little Indian boys on the table.*"

15

THREE PEOPLE SAT eating breakfast in the kitchen. Outside, the sun shone. It was a lovely day. The storm was a thing of the past. And with the change in the weather, a change had come in the mood of the prisoners on the island. They felt now like people just awakening from a nightmare. There was danger, yes, but it was danger in daylight. That paralyzing atmosphere of fear that had wrapped them round like a blanket yesterday while the wind howled outside was gone.

Lombard said, "We'll try heliographing today with a mirror from the highest point of the island. Some bright lad wandering on the cliff will recognize SOS when he sees it, I hope. In the evening we could try a bonfire—only there isn't much wood—and anyway they might just think it was song and dance and merriment."

Vera said, "Surely someone can read Morse. And then they'll come to take us off. Long before this evening."

Lombard said, "The weather's cleared all right, but the sea hasn't gone down yet. Terrific swell on! They won't be able to get a boat near the island before tomorrow."

Vera cried, "Another night in this place!"

Lombard shrugged his shoulders. "May as well face it! Twenty-four hours will do it, I think. If we can last out that, we'll be all right."

Blore cleared his throat. He said, "We'd better come to a clear understanding. *What's happened to Armstrong?*"

Lombard said, "Well, we've got one piece of evidence. Only three little Indian boys left on the dinner table. It looks as though Armstrong had got his quietus."

Vera said, "Then why haven't you found his dead body?"

Blore said, "Exactly."

Lombard shook his head. He said, "It's damned odd—no getting over it."

Blore said doubtfully, "It might have been thrown into the sea."

Lombard said sharply, "By whom? You? Me? You saw him go out of the front door. You come along and find me in my room. We go out and search together. When the devil had I time to kill him and carry his body round the island?"

Blore said, "I don't know. But I do know one thing."

Lombard said, "What's that?"

Blore said, "The revolver. It was your revolver. It's in your possession now. There's nothing to show that it hasn't been in your possession all along."

"Come now, Blore, we were all searched."

"Yes, you'd hidden it away before that happened. Afterwards you just took it back again."

"My good blockhead, I swear to you that it was put back in my drawer. Greatest surprise I ever had in my life when I found it there."

Blore said, "You ask us to believe a thing like that! Why the devil should Armstrong, or anyone else for that matter, put it back?"

Lombard raised his shoulders hopelessly. "I haven't the least idea.

It's just crazy. The last thing one would expect. There seems no point in it."

Blore agreed. "No, there isn't. You might have thought of a better story."

"Rather proof that I'm telling the truth, isn't it?"

"I don't look at it that way."

Philip said, "You wouldn't."

Blore said, "Look here, Mr. Lombard, if you're an honest man, as you pretend—"

Philip murmured, "When did I lay claims to being an honest man? No, indeed, I never said that."

Blore went on stolidly, "If you're speaking the truth—there's only one thing to be done. As long as you have that revolver, Miss Claythorne and I are at your mercy. The only fair thing is to put that revolver with the other things that are locked up—and you and I will hold the two keys still."

Philip Lombard lit a cigarette. As he puffed smoke, he said, "Don't be an ass."

"You won't agree to that?"

"No, I won't. That revolver's mine. I need it to defend myself—and I'm going to keep it."

Blore said, "In that case we're bound to come to one conclusion."

"That I'm U.N. Owen? Think what you damned well please. But I'll ask you, if that's so, why I didn't pot you with the revolver last night? I could have, about twenty times over."

Blore shook his head. He said, "I don't know—and that's a fact. You must have had some reason."

Vera had taken no part in the discussion. She stirred now and said, "I think you're both behaving like a pair of idiots."

Lombard looked at her, "What's this?"

Vera said, "You've forgotten the nursery rhyme. Don't you see there's a clue there?"

She recited in a meaning voice:

> *Four little Indian boys going out to sea;*
> *A red herring swallowed one and then there were three.*

She went on: "*A red herring*—that's the vital clue. *Armstrong's not dead.* . . . He took away the china Indian to make you think he was. You may say what you like—Armstrong's on the island still. His disappearance is just a red herring across the track. . . ."

Lombard sat down again. He said, "You know, you may be right."

Blore said, "Yes, but if so, where is he? We've searched the place. Outside and inside."

Vera said scornfully, "We all searched for the revolver, didn't we, and couldn't find it? But it was somewhere all the time!"

Lombard murmured, "There's a slight difference in size, my dear, between a man and a revolver."

Vera said, "I don't care—I'm sure I'm right."

Blore murmured, "Rather giving himself away, wasn't it? Actually mentioning a red herring in the verse. He could have written it up a bit different."

Vera cried, "But don't you *see*, he's *mad*? It's all mad! The whole thing of going by the rhyme is mad! Dressing up the judge, killing Rogers when he was chopping sticks—drugging Mrs. Rogers so that she overslept herself—arranging for a bumblebee when Miss Brent died! It's like some horrible child playing a game. It's all got to fit in."

Blore said, "Yes, you're right." He thought a minute. "At any rate there's no Zoo on the island. He'll have a bit of trouble getting over that."

Vera cried, "Don't you see? *We're the Zoo....* Last night, we were hardly human any more. *We're the Zoo....*"

ii

They spent the morning on the cliffs, taking it in turns to flash a mirror at the mainland. There were no signs that anyone saw them. No answering signals. The day was fine, with a slight haze. Below the sea heaved in a gigantic swell. There were no boats out. They had made another abortive search of the island. There was no trace of the missing physician.

Vera looked up at the house from where they were standing. She said, her breath coming with a slight catch in it, "One feels safer here, out in the open.... Don't let's go back into the house again."

Lombard said, "Not a bad idea. We're pretty safe here; no one can get at us without our seeing him a long time beforehand."

Vera said, "We'll stay here."

Blore said, "Have to pass the night somewhere. We'll have to go back to the house then."

Vera shuddered. "I can't bear it. I *can't* go through another night!"

Philip said, "You'll be safe enough—locked in your room."

Vera murmured, "I suppose so." She stretched out her hands, murmuring, "It's lovely—to feel the sun again...." She thought, "How odd ... I'm almost happy. And yet I suppose I'm actually in danger...."

Somehow—now—nothing seems to matter ... not in daylight. ... I feel full of power—I feel that I can't die. ..."

Blore was looking at his wristwatch. He said, "It's two o'clock. What about lunch?"

Vera said obstinately, "I'm not going back to the house. I'm going to stay here—in the open."

"Oh, come now, Miss Claythorne. Got to keep your strength up, you know."

Vera said, "If I even see a tinned tongue, I shall be sick! I don't want any food. People go days on end with nothing sometimes when they're on a diet."

Blore said, "Well, I need my meals regular. What about you, Mr. Lombard?"

Philip said, "You know, I don't relish the idea of tinned tongue particularly. I'll stay here with Miss Claythorne."

Blore hesitated. Vera said, "I shall be quite all right. I don't think he'll shoot me as soon as your back is turned if that's what you're afraid of."

Blore said, "It's all right if you say so. But we agreed we ought not to separate."

Philip said, "You're the one who wants to go into the lion's den. I'll come with you if you like."

"No, you won't," said Blore. "You'll stay here."

Philip laughed. "So you're still afraid of me? Why, I could shoot you both this minute if I liked."

Blore said, "Yes, but that wouldn't be according to plan. It's one at a time, and it's got to be done in a certain way."

"Well," said Philip, "you seem to know all about it."

"Of course," said Blore, "it's a bit jumpy going up to the house alone—"

Philip said softly, "And therefore, *will I lend you my revolver*? Answer, no, I will *not*! Not quite so simple as that, thank you."

Blore shrugged his shoulders and began to make his way up the steep slope to the house. Lombard said softly, "Feeding time at the Zoo! The animals are very regular in their habits!"

Vera said anxiously, "Isn't it very risky, what he's doing?"

"In the sense you mean—no, I don't think it is! Armstrong's not armed, you know, and anyway Blore is twice a match for him in physique and he's very much on his guard. And anyway it's a sheer impossibility that Armstrong can be in the house. I *know* he's not there."

"But—what other solution is there?"

Philip said softly, "There's Blore."

"Oh—do you really think—?"

"Listen, my girl. You heard Blore's story. You've got to admit that if it's true, *I can't possibly have had anything to do with Armstrong's disappearance.* His story clears me. *But it doesn't clear him.* We've only *his* word for it that he heard footsteps and saw a man going downstairs and out at the front door. The whole thing may be a lie. He may have got rid of Armstrong a couple of hours before that."

"How?"

Lombard shrugged his shoulders. "That we don't know. But if you ask me, we've only one danger to fear—and that danger is Blore! What do we know about the man? Less than nothing! All this ex-policeman story may be bunkum! He may be anybody—a mad millionaire—a crazy businessman—an escaped inmate of Broadmoor. One thing's certain. He *could* have done every one of these crimes."

Vera had gone rather white. She said in a slightly breathless voice, "And supposing he gets—us?"

Lombard said softly, patting the revolver in his pocket, "I'm going to take very good care he doesn't." Then he looked at her curiously. "Touching faith in me, haven't you, Vera? Quite sure I wouldn't shoot you?"

Vera said, "One has got to trust someone. . . . As a matter of fact I think you're wrong about Blore. I still think it's Armstrong." She turned to him suddenly. "Don't you feel—all the time—that there's *someone.* Someone watching and waiting?"

Lombard said slowly, "That's just nerves."

Vera said eagerly, "Then you *have* felt it?" She shivered. She bent a little closer. "Tell me—you don't think—" She broke off, went on, "I read a story once—about two judges that came to a small American town—from the Supreme Court. They administered justice—Absolute Justice. *Because—they didn't come from this world at all. . . .*"

Lombard raised his eyebrows. He said, "Heavenly visitants, eh? No, I don't believe in the supernatural. This business is human enough."

Vera said, in a low voice, "Sometimes—I'm not sure. . . ."

Lombard looked at her. He said, "That's conscience. . . ." After a moment's silence he said very quietly, "So you *did* drown that kid after all?"

"I didn't! I didn't! You've no right to say that!"

He laughed easily. "Oh, yes, you did, my good girl! I don't know why. Can't imagine. There was a man in it probably. Was that it?"

A sudden feeling of lassitude, of intense weariness, spread over Vera's limbs. She said in a dull voice, "Yes—there was a man in it. . . ."

Lombard said softly, "Thanks. That's what I wanted to know. . . ."

Vera sat up suddenly. She exclaimed, "What was that? It wasn't an earthquake?"

Lombard said, "No, no. Queer, though—a thud shook the ground. And I thought—did you hear a sort of cry? I did."

They stared up at the house. Lombard said, "It came from there. We'd better go up and see."

"No, no, I'm not going."

"Please yourself. I am."

Vera said desperately, "All right, I'll come with you."

They walked up the slope to the house. The terrace was peaceful and innocuous looking in the sunshine. They hesitated there a minute; then instead of entering by the front door, they made a cautious circuit of the house. They found Blore. He was spreadeagled on the stone terrace on the east side, his head crushed and mangled by a great block of white marble.

Philip looked up. He said, "Whose is that window just above?"

Vera said in a low, shuddering voice, "It's mine—and *that's the clock from my mantelpiece*. . . . I remember now. It was—shaped like a bear. . . . " She repeated and her voice shook and quavered, "It was shaped like a bear. . . ."

iii

Philip grasped her shoulder. He said, and his voice was urgent and grim, "This settles it. Armstrong is in hiding somewhere in that house. I'm going to get him."

But Vera clung to him. She cried, "Don't be a fool. It's *us* now! We're next! He *wants* us to look for him! He's *counting* on it!"

Philip stopped. He said thoughtfully, "There's something in that."

Vera cried, "At any rate, you do admit now I was right."

He nodded. "Yes—you win! It's Armstrong all right. But where the devil did he hide himself? We went over the place with a fine-tooth comb."

Vera said urgently, "If you didn't find him last night, you *won't find him now*. . . . That's common sense."

Lombard said reluctantly, "Yes, but—"

"He must have prepared a secret place beforehand—naturally—of course it's just what he would do. You know, like a Priest's Hole in old manor houses."

"This isn't an old house of that kind."

"He could have had one made."

Philip Lombard shook his head. He said, "We measured the

place—that first morning. I'll swear there's no space unaccounted for."

Vera said, "There must be. . . ."

Lombard said, "I'd like to see—"

Vera cried, "Yes, you'd like to see! And he knows that! He's in there—waiting for you."

Lombard said, half bringing out the revolver from his pocket, "I've got this, you know."

"You said Blore was all right—that he was more than a match for Armstrong. So he was physically, and he was on the lookout too. But what you don't seem to realize is that Armstrong is *mad*! And a madman has all the advantages on his side. He's twice as cunning as anyone sane can be."

Lombard put back the revolver in his pocket. He said, "Come on, then."

iv

Lombard said at last, "What are we going to do when night comes?"

Vera didn't answer. He went on accusingly, "You haven't thought of that?"

She said helplessly, "What *can* we do? Oh, my God, I'm *frightened.* . . ."

Philip Lombard said thoughtfully, "It's fine weather. There will be a moon. We must find a place—up by the top cliffs perhaps. We can sit there and wait for the morning. *We mustn't go to sleep.* . . . We must watch the whole time. And if anyone comes up towards us, I shall shoot!" He paused, "You'll be cold, perhaps, in that thin dress?"

Vera said with a raucous laugh, "Cold? I should be colder if I were dead!"

Philip Lombard said quietly, "Yes, that's true. . . ."

Vera moved restlessly. She said, "I shall go mad if I sit here any longer. Let's move about."

"All right."

They paced slowly up and down, along the line of the rocks overlooking the sea. The sun was dropping towards the west. The light was golden and mellow. It enveloped them in a golden glow. Vera said, with a sudden nervous little giggle, "Pity we can't have a bathe. . . ."

Philip was looking down towards the sea. He said abruptly, "What's that, there? You see—by that big rock? No—a little further to the right."

Vera stared. She said, "It looks like somebody's clothes!"

"A bather, eh?" Lombard laughed. "Queer. I suppose it's only sea-weed."

Vera said, "Let's go and look."

"It is clothes," said Lombard as they drew nearer. "A bundle of them. That's a boot. Come on, let's scramble along here."

They scrambled over the rocks. Vera stopped suddenly. She said, "*It's not clothes—it's a man. . . .*"

The man was wedged between two rocks, flung there by the tide earlier in the day. Lombard and Vera reached it in a last scramble. They bent down. *A purple discolored face—a hideous, drowned face. . . .* Lombard said, "My God! It's *Armstrong. . . .*"

16

Eons passed . . . worlds spun and whirled. . . . Time was motion-less. . . . It stood still—it passed through a thousand ages. . . . No, it was only a minute or so. . . . Two people were standing looking down on a dead man. . . . Slowly, very slowly, Vera Claythorne and Philip Lombard lifted their heads and looked into each other's eyes. . . .

ii

Lombard laughed. He said, "So that's it, is it, Vera?"

Vera said, "There's no one on the island—no one at all—*except us two. . . .*" Her voice was a whisper—nothing more.

Lombard said, "Precisely. So we know where we are, don't we?"

Vera said, "How was it worked—that trick with the marble bear?"

He shrugged his shoulders. "A conjuring trick, my dear—a very good one. . . ."

Their eyes met again. Vera thought, *Why did I never see his face properly before. A wolf—that's what it is—a wolf's face. . . . Those horrible teeth. . . .*

Lombard said, and his voice was a snarl—dangerous—menacing, "This is the end, you understand. We've come to the truth now. *And it's the end. . . .*"

Vera said quietly, "I understand. . . ." She stared out to sea. General Macarthur had stared out to sea—when—only yesterday? Or was it

the day before? He too had said, "*This is the end.* . . ." He had said it
with acceptance—almost with welcome. But to Vera the words—the
thought—brought rebellion. No, it should not be the end. She looked
down at the dead man. She said, "Poor Dr. Armstrong. . . ."

Lombard sneered. "What's this? Womanly pity?"

Vera said, "Why not? Haven't *you* any pity?"

He said, "I've no pity for you. Don't expect it!"

Vera looked down again at the body. She said, "We must move him.
Carry him up to the house."

"To join the other victims, I suppose? All neat and tidy. As far as
I'm concerned he can stay where he is."

Vera said, "At any rate, let's get him out of reach of the sea."

Lombard laughed. He said, "If you like."

He bent—tugging at the body. Vera leaned against him, helping him.
She pulled and tugged with all her might. Lombard panted. "Not such
an easy job."

They managed it, however, drawing the body clear of high-water
mark. Lombard said as he straightened up, "Satisfied?"

Vera said, "Quite."

Her tone warned him. He spun round. Even as he clapped his hand
to his pocket he knew that he would find it empty. She had moved a
yard or two away and was facing him, revolver in hand.

Lombard said, "So that's the reason for your womanly solicitude!
You wanted to pick my pocket."

She nodded. She held it steadily and unwaveringly.

Death was very near to Philip Lombard now. It had never, he knew,
been nearer. Nevertheless he was not beaten yet. He said
authoritatively, "Give that revolver to me."

Vera laughed.

Lombard said, "Come on, hand it over."

His quick brain was working. Which way—which method—talk her
over—lull her into security—or a swift dash—All his life Lombard had
taken the risky way. He took it now. He spoke slowly, argumen-
tatively. "Now look here, my dear girl, you just listen—"

And then he sprang. Quick as a panther—as any other feline
creature. . . . Automatically Vera pressed the trigger. . . . Lombard's
leaping body stayed poised in mid-spring, then crashed heavily to the
ground.

Vera came warily forward, the revolver ready in her hand. But there
was no need for caution. Philip Lombard was dead—shot through the
heart. . . .

iii

Relief possessed Vera—enormous, exquisite relief. At last it was over. There was no more fear—no more steeling of her nerves. . . . She was alone on the island. . . . Alone with nine dead bodies. . . . But what did that matter? *She* was alive. . . . She sat there—exquisitely happy—exquisitely at peace. . . . No more fear. . . .

iv

The sun was setting when Vera moved at last. Sheer reaction had kept her immobile. There had been no room in her for anything but the glorious sense of safety.

She realized now that she was hungry and sleepy. Principally sleepy. She wanted to throw herself on her bed and sleep and sleep and sleep. . . . Tomorrow, perhaps, they would come and rescue her—but she didn't really mind. She didn't mind staying here. Not now that she was alone. . . . Oh! blessed, blessed peace. . . .

She got to her feet and glanced up at the house. Nothing to be afraid of any longer! No terrors waiting for her! Just an ordinary well-built modern house. And yet, a little earlier in the day, she had not been able to look at it without shivering. . . .

Fear—what a strange thing fear was. . . . Well, it was over now. She had conquered—had triumphed over the most deadly peril. By her own quick-wittedness and adroitness she had turned the tables on her would-be destroyer.

She began to walk up towards the house. The sun was setting, the sky to the west was streaked with red and orange. It was beautiful and peaceful. . . . Vera thought: The whole thing might be a dream. . . .

How tired she was—terribly tired. Her limbs ached, her eyelids were drooping. Not to be afraid any more. . . . To sleep. Sleep . . . sleep . . . sleep . . . To sleep safely since she was alone on the island. One little Indian boy left all alone. She smiled to herself.

She went in at the front door. The house, too, felt strangely peaceful. Vera thought: ordinarily one wouldn't care to sleep where there's a dead body in practically every bedroom!

Should she go to the kitchen and get herself something to eat? She hesitated a moment, then decided against it. She was really too tired. . . . She paused by the dining-room door. There were still three little china figures in the middle of the table. Vera laughed. She said, "You're behind the times, my dears."

She picked up two of them and tossed them out through the window.

She heard them crash on the stone of the terrace. The third little figure she picked up and held in her hand. She said, "You can come with me. We've won, my dear! We've won!"

The hall was dim in the dying light. Vera, the little Indian clasped in her hand, began to mount the stairs. Slowly, because her legs were suddenly very tired. *One little Indian boy left all alone.* How did it end? Oh, yes! *He got married and then there were none.*

Married. . . . Funny, how she suddenly got the feeling again that Hugo was in the house. . . . Very strong. Yes, Hugo was upstairs waiting for her. Vera said to herself: Don't be a fool. You're so tired that you're imagining the most fantastic things. . . .

Slowly up the stairs. . . . At the top of them something fell from her hand, making hardly any noise on the soft-pile carpet. She did not notice that she had dropped the revolver. She was only conscious of clasping a little china figure. How very quiet the house was. And yet—it didn't seem like an empty house. . . . Hugo, upstairs, waiting for her. . . .

One little Indian boy left all alone. What was the last line again? Something about being married—or was it something else? She had come now to the door of her room. Hugo was waiting for her inside—she was quite sure of it.

She opened the door. . . . She gave a gasp. . . . *What was that—* hanging from the hook in the ceiling? *A rope with a noose all ready? And a chair to stand upon—a chair that could be kicked away. . . . That was what Hugo wanted. . . .* And of course that was the last line of the rhyme. *He went and hanged himself and then there were none. . . .*

The little china figure fell from her hand. It rolled unheeded and broke against the fender. Like an automaton Vera moved forward. This was the end—here where the cold wet hand (Cyril's hand, of course) had touched her throat. . . .

"You can go to the rock, Cyril. . . ."

That was what murder was—as easy as that! But afterwards you went on remembering. . . .

She climbed up on the chair, her eyes staring in front of her like a sleepwalker's. . . . She adjusted the noose round her neck. Hugo was there to see she did what she had to do.

She kicked away the chair. . . .

Epilogue

Sir Thomas Legge, Assistant Commissioner at Scotland Yard, said irritably, "But the whole thing's incredible!"

Inspector Maine said respectfully, "I know, sir."

The A.C. went on, "Ten people dead on an island and not a living soul on it. It doesn't make sense!"

Inspector Maine said stolidly, "Nevertheless, it *happened*, sir."

Sir Thomas Legge said, "Damn it all, Maine, somebody must have killed 'em."

"That's just our problem, sir."

"Nothing helpful in the doctor's report?"

"No, sir. Wargrave and Lombard were shot, the first through the head, the second through the heart. Miss Brent and Marston died of cyanide poisoning. Mrs. Rogers died of an overdose of chloral. Rogers' head was split open. Blore's head was crushed in. Armstrong died of drowning. Macarthur's skull was fractured by a blow on the back of the head and Vera Claythorne was hanged."

The A.C. winced. He said, "Nasty business—all of it." He considered for a minute or two. He said irritably, "Do you mean to say that you haven't been able to get anything helpful out of the Sticklehaven people? Dash it, they must know something."

Inspector Maine shrugged his shoulders. "They're ordinary decent seafaring folk. They know that the island was bought by a man called Owen—and that's about all they do know."

"Who provisioned the island and made all the necessary arrangements?"

"Man called Morris. Isaac Morris."

"And what does he say about it all?"

"He can't say anything, sir, he's dead."

The A.C. frowned. "Do we know anything about this Morris?"

"Oh, yes, sir, we know about him. He wasn't a very savory gentleman, Mr. Morris. He was implicated in that share-pushing fraud of Bennito's three years ago—we're sure of that though we can't prove it. And he was mixed up in the dope business. And again we can't prove it. He was a very careful man, Morris."

"And he was behind this island business?"

"Yes, sir, he put through the sale—though he made it clear that he was buying Indian Island for a third party, unnamed."

"Surely there's something to be found out on the financial angle, there?"

579

Inspector Maine smiled. "Not if you knew Morris! He can wangle figures until the best chartered accountant in the country wouldn't know if he was on his head or his heels! We've had a taste of that in the Bennito business. No, he covered his employer's tracks all right."

The other man sighed. Inspector Maine went on, "It was Morris who made all the arrangements down at Sticklehaven. Represented himself as acting for 'Mr. Owen'. And it was he who explained to the people down there that there was some experiment on—some bet about living on a 'desert island' for a week—and that no notice was to be taken of any appeal for help from out there."

Sir Thomas Legge stirred uneasily. He said, "And you're telling me that those people didn't smell a rat? Not even then?"

Maine shrugged his shoulders. He said, "You're forgetting, sir, that Indian Island previously belonged to young Elmer Robson, the American. He had the most extraordinary parties down there. I've no doubt the local people's eyes fairly popped out over them. But they got used to it and they'd begun to feel that anything to do with Indian Island would necessarily be incredible. It's natural, that, sir, when you come to think of it."

The Assistant Commissioner admitted gloomily that he supposed it was.

Maine said, "Fred Narracott—that's the man who took the party out there—did say one thing that was illuminating. He said he was surprised to see what sort of people these were. 'Not at all like Mr. Robson's parties.' I think it was the fact that they were all so normal and so quiet that made him override Morris' orders and take out a boat to the island after he'd heard about the SOS signals."

"When did he and the other men go?"

"The signals were seen by a party of boy scouts on the morning of the 11th. There was no possibility of getting out there that day. The men got there on the afternoon of the 12th at the first moment possible to run a boat ashore there. They're all quite positive that nobody could have left the island before they got there. There was a big sea on after the storm."

"Couldn't someone have swum ashore?"

"It's over a mile to the coast and there were heavy seas and big breakers inshore. And there were a lot of people, boy scouts and others on the cliffs looking out towards the island and watching."

The A.C. sighed. He said, "What about that gramophone record you found in the house? Couldn't you get hold of anything there that might help?"

Inspector Maine said, "I've been into that. It was supplied by a firm that does a lot of theatrical stuff and film effects. It was sent to U.N.

Owen, Esq., c/o Isaac Morris, and was understood to be required for the amateur performance of a hitherto unacted play. The typescript of it was returned with the record."

Legge said, "And what about the subject matter, eh?"

Inspector Maine said gravely, "I'm coming to that, sir." He cleared his throat. "I've investigated those accusations as thoroughly as I can. Starting with the Rogerses who were the first to arrive on the island. They were in service with a Miss Brady who died suddenly. Can't get anything definite out of the doctor who attended her. He says they certainly didn't poison her, or anything like that, but his personal belief is that there *was* some funny business—that she died as the result of neglect on their part. Says it's the sort of thing that's quite impossible to prove.

"Then there is Mr. Justice Wargrave. That's O.K. He was the judge who sentenced Seton. By the way, Seton was guilty—unmistakably guilty. Evidence turned up later after he was hanged which proved that beyond any shadow of doubt. But there was a good deal of comment at the time—nine people out of ten thought Seton was innocent and that the judge's summing up had been vindictive.

"The Claythorne girl, I find, was governess in a family where a death occurred by drowning. However, she doesn't seem to have had anything to do with it, and as a matter of fact she behaved very well, swam out to the rescue and was actually carried out to sea and only just rescued in time."

"Go on," said the A.C. with a sigh.

Maine took a deep breath. "Dr. Armstrong now. Well-known man. Had a consulting room in Harley Street. Absolutely straight and aboveboard in his profession. Haven't been able to trace any record of an illegal operation or anything of that kind. It's true that there was a woman called Clees who was operated on by him way back in 1925 at Leithmore, when he was attached to the hospital there. Peritonitis and she died on the operating table. Maybe he wasn't very skillful over the op.—after all he hadn't much experience—but after all clumsiness isn't a criminal offense. There was certainly no motive.

"Then there's Miss Emily Brent. Girl, Beatrice Taylor, was in service with her. Got pregnant, was turned out by her mistress and went and drowned herself. Not a nice business—but again not criminal."

"That," said the A.C., "seems to be the point. U.N. Owen dealt with cases that the law couldn't touch."

Maine went stolidly on with his list. "Young Marston was a fairly reckless car driver—had his license endorsed twice and he ought to have been prohibited from driving, in my opinion. That's all there is to him. The two names John and Lucy Combes were those of two kids he knocked down and killed near Cambridge. Some friends of his gave evidence for him and he was let off with a fine.

"Can't find anything definite about General Macarthur. Fine record—war service—all the rest of it. Arthur Richmond was serving under him in France and was killed in action. No friction of any kind between him and the General. They were close friends as a matter of fact. There were some blunders made about that time—commanding officers sacrificed men unnecessarily—possibly this was a blunder of that kind."

"Possibly," said the A.C.

"Now, Philip Lombard. Lombard has been mixed up in some very curious shows abroad. He's sailed very near the law once or twice. Got a reputation for daring and for not being overscrupulous. Sort of fellow who might do several murders in some quiet out-of-the-way spot.

"Then we come to Blore." Maine hesitated. "He of course was one of our lot."

The other man stirred. "Blore," said the Assistant Commissioner forcibly, "was a bad hat!"

"You think so, sir?"

The A.C. said, "I always thought so. But he was clever enough to get away with it. It's my opinion that he committed black perjury in the Landor case. I wasn't happy about it at the time. But I couldn't find anything. I put Harris onto it and *he* couldn't find anything, but I'm still of the opinion that there was something to find if we'd known how to set about it. The man wasn't straight."

There was a pause, then Sir Thomas Legge said, "And Isaac Morris is dead, you say? When did he die?"

"I thought you'd soon come to that, sir. Isaac Morris died on the night of August 8th. Took an overdose of sleeping stuff—one of the barbiturates, I understand. There wasn't anything to show whether it was accident or suicide."

Legge said slowly, "Care to know what I think, Maine?"

"Perhaps I can guess, sir."

Legge said heavily, "That death of Morris' is a damned sight too opportune!"

Inspector Maine nodded. He said, "I thought you'd say that, sir."

The Assistant Commissioner brought down his fist with a bang on the table. He cried out, "The whole thing's fantastic—impossible. Ten people killed on a bare rock of an island—and we don't know who did it, or why, or how."

Maine coughed. He said, "Well, it's not quite like that, sir. We do know *why*, more or less. Some fanatic with a bee in his bonnet about justice. He was out to get people who were beyond the reach of the law. He picked ten people—whether they were really guilty or not doesn't matter—"

The Commissioner stirred. He said sharply, "Doesn't it? It seems to me—" He stopped. Inspector Maine waited respectfully. With a sigh Legge shook his head. "Carry on," he said. "Just for a minute I felt I'd got somewhere. Got, as it were, the clue to the thing. It's gone now. Go ahead with what you were saying."

Maine went on, "There were ten people to be—executed, let's say. They *were* executed. U.N. Owen accomplished his task. And somehow or other he spirited himself off that island into thin air."

The A.C. said, "First-class vanishing trick. But you know, Maine, there must be an explanation."

Maine said, "You're thinking, sir, that if the man wasn't on the island, he couldn't have left the island, and according to the account of the interested parties he never was on the island. Well, then the only explanation possible is that he was actually one of the ten." The A.C. nodded. Maine said earnestly, "We thought of that, sir. We went into it. Now, to begin with, we're not quite in the dark as to what happened on Indian Island. Vera Claythorne kept a diary, so did Emily Brent. Old Wargrave made some notes—dry legal cryptic stuff, but quite clear. And Blore made notes too. All those accounts tally. The deaths occurred in this order: Marston, Mrs. Rogers, Macarthur, Rogers, Miss Brent, Wargrave. After his death Vera Claythorne's diary states that Armstrong left the house in the night and that Blore and Lombard had gone after him. Blore has one more entry in his notebook. Just two words: 'Armstrong disappeared.'

"Now, sir, it seemed to me, taking everything into account, that we might find here a perfectly good solution. Armstrong was drowned, you remember. Granting that Armstrong was mad, what was to prevent him having killed off all the others and then committed suicide by throwing himself over the cliff, or perhaps while trying to swim to the mainland?

"That was a good solution—but it won't do. No, sir, it won't do. First of all there's the police surgeon's evidence. He got to the island early on the morning of August 13th. He couldn't say much to help us. All he could say was that all the people had been dead at least thirty-six hours and probably a good deal longer. But he was fairly definite about Armstrong. Said he must have been from eight to ten hours in the water before his body was washed up. That works out at this, that Armstrong must have gone into the sea sometime during the night of the 10th-11th—and I'll explain why. We found the point where the body was washed up—it had been wedged between two rocks and there were bits of cloth, hair, etc., on them. It must have been deposited there at high water on the 11th—that's to say round about 11 o'clock A.M. After that, the storm subsided, and succeeding high-water marks are considerably lower.

"You might say, I suppose, that Armstrong managed to polish off the other three *before* he went into the sea that night. But there's another point and one you can't get over. *Armstrong's body had been dragged above highwater mark*. We found it well above the reach of any tide. And it was laid out straight on the ground—all neat and tidy. So that settles one point definitely. *Someone* was alive on the island after Armstrong was dead."

He paused and then went on. "And that leaves—just what exactly? Here's the position early on the morning of the 11th. Armstrong has 'disappeared' *(drowned)*. That leaves us three people. Lombard, Blore and Vera Claythorne. Lombard was shot. His body was down by the sea—near Armstrong's. Vera Claythorne was found hanged in her own bedroom. Blore's body was on the terrace. His head was crushed in by a heavy marble block that it seems reasonable to suppose fell on him from the window above."

The A.C. said sharply, "Whose window?"

"Vera Claythorne's. Now, sir, let's take each of these cases separately. First Philip Lombard. Let's say *he* pushed over that lump of marble onto Blore—then he doped Vera Claythorne and strung her up. Lastly, he went down to the seashore and shot himself. But if so, *who took away the revolver from him?* For that revolver was found up in the house just inside the door at the top of the stairs—Wargrave's room."

The A.C. said, "Any fingerprints on it?"

"Yes, sir, Vera Claythorne's."

"But, man alive, then—"

"I know what you're going to say, sir. That it was Vera Claythorne. That she shot Lombard, took the revolver back to the house, toppled the marble block onto Blore and then—hanged herself. And that's quite all right—up to a point. There's a chair in her bedroom and on the seat of it there are marks of seaweed same as on her shoes. Looks as though she stood on the chair, adjusted the rope round her neck and kicked away the chair.

"*But that chair wasn't found kicked over*. It was, like all the other chairs, neatly put back against the wall. That was done *after Vera Claythorne's death—by someone else*.

"That leaves us with Blore and if you tell me that after shooting Lombard and inducing Vera Claythorne to hang herself he then went out and pulled down a whacking great block of marble on himself by tying a string to it or something like that—well, I simply don't believe you. Men don't commit suicide that way—and what's more Blore wasn't that kind of man. *We* knew Blore—and he was not the man that you'd ever accuse of a desire for abstract justice."

The Assistant Commissioner said, "I agree.".

Inspector Maine said, "And therefore, sir, there must have been *someone* else on the island. Someone who tidied up when the whole business was over. But where was he all the time—and where did he go to? The Sticklehaven people are absolutely certain that no one could have left the island before the rescue boat got there. But in that case—"

He stopped. The Assistant Commissioner said, "In that case—"

He sighed. He shook his head. He leaned forward. "But in that case," he said, "*who killed them?*"

A manuscript document sent to
Scotland Yard by the master of the
Emma Jane, *fishing trawler*

FROM MY EARLIEST youth I realized that my nature was a mass of contradictions. I have, to begin with, an incurably romantic imagination. The practice of throwing a bottle into the sea with an important document inside was one that never failed to thrill me when reading adventure stories as a child. It thrills me still—and for that reason I have adopted this course—writing my confession, enclosing it in a bottle, sealing the latter, and casting it into the waves. There is, I suppose, a hundred-to-one chance that my confession may be found—and then (or do I flatter myself?) a hitherto unsolved murder mystery will be explained.

I was born with other traits besides my romantic fancy. I have a definite sadistic delight in seeing or causing death. I remember experiments with wasps—with various garden pests. . . . From an early age I knew very strongly the lust to kill. But side by side with this went a contradictory trait—a strong sense of justice. It is abhorrent to me that an innocent person or creature should suffer or die by an act of mine. I have always felt strongly that right should prevail.

It may be understood—I think a psychologist would understand—that with my mental make-up being what it was, I adopted the law as a profession. The legal profession satisfied nearly all my instincts.

Crime and its punishment have always fascinated me. I enjoy

reading every kind of detective story and thriller. I have devised for my own private amusement the most ingenious ways of carrying out a murder.

When in due course I came to preside over a court of law, that other secret instinct of mine was encouraged to develop. To see a wretched criminal squirming in the dock, suffering the tortures of the damned, as his doom came slowly and slowly nearer, was to me an exquisite pleasure. Mind you, I took no pleasure in seeing an *innocent* man there. On at least two occasions I stopped cases where to my mind the accused was palpably innocent, directing the jury that there was no case. Thanks, however, to the fairness and efficiency of our police force, the majority of the accused persons who have come before me to be tried for murder have been guilty.

I will say here that such was the case with the man Edward Seton. His appearance and manner were misleading and he created a good impression on the jury. But not only the evidence, which was clear, though unspectacular, but my own knowledge of criminals told me without any doubt that the man had actually committed the crime with which he was charged, the brutal murder of an elderly woman who trusted him.

I have a reputation as a hanging judge, but that is unfair. I have always been strictly just and scrupulous in my summing up of a case. All I have done is to protect the jury against the emotional effect of emotional appeals by some of our more emotional counsel. I have drawn their attention to the actual evidence.

For some years past I have been aware of a change within myself, a lessening of control—a desire to act instead of to judge. I have wanted—let me admit it frankly—*to commit a murder myself.* I recognized this as the desire of the artist to express himself! I was, or could be, an artist in crime! My imagination, sternly checked by the exigencies of my profession, waxed secretly to colossal force. I must—I must—I *must*—commit a murder! And what is more, it must be no ordinary murder! It must be a fantastical crime—something stupendous—out of the common! In that one respect, I have still, I think, an adolescent's imagination. I wanted something theatrical, impossible! I wanted to kill. . . . Yes, I wanted to kill. . . . But— incongruous as it may seem to some—I was restrained and hampered by my innate sense of justice. The innocent must not suffer.

And then, quite suddenly, the idea came to me—started by a chance remark uttered during casual conversation. It was a doctor to whom I was talking—some ordinary undistinguished G.P. He mentioned casually how often murder must be committed which the law was unable to touch. And he instanced a particular case—that of an old lady, a patient of his who had recently died. He was, he said, himself convinced that her death was due to the withholding of a restorative drug by a married couple who attended on her and who stood to benefit very substantially by her death. That sort of thing, he explained, was quite impossible to prove, but he was nevertheless quite sure of it in his own mind. He added that there were many cases of a similar nature going on all the time—cases of deliberate murder—and all quite untouchable by the law.

That was the beginning of the whole thing. I suddenly saw my way clear. And I determined to commit not one murder, but murder on a grand scale.

A childish rhyme of my infancy came back into my mind—the rhyme of the ten little Indian boys. It had fascinated me as a child of two—the inexorable diminishment—the sense of inevitability. I began, secretly, to collect victims. . . . I will not take up space here by going into details of how this was accomplished. I had a certain routine line of conversation which I employed with nearly everyone I met—and the results I got were really surprising. During the time I was in a nursing home I collected the case of Dr. Armstrong—a violently teetotal sister who attended on me being anxious to prove to me the evils of drink by recounting to me a case many years ago in hospital when a doctor under the influence of alcohol had killed a patient on whom he was operating. A careless question as to where the sister in question had trained, etc., soon gave me the necessary data. I tracked down the doctor and the patient mentioned without difficulty.

A conversation between two old military gossips in my club put me on the track of General Macarthur. A man who had recently returned from the Amazon gave me a devastating résumé of the activities of one Philip Lombard. An indignant *mem sahib* in Majorca recounted the tale of the Puritan Emily Brent and her wretched servant girl. Anthony Marston I selected from a large group of people who had committed similar offenses. His complete callousness and his inability to feel any responsibility for the lives he had taken made him, I considered, a type dangerous to the community and unfit to live. Ex-Inspector Blore came my way quite naturally, some of my professional brethren discussing the Landor case with freedom and vigor. I took a serious view of his offense. The police, as servants of the law, must be of a high order of integrity. For their word is perforce believed by virtue of their profession.

Finally there was the case of Vera Claythorne. It was when I was crossing the Atlantic. At a late hour one night the sole occupants of the smoking room were myself and a good-looking young man called Hugo Hamilton. Hugo Hamilton was unhappy. To assuage that unhappiness he had taken a considerable quantity of drink. He was in the maudlin confidential stage. Without much hope of any result I automatically started my routine conversational gambit. The response was startling. I can remember his words now. He said:

"You're right. Murder isn't what most people think—giving someone a dollop of arsenic—pushing them over a cliff—that sort of stuff." He leaned forward, thrusting his face into mine. He said, "I've known a murderess—known her, I tell you. And what's more I was crazy about her. . . . God help me, sometimes I think I still am. . . . It's hell, I tell you—hell— You see, she did it more or less for me. . . . Not that I ever dreamed. Women are fiends—absolute fiends—you wouldn't think a girl like that—a nice straight jolly girl—you wouldn't think she'd do that, would you? That she'd take a kid out to sea and let it drown—you wouldn't think a *woman* could do a thing like that?"

I said to him, "Are you sure she did do it?"

He said and in saying it he seemed suddenly to sober up, "I'm quite sure. Nobody else ever thought of it. But I knew the moment I looked at her—when I got back—after. . . . And she knew I knew. . . . What she didn't realize was that I loved that kid. . . ." He didn't say any more, but it was easy enough for me to trace back the story and reconstruct it.

I needed a tenth victim. I found him in a man named Morris. He was a shady little creature. Amongst other things he was a dope peddler and he was responsible for inducing the daughter of friends of mine to take to drugs. She committed suicide at the age of twenty-one.

During all this time of search my plan had been gradually maturing in my mind. It was now complete and the coping stone to it was an interview I had with a doctor in Harley Street. I have mentioned that I underwent an operation. My interview in Harley Street told me that another operation would be useless. My medical adviser wrapped up the information very prettily, but I am accustomed to getting at the truth of a statement.

I did not tell the doctor of my decision—that my death would not be a slow and protracted one as it would be in the course of nature. No, my death should take place in a blaze of excitement. I would *live* before I died.

And now to the actual mechanics of the crime of Indian Island. To acquire the island, using the man Morris to cover my tracks, was easy enough. He was an expert in that sort of thing. Tabulating the information I had collected about my prospective victims, I was able to concoct a suitable bait for each. None of my plans miscarried. All my guests arrived at Indian Island on the 8th of August. The party included myself.

Morris was already accounted for. He suffered from indigestion.

Before leaving London I gave him a capsule to take last thing at night which had, I said, done wonders for my own gastric juices. He accepted it unhesitatingly—the man was a slight hypochondriac. I had no fear that he would leave any compromising documents or memoranda behind. He was not that sort of man.

The order of death upon the island had been subjected by me to special thought and care. There were, I considered, amongst my guests, varying degrees of guilt. Those whose guilt was the lightest should, I decided, pass out first, and not suffer the prolonged mental strain and fear that the more cold-blooded offenders were to suffer. Anthony Marston and Mrs. Rogers died first, the one instantaneously, the other in a peaceful sleep. Marston, I recognized, was a type born without that feeling of moral responsibility which most of us have. He was amoral—pagan. Mrs. Rogers, I had no doubt, had acted very largely under the influence of her husband.

I need not describe closely how those two met their deaths. The police will have been able to work that out quite easily. Potassium cyanide is easily obtained by householders for putting down wasps. I had some in my possession and it was easy to slip it into Marston's almost empty glass during the tense period after the gramophone recital.

I may say that I watched the faces of my guests closely during that indictment and I had no doubt whatever, after my long court experience, that one and all were guilty.

During recent bouts of pain, I had been ordered a sleeping draught—chloral hydrate. It had been easy for me to suppress this until I had a lethal amount in my possession. When Rogers brought up some brandy for his wife, he set it down on a table and in passing that table I put the stuff into the brandy. It was easy, for at that time suspicion had not begun to set in.

General Macarthur met his death quite painlessly. He did not hear me come up behind him. I had, of course, to choose my time for leaving the terrace very carefully, but everything was successful.

As I had anticipated, a search was made of the island and it was discovered that there was no one on it but our seven selves. That at once created an atmosphere of suspicion. According to my plan I should shortly need an ally. I selected Dr. Armstrong for that part. He was a gullible sort of man, he knew me by sight and reputation and it was inconceivable to him that a man of my standing should actually be a murderer! All his suspicions were directed against Lombard and I pretended to concur in these. I hinted to him that I had a scheme by which it might be possible to trap the murderer into incriminating himself.

Though a search had been made of everyone's room, no search had as yet been made of the persons themselves. But that was bound to come soon.

I killed Rogers on the morning of August 10th. He was chopping sticks for lighting the fire and did not hear me approach. I found the key to the dining-room door in his pocket. He had locked it the night before.

In the confusion attending the finding of Rogers' body I slipped into Lombard's room and abstracted his revolver. I knew that he would have one with him—in fact, I had instructed Morris to suggest as much when he interviewed him.

At breakfast I slipped my last dose of chloral into Miss Brent's coffee when I was refilling her cup. We left her in the dining room. I slipped in there a little while later—she was nearly unconscious and it was easy to inject a strong solution of cyanide into her. The bumblebee business was really rather childish—but somehow, you know, it pleased me. I liked adhering as closely as possible to the nursery rhyme.

Immediately after this what I had already foreseen happened—indeed I believe I suggested it myself. We all submitted to a rigorous search. I had safely hidden away the revolver, and had no more cyanide or chloral in my possession.

It was then that I intimated to Armstrong that we must carry our plan into effect. It was simply this—*I* must appear to be the next victim. That would perhaps rattle the murderer—at any rate once I was supposed to be dead I could move about the house and spy upon the unknown murderer. Armstrong was keen on the idea. We carried it out that evening. A little plaster of red mud on the forehead—the red curtain and the wool and the stage was set. The lights of the candles were very flickering and uncertain and the only person who would examine me closely was Armstrong. It worked perfectly. Miss Claythorne screamed the house down when she found the seaweed which I had thoughtfully arranged in her room. They all rushed up, and I took up my pose of a murdered man.

The effect on them when they found me was all that could be desired. Armstrong acted his part in the most professional manner. They carried me upstairs and laid me on my bed. Nobody worried about me, they were all too deadly scared and terrified of each other.

I had a rendezvous with Armstrong outside the house at a quarter to two. I took him up a little way behind the house on the edge of the cliff. I said that here we could see if anyone else approached us, and we should not be seen from the house as the bedrooms faced the other way. He was still quite unsuspicious—and yet he ought to have been warned— If he had only remembered the words of the nursery rhyme, "A red herring swallowed one. . . ." He took the red herring all right.

It was quite easy. I uttered an exclamation, leant over the cliff, told him to look, wasn't that the mouth of a cave? He leant right over. A quick vigorous push sent him off his balance and splash into the heaving sea below. I returned to the house. It must have been my footfall that Blore heard. A few minutes after I had returned to Armstrong's room I left it, this time making a certain amount of noise so that someone *should* hear me. I heard a door open as I got to the bottom of the stairs. They must have just glimpsed my figure as I went out of the front door. It was a minute or two before they followed me. I had gone straight round the house and in at the dining-room window which I had left open. I shut the window and later I broke the glass. Then I went upstairs and laid myself out again on my bed.

I calculated that they would not look closely at any of the corpses, a mere twitch aside of the sheet to satisfy themselves that it was not Armstrong masquerading as a body. This is exactly what occurred.

I forgot to say that I returned the revolver to Lombard's room. It may be of interest to someone to know where it was hidden during the search. There was a big pile of tinned food in the larder. I opened the bottommost of the tins—biscuits I think it contained—bedded in the revolver and replaced the strip of adhesive tape. I calculated, and rightly, that no one would think of working their way through a pile of apparently untouched foodstuffs, especially as all the top tins were soldered. The red curtain I had concealed by laying it flat on the seat of one of the drawing-room chairs under the chintz cover and the wool in the seat cushion, cutting a small hole.

And now came the moment that I had anticipated—three people who were so frightened of each other that anything might happen— *and one of them had a revolver.* I watched them from the windows of the house. When Blore came up alone I had the big marble block poised ready. *Exit Blore.*

From my window I saw Vera Claythorne shoot Lombard. A daring and resourceful young woman. I always thought she was a match for him and more. As soon as that had happened I set the stage in her bedroom.

It was an interesting psychological experiment. Would the consciousness of her own guilt, the state of nervous tension consequent on having just shot a man, be sufficient, together with the hypnotic suggestion of the surroundings, to cause her to take her own life? I thought it would. I was right. Vera Claythorne hanged herself before my eyes where I stood in the shadow of the wardrobe.

And now for the last stage. I came forward, picked up the chair and set it against the wall. I looked for the revolver and found it at the top of the stairs where the girl had dropped it. I was careful to preserve her fingerprints on it.

And now? I shall finish writing this. I shall enclose it and seal it in a bottle and I shall throw the bottle into the sea. Why? Yes, why? . . . It was my ambition to *invent* a murder mystery that no one could solve. But no artist, I now realize, can be satisfied with art alone. There is a natural craving for recognition which cannot be gainsaid. I have, let me confess it in all humility, a pitiful human wish that someone should know just how clever I have been. . . .

In all this, I have assumed that the mystery of Indian Island will remain unsolved. It may be, of course, that the police will be cleverer than I think. There are, after all, three clues. One: the police are perfectly aware that Edward Seton was guilty. They know, therefore, that one of the ten people on the island was not a murderer in any sense of the word, and it follows, paradoxically, that that person must logically be the murderer. The second clue lies in the seventh verse of the nursery rhyme. Armstrong's death is associated with a "red herring" which he swallowed—or rather which resulted in swallowing him! That is to say that at that stage of the affair some hocus-pocus is clearly indicated—and that Armstrong was deceived by it and sent to his death. That might start a promising line of inquiry. For at that period there are only four persons and of those four I am clearly the only one likely to inspire him with confidence. The third is symbolical. The manner of my death marking me on the forehead. The brand of Cain.

There is, I think, little more to say. After entrusting my bottle and its message to the sea I shall go to my room and lay myself down on the bed. To my eyeglasses is attached what seems a length of fine black cord—but it is elastic cord. I shall lay the weight of my body on the glasses. The cord I shall loop around the door handle and attach it, not too solidly, to the revolver. What I think will happen is this. My hand, protected with a handkerchief, will press the trigger. My hand will fall to my side, the revolver, pulled by the elastic, will recoil to the door, jarred by the door handle it will detach itself from the elastic and fall. The elastic, released, will hang down innocently from the eyeglasses on which my body is lying. A handkerchief lying on the floor will cause no comment whatever. I shall be found, laid neatly on my bed, shot through the forehead in accordance with the record kept by my fellow victims. Times of death cannot be stated with any accuracy by the time our bodies are examined.

When the sea goes down, there will come from the mainland boats and men. And they will find ten dead bodies and an unsolved problem on Indian Island.

(Signed) LAWRENCE WARGRAVE

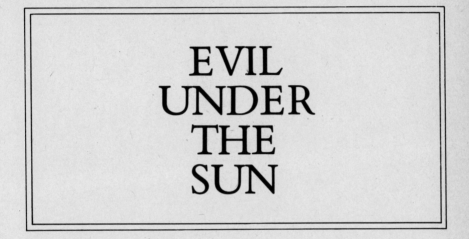

EVIL
UNDER
THE
SUN

Cast of Characters

HERCULE POIROT—The famous Belgian detective with the magnificent moustaches and the "little grey cells."

MRS. GARDENER—A garrulous American tourist.

ODELL C. GARDENER—Who found it simpler to be his wife's echo.

EMILY BREWSTER—A tough, uncompromising, and athletic spinster.

ROSAMUND DARNLEY—A fashionable dressmaker, who embroidered the truth as well as her gowns.

MAJOR BARRY—A retired army officer, whose interest in gossip was a bit abnormal.

REVEREND STEPHEN LANE—Whose reactions were strangely at variance with his cloth.

CHRISTINE REDFERN—Young, and too recently married to be so concerned about—.

PATRICK REDFERN—Christine's errant husband, obviously bewitched by—.

ARLENA STUART MARSHALL—A very beautiful young woman, who wore her heart on her sleeve.

CAPTAIN KENNETH MARSHALL—Arlena's present husband, fortyish and proud as Lucifer.

LINDA MARSHALL—Kenneth Marshall's sixteen-year-old daughter by a previous marriage; a curious mixture of precocity and naïveté.

HORACE BLATT—An almost too blatantly "self-made" man.

1

WHEN CAPTAIN ROGER ANGMERING built himself a house in the year 1782 on the island off Leathercombe Bay, it was thought the height of eccentricity on his part. A man of good family such as he was should have had a decorous mansion set in wide meadows with, perhaps, a running stream and good pasture. But Captain Angmering had only one great love, the sea. So he built his house—a sturdy house too, as it needed to be, on the little windswept gull-haunted promontory—cut off from land at each high tide. He did not marry, the sea was his first and last spouse, and at his death the house and island went to a distant cousin. That cousin and his descendants thought little of the bequest. Their own acres dwindled, and their heirs grew steadily poorer.

In 1922 when the great cult of the Seaside for Holidays was finally established and the coast of Devon and Cornwall was no longer thought too hot in the summer, Arthur Angmering found his vast inconvenient late Georgian house unsaleable, but he got a good price for the odd bit of property acquired by the seafaring Captain Roger. The sturdy house was added to and embellished. A concrete causeway was laid down from the mainland to the island. "Walks" and "Nooks" were cut and devised all round the island. There were two tennis courts, sunterraces leading down to a little bay embellished with rafts and divingboards. The Jolly Roger Hotel, Smugglers' Island, Leather-combe Bay came triumphantly into being. And from June till September (with a short season at Easter) the Jolly Roger Hotel was usually packed to the attics. It was enlarged and improved in 1934 by the addition of a cocktail bar, a bigger dining-room and some extra bathrooms. The prices went up. People said: "Ever been to Leathercombe Bay? Awfully jolly hotel there, on a sort of island. Very comfortable and no trippers or charabancs. Good cooking and all that. You ought to go." And people did go.

There was one very important person (in his own estimation at least) staying at the Jolly Roger. Hercule Poirot, resplendent in a white duck suit, with a Panama hat tilted over his eyes, his mustaches magnificently befurled, lay back in an improved type of deck-chair and surveyed the bathing beach. A series of terraces led down to it from the hotel. On the beach itself were floats, lilos, rubber and canvas boats, balls and rubber toys. There were a long springboard and three rafts at varying distances from the shore. Of the bathers, some were in the sea, some were lying stretched out in the sun, and some were anointing themselves carefully with oil. On the terrace immediately above, the non-bathers sat and commented on the weather, the scene in front of them, the news in the morning papers and any other subject that appealed to them.

On Poirot's left a ceaseless flow of conversation poured in a gentle monotone from the lips of Mrs. Gardener while at the same time her needles clacked as she knitted vigorously. Beyond her, her husband, Odell C. Gardener, lay in a hammock chair, his hat tilted forward over his nose, and occasionally uttered a brief statement when called upon to do so. On Poirot's right, Miss Brewster, a tough athletic woman with grizzled hair and a pleasant weatherbeaten face, made gruff comments. The result sounded rather like a sheepdog whose short stentorian barks interrupted the ceaseless yapping of a Pomeranian. Mrs. Gardener was saying: "And so I said to Mr. Gardener, why, I said, sightseeing is all very well, and I do like to do a place thoroughly. But, after all, I said, we've done England pretty well and all I want now is to get to some quiet spot by the seaside and just relax. That's what I said, wasn't it, Odell? Just *relax*. I feel I must relax, I said. That's so, isn't it, Odell?"

Mr. Gardener, from behind his hat, murmured: "Yes, darling."

Mrs. Gardener pursued the theme. "And so, when I mentioned it to Mr. Kelso, at Cook's (he's arranged all our itinerary for us and been *most* helpful in every way. I don't really know what we'd have done without him!)—Well, as I say, when I mentioned it to him, Mr. Kelso said that we couldn't do better than come here. A most picturesque spot, he said, quite out of the world, and at the same time very comfortable and most exclusive in every way. And of course Mr. Gardener, he chipped in there and said what about the sanitary arrangements? Because, if you'll believe me, Mr. Poirot, a sister of Mr. Gardener's went to stay at a guesthouse once, very exclusive they said it was, and in the heart of the moors, but would you believe me, *nothing but an earth closet*! So naturally that made Mr. Gardener suspicious of these out-of-the-world places, didn't it, Odell?"

"Why, yes, darling," said Mr. Gardener.

"But Mr. Kelso reassured us at once. The sanitation, he said, was absolutely the latest word, and the cooking was excellent. And I'm sure that's so. And what I like about it is, it's *intime* if you know what I mean. Being a small place we all talk to each other and everybody knows everybody. If there is a fault about the British it is that they're inclined to be a bit stand-offish until they've known you a couple of years. After that nobody could be nicer. Mr. Kelso said that interesting people came here and I see he was right. There's you, Mr. Poirot and Miss Darnley. Oh! I was just tickled to death when I found out who you were, wasn't I, Odell?"

"You were, darling."

"Ha!" said Miss Brewster, breaking in explosively. "What a thrill, eh, M. Poirot?"

Hercule Poirot raised his hands in deprecation. But it was no more than a polite gesture. Mrs. Gardener went smoothly on. "You see, M. Poirot, I'd heard a lot about you from Cornelia Robson who was. Mr. Gardener and I were at Badenhof in May. And of course Cornelia told us all about that business in Egypt when Linnet Ridgeway was killed. She said you were wonderful and I've always been simply crazy to meet you, haven't I, Odell?"

"Yes, darling."

"And then Miss Darnley, too. I get a lot of my things at Rose Mond's and of course she *is* Rose Mond, isn't she? I think her clothes are ever so clever. Such a marvellous line. That dress I had on last night was one of hers. She's just a lovely woman in every way, I think."

From beyond Miss Brewster, Major Barry who had been sitting with protuberant eyes glued to the bathers grunted out: "Distinguished lookin' gal!"

Mrs. Gardener clacked her needles. "I've just got to confess one thing, M. Poirot. It gave me a kind of a *turn* meeting you here—not that I wasn't just thrilled to meet you, because I was. Mr. Gardener knows that. But it just came to me that you might be here—well, *professionally*. You know what I mean? Well, I'm just terribly sensitive, as Mr. Gardener will tell you, and I just couldn't bear it if I was to be mixed up in crime of any kind. You see—"

Mr. Gardener cleared his throat. He said: "You see, M. Poirot, Mrs. Gardener is very sensitive."

The hands of Hercule Poirot shot into the air. "But let me assure you, Madame, that I am here simply in the same way that you are here yourselves—to enjoy myself— to spend the holiday. I do not think of crime even."

Miss Brewster said again giving her short gruff bark: "No bodies on Smugglers' Island."

Hercule Poirot said: "Ah! but that, it is not strictly true." He pointed downward. "Regard them there, lying out in rows. What are they? They are not men and women. There is nothing personal about them. They are just—bodies!"

Major Barry said appreciatively: "Good-looking fillies, some of 'em. Bit on the thin side, perhaps."

Poirot cried: "Yes, but what appeal is there? What mystery? I, I am old, of the old school. When I was young, one saw barely the ankle. The glimpse of a foamy petticoat, how alluring! The gentle swelling of the calf—a knee—a beribboned garter—"

"Naughty, naughty!" said Major Barry hoarsely.

"Much more sensible—the things we wear nowadays," said Miss Brewster.

"Why, yes, M. Poirot," said Mrs. Gardener. "I do think, you know, that our girls and boys nowadays lead a much more natural healthy life. They just romp about together and they—well, they—" Mrs. Gardener blushed slightly for she had a nice mind—"they think nothing of it, if you know what I mean?"

"I do know," said Hercule Poirot. "It is deplorable!"

"Deplorable?" squeaked Mrs. Gardener.

"To remove all the romance—all the mystery! Today everything is standardized!" He waved a hand towards the recumbent figures. "That reminds me very much of the Morgue in Paris."

"M. Poirot!" Mrs. Gardener was scandalized.

"Bodies—arranged on slabs—like butcher's meat!"

"But M. Poirot, isn't that too far-fetched for words?"

Hercule Poirot admitted: "It may be, yes."

"All the same," Mrs. Gardener knitted with energy, "I'm inclined to agree with you on one point. These girls that lie out like that in the sun will grow hair on their legs and arms. I've said so to Irene—that's my daughter, M. Poirot. Irene, I said to her, if you lie out like that in the sun, you'll have hair all over you, hair on your arms and hair on your legs and hair on your bosom, and what will you look like then? I said to her. Didn't I, Odell?"

"Yes, darling," said Mr. Gardener.

Every one was silent, perhaps making a mental picture of Irene when the worst had happened. Mrs. Gardener rolled up her knitting and said: "I wonder now—"

Mr. Gardener said: "Yes, darling?" He struggled out of the hammock chair and took Mrs. Gardener's knitting and her book. He asked: "What about joining us for a drink, Miss Brewster?"

"Not just now, thanks."

The Gardeners went up to the hotel. Miss Brewster said: "American husbands are wonderful!"

Mrs. Gardener's place was taken by the Reverend Stephen Lane. Mr. Lane was a tall vigorous clergyman of fifty odd. His face was tanned and his dark grey flannel trousers were holidayfied and disreputable. He said with enthusiasm: "Marvelous country! I've been from Leathercombe Bay to Harford and back over the cliffs."

"Warm work walking to-day," said Major Barry who never walked.

"Good exercise," said Miss Brewster. "I haven't been for my row yet. Nothing like rowing for your stomach muscles." The eyes of Hercule Poirot dropped somewhat ruefully to a certain protuberance in his middle. Miss Brewster, noting the glance, said kindly: "You'd soon get that off, M. Poirot, if you took a rowing-boat out every day."

"*Merci, Mademoiselle*. I detest boats!"

"You mean small boats?"

"Boats of all sizes!" He closed his eyes and shuddered. "The movement of the sea, it is not pleasant."

"Bless the man, the sea is as calm as a mill pond to-day."

Poirot replied with conviction: "There is no such thing as a really calm sea. Always, always, there is motion."

"If you ask me," said Major Barry, "seasickness is nine-tenths nerves."

"There," said the clergyman, smiling a little, "speaks the good sailor—eh, Major?"

"Only been ill once—and that was crossing the channel! Don't think about it, that's my motto."

"Seasickness is really a very odd thing," mused Miss Brewster. "Why should some people be subject to it and not others? It seems so unfair. And nothing to do with one's ordinary health. Quite sickly people are good sailors. Some one told me once it was something to do with one's spine. Then there's the way some people can't stand heights. I'm not very good myself, but Mrs. Redfern is far worse. The other day, on the cliff path to Harford, she turned quite giddy and simply clung to me. She told me she once got stuck halfway down that outside staircase on Milan Cathedral. She'd gone up without thinking but coming down did for her."

"She'd better not go down the ladder to Pixy Cove, then," observed Lane.

Miss Brewster made a face. "I funk that myself. It's all right for the young. The Cowan boys and the young Mastermans, they run up and down it and enjoy it."

Lane said: "Here comes Mrs. Redfern now coming up from her bathe."

Miss Brewster remarked: "M. Poirot ought to approve of her. She's no sun bather."

Young Mrs. Redfern had taken off her rubber cap and was shaking out her hair. She was an ash blonde and her skin was of that dead fairness that goes with that colouring. Her legs and arms were very white. With a hoarse chuckle, Major Barry said: "Looks a bit uncooked among the others, doesn't she?"

Wrapping herself in a long bath-robe Christine Redfern came up the beach and mounted the steps towards them. She had a fair serious face, pretty in a negative way, and small dainty hands and feet. She smiled at them and dropped down beside them, tucking her bath-wrap round her. Miss Brewster said: "You have earned M. Poirot's good opinion. He doesn't like the sun-tanning crowd. Says they're like joints of butcher's meat or words to that effect."

Christine Redfern smiled ruefully. She said: "I wish I *could* sun-bathe! But I don't brown. I only blister and get the most frightful freckles all over my arms."

"Better than getting hair all over them like Mrs. Gardener's Irene," said Miss Brewster. In answer to Christine's inquiring glance she went on: "Mrs. Gardener's been in grand form this morning. Absolutely non stop. 'Isn't that so, Odell?' 'Yes, darling.'" She paused and then said: "I wish, though, M. Poirot, that you'd played up to her a bit. Why didn't you tell her that you were down here investigating a particularly gruesome murder, and that the murderer, a homicidal maniac, was certainly to be found among the guests of the hotel?"

Hercule Poirot sighed. He said: "I very much fear she would have believed me."

Major Barry gave a wheezy chuckle. He said: "She certainly would."

Emily Brewster said: "No, I don't believe even Mrs. Gardener would have believed in a crime staged here. This isn't the sort of place you'd get a body!"

Hercule Poirot stirred a little in his chair. He protested. He said: "But why not, Mademoiselle? Why should there not be what you call a 'body' here on Smugglers' Island?"

Emily Brewster said: "I don't know. I suppose some places *are* more unlikely than others. This isn't the kind of spot—" She broke off, finding it difficult to explain her meaning.

"It is romantic, yes," agreed Hercule Poirot. "It is peaceful. The sun shines. The sea is blue. But you forget, Miss Brewster, there is evil everywhere under the sun."

The clergyman stirred in his chair. He leaned forward. His intensely blue eyes lighted up. Miss Brewster shrugged her shoulders. "Oh! of course I realize that, but all the same—"

"But all the same this still seems to you an unlikely setting for crime? You forget one thing, Mademoiselle."

"Human nature, I suppose?"

"That, yes. That, always. But that was not what I was going to say. I was going to point out to you that here every one is on holiday."

Emily Brewster turned a puzzled face to him. "I don't understand."

Hercule Poirot beamed kindly at her. He made dabs in the air with an emphatic forefinger. "Let us say, you have an enemy. If you seek him out in his flat, in his office, in the street—*eh bien*, you must have a *reason*—you must account for yourself. But here at the seaside it is necessary for no one to account for himself. You are at Leathercombe Bay, why? *Parbleu*! it is August—one goes to the seaside in August—one is on one's holiday. It is quite natural, you see, for you to be here and for Mr. Lane to be here and for Major Barry to be here and for Mrs. Redfern and her husband to be here. Because it is the custom in England to go to the seaside in August."

"Well," admitted Miss Brewster, "that's certainly a very ingenious idea. But what about the Gardeners? They're American."

Poirot smiled. "Even Mrs. Gardener, as she told us, feels the need to *relax*. Also, since she is 'doing' England, she must certainly spend a fortnight at the seaside—as a good tourist, if nothing else. She enjoys watching people."

Mrs. Redfern murmured: "You like watching the people too, I think?"

"Madame, I will confess it. I do."

She said thoughtfully: "You see—a good deal."

There was a pause. Stephen Lane cleared his throat and said with a trace of self-consciousness: "I was interested, M. Poirot, in something you said just now. You said that there was evil done everywhere under the sun. It was almost a quotation from Ecclesiastes." He paused and then quoted himself. "*Yea, also the heart of the sons of men is full of evil, and madness is in their heart while they live.*" His face lit up with an almost fanatical light. "I was glad to hear you say that. Nowadays, no one believes in evil. It is considered, at most, a mere negation of good. Evil, people say, is done by those who know no better—who are undeveloped—who are to be pitied rather than blamed. But, M. Poirot, evil is *real*! It is a *fact*! I believe in Evil as I believe in Good. It exists! It is powerful! It walks the earth!" He stopped. His breath was coming fast. He wiped his forehead with his handkerchief and looked suddenly apologetic. "I'm sorry. I got carried away."

Poirot said calmly: "I understand your meaning. Up to a point I agree with you. Evil does walk the earth and can be recognized as such."

Major Barry cleared his throat. "Talking of that sort of thing, some of these fakir fellers in India—"

Major Barry had been long enough at the Jolly Roger for every one to be on their guard against his fatal tendency to embark on long India stories. Both Miss Brewster and Mrs. Redfern burst into speech. "That's your husband swimming in now, isn't it, Mrs. Redfern? How magnificent his crawl stroke is. He's an awfully good swimmer." At the same moment Mrs. Redfern said: "Oh, look! What a lovely little boat that is out there with the red sails. It's Mr. Blatt's, isn't it?" The sailing boat with the red sails was just crossing the end of the bay.

Major Barry grunted: "Fanciful idea, red sails," but the menace of the story about the fakir was avoided.

Hercule Poirot looked with appreciation at the young man who had just swum to shore. Patrick Redfern was a good specimen of humanity. Lean, bronzed, with broad shoulders and narrow thighs, there was about him a kind of infectious enjoyment and gaiety—a native simplicity that endeared him to all women and most men. He stood there shaking the water from him and raising a hand in gay salutation to his wife. She waved back, calling out: "Come up here, Pat."

"I'm coming."

He went a little way along the beach to retrieve the towel he had left there. It was then that a woman came down past them from the hotel to the beach. Her arrival had all the importance of a stage entrance. Moreover, she walked as though she knew it. There was no self-consciousness apparent. It would seem that she was too used to the invariable effect her presence produced. She was tall and slender. She wore a simple backless white bathing dress and every inch of her exposed body was tanned a beautiful even shade of bronze. She was as perfect as a statue. Her hair was a rich flaming auburn curling richly and intimately into her neck. Her face had that slight hardness which is seen when thirty years have come and gone, but the whole effect of her was one of youth—of superb and triumphant vitality. There was a Chinese immobility about her face, and an upward slant of the dark blue eyes. On her head she wore a fantastic Chinese hat of jade-green cardboard. There was that about her which made every other woman on the beach seem faded and insignificant. And with equal inevitability, the eye of every male present was drawn and rivetted on her.

The eyes of Hercule Poirot opened, his mustache quivered appreciatively, Major Barry sat up and his protuberant eyes bulged even further with excitement; on Poirot's left the Reverend Stephen Lane drew in his breath with a little hiss and his figure stiffened. Major Barry said in a hoarse whisper: "Arlena Stuart (that's who she was before she married Marshall)—I saw her in *Come and Go* before she left the stage. Something worth looking at, eh?"

Christine Redfern said slowly and her voice was cold: "She's handsome—yes. I think—she looks rather a beast!"

Emily Brewster said abruptly: "You talked about evil just now, M. Poirot. Now to my mind that woman's a personification of evil! She's a bad lot through and through. I happen to know a good deal about her."

Major Barry said reminiscently: "I remember a gal out in Simla. *She* had red hair too. Wife of a subaltern. Did she set the place by the ears? I'll say she did! Men went mad about her! All the women, of course, would have liked to gouge her eyes out! She upset the apple cart in more homes than one." He chuckled reminiscently. "Husband was a nice quiet fellow. Worshipped the ground she walked on. Never saw a thing—or made out he didn't."

Stephen Lane said in a low voice full of intense feeling: "Such women are a menace—a menace to—" He stopped.

Arlena Stuart had come to the water's edge. Two young men, little more than boys, had sprung up and come eagerly toward her. She stood smiling at them. Her eyes slid past them to where Patrick Redfern was coming along the beach. It was, Hercule Poirot thought, like watching the needle of a compass. Patrick Redfern was deflected, his feet changed their direction. The needle, do what it will, must obey the law of magnetism and turn to the North. Patrick Redfern's feet brought him to Arlena Stuart. She stood smiling at him. Then she moved slowly along the beach by the side of the waves. Patrick Redfern went with her. She stretched herself out by a rock. Redfern dropped to the shingle beside her. Abruptly, Christine Redfern got up and went into the hotel.

There was an uncomfortable little silence after she had left. Then Emily Brewster said: "It's rather too bad. She's a nice little thing. They've only been married a year or two."

"Gal I was speaking of," said Major Barry, "The one in Simla. She upset a couple of really happy marriages. Seemed a pity, what?"

"There's a type of woman," said Miss Brewster, "who *likes* smashing up homes." She added after a minute or two, "Patrick Redfern's a fool!" Hercule Poirot said nothing. He was gazing down the beach, but he was not looking at Patrick Redfern and Arlena Stuart. Miss Brewster said: "Well, I'd better go and get hold of my boat." She left them.

Major Barry turned his boiled gooseberry eyes with mild curiosity on Poirot. "Well, Poirot," he said. "What are you thinking about?

You've not opened your mouth. What do you think of the siren? Pretty hot?"

Poirot said: "*C'est possible.*"

"Now then, you old dog. I know you Frenchmen!"

Poirot said coldly: "I am *not* a Frenchman!"

"Well, don't tell me you haven't got an eye for a pretty girl! What do you think of her, eh?"

Hercule Poirot said: "She is not young."

"What does that matter? A woman's as old as she looks! *Her* looks are all right."

Hercule Poirot nodded. He said: "Yes, she is beautiful. But it is not beauty that counts in the end. It is not beauty that makes every head (except one) turn on the beach to look at her."

"It's IT, my boy," said the Major. "That's what it is—IT." Then he said with sudden curiosity: "What are you looking at so steadily?"

Hercule Poirot replied: "I am looking at the exception. At the one man who did not look up when she passed."

Major Barry followed his gaze to where it rested on a man of about forty, fair-haired and sun-tanned. He had a quiet, pleasant face and was sitting on the beach smoking a pipe and reading the *Times*. "Oh, *that*!" said Major Barry. "That's the husband, my boy. That's Marshall."

Hercule Poirot said: "Yes, I know."

Major Barry chuckled. He himself was a bachelor. He was accustomed to think of The Husband in three lights only—as "the Obstacle," "the Inconvenience" or "the Safeguard." He said: "Seems a nice fellow. Quiet. Wonder if my *Times* has come?" He got up and went up towards the hotel.

Poirot's glance shifted slowly to the face of Stephen Lane. Stephen Lane was watching Arlena Marshall and Patrick Redfern. He turned suddenly to Poirot. There was a stern fanatical light in his eyes. He said: "That woman is evil through and through. Do you doubt it?"

Poirot said slowly: "It is difficult to be sure."

Stephen Lane said: "But, man alive, don't you feel it in the air? All round you? The presence of Evil."

Slowly, Hercule Poirot nodded his head.

2

WHEN ROSAMUND DARNLEY came and sat down by him, Hercule Poirot
made no attempt to disguise his pleasure. As he has since admitted, he
admired Rosamund Darnley as much as any woman he had ever met.
He liked her distinction, the graceful lines of her figure, the alert proud
carriage of her head. He liked the neat sleek waves of her dark hair and
the ironic quality of her smile. She was wearing a dress of some navy
blue material with touches of white. It looked very simple owing to the
expensive severity of its line. Rosamund Darnley as Rose Mond Ltd.
was one of London's best-known dressmakers. She said: "I don't think
I like this place. I'm wondering why I came here!"

"You have been here before, have you not?"

"Yes, two years ago, at Easter. There weren't so many people
then."

Hercule Poirot looked at her. He said gently: "Something has
occurred to worry you. That is right, is it not?"

She nodded. Her foot swung to and fro. She stared down at it. She
said: "I've met a ghost. That's what it is."

"A ghost, Mademoiselle?"

"Yes."

"The ghost of what? Or of whom?"

"Oh, the ghost of myself."

Poirot asked gently: "Was it a painful ghost?"

"Unexpectedly painful. It took me back, you know." She paused,
musing. Then she said: "Imagine my childhood—No, you can't!
You're not English!"

Poirot asked: "Was it a very English childhood?"

"Oh, incredibly so! The country—a big shabby house—horses,
dogs—walks in the rain—wood fires—apples in the orchard—lack of
money—old tweeds—evening dresses that went on from year to
year—a neglected garden—with Michaelmas daisies coming out like
great banners in the Autumn . . ."

Poirot asked gently: "And you want to go back?"

Rosamund Darnley shook her head. She said: "One can't go back,
can one? That—never. But I'd like to have gone on—a different way."

Poirot said: "I wonder."

Rosamund Darnley laughed. "So do I really!"

Poirot said: "When I was young (and that, Mademoiselle, is indeed
a long time ago) there was a game entitled '*If not yourself, who would*

you be?' One wrote the answer in young ladies' albums. They had gold edges and were bound in blue leather. The answer, Mademoiselle, is not really very easy to find.''

Rosamund said: "No—I suppose not. It would be a big risk. One wouldn't like to take on being Mussolini or Princess Elizabeth. As for one's friends, one knows too much about them. I remember once meeting a charming husband and wife. They were so courteous and delightful to one another and seemed on such good terms after years of marriage that I envied the woman. I'd have changed places with her willingly. Somebody told me afterwards that in private they'd never spoken to each other for eleven years!" She laughed. "That shows, doesn't it, that you never know?"

After a moment or two Poirot said: "Many people, Mademoiselle, must envy you."

Rosamund Darnley said coolly: "Oh, yes. Naturally." She thought about it, her lips curved upward in their ironic smile. "Yes, I'm really the perfect type of the successful woman! I enjoy the artistic satisfaction of the successful creative artist (I really do like designing clothes) and the financial satisfaction of the successful business woman. I'm very well off, I've a good figure, a passable face, and a not too malicious tongue." She paused. Her smile widened. "Of course—I haven't got a husband! I've failed there, haven't I, M. Poirot?"

Poirot said gallantly: "Mademoiselle, if you are not married, it is because none of my sex have been sufficiently eloquent. It is from choice, not necessity, that you remain single."

Rosamund Darnley said: "And yet, like all men, I'm sure you believe in your heart that no woman is content unless she is married and has children."

Poirot shrugged his shoulders. "To marry and have children, that is the common lot of women. Only one woman in a hundred—more, in a thousand—can make for herself a name and a position as you have done."

Rosamund grinned at him. "And yet, all the same, I'm nothing but a wretched old maid! That's what I feel today, at any rate. I'd be happier with a twopence a year and a big silent brute of a husband and a brood of brats running after me. That's true, isn't it?"

Poirot shrugged his shoulders. "Since you say so, then, yes, Mademoiselle."

Rosamund laughed, her equilibrium suddenly restored. She took out a cigarette and lit it. She said: "You certainly know how to deal with women, M. Poirot. I now feel like taking the opposite point of view and arguing with you in favour of careers for women. Of course I'm damned well off as I am—and I know it!"

"Then everything in the garden—or shall we say at the seaside?—is lovely, Mademoiselle."

"Quite right."

Poirot, in his turn, extracted his cigarette case and lit one of those tiny cigarettes which it was his affectation to smoke. Regarding the ascending haze with a quizzical eye, he murmured: "So Mr.—no, Captain—Marshall is an old friend of yours, Mademoiselle?"

Rosamund sat up. She said: "Now how do you know that? Oh, I suppose Ken told you."

Poirot shook his head. "Nobody has told me anything. After all, Mademoiselle, I am a detective. It was the obvious conclusion to draw."

Rosamund Darnley said: "I don't see it."

"But consider!" The little man's hands were eloquent. "You have been here a week. You are lively, gay, without a care. To-day, suddenly, you speak of ghosts, of old times. What has happened? For several days there have been no new arrivals until last night when Captain Marshall and his wife and daughter arrive. To-day the change! It is obvious!"

Rosamund Darnley said: "Well, it's true enough. Kenneth Marshall and I were more or less children together. The Marshalls lived next door to us. Ken was always nice to me—although condescending, of course, since he was four years older. I've not seen anything of him for a long time. It must be—fifteen years at least."

Poirot said thoughtfully: "A long time." Rosamund nodded. There was a pause and then Hercule Poirot said: "He is sympathetic, yes?"

Rosamund said warmly: "Ken's a dear. One of the best. Frightfully quiet and reserved. I'd say his only fault is a *penchant* for making unfortunate marriages."

Poirot said in a tone of great understanding: "Ah. . . ."

Rosamund Darnley went on. "Kenneth's a fool—an utter fool where women are concerned! Do you remember the Martingdale case?"

Poirot frowned. "Martingdale? Martingdale? Arsenic, was it not?"

"Yes. Seventeen or eighteen years ago. The woman was tried for the murder of her husband."

"And he was proved to have been an arsenic eater and she was acquitted?"

"That's right. Well, after her acquittal, Ken married her. That's the sort of damn silly thing he does."

Hercule Poirot murmured: "But if she was innocent?"

Rosamund Darnley said impatiently: "Oh, I daresay she *was* innocent. Nobody really knows! But there are plenty of women to marry in the world without going out of your way to marry one who's stood her trial for murder." Poirot said nothing. Perhaps he knew that if he kept silence Rosamund Darnley would go on. She did so. "He was very young, of course, only just twenty-one. He was crazy about her. She died when Linda was born—a year after their marriage. I believe Ken was terribly cut up by her death. Afterwards he racketed around a lot—trying to forget, I suppose." She paused. "And then came this business of Arlena Stuart. She was in Revue at the time. There was the Codrington divorce case. Lady Codrington divorced Codrington citing Arlena Stuart. They say Lord Codrington was absolutely infatuated with her. It was understood they were to be married as soon as the decree was made absolute. Actually, when it came to it, he didn't marry her. Turned her down flat. I believe she actually sued him for breach of promise. Anyway, the thing made a big stir at the time. The next thing that happens is that Ken goes and marries her. The fool—the complete fool!"

Hercule Poirot murmured: "A man might be excused such a folly—she is beautiful, Mademoiselle."

"Yes, there's no doubt of that. There was another scandal about three years ago. Old Sir Roger Erskine left her every penny of his money. I should have thought that would have opened Ken's eyes if anything would."

"And did it not?"

Rosamund Darnley shrugged her shoulders. "I tell you I've seen nothing of him for years. People say though, that he took it with absolute equanimity. Why I should like to know? Has he got an absolutely blind belief in her?"

"There might be other reasons."

"Yes. Pride! Keeping a stiff upper lip! I don't know what he really feels about her. Nobody does."

"And she? What does she feel about him?"

Rosamund stared at him. She said: "She? She's the world's first gold-digger. And a man eater as well! If anything personable in trousers comes within a hundred yards of her, it's fresh sport for Arlena! She's that kind."

Poirot nodded his head slowly in complete agreement. "Yes," he said. "That is true what you say. . . . Her eyes look for one thing only —men."

Rosamund said: "She's got her eye on Patrick Redfern now. He's a good-looking man—and rather the simple kind—you know, fond of his wife, and not a philanderer. That's the kind that's meat and drink to Arlena. I like little Mrs. Redfern—she's nice-looking in her fair washed-out way—but I don't think she'll stand a dog's chance against that man-eating tiger, Arlena."

Poirot said: "No, it is as you say." He looked distressed.

Rosamund said: "Christine Redfern was a school teacher, I believe. She's the kind that thinks that mind has a pull over matter. She's got a rude shock coming to her." Poirot shook his head vexedly. Rosamund got up. She said: "It's a shame, you know." She added vaguely: "Somebody ought to do something about it."

Linda Marshall was examining her face dispassionately in her bedroom mirror. She disliked her face very much. At this minute it seemed to her to be mostly bones and freckles. She noted with distaste her heavy bush of red-brown hair (mouse, she called it in her own mind), her greenish-grey eyes, her high cheek-bones and the long aggressive line of the chin. Her mouth and teeth weren't perhaps quite so bad—but what were teeth after all? And was that a spot coming on the side of her nose? She decided with relief that it wasn't a spot. She thought to herself: "It's awful to be sixteen—simply *awful*."

One didn't, somehow, know where one was. Linda was as awkward as a young colt and as prickly as a hedgehog. She was conscious the whole time of her ungainliness and of the fact that she was neither one thing nor the other. It hadn't been so bad at school. But now she had left school. Nobody seemed to know quite what she was going to do next. Her father talked vaguely of sending her to Paris next winter. Linda didn't want to go to Paris—but then she didn't want to be at home either. She'd never realized properly, somehow, until now, how very much she disliked Arlena.

Linda's young face grew tense, her green eyes hardened. Arlena. . . . She thought to herself: "She's a beast—a *beast*. . . ." Stepmothers! It was rotten to have a stepmother, everybody said so. And it was true! Not that Arlena was unkind to her. Most of the time she hardly noticed the girl. But when she did, there was a contemptuous amusement in her glance, in her words. The finished grace and poise of Arlena's movements emphasized Linda's own adolescent clumsiness. With Arlena about, one felt, shamingly, just how immature and crude one was. But it wasn't that only. No, it wasn't only that. Linda groped haltingly in the recesses of her mind. She wasn't very good at sorting out her emotions and labeling them. It was something that Arlena *did* to people—to the house—"She's bad," thought Linda with decision. "She's quite, quite bad."

But you couldn't even leave it at that. You couldn't just elevate your nose with a sniff of moral superiority and dismiss her from your mind. It was something she did to people. Father, now, Father was quite different. . . . She puzzled over it. Father coming down to take her out from school. Father taking her once for a cruise. And Father at home—with Arlena there. All—all sort of bottled up and not—and not *there*. Linda thought: "And it'll go on like this. Day after day—month after month. I can't bear it."

Life stretched before her—endless—in a series of days darkened and poisoned by Arlena's presence. She was childish enough still to have little sense of proportion. A year, to Linda, seemed like an eternity. A big dark burning wave of hatred against Arlena surged up in her mind. She thought: "I'd like to kill her. Oh! I wish she'd die. . . ."

She looked out above the mirror onto the sea below. This place was really rather fun. Or it could be fun. All those beaches and coves and queer little paths. Lots to explore. And places where one could go off by oneself and muck about. There were caves, too, so the Cowan boys had told her. Linda thought: "If only Arlena would go away, I could enjoy myself."

Her mind went back to the evening of their arrival. It had been exciting coming from the mainland. The tide had been up over the causeway. They had come in a boat. The hotel had looked exciting, unusual. And then on the terrace a tall dark woman had jumped up and said: "Why, Kenneth!"

And her father, looking frightfully surprised, had exclaimed: "Rosamund!"

Linda considered Rosamund Darnley severely and critically in the manner of youth. She decided that she approved of Rosamund. Rosamund, she thought, was sensible. And her hair grew nicely—as though it fitted her—most people's hair didn't fit them. And her clothes were nice. And she had a kind of funny amused face—as though it were amused at herself not at you. Rosamund had been nice to her, Linda. She hadn't been gushing or *said* things. (Under the term of "saying things" Linda grouped a mass of miscellaneous dislikes.) And Rosamund hadn't looked as though she thought Linda a fool. In fact she'd treated Linda as though she were a real human being. Linda so seldom felt like a real human being that she was deeply grateful when any one appeared to consider her one.

Father, too, had seemed pleased to see Miss Darnley. Funny—he'd looked quite different, all of a sudden. He'd looked—he'd looked—Linda puzzled it out—why, *young*, that was it! He'd laughed—a queer boyish laugh. Now Linda came to think of it, she'd very seldom heard him laugh. She felt puzzled. It was as though she'd got a glimpse of quite a different person. She thought: "I wonder what Father was like when he was my age. . . ." But that was too difficult. She gave it up.

An idea just flashed across her mind. What fun it would have been if they'd come here and found Miss Darnley here—just she and Father. A vista opened out just for a minute. Father, boyish and laughing, Miss

Darnley, herself—and all the fun one could have on the island—bathing—caves—The blackness shut down again.

Arlena. One couldn't enjoy oneself with Arlena about. Why not? Well, she, Linda, couldn't, anyway. You couldn't be happy when there was a person there you—hated. Yes, hated. She hated Arlena. Very slowly that black burning wave of hatred rose up again. Linda's face went very white. Her lips parted a little. The pupils of her eyes contracted. And her fingers stiffened and clenched themselves. . . .

Kenneth Marshall tapped on his wife's door. When her voice answered, he opened the door and went in. Arlena was just putting the finishing touches to her toilet. She was dressed in glittering green and looked a little like a mermaid. She was standing in front of the glass applying mascara to her eyelashes. She said: "Oh, it's you, Ken."

"Yes. I wondered if you were ready."

"Just a minute."

Kenneth Marshall strolled to the window. He looked out on the sea. His face, as usual, displayed no emotion of any kind. It was pleasant and ordinary. Turning around, he said: "Arlena?"

"Yes?"

"You've met Redfern before, I gather?"

Arlena said easily: "Oh, yes, darling. At a cocktail party somewhere. I thought he was rather a pet."

"So I gather. Did you know that he and his wife were coming down here?"

Arlena opened her eyes very wide. "Oh, no, darling. It was the *greatest* surprise!"

Kenneth Marshall said quietly: "I thought, perhaps, that that was what put the idea of this place into your head. You were very keen we should come here."

Arlena put down the mascara. She turned towards him. She smiled—a soft seductive smile. She said: "Somebody told me about this place. I think it was the Rylands. They said it was simply too marvelous—so unspoilt! Don't you like it?"

Kenneth Marshall said: "I'm not sure."

"Oh, darling, but you adore bathing and lazing about. I'm sure you'll simply adore it here."

"I can see that you mean to enjoy yourself." Her eyes widened a little. She looked at him uncertainly. Kenneth Marshall said: "I suppose the truth of it is that you told young Redfern that you were coming here?"

Arlena said: "Kenneth darling, you're not going to be horrid, are you?"

Kenneth Marshall said: "Look here, Arlena. I know what you're like. That's rather a nice young couple. That boy's fond of his wife really. Must you upset the whole blinking show?"

Arlena said: "It's so unfair blaming *me*. I haven't done anything— anything at all. I can't help it if—"

He prompted her. "If what?"

Her eyelids fluttered. "Well, of course, I know people do go crazy about me. But it's not my doing. They just get like that."

"So you do admit that young Redfern is crazy about you?"

Arlena murmured: "It's really rather stupid of him." She moved a step towards her husband. "But you know, don't you, Ken, that I don't really care for any one but you?"

She looked up at him through her darkened lashes. It was a marvelous look—a look that few men could have resisted. Kenneth Marshall looked down at her gravely. His face was composed. His voice quiet. He said: "I think I know you pretty well, Arlena. . . ."

When you came out of the hotel on the south side the terraces and the bathing beach were immediately below you. There was also a path that led off round the cliff on the southwest side of the island. A little way along it, a few steps led down to a series of recesses cut into the cliff and labelled on the hotel map of the island as Sunny Ledge. Here cut out of the cliff were niches with seats in them. To one of these, immediately after dinner, came Patrick Redfern and his wife. It was a lovely clear night with a bright moon. The Redferns sat down. For a while they were silent. At last Patrick Redfern said: "It's a glorious evening, isn't it, Christine?"

"Yes." Something in her voice may have made him uneasy. He sat without looking at her. Christine Redfern asked in her quiet voice: "Did you know that woman was going to be here?"

He turned sharply. He said: "I don't know what you mean."

"I think you do."

"Look here, Christine. I don't know what has come over you—"

She interrupted. Her voice held feeling now. It trembled. "Over *me*? It's what has come over *you*!"

"Nothing's come over me."

"Oh! Patrick! It *has*! You insisted so on coming here. You were quite vehement. I wanted to go to Tintagel again where—where we had our honeymoon. You were bent on coming here."

"Well, why not? It's a fascinating spot."

"Perhaps. But you wanted to come here because *she* was going to be here."

"She? Who is she?"

"Mrs. Marshall. You—you're infatuated with her."

"For God's sake, Christine, don't make a fool of yourself. It's not like you to be jealous." His bluster was a little uncertain. He exaggerated it.

She said: "We've been happy!"

"Happy? Of course we've been happy! We *are* happy. But we shan't go on being happy if I can't even speak to another woman without you kicking up a row."

"It's not like that."

"Yes, it is. In marriage one has got to have—well—friendships with other people. This suspicious attitude is all wrong. I—I can't speak to a pretty woman without your jumping to the conclusion that I'm in love with her—" He stopped. He shrugged his shoulders.

Christine Redfern said: "You *are* in love with her. . . ."

"Oh, don't be a fool, Christine! I've—I've barely spoken to her."

"That's not true."

"Don't for goodness' sake get into the habit of being jealous of every pretty woman we come across."

Christine Redfern said: "She's not just any pretty woman! She's—she's *different*! She's a bad lot! Yes, she is. She'll do you harm. Patrick, please, *give it up*. Let's go away from here."

Patrick Redfern stuck out his chin mutinously. He looked somehow very young as he said defiantly: "Don't be ridiculous, Christine. And—and don't let's quarrel about it."

"I don't want to quarrel."

"Then behave like a reasonable human being. Come on, let's go back to the hotel."

He got up. There was a pause, then Christine Redfern got up too. She said: "Very well . . ."

In the recess adjoining, on the seat there, Hercule Poirot sat and shook his head sorrowfully. Some people might have scrupulously removed themselves from earshot of a private conversation. But not Hercule Poirot. He had no scruples of that kind. "Besides," as he explained to his friend Hastings at a later date, "it was a question of murder."

Hastings said, staring: "But the murder hadn't happened, then."

Hercule Poirot sighed. He said: "But already, *mon cher*, it was very clearly indicated."

"Then why didn't you stop it?"

And Hercule Poirot, with a sigh, said, as he had said once before in Egypt, that if a person is determined to commit murder it is not easy to prevent them. He does not blame himself for what happened. It was, according to him, inevitable.

3

ROSAMUND DARNLEY AND KENNETH MARSHALL sat on the short springy turf of the cliff overlooking Gull Cove. This was on the east side of the island. People came here in the morning sometimes to bathe when they wanted to be peaceful. Rosamund said: "It's nice to get away from people."

Marshall murmured inaudibly: "M-m, yes." He rolled over sniffing at the short turf. "Smells good. Remember the downs at Shipley?"

"Rather."

"Pretty good, those days."

"Yes."

"You're not changed much, Rosamund."

"Yes, I have. I've changed enormously."

"You've been very successful and you're rich and all that, but you're the same old Rosamund."

Rosamund murmured: "I wish I were."

"What's that?"

"Nothing. It's a pity, isn't it, Kenneth, that we can't keep the nice natures and high ideals that we had when we were young?"

"I don't know that your nature was ever particularly nice, my child. You used to get into the most frightful rages. You half choked me once when you flew at me in a temper."

Rosamund laughed. She said: "Do you remember the day that we took Toby down to get water rats?"

They spent some minutes in recalling old adventures. Then there came a pause. Rosamund's fingers played with the clasp of her bag. She said at last: "Kenneth?"

"Um." His reply was indistinct. He was still lying on his face on the turf.

"If I say something to you that is probably outrageously impertinent, will you never speak to me again?"

He rolled over and sat up. "I don't think," he said seriously, "that I would ever regard anything you said as impertinent. You see, you *belong*."

She nodded in acceptance of all that last phrase meant. She concealed only the pleasure it gave her. "Kenneth, why don't you get a divorce from your wife?"

His face altered. It hardened—the happy expression died out of it. He took a pipe from his pocket and began filling it. Rosamund said: "I'm sorry if I've offended you."

618

He said quietly: "You haven't offended me."

"Well, then, why don't you?"

"You don't understand, my dear girl."

"Are you—so frightfully fond of her?"

"It's not just a question of that. You see, I married her."

"I know. But she's—pretty notorious."

He considered that for a moment, ramming in the tobacco carefully. "Is she? I suppose she is."

"You *could* divorce her, Ken."

"My dear girl, you've got no business to say a thing like that. Just because men lose their heads about her a bit isn't to say that she loses hers."

Rosamund bit off a rejoinder. Then she said: "You could fix it so that she divorced you—if you prefer it that way."

"I daresay I could."

"You ought to, Ken. Really, I mean it. There's the child."

"Linda?"

"Yes, Linda."

"What's Linda to do with it?"

"Arlena's not good for Linda. She isn't really. Linda, I think, *feels* things a good deal."

Kenneth Marshall applied a match to his pipe. Between puffs he said: "Yes—there's something in that. I suppose Arlena and Linda aren't very good for each other. Not the right thing for a girl perhaps. It's a bit worrying."

Rosamund said: "I like Linda—very much. There's something— fine about her."

Kenneth said: "She's like her mother. She takes things hard like Ruth did."

Rosamund said: "Then don't you think—really—that you ought to get rid of Arlena?"

"Fix up a divorce?"

"Yes. People are doing that all the time."

Kenneth Marshall said with sudden vehemence: "Yes, and that's just what I hate."

"Hate?" She was startled.

"Yes. Sort of attitude to life there is nowadays. If you take on a thing and don't like it, then you get yourself out of it as quick as possible! Dash it all, there's got to be such a thing as good faith. If you marry a woman and engage yourself to look after her, well, it's up to you to do it. It's your show. You've taken it on. I'm sick of quick marriage and easy divorce. Arlena's my wife, that's all there is to it."

Rosamund leaned forward. She said in a low voice: "So it's like that with you? 'Till death do us part'?"

Kenneth Marshall nodded his head. He said: "That's just it."

Rosamund said: "I see."

Mr. Horace Blatt, returning to Leathercombe Bay down a narrow twisting lane, nearly ran down Mrs. Redfern at a corner. As she flattened herself into the hedge, Mr. Blatt brought his Sunbeam to a halt by applying the brakes vigorously. "Hullo-ullo-ullo," said Mr. Blatt cheerfully. He was a large man with a red face and a fringe of reddish hair round a shining bald spot. It was Mr. Blatt's apparent ambition to be the life and soul of any place he happened to be in. The Jolly Roger Hotel, in his opinion, given somewhat loudly, needed brightening up. He was puzzled at the way people seemed to melt and disappear when he himself arrived on the scene. "Nearly made you into strawberry jam, didn't I?" said Mr. Blatt gaily.

Christine Redfern said: "Yes, you did."

"Jump in," said Mr. Blatt.

"Oh, thanks—I think I'll walk."

"Nonsense," said Mr. Blatt. "What's a car for?"

Yielding to necessity Christine Redfern got in. Mr. Blatt restarted the engine which had stopped owing to the suddenness with which he had previously pulled up. Mr. Blatt inquired: "And what are you doing walking about all alone? That's all wrong, a nice-looking girl like you."

Christine said hurriedly: "Oh! I like being alone."

Mr. Blatt gave her a terrific dig with his elbow, nearly sending the car into the hedge at the same time. "Girls always say that," he said. "They don't mean it. You know, that place, the Jolly Roger, wants a bit of livening up. Nothing jolly about it. No *life* in it. Of course there's a good amount of duds staying there. A lot of kids, to begin with, and a lot of old fogeys too. There's that old Anglo-Indian bore and that athletic parson and those yapping Americans and that foreigner with the mustache—makes me laugh that mustache of his! I should say he's a hair-dresser, something of that sort."

Christine shook her head. "Oh, no, he's a detective."

Mr. Blatt nearly let the car go into the hedge again. "A detective? D'you mean he's in *disguise*?"

Christine smiled faintly. She said: "Oh, no, he really *is* like that. He's Hercule Poirot. You must have heard of him."

Mr. Blatt said: "Didn't catch his name properly. Oh, yes, I've *heard* of him. But I thought he was dead.... Dash it, he *ought* to be dead. What's he after down here?"

"He's not after anything—he's just on a holiday."

"Well, I suppose that might be so." Mr. Blatt seemed doubtful about it. "Looks a bit of a bounder, doesn't he?"

"Well," said Christine and hesitated. "Perhaps a little peculiar."

"What I say is," said Mr. Blatt, "what's wrong with Scotland Yard? Buy British every time for me." He reached the bottom of the hill and with a triumphant fanfare of the horn ran the car into the Jolly Roger's garage which was situated, for tidal reasons, on the mainland opposite the hotel.

Linda Marshall was in the small shop which catered to the wants of visitors to Leathercombe Bay. One side of it was devoted to shelves on which were books which could be borrowed for the sum of twopence. The newest of them was ten years old, some were twenty years old and others older still. Linda took first one and then another doubtfully from the shelf and glanced into it. She decided that she couldn't possibly read *The Four Feathers or Vice Versa*. She took out a small squat volume in brown calf. The time passed. . . . With a start Linda shoved the book back in the shelf as Christine Redfern's voice said: "What are you reading, Linda?"

Linda said hurriedly: "Nothing. I'm looking for a book." She pulled out *The Marriage of William Ashe* at random and advanced to the counter fumbling for twopence.

Christine said: "Mr. Blatt just drove me home—after nearly running over me first, I really felt I couldn't walk all across the causeway with him, so I said I had to buy some things."

Linda said: "He's awful, isn't he? Always saying how rich he is and making the most terrible jokes."

Christine said: "Poor man. One really feels rather sorry for him."

Linda didn't agree. She didn't see anything to be sorry for in Mr. Blatt. She was young and ruthless. She walked with Christine Redfern out of the shop and down towards the causeway. She was busy with her own thoughts. She like Christine Redfern. She and Rosamund Darnley were the only bearable people on the island in Linda's opinion. Neither of them talked much to her for one thing. Now, as they walked, Christine didn't say anything. That, Linda thought, was sensible. If you hadn't anything worth saying why go chattering all the time? She lost herself in her own perplexities.

She said suddenly: "Mrs. Redfern, have you ever felt that everything's so awful—so terrible—that you'll—oh, *burst*. . .?"

The words were almost comic, but Linda's face, drawn and anxious, was not. Christine Redfern, looking at her at first vaguely, with scarcely comprehending eyes, certainly saw nothing to laugh at. . . . She caught her breath sharply. She said: "Yes—yes—I have felt—just that. . . ."

Mr. Blatt said: "So you're the famous sleuth, eh?" They were in the cocktail bar, a favorite haunt of Mr. Blatt's.

Hercule Poirot acknowledged the remark with his usual lack of modesty. Mr. Blatt went on. "And what are you doing down here—on a job?"

"No, no. I repose myself. I take the holiday."

Mr. Blatt winked. "You'd say that anyway, wouldn't you?"

Poirot replied: "Not necessarily."

Horace Blatt said: "Oh! come now. As a matter of fact you'd be safe enough with *me*. I don't repeat all I hear! Learnt to keep my mouth shut years ago. Shouldn't have got on the way I have if I hadn't known how to do that. But you know what most people are—yap, yap, yap, about everything they hear! Now you can't afford that in your trade! That's why you've got to keep it up that you're here holiday-making and nothing else."

Poirot asked: "And why should you suppose the contrary?"

Mr. Blatt closed one eye. He said: "I'm a man of the world. I know the cut of a fellow's jib. A man like you would be at Deauville or Le Touquet or down at Juan les Pins. That's your—what's the phrase?—spiritual home."

Poirot sighed. He looked out of the window. Rain was falling and mist encircled the island. He said: "It is possible that you are right! There, at least, in wet weather there are the distractions."

"Good old Casino!" said Mr. Blatt. "You know, I've had to work pretty hard most of my life. No time for holidays or kickshaws. I meant to make good and I have made good. Now I can do what I please. My money's as good as any man's. I've seen a bit of life in the last few years, I can tell you."

Poirot murmured: "Ah, yes?"

"Don't know why I came to this place," Mr. Blatt continued.

Poirot observed: "I, too, wondered."

"Eh, what's that?"

Poirot waved an eloquent hand. "I, too, am not without observation. I should have expected *you* most certainly to choose Deauville or Biarritz."

"Instead of which, we're both here, eh?" Mr. Blatt gave a hoarse chuckle. "Don't really know why I came here," he mused. "I think, you know, it sounded *romantic*. Jolly Roger Hotel, Smugglers' Island. That kind of address tickles you up, you know. Makes you think of when you were a boy. Pirates, smuggling, all that." He laughed rather self-consciously. "I used to sail quite a bit as a boy. Not this part of the world. Off the East coast. Funny how a taste for that sort of thing never leaves you. I could have a tiptop yacht if I liked, but somehow I don't really fancy it. I like mucking about in that little yawl of mine. Redfern's keen on sailing, too. He's been out with me once or twice. Can't get hold of him now—always hanging round that redhaired wife of Marshall's." He paused, then lowering his voice, he went on. "Mostly a dried-up lot of sticks in this hotel! Mrs. Marshall's about the only lively spot! I should think Marshall's got his hands full looking after her. All sorts of stories about her in her stage days—*and* after! Men go crazy about her. You'll see, there'll be a spot of trouble one of these days."

Poirot asked: "What kind of trouble?"

Horace Blatt replied: "That depends. I'd say, looking at Marshall, that he's a man with a funny kind of temper. As a matter of fact, I know he is. Heard something about him. I've met that quiet sort. Never know where you are with that kind. Redfern had better look out—"

He broke off, as the subject of his words came into the bar. He went on speaking loudly and self-consciously. "And, as I say, sailing round this coast is good fun. Hullo, Redfern, have one with me? What'll you have? Dry Martini? Right. What about you, Mr. Poirot?"

Poirot shook his head. Patrick Redfern sat down and said: "Sailing? It's the best fun in the world. Wish I could do more of it. Used to spend most of my time as a boy in a sailing dinghy round this coast."

Poirot said: "Then you know this part of the world well?"

"Rather! I knew this place before there was a hotel on it. There were just a few fishermen's cottages at Leathercombe Bay and a tumble-down old house, all shut up, on the island."

"There was a house here?"

"Oh, yes, but it hadn't been lived in for years. Was practically falling down. There used to be all sorts of stories of secret passages from the house to Pixy's Cave. We were always looking for that secret passage, I remember."

Horace Blatt spilt his drink. He cursed, mopped himself and asked: "What is this Pixy's Cave?"

Patrick said: "Oh, don't you know it? It's on Pixy Cove. You can't find the entrance to it easily. It's among a lot of piled-up boulders at one end. Just a long thin crack. You can just squeeze through it. Inside it widens out into quite a big cave. You can imagine what fun it was to a boy! An old fisherman showed it to me. Nowadays, even the fishermen don't know about it. I asked one the other day why the place was called Pixy Cove and he couldn't tell me."

Hercule Poirot said: "But I still do not understand. What is this Pixy?"

Patrick Redfern said: "Oh! that's typically Devonshire. There's the Pixy's Cave at Sheepstor on the Moor. You're supposed to leave a pin, you know, as a present for the Pixy. A Pixy is a kind of moor spirit."

Hercule Poirot said: "Ah! but it is interesting, that."

Patrick Redfern went on. "There's a lot of pixy lore on Dartmoor still. There are Tors that are said to be pixy-ridden, and I expect that farmers coming home after a thick night still complain of being pixy-led."

Horace Blatt said: "You mean when they've had a couple?"

Patrick Redfern said with a smile: "That's certainly the commonsense explanation!"

Blatt looked at his watch. He said: "I'm going in to dinner. On the whole, Redfern, pirates are my favorites, not pixies."

Patrick Redfern said with a laugh as the other went out: "Faith, I'd like to see the old boy pixy-led himself!"

Poirot observed meditatively: "For a hard-bitten business man, M. Blatt seems to have a very romantic imagination."

Patrick Redfern said: "That's because he's only half educated. Or so my wife says. Look at what he reads! Nothing but thrillers or Wild West stories."

Poirot said: "You mean that he has still the mentality of a boy?"

"Well, don't you think so, sir?"

"Me, I have not seen very much of him."

"I haven't really, either. I've been out sailing with him once or twice—but he doesn't really like having any one with him. He prefers to be on his own."

Hercule Poirot said: "That is indeed curious. It is singularly unlike his practice on land."

Redfern laughed. He said: "I know. We all have a bit of trouble keeping out of his way. He'd like to turn this place into a cross between Margate and Le Touquet."

Poirot said nothing for a minute or two. He was studying the laughing face of his companion very attentively. He said suddenly and unexpectedly: "I think, Mr. Redfern, that you enjoy living."

Patrick stared at him, surprised. "Indeed I do. Why not?"

"Why not indeed," agreed Poirot. "I make you my felicitation on the fact."

Smiling a little Patrick Redfern said: "Thank you, sir."

"That is why, as an older man, a very much older man, I venture to offer you a piece of advice."

"Yes, sir?"

"A very wise friend of mine in the Police Force said to me years ago: 'Hercule, my friend, if you would know tranquillity, avoid women.'"

Patrick Redfern said: "I'm afraid it's a bit late for that, sir. I'm married, you know."

"I do know. Your wife is a very charming, a very accomplished woman. She is, I think, very fond of you."

Patrick Redfern said sharply: "I'm very fond of her."

"Ah," said Hercule Poirot, "I am delighted to hear it."

Patrick's brow was suddenly like thunder. "Look here, M. Poirot, what are you getting at?"

"*Les femmes.*" Poirot leaned back and closed his eyes. "I know something of them. They are capable of complicating life unbearably. And the English, they conduct their affairs indescribably. If it was necessary for you to come here, Mr. Redfern, why, in the name of Heaven, did you bring your wife?"

Patrick Redfern said angrily: "I don't know what you mean."

Hercule Poirot said calmly: "You know perfectly. I am not so foolish as to argue with an infatuated man. I utter only the word of caution."

"You've been listening to these damned scandalmongers. Mrs. Gardener, the Brewster woman—nothing to do but to clack their tongues all day. Just because a woman's good-looking—they're down on her like a sack of coals."

Hercule Poirot got up. He murmured: "Are you really as young as all that?" Shaking his head, he left the bar. Patrick Redfern stared angrily after him.

Hercule Poirot paused in the hall on his way from the dining-room. The doors were open—a breath of soft night air came in. The rain had stopped and the mist had dispersed. It was a fine night again. Hercule Poirot found Mrs. Redfern in her favourite seat on the cliff ledge. He stopped by her and said: "This seat is damp. You should not sit here. You will catch the chill."

"No, I shan't. And what does it matter anyway."

"Tscha, tscha, you are not a child! You are an educated woman. You must look at things sensibly."

She said coldly: "I can assure you I never take cold."

Poirot said: "It has been a wet day. The wind blew, the rain came down, and the mist was everywhere so that one could not see through it. *Eh bien*, what is it like now? The mists have rolled away, the sky is clear and up above the stars shine. That is like life, Madame."

Christine said in a low fierce voice: "Do you know what I am most sick of in this place?"

"What, Madame?"

"Pity." She brought the word out like the flick of a whip. She went on: "Do you think I don't know? That I can't see? All the time people are saying: 'Poor Mrs. Redfern—that poor little woman.' And anyway I'm not little, I'm tall. They say little because they are sorry for me. And I can't bear it!"

Cautiously Hercule Poirot spread his handkerchief on the seat and sat down. He said thoughtfully: "There is something in that."

She said: "That woman—" and stopped.

Poirot said gravely: "Will you allow me to tell you something, Madame? Something that is as true as the stars above us? The Arlena Stuarts—or Arlena Marshalls—of this world—do not count."

Christine Redfern said: "Nonsense."

"I assure you, it is true. Their Empire is of the moment and for the moment. To count—really and truly to count—a woman must have goodness or brains."

Christine said scornfully: 'Do you think men care for goodness or brains?"

Poirot said gravely: "Fundamentally, yes."

Christine laughed shortly. She said: "I don't agree with you."

Poirot said: "Your husband loves you, Madame, I know it."

"You can't know it."

"Yes, yes. I know it. I have seen him looking at you."

Suddenly she broke down. She wept stormily and bitterly against Poirot's accommodating shoulder. She said: "I can't bear it. . . . I can't bear it. . . ."

Poirot patted her arm. He said soothingly: "Patience—only patience."

She sat up and pressed her handkerchief to her eyes. She said in a stifled voice: "It's all right. I'm better now. Leave me. I'd—I'd rather be alone."

He obeyed and left her sitting there while he himself followed the winding path down to the hotel. He was nearly there when he heard the murmur of voices. He turned a little aside from the path. There was a gap in the bushes. He saw Arlena Marshall and Patrick Redfern beside her. He heard the man's voice, with the throb in it of emotion. "I'm crazy about you—crazy—you've driven me mad. . . You do care a little—you do care?"

He saw Arlena Marshall's face—it was, he thought, like a sleek happy cat—it was animal, not human. She said softly: "Of course, Patrick darling, I adore you. You know that. . . . ' '

For once Hercule Poirot cut his eavesdropping short. He went back to the path and on down to the hotel.

A figure joined him suddenly. It was Captain Marshall. Marshall said: "Remarkable night, what? After that foul day." He looked up at the sky. "Looks as though we should have fine weather to-morrow."

4

THE MORNING OF THE 25 TH OF AUGUST dawned bright and cloudless. It was a morning to tempt even an inveterate sluggard to rise early. Several people rose early that morning at the Jolly Roger.

It was eight o'clock when Linda, sitting at her dressing-table, turned a little thick calf-bound volume face downwards, sprawling it open, and looked at her own face in the mirror. Her lips were set tight together and the pupils of her eyes contracted. She said below her breath: "I'll do it. . . ."

She slipped out of her pyjamas and into her bathing dress. Over it she flung on a bath-robe and laced espadrilles on her feet. She went out of her room and along the passage. At the end of it a door on to the balcony led to an outside staircase leading directly down to the rocks below the hotel. There was a small iron ladder clamped onto the rocks leading down into the water which was used by many of the hotel guests for a before breakfast dip as taking up less time than going down to the main bathing beach. As Linda started down from the balcony she met her father coming up. He said: "You're up early. Going to have a dip?"

Linda nodded. They passed each other. Instead of going on down to the rocks, however, Linda skirted round the hotel to the left until she came to the path down to the causeway connecting the hotel with the mainland. The tide was high and the causeway under water, but the boat that took hotel guests across was tied to a little jetty. The man in charge of it was absent at the moment. Linda got in, untied it and rowed herself across.

She tied up the boat on the other side, walked up the slope past the hotel garage and along until she reached the general shop. The woman had just taken down the shutters and was engaged in sweeping the floor. She looked amazed at the sight of Linda. "Well, Miss, you *are* up early."

Linda put her hand in the pocket of her bath-wrap and brought out some money. She proceeded to make her purchases.

Christine Redfern was standing in Linda's room when the girl returned. "Oh, there you are," Christine exclaimed. "I thought you couldn't be really up yet."

Linda said: "No, I've been bathing."

Noticing the parcel in her hand, Christine said with surprise: "The post has come early to-day." Linda flushed. With her habitual nervous clumsiness the parcel slipped from her hand. The flimsy string broke and some of the contents rolled over the floor. Christine exclaimed: "What have you been buying *candles* for?" But to Linda's relief she did not wait for an answer, but went on, as she helped to pick the things up from the floor: "I came in to ask whether you would like to come with me to Gull Cove this morning. I want to sketch there."

Linda accepted with alacrity. In the last few days she had accompanied Christine Redfern more than once on sketching expeditions. Christine was a most indifferent artist but it is possible that she found the excuse of painting a help to her pride since her husband now spent most of his time with Arlena Marshall.

Linda Marshall had been increasingly morose and bad-tempered. She liked being with Christine who, intent on her work, spoke very little. It was, Linda felt, nearly as good as being by oneself, and in a curious way she craved for company of some kind. There was a subtle kind of sympathy between her and the elder woman, probably based on the fact of their mutual dislike of the same person. Christine said: "I'm playing tennis at twelve, so we'd better start fairly early. Half past ten?"

"Right. I'll be ready. Meet you in the hall."

Rosamund Darnley, strolling out of the dining-room after a very late breakfast, was cannoned into by Linda as the latter came tearing down the stairs. "Oh! sorry, Miss Darnley."

Rosamund said: "Lovely morning, isn't it? One can hardly believe it after yesterday."

"I know. I'm going with Mrs. Redfern to Gull Cove. I said I'd meet her at half past ten. I thought I was late."

"No, it's only twenty-five past."

"Oh! good."

She was panting a little and Rosamund looked at her curiously. "You're not feverish, are you, Linda?"

The girl's eyes were very bright and she had a vivid patch of colour in each cheek. "Oh! *no*. I'm never feverish."

Rosamund smiled and said: "It's such a lovely day I got up for breakfast. Usually I have it in bed. But to-day I came down and faced eggs and bacon like a man."

"I know—it's heavenly after yesterday. Gull Cove is nice in the morning. I shall put a lot of oil on and get really brown."

Rosamund said: "Yes, Gull Cove is nice in the morning. And it's more peaceful than the beach here."

Linda said, rather shyly: "Come too."

Rosamund shook her head. She said: "Not this morning. I've other fish to fry."

Christine Redfern came down the stairs. She was wearing beach pajamas of a loose floppy pattern with long sleeves and wide legs. They were made of some green material with a yellow design. Rosamund's tongue itched to tell her that yellow and green were the most unbecoming colours possible for her fair, slightly anaemic complexion. It always annoyed Rosamund when people had no clothes sense. She thought: "If I dressed that girl, *I*'d soon make her husband sit up and take notice. However much of a fool Arlena is, she does know how to dress. This wretched girl looks just like a wilting lettuce." Aloud she said: "Have a nice time. I'm going to Sunny Ledge with a book."

Hercule Poirot breakfasted in his room as usual off coffee and rolls. The beauty of the morning, however, tempted him to leave the hotel earlier than usual. It was ten o'clock, at least half an hour before his usual appearance, when he descended to the bathing beach. The beach itself was empty save for one person.

That person was Arlena Marshall. Clad in her white bathing-dress, the green Chinese hat on her head, she was trying to launch a white wooden float. Poirot came gallantly to the rescue, completely immersing a pair of white suède shoes in doing so. She thanked him with one of those sideways glances of hers. Just as she was pushing off, she called him. "M. Poirot?"

Poirot leaped to the water's edge. "Madame."

Arlena Marshall said: "Do something for me, will you?"

"Anything."

She smiled at him. She murmured: "Don't tell any one where I am." She made her glance appealing. "Every one *will* follow me about so. I just want for once to be *alone*." She paddled off vigorously.

Poirot walked up the beach. He murmured to himself: *"Ah ça, Jamais!* That, *par exemple,* I do not believe."

He doubted if Arlena Stuart, to give her stage name, had ever wanted to be alone in her life. Hercule Poirot, that man of the world, knew better. Arlena Marshall was doubtless keeping a rendezvous, and Poirot had a very good idea with whom. Or thought he had, but there he found himself proved wrong. For just as the float rounded the point of the bay and disappeared out of sight Patrick Redfern closely followed by Kenneth Marshall came striding down the beach from the hotel.

Marshall nodded to Poirot. "Morning, Poirot. Seen my wife anywhere about?"

Poirot's answer was diplomatic. "Has Madame then risen so early?"

Marshall said: "She's not in her room." He looked up at the sky. "Lovely day. I shall have a bathe right away. Got a lot of typing to do this morning."

Patrick Redfern, less openly, was looking up and down the beach. He sat down near Poirot and prepared to wait for the arrival of his lady. Poirot said: "And Madame Redfern? Has she too risen early?"

Patrick Redfern said: "Christine? Oh, she's going off sketching. She's rather keen on art just now." He spoke impatiently, his mind clearly elsewhere. As time passed he displayed his impatience for Arlena's arrival only too crudely. At every footstep he turned an eager head to see who it was coming down from the hotel.

Disappointment followed disappointment. First Mr. and Mrs. Gardener complete with knitting and book and then Miss Brewster arrived. Mrs. Gardener, industrious as ever, settled herself in her chair, and began to knit vigorously and talk at the same time. "Well, M. Poirot. The beach seems very deserted this morning. Where *is* everybody?"

Poirot replied that the Mastermans and the Cowans, two families with young people in them, had gone off on an all-day sailing excursion.

"Why, that certainly does make all the difference, not having them about laughing and calling out. And only one person bathing, Captain Marshall."

Marshall had just finished his swim. He came up the beach swinging his towel. "Pretty good in the sea this morning," he said. "Unfortunately I've got a lot of work to do. Must go and get on with it."

"Why, if that isn't too bad, Captain Marshall. On a beautiful day like this, too. My, wasn't yesterday too terrible? I said to Mr. Gardener that if the weather was going to continue like that, we'd just have to leave. It's so melancholy, you know, with the mist right up around the island. Gives you a kind of ghostly feeling, but then I've always been very susceptible to atmosphere ever since I was a child. Sometimes, you know, I'd feel I just had to scream and scream. And that, of course, was very trying to my parents. But my mother was a lovely woman and she said to my father, 'Sinclair, if the child feels like that, we must let her do it. Screaming is her way of expressing herself.' And of course my father agreed. He was devoted to my mother and just did everything she said. They were a perfectly lovely couple, as I'm sure Mr. Gardener will agree. They were a very remarkable couple, weren't they, Odell?"

"Yes, darling," said Mr. Gardener.

"And where's your girl this morning, Captain Marshall?"

"Linda? I don't know. I expect she's mooning round the island somewhere."

"You know, Captain Marshall, that girl looks kind of peaky to me. She needs feeding up and very, very sympathetic treatment."

Kenneth Marshall said curtly: "Linda's all right."

He went up to the hotel. Patrick Redfern did not go into the water. He sat about, frankly looking up towards the hotel. He was beginning to look a shade sulky. Miss Brewster was brisk and cheerful when she arrived.

The conversation was much as it had been on a previous morning. Gentle yapping from Mrs. Gardener and short staccato barks from Miss Brewster. She remarked at last: "Beach seems a bit empty. Every one off on excursions?"

Mrs. Gardener said: "I was saying to Mr. Gardener only this morning that we simply must make an excursion to Dartmoor. It's quite near and the associations are all so romantic. And I'd like to see that convict prison—Princetown, isn't it? I think we'd better fix up right away and go there to-morrow, Odell."

Mr. Gardener said: "Yes, darling."

Hercule Poirot said to Miss Brewster: "You are going to bathe, Mademoiselle?"

"Oh, I've had my morning dip before breakfast. Somebody nearly brained me with a bottle, too. Chucked it out of one of the hotel windows."

"Now that's a very dangerous thing to do," said Mrs. Gardener. "I had a very dear friend who got concussion by a toothpaste tin falling on him in the street—thrown out of a thirty-fifth storey window it was. A most dangerous thing to do. He got very substantial damages." She began to hunt among her skeins of wool. "Why, Odell, I don't believe I've got that second shade of purple wool. It's in the second drawer of the bureau in our bedroom or it might be the third."

"Yes, darling."

Mr. Gardener rose obediently and departed on his search. Mrs. Gardener went on: "Sometimes, you know, I do think that maybe we're going a little too far nowadays. What with all our great discoveries and all the electrical waves there must be in the atmosphere, I do think it leads to a great deal of mental unrest and I just feel that maybe the time has come for a new message to humanity. I don't know, M. Poirot, if you've ever interested yourself in the prophecies from the Pyramids."

"I have not," said Poirot.

"Well, I do assure you that they're very, very interesting. What with Moscow being exactly a thousand miles due North of—now what was it?—Would it be Nineveh?—but anyway you take a circle and it just shows the most surprising things—and one can just see that there must have been special guidance, and that those ancient Egyptians couldn't have thought of what they did all by themselves. And when you've gone into the theory of the numbers and their repetition, why, it's all just so clear that I can't see how any one can doubt the truth of it for a moment." Mrs. Gardener paused triumphantly but neither Poirot nor Miss Emily Brewster felt moved to argue the point.

Poirot studied his white suède shoes ruefully. Emily Brewster said: "You been paddling with your shoes on, M. Poirot?"

Poirot murmured: "Alas! I was precipitate."

Emily Brewster lowered her voice. She said: "Where's our Vamp this morning? She's late."

Mrs. Gardener, raising her eyes from her knitting to study Patrick Redfern, murmured: "He looks just like a thundercloud. Oh! dear, I do feel the whole thing is such a pity. I wonder what Captain Marshall thinks about it all. He's such a nice quiet man—very British and unassuming. You just never know what he's thinking about things."

Patrick Redfern rose and began to pace up and down the beach. Mrs. Gardener murmured: "Just like a tiger."

Three pairs of eyes watched his pacing. Their scrutiny seemed to make Patrick Redfern uncomfortable. He looked more than sulky now. He looked in a flaming temper. In the stillness a faint chime from the mainland came to their ears. Emily Brewster murmured: "Wind's from the East again. That's a good sign when you can hear the church clock strike."

Nobody said any more until Mr. Gardener returned with a skein of brilliant magenta wool. "Why, Odell, what a long time you have been!"

"Sorry, darling, but you see it wasn't in your bureau at all. I found it on your wardrobe shelf."

"Why, isn't that too extraordinary? I could have declared I put it in that bureau drawer. I do think it's fortunate that I've never had to give evidence in a court case. I'd just worry myself to death in case I wasn't remembering a thing just right."

Mr. Gardener said: "Mrs. Gardener is very conscientious."

It was some five minutes later that Patrick Redfern said: "Going for your row this morning, Miss Brewster? Mind if I come with you?"

Miss Brewster said heartily: "Delighted."

"Let's row right round the island," proposed Redfern.

Miss Brewster consulted her watch. "Shall we have time? Oh, yes, it's not half past eleven yet. Come on, then, let's start."

They went down the beach together. Patrick Redfern took first turn at the oars. He rowed with a powerful stroke. The boat leapt forward. Emily Brewster said approvingly: "Good. We'll see if you can keep that up."

He laughed into her eyes. His spirits had improved. "I shall probably have a fine crop of blisters by the time we get back." He threw up his head tossing back his black hair. "God, it's a marvellous day! If you do get a real summer's day in England there's nothing to beat it."

Emily Brewster said gruffly: "Can't beat England anyway in my opinion. Only place in the world to live in."

"I'm with you."

They rounded the point of the bay to the west and rowed under the cliffs. Patrick Redfern looked up. "Any one on Sunny Ledge this morning? Yes, there's a sunshade. Who is it, I wonder?"

Emily Brewster said: "It's Miss Darnley, I think. She's got one of those Japanese affairs."

They rowed up the coast. On their left was the open sea. Emily Brewster said: "We ought to have gone the other way round. This way we've got the current against us."

"There's very little current. I've swum out here and not noticed it. Anyway we couldn't go the other way. The causeway wouldn't be covered."

"Depends on the tide, of course. But they always say that bathing from Pixy Cove is dangerous if you swim out too far."

Patrick was rowing vigorously still. At the same time he was scanning the cliffs attentively. Emily Brewster thought suddenly: "He's looking for the Marshall woman. That's why he wanted to come with me. She hasn't shown up this morning and he's wondering what she's up to. Probably she's done it on purpose. Just a move in the game—to make him keener."

They rounded the jutting point of rock to the south of the little bay named Pixy's Cove. It was quite a small cove, with rocks dotted fantastically about the beach. It faced nearly northwest and the cliff overhung it a good deal. It was a favourite place for picnic teas. In the morning, when the sun was off it, it was not popular and there was seldom any one there. On this occasion, however, there was a figure on the beach. Patrick Redfern's stroke checked and recovered. He said in a would-be casual tone: "Hullo, who's that?"

Miss Brewster said drily: "It looks like Mrs. Marshall."

Patrick Redfern said as though struck by the idea: "So it does."

He altered his course, rowing inshore. Emily Brewster protested. "We don't want to land here, do we?"

Patrick Redfern said quickly: "Oh, plenty of time."

His eyes looked into hers—something in them, a naïve pleading look rather like that of an importunate dog, silenced Emily Brewster. She thought to herself: "Poor boy, he's got it badly. Oh, well, it can't be helped. He'll get over it in time."

The boat was fast approaching the beach. Arlena Marshall was lying face downwards on the shingle her arms outstretched. The white float was drawn up near by. Something was puzzling Emily Brewster. It was as though she was looking at something she knew quite well but which was in one respect quite wrong. It was a minute or two before it came to her. Arlena Marshall's attitude was the attitude of a sun-bather. So had she lain many a time on the beach by the hotel, her bronzed body outstretched and the green cardboard hat protecting her head and neck.

But there was no sun on Pixy's Beach and there would be none for some hours yet. The overhanging cliff protected the beach from the sun in the morning. A vague feeling of apprehension came over Emily Brewster.

The boat grounded on the shingle. Patrick Redfern called: "Hullo, Arlena."

And then Emily Brewster's foreboding took definite shape. For the recumbent figure did not move or answer.

Emily saw Patrick Redfern's face change. He jumped out of the boat and she followed him. They dragged the boat ashore then set off up the beach to where that white figure lay so still and unresponsive near the bottom of the cliff. Patrick Redfern got there first but Emily Brewster was close behind him.

She saw, as one sees in a dream, the bronzed limbs, the white backless bathing dress—the red curl of hair escaping under the jade-green hat—saw something else too—the curious unnatural angle of the outspread arms. Felt, in that minute, that this body had not *lain* down but had been *thrown*. . . . She heard Patrick's voice—a mere frightened whisper. He knelt down beside that still form—touched the hand—the arm. . . . He said in a low shuddering whisper: *"My God, she's dead. . . ."*

And then, as he lifted the hat a little, peered at the neck: *"Oh, God, she's been strangled . . . murdered."*

It was one of those moments when time stands still. With an odd feeling of unreality Emily Brewster heard herself saying: "We mustn't touch anything. . . . Not until the police come."

Redfern's answer came mechanically: "No—no—of course not." And then in a deep agonized whisper: "Who? *Who?* Who could have done that to Arlena. She can't have—have been murdered. It can't be true!" Emily Brewster shook her head, not knowing quite what to answer. She heard him draw in his breath—heard the low controlled rage in his voice as he said: "My God, if I get my hands on the foul fiend who did this."

Emily Brewster shivered. Her imagination pictured a lurking murderer behind one of the boulders. Then she heard her voice saying: "Whoever did it wouldn't be hanging about. We must get the police. Perhaps"—she hesitated—"one of us ought to stay with—with the body."

Patrick Redfern said: "I'll stay."

Emily Brewster drew a little sigh of relief. She was not the kind of woman who would ever admit to feeling fear, but she was secretly thankful not to have to remain on that beach alone with the faint possibility of a homicidal maniac lingering close at hand. She said: "Good. I'll be as quick as I can. I'll go in the boat. Can't face that ladder. There's a constable at Leathercombe Bay."

Patrick Redfern murmured mechanically: "Yes—yes, whatever you think best."

As she rowed vigorously away from the shore, Emily Brewster saw Patrick drop down beside the dead woman and bury his head in his hands. There was something so forlorn about his attitude that she felt an unwilling sympathy. He looked like a dog watching by its dead master. Nevertheless her robust common sense was saying to her: "Best thing that could have happened for him and his wife—and for Marshall and the child—but I don't suppose *he* can see it that way, poor devil."

Emily Brewster was a woman who could always rise to an emergency.

5

Inspector Colgate stood back by the cliff waiting for the police surgeon to finish with Arlena's body. Patrick Redfern and Emily Brewster stood a little to one side. Dr. Neasdon rose from his knees with a quick deft movement. He said: "Strangled—and by a pretty powerful pair of hands. She doesn't seem to have put up much of a struggle. Taken by surprise. H'm—well—nasty business."

Emily Brewster had taken one look and then quickly averted her eyes from the dead woman's face. That horrible purple convulsed countenance. Inspector Colgate asked: "What about the time of death?"

Neasdon said irritably: "Can't say definitely without knowing more about her. Lots of factors to take into account. Let's see, it's quarter to one now. What time was it when you found her?"

Patrick Redfern, to whom the question was addressed, said vaguely: "Some time before twelve. I don't know exactly."

Emily Brewster said: "It was exactly a quarter to twelve when we found she was dead."

"Ah, and you came here in the boat. What time was it when you caught sight of her lying here?"

Emily Brewster considered. "I should say we rounded the point about five or six minutes earlier." She turned to Redfern. "Do you agree?"

He said vaguely: "Yes—yes—about that, I should think."

Neasdon asked the Inspector in a low voice: "This the husband? Oh! I see, my mistake. Thought it might be. He seems rather done in over it." He raised his voice officially. "Let's put it at twenty minutes to twelve. She cannot have been killed very long before that. Say between then and eleven—quarter to eleven at the earliest outside limit."

The Inspector shut his notebook with a snap. "Thanks," he said. "That ought to help us considerably. Puts it within very narrow limits—less than an hour all told." He turned to Miss Brewster. "Now then, I think it's all clear so far. You're Miss Emily Brewster and this is Mr. Patrick Redfern, both staying at the Jolly Roger Hotel. You identify this lady as a fellow guest of yours at the hotel—the wife of a Captain Marshall?"

Emily Brewster nodded.

"Then, I think," said Inspector Colgate, "that we'll adjourn to the hotel." He beckoned to a constable. "Hawkes, you stay here and don't allow any one onto this cove. I'll be sending Phillips along later."

636

"Upon my soul!" said Colonel Weston. "This is a surprise finding you here!"

Hercule Poirot replied to the Chief Constable's greeting in a suitable manner. He murmured: "Ah, yes, many years have passed since that affair at St. Loo."

"I haven't forgotten it, though," said Weston. "Biggest surprise of my life. The thing I've never got over, though, is the way you got round me about that funeral business. Absolutely unorthodox, the whole thing, fantastic!"

"*Tout de même, mon Colonel,*" said Poirot. "It produced the goods, did it not?"

"Er—well, possibly. I daresay we should have got there by more orthodox methods."

"It is possible," agreed Poirot diplomatically.

"And here you are in the thick of another murder," said the Chief Constable. "Any ideas about this one?"

Poirot said slowly: "Nothing definite—but it is interesting."

"Going to give us a hand?"

"You would permit it, yes?"

"My dear fellow, delighted to have you. Don't know enough yet to decide whether it's a case for Scotland Yard or not. Offhand it looks as though our murderer must be pretty well within a limited radius. On the other hand , all these people are strangers down here. To find out about them and their motives you've got to go to London."

Poirot said: "Yes, that is true."

"First of all," said Weston, "we've got to find out who last saw the dead woman alive. Chambermaid took her her breakfast at nine. Girl in the bureau downstairs saw her pass through the lounge and go out about ten."

"My friend," said Poirot, "I suspect that I am the man you want."

"You saw her this morning? What time?"

"At five minutes past ten. I assisted her to launch her float from the bathing beach."

"And she went off on it?"

"Yes."

"Alone?"

"Yes."

"Did you see which direction she took?"

"She paddled round that point there to the right."

"In the direction of Pixy's Cove, that is?"

"Yes."

"And the time then was—"

"I should say she actually left the beach at a quarter past ten."

Weston considered. "That fits in well enough. How long should you say that it would take her to paddle round to the Cove?"

"Ah, me, I am not an expert. I do not go in boats or expose myself on floats. Perhaps half an hour?"

"That's about what I think," said the Colonel. "She wouldn't be hurrying, I presume. Well, if she arrived there at a quarter to eleven, that fits in well enough."

"At what time does your doctor suggest she died?"

"Oh, Neasdon doesn't commit himself. He's a cautious chap. A quarter to eleven is his earliest outside limit."

Poirot nodded. He said: "There is one other point that I must mention. As she left Mrs. Marshall asked me not to say I had seen her."

Weston stared. He said: "H'm, that's rather suggestive, isn't it?"

Poirot murmured: "Yes, I thought so myself."

Weston tugged at his mustache. He said: "Look here, Poirot. You're a man of the world. What sort of a woman was Mrs. Marshall?"

A faint smile came to Poirot's lips. He asked: "Have you not already heard?"

The Chief Constable said drily: "I know what the women say of her. They would. How much truth is there in it? *Was* she having an affair with this fellow Redfern?"

"I should say undoubtedly *yes*."

"He followed her down here, eh?"

"There is reason to suppose so."

"And the husband? Did he know about it? What did he feel?"

Poirot said slowly: "It is not easy to know what Captain Marshall feels or thinks. He is a man who does not display his emotions."

Weston said sharply: "But he might have 'em, all the same."

Poirot nodded. He said: "Oh, yes, he might have them."

The Chief Constable was being as tactful as it was in his nature to be with Mrs. Castle. Mrs. Castle was the owner and proprietress of the Jolly Roger Hotel. She was a woman of forty odd with a large bust, rather violent henna-red hair, and an almost offensively refined manner of speech. She was saying: "That such a thing should happen in my Hotel! Ay am sure it has always been the quayettest place imaginable! The people who come here are such nice people. No *rowdiness*—if you know what Ay mean. Not like the big hotels in St. Loo."

"Quite so, Mrs. Castle," said Colonel Weston. "But accidents happen in the best-regulated—er households."

"Ay'm sure Inspector Colgate will bear me out," said Mrs. Castle, sending an appealing glance towards the Inspector who was sitting looking very official. "As to the laycensing laws, Ay am *most* particular. There has never been *any* irregularity!"

"Quite, quite," said Weston. "We're not blaming you in any way, Mrs. Castle."

"But it does so reflect upon an establishment," said Mrs. Castle, her large bust heaving. "When Ay think of the noisy gaping crowds. Of course no one but hotel guests are allowed upon the island—but all the same they will no doubt come and *point* from the shore." She shuddered.

Inspector Colgate saw his chance to turn the conversation to good account. He said: "In regard to that point you've just raised. Access to the island. How do you keep people off?"

"Ay am *most* particular about it."

"Yes, but what measures do you take? *What* keeps 'em off? Holiday crowds in summer-time swarm everywhere like flies."

Mrs. Castle shuddered slightly again. She said: "That is the fault of the charabancs. Ay have seen eighteen at one time parked by the quay at Leathercombe Bay. Eighteen!"

"Just so. How do you stop them coming here?"

"There are notices. And then, of course, at high tide, we are cut off."

"Yes, but at low tide?"

Mrs. Castle explained. At the island end of the causeway there was a gate. This said, "Jolly Roger Hotel. Private. No entry except to Hotel." The rocks rose sheer out of the sea on either side there and could not be climbed.

"Any one could take a boat, though, I suppose, and row round and land on one of the coves? You couldn't stop them doing that. There's a right of access to the foreshore. You can't stop people being on the beach between low and high watermark."

But this, it seemed, very seldom happened. Boats could be obtained at Leathercombe Bay harbour but from there it was a long row to the island and there was also a strong current just outside Leathercombe Bay harbour. There were notices, too, on both Gull Cove and Pixy Cove by the ladder. She added that George or William was always on the lookout at the bathing beach proper which was the nearest to the mainland.

"Who are George and William?"

"George attends to the bathing beach. He sees to the costumes and the floats. William is the gardener. He keeps the paths and marks the tennis courts and all that."

Colonel Weston said impatiently: "Well, that seems clear enough. That's not to say that nobody could have come from outside, but any one who did so took a risk—the risk of being noticed. We'll have a word with George and William presently."

Mrs. Castle said: "Ay do not care for trippers—a very noisy crowd and they frequently leave orange peel and cigarette boxes on the causeway and down by the rocks, but all the same Ay never thought one of them would turn out to be a murderer. Oh, dear! it really is too terrible for words. A lady like Mrs. Marshall murdered and what's so horrible, actually—er—strangled. . . ." Mrs. Castle could hardly bring herself to say the word. She brought it out with the utmost reluctance.

Inspector Colgate said soothingly: "Yes, it's a nasty business."

"And the newspapers. *My* hotel in the newspapers!"

Colgate said, with a faint grin: "Oh, well, it's advertisement, in a way."

Mrs. Castle drew herself up. Her bust heaved and whalebone creaked. She said icily: "That is not the kind of advertisement Ay care about, Mr. Colgate."

Colonel Weston broke in. He said: "Now then, Mrs. Castle, you've got a list of the guests staying here, as I asked you?"

"Yes, sir."

Colonel Weston pored over the hotel register. He looked over to Poirot who made the fourth member of the group assembled in the Manageress's office. "This is where you'll probably be able to help us presently." He read down the names. "What about servants?"

Mrs. Castle produced a second list. "There are four chambermaids, the head waiter and three under him and Henry in the bar. William does the boots and shoes. Then there's the cook and two under her."

"What about the waiters?"

"Well, sir, Albert, the Mater Dotel, came to me from the Vincent at Plymouth. He was there for some years. The three under him have been here for three years—one of them four. They are very naice lads and most respectable. Henry has been here since the hotel opened. He is quite an institution."

Weston nodded. He said to Colgate: "Seems all right. You'll check up on them, of course. Thank you, Mrs. Castle."

"That will be all you require?"

"For the moment, yes."

Mrs. Castle creaked out of the room. Weston said: "First thing to do is to talk with Captain Marshall."

Kenneth Marshall sat quietly answering the questions put to him. Apart from a slight hardening of his features he was quite calm. Seen here, with the sunlight falling on him from the window, you realized that he was a handsome man. Those straight features, the steady blue eyes, the firm mouth. His voice was low and pleasant. Colonel Weston was saying: "I quite understand, Captain Marshall, what a terrible shock this must be to you. But you realize that I am anxious to get the fullest information as soon as possible."

Marshall nodded. He said: "I quite understand. Carry on."

"Mrs. Marshall was your second wife?"

"Yes."

"And you have been married, how long?"

"Just over four years."

"And her name before she was married?"

"Helen Stuart. Her acting name was Arlena Stuart."

"She was an actress?"

"She appeared in Revue and musical shows."

"Did she give up the stage on her marriage?"

"No. She continued to appear. She actually retired only about a year and half ago."

"Was there any special reason for her retirement?"

Kenneth Marshall appeared to consider. "No," he said. "She simply said that she was tired of it all."

"It was not—er—in obedience to your special wish?"

Marshall raised his eyebrows. "Oh, no."

"You were quite content for her to continue acting after your marriage?"

Marshall smiled very faintly. "I should have preferred her to give it up—that, yes. But I made no fuss about it."

"It caused no point of dissension between you?"

"Certainly not. My wife was free to please herself."

"And—the marriage was a happy one?"

Kenneth Marshall said coldly: "Certainly."

Colonel Weston paused a minute. Then he said: "Captain Marshall, have you any idea who could possibly have killed your wife?"

The answer came without the least hesitation. "None whatever."

"Had she any enemies?"

"Possibly."

"Ah?"

The other went on quickly. He said: "Don't misunderstand me, sir. My wife was an actress. She was also a very good-looking woman. In both capacities she aroused a certain amount of envy and jealousy. There were fusses over parts—there was rivalry from other women—there was a good deal, shall we say, of general envy, hatred, malice, and all uncharitableness! But that is not to say that there was any one who was capable of deliberately murdering her."

Hercule Poirot spoke for the first time. He said: "What you really mean, Monsieur, is that her enemies were mostly, or entirely, *women*?"

Kenneth Marshall looked across at him. "Yes," he said. "That is so."

The Chief Constable said: "You know of no man who had a grudge against her?"

"No."

"Was she previously acquainted with any one in this hotel?"

"I believe she had met Mr. Redfern before—at some cocktail party. Nobody else to my knowledge."

Weston paused. He seemed to deliberate as to whether to pursue the subject. Then he decided against that course. He said: "We now come to this morning. When was the last time you saw your wife?"

Marshall paused a minute, then he said: "I looked in on my way down to breakfast—"

"Excuse me, you occupied separate rooms?"

"Yes."

"And what time was that?"

"It must have been about nine o'clock."

"What was she doing?"

"She was opening her letters."

"Did she say anything?"

"Nothing of any particular interest. Just Good-morning—and that it was a nice day—that sort of thing."

"What was her manner? Unusual at all?"

"No, perfectly normal."

"She did not seem excited, or depressed, or upset in any way?"

"I certainly didn't notice it."

Hercule Poirot said: "Did she mention at all what were the contents of her letters?"

Again a faint smile appeared on Marshall's lips. He said: "As far as I can remember, she said they were all bills."

"Your wife breakfasted in bed?"

"Yes."

"Did she always do that?"

"Invariably."

Hercule Poirot said: "What time did she usually come downstairs?"

"Oh! between ten and eleven—usually nearer eleven."

Poirot went on: "If she were to descend at ten o'clock exactly, that would be rather surprising?"

"Yes. She wasn't often down as early as that."

"But she was this morning. Why do you think that was, Captain Marshall?"

Marshall said unemotionally: "Haven't the least idea. Might have been the weather—extra fine day and all that."

"You missed her?"

Kenneth Marshall shifted a little in his chair. He said: "Looked in on her again after breakfast. Room was empty. I was a bit surprised."

"And then you came down on the beach and asked me if I had seen her?"

"Er—yes." He added with a faint emphasis in his voice. "And you said you hadn't. . . ."

The innocent eyes of Hercule Poirot did not falter. Gently, he caressed his large and flamboyant mustache.

Weston asked: "Had you any special reason for wanting to find your wife this morning?"

Marshall shifted his glance amiably to the Chief Constable. He said: "No, just wondered where she was, that's all."

Weston paused. He moved his chair slightly. His voice fell into a different key. He said: "Just now, Captain Marshall, you mentioned that your wife had a previous acquaintance with Mr. Patrick Redfern. How well did your wife know Mr. Redfern?"

Kenneth Marshall said: "Mind if I smoke?" He felt through his pockets. "Dash! I've mislaid my pipe somewhere."

Poirot offered him a cigarette which he accepted. Lighting it, he said: "You were asking about Redfern. My wife told me she had come across him at some cocktail party or other."

"He was, then, just a casual acquaintance?"

"I believe so."

"Since then—" the Chief Constable paused. "I understand that that acquaintanceship has ripened into something rather closer."

Marshall said sharply: "You understand that, do you? Who told you so?"

"It is the common gossip of the hotel."

For a moment Marshall's eyes went to Hercule Poirot. They dwelt on him with a kind of cold anger. He said: "Hotel gossip is usually a tissue of lies!"

"Possibly. But I gather that Mr. Redfern and your wife gave some grounds for the gossip."

"What grounds?"

"They were constantly in each other's company."

"Is that all?"

"You do not deny that that was so?"

"May have been. I really didn't notice."

"You did not—excuse me, Captain Marshall—object to your wife's friendship with Mr. Redfern?"

"I wasn't in the habit of criticizing my wife's conduct."

"You did not protest or object in any way?"

"Certainly not."

"Not even though it was becoming a subject of scandal and an estrangement was growing up between Mr. Redfern and his wife?"

Kenneth Marshall said coldly: "I mind my own business and I expect other people to mind theirs. I don't listen to gossip and tittle tattle."

"You won't deny that Mr. Redfern admired your wife?"

"He probably did. Most men did. She was a very beautiful woman."

"But you yourself were persuaded that there was nothing serious in the affair?"

"I never thought about it, I tell you."

"And suppose we have a witness who can testify that they were on terms of the greatest intimacy?"

Again those blue eyes went to Hercule Poirot. Again an expression of dislike showed on that usually impassive face. Marshall said: "If you want to listen to tales, listen to 'em. My wife's dead and can't defend herself."

"You mean that you, personally, don't believe them?"

For the first time a faint dew of sweat was observable on Marshall's brow. He said: "I don't propose to believe anything of the kind." He went on: "Aren't you getting a good way from the essentials of this business? What I believe or don't believe is surely not relevant to the plain fact of murder?"

Hercule Poirot answered before either of the others could speak. He said: "You do not comprehend, Captain Marshall. There is no such thing as a plain fact of murder. Murder springs, nine times out of ten, out of the character and circumstances of the murdered person. *Because* the victim was the kind of person he or she was, *therefore* was he or she murdered! Until we can understand fully and completely *exactly what kind of person Arlena Marshall was*, we shall not be able to see clearly exactly *the kind of person who murdered her*. From that springs the necessity of our questions."

Marshall turned to the Chief Constable. He said: "That your view, too?"

Weston boggled a little. He said: "Well, up to a point—that is to say—"

Marshall gave a short laugh. He said: "Thought you wouldn't agree. This character stuff is M. Poirot's specialty, I believe."

Poirot said, smiling: "You can at least congratulate yourself on having done nothing to assist me!"

"What do you mean?"

"What have you told us about your wife? Exactly nothing at all. You have told us only what every one could see for themselves. That she was beautiful and admired. Nothing more."

Kenneth Marshall shrugged his shoulders. He said simply: "You're crazy." He looked towards the Chief Constable and said with emphasis: "Anything else, sir that *you'd* like me to tell you?"

"Yes, Captain Marshall, your own movements this morning, please."

Kenneth Marshall nodded. He had clearly expected this. He said: "I breakfasted downstairs about nine o'clock as usual and read the paper. As I told you I went up to my wife's room afterwards and found she had gone out. I came down to the beach, saw M. Poirot and asked if he had seen her. Then I had a quick bathe and went up to the hotel again. It was then, let me see, about twenty to eleven—yes, just about that. I saw the clock in the lounge. It was just after twenty minutes to. I went up to my room, but the chambermaid hadn't quite finished it. I asked her to finish as quickly as she could. I had some letters to type which I wanted to get off by the post. I went downstairs again and had a word or two with Henry in the bar. I went up again to my room at ten minutes to eleven. There I typed my letters. I typed until ten minutes to twelve. I then changed into tennis kit as I had a date to play tennis at twelve. We'd booked the court the day before."

"Who was we?"

"Mrs. Redfern, Miss Darnley, Mr. Gardener and myself. I came down at twelve o'clock and went up to the court. Miss Darnley was there and Mr. Gardener. Mrs. Redfern arrived a few minutes later. We played tennis for an hour. Just as we came into the hotel afterwards I—I—got the news."

"Thank you, Captain Marshall. Just as a matter of form, is there any one who can corroborate the fact that you were typing in your room between—er—ten minutes to eleven and ten minutes to twelve?"

Kenneth Marshall said with a faint smile: "Have you got some idea that I killed my own wife? Let me see now. The chambermaid was about doing the rooms. She must have heard the typewriter going. And then there are the letters themselves. With all this upset I haven't posted them. I should imagine they are as good evidence as anything."

He took three letters from his pocket. They were addressed, but not stamped. He said: "Their contents, by the way, are strictly confidential. But when it's a case of murder, one is forced to trust in the discretion of the police. They contain lists of figures and various financial statements. I think you will find that if you put one of your men on to type them out, he won't do it in much under an hour." He paused. "Satisfied, I hope?"

Weston said smoothly: "It is no question of suspicion. Every one on the island will be asked to account for his or her movements between a quarter to eleven and twenty minutes to twelve this morning."

Kenneth Marshall said: "Quite."

Weston said: "One more thing, Captain Marshall. Do you know anything about the way your wife was likely to have disposed of any property she had?"

"You mean a will? I don't think she ever made a will."

"But you are not sure?"

"Her solicitors are Barkett, Markett & Applegood, Bedford Square. They saw to all her contracts, etc. But I'm fairly certain she never made a will. She said once that doing a thing like that would give her the shivers."

"In that case, if she has died intestate, you, as her husband, succeed to her property."

"Yes, I suppose I do."

"Had she any near relatives?"

"I don't think so. If she had, she never mentioned them. I know that her father and mother died when she was a child and she had no brothers or sisters."

"In any case, I suppose, she had nothing very much to leave?"

Kenneth Marshall said coolly: "On the contrary. Only two years ago, Sir Robert Erskine, who was an old friend of hers, died and left her a good deal of his fortune. It amounted, I think, to about fifty thousand pounds."

Inspector Colgate looked up. An alertness came into his glance. Up to now he had been silent. Now he asked: "Then actually, Captain Marshall, your wife was a rich woman?"

Kenneth Marshall shrugged his shoulders. "I suppose she was really."

"And you still say she did not make a will?"

"You can ask the solicitors. But I'm pretty certain she didn't. As I tell you, she thought it unlucky." There was a pause then Marshall added: "Is there anything further?"

Weston shook his head. "Don't think so—eh, Colgate? No. Once more, Captain Marshall, let me offer you all my sympathy in your loss."

Marshall blinked. He said jerkily: "Oh—thanks." He went out.

The three men looked at each other. Weston said: "Cool customer. Not giving anything away, is he? What do you make of him, Colgate?"

The Inspector shook his head. "It's difficult to tell. He's not the kind that shows anything. That sort makes a bad impression in the witness box, and yet it's a bit unfair on them really. Sometimes they're as cut up as anything and yet can't show it. That kind of manner made the jury bring a verdict of Guilty against Wallace. It wasn't the evidence. They just couldn't believe that a man could lose his wife and talk and act so coolly about it."

Weston turned to Poirot. "What do you think, Poirot?"

Hercule Poirot raised his hands. He said: "What can one say? He is the closed box—the fastened oyster. He has chosen his rôle. He has heard nothing, he has seen nothing, he knows nothing!"

"We've got a choice of motives," said Colgate. "There's jealousy and there's the money motive. Of course, in a way, a husband's the obvious suspect. One naturally thinks of him first. If he knew his missus was carrying on with the other chap—"

Poirot interrupted. He said: "I think he knew that."

"Why do you say so?"

"Listen, my friend. Last night I had been talking with Mrs. Redfern on Sunny Ledge. I came down from there to the hotel and on my way I saw those two together—Mrs. Marshall and Patrick Redfern. And a moment or two after I met Captain Marshall. His face was very stiff. It says nothing—but nothing at all! It is almost *too* blank, if you understand me. Oh! he knew all right."

Colgate grunted doubtfully. He said: "Oh, well, if you think so—"

"I am sure of it! But even then, what does that tell us? What did Kenneth Marshall *feel* about his wife?"

Colonel Weston said: "Takes her death coolly enough."

Poirot shook his head in a dissatisfied manner. Inspector Colgate said: "Sometimes these quiet ones are the most violent underneath, so to speak. It's all bottled up. He may have been madly fond of her—and madly jealous. But he's not the kind to show it."

Poirot said slowly: "That is possible—yes. He is a very interesting character, this Captain Marshall. I interest myself in him greatly. And in his *alibi*."

"Alibi by typewriter," said Weston with a short bark of a laugh. "What have you got to say about that, Colgate?"

Inspector Colgate screwed up his eyes. He said: "Well, you know, sir, I rather fancy that alibi. It's not too good, if you know what I mean. It's—well, it's *natural*. And if we find the chambermaid was about, and did hear the typewriter going, well then, it seems to me that it's all right and that we'll have to look elsewhere."

"H'm," said Colonel Weston. "Where are you going to look?"

For a minute or two the three men pondered the question. Inspector Colgate spoke first. He said: "It boils down to this—was it an outsider, or a guest at the hotel? I'm not eliminating the servants entirely, mind, but I don't expect for a minute that we'll find any of them had a hand in it. No, it's a hotel guest, or it's some one from right outside. We've got to look at it this way. First of all—motive. There's gain. The only person to gain by her death was the lady's husband, it seems. What other motives are there? First and foremost—jealousy. It seems to me—just looking at it—that if ever you've got a *crime passionnel* (he bowed to Poirot) this is one."

Poirot murmured as he looked up at the ceiling: "There are so many passions."

Inspector Colgate went on: "Her husband wouldn't allow that she had any enemies—real enemies, that is, but I don't believe for a minute that that's so! I should say that a lady like her would—well, would make some pretty bad enemies—eh, sir, what do you say?"

Poirot responded. He said: "*Mais oui*, that is so. Arlena Marshall would make enemies. But in my opinion, the enemy theory is not tenable, for you see, Inspector, Arlena Marshall's enemies would, I think, as I said just now, always be *women*."

Colonel Weston grunted and said: "Something in that. It's the women who've got their knives into her here all right."

Poirot went on: "It seems to be hardly possible that this crime was committed by a woman. What does the medical evidence say?"

Weston grunted again. He said: "Neasdon's pretty confident that she was strangled by a man. Big hands—powerful grip. It's just possible, of course, that an unusually athletic woman might have done it—but it's damned unlikely."

Poirot nodded. "Exactly. Arsenic in a cup of tea—a box of poisoned chocolates—a knife—even a pistol—but strangulation—no! It is a man we have to look for. And immediately," he went on, "it becomes more difficult. There are two people here in this hotel who have a motive for wishing Arlena Marshall out of the way—but both of them are women."

Colonel Weston asked: "Redfern's wife is one of them, I suppose?"

"Yes. Mrs. Redfern might have made up her mind to kill Arlena Stuart. She had, let us say, ample cause. I think, too, that it would be possible for Mrs. Redfern to commit a murder. But not this kind of murder. For all her unhappiness and jealousy, she is not, I should say, a woman of strong passions. In love, she would be devoted and loyal—not passionate. As I said just now—arsenic in the teacup—possibly—strangulation, no. I am sure, also, that she is physically incapable of committing this crime and her hands and feet are small below the average."

Weston nodded. He said: "This isn't a woman's crime. No, a man did this."

Inspector Colgate coughed. "Let me put forward a solution, sir. Say that prior to meeting this Mr. Redfern the lady had had another affair with some one—call him X. She turns down X for Mr. Redfern. X is mad with rage and jealousy. He follows her down here, stays somewhere in the neighbourhood, comes over to the island and does her in. It's a possibility!"

Weston said: "It's *possible*, all right. And if it's true, it ought to be easy to prove. Did he come on foot or in a boat? The latter seems more likely. If so, he must have hired a boat somewhere. You'd better make inquiries." He looked across at Poirot. "What do you think of Colgate's suggestion?"

Poirot said slowly: "It leaves, somehow, too much to chance. And besides—somewhere the picture is not true. I cannot, you see, imagine this man . . . the man who is mad with rage and jealousy."

Colgate said: "People *did* go potty about her, though, sir. Look at Redfern."

"Yes, yes. . . . But all the same—" Colgate looked at his questioningly. Poirot shook his head. He said frowning: "Somewhere, there is something we have missed. . . ."

6

COLONEL WESTON was poring over the hotel register.
   He read aloud.

"Major and Mrs. Cowan,
   Miss Pamela Cowan,   Rydal's Mount,
   Master Robert Cowan,   Leatherhead.
   Master Evan Cowan.

Mr. and Mrs. Masterman,
Mr. Edward Masterman,
Miss Jennifer Masterman,   5 Malborough Avenue,
Mr. Roy Masterman,   London, N.W.
Master Frederick Masterman.

Mr. and Mrs. Gardener.   New York.

Mr. and Mrs. Redfern.   Crossgates, Seldon,
                                               Princes Risborough.

Major Barry.   18 Cardon Street,
                                               St. James, London, S.W.1.

Mr. Horace Blatt.	5 Pickersgill Street, London, E.C.2.
M. Hercule Poirot.	Whitehaven Mansions, London, W.1.
Miss Rosamund Darnley.	8 Cardigan Court, W. 1.
Miss Emily Brewster.	Southgates, Sunbury-on-Thames.
Rev. Stephen Lane.	London.
Captain and Mrs. Marshall, Miss Linda Marshall.	73 Upcott Mansions, London, S.W.7."

He stopped. Inspector Colgate said: "I think, sir, that we can wash out the first two entries. Mrs. Castle tells me that the Mastermans and the Cowans come here regularly every summer with their children. This morning they went off on an all-day excursion sailing, taking lunch with them. They left just after nine o'clock. A man called Andrew Baston took them. We can check up for him, but I think we can put them right out of it."

Weston nodded. "I agree. Let's eliminate every one we can. Can you give us a pointer on any of the rest of them, Poirot?"

Poirot said: "Superficially, that is easy. The Gardeners are a middle-aged married couple, pleasant, travelled. All the talking is done by the lady. The husband is acquiescent. He plays tennis and golf and has a form of dry humour that is attractive when one gets him to oneself."

"Sounds quite O.K."

"Next—the Redferns. Mr. Redfern is young, attractive to women, a magnificent swimmer, a good tennis player and accomplished dancer. His wife I have already spoken of to you. She is quiet, pretty in a washed-out way. She is, I think, devoted to her husband. She has something that Arlena Marshall did not have."

"What is that?"

"Brains."

Inspector Colgate sighed. He said: "Brains don't count for much when it comes to an infatuation, sir."

"Perhaps not. And yet I do truly believe that in spite of his infatuation for Mrs. Marshall, Patrick Redfern really cares for his wife."

"That may be, sir. It wouldn't be the first time that's happened."

Poirot murmured: "That is the pity of it! It is always the thing women find it hardest to believe." He went on: "Major Barry, Retired Indian Army. An admirer of women. A teller of long and boring stories."

Inspector Colgate sighed. "You needn't go on. I've met a few, sir."

"Mr. Horace Blatt. He is, apparently, a rich man. He talks a good deal—about Mr. Blatt. He wants to be everybody's friend. It is sad. For nobody likes him very much. And there is something else. Mr. Blatt last night asked me a good many questions. Mr. Blatt was uneasy. Yes, there is something not quite right about Mr. Blatt." He paused and went on with a change of voice: "Next comes Miss Rosamund Darnley. Her business name is Rose Mond, Ltd. She is a celebrated dressmaker. What can I say of her? She has brains and charm and chic. She is very pleasing to look at." He paused and added, "And she is a very old friend of Captain Marshall's."

Weston sat up in his chair. "Oh, she is, is she?"

"Yes. They had not met for some years."

Weston asked: "Did she know he was going to be down here?"

"She says not." Poirot paused and then went on: "Who comes next? Miss Brewster. I find her just a little alarming." He shook his head. "She has a voice like a man's. She is gruff and what you call hearty. She rows boats and has a handicap of four at golf." He paused. "I think, though, that she has a good heart."

Weston said: "That leaves only the Reverend Stephen Lane. Who's the Reverend Stephen Lane?"

"I can only tell you one thing. He is a man who is in a condition of great nervous tension. Also he is, I think, a fanatic."

Inspector Colgate said: "Oh, that kind of person."

Weston said: "And that's the lot!" He looked at Poirot. "You seem very lost in thought, my friend."

Poirot said: "Yes. Because, you see, when Mrs. Marshall went off this morning and asked me not to tell any one I had seen her, I jumped at once in my own mind to a certain conclusion. I thought that her friendship with Patrick Redfern had made trouble between her and her husband. I thought that she was going to meet Patrick Redfern somewhere and that she did not want her husband to know where she was."

He paused. "But that, you see, was where I was wrong. Because, although her husband appeared almost immediately on the beach and asked if I had seen her, Patrick Redfern arrived also—and was most patently and obviously looking for her! And therefore, my friends, I am asking myself, *Who was it that Arlena Marshall went off to meet?*"

Inspector Colgate said: "That fits in with *my* idea. A man from London or somewhere."

Hercule Poirot shook his head. He said: "But, my friend, according to your theory, Arlena Marshall had broken with this mythical man. Why, then, should she take such trouble and pains to meet him?"

Inspector Colgate shook his head. He said: "Who do *you* think it was?"

"That is just what I cannot imagine. We have just read through the list of hotel guests. They are all middle-aged—dull. Which of them would Arlena Marshall prefer to Patrick Redfern? No, that is impossible. And yet, all the same, she *did* go to meet some one—and that some one was not Patrick Redfern."

Weston murmured: "You don't think she just went off by herself?"

Poirot shook his head. "*Mon cher*," he said. "It is very evident that you never met the dead woman. Somebody once wrote a learned treatise on the difference that solitary confinement would mean to Beau Brummell or a man like Newton. Arlena Marshall, my dear friend, would practically not exist in solitude. She only lived in the light of a man's admiration. No, Arlena Marshall went to meet *some one* this morning. *Who was it?*"

Colonel Weston sighed, shook his head and said: "Well, we can go into theories later. Got to get through these interviews now. Got to get it down in black and white where everyone was. I suppose we'd better see the Marshall girl now. She might be able to tell us something useful."

Linda Marshall came into the room clumsily, knocking against the doorpost. She was breathing quickly and the pupils of her eyes were dilated. She looked like a startled young colt. Colonel Weston felt a kindly impulse towards her. He thought: "Poor kid—she's nothing but a kid after all. This must have been a pretty bad shock to her." He drew up a chair and said in a reassuring voice: "Sorry to put you through this, Miss—Linda, isn't it?"

"Yes, Linda."

Her voice had that indrawn breathy quality that is often characteristic of schoolgirls. Her hands rested helplessly on the table in front of him—pathetic hands, big and red, with large bones and long wrists. Weston thought: "A kid oughtn't to be mixed up in this sort of thing." He said reassuringly: "There's nothing very alarming about all this. We just want you to tell us anything you know that might be useful, that's all."

Linda said: "You mean—about Arlena?"

"Yes. Did you see her this morning at all?"

The girl shook her head. "No. Arlena always gets down rather late. She has breakfast in bed."

Hercule Poirot said: "And you, Mademoiselle?"

"Oh, I get up. Breakfast in bed's so *stuffy*."

Weston said: "Will you tell us just what you did this morning?"

"Well, I had a bathe first and then breakfast and then I went with Mrs. Redfern to Gull Cove."

Weston said: "What time did you and Mrs. Redfern start?"

"She said she'd be waiting for me in the hall at half past ten. I was afraid I was going to be late, but it was all right. We started off at about three minutes to the half hour."

Poirot said: "And what did you do at Gull Cove?"

"Oh, I oiled myself and sunbathed and Mrs. Redfern sketched. Then, later, I went into the sea and Christine went back to the hotel to get changed for tennis."

Weston said, keeping his voice quite casual: "Do you remember what time that was?"

"When Mrs. Redfern went back to the hotel? Quarter to twelve."

"Sure of that time—quarter to twelve?"

Linda, opening her eyes wide, said: "Oh, *yes*. I looked at my watch."

"The watch you have on now?"

Linda glanced down at her wrist. "Yes."

Weston said: "Mind if I see?"

She held out her wrist. He compared the watch with his own and with the hotel clock on the wall. He said, smiling: "Correct to a second. And after that you had a bathe?"

"Yes."

"And you got back to the hotel—when?"

"Just about one o'clock. And—and then—I heard—about Arlena. . . ." Her voice changed.

Colonel Weston said: "Did you—er—get on with your stepmother all right?"

She looked at him for a minute without replying. Then she said: "Oh, yes."

Poirot asked: "Did you like her, Mademoiselle?"

Linda said again: "Oh, yes." She added: "Arlena was quite kind to me."

Weston said with rather uneasy facetiousness: "Not the cruel stepmother, eh?"

Linda shook her head without smiling.

Weston said: "That's good. That's good. Sometimes, you know, there's a bit of difficulty in families—jealousy—all that. Girl and her father great pals and then she resents it a bit when he's all wrapped up in the new wife. You didn't feel like that, eh?"

Linda stared at him. She said with obvious sincerity: "Oh, no."

Weston said: "I suppose your father was—er—very wrapped up in her?"

Linda said simply: "I don't know."

Weston went on: "All sorts of difficulties, as I say, arise in families. Quarrels—rows—that sort of thing. If husband and wife get ratty with each other, that's a bit awkward for a daughter, too. Anything of that sort?"

Linda said clearly: "Do you mean, did Father and Arlena quarrel?"

"Well—yes." Weston thought to himself: "Rotten business— questioning a child about her father. Why is one a policeman? Damn it all, it's got to be done, though."

Linda said positively: "Oh, no." She added: "Father doesn't quarrel with people. He's not like that at all."

Weston said: "Now, Miss Linda, I want you to think very carefully. Have you any idea at all who might have killed your stepmother? Is there anything you've ever heard or anything you know that could help us on that point?"

Linda was silent a minute. She seemed to be giving the question a serious unhurried consideration. She said at last: "No, I don't know who could have wanted to kill Arlena." She added, "Except, of course, Mrs. Redfern."

Weston said: "You think Mrs. Redfern wanted to kill her? Why?"

Linda said: "Because her husband was in love with Arlena. But I don't think she would really want to *kill* her. I mean she'd just feel that she wished she was dead—and that isn't the same thing at all, is it?"

Poirot said gently: "No, it is not at all the same."

Linda nodded. A queer sort of spasm passed across her face. She said: "And anyway, Mrs. Redfern could never do a thing like that—kill anybody. She isn't—she isn't *violent*, if you know what I mean."

Weston and Poirot nodded. The latter said: "I know exactly what you mean, my child, and I agree with you. Mrs. Redfern is not of those who, as your saying goes, 'sees red.' She would not be—" He leaned back half closing his eyes, picking his words with care—"shaken by a storm of feeling—seeing life narrowing in front of her—seeing a hated face—a hated white neck—feeling her hands clench—longing to feel them press into flesh—"

He stopped. Linda moved jerkily back from the table. She said in a trembling voice: "Can I go now? Is that all?"

Colonel Weston said: "Yes, yes, that's all. Thank you, Miss Linda." He got up to open the door for her. Then came back to the table and lit a cigarette. "Phew," he said. "Not a nice job, ours. I can tell you I felt a bit of a cad questioning that child about the relations between her father and her stepmother. More or less inviting a daughter to put a rope round her father's neck. All the same, it had to be done. Murder is murder. And she's the person most likely to know the truth of things. I'm rather thankful, though, that she'd nothing to tell us in that line."

Poirot said: "Yes, I thought you were."

Weston said with an embarrassed cough: "By the way, Poirot, you went a bit far, I thought, at the end. All that hands-sinking-into-flesh business! Not quite the sort of idea to put into a kid's head."

Hercule Poirot looked at him with thoughtful eyes. He said: "So you thought I put ideas into her head?"

"Well, didn't you? Come now." Poirot shook his head. Weston sheered away from the point. He said: "On the whole we got very little useful stuff out of her. Except a more or less complete *alibi* for the Redfern woman. If they were together from half past ten to a quarter to twelve that lets Christine Redfern out of it. Exit the jealous wife suspect."

Poirot said: "There are better reasons than that for leaving Mrs. Redfern out of it. It would, I am convinced, be physically impossible and mentally impossible for her to strangle any one. She is cold rather than warm blooded, capable of deep devotion and unswerving constancy, but not of hot-blooded passion or rage. Moreover, her hands are far too small and delicate."

Colgate said: "I agree with Mr. Poirot. She's out of it. Dr. Neasdon says it was a full-sized pair of hands throttled that dame."

Weston said: "Well, I suppose we'd better see the Redferns next. I expect he's recovered a bit from the shock now."

Patrick Redfern had recovered full composure by now. He looked pale and haggard and suddenly very young, but his manner was quite composed.

"You are Mr. Patrick Redfern of Crossgates, Seldon, Princes Risborough?"

"Yes."

"How long had you known Mrs. Marshall?"

Patrick Redfern hesitated, then said: "Three months."

Weston went on: "Captain Marshall has told us that you and she met casually at a cocktail party. Is that right?"

"Yes, that's how it came about."

Weston said: "Captain Marshall has implied that until you both met down here you did not know each other well. Is that the truth, Mr. Redfern?"

Again Patrick Redfern hesitated a minute. Then he said, "Well—not exactly. As a matter of fact I saw a fair amount of her one way and another."

"Without Captain Marshall's knowledge?"

Redfern flushed slightly. He said: "I don't know whether he knew about it or not."

Hercule Poirot spoke. He murmured: "And was it also without your wife's knowledge, Mr. Redfern?"

"I believe I mentioned to my wife that I had met the famous Arlena Stuart."

Poirot persisted. "But she did not know how often you were seeing her?"

"Well, perhaps not."

Weston said: "Did you and Mrs. Marshall arrange to meet down here?"

Redfern was silent a minute or two. Then he shrugged his shoulders. "Oh, well," he said. "I suppose it's bound to come out now. It's no good my fencing with you. I was crazy about the woman— mad—infatuated—anything you like. She wanted me to come down here. I demurred a bit and then I agreed. I—I—well, I would have agreed to do any mortal thing she liked. She had that kind of effect on people."

Hercule Poirot murmured: "You paint a very clear picture of her. She was the eternal Circe. Just that!"

Patrick Redfern said bitterly: "She turned men into swine all right!" He went on: "I'm being frank with you, gentlemen. I'm not going to hide anything. What's the use? As I say, I was infatuated with her. Whether she cared for me or not, I don't know. She pretended to, but I think she was one of those women who lose interest in a man once they've got him body and soul. She knew she'd got me all right. This morning, when I found her there on the beach, dead, it was as though—" he paused— "as though something had hit me straight between the eyes. I was dazed—knocked out!"

Poirot leaned forward. "And now?"

Patrick Redfern met his eyes squarely. He said: "I've told you the truth. What I want to ask is this—*how much of it has got to be made public*? It's not as though it could have any bearing on her death. And if it all comes out, it's going to be pretty rough on my wife. Oh, I know," he went on quickly. "You think I haven't thought much about her up to now? Perhaps that's true. But, though I may sound the worst kind of hypocrite, the real truth is that I care for my wife—care for her very deeply. The other—" he twitched his shoulders—"it was a madness—the kind of idiotic fool thing men do—but Christine is different. She's *real*. Badly as I've treated her, I've known all along, deep down, that she was the person who really counted." He paused—sighed—and said rather pathetically: "I wish I could make you believe that."

Hercule Poirot leant forward. He said: "But I do believe it. Yes, yes, I do believe it!"

Patrick Redfern looked at him gratefully. He said: "Thank you."

Colonel Weston cleared his throat. He said: "You may take it, Mr.

Redfern, that we shall not go into irrelevancies. If your infatuation for Mrs. Marshall played no part in the murder then there will be no point in dragging it into the case. But what you don't seem to realize is that that—er—intimacy—may have a very direct bearing on the murder. It might establish, you understand, a *motive* for the crime."

Patrick Redfern said: "Motive?"

Weston said: "Yes, Mr. Redfern, *motive*! Captain Marshall, perhaps, was unaware of the affair. Suppose that he suddenly found out."

Redfern said: "Oh, God! You mean he got wise and—and killed her?"

The Chief Constable said rather drily: "That solution had not occurred to you?"

Redfern shook his head. He said: "No—funny. I never thought of it. You see, Marshall's such a quiet chap. I—oh, it doesn't seem likely."

Weston said: "What was Mrs. Marshall's attitude to her husband in all this? Was she—well, uneasy—in case it should come to his ears? Or was she indifferent?"

Redfern said slowly: "She was—a bit nervous. She didn't want him to suspect anything."

"Did she seem afraid of him?"

"Afraid? No, I wouldn't say that."

Poirot murmured: "Excuse me, Mr. Redfern, there was not, at any time, the question of a divorce?"

Patrick Redfern shook his head decisively. "Oh, no, there was no question of anything like that. There was Christine, you see. And Arlena, I am sure, never thought of such a thing. She was perfectly satisfied married to Marshall. He's—well, rather a big bug in his way—" He smiled suddenly. "County—all that sort of thing, and quite well off. She never thought of me as a possible *husband*. No, I was just one of a succession of poor mutts—just something to pass the time with. I knew that all along, and yet, queerly enough, it didn't alter my feeling towards her. . . ."

His voice trailed off. He sat there thinking. Weston recalled him to the needs of the moment. "Now, Mr. Redfern, had you any particular appointment with Mrs. Marshall this morning?"

Patrick Redfern looked slightly puzzled. He said: "Not a particular appointment, no. We usually met every morning on the beach. We used to paddle about on floats."

"Were you surprised not to find Mrs. Marshall there this morning?"

"Yes, I was. Very surprised. I couldn't understand it at all."

"What did you think?"

"Well, I didn't know what to think. I mean, all the time I thought she would be coming."

"If she were keeping an appointment elsewhere you had no idea with whom that appointment might be?" Patrick Redfern merely stared and shook his head. "When you had a *rendezvous* with Mrs. Marshall, where did you meet?"

"Well, sometimes I'd meet her in the afternoon down at Gull Cove. You see the sun is off Gull Cove in the afternoon and so there aren't usually many people there. We met there once or twice."

"Never on the other cove? Pixy Cove?"

"No. You see Pixy Cove faces west and people go round there in boats or on floats in the afternoon. We never tried to meet in the morning. It would have been too noticeable. In the afternoon people go and have a sleep or mouch around and nobody knows much where any one else is." Weston nodded. Patrick Redfern went on: "After dinner, of course, on the fine nights, we used to go off for a stroll together to different parts of the island."

Hercule Poirot murmured: "Ah, yes!" and Patrick Redfern shot him an inquiring glance.

Weston said: "Then you can give us no help whatsoever as to the cause that took Mrs. Marshall to Pixy Cove this morning?"

Redfern shook his head. He said, and his voice sounded honestly bewildered: "I haven't the faintest idea! It wasn't *like* Arlena."

Weston said: "Had she any friends down here staying in the neighbourhood?"

"Not that I know of. Oh, I'm sure she hadn't."

"Now, Mr. Redfern, I want you to think very carefully. You knew Mrs. Marshall in London. You must be acquainted with various members of her circle. Is there any one you know of who could have had a grudge against her? Someone, for instance, whom you may have supplanted in her fancy?"

Patrick Redfern thought for some minutes. Then he shook his head. "Honestly," he said. "I can't think of any one."

Colonel Weston drummed with his fingers on the table. He said at last: "Well, that's that. We seem to be left with three possibilities. That of an unknown killer—some monomaniac—who happened to be in the neighborhood—and that's a pretty tall order—"

Redfern said, interrupting: "And yet surely, it's by far the most likely explanation."

Weston shook his head. He said: "This isn't one of the 'lonely copse' murders. This cove place was pretty inaccessible. Either a man would have to come up from the causeway past the hotel, over the top of the island and down by that ladder contraption, or else he came there by boat. Either way is unlikely for a casual killing."

Patrick Redfern said: "You said there were three possibilities."

"Um—yes," said the Chief Constable. "That's to say, there were two people on this island who had a motive for killing her. Her husband, for one, and your wife for another."

Redfern stared at him. He looked dumbfounded. He said: "My wife? Christine? D'you mean that *Christine* had anything to do with this?" He got up and stood there stammering slightly in his incoherent haste to get the words out. "You're mad—quite mad—Christine? Why, it's *impossible*. It's laughable!"

Weston said: "All the same, Mr. Redfern, jealousy is a very powerful motive. Women who are jealous lose control of themselves completely."

Redfern said earnestly: "Not Christine. She's—oh, she's not like that. She was unhappy, yes. But she's not the kind of person to—Oh, there's no violence in her."

Hercule Poirot nodded thoughtfully. Violence. The same word that Linda Marshall had used. As before, he agreed with the sentiment. "Besides," went on Redfern confidently. "It would be absurd. Arlena was twice as strong physically as Christine. I doubt if Christine could strangle a kitten—certainly not a strong wiry creature like Arlena. And then Christine could never have got down that ladder to the beach. She has no head for that sort of thing. And—oh, the whole thing is fantastic!"

Colonel Weston scratched his ear tentatively. "Well," he said. "Put like that it doesn't seem likely. I grant you that. But motive's the first thing we've go to look for." He added: "Motive and opportunity."

When Redfern had left the room, the Chief Constable observed with a slight smile: "Didn't think it necessary to tell the fellow his wife had got an alibi. Wanted to hear what he'd have to say to the idea. Shook him up a bit, didn't it?"

Hercule Poirot murmured: "The arguments he advanced were quite as strong as any alibi."

"Yes. Oh! she didn't do it! She couldn't have done it—physically impossible as you said. Marshall *could* have done it—but apparently he didn't."

Inspector Colgate coughed. He said: "Excuse me, sir, I've been thinking about that alibi. It's possible, you know, if he'd thought this thing out, that those letters were got ready *beforehand*."

Weston said: "That's a good idea. We must look into—"

He broke off as Christine Redfern entered the room. She was, as always, calm and a little precise in manner. She was wearing a white tennis frock and a pale blue pullover. It accentuated her fair, rather anemic prettiness. Yet, Hercule Poirot thought to himself, it was neither a silly face nor a weak one. It had plenty of resolution, courage and good sense. He nodded appreciatively. Colonel Weston thought: "Nice little woman. Bit wishy-washy, perhaps. A lot too good for that philandering young ass of a husband of hers. Oh, well, the boy's young. Women usually make a fool of you once!" He said: "Sit down, Mrs. Redfern. We've got to go through a certain amount of routine, you see. Asking everybody for an account of their movements this morning. Just for our records."

Christine Redfern nodded. She said in her quiet precise voice: "Oh, yes, I quite understand. Where do you want me to begin?"

Hercule Poirot said: "As early as possible, Madame. What did you do when you first got up this morning?"

Christine said: "Let me see. On my way down to breakfast I went into Linda Marshall's room and fixed up with her to go to Gull Cove this morning. We agreed to meet in the lounge at half past ten."

Poirot asked: "You did not bathe before breakfast, Madame?"

"No. I very seldom do." She smiled. "I like the sea well warmed before I get into it. I'm rather a chilly person."

"But your husband bathes then?"

"Oh, yes. Nearly always."

"And Mrs. Marshall, she also?"

A change came over Christine's voice. It became cold and almost acrid. She said: "Oh, no, Mrs. Marshall was the sort of person who never made an appearance before the middle of the morning."

With an air of confusion, Hercule Poirot said: "Pardon, Madame, I interrupted you. You were saying that you went to Miss Linda Marshall's room. What time was that?"

"Let me see—half past eight—no, a little later."

"And was Miss Marshall up then?"

"Oh, yes, she had been out."

"Out?"

"Yes, she said she'd been bathing."

There was a faint—a very faint note of embarrassment in Christine's voice. It puzzled Hercule Poirot.

Weston said: "And then?"

"Then I went down to breakfast."

"And after breakfast?"

"I went upstairs, collected my sketching box, and sketching book and we started out."

"You and Miss Linda Marshall?"

"Yes."

"What time was that?"

"I think it was just on half past ten."

"And what did you do?"

"We went to Gull Cove. You know, the cove on the east side of the island. We settled ourselves there. I did a sketch and Linda sunbathed."

"What time did you leave the cove?"

"At a quarter to twelve. I was playing tennis at twelve and had to change."

"You had your watch with you?"

"No, as a matter of fact I hadn't. I asked Linda the time."

"I see. And then?"

"I packed up my sketching things and went back to the hotel."

Poirot said: "And Mademoiselle Linda?"

"Linda? Oh, Linda went into the sea."

Poirot said: "Were you far from the sea where you were sitting?"

"Well, we were well above high-water mark. Just under the cliff—so that I could be a little in the shade and Linda the sun."

Poirot said: "Did Linda Marshall actually enter the sea before you left the beach?"

Christine frowned a little in the effort to remember. She said: "Let me see. She ran down the beach—I fastened my box—Yes, I heard her splashing in the waves as I was on the path up the cliff."

"You are quite sure of that, Madame? That she really entered the sea?"

"Oh, yes." She stared at him in surprise.

Colonel Weston also stared at him. Then he said: "Go on, Mrs. Redfern."

"I went back to the hotel, changed, and went to the tennis courts where I met the others."

"Who were?"

"Captain Marshall, Mr. Gardener and Miss Darnley. We played two sets. We were just going in again when the news came about—about Mrs. Marshall."

Hercule Poirot leant forward. He said: "And what did you think, Madame, when you heard that news?"

"What did I think?" Her face showed a faint distaste for the question.

"Yes."

Christine Redfern said slowly: "It was—a horrible thing to happen."

"Ah, yes, your fastidiousness was revolted. I understand that. But what did it mean to *you*—personally?"

She gave him a quick look—a look of appeal. He responded to it. He said in a matter-of-fact voice: "I am appealing to you, Madame, as a woman of intelligence with plenty of good sense and judgment. You had doubtless during your stay here formed an opinion of Mrs. Marshall, of the kind of woman she was?"

Christine said cautiously: "I suppose one always does that more or less when one is staying in hotels."

"Certainly, it is the natural thing to do. So I ask you, Madame, were you really very surprised at the manner of her death?"

Christine said slowly: "I think I see what you mean. No, I was not, perhaps, surprised. Shocked, yes. But she was the kind of woman—"

Poirot finished the sentence for her. "She was the kind of woman to whom such a thing might happen. . . . Yes, Madame, that is the truest and most significant thing that has been said in this room this morning. Laying all—er—[he stressed it carefully] *personal* feeling aside, what did you really think of the late Mrs. Marshall?"

Christine Redfern said calmly: "Is it really worth while going into all that now?"

"I think it might be, yes."

"Well, what shall I say?" Her fair skin was suddenly suffused with colour. The careful poise of her manner was relaxed. For a short space the natural raw woman looked out. "She's the kind of woman that to my mind is absolutely worthless! She did nothing to justify her existence. She had no mind—no brains. She thought of nothing but men and clothes and admiration. Useless, a parasite! She was attractive to men, I suppose—Oh, of course she was. And she lived for that kind of life. And so, I suppose, I wasn't really surprised at her coming to a sticky end. She was the sort of woman who would be mixed up with everything sordid—blackmail—jealousy—every kind of crude emotion. She—she appealed to the worst in people."

She stopped, panting a little. Her rather short top lip lifted itself in a kind of fastidious disgust. It occurred to Colonel Weston that you could not have found a more complete contrast to Arlena Stuart than Christine Redfern. It also occurred to him that if you were married to Christine Redfern, the atmosphere might be so rarefied that the Arlena Stuarts of this world would hold a particular attraction for you. And then, immediately following on these thoughts, a single word out of the words she had spoken fastened on his attention with particular intensity. He leaned forward and said: "Mrs. Redfern, why in speaking of her, did you mention the word *blackmail*?"

7

CHRISTINE STARED at him, not seeming at once to take in what he meant. She answered almost mechanically. "I suppose—because she *was* being blackmailed. She *was* the sort of person who would be."

Colonel Weston said earnestly: "But—do you know she was being blackmailed?"

A faint colour rose in the girl's cheeks. She said rather awkwardly: "As a matter of fact I do happen to know it. I—I overheard something."

"Will you explain, Mrs. Redfern?"

Flushing still more, Christine Redfern said: "I—I didn't mean to overhear. It was an accident. It was two—no, three nights ago. We were playing bridge." She turned towards Poirot. "You remember? My husband and I, M. Poirot and Miss Darnley. I was dummy. It was very stuffy in the card room, and I slipped out of the window for a breath of fresh air. I went down towards the beach and I suddenly heard voices. One—it was Arlena Marshall's—I knew it at once—said: 'It's no good pressing me. I can't get any more money now. My husband will suspect something.' And then a man's voice said: 'I'm not taking any excuses. You've got to cough up.' And then Arlena Marshall said: 'You blackmailing brute!' And the man said: 'Brute or not, you'll pay up, my lady.'" Christine paused. "I'd turned back and a minute after Arlena Marshall rushed past me. She looked—well, frightfully upset."

Weston said: "And the man? Do you know who he was?"

Christine Redfern shook her head. She said: "He was keeping his voice low. I barely heard what he said."

"It didn't suggest the voice to you of any one you knew?"

She thought again, but once more shook her head. She said: "No, I don't know. It was gruff and low. It—oh, it might have been anybody's."

Colonel Weston said: "Thank you, Mrs. Redfern."

When the door had closed behind Christine Redfern Inspector Colgate said: "Now we are getting somewhere!"

Weston said: "You think so, eh?"

"Well, it's suggestive, sir, you can't get away from it. Somebody in this hotel was blackmailing the lady."

Poirot murmured: "But it is not the wicked blackmailer who lies dead. It is the victim."

"That's a bit of a setback, I agree," said the Inspector. "Blackmailers aren't in the habit of bumping off their victims. But what it does give us is this, it suggests a reason for Mrs. Marshall's curious behaviour this morning. She'd got a *rendezvous* with this fellow who was blackmailing her, and she didn't want either her husband or Redfern to know about it."

"It certainly explains that point," agreed Poirot.

Inspector Colgate went on: "And think of the place chosen. The very spot for the purpose. The lady goes off on her float. That's natural enough. It's what she does every day. She goes round to Pixy Cove where no one ever goes in the morning and which will be a nice quiet place for an interview."

Poirot said: "But yes, I too was struck by that point. It is, as you say, an ideal spot for a *rendezvous*. It is deserted, it is only accessible from the land side by descending a vertical steel ladder which is not everybody's money, *bien entendu*. Moreover, most of the beach is invisible from above because of the overhanging cliff. And it has another advantage. Mr. Redfern told me of that one day. There is a cave on it, the entrance to which is not easy to find but where any one could wait unseen."

Weston said: "Of course, the Pixy's Cave—remember hearing about it."

Inspector Colgate said: "Haven't heard it spoken of for years, though. We'd better have a look inside it. Never know, we might find a pointer of some kind."

Weston said: "Yes, you're right, Colgate, we've got the solution to part one of the puzzle. *Why did Mrs. Marshall go to Pixy's Cove*? We want the other half of that solution, though. *Who did she go there to meet*? Presumably someone staying in this hotel. None of them fitted as a lover—but a blackmailer's a different proposition." He drew the register towards him. "Excluding the waiters, boots, etc., whom I don't think likely, we've got the following. The American—Gardener, Major Barry, Mr. Horace Blatt, and the Reverend Stephen Lane."

Inspector Colgate said: "We can narrow it down a bit, sir. We might almost rule out the American, I think. He was on the beach all the morning. That's so, isn't it, M. Poirot?"

Poirot replied: "He was absent for a short time when he fetched a skein of wool for his wife."

Colgate said: "Oh, well, we needn't count that."

Weston said: "And what about the other three?"

"Major Barry went out at ten o'clock this morning. He returned at one-thirty. Mr. Lane was earlier still. He breakfasted at eight. Said he was going for a tramp. Mr. Blatt went off for a sail at nine-thirty same as he does most days. Neither of them is back yet?"

"A sail, eh?" Colonel Weston's voice was thoughtful.

Inspector Colgate's voice was responsive. He said: "Might fit in rather well, sir."

Weston said: "Well, we'll have a word with this Major bloke—and let me see, who else is there? Rosamund Darnley. And there's the Brewster woman who found the body with Redfern. What's she like, Colgate?"

"Oh, a sensible party, sir. No nonsense about her."

"She didn't express any opinions on the death?"

The inspector shook his head. "I don't think she'll have anything more to tell us, sir, but we'll have to make sure. Then there are the Americans."

Colonel Weston nodded. He said: "Let's have 'em all in and get it over as soon as possible. Never know, might learn something. About the blackmailing stunt if about nothing else."

Mr. and Mrs. Gardener came into the presence of authority together. Mrs. Gardener explained immediately. "I hope you'll understand how it is, Colonel Weston (that is the name, I think?)." Reassured on this point she went on: "But this has been a very bad shock to me and Mr. Gardener is always very, very careful of my health—"

Mr. Gardener here interpolated. "Mrs. Gardener," he said, "is very sensitive."

"—and he said to me, 'Why, Carrie,' he said, 'naturally I'm coming right along with you.' It's not that we haven't the highest admiration for British police methods, because we have. I've been told that British police procedure is most refined and delicate and I've never doubted it and certainly when I once had a bracelet missing at the Savoy Hotel nothing could have been more lovely and sympathetic than the young man who came to see me about it, and of course I hadn't really lost the bracelet at all, but just mislaid it, that's the worst of rushing about so much, it makes you kind of forgetful where you put things—" Mrs. Gardener paused, inhaled gently and started off again. "And what I say is, and I know Mr. Gardener agrees with me, that we're only too anxious to do anything to help the British police in every way. So go right ahead and ask me anything at all you want to know—"

Colonel Weston opened his mouth to comply with this invitation but had momentarily to postpone speech while Mrs. Gardener went on. "That's what I said, Odell, isn't it? And that's so, isn't it?"

"Yes, darling," said Mr. Gardener.

Colonel Weston spoke hastily. "I understand, Mrs. Gardener, that you and your husband were on the beach all the morning?"

For once Mr. Gardener was able to get in first. "That's so," he said.

"Why, certainly we were," said Mrs. Gardener. "And a lovely peaceful morning it was, just like any other morning, if you get me, perhaps even more so, and not the slightest idea in our minds of what was happening round the corner on that lonely beach."

"Did you see Mrs. Marshall at all to-day?"

"We did not. And I said to Odell, Why, wherever can Mrs. Marshall have got to this morning? I said. And first her husband coming looking for her and then that good-looking young man, Mr. Redfern, and so impatient he was, just sitting there on the beach scowling at every one and everything. And I said to myself, Why, when he has that nice pretty little wife of his own, must he go running after that dreadful woman? Because that's just what I felt she was. I always felt that about her, didn't I, Odell?"

"Yes, darling."

"However that nice Captain Marshall came to marry such a woman I just cannot imagine—and with that nice young daughter growing up, and it's so important for girls to have the right influence. Mrs. Marshall was not at all the right person—no breeding at all—and I should say a very animal nature. Now if Captain Marshall had had any sense he'd have married Miss Darnley who's a very, very charming woman and a very distinguished one. I must say I admire the way she's gone straight ahead and built up a first-class business as she has. It takes brains to do a thing like that—and you've only to look at Rosamund Darnley to see she's just frantic with brains. She could plan and carry out any mortal thing she liked. I just admire that woman more than I can say. And I said to Mr. Gardener the other day that any one could see she was very much in love with Captain Marshall—crazy about him was what I said, didn't I, Odell?"

"Yes, darling."

"It seems they knew each other as children, and, why, now, who knows, it may all come right after all with that woman out of the way. I'm not a narrow-minded woman, Colonel Weston, and it isn't that I disapprove of the stage as such—why, quite a lot of my best friends are actresses—but I've said to Mr. Gardener all along that there was something evil about that woman. And you see, I've been proved right."

She paused triumphantly. The lips of Hercule Poirot quivered in a little smile. His eyes met for a minute the shrewd grey eyes of Mr. Gardener. Colonel Weston said rather desperately: "Well, thank you, Mrs. Gardener. I suppose there's nothing that either of you has noticed since you've been here that might have a bearing upon the case?"

"Why, no, I don't think so." Mr. Gardener spoke with a slow drawl.

"Mrs. Marshall was around with young Redfern most of the time—but everybody can tell you that."

"What about her husband? Did he mind, do you think?"

Mr. Gardener said cautiously: "Captain Marshall is a very reserved man."

Mrs. Gardener confirmed this by saying: "Why, yes, he is a real Britisher!"

On the slightly apoplectic countenance of Major Barry various emotions seemed contending for mastery. He was endeavouring to look properly horrified but could not subdue a kind of shamefaced gusto. He was saying in his hoarse slightly wheezy voice: "Glad to help you any way I can. 'Course I don't know anythin' about it—nothin' at all. Not acquainted with the parties. But I've knocked about a bit in my time. Lived a lot in the East, you know. And I can tell you that after being in an Indian hill station what you don't know about human nature isn't worth knowin'." He paused, took a breath and was off again. "Matter of fact this business reminds me of a case in Simla. Fellow called Robinson or was it Falconer? Anyway he was in the East Wilts or was it the North Surreys? Can't remember now and anyway it doesn't matter. Quiet chap, you know, great reader—mild as milk you'd have said. Went for his wife one evening in their bungalow. Got her by the throat. She'd been carryin' on with some feller or other and he'd got wise to it. By Jove, he nearly did for her! It was touch and go. Surprised us all! Didn't think he had it in him."

Hercule Poirot murmured: "And you see there an analogy to the death of Mrs. Marshall?"

"Well, what I mean to say—strangled, you know. Same idea. Feller suddenly sees red!"

Poirot said: "You think that Captain Marshall felt like that?"

"Oh, look here, I never said that." Major Barry's face went even redder. "Never said anything about Marshall. Thoroughly nice chap. Wouldn't say a word against him for the world."

Poirot murmured: "Ah, *pardon*, but you *did* refer to the natural reactions of a husband."

Major Barry said: "Well, I mean to say, I should think she'd been pretty hot stuff. Eh? Got young Redfern on a string all right. And there were probably others before him. But the funny thing is, you know, that husbands are a dense lot. Amazin'. I've been surprised by it again and again. They see a feller sweet on their wife but they don't see that *she's* sweet on *him*! Remember a case like that in Poona. Very pretty woman. Jove, she led her husband a dance—"

Colonel Weston stirred a little restively. He said: "Yes, yes, Major Barry. For the moment we've just got to establish the facts. You don't know of anything personally—that you've seen or noticed that might help us in this case?"

"Well, really, Weston, I can't say I do. Saw her and young Redfern one afternoon on Gull Cove—" Here he winked knowingly and gave a deep hoarse chuckle—"Very pretty it was, too. But it's not evidence of that kind you're wanting. Ha, ha."

"You did not see Mrs. Marshall at all this morning?"

"Didn't see anybody this morning. Went over to St. Loo. Just my luck. Sort of place here where nothin' happens for months and when it does you miss it!"

The Major's voice held a ghoulish regret. Colonel Weston prompted him. "You went to St. Loo, you say?"

"Yes, wanted to do some telephonin'. No telephone here and that post office place at Leathercombe Bay isn't very private."

"Were your telephone calls of a very private nature?"

The Major winked again cheerfully. "Well, they were and they weren't. Wanted to get through to a pal of mine and get him to put somethin' on a horse. Couldn't get through to him, worse luck."

"Where did you telephone from?"

"Call box in the G.P.O. at St. Loo. Then on the way back I got lost—these confounded lanes—twistin' and turnin' all over the place. Must have wasted an hour over that at least. Damned confusing part of the world. I only got back half an hour ago."

Colonel Weston said: "Speak to any one or meet any one in St. Loo?"

Major Barry said with a chuckle: "Wantin' me to prove an alibi? Can't think of anythin' useful. Saw about fifty thousand people in St. Loo—but that's not to say they'll remember seein' me."

The Chief Constable said: "We have to ask these things, you know."

"Right you are. Call on me at any time. Glad to help you. Very fetchin' woman, the deceased. Like to help you catch the feller who did it. The Lonely Beach Murder—bet you that's what the papers will call it. Reminds me of the time—"

It was Inspector Colgate who firmly nipped this latest reminiscence in the bud and maneuvered the garrulous Major out of the door. Coming back he said: "Difficult to check up on anything in St. Loo. It's the middle of the holiday season."

The Chief Constable said: "Yes, we can't take him off the list. Not that I seriously believe he's implicated. Dozens of old bores like him going about. Remember one or two of them in my Army days.

Still—he's a possibility. I leave all that to you, Colgate. Check what time he took the car out—petrol—all that. It's humanly possible that he parked the car somewhere in a lonely spot, walked back here and went to the cove. But it doesn't seem feasible to me. He'd have run too much risk of being seen."

Colgate nodded. He said: "Of course there are a good many charabancs here to-day. Fine day. They start arriving round about half past eleven. High tide was at seven. Low tide would be about one o'clock. People would be spread out over the sands and the causeway."

Weston said: "Yes. But he'd have to come up from the causeway past the hotel."

"Not right past it. He could branch off on the path that leads up over the top of the island."

Weston said doubtfully: "I'm not saying that he mightn't have done it without being seen. Practically all the hotel guests were on the bathing beach except for Mrs. Redfern and the Marshall girl who were down in Gull Cove, and the beginning of that path would only be overlooked by a few rooms of the hotel and there are plenty of chances against any one looking out of those windows just at that moment. For the matter of that, I daresay it's possible for a man to walk up to the hotel, through the lounge and out again without any one happening to see him. But what I say is, he couldn't *count* on no one seeing him."

Colgate said: "He could have gone round to the cove by boat."

Weston nodded. He said: "That's much sounder. If he'd had a boat handy in one of the coves near by, he could have left the car, rowed or sailed to Pixy's Cove, done the murder, rowed back, picked up the car and arrived back with this tale about having been to St. Loo and lost his way—a story that he'd know would be pretty hard to disprove."

"You're right, sir."

The Chief Constable said: "Well, I leave it to you, Colgate. Comb the neighborhood thoroughly. You know what to do. We'd better see Miss Brewster now."

Emily Brewster was not able to add anything of material value to what they already knew. Weston said after she had repeated her story: "And there's nothing you know of that could help us in any way?"

Emily Brewster said shortly: "Afraid not. It's a distressing business. However I expect you'll soon get to the bottom of it."

Weston said: "I hope so too."

Emily Brewster said drily: "Ought not to be difficult."

"Now what do you mean by that, Miss Brewster?"

"Sorry. Wasn't attempting to teach you your business. All I meant was that with a woman of that kind it ought to be easy enough."

Hercule Poirot murmured: "That is your opinion?"

Emily Brewster snapped out: "Of course. *De mortuis nil nisi bonum* and all that, but you can't get away from *facts*. That woman was a bad lot through and through. You've only got to hunt round a bit in her unsavoury past."

Hercule Poirot said gently: "You did not like her?"

"I know a bit too much about her." In answer to the inquiring looks she went on. "My first cousin married one of the Erskins. You've probably heard that that woman induced old Sir Robert when he was in his dotage to leave most of his fortune to her away from his own family."

Colonel Weston said: "And the family—er—resented that?"

"Naturally. His association with her was a scandal anyway and on top of that to leave her a sum like fifty thousand pounds shows just the kind of woman she was. I daresay I sound hard, but in my opinion the Arlena Stuarts of this world deserve very little sympathy. I know of something else too—a young fellow who lost his head about her completely—he'd always been a bit wild, naturally his association with her pushed him over the edge. He did something rather fishy with some shares—solely to get money to spend on her—and only just managed to escape prosecution. That woman contaminated every one she met. Look at the way she was ruining young Redfern. No, I'm afraid I can't have any regret for her death—though of course it would have been better if she'd drowned herself, or fallen over a cliff. Strangling is rather unpleasant."

"And you think the murderer was some one out of her past?"

"Yes, I do."

"Some one who came from the mainland with no one seeing him?"

"Why should any one see him? We were all on the beach. I gather the Marshall child and Christine Redfern were down on Gull Cove out of the way. Captain Marshall was in his room in the hotel. Then who on earth was there to see him except possibly Miss Darnley."

"Where was Miss Darnley?"

"Sitting up on the cutting at the top of the cliff. Sunny Ledge it's called. We saw her there, Mr. Redfern and I, when we were rowing round the island."

Colonel Weston said: "You may be right, Miss Brewster."

Emily Brewster said positively: "I'm sure I'm right. When a woman's neither more nor less than a nasty mess, then she herself will provide the best possible clue. Don't you agree with me, M. Poirot?"

Hercule Poirot looked up. His eyes met her confident grey ones. He said: "Oh, yes—I agree with that which you have just this minute said.

Arlena Marshall herself is the best, the only clue, to her own death."

Miss Brewster said sharply: "Well, then!" She stood there, an erect sturdy figure, her cool self-confident glance going from one man to the other.

Colonel Weston said: "You may be sure, Miss Brewster, that any clue there may be in Mrs. Marshall's past life will not be overlooked."

Emily Brewster went out.

Inspector Colgate shifted his position at the table. He said in a thoughtful voice: "She's a determined one, she is. And she'd got her knife in to the dead lady, proper, she had." He stopped a minute and said reflectively: "It's a pity in a way that she's got a castiron alibi for the whole morning. Did you notice her hands, sir? As big as a man's. And she's a hefty woman—as strong and stronger than many a man I'd say. . . ." He paused again. His glance at Poirot was almost pleading. "And you say she never left the beach this morning, M. Poirot?"

Slowly Poirot shook his head. He said: "My dear Inspector, she came down to the beach before Mrs. Marshall could have reached Pixy's Cove; and she was within my sight until she set off with Mr. Redfern in the boat."

Inspector Colgate said gloomily: "Then that washes her out." He seemed upset about it.

As always, Hercule Poirot felt a keen sense of pleasure at the sight of Rosamund Darnley. Even to a bare police inquiry into the ugly facts of murder she brought a distinction of her own. She sat down opposite Colonel Weston and turned a grave and intelligent face on him. She said: "You want my name and address? Rosamund Anne Darnley. I carry on a dressmaking business under the name of Rose Mond, Ltd. at 622 Brook Street."

"Thank you, Miss Darnley. Now can you tell us anything that may help us?"

"I don't really think I can."

"Your own movements—"

"I had breakfast about nine-thirty. Then I went up to my room and collected some books and my sunshade and went out to Sunny Ledge. That must have been about twenty-five past ten. I came back to the hotel about ten minutes to twelve, went up and got my tennis racquet and went out to the tennis courts where I played tennis until lunch-time."

"You were in the cliff recess, called by the hotel, Sunny Ledge, from about half past ten until ten minutes to twelve?"

"Yes."

"Did you see Mrs. Marshall at all this morning?"

"No."

"Did you see her from the cliff as she paddled her float around to Pixy's Cove?"

"No, she must have gone by before I got there."

"Did you notice any one on a float or in a boat at all this morning?"

"No, I don't think I did. You see I was reading. Of course I looked up from my book from time to time but as it happened the sea was quiet each time I did so."

"You didn't even notice Mr. Redfern and Miss Brewster when they went round?"

"No."

"You were, I think acquainted with Mr. Marshall?"

"Captain Marshall is an old family friend. His family and mine lived next door to each other. I had not seen him, however, for a good many years—it must be something like twelve years."

"And Mrs. Marshall?"

"I'd never exchanged half a dozen words with her until I met her here."

"Were Captain and Mrs. Marshall, as far as you knew, on good terms with each other?"

"On perfectly good terms, I should say."

"Was Captain Marshall very devoted to his wife?"

Rosamund said: "He may have been. I can't really tell you anything about that. Captain Marshall is rather old-fashioned—but he hasn't got the modern habit of shouting matrimonial woes upon the house-top."

"Did you like Mrs. Marshall, Miss Darnley?"

"No." The monosyllable came quietly and evenly. It sounded what it was—a simple statement of fact.

"Why was that?"

A half smile came to Rosamund's lips. She said: "Surely you've discovered that Arlena Marshall was not popular with her own sex? She was bored to death with women and showed it. Nevertheless I should like to have had the dressing of her. She had a great gift for clothes. Her clothes were always just right and she wore them well. I should like to have had her as a client."

"She spent a good deal on clothes?"

"She must have done. But then she had money of her own and of course Captain Marshall is quite well off."

"Did you ever hear or did it ever occur to you that Mrs. Marshall was being blackmailed, Miss Darnley?"

A look of intense astonishment came over Rosamund Darnley's expressive face. She said: "Blackmailed? Arlena?"

"The idea seems to surprise you."

"Well, yes, it does rather. It seems so incongruous."

"But surely it is possible?"

"Everything's possible, isn't it? The world soon teaches one that. But I wondered what any one could blackmail Arlena about?"

"There are certain things, I suppose, that Mrs. Marshall might be anxious should not come to her husband's ears?"

"We-ll, yes." She explained the doubt in her voice by saying with a half smile: "I sound sceptical, but then, you see, Arlena was rather notorious in her conduct. She never made much of a pose of respectability."

"You think, then, that her husband was aware of her—intimacies with other people?"

There was a pause. Rosamund was frowning. She spoke at last in a slow reluctant voice. She said: "You know, I don't really know what to think. I've always assumed that Kenneth Marshall accepted his wife, quite frankly, for what she was. That he had no illusions about her. But it may not be so."

"He may have believed in her absolutely?"

Rosamund said with semi-exasperation: "Men are such fools. And Kenneth Marshall is unworldly under his sophisticated manner. He *may* have believed in her blindly. He may have thought she was just—admired."

"And you know of no one—that is you have heard of no one who was likely to have had a grudge against Mrs. Marshall?"

Rosamund Darnley smiled. She said: "Only resentful wives. And I presume since she was strangled, that it was a man who killed her."

"Yes."

Rosamund said thoughtfully: "No, I can't think of any one. But then I probably shouldn't know. You'll have to ask some one in her own intimate set."

"Thank you, Miss Darnley."

Rosamund turned a little in her chair. She said: "Hasn't M. Poirot any questions to ask?" Her faintly ironic smile flashed out at him.

Hercule Poirot smiled and shook his head. He said: "I can think of nothing."

Rosamund Darnley got up and went out.

8

THEY WERE STANDING in the bedroom that had been Arlena Marshall's.
Two big bay windows gave onto a balcony that overlooked the bathing
beach and the sea beyond. Sunshine poured into the room flashing over
the bewildering array of bottles and jars on Arlena's dressing-table.
Here there was every kind of cosmetic and unguent known to beauty
parlors. Amongst this panoply of women's affairs three men moved
purposefully. Inspector Colgate went about shutting and opening
drawers. Presently he gave a grunt. He had come upon a packet of
folded letters. He and Weston ran through them together.

Hercule Poirot had moved to the wardrobe. He opened the door of
the hanging cupboard and looked at the multiplicity of gowns and
sports suits that hung there. He opened the other side. Foamy lingerie
lay in piles. On a wide shelf were hats. Two more beach cardboard hats
in lacquer red and pale yellow—a big Hawaiian straw hat—another of
drooping dark blue linen and three or four little absurdities for which,
no doubt, several guineas had been paid apiece—a kind of beret in dark
blue—a tuft, no more, of black velvet—a pale grey turban. Hercule
Poirot stood scanning them—a faintly indulgent smile came to his lips.
He murmured, "*Les femmes!*"

Colonel Weston was refolding the letters. "Three from young
Redfern," he said. "Damned young ass. He'll learn not to write letters
to women in a few more years. Women always keep letters and then
swear they've burnt them. There's one other letter here. Same line of
country." He held it out and Poirot took it.

> "Darling Arlena,
> "God, I feel blue. To be going out to China—and perhaps
> not seeing you again for years and years. I didn't know any man
> could go on feeling crazy about a woman like I feel about you.
> Thanks for the cheque. They won't prosecute now. It was a
> near shave, though, and all because I wanted to make big
> money for you. Can you forgive me? I wanted to set diamonds
> in your ears—Your lovely lovely ears and clasp great milk-
> white pearls round your throat only they say pearls are no good
> nowadays. A fabulous emerald, then? Yes, that's the thing. A
> great emerald, cool and green and full of hidden fire. Don't
> forget me—but you won't, I know. You're mine—always.
> "Good-bye—good-bye—good-bye.
>   "J.N."

Inspector Colgate said: "Might be worth while to find out if J.N. really did go to China. Otherwise—well, he might be the person we're looking for. Crazy about the woman, idealizing her, suddenly finding out he'd been played for a sucker. It sounds to me as though this is the boy Miss Brewster mentioned. Yes, I think this might be useful."

Hercule Poirot nodded. He said: "Yes, that letter is important. I find it very important."

He turned round and stared at the room—at the bottles on the dressing-table—at the open wardrobe and at a big Pierrot doll that lolled insolently on the bed. They went into Kenneth Marshall's room. It was next door to his wife's but with no communicating door and no balcony. It faced the same way and had two windows, but it was much smaller. Between the two windows a gilt mirror hung on the wall. In the corner beyond the right-hand window was the dressing-table. On it were two ivory brushes, a clothes brush and a bottle of hair lotion. In the corner by the left-hand window was a writing-table. An open typewriter stood on it and papers were ranged in a stack beside it.

Colgate went through them rapidly. He said, "All seems straightforward enough. Ah, here's the letter he mentioned this morning. Dated the 24th—that's yesterday. And here's the envelope—postmarked Leathercombe Bay this morning. Seems all square. Now we'll have an idea if he could have prepared that answer of his beforehand."

He sat down. Colonel Weston said: "We'll leave you to it, for a moment. We'll just glance through the rest of the rooms. Every one's been kept out of this corridor until now and they're getting a bit restive about it." They went next into Linda Marshall's room. It faced east, looking out over the rocks down to the sea below.

Weston gave a glance round. He murmured: "Don't suppose there's anything to see here. But it's possible Marshall might have put something in his daughter's room that he didn't want us to find. Not likely, though. It isn't as though there had been a weapon or anything to get rid of." He went out again.

Hercule Poirot stayed behind. He found something that interested him in the grate. Something had been burnt there recently. He knelt down, working patiently. He laid out his finds on a sheet of paper. A large irregular blob of candle grease—some fragments of green paper or cardboard, possibly a pull-off calendar, for with it was an unburnt fragment bearing a large figure 5 and a scrap of printing... *noble deeds*. ... There was also an ordinary pin and some burnt animal matter which might have been hair. Poirot arranged them neatly in a row and stared at them. He murmured. "'*Do noble deeds, not dream them all day long.' C'est possible.* But what is one to make of this collection? *C'est fantastique!"* And then he picked up the pin and his eyes grew sharp and green. He murmured: *"Pour l'amour de Dieu!* Is it possible?"

Hercule Poirot got up from where he had been kneeling by the grate. Slowly he looked round the room and this time there was an entirely new expression on his face. It was grave and almost stern. To the left of the mantelpiece there were some shelves with a row of books. Hercule Poirot looked thoughtfully along the titles. A Bible, a battered copy of Shakespeare's plays. *The Marriage of William Ashe* by Mrs. Humphry Ward. *The Young Stepmother* by Charlotte Yonge. *The Shropshire Lad.* Eliot's *Murder in the Cathedral.* Bernard Shaw's *St. Joan. Gone with the Wind* by Margaret Mitchell. *The Burning Court* by Dickson Carr.

Poirot took out two books, *The Young Stepmother* and *William Ashe,* and glanced inside at the blurred stamp affixed to the title page. As he was about to replace them, his eye caught sight of a book that had been shoved behind the other books. It was a small dumpy volume bound in brown calf. He took it out and opened it. Very slowly he nodded his head. He murmured: *"So I was right. . . .* Yes, I was right. But for the other—is that possible too? No, it is not possible, unless. . . ."

He stayed there, motionless, stroking his mustaches whilst his mind ranged busily over the problem. He said again softly: *"Unless—?"*

Colonel Weston looked in at the door. "Hullo, Poirot, still there?"

"I arrive. I arrive," cried Poirot. He hurried out into the corridor. The room next to Linda's was that of the Redferns. Poirot looked into it, noting automatically the traces of two different individualities—a neatness and tidiness which he associated with Christine and a picturesque disorder which was characteristic of Patrick. Apart from these sidelights on personality the room did not interest him. Next to it again was Rosamund Darnley's room and here he lingered for a moment in the sheer pleasure of the owner's personality. He noted the few books that lay on the table next to the bed, the expensive simplicity of the toilet set on the dressing-table. And there came gently to his nostrils the elusive expensive perfume that Rosamund Darnley used.

Next to Rosamund Darnley's room at the northern end of the corridor was an open window leading to a balcony from which an outside stair led down to the rocks below. Weston said: "That's the way people go down to bathe before breakfast—that is, if they bathe off the rocks as most of them do."

Interest came into Hercule Poirot's eyes. He stepped outside and looked down. Below, a path led to steps cut zigzag leading down the rocks to the sea. There was also a path that led round the hotel to the left. He said: "One could go down these stairs, go to the left round the hotel and join the main path up from the causeway."

Weston nodded. He amplified Poirot's statement. "One could go right across the island without going through the hotel at all." He added: "But one might still be seen from a window."

"What window?"

"Two of the public bathrooms look out that way—north—and the staff bathroom, and the cloakroom on the ground floor. Also the billiard room."

Poirot nodded. He said: "And all the former have frosted glass windows and one does not play billiards on a fine morning."

"Exactly." Weston paused and said: "If he did it, that's the way he went."

"You mean Captain Marshall?"

"Yes. Blackmail or no blackmail, I still feel it points to him. And his manner—well, his manner is unfortunate."

Hercule Poirot said drily: "Perhaps—but a manner does not make a murderer!"

Weston said: "Then you think he's out of it?"

Poirot shook his head. He said: "No, I would not say that."

Weston said: "We'll see what Colgate can make out of the type-writing alibi. In the meantime I've got the chambermaid of this floor waiting to be interviewed. A good deal may depend on her evidence."

The chambermaid was a woman of thirty, brisk, efficient and intelligent. Her answers came readily. Captain Marshall had come up to his room not long after ten-thirty. She was then finishing the room. He had asked her to be as quick as possible. She had not seen him come back but she had heard the sound of the typewriter a little later. She put it at about five minutes to eleven. She was then in Mr. and Mrs. Redfern's room. After she had done that she moved on to Miss Darnley's room at the end of the corridor. She could not hear the typewriter from there. She went to Miss Darnley's room, as near as she could say, at just after eleven o'clock. She remembered hearing Leathercombe Church strike the hour as she went in. At a quarter past eleven she had gone downstairs for her eleven o'clock cup of tea and "snack." Afterwards she had gone to do the rooms in the other wing of the hotel. In answer to the Chief Constable's question she explained that she had done the rooms in this corridor in the following order: Miss Linda Marshall's, the two public bathrooms, Mrs. Marshall's room and private bath, Captain Marshall's room. Mr. and Mrs. Redfern's room and private bath, Miss Darnley's room and private bath. Captain Marshall's and Miss Marshall's rooms had no adjoining bathrooms. During the time she was in Miss Darnley's room and bathroom she had not heard any one pass the door or go out by the staircase to the rocks, but it was quite likely she wouldn't have heard if any one went quietly.

Weston then directed his questions to the subject of Mrs. Marshall.

No, Mrs. Marshall wasn't one for rising early as a rule. She, Gladys Narracott, had been surprised to find the door open and Mrs. Marshall gone down at just after ten. Something quite unusual, that was:

"Did Mrs. Marshall always have her breakfast in bed?"

"Oh, yes, sir, always. Not very much of it either. Just tea and orange juice and one piece of toast. Slimming like so many ladies." No, she hadn't noticed anything unusual in Mrs. Marshall's manner that morning. She'd seemed quite as usual.

Hercule Poirot murmured: "What did you think of Mrs. Marshall, Mademoiselle?"

Gladys Narracott stared at him. She said: "Well, that's hardly for me to say, is it, sir?"

"But yes, it is for you to say. We are anxious—very anxious—to hear your impression."

Gladys gave a slightly uneasy glance towards the Chief Constable who endeavored to make his face sympathetic and approving, though actually he felt slightly embarrassed by his foreign colleague's methods of approach. He said: "Er—yes, certainly. Go ahead."

For the first time Gladys Narracott's brisk efficiency deserted her. Her fingers fumbled with her print dress. She said: "Well, Mrs. Marshall—she wasn't exactly a lady, as you might say. What I mean is she was more like an actress."

Colonel Weston said: "She was an actress."

"Yes, sir, that's what I'm saying. She just went on exactly as she felt like it. She didn't—well, she didn't trouble to be polite if she wasn't feeling polite. And she'd be all smiles one minute and then if she couldn't find something or the bell wasn't answered at once or her laundry wasn't back, well, she'd be downright rude or nasty about it. None of us as you might say *liked* her. But her clothes were beautiful, and of course she was a very handsome lady, so it was only natural she should be admired."

Colonel Weston said: "I am sorry to have to ask you what I am going to ask you, but it is a very vital matter. Can you tell me how things were between her and her husband?"

Gladys Narracott hesitated a minute. She said: "You don't—it wasn't—you don't think as *he* did it?"

Hercule Poirot said quickly: "Do you?"

"Oh! I wouldn't like to think so. He's such a nice gentleman,

Captain Marshall. He couldn't do a thing like that—I'm sure he couldn't."

"But you are *not* very sure—I hear it in your voice."

Gladys Narracott said reluctantly: "You do read things in the papers! When there's jealousy. If there's been goings on—and of course every one's been talking about it—about her and Mr. Redfern, I mean. And Mrs. Redfern's such a nice quiet lady! It does seem a shame! And Mr. Redfern's a nice gentleman too, but it seems men can't help themselves when it's a lady like Mrs. Marshall—one who's used to having her own way. Wives have to put up with a lot, I'm sure." She sighed and paused. "But if Captain Marshall found out about it—"

Colonel Weston said sharply: "Well?"

Gladys Narracott said slowly: "I did think sometimes that Mrs. Marshall was frightened of her husband knowing."

"What makes you say that?"

"It wasn't anything definite, sir. It was only I felt—that sometimes she was—afraid of him. He was a very quiet gentleman but he wasn't—he wasn't *easy*."

Weston said: "But you've nothing definite to go on? Nothing either of them ever said to each other." Slowly Gladys Narracott shook her head. Weston sighed. He went on: "Now, as to letters received by Mrs. Marshall this morning. Can you tell us anything about those?"

"There were about six or seven, sir. I couldn't say exactly."

"Did you take them up to her?"

"Yes, sir. I got them from the office as usual and put them on her breakfast tray."

"Do you remember anything about the look of them?"

The girl shook her head. "They were just ordinary looking letters. Some of them were bills and circulars, I think, because they were torn up on the tray."

"What happened to them?"

"They went into the dustbin, sir. One of the police gentlemen is going through that now."

Weston nodded. "And the contents of the wastepaper baskets, where are they?"

"They'll be in the dustbin too."

Weston said: "H'm—well, I think that is all at present." He looked inquiringly at Poirot.

Poirot leaned forward. "When you did Miss Linda Marshall's room this morning, did you do the fireplace?"

"There wasn't anything to do, sir. There had been no fire lit."

"And there was nothing in the fireplace itself?"

"No, sir, it was perfectly all right."

"What time did you do her room?"

"About a quarter past nine, sir, when she'd gone down to breakfast."

"Did she come up to her room after breakfast, do you know?"

"Yes, sir. She came up about a quarter to ten."

"Did she stay in her room?"

"I think so, sir. She came out, hurrying rather, just before half past ten."

"You didn't go into her room again?"

"No, sir. I had finished with it."

Poirot nodded. He said: "There is another thing I want to know. What people bathed before breakfast this morning?"

"I couldn't say about the other wing and the floor above. Only about this one."

"That is all I want to know."

"Well, sir, Captain Marshall and Mr. Redfern were the only ones up this morning, I think. They always go down for an early dip."

"Did you see them?"

"No, sir, but their wet bathing things were hanging over the balcony rail as usual."

"Miss Linda Marshall did not bathe this morning?"

"No, sir. All her bathing dresses were quite dry."

"Ah," said Poirot. "That is what I wanted to know."

Gladys Narracott volunteered: "She does most mornings, sir."

"And the other three, Miss Darnley, Mrs. Redfern and Mrs. Marshall?"

"Mrs. Marshall never, sir. Miss Darnley has once or twice, I think. Mrs. Redfern doesn't often bathe before breakfast—only when it's very hot, but she didn't this morning."

Again Poirot nodded. Then he asked: "I wonder if you have noticed whether a bottle is missing from any of the rooms you look after in this wing?"

"A bottle, sir? What kind of a bottle?"

"Unfortunately I do not know. But have you noticed—if one had gone?"

Gladys said frankly: "I shouldn't from Mrs. Marshall's room, sir, and that's a fact. She has ever so many."

"And the other rooms?"

"Well, I'm not sure about Miss Darnley. She has a good many creams and lotions. But from the other rooms, yes, I would, sir. I mean if I were to look special. If I were noticing, so to speak."

"But you haven't actually noticed?"

"No, because I wasn't looking special, as I say."

"Perhaps you would go and look now, then."

"Certainly, sir."

She left the room, her print dress rustling. Weston looked at Poirot. He said: "What's all this?"

Poirot murmured, "My orderly mind, that is vexed by trifles! Miss Brewster, this morning, was bathing off the rocks before breakfast, and she says that a bottle was thrown from above and nearly hit her. *Eh bien*, I want to know who threw that bottle and why?"

"My dear man, any one may have chucked a bottle away."

"Not at all. To begin with, it could only have been thrown from a window on the east side of the hotel—that is, one of the windows of the rooms we have just examined. Now I ask you, if you have an empty bottle on your dressing-table or in your bathroom, what do you do with it? I will tell you, you drop it into the wastepaper basket. You do not take the trouble to go out on your balcony and hurl it into the sea! For one thing you might hit some one, for another it would be too much trouble. No, you would only do that *if you did not want any one to see that particular bottle*."

Weston stared at him. Weston said: "I know that Chief Inspector Japp, whom I met over a case not long ago, always says you have a damned tortuous mind. You're not going to tell me now that Arlena Marshall wasn't strangled at all, but poisoned out of some mysterious bottle with a mysterious drug?"

"No, no, I do not think there was poison in that bottle."

"Then what was there?"

"I do not know at all. That's why I am interested."

Gladys Narracott came back. She was a little breathless. She said: "I'm sorry, sir, but I can't find anything missing. I'm sure there's nothing gone from Captain Marshall's room, or Miss Linda Marshall's room or Mr. and Mrs. Redfern's room and I'm pretty sure there's nothing gone from Miss Darnley's either. But I couldn't say about Mrs. Marshall's. As I say, she's got such a lot."

Poirot shrugged his shoulders. He said: "No matter. We will leave it."

Gladys Narracott said: "Is there anything more, sir?" She looked from one to the other of them.

Weston said: "Don't think so. Thank you."

Poirot said: "I thank you, no. You are sure, are you not, that there is nothing—nothing at all, that you have forgotten to tell us?"

"About Mrs. Marshall, sir?"

"About anything at all. Anything unusual, out of the way, unexplained, slightly peculiar, rather curious—*enfin*, something that has made you say to yourself or to one of your colleagues: 'That's funny!'?"

Gladys said doubtfully: "Well, not the sort of thing that you would mean, sir?"

Hercule Poirot said: "Never mind what I mean. You do not know what I mean. It is true, then, that you have said to yourself or to a colleague to-day: 'That is funny!'?" He brought out the three words with ironic detachment.

Gladys said: "It was nothing really. Just a bath being run. And I did pass the remark to Elsie, downstairs, that it was funny somebody having a bath round about twelve o'clock."

"Whose bath, who had a bath?"

"That I couldn't say, sir. We heard it going down the waste from this wing that's all, and that's when I said what I did to Elsie."

"You are sure it was a bath? Not one of the handbasins?"

"Oh! quite sure, sir. You can't mistake bath-water running away."

Poirot displaying no further desire to keep her, Gladys Narracott was permitted to depart.

Weston said: "You don't think this bath question is important, do you, Poirot? I mean, there's no point to it. No bloodstains or anything like that to wash off. That's the—" he hesitated.

Poirot cut in: "That, you would say, is the advantage of strangulation! No bloodstains, no weapon—nothing to get rid of or conceal! Nothing is needed but physical strength—*and the soul of a killer!*" His voice was so fierce, so charged with feeling, that Weston recoiled a little. Hercule Poirot smiled at him apologetically. "No, no," he said, "the bath is probably of no importance. Any one may have had a bath. Mrs. Redfern before she went to play tennis, Captain Marshall, Miss Darnley. As I say, any one. There is nothing in that."

A Police Constable knocked at the door, and put in his head. "It's Miss Darnley, sir. She says she'd like to see you again for a minute. There's something she forgot to tell you, she says."

Weston said: "We're coming down—now."

The first person they saw was Colgate. His face was gloomy. "Just a minute, sir." Weston and Poirot followed him into Mrs. Castle's office. Colgate said: "I've been checking up with Heald on this typewriting business. Not a doubt of it, it couldn't be done under an hour. Longer, if you had to stop and think here and there. That seems to me pretty well to settle it. And look at this letter." He held it out.

"My Dear Marshall,
"Sorry to worry you on your holiday but an entirely unforeseen situation has arisen over the Burley and Tender contracts. . . ."

"Etcetera, etcetera," said Colgate. "Dated the 24th—that's yesterday. Envelope postmarked yesterday evening E.C.1 and Leathercombe Bay this morning. Same typewriter used on envelope and in letter. And by the contents it was clearly impossible for Marshall to prepare his answer beforehand. The figures arise out of the ones in the letter—the whole thing is quite intricate."

"H'm," said Weston gloomily. "That seems to let Marshall out. We'll have to look elsewhere." He added: "I've got to see Miss Darnley again. She's waiting now."

Rosamund came in crisply. Her smile held an apologetic *nuance*. She said: "I'm frightfully sorry. Probably it isn't worth bothering about. But one does forget things so."

"Yes, Miss Darnley?" The Chief Constable indicated a chair.

She shook her shapely black head. "Oh, it isn't worth sitting down. It's simply this. I told you that I spent the morning lying out on Sunny Ledge. That isn't quite accurate. I forgot that once during the morning I went back to the hotel and out again."

"What time was that, Miss Darnley?"

"It must have been about a quarter past eleven."

"You went back to the hotel, you said?"

"Yes, I'd forgotten my glare glasses. At first I thought I wouldn't bother and then my eyes got tired and I decided to go in and get them."

"You went straight to your room and out again."

"Yes. At least, as a matter of fact, I just looked in on Ken—Captain Marshall. I heard his machine going and I thought it was so stupid of him to stay indoors typing on such a lovely day. I thought I'd tell him to come out."

"And what did Captain Marshall say?"

Rosamund smiled rather shamefacedly. "Well, when I opened the door he was typing so vigorously, and frowning and looking so concentrated that I just went away quietly. I don't think he even saw me come in."

"And that was—at what time, Miss Darnley?"

"Just about twenty past eleven, I noticed the clock in the hall as I went out again."

"And that puts the lid on it finally," said Inspector Colgate. "The chambermaid heard him typing up till five minutes to eleven. Miss Darnley saw him at twenty minutes past, and the woman was dead at a quarter to twelve. He says he spent that hour typing in his room and it seems quite clear that he *was* typing in his room. That washes Captain Marshall right out." He stopped, then looking at Poirot with some curiosity he asked: "M. Poirot's looking very serious over something."

Poirot said thoughtfully: "I was wondering why Miss Darnley suddenly volunteered this extra evidence."

Inspector Colgate cocked his head alertly. "Think there's something fishy about it? That it isn't just a question of 'forgetting'?" He considered for a minute or two, then he said slowly: "Look here, sir, let's look at it this way. Supposing Miss Darnley wasn't on Sunny Ledge this morning as she says. That story's a lie. Now suppose that *after* telling us her story, she finds that somebody saw her somewhere else or alternatively that some one went to the Ledge and didn't find her there. Then she thinks up this story quick and comes and tells it to us to account for her absence. You'll notice that she was careful to say Captain Marshall didn't *see* her when she looked into his room."

Poirot murmured: "Yes, I noticed that."

Weston said incredulously: "Are you suggesting that Miss Darnley's mixed up in this? Nonsense, seems absurd to me. Why should she be?"

Inspector Colgate coughed. He said: "You'll remember what the American lady, Mrs. Gardener, said. She sort of hinted that Miss Darnley was sweet on Captain Marshall. There'd be a motive there, sir."

Weston said impatiently: "Arlena Marshall wasn't killed by a woman. It's a man we've got to look for. We've got to stick to the men in the case."

Inspector Colgate sighed. He said: "Yes, that's true, sir. We always come back to that, don't we?"

Weston went on: "Better put a constable on to timing one or two things. From the hotel across the island to the top of the ladder. Let him do it running and walking. Same thing with the ladder itself. And somebody had better check the time it takes to go on a float from the bathing beach to the cove."

Inspector Colgate nodded, "I'll attend to all that, sir," he said confidently.

The Chief Constable said: "Think I'll go along to the cove now. See if Phillips has found anything. Then there's that Pixy's cave we've been hearing about. Ought to see if there are any traces of a man waiting in there. Eh? Poirot. What do you think?"

"By all means. It is a possibility."

Weston said: "If somebody from outside had nipped over to the island that would be a good hiding-place—if he knew about it. I suppose the locals know?"

Colgate said; "Don't believe the younger generation would. You see, ever since this hotel was started the coves have been private property. Fishermen don't go there, or picnic parties. And the hotel people aren't local. Mrs. Castle's a Londoner."

Weston said: "We might take Redfern with us. He told us about it. What about you, M. Poirot?"

Hercule Poirot hesitated. He said, his foreign intonation very pronounced: "No, I am like Miss Brewster and Mrs. Redfern, I do not like to descend perpendicular ladders."

Weston said: "You can go round by boat."

Again Hercule Poirot sighed. "My stomach, it is not happy on the sea."

"Nonsense, man, it's a beautiful day. Calm as a mill pond. You can't let us down, you know."

Hercule Poirot hardly looked like responding to this British adjuration. But at that moment, Mrs. Castle poked her ladylike face and elaborate coiffure round the door. "Ay'm sure Ay hope Ay am not intruding," she said. "But Mr. Lane, the clergyman, you know, has just returned. Ay thought you might like to know."

"Ah, yes, thanks, Mrs. Castle. We'll see him right away."

Mrs. Castle came a little further into the room. She said: "Ay don't know if it is worth mentioning, but Ay *have* heard that the smallest incident should not be ignored—"

"Yes, yes?" said Weston impatiently.

"It is only that there was a lady and gentleman here about one o'clock. Came over from the mainland. For luncheon. They were informed that there had been an accident and that under the circumstances no luncheon could be served."

"Any idea who they were?"

"Ay couldn't say at all. Naturally no name was given. They expressed disappointment and a certain amount of curiosity as to the nature of the accident. Ay couldn't tell them anything, of course. Ay should say, myself, they were summer visitors of the better class."

Weston said brusquely: "Ah, well, thank you for telling us. Probably not important but quite right—er—to remember everything."

"Naturally," said Mrs. Castle, "Ay wish to do my Duty!"

"Quite, quite. Ask Mr. Lane to come here."

Stephen Lane strode into the room with his usual vigour. Weston said: "I'm the Chief Constable of the County, Mr. Lane. I suppose you've been told what has occurred here?"

"Yes—oh, yes—I heard as soon as I got here. Terrible . . . Terrible. . . ." His thin frame quivered. He said in a low voice, "All along—ever since I arrived here—I have been conscious—very conscious—of

the forces of evil close at hand." His eyes, burning eager eyes, went to
Hercule Poirot. He said: "You remember, M. Poirot? Our
conversation some days ago? About the reality of evil?"

Weston was studying the tall gaunt figure in some perplexity. He
found it difficult to make this man out. Lane's eyes came back to him.
The clergyman said with a slight smile: "I daresay that seems fantastic
to you, sir. We have left off believing in evil in these days. We have
abolished Hell fire! We no longer believe in the Devil! But Satan and
Satan's emissaries were never more powerful than they are to-day!"

Weston said: "Er—er—yes, perhaps. That, Mr. Lane, is your
province. Mine is more prosaic—to clear up a case of murder."

Stephen Lane said: "An awful word. Murder! One of the earliest
sins known on earth—the ruthless shedding of an innocent brother's
blood. . . ." He paused, his eyes half closed. Then, in a more ordinary
voice he said; "In what way can I help you?"

"First of all, Mr. Lane, will you tell me your own movements
to-day?"

"Willingly. I started off early on one of my usual tramps. I am fond
of walking. I have roamed over a good deal of the countryside round
here. To-day I went to St. Petrock-in-the-Combe. That is about seven
miles from here—a very pleasant walk along winding lanes, up and
down the Devon hills and valleys. I took some lunch wih me and ate it
in a spinney. I visited the Church—it has some fragments—only
fragments, alas, of early glass—also a very interesting painted screen."

"Thank you, Mr. Lane. Did you meet any one on your walk?"

"Not to speak to. A cart passed me once and a couple of boys on
bicycles and some cows. However," he smiled, "if you want proof of
my statement I wrote my name in the book at the Church. You will find
it there."

"You did not see any one at the Church itself—the Vicar, or the
verger?"

Stephen Lane shook his head. He said: "No, there was no one about
and I was the only visitor. St. Petrock is a very remote spot. The village
itself lies on the far side of it about half a mile further on."

Colonel Weston said pleasantly: "You mustn't think we're—er—
doubting what you say. Just a matter of checking up on everybody.
Just routine, you know, routine. Have to stick to routine in cases of this
kind."

Stephen Lane said gently: "Oh, yes, I quite understand."

Weston went on: "Now the next point. Is there anything you know
that would assist us at all? Anything about the dead woman? Anything
that could give us a pointer as to who murdered her? Anything you
heard or saw?"

Stephen Lane said: "I heard nothing. All I can tell you is this; that I knew instinctively as soon as I saw her that Arlena Marshall was a focus of evil. She *was* Evil! Evil personified! Woman can be man's help and inspiration in life—she can also be man's downfall. She can drag a man down to the level of the beast. The dead woman was just such a woman. She appealed to everything base in a man's nature. She was a woman such as Jezebel and Aholibah. Now—she has been struck down in the middle of her wickedness!"

Hercule Poirot stirred. He said: "Not struck down—*strangled*! Strangled, Mr. Lane, by a pair of human hands."

The clergyman's own hands trembled. The fingers writhed and twitched. He said, and his voice came low and choked: "That's horrible—horrible—Must you put it like that?"

Hercule Poirot said: "It is the simple truth. Have you any idea, Mr. Lane, whose hands those were?"

The other shook his head. He said: "I know nothing—nothing. . . ."

Weston got up. He said, after a glance at Colgate to which the latter replied by an almost imperceptible nod, "Well, we must get on to the Cove."

Lane said: "Is that where—it happened?"

Weston nodded. Lane said: "Can—can I come with you?"

About to return a curt negative, Weston was forestalled by Poirot. "But certainly," said Poirot. "Accompany me there in a boat, Mr. Lane. We start immediately."

9

FOR THE SECOND time that morning Patrick Redfern was rowing a boat into Pixy's Cove. The other occupants of the boat were Hercule Poirot, very pale with a hand to his stomach, and Stephen Lane. Colonel Weston had taken the land route. Having been delayed on the way he arrived on the beach at the same time as the boat grounded. A Police Constable and a plain clothes sergeant were on the beach already. Weston was questioning the latter as the three from the boat walked up and joined him.

Sergeant Phillips said: "I think I've been over every inch of the beach, sir."

"Good, what did you find?"

"It's all together here, sir, if you like to come and see." A small collection of objects was laid out neatly on a rock. There were a pair of scissors, an empty Gold Flake packet, five patent bottle tops, a number of used matches, three pieces of string, one or two fragments of newspaper, a fragment of a smashed pipe, four buttons, the drumstick bone of a chicken and an empty bottle of sun-bathing oil.

Weston looked down appraisingly on the objects. "H'm," he said. "Rather moderate for a beach nowadays! Most people seem to confuse a beach with a public rubbish dump! Empty bottle's been here some time by the way the label's blurred—so have most of the other things, I should say. The scissors are new, though. Bright and shining. *They* weren't out in yesterday's rain! Where were they?"

"Close by the bottom of the ladder, sir. Also this bit of pipe."

"H'm, probably dropped by some one going up or down. Nothing to say who they belong to?"

"No, sir. Quite an ordinary pair of nail scissors. Pipe's a good quality briar—expensive."

Poirot murmured thoughtfully: "Captain Marshall told us, I think, that he had mislaid his pipe."

Weston said: "Marshall's out of the picture. Anyway he's not the only person who smokes a pipe."

Hercule Poirot was watching Stephen Lane as the latter's hand went to his pocket and away again. He said pleasantly: "You also smoke a pipe, do you not, Mr. Lane?"

The clergyman started. He looked at Poirot. He said: "Yes. Oh, yes. My pipe is an old friend and companion." Putting his hand into his pocket again he drew out a pipe, filled it with tobacco and lighted it.

Hercule Poirot moved away to where Redfern was standing, his eyes blank. He said in a low voice: "I'm glad—they've taken *her* away. . . ."

Stephen Lane asked: "Where was she found?"

The Sergeant said cheerfully: "Just about where you're standing, sir."

Lane moved swiftly aside. He stared at the spot he had just vacated. The Sergeant went on: "Place where the float was drawn up agrees with putting the time she arrived here at 10:45. That's going by the tide. It's turned now."

Weston said: "Photography all done?"

"Yes, sir."

Weston turned to Redfern. "Now then, man, where's the entrance to this cave of yours?"

Patrick Redfern was still staring down at the beach where Lane had been standing. It was as though he was seeing that sprawling body that was no longer there. Weston's words recalled him to himself. He said: "It's over here." He led the way to where a great mass of tumbled down rocks were massed picturesquely against the cliffside. He went straight to where two big rocks, side by side, showed a straight narrow cleft between them. He said: "The entrance is here."

Weston said: "Here? Doesn't look as though a man could squeeze through."

"It's deceptive, you'll find, sir. It can just be done."

Weston inserted himself gingerly into the cleft. It was not as narrow as it looked. Inside, the space widened and proved to be a fairly roomy recess with room to stand upright and to move about. Hercule Poirot and Stephen Lane joined the Chief Constable. The others stayed outside. Light filtered in through the opening, but Weston had also got a powerful torch which he played freely over the interior. He observed: "Handy place. You'd never suspect it from the outside." He played the torch carefully over the floor.

Hercule Poirot was delicately sniffing the air. Noticing this, Weston said: "Air quite fresh, not fishy or seaweedy, but of course this place is well above highwater mark."

But to Poirot's sensitive nose, the air was more than fresh. It was delicately scented. He knew two people who used that elusive Perfume. . . . Weston's torch came to rest. He said: "Don't see anything out of the way in here."

Poirot's eyes rose to a ledge a little way above his head. He murmured: "One might perhaps see that there is nothing up there?"

Weston said: "If there's anything up there it would have to be deliberately put there. Still, we'd better have a look."

Poirot said to Lane: "You are, I think, the tallest of us, Monsieur. Could we venture to ask you to make sure there is nothing resting on that ledge?"

Lane stretched up, but he could not quite reach to the back of the shelf. Then, seeing a crevice in the rock, he inserted a toe in it and pulled himself up by one hand. He said: "Hullo, there's a box up here."

In a minute or two they were out in the sunshine examining the clergyman's find. Weston said: "Careful, don't handle it more than you can help. May be fingerprints."

It was a dark green tin box and bore the word Sandwiches on it. Sergeant Phillips said: "Left from some picnic or other, I suppose." He opened the lid with his handkerchief. Inside were small tin containers marked salt, pepper, mustard, and two larger square tins evidently for sandwiches. Sergeant Phillips lifted the lid of the salt container. It was full to the brim. He raised the next one, commenting: "H'm, got salt in the pepper one too." The mustard compartment also contained salt. His face suddenly alert, the police sergeant opened one of the bigger square tins. That, too, contained the same white crystalline powder.

Very gingerly, Sergeant Phillips dipped a finger in and applied it to his tongue. His face changed. He said—and his voice was excited: "This isn't *salt*, sir. Not by a long way! Bitter taste! Seems to me it's some kind of *drug*."

"The third angle," said Colonel Weston with a groan. They were back at the hotel again. The Chief Constable went on: "If by any chance there's a dope gang mixed up in this, it opens up several possibilities. First of all, the dead woman may have been in with the gang herself. Think that's likely?"

Hercule Poirot said cautiously: "It is possible."

"She may have been a drug addict?"

Poirot shook his head. He said: "I should doubt that. She had steady nerves, radiant health, there were no marks of hypodermic injections (not that that proves anything. Some people sniff the stuff). No, I do not think she took drugs."

"In that case," said Weston, "She may have run into the business accidentally and she was deliberately silenced by the people running the show. We'll know presently just what the stuff is. I've sent it to Neasdon. If we're on to some dope ring, they're not the people to stick at trifles—"

He broke off as the door opened and Mr. Horace Blatt came briskly into the room. Mr. Blatt was looking hot. He was wiping the perspiration from his forehead. His big hearty voice billowed out and filled the small room. "Just this minute got back and heard the news! You the Chief Constable? They told me you were in here. My name's Blatt—Horace Blatt. Any way I can help you? Don't suppose so. I've been out in my boat since early this morning. Missed the whole blinking show. The one day that something *does* happen in this out-of-the-way spot, I'm not there. Just like life, that, isn't it? Hullo, Poirot, didn't see you at first. So you're in on this? Oh, well, I suppose you would be. Sherlock Holmes v. the local police, is that it? Ha, ha! Lestrade—all that stuff. I'll enjoy seeing you do a bit of fancy sleuthing."

Mr. Blatt came to anchor in a chair, pulled out a cigarette case and offered it to Colonel Weston who shook his head. He said, with a slight smile: "I'm an inveterate pipe smoker."

"Same here. I smoke cigarettes as well—but nothing beats a pipe."

Colonel Weston said with sudden geniality: "Then light up, man."

Blatt shook his head. "Not got my pipe on me at the moment. But put me wise about all this. All I've heard so far is that Mrs. Marshall was found murdered on one of the beaches here."

"On Pixy Cove," said Colonel Weston, watching him.

But Mr. Blatt merely asked excitedly: "And she was strangled?"

"Yes, Mr. Blatt."

"Nasty—very nasty. Mind you, she asked for it! Hot stuff—*très moutarde*—eh, M. Poirot? Any idea who did it, or mustn't I ask that?"

With a faint smile Colonel Weston said: "Well, you know, it's we who are supposed to ask the questions."

Mr. Blatt waved his cigarette. "Sorry—sorry—my mistake. Go ahead."

"You went out sailing this morning. At what time?"

"Left here at a quarter to ten."

"Was any one with you?"

"Not a soul. All on my little lonesome."

"And where did you go?"

"Along the coast in the direction of Plymouth. Took lunch with me. Not much wind so I didn't actually get very far."

After another question or two, Weston asked: "Now about the Marshalls? Do you know anything that might help us?"

"Well, I've given you my opinion. *Crime passionnel*! All I can tell you is, it wasn't *me*! The fair Arlena had no use for me. Nothing doing in that quarter. She had her own blue-eyed boy! And if you ask me, Marshall was getting wise to it."

"Have you any evidence for that?"

"Saw him give young Redfern a dirty look once or twice. Dark horse, Marshall. Looks very meek and mild and as though he were half asleep all the time—but that's not his reputation in the City. I've heard a thing or two about him. Nearly had up for assault once. Mind you, the fellow in question had put up a pretty dirty deal. Marshall had trusted him and the fellow had let him down cold. Particularly dirty business, I believe. Marshall went for him and half killed him. Fellow didn't prosecute—too afraid of what might come out. I give you that for what it's worth."

"So you think it possible," said Poirot, "that Captain Marshall strangled his wife?"

"Not at all. Never said anything of the sort. Just letting you know that he's the sort of fellow who could go berserk on occasions."

Poirot said: "Mr. Blatt, there is reason to believe that Mrs. Marshall went this morning to Pixy Cove to meet some one. Have you any idea who that some one might be?"

Mr. Blatt winked. "It's not a guess. It's a certainty. Redfern!"

"It was not Mr. Redfern."

Mr. Blatt seemed taken aback. He said hesitatingly: "Then I don't know. . . . No, I can't imagine. . . ." He went on, regaining a little of his aplomb, "As I said before, it wasn't *me*! No such luck! Let me see,

couldn't have been Gardener—his wife keeps far too sharp an eye on
him! That old ass Barry? Rot! And it would hardly be the parson.
Although, mind you, I've seen his Reverence watching her a good bit.
All holy disapproval, but perhaps an eye for the contours all the same!
Eh? Lot of hypocrites, most parsons. Did you read that case last
month? Parson and the Churchwarden's daughter? Bit of an
eyeopener." Mr. Blatt chuckled.

Colonel Weston said coldly: "There is nothing you can think of that
might help us?"

The other shook his head. "No. Can't think of a thing." He added:
"This will make a bit of a stir, I imagine. The press will be on to it like
hot cakes. There won't be quite so much of this high-toned
exclusiveness about the Jolly Roger in future. Jolly Roger indeed.
Precious little jollity about it."

Hercule Poirot murmured: "You have not enjoyed your stay here?"

Mr. Blatt's red face got slightly redder. He said: "Well, no, I
haven't. The sailing's all right and the scenery and the service and the
food—but there's no *mateyness* in the place, you know what I mean!
What I say is, my money's as good as another man's. We're all here to
enjoy ourselves. Then why not get together and *do* it? All these cliques
and people sitting by themselves and giving you frosty Good-
mornings—and Good-evenings—and Yes, very pleasant weather. No
joy de viver. Lot of stuck-up dummies!" Mr. Blatt paused—by now
very red indeed. He wiped his forehead once more and said
apologetically: "Don't pay any attention to me. I get all worked up."

Hercule Poirot murmured: "And what do we think of Mr. Blatt?"

Colonel Weston grinned and said: "What do *you* think of him?
You've seen more of him than I have."

Poirot said softly: "There are many of your English idioms that
describe him. The rough diamond! The self-made man! The social
climber! He is, as you choose to look at it, pathetic, ludicrous, blatant!
It is a matter of opinion. But I think, too, that he is something else."

"And what is that?"

Hercule Poirot, his eyes raised to the ceiling, murmured: "I think
that he is—*nervous!*"

Inspector Colgate said: "I've got those times worked out. From the
hotel to the ladder down to Pixy Cove three minutes. That's walking
till you are out of sight of the hotel and then running like hell."

Weston raised his eyebrows. He said: "That's quicker than I
thought."

"Down ladder to beach one minute and three quarters. Up same two
minutes. That's P.C. Flint. He's a bit of an athlete. Walking and taking

the ladder in the normal way the whole business takes close to a quarter of an hour."

Weston nodded. He said: "There's another thing we must go into, the pipe question."

Colgate said: "Blatt smokes a pipe, so does Marshall, so does the parson. Redfern smokes cigarettes, the American prefers a cigar. Major Barry doesn't smoke at all. There's one pipe in Marshall's room, two in Blatt's, and one in the parson's. Chambermaid says Marshall has two pipes. The other chambermaid isn't a very bright girl. Doesn't know how many pipes the other two have. Says vaguely she's noticed two or three about in their rooms."

Weston nodded. "Anything else?"

"I've checked up on the staff. They all seem quite O.K. Henry, in the bar, checks Marshall's statement about seeing him at ten to eleven. William, the beach attendant, was down repairing the ladder on the rocks most of the morning. He seems all right. George marked the tennis court and then bedded out some plants round by the dining-room. Neither of them would have seen any one who came across the causeway to the island."

"When was the causeway uncovered?"

"Round about 9.30, sir."

Weston pulled at his mustache. "It's possible somebody did come that way. We've got a new angle, Colgate." He told of the discovery of the sandwich box in the cave.

There was a tap on the door.

"Come in," said Weston.

It was Captain Marshall. He said: "Can you tell me what arrangements I can make about the funeral?"

"I think we shall manage the inquest for the day after tomorrow, Captain Marshall."

"Thank you."

Inspector Colgate said: "Excuse me, sir, allow me to return you these." He handed over the three letters.

Kenneth Marshall smiled rather sardonically. He said: "Has the police department been testing the speed of my typing? I hope my character is cleared."

Colonel Weston said pleasantly: "Yes, Captain Marshall, I think we can give you a clean bill of health. Those sheets take fully an hour to type. Moreover, you were heard typing them by the chambermaid up till five minutes to eleven and you were seen by another witness at twenty minutes past."

Captain Marshall murmured: "Really? That all seems very satisfactory!"

"Yes. Miss Darnley came to your room at twenty minutes past eleven. You were so busy typing that you did not observe her entry."

Kenneth Marshall's face took on an impassive expression. He said: "Does Miss Darnley say that?" He paused. "As a matter of fact she is wrong. I *did* see her, though she may not be aware of the fact. I saw her in the mirror."

Poirot murmured: "But you did not interrupt your typing?"

Marshall said shortly: "No. I wanted to get finished." He paused a minute, then in an abrupt voice, he said: "Nothing more I can do for you?"

"No, thank you, Captain Marshall."

Kenneth Marshall nodded and went out. Weston said with a sigh: "There goes our most hopeful suspect—cleared! Hullo, here's Neasdon."

The doctor came in with a trace of excitement in his manner. He said: "That's a nice little death lot you sent me along."

"What is it?"

"What is it? Diamorphine hydrochloride. Stuff that's usually called heroin."

Inspector Colgate whistled. He said: "Now we're getting places, all right! Depend upon it, this dope stunt is at the bottom of the whole business."

10

THE LITTLE CROWD of people flocked out of The Red Bull. The brief inquest was over—adjourned for a fortnight. Rosamund Darnley joined Captain Marshall. She said in a low voice: "That wasn't so bad, was it, Ken?"

He did not answer at once. Perhaps he was conscious of the staring eyes of the villagers, the fingers that nearly pointed to him and only just did not quite do so!

"That's 'im, my dear." "See, that's 'er 'usband." "That be the 'usband." "Look, there 'e goes. . . ."

The murmurs were not loud enough to reach his ears, but he was none the less sensitive to them. This was the modern day pillory. The press he had already encountered—self-confident, persuasive young men, adepts at battering down his wall of silence, of "Nothing to say"

that he had endeavored to erect. Even the curt monosyllables that he
had uttered thinking that they at least could not lead to
misapprehension had reappeared in this morning's papers in a totally
different guise. "Asked whether he agreed that the mystery of his
wife's death could only be explained on the assumption that a
homocidal murderer had found his way on to the island, Captain
Marshall declared that—" and so on and so forth.

Cameras had clicked ceaselessly. Now, at this minute, the
well-known sound caught his ear. He half turned—a smiling young
man was nodding cheerfully, his purpose accomplished.

Rosamund murmured: *"Captain Marshall and a friend leaving
The Red Bell after the inquest."* Marshall winced. Rosamund said:
"It's no use, Ken! You've got to face it! I don't mean just the fact of
Arlena's death—I mean all the attendant beastliness. The staring eyes
and gossiping tongues, the fatuous interviews in the papers—and the
best way to meet it is to find it funny! Come out with all the old inane
clichés and curl a sardonic lip at them."

He said: "Is that your way?"

"Yes." She paused. "It isn't yours, I know. Protective colouring is
your line. Remain rigidly non-active and fade into the background! But
you can't do that here—you've no background to fade into. You stand
out clear for all to see—like a striped tiger against a white backcloth.
The husband of the murdered woman!"

"For God's sake, Rosamund—"

She said gently: "My dear, I'm trying to be good for you!"

They walked for a few steps in silence. Then Marshall said in a
different voice; "I know you are. I'm not really ungrateful, Rosamund."

They had progressed beyond the limits of the village. Eyes followed
them but there was no one very near. Rosamund Darnley's voice
dropped as she repeated a variant of her first remark. "It didn't really
go so badly, did it?"

He was silent for a moment, then he said: "I don't know."

"What do the police think?"

"They're non-committal."

After a minute Rosamund said: "That little man—Poirot—is he
really taking an active interest?"

Kenneth Marshall said: "Seemed to be sitting in the Chief
Constable's pocket all right the other day."

"I know—but is he *doing* anything?"

"How the hell should I know, Rosamund?"

She said thoughtfully: "He's pretty old. Probably more or less ga
ga."

"Perhaps."

They came to the causeway. Opposite them, serene in the sun, lay the island. Rosamund said suddenly: "Sometimes—things seem unreal. I can't believe, this minute, that it ever happened. . . ."

Marshall said slowly; "I think I know what you mean. Nature is so—regardless! One ant the less—that's all it is in Nature!"

Rosamund said: "Yes—and that's the proper way to look at it really."

He gave her one very quick glance. Then he said in a low voice: "Don't worry, my dear. It's all right. *It's all right*."

Linda came down to the causeway to meet them. She moved with the spasmodic jerkiness of a nervous colt. Her young face was marred by deep black shadows under her eyes. Her lips were dry and rough. She said breathlessly: "What happened—what—what did they say?"

Her father said abruptly: "Inquest adjourned for a fortnight."

"That means they—they haven't decided?"

"Yes. More evidence is needed."

"But—but what do they think?"

Marshall smiled a little in spite of himself. "Oh, my dear child—who knows? And whom do you mean by they? The Coroner, the jury, the police, the newspaper reporters, the fishing folk of Leathercombe Bay?"

Linda said slowly: "I suppose I mean—the police."

Marshall said drily: "Whatever the police think, they're not giving it away at present." His lips closed tightly after the sentence. He went into the hotel.

As Rosamund Darnley was about to follow suit, Linda said: "Rosamund!"

Rosamund turned. The mute appeal in the girl's unhappy face touched her. She linked her arm through Linda's and together they walked away from the hotel, taking the path that led to the extreme end of the island.

Rosamund said gently: "Try not to mind so much, Linda. I know it's all very terrible and a shock and all that, but it's no use brooding over these things. And it can be only the—the horror of it, that is worrying you. You weren't in the least *fond* of Arlena, you know."

She felt the tremor that ran through the girl's body as Linda answered: "No, I wasn't fond of her. . . . "

Rosamund went on: "Sorrow for a person is different—one can't put *that* behind one. But one *can* get over shock and horror by just not letting your mind *dwell* on it all the time."

Linda said sharply: "You don't understand."

"I think I do, my dear."

Linda shook her head. "No, you don't. You don't understand in the least—and Christine doesn't understand either! Both of you have been nice to me, but you can't understand what I'm feeling. You just think it's morbid—that I'm dwelling on it all when I needn't." She paused. "But it isn't that at all. If you knew what I know—"

Rosamund stopped dead. Her body did not tremble—on the contrary it stiffened. She stood for a minute or two, then she disengaged her arm from Linda's. She said: "What is it that you know, Linda?"

The girl gazed at her. Then she shook her head. She muttered: "Nothing."

Rosamund caught her by the arm. The grip hurt and Linda winced slightly. Rosamund said: "Be careful, Linda. Be damned careful."

Linda had gone dead white. She said: "I *am* very careful—all the time."

Rosamund said urgently: "Listen, Linda, what I said a minute or two ago applies just the same—only a hundred times more so. *Put the whole business out of your mind*. Never think about it. Forget—forget ... You can if you try! Arlena is dead and nothing can bring her back to life. . . . Forget everything and live in the future. And above all, *hold your tongue*."

Linda shrank a little. She said: "You—you seem to know all about it?"

Rosamund said energetically: "I don't know *anything*! In my opinion a wandering maniac got onto the island and killed Arlena. That's much the most probable solution. I'm fairly sure that the police will have to accept that in the end. That's what *must* have happened! That's what *did* happen!"

Linda said: "If Father—"

Rosamund interrupted her. "Don't talk about it."

Linda said: "I've got to say one thing. My Mother—"

"Well, what about her?"

"She—she was tried for murder, wasn't she?"

"Yes."

Linda said slowly: "And then Father married her. That looks, doesn't it, as though Father didn't really think murder was very wrong—not always, that is."

Rosamund said sharply: "Don't say things like that—even to me! The police haven't got anything against your father. He's got an alibi—an alibi that they can't break. He's perfectly safe."

Linda whispered: "Did they think at first that Father—?"

Rosamund cried: "I don't know what they thought! But they know now *that he couldn't have done it*. Do you understand? He couldn't have done it." She spoke with authority, her eyes commanded Linda's acquiescence. The girl uttered a long fluttering sigh. Rosamund said: "You'll be able to leave here soon. You'll forget everything—everything!"

Linda said with sudden unexpected violence: "*I shall never forget.*" She turned abruptly and ran back to the hotel. Rosamund stared after her.

"There is something I want to know, Madame?"

Christine Redfern glanced up at Poirot in a slightly abstracted manner. She said: "Yes?"

Hercule Poirot took very little notice of her abstraction. He had noted the way her eyes followed her husband's figure where he was pacing up and down on the terrace outside the bar, but for the moment he had no interest in purely conjugal problems. He wanted information. He said: "Yes, Madame. It was a phrase—a chance phrase of yours the other day which roused my attention."

Christine, her eyes still on Patrick, said: "Yes? What did I say?"

"It was in answer to a question from the Chief Constable. You described how you went into Miss Linda Marshall's room on the morning of the crime and how you found her absent from it and how she returned there and it was then that the Chief Constable asked you where she had been."

Christine said rather impatiently: "And I said she had been bathing? Is that it?"

"Ah, but you did not say quite that. You did not say 'she had been bathing.' Your words were 'she said she had been bathing.'"

Christine said: "It's the same thing, surely."

"No, it is not the same! The form of your answer suggests a certain attitude of mind on your part. Linda Marshall came into the room—she was wearing a bathing-wrap and yet—for some reason—you did not at once assume she had been bathing. That is shown by your words 'she *said* she had been bathing.' What was there about her appearance—was it her manner, or something that she was wearing or something she said, that led you to feel surprised when she said she had been bathing?"

Christine's attention left Patrick and focused itself entirely on Poirot. She was interested. She said: "That's clever of you. It's quite true, now I remember. . . . I *was*, just faintly, surprised when Linda said she had been bathing."

"But why, Madame, why?"

"Yes, why? That's just what I'm trying to remember. Oh, yes, I think it was the parcel in her hand."

"She had a parcel?"

"Yes."

"You do not know what was in it?"

"Oh, yes, I do. The string broke. It was loosely done up in the way they do in the village. It was *candles*—they were scattered on the floor. I helped her to pick them up."

"Ah," said Poirot. "Candles."

Christine stared at him. She said: "You seem excited, M. Poirot."

Poirot asked: "Did Linda say why she had bought candles?"

Christine reflected. "No, I don't think she did. I suppose it was to read by at night—perhaps the electric light wasn't good."

"On the contrary, Madame, there was a bedside electric lamp in perfect order."

Christine said: "Then I don't know what she wanted them for."

Poirot said: "What was her manner—when the string broke and the candles fell out of the parcel?"

Christine said slowly: "She was—upset—embarrassed."

Poirot nodded his head. Then he asked: "Did you notice a calendar in her room?"

"A calendar? What kind of a calendar?"

Poirot said: "Possibly a green calendar—with tear-off leaves"

Christine screwed up her eyes in an effort of memory. "A green calendar—rather a bright green. Yes, I have seen a calendar like that—but I can't remember where. It may have been in Linda's room, but I can't be sure."

"But you have definitely seen such a thing."

"Yes." Again Poirot nodded. Christine said rather sharply: "What are you hinting at, M. Poirot? What is the meaning of all this?"

For answer Poirot produced a small volume bound in faded brown calf. He said: "Have you ever seen this before?"

"Why—I think—I'm not sure—yes, Linda was looking into it in the village lending library the other day. But she shut it up and thrust it back quickly when I came up to her. It made me wonder what it was."

Silently Poirot displayed the title. *A History of Witchcraft, Sorcery and of the Compounding of Untraceable Poisons.*

Christine said: "I don't understand. What does all this mean?"

Poirot said gravely: "It may mean, Madame, a good deal."

She looked at him inquiringly, but he did not go on. Instead he asked: "One more question, Madame. Did you take a bath that morning before you went out to play tennis?"

Christine stared again. "A bath? No. I would have had no time and anyway I didn't want a bath—not before tennis. I might have had one after."

"Did you use your bathroom at all when you came in?"

"I sponged my face and hands, that's all."

"You did not turn on the bath at all?"

"No, I'm sure I didn't."

Poirot nodded. He said: "It is of no importance."

Hercule Poirot stood by the table where Mrs. Gardener was wrestling with a jigsaw. She looked up and jumped. "Why M. Poirot, how very quietly you came up beside me! I never heard you. Have you just come back from the inquest? You know, the very thought of that inquest makes me so nervous, I don't know what to do. That's why I'm doing this puzzle. I just felt I couldn't sit outside on the beach as usual. As Mr. Gardener knows, when my nerves are all upset, there's nothing like one of these puzzles for calming me. There now, where *does* this white piece fit in? It must be part of the fur rug, but I don't seem to see. . . . "

Gently Poirot's hand took the piece from her. He said: "It fits, Madame, *here*. It is part of the cat."

"It can't be. It's a black cat."

"A black cat, yes, but you see the tip of the black cat's tail happens to be white."

"Why, so it does! How clever of you! But I do think the people who make puzzles are kind of mean. They just go out of their way to deceive you." She fitted in another piece and then resumed: " You know, M. Poirot, I've been watching you this last day or two. I just wanted to watch you detecting if you know what I mean—not that it doesn't sound rather heartless put like that, as though it were all a game—and a poor creature killed. Oh, dear, every time I think of it I get the shivers! I told Mr. Gardener this morning I'd just *got* to get away from here, and now the inquest's over he says he thinks we'll be able to leave to-morrow, and that's a blessing, I'm sure. But about detecting, I would so like to know your methods—you know, I'd feel privileged if you'd just *explain* it to me."

Hercule Poirot said: "It is a little like your puzzle, Madame. One assembles the pieces. It is like a mosaic—many colours and patterns—and every strange-shaped little piece must be fitted into its own place."

"Now isn't that interesting? Why, I'm sure you explain it just too beautifully."

Poirot went on: "And sometimes it is like that piece of your puzzle just now. One arranges very methodically the pieces of the puzzle— one sorts the colours—and then perhaps a piece of one colour that should fit in with—say, the fur rug, fits in instead in a black cat's tail."

"Why, if that doesn't sound too fascinating! And are there a great many pieces, M. Poirot?"

"Yes, Madame. About every one here in this hotel has given me a piece for my puzzle. You amongst them."

"Me?" Mrs. Gardener's tone was shrill.

"Yes, a remark of yours, Madame, was exceedingly helpful. I might say it was illuminating."

"Well, if that isn't too lovely! Can't you tell me some more, M. Poirot?"

"Ah! Madame, I reserve the explanations for the last chapter."

Mrs. Gardener murmured: "If that isn't just too bad!"

Hercule Poirot tapped gently on the door of Captain Marshall's room. Inside there was the sound of a typewriter. A curt "Come in" came from the room and Poirot entered. Captain Marshall's back was turned to him. He was sitting typing at the table between the windows. He did not turn his head but his eyes met Poirot's in the mirror that hung on the wall directly in front of him. He said irritably: "Well, M. Poirot, what is it?"

Poirot said quickly: "A thousand apologies for intruding. You are busy?"

Marshall said shortly: "I am rather."

Poirot said: "It is one little question that I would like to ask you."

Marshall said: "My God, I'm sick of answering questions. I've answered the police questions. I don't feel called upon to answer yours."

Poirot said: "Mine is very simple one. Only this. On the morning of your wife's death, did you have a bath after you finished typing and before you went out to play tennis?"

"A bath? No of course I didn't! I'd had a bath only an hour earlier!"

Hercule Poirot said: "Thank you. That is all."

"But look here—Oh—" the other paused irresolutely. Poirot withdrew gently closing the door. Kenneth Marshall said: "The fellow's crazy!"

Just outside the bar Poirot encountered Mr. Gardener. He was carrying two cocktails and was clearly on his way to where Mrs. Gardener was ensconced with her jigsaw. He smiled at Poirot in genial fashion. "Care to join us, M. Poirot?"

Poirot shook his head. He said: "What did you think of the inquest, Mr. Gardener?"

Mr. Gardener lowered his voice. He said: "Seemed kind of

indeterminate to me. Your police, I gather, have got something up their sleeves."

"It is possible," said Hercule Poirot.

Mr. Gardener lowered his voice still further. "I shall be glad to get Mrs. Gardener away. She's a very, very sensitive woman, and this affair has got on her nerves. She's very highly strung."

Hercule Poirot said: "Will you permit me, Mr. Gardener, to ask you one question?"

"Why, certainly, M. Poirot. Delighted to assist in any way I can."

Hercule Poirot said: "You are a man of the world—a man, I think, of considerable acumen. What, frankly, was your opinion of the late Mrs. Marshall?"

Mr. Gardener's eyebrows rose in surprise. He glanced cautiously round and lowered his voice. "Well, M. Poirot, I've heard a few things that have been kind of going around, if you get me, especially among the women." Poirot nodded. "But if you ask me I'll tell you my candid opinion and that is that that woman was pretty much of a darned fool!"

Hercule Poirot said thoughtfully: "Now that is very interesting."

Rosamund Darnley said: "So it's my turn, is it?"

"Pardon?"

She laughed. "The other day the Chief Constable held his inquisition. You sat by. To-day, I think, you are conducting your own unofficial inquiry. I've been watching you. First Mrs. Redfern, then I caught a glimpse of you through the lounge window where Mrs. Gardener is doing her hateful jigsaw puzzle. Now it's my turn."

Hercule Poirot sat down beside her. They were on Sunny Ledge. Below them the sea showed a deep glowing green. Further out it was a pale dazzling blue. Poirot said: "You are very intelligent, Mademoiselle. I have thought so ever since I arrived here. It would be a pleasure to discuss this business with you."

Rosamund Darnley said softly: "You want to know what I think about the whole thing?"

"It would be most interesting."

Rosamund said: "I think it's really very simple. The clue is in the woman's past."

"The past? Not the present?"

"Oh! not necessarily the very remote past. I look at it like this. Arlena Marshall was attractive, fatally attractive, to men. It's possible, I think, that she also tired of them rather quickly. Amongst her—followers, shall we say—was one who resented that. Oh, don't misunderstand me, it won't be someone who sticks out a mile. Probably some tepid little man, vain and sensitive—the kind of man who broods. I think he followed her down here, waited his opportunity and killed her."

"You mean that he was an outsider, that he came from the main-land?"

"Yes. He probably hid in that cave until he got his chance."

Poirot shook his head. He said: "Would she go there to meet such a man as you describe? No, she would laugh and not go."

Rosamund said: "She mayn't have know she was going to meet him. He may have sent her a message in some other person's name."

Poirot murmured: "That is possible." Then he said: "But you forget one thing, Mademoiselle. A man bent on murder could not risk coming in broad daylight across the causeway and past the hotel. Some one might have seen him."

"They might have—but I don't think that it's certain. I think it's quite possible that he could have come without any one noticing him at all."

"It would be *possible*, yes, that I grant you. But the point is that he could not *count* on the possibility."

Rosamund said: "Aren't you forgetting something? The weather."

"The weather?"

"Yes. The day of the murder was a glorious day but the day before, remember, there was rain and thick mist. Any one could come onto the island then without being seen. He had only to go down to the beach and spend the night in the cave. That mist, M. Poirot, is important."

Poirot looked at her thoughtfully for a minute or two. He said: "You know, there is a good deal in what you have just said."

Rosamund flushed. She said: "That's my theory, for what it is worth. Now tell me yours."

"Ah," said Hercule Poirot. He stared down at the sea. "*Eh bien*, Mademoiselle. I am a very simple person. I always incline to the belief that the most likely person committed the crime. At the very beginning it seemed to me that one person was very clearly indicated."

Rosamund's voice hardened a little. She said: "Go on."

Hercule Poirot went on. "But you see, there is what you call a snag in the way! It seems that it was *impossible* for that person to have committed the crime."

He heard the quick expulsion of her breath. She said rather breathlessly: "Well?"

Hercule Poirot shrugged his shoulders. "Well, what do we do about it? That is my problem." He paused and then went on. "May I ask you a question?"

"Certainly."

She faced him, alert and vigilant. But the question that came was an unexpected one. "When you came in to change for tennis that morning, did you have a bath?"

Rosamund stared at him. "A bath? What do you mean?"

"That is what I mean. A bath! The receptacle of porcelain, one turns the taps and fills it, one gets in, one gets out and ghoosh—ghoosh—ghoosh, the water goes down the waste pipe!"

"M. Poirot, are you quite mad?"

"No, I am extremely sane."

"Well, anyway, I *didn't* take a bath."

"Ha!" said Poirot. "So nobody took a bath. That is extremely interesting."

"But why should anyone take a bath?"

Hercule Poirot said: "Why, indeed?"

Rosamund said with some exasperation: "I suppose this is the Sherlock Holmes touch!"

Hercule Poirot smiled. Then he sniffed the air delicately. "Will you permit me to be impertinent, Mademoiselle?"

"I'm sure you couldn't be impertinent, M. Poirot."

"That is very kind of you. Then may I venture to say that the scent you use is delicious—it has a *nuance*—a delicate elusive charm." He waved his hands, and then added in a practical voice, "Gabrielle, No. 8, I think?"

"How clever you are. Yes, I always use it."

"So did the late Mrs. Marshall. It is chic, eh? And very expensive?" Rosamund shrugged her shoulders with a faint smile. Poirot said: "You sat here where we are now, Mademoiselle, on the morning of the crime. You were seen here, or at least your sunshade was seen by Miss Brewster and Mr. Redfern as they passed on the sea. During the morning, Mademoiselle, are you sure you did not happen to go down to Pixy's Cove and enter the cave there—the famous Pixy's Cave?"

Rosamund turned her head and stared at him. She said in a quiet voice: "Are you asking me if I killed Arlena Marshall?"

"No. I am asking you if you went into the Pixy's Cave?"

"I don't even know where it is. Why should I go into it? For what reason?"

"On the day of the crime, Mademoiselle, somebody had been in that cave who used Gabrielle No. 8."

Rosamund said sharply: "You've just said yourself, M. Poirot, that Arlena Marshall used Gabrielle No. 8. She was on the beach there that day. Presumably she went into the cave."

"Why should she go into the cave? It is dark there and narrow and very uncomfortable."

Rosamund said impatiently: "Don't ask me for reasons. Since she was actually at the cove she was by far the most likely person, I've told you already I never left this place the whole morning."

"Except for the time when you went into the hotel to Captain Marshall's room," Poirot reminded her.

"Yes, of course. I'd forgotten that."

Poirot said: "And you were wrong, Mademoiselle, when you thought that Captain Marshall did not see you."

Rosamund said incredulously: "Kenneth did see me? Did—did he say so?"

Poirot nodded. "He saw you, Mademoiselle, in the mirror that hangs over the table."

Rosamund caught her breath. She said: "Oh! I see."

Poirot was no longer looking out to sea. He was looking at Rosamund Darnley's hands as they lay folded in her lap. They were well-shaped hands, beautifully molded with very long fingers. Rosamund, shooting a quick look at him, followed the direction of his eyes. She said sharply: "What are you looking at my hands for? Do you think—do you think—?"

Poirot said: "Do I think—what, Mademoiselle?"

Rosamund Darnley said: "Nothing."

It was perhaps an hour later that Hercule Poirot came to the top of the path leading to Gull Cove. There was some one sitting on the beach. A slight figure in a red shirt and dark blue shorts. Poirot descended the path, stepping carefully in his tight smart shoes. Linda Marshall turned her head sharply. He thought that she shrank a little. Her eyes, as he came and lowered himself gingerly to the shingle beside her, rested on him with the suspicion and alertness of a trapped animal. He realized, with a pang, how young and vulnerable she was. She said: "What is it? What do you want?"

Hercule Poirot did not answer for a minute or two. Then he said: "The other day you told the Chief Constable that you were fond of your stepmother and that she was kind to you."

"Well?"

"That was not true, was it, Mademoiselle?"

"Yes, it was."

Poirot said: "She may not have been actively unkind—that I will grant you. But you were not fond of her—oh, no—I think you disliked her very much. That was very plain to see."

Linda said: "Perhaps I didn't like her very much. But one can't say that when a person is dead. It wouldn't be decent."

Poirot sighed. He said: "They taught you that at your school?"

"More or less, I suppose."

Hercule Poirot said: "When a person has been murdered, it is more important to be truthful than to be decent."

Linda said: "I suppose you *would* say a thing like that."

"I would say it and I do say it. It is my business, you see, to find out who killed Arlena Marshall."

Linda muttered: "I want to forget it all. It's so horrible.'"

Poirot said gently: "*But you can't forget, can you?*"

Linda said: "I suppose some beastly madman killed her."

Hercule Poirot murmured: "No, I do not think it was quite like that."

Linda caught her breath. She said: "You sound—as though you *knew*?"

Poirot said: "Perhaps I do know." He paused and went on, "Will you trust me, my child, to do the best I can for you in your bitter trouble?"

Linda sprang up. She said: "I haven't any trouble. There is nothing you can do for me. I don't know what you are talking about."

Poirot said, watching her: "I am talking about *candles*. . . ."

He saw the terror leap into her eyes. She cried: "I won't listen to you. I won't listen." She ran across the beach, swift as a young gazelle, and went flying up the zigzag path.

Poirot shook his head. He looked grave and troubled.

11

INSPECTOR COLGATE was reporting to the Chief Constable.

"I've got on to one thing, sir, and something pretty sensational. It's about Mrs. Marshall's money. I've been into it with her lawyers. I'd say it's a bit of a shock to them. I've got proof of the blackmail story. You remember she was left fifty thousand pounds by old Erskine? Well, all that's left of that is about fifteen thousand."

The Chief Constable whistled. "Whew, what's become of the rest?"

"That's the interesting part, sir. She's sold out stuff from time to time, and each time she's handled it in cash or negotiable securities—that's to say she's handed out money to some one that she didn't want traced. Blackmail all right."

The Chief Constable nodded. "Certainly looks like it. And the blackmailer is here in this hotel. That means it must be one of those three men. Got anything fresh on any of them?"

"Can't say I've got anything definite, sir. Major Barry's a retired Army man, as he says. Lives in a small flat, has a pension and a small income from stocks. *But* he's paid in pretty considerable sums into his account in the last year."

"That sounds promising. What's his explanation?"

"Says they're betting gains. It's perfectly true that he goes to all the large race meetings. Places his bets on the course too, doesn't run an account."

The Chief Constable nodded. "Hard to disprove that," he said. "But it's suggestive."

Colgate went on: "Next, the Reverend Stephen Lane. He's *bona fide* all right—had a living at St. Helen's, Whiteridge, Surrey— resigned his living just over a year ago owing to ill-health. His ill-health amounted to his going into a nursing home for mental patients. He was there for over a year."

"Interesting," said Weston.

"Yes, sir. I tried to get as much as I could out of the doctor in charge but you know what these medicos are—it's difficult to pin them down to anything you can get hold of. But as far as I can make out, his Reverence's trouble was an obsession about the Devil—especially the Devil in the guise of woman—scarlet woman—whore of Babylon."

"H'm," said Weston. "There have been precedents for murder there."

"Yes, sir. It seems to me that Stephen Lane is at least a possibility. The late Mrs. Marshall was a pretty good example of what a clergyman would call a Scarlet Woman—hair and goings on and all. Seems to me it's not impossible he may have felt it his appointed task to dispose of her. That is if he is really batty."

"Nothing to fit in with the blackmail theory?"

"No, sir, I think we can wash him out as far as that's concerned. Has some private means of his own, but not very much, and no sudden increase lately."

"What about his story of his movements on the day of the crime?"

"Can't get any confirmation of them. Nobody remembers meeting a parson in the lanes. As to the book at the church, the last entry was three days before and nobody had looked at it for about a fortnight. He could have quite easily gone over the day before, say, or even a couple of days before, and dated his entry the 25th."

Weston nodded. He said: "And the third man?"

"Horace Blatt? It's my opinion, sir, that there's definitely something fishy there. Pays income tax on a sum far exceeding what he makes out of his hardware business. And mind you, he's a slippery customer. He could probably cook up a reasonable statement—he gambles a bit on the Stock Exchange and he's in with one or two shady deals. Oh, yes, there may be plausible explanations, but there's no getting away from it that he's been making pretty big sums from unexplained sources for some years now."

"In fact," said Weston, "the idea is that Mr. Horace Blatt is a successful blackmailer by profession?"

"Either that, sir, or it's dope. I saw Chief Inspector Ridgeway who's in charge of the dope business, and he was no end keen. Seems there's been a good bit of heroin coming in lately. They're on to the small distributors and they know more or less who's running it the other end, but it's the way it's coming into the country that's baffled them so far."

Weston said: "If the Marshall woman's death is the result of her getting mixed up, innocently or otherwise, with the dope-running stunt, then we'd better hand the whole thing over to Scotland Yard. It's their pigeon. Eh? What do you say?"

Inspector Colgate said rather regretfully: "I'm afraid you're right, sir. If it's dope, then it's a case for the Yard."

Weston said after a moment or two's thought: "It really seems the most likely explanation."

Colgate nodded gloomily. "Yes, it does. Marshall's right out of it—though I did get some information that might have been useful if his alibi hadn't been so good. Seems his firm is very near the rocks. Not his fault or his partner's, just the general result of the crisis last year and the general state of trade and finance. And so far as he knew, he'd come into fifty thousand pounds if his wife died. And fifty thousand would have been a very useful sum." He sighed. "Seems a pity when a man's got two perfectly good motives for murder, that he can be proved to have had nothing to do with it!"

Weston smiled. "Cheer up, Colgate. There's still a chance we may distinguish ourselves. There's the blackmail angle still and there's the batty parson, but personally I think the dope solution is far the most likely." He added: "And if it was one of the dope gang who put her out we'll have been instrumental in helping Scotland Yard to solve the dope problem. In fact, take it all round, one way or another, we've done pretty well."

An unwilling smile showed on Colgate's face. He said: "Well, that's the lot, sir. By the way, I checked up on the writer of that letter we found in her room. The one signed J. N. Nothing doing. He's in China safe enough. Same chap as Miss Brewster was telling us about. Bit of a young scallywag. I've checked up on the rest of Mrs. Marshall's friends. No leads there. Everything there is to get, we've got, sir."

Weston said: "So now it's up to us." He paused and then added: "Seen anything of our Belgian colleague? Does he know all you've told me?"

Colgate said with a grin: "He's a queer little cuss, isn't he? D'you know what he asked me day before yesterday? He wanted particulars of any cases of strangulation in the last three years."

Colonel Weston sat up. "He did, did he? Now I wonder—" he paused a minute. "When did you say the Reverend Stephen Lane went into that mental home?"

"A year ago last Easter, sir."

Colonel Weston was thinking deeply. He said: "There was a case—body of a young woman found somewhere near Bagshot. Going to meet her husband somewhere and never turned up. And there was what the papers called the Lonely Copse Mystery. Both in Surrey if I remember rightly."

His eyes met those of his Inspector. Colgate said: "Surrey? My word, sir, it fits, doesn't it? I wonder. . . ."

Hercule Poirot sat on the turf on the summit of the island. A little to his left was the beginning of the steel ladder that led down to Pixy's Cove. There were several rough boulders near the head of the ladder, he noted, forming easy concealment for any one who proposed to descend to the beach below. Of the beach itself little could be seen from the top owing to the overhang of the cliff.

Hercule Poirot nodded his head gravely. The pieces of his mosaic were fitting into position. Mentally he went over those pieces considering each as a detached item.

A morning on the bathing beach some few days before Arlena Marshall's death.

One, two, three, four, five, separate remarks uttered on that morning.

The evening of a bridge game. He, Patrick Redfern and Rosamund Darnley had been at the table. Christine had wandered out while dummy and had overheard a certain conversation. Who else had been in the lounge at that time? Who had been absent?

The evening before the crime. The conversation he had had with Christine on the cliff and the scene he had witnessed on his way back to the hotel.

Gabrielle No. 8.

A pair of scissors.

A broken pipe.

A bottle thrown from a window.

A green calendar.

A packet of candles.

A mirror and a typewriter.

A skein of magenta wool.

A girl's wrist-watch.

Bath-water rushing down the waste-pipe.

Each of these unrelated facts must fit into its appointed place. There must be no loose ends. And then, with each concrete fact fitted into position, on to the next step: his own belief in the presence of evil on the island. . . . Evil . . . He looked down at a typewritten list in his hands. *Nellie Parsons—found strangled in a lonely copse near Chobham. No clue to her murderer ever discovered.* Nellie Parsons? *Alice Corrigan.* He read very carefully the details of Alice Corrigan's death.

To Hercule Poirot, sitting on the ledge overlooking the sea, came Inspector Colgate. Poirot liked Inspector Colgate. He liked his rugged face, his shrewd eyes, and his slow unhurried manner. Inspector Colgate sat down. He said, glancing down at the typewritten sheets in Poirot's hand: "Done anything with those cases, sir?"

"I have studied them—yes."

Colgate got up, he walked along and peered into the next niche. He came back, saying: "One can't be too careful. Don't want to be overheard."

Poirot said: "You are wise."

Colgate said: "I don't mind telling you, M. Poirot, that I've been interested in those cases myself—though perhaps I shouldn't have thought about them if you hadn't asked for them." He paused. "I've been interested in one case in particular."

"Alice Corrigan?"

"Alice Corrigan." He paused. "I've been on to the Surrey police about that case—wanted to get all the ins and outs of it."

"Tell me, my friend. I am interested—very interested."

"I thought you might be. Alice Corrigan was found strangled in Caesar's Grove on Blackridge Heath—not ten miles from Marley Copse where Nellie Parsons was found—and both those places are within twelve miles of Whiteridge where Mr. Lane was vicar."

Poirot said: "Tell me more about the death of Alice Corrigan."

Colgate said: "The Surrey police didn't at first connect her death with that of Nellie Parsons. That's because they'd pitched on the husband as the guilty party. Don't quite know why except that he was a bit of what the press calls a 'mystery man'—not much known about him—who he was or where he came from. She'd married him against her people's wishes, she'd a bit of money of her own—and she'd insured her life in his favour—all that was enough to raise suspicion, as I think you'll agree, sir?" Poirot nodded.

"But when it came down to brass tacks the husband was washed right out of the picture. The body was discovered by one of these women hikers—hefty young woman in shorts. She was an absolutely competent and reliable witness—games mistress at a school in

Lancashire. She noted the time when she found the body—it was exactly four fifteen—and gave it as her opinion that the woman had been dead quite a short time—not more than ten minutes. That fitted in well enough with the police surgeon's view when he examined the body at 5:45. She left everything as it was and tramped across country to Bagshot police station where she reported the death. Now from three o'clock to four ten, Edward Corrigan was in the train coming down from London where he'd gone up for the day on business. Four other people were in the carriage with him. From the station he took the local bus, two of his fellow passengers travelling by it also. He got off at the Pine Ridge Café where he'd arranged to meet his wife for tea. Time then was four twenty-five. He ordered tea for them both, but said not to bring it till she came. Then he walked about outside waiting for her. When, by five o'clock she hadn't turned up, he was getting alarmed—thought she might have sprained her ankle. The arrangement was that she was to walk across the moors from the village where they were staying to the Pine Ridge Café and go home by bus. Caesar's Grove is not far from the café and it's thought that as she was ahead of time she sat down there to admire the view for a bit before going on, and that some tramp or madman come upon her there and caught her unawares. Once the husband was proved to be out of it, naturally they connected up her death with that of Nellie Parsons—that rather flighty servant girl who was found strangled in Marley Copse. They decided that the same man was responsible for both crimes but they never caught him—and what's more they never came near to catching him! Drew a blank everywhere."

He paused and then he said slowly: "And now—here's a third woman strangled—and a certain gentleman we won't name right on the spot." He stopped. His small shrewd eyes came round to Poirot. He waited hopefully.

Poirot's lips moved. Inspector Colgate leaned forward. Poirot was murmuring: "—so difficult to know what pieces are part of the fur rug and which are the cat's tail."

"I *beg* pardon, sir?" said Inspector Colgate, startled. Poirot said quickly: "I apologize. I was following a train of thought of my own."

"What's this about a fur rug and a cat?"

"Nothing—nothing at all." He paused. "Tell me, Inspector Colgate, if you suspected some one of telling lies—many, many lies, but you had no proof, what would you do?"

Inspector Colgate considered. "It's difficult, that is. But it's my opinion that if any one tells enough lies, they're bound to trip up in the end."

Poirot nodded. "Yes, that is very true. You see, it is only in my mind that certain statements are lies. I *think* that they are lies, but I cannot *know* that they are lies. But one might perhaps make a test—a test of one little not very noticeable lie. And if that were proved to be a lie—why then, one would know that all the rest were lies, too!"

Inspector Colgate looked at him curiously. "Your mind works a funny way, doesn't it, sir? But I daresay it comes out all right in the end. If you'll excuse me asking, what put you on to asking about strangulation cases in general?"

Poirot said slowly: "You have a word in your language—*slick*. This crime seemed to me a very slick crime! It made me wonder, if, perhaps, it was not a first attempt."

Inspector Colgate said: "I see."

Poirot went on: "I said to myself, let us examine past crimes of a similar kind and if there is a crime that closely resembles this one—*eh bien*, we shall have there a very valuable clue."

"You mean using the same method of death, sir?"

"No, no, I mean more than that. The death of Nellie Parsons for instance tells me nothing. But the death of Alice Corrigan—tell me, Inspector Colgate, do you not notice one striking form of similarity to this crime?"

Inspector Colgate turned the problem over in his mind. He said at last: "No, sir, I can't say that I do really. Unless it's that in each case the husband has got a cast-iron alibi."

Poirot said softly: "Ah, so you *have* noticed that?"

"Ha, Poirot. Glad to see you. Come in. Just the man I want." Hercule Poirot responded to the invitation. The Chief Constable pushed over a box of cigarettes, took one himself and lighted it. Between puffs he said: "I've decided, more or less, on a course of action. But I'd like your opinion on it before I act decisively."

Hercule Poirot said: "Tell me, my friend."

Weston said: "I've decided to call in Scotland Yard and hand the case over to them. In my opinion, although there have been grounds for suspicion against one or two people, the whole case hinges on dope smuggling. It seems clear to me that that place, Pixy's Cove, was a definite rendezvous for the stuff."

Poirot nodded. "I agree."

"Good man. And I'm pretty certain who our dope smuggler is. Horace Blatt."

Again Poirot assented. He said: "That, too, is indicated."

"I see our minds have both worked the same way. Blatt used to go sailing in that boat of his. Sometimes he'd invite people to go with him, but most of the time he went out alone. He had some rather conspicuous red sails on that boat but we've found that he had some white sails as well stowed away. I think he sailed out on a good day to an appointed spot, and was met by another boat—sailing boat or motor yacht—something of the kind, and the stuff was handed over. Then Blatt would run ashore into Pixy's Cove at a suitable time of day—"

Hercule Poirot smiled: "Yes, yes, at half past one. The hour of the British lunch when every one is quite sure to be in the dining-room. The island is private. It is not a place where outsiders come for picnics. People take their tea sometimes from the hotel to Pixy's Cove in the afternoon when the sun is on it, or if they want a picnic they would go somewhere far afield, many miles away."

The Chief Constable nodded. "Quite," he said. "Therefore Blatt ran ashore there and stowed the stuff on that ledge in the cave. Somebody else was to pick it up there in due course."

Poirot murmured: "There was a couple, you remember, who came to the island for lunch on the day of the murder? That would be a way of getting the stuff. Some summer visitors from a hotel on the Moor or at St. Loo come over to Smuggler's Island. They announce that they will have lunch. They walk round the island first. How easy to descend to the beach, pick up the sandwich box, place it, no doubt, in Madame's bathing bag which she carries—and return for lunch to the hotel—a little late, perhaps, say at ten minutes to two, having enjoyed their walk whilst every one else was in the dining-room."

Weston said: "Yes, it all sounds practicable enough. Now these dope organizations are pretty ruthless. If any one blundered in and got wise to things they wouldn't make any bones about silencing that person. It seems to me that that is the right explanation of Arlena Marshall's death. It's possible that on that morning Blatt was actually at the cove stowing the stuff away. His accomplices were to come for it that very day. Arlena arrives on her float and sees him going into the cave with the box. She asks him about it and he kills her then and there and sheers off in his boat as quick as possible."

Poirot said: "You think definitely that Blatt is the murderer?"

"It seems the most probable solution. Of course it's possible that Arlena might have got on to the truth earlier, said something to Blatt about it and some other member of the gang fixed a fake appointment with her and did her in. As I say, I think the best course is to hand the case over to Scotland Yard. They've a far better chance than we have of proving Blatt's connection with the gang."

Hercule Poirot nodded thoughtfully. Weston said: "You think that's the wise thing to do—eh?"

Poirot was thoughtful. He said at last: "It may be."

"Dash it all, Poirot, have you got something up your sleeve, or haven't you?"

Poirot said gravely: "If I have, I am not sure that I can prove it."

Weston said: "Of course, I know that you and Colgate have other ideas. Seems a bit fantastic to me but I'm bound to admit there may be something in it. But even if you're right, I still think it's a case for the Yard. We'll give them the facts and they can work in with the Surrey police. What I feel is that it isn't really a case for us. It's not sufficiently localized." He paused. "What do you think, Poirot? What do you feel ought to be done about it?"

Poirot seemed lost in thought. At last he said: "I know what I should like to do."

"Yes, man."

Poirot murmured: "I should like to go for a picnic."

Colonel Weston stared at him.

12

"A PICNIC, M. POIROT?" Emily Brewster stared at him as though he were out of his senses.

Poirot said engagingly: "It sounds to you, does it not, very outrageous? But indeed it seems to me a most admirable idea. We need something of the everyday, the usual, to restore life to the normal. I am most anxious to see something of Dartmoor, the weather is good. It will—how shall I say, it will cheer everybody up! So aid me in this matter. Persuade every one."

The idea met with unexpected success. Every one was at first dubious and then grudgingly admitted it might not be such a bad idea after all. It was not suggested that Captain Marshall should be asked. He had himself announced that he had to go to Plymouth that day. Mr. Blatt was of the party, enthusiastically so. He was determined to be the life and soul of it. Besides him, there were Emily Brewster, the Redferns, Stephen Lane, the Gardeners who were persuaded to delay their departure by one day, Rosamund Darnley and Linda.

Poirot had been eloquent to Rosamund and had dwelt on the advantage it would be to Linda to have something to take her out of herself. To this Rosamund agreed. She said: "You're quite right. The shock has been very bad for a child of that age. It has made her terribly jumpy."

"That is only natural, Mademoiselle. But at that age one soon forgets. Persuade her to come. You can, I know."

Major Barry had refused firmly. He said he didn't like picnics. "Lots of baskets to carry," he said. "And darned uncomfortable. Eating my food at a table's good enough for me."

The party assembled at ten o'clock. Three cars had been ordered. Mr. Blatt was loud and cheerful imitating a tourist guide. "This way, ladies and gentlemen—this way for Dartmoor. Heather and bilberries, Devonshire cream and convicts. Bring your wives, gentlemen, or bring the other thing! Every one welcome! Scenery guaranteed. Walk up. Walk up."

At the last minute Rosamund Darnley came down looking concerned. She said: "Linda's not coming. She says she's got a frightful headache."

Poirot cried: "But it will do her good to come. Persuade her, Mademoiselle."

Rosamund said firmly: "It's no good. She's absolutely determined. I've given her some aspirin and she's gone to bed." She hesitated and said: "I think, perhaps, I won't go, either."

"Can't allow that, dear lady, can't allow that," cried Mr. Blatt, seizing her facetiously by the arm. "*La haute Mode* must grace the occasion. No refusals! I've taken you into custody, ha, ha. Sentenced to Dartmoor."

He led her firmly to the first car. Rosamund threw a black look at Hercule Poirot. "I'll stay with Linda," said Christine Redfern. "I don't mind a bit."

Patrick said: "Oh, come on, Christine."

And Poirot said: "No, no, you must come, Madame. With a headache one is better alone. Come, let us start."

The three cars drove off. They went first to the real Pixy's Cave on Sheepstor and had a good deal of fun looking for the entrance and at last finding it, aided by a picture postcard. It was precarious going on the big boulders and Hercule Poirot did not attempt it. He watched indulgently while Christine Redfern sprang lightly from stone to stone and observed that her husband was never far from her. Rosamund Darnley and Emily Brewster had joined in the search though the latter slipped once and gave a slight twist to her ankle. Stephen Lane was indefatigable, his long lean figure turning and twisting among the boulders. Mr. Blatt contented himself with going a little way and shouting encouragement, also taking photographs of the searchers.

The Gardeners and Poirot remained staidly sitting by the wayside whilst Mrs. Gardener's voice upraised itself in a pleasant even-toned monologue punctuated now and then by the obedient "Yes, darlings" of her spouse. "—and what I always have felt, Mr. Poirot, and Mr. Gardener agrees with me—is that snapshots can be very annoying. Unless, that is to say, they are taken among friends. That Mr. Blatt has just no sensitiveness of any kind. He just comes right up to every one and talks away and takes pictures of you and, as I said to Mr. Gardener, that really is very ill-bred. That's what I said, Odell, wasn't it?"

"Yes, darling."

"That group he took of us all sitting on the beach. Well, that's all very well, but he should have asked first. As it was, Miss Brewster was just getting up from the beach and it certainly makes her look a very peculiar shape."

"I'll say it does," said Mr. Gardener with a grin.

"And there's Mr. Blatt giving round copies to everyone without so much as asking first. He gave one to you, M. Poirot, I noticed."

Poirot nodded. He said: "I value that group very much."

Mrs. Gardener went on: "And look at his behavior to-day—so loud and noisy and common. Why, it just makes me shudder. You ought to have arranged to leave that man at home, M. Poirot."

Hercule Poirot murmured: "Alas, Madame, that would have been difficult."

"I should say it would. That man just pushes his way in anywhere. He's just not sensitive at all."

At this moment the discovery of the Pixy's Cave was hailed from below with loud cries. The party now drove on, under Hercule Poirot's directions, to a spot where a short walk from the car down a hillside of heather led to a delightful spot by a small river. A narrow plank bridge crossed the river and Poirot and her husband induced Mrs. Gardener to cross it to where a delightful heathery spot free from prickly furze looked an ideal spot for a picnic lunch. Talking volubly about her sensations when crossing on a plank bridge Mrs. Gardener sank down. Suddenly there was a slight outcry. The others had run across the bridge lightly enough, but Emily Brewster was standing in the middle of the plank, her eyes shut, swaying to and fro. Poirot and Patrick Redfern rushed to the rescue. Emily Brewster was gruff and ashamed. "Thanks, thanks. Sorry. Never was good at crossing running water. Get giddy. Stupid, very."

Lunch was spread out and the picnic began. All the people concerned were secretly surprised to find how much they enjoyed this interlude. It was, perhaps, because it afforded an escape from an atmosphere of suspicion and dread. Here, with the trickling of the water, the soft peaty smell in the air and the warm colouring of bracken and heather, a world of murder and police inquiries and suspicion seemed blotted out as though it had never existed. Even Mr. Blatt forgot to be the life and soul of the party. After lunch he went to sleep a little distance away and subdued snores testified to his blissful unconsciousness.

It was quite a grateful party of people who packed up the picnic baskets and congratulated Hercule Poirot on his good idea. The sun was sinking as they returned along the narrow winding lanes. From the top of the hill above Leathercombe Bay they had a brief glimpse of the island with the white Hotel on it. It looked peaceful and innocent in the setting sun. Mrs. Gardener, not loquacious for once, sighed and said: "I really do thank you, M. Poirot. I feel so calm. It's just wonderful."

Major Barry came out to greet them on arrival. "Hullo," he said. "Had a good day?"

Mrs. Gardener said: "Indeed we did. The moors were just too lovely for anything. So English and old world. And the air delicious and invigorating. You ought to be ashamed of yourself for being so lazy as to stay behind."

The Major chuckled. "I'm too old for that kind of thing—sitting on a patch of bog and eating sandwiches."

A chambermaid had come out of the hotel. She was a little out of breath. She hesitated for a a moment, then came swiftly up to Christine Redfern. Hercule Poirot recognized her as Gladys Narrracott. Her voice came quick and uneven. "Excuse me, Madam, but I'm worried about the young lady. About Miss Marshall. I took her up some tea just now and I couldn't get her to wake and she looks so—so queer somehow."

Christine looked round helplessly. Poirot was at her side in a moment. His hand under her elbow he said quietly: "We will go up and see."

They hurried up the stairs and along the passage to Linda's room. One glance at her was enough to tell them both that something was very wrong. She was an odd colour and her breathing was hardly perceptible. Poirot's hand went to her pulse. At the same time he noticed an envelope stuck up against the lamp on the bedside table. It was addressed to himself.

Captain Marshall came quickly into the room. He said: "What's this about Linda? What's the matter with her?"

A small frightened sob came from Christine Redfern. Hercule Poirot turned from the bed. He said to Marshall: "Get a doctor—as quick as you possibly can. But I'm afraid—very much afraid—it may be too late."

He took the letter with his name on it and ripped open the envelope.

Inside were a few lines of writing in Linda's prim schoolgirl hand. *I think this is the best way out. Ask Father to try and forgive me. I killed Arlena. I thought I should be glad—but I'm not. I am very sorry for everything. . . .*

They were assembled in the lounge—Marshall, the Redferns, Rosamund Darnley and Hercule Poirot. They sat there silent— waiting. . . . The door opened and Dr. Neasdon came in. He said curtly: "I've done all I can. She may pull through—but I'm bound to tell you that there's not much hope."

He paused. Marshall, his face stiff, his eyes a cold frosty blue, asked: "How did she get hold of the stuff?"

Neasdon opened the door again and beckoned. The chambermaid came into the room. She had been crying. Neasdon said: "Just tell us again what you saw?"

Sniffing, the girl said: "I never thought—I never thought for a minute there was anything wrong—though the young lady did seem rather strange about it." A slight gesture of impatience from the doctor started her off again. "She was in the other lady's room. Mrs. Redfern's. Your room, Madam. Over at the washstand and she took up a little bottle. She did give a bit of a jump when I came in and I thought it was queer her taking things from your room, but then of course it might be something she'd lent you. She just said: 'Oh, this is what I'm looking for—' and went out."

Christine said almost in a whisper: "My sleeping tablets."

The doctor said brusquely: "How did she know about them?"

Christine said: "I gave her one. The night after it happened. She told me she couldn't sleep. She—I remember her saying—'Will one be enough?'—and I said, Oh, yes, they were very strong—that I'd been cautioned never to take more than two at most."

Neasdon nodded. "She made pretty sure," he said. "She took six of them."

Christine sobbed again. "Oh, dear, I feel it's my fault. I should have kept them locked up."

The doctor shrugged his shoulders. "It might have been wiser, Mrs. Redfern."

Christine said despairingly: "She's dying—and it's my fault. . . ."

Kenneth Marshall stirred in his chair. He said: "No, you can't blame yourself. Linda knew what she was doing. She took them deliberately. Perhaps—perhaps it was best." He looked down at the crumpled note in his hand—the note that Poirot had silently handed to him.

Rosamund Darnley cried out: "I don't believe it. I don't believe Linda killed her. Surely it's impossible—on the evidence!"

Christine said eagerly: "Yes, she *can't* have done it! She must have got overwrought and imagined it all."

The door opened and Colonel Weston came in. He said: "What's all this I hear?"

Dr. Neasdon took the note from Marshall's hand and handed it to the Chief Constable. The latter read it. He exclaimed incredulously: "What? But this is nonsense—absolute nonsense! It's impossible." He repeated with assurance, "Impossible! isn't it, Poirot?"

Hercule Poirot moved for the first time. He said in a slow sad voice: "No, I'm afraid it is not impossible."

Christine Redfern said: "But I was with her, M. Poirot. I was with her up to a quarter to twelve. I told the police so."

Poirot said: "Your evidence gave her an alibi—yes. But what was your evidence based on? It was based on *Linda Marshall's own wrist-watch.* You do not know *of your own knowledge* that it was a quarter to twelve when you left her—you only know that she told you so. You said yourself the time seemed to have gone very fast."

She stared at him stricken. He said: "Now think, Madame, when you left the beach, did you walk back to the hotel fast or slow?"

"I—well, fairly slowly, I think."

"Do you remember much about that walk back?"

"Not very much, I'm afraid. I—I was thinking."

Poirot said: "I am sorry to ask you this, but will you tell us just what you were thinking about during that walk?"

Christine flushed. "I suppose—if it is necessary. . . . I was just considering the question of—of leaving here. Just going away without telling my husband. I—I was very unhappy just then, you see."

Patrick Redfern cried: "Oh, Christine! I know. . . . I know. . . ."

Poirot's precise voice cut in: "Exactly. You were concerned over taking a step of some importance. You were, I should say, deaf and blind to your surroundings. You probably walked very slowly and occasionally stopped for some minutes whilst you puzzled things out."

Christine nodded. "How clever you are. It was just like that. I woke up from a kind of dream just outside the hotel and hurried in thinking I should be very late but when I saw the clock in the lounge I realized I had plenty of time."

Hercule Poirot said again: "Exactly." He turned to Marshall: "I must now describe to you certain things I found in your daughter's room after the murder. In the grate was a large blob of melted wax, some burnt hair, fragments of cardboard and paper and an ordinary household pin. The paper and the cardboard might not be relevant but the other three things were suggestive—particularly when I found tucked away in the bookshelf a volume from the local library here dealing wth witchcraft and magic. It opened very easily at a certain page. On that page were described various methods of causing death by moulding in wax a figure supposed to represent the victim. This was then slowly roasted till it melted away—or alternatively you would pierce the wax figure to the heart with a pin. Death of the victim would ensue. I later heard from Mrs. Redfern that Linda Marshall had been out early that morning and had bought a packet of candles and had seemed embarrassed when her purchase was revealed. I had no doubt what had happened after that. Linda had made a crude figure of the candle wax—possibly adorning it with a snip of Arlena's red hair to give the magic force—had then stabbed it to the heart with a pin and finally melted the figure away by lighting strips of cardboard under it.

"It was crude, childish, superstitious, but it revealed one thing: the desire to kill. Was there any possibility that there had been more than a desire? Could Linda Marshall have *actually* killed her stepmother? At first sight it seemed as though she had a perfect alibi—but in actuality, as I have just pointed out, the time evidence was supplied by *Linda herself*. She could easily have declared the time to be a quarter of an hour later than it really was.

"It was quite possible once Mrs. Redfern had left the beach for Linda to follow her up and then strike across the narrow neck of land to the ladder, hurry down it, meet her stepmother there, strangle her and return up the ladder before the boat containing Miss Brewster and Patrick Redfern came in sight. She could then return to Gull Cove, take her bath and return to the hotel at her leisure.

"But that entailed two things. She must have definite knowledge that Arlena Marshall would be at Pixy Cove and she must be physically capable of the deed. Well, the first was quite possible—if Linda Marshall had written a note to Arlena herself in some one else's name. As to the second, Linda has very large strong hands. They are as large as a man's. As to the strength she is at the age when one is prone to be mentally unbalanced. Mental derangement often is accompanied by unusual strength. There was one other small point. Linda Marshall's mother had actually been accused and tried for murder."

Kenneth Marshall lifted his head. He said fiercely: "She was also acquitted."

"She was acquitted," Poirot agreed.

Marshall said: "And I'll tell you this, M. Poirot. Ruth—my wife—was innocent. That I know with complete and absolute certainty. In the intimacy of our life I could not have been deceived, She was an innocent victim of circumstances." He paused: "And I don't believe that Linda killed Arlena. It's ridiculous—absurd!"

Poirot said: "Do you believe that letter, then, to be a forgery?"

Marshall held out his hand for it and Weston gave it to him. Marshall studied it attentively. Then he shook his head. "No," he said unwillingly. "I believe Linda did write this."

Poirot said: "Then if she wrote it, there are only two explanations. Either she wrote it in all good faith, knowing herself to be the murderess or—or, I say—*she wrote it deliberately to shield some one else*, some one whom she feared was suspected."

Kenneth Marshall said: "You mean me?"

"It is possible, is it not?"

Marshall considered for a moment or two, then he said quietly: "No, I think that idea is absurd. Linda may have realized that I was regarded with suspicion at first. But she knew definitely by now that that was over and done with—that the police had accepted my alibi and turned their attention elsewhere."

Poirot said: "And supposing that it was not so much that she thought that you were suspected as that she *knew* you were guilty."

Marshall stared at him. He gave a short laugh. "That's absurd."

Poirot said: "I wonder. There are, you know, several possibilities about Mrs. Marshall's death. There is the theory that she was being blackmailed, that she went that morning to meet the blackmailer and that the blackmailer killed her. There is the theory that Pixy Cove and Cave were being used for drug-running and that she was killed because she accidentally learned something about that. There is a third possibility—that she was killed by a religious maniac. And there is a fourth possibility—you stood to gain a lot of money by your wife's death, Captain Marshall?"

"I've just told you—"

"Yes, yes—I agree that it is impossible that you could have killed your wife—if you were acting alone. But supposing someone helped you?"

"What the devil do you mean?" The quiet man was roused at last. He half rose from his chair. His voice was menacing. There was a hard angry light in his eyes.

Poirot said: "I mean that this is not a crime that was committed single-handed. Two people were in it. It is quite true that you could not have typed that letter and at the same time gone to the cove—but there would have been time for you to have jotted down that letter in shorthand—and for *some one else* to have typed it in your room while you yourself were absent on your murderous errand."

Hercule Poirot looked towards Rosamund Darnley. He said: "Miss Darnley states that she left Sunny Ledge at ten minutes past eleven and saw you typing in your room. But just about that time Mr. Gardener went up to the hotel to fetch a skein of wool for his wife. He did not meet Miss Darnley or see her. That is rather remarkable. It looks as though either Miss Darnley never left Sunny Ledge, or else she had left it much earlier and was in your room typing industriously. Another point, you stated that when Miss Darnley looked into your room at a quarter past eleven *you saw her in the mirror*. But on the day of the murder your typewriter and papers were all on the writing-desk across the corner of the room, whereas the mirror was between the windows. So that that statement was a deliberate lie. Later, you moved your typewriter to the table under the mirror so as to substantiate your story—but it was too late. I was aware that both you and Miss Darnley had lied."

Rosamund Darnley spoke. Her voice was low and clear. She said: "How devilishly ingenious you are!"

Hercule Poirot said, raising his voice: "But not so devilish and so ingenious as the man who killed Arlena Marshall! Think back for a moment. Who did I think—who did everybody think—that Arlena Marshall had gone to meet that morning? We all jumped to the same conclusion. *Patrick Redfern*. It was not to meet a blackmailer that she went. Her face alone would have told me that. Oh, no, it was a lover she was going to meet—or thought she was going to meet. Yes, I was quite sure of that. Arlena Marshall was going to meet Patrick Redfern. But a minute later Patrick Redfern appeared on the beach and was obviously looking for her. So what then?"

Patrick Redfern said with subdued anger: "Some devil used my name."

Poirot said: "You were very obviously upset and surprised by her non-appearance. Almost too obviously, perhaps. It is *my* theory, Mr. Redfern, that she went to Pixy Cove to meet *you* and that she *did* meet you and that *you killed her there as you had planned to do*."

Patrick Redfern stared. He said in his high good-humoured Irish voice: "Is it daft you are? I was with you on the beach until I went round in the boat with Miss Brewster and found her dead."

Hercule Poirot said: "You killed her after Miss Brewster had gone off in the boat to fetch the police. Arlena Marshall was not dead when you got to the beach. She was waiting hidden in the Cave until the coast should be clear."

"But the body! Miss Brewster and I both saw the body."

"A body—yes. But not a *dead* body. The *live* body of the woman who helped you, her arms and legs stained with tan, her face hidden by a green cardboard hat. Christine, your wife (or possibly not your wife—but still your partner), helping you to commit this crime as she helped you to commit that crime in the past when she 'discovered' the body of Alice Corrigan at least twenty minutes before Alice Corrigan died—killed by her husband Edward Corrigan—you!"

Christine spoke. Her voice was sharp—cold. She said: "Be careful, Patrick, don't lose your temper."

Poirot said: "You will be interested to hear that both you and your wife Christine were easily recognized and picked out by the Surrey police from a group of people photographed here. They identified you both at once as Edward Corrigan and Christine Deverill, the young woman who found the body."

Patrick Redfern had risen. His handsome face was transformed, suffused with blood, blind with rage. It was the face of a killer—of a tiger. He yelled: "You damned interfering murdering lousy little worm!"

He hurled himself forward, his fingers stretching and curling, his voice raving curses, as he fastened his fingers round Hercule Poirot's throat. . . .

13

POIROT SAID REFLECTIVELY: "It was on a morning when we were sitting out here that we talked of suntanned bodies lying like meat upon a slab and it was then that I reflected how little difference there was between one body and another. If one looked closely and appraisingly—yes —but to the casual glance? One moderately wellmade young woman is very like another. Two brown legs, two brown arms, a little piece of bathing suit in between—just a body lying out in the sun. When a woman walks, when she speaks, laughs, turns her head, moves a hand—then, yes, then, there is personality—individuality. But in the sun ritual—no.

"It was that day we spoke of evil—*evil under the sun*, as Mr. Lane put it. Mr. Lane is a very sensitive person—evil affects him—he perceives its presence—but though he is a good recording instrument, he did not really know exactly where the evil was. To him, evil was focused in the person of Arlena Marshall and practically every one present agreed with him.

"But to my mind, though evil was present, it was not centralized in Arlena Marshall at all. It was connected with her, yes—but in a totally different way. I saw her, first, last and all the time, as an eternal and predestined *victim.* Because she was beautiful, because she had glamor, because men turned their heads to look at her, it was assumed that she was the type of woman who wrecked lives and destroyed souls. But I saw her very differently. It was not she who fatally attracted men—it was men who fatally attracted her. She was the type of woman whom men care for easily and of whom they as easily tire. And everything that I was told or found out about her strengthened my conviction on this point. The first thing that was mentioned about her was how the man in whose divorce case she had been cited refused to marry her. It was then that Captain Marshall, one of those incurably chivalrous men, stepped in and asked her to marry him. To a shy retiring man of Captain Marshall's type, a public ordeal of any kind would be the worst torture—hence his love and pity for his first wife who was publicly accused and tried for a murder she had not committed. He married her and found himself amply justified in his estimate of her character. After her death another beautiful woman, perhaps something of the same type (since Linda has red hair which she probably inherited from her mother) is held up to public ignominy. Again Marshall performs a rescue act. But this time he finds little to sustain his infatuation. Arlena is stupid, unworthy of his sympathy and protection, mindless. Nevertheless I think he always had a fairly true vision of her. Long after he ceased to love her and was irked by her presence, he remained sorry for her. She was to him like a child who cannot get farther than a certain page in the book of life.

"I saw in Arlena Marshall with her passion for men, a predestined prey for an unscrupulous man of a certain type. In Patrick Redfern, with his good looks, his easy assurance, his undeniable charm for women, I recognized at once that type. The adventurer who makes his living, one way or another, out of women. Looking on from my place on the beach I was quite certain that Arlena was Patrick's victim, not the other way about. And I associated that focus of evil with Patrick Redfern not with Arlena Marshall.

"Arlena had recently come into a large sum of money, left her by an elderly admirer who had not had time to grow tired of her. She was the type of woman who is invariably defrauded of money by some man or another. Miss Brewster mentioned a young man who had been 'ruined' by Arlena, but a letter from him which was found in her room, though it expressed a wish (which cost nothing) to cover her with jewels, in actual *fact* acknowledged a cheque from *her* by means of which he hoped to escape prosecution. A clear case of a young waster sponging on her. I have no doubt that Patrick Redfern found it easy to induce her to hand him large sums from time to time 'for investment.' He probably dazzled her with stories of great opportunities—how he would make her fortune and his own. Unprotected women, living alone, are easy preys to that type of man—and he usually escapes scot-free with the booty. If, however, there is a husband, or a brother, or a father about, things are apt to take an unpleasant turn for the swindler. Once Captain Marshall was to find out what had happened to his wife's fortune, Patrick Redfern might expect short shrift. That did not worry him, however, because he contemplated quite calmly doing away with her when he judged it necessary—encouraged by having already got away with one murder—that of a young woman whom he had married in the name of Corrigan and whom he had persuaded to insure her life for a large sum.

"In his plans he was aided and abetted by the young woman who down here passed as his wife and to whom he was genuinely attached. A young woman as unlike the type of his victims as could well be imagined—cool, calm, passionless, but steadfastly loyal to him and an actress of no mean ability. From the time of her arrival here Christine Redfern played the part, the part of the 'poor little wife'—frail, helpless, an intellectual rather than athletic. Think of the points she made one after another. Her tendency to blister in the sun and her consequent white skin, her giddiness at heights—stories of getting stuck on Milan Cathedral, etc. An emphasis on her frailty and delicacy—nearly every one spoke of her as a 'little woman.' She was actually as tall as Arlena Marshall but with very small hands and feet. She spoke of herself as a former school-teacher and thereby emphasized an impression of book learning and lack of athletic prowess. Actually it is quite true that she had worked in a school, but the position she held there was that of *games mistress* and she was an extremely active young woman who could climb like a cat and run like an athlete.

"The crime itself was perfectly planned and timed. It was, as I mentioned before, a very slick crime. The timing was a work of genius. First of all there were certain preliminary scenes—one played on the cliff ledge when they knew me to be occupying the next recess—a conventional jealous wife dialogue between her and her husband. Later she played the same part in a scene with me. At the time I remember a vague feeling of having read all this in a book. It did not seem *real*. Because, of course, it was *not* real. Then came the day of the crime. It was a fine day—an essential. Redfern's first act was to slip out very early—by the balcony door which he unlocked from the inside (if found open it would only be thought some one had gone for an early bathe). Under his bathing-wrap he concealed a green Chinese hat, the duplicate of the one Arlena was in the habit of wearing. He slipped across the island, down the ladder and stowed it away in an appointed place behind some rocks. Part I.

"On the previous evening he had arranged a rendezvous with Arlena. They were exercising a good deal of caution about meeting as Arlena was slightly afraid of her husband. She agreed to go round to Pixy Cove early. Nobody went there in the morning. Redfern was to join her there, taking a chance to slip away unobtrusively. If she heard any one descending the ladder or a boat came in sight she was to slip inside the Pixy's Cave, the secret of which he had told her, and wait there until the coast was clear. Part II.

"In the meantime Christine went to Linda's room at a time when she judged Linda would have gone for an early morning dip. She would then alter Linda's watch, putting it on twenty minutes. There was, of course, a risk that Linda might notice her watch was wrong, but it did not much matter if she did. Christine's real alibi was the size of her hands which made it a physical impossibility for her to have committed the crime. Nevertheless an additional alibi would be desirable. When in Linda's room she noticed the book on witchcraft and magic, open at a certain page. She read it and when Linda came in and dropped a parcel of candles she realized what was in Linda's mind. It opened up some new ideas to her. The original idea of the guilty pair had been to cast a reasonable amount of suspicion on Kenneth Marshall, hence the abstracted pipe, a fragment of which was to be planted at the cove underneath the ladder. On Linda's return Christine easily arranged an outing together to Gull Cove. She then returned to her own room, took out from a locked suitcase a bottle of artificial suntan, applied it carefully and threw the empty bottle out of the window where it narrowly escaped hitting Emily Brewster who was bathing. Part III successfully accomplished.

"Christine then dressed herself in a white bathing-suit and over it a pair of beach trousers and coat with long floppy sleeves which effectually concealed her newly browned arms and legs. At 10.15 Arlena departed for her rendezvous, a minute or two later Patrick Redfern came down and registered surprise, annoyance, etc. Christine's task was easy enough. Keeping her own watch concealed she asked Linda at twenty-five past eleven what time it was. Linda looked at her watch and replied that it was a quarter to twelve. She then starts down to the sea and Christine packs up her sketching things. As soon as Linda's back is turned Christine picks up the girl's watch which she has necessarily discarded before going into the sea and alters it back to the correct time. Then she hurries up the cliff path, runs across the narrow neck of land to the top of the ladder, strips off her pajamas and shoves them and her sketching box behind a rock and swarms rapidly down the ladder in her best gymnastic fashion.

"Arlena is on the beach below wondering why Patrick is so long in coming. She sees or hears some one on the ladder, takes a cautious observation and to her annoyance sees that inconvenient person—the wife! She hurries along the beach and into the Pixy's Cave.

"Christine takes the hat from its hiding-place, a false red curl pinned underneath the brim at the back, and disposes herself in a sprawling attitude with the hat and curl shielding her face and neck. The timing is perfect. A minute or two later the boat containing Patrick and Emily Brewster comes round the point. Remember it is *Patrick* who bends down and examines the body, *Patrick* who is stunned—shocked—broken down by the death of his lady love! His witness has been carefully chosen. Miss Brewster has not got a good head, she will not attempt to go up the ladder. She will leave the cove by boat, Patrick naturally being the one to remain with the body—'in case the murderer may be still about'. Miss Brewster rows off to fetch the police. Christine, as soon as the boat has disappeared, springs up, cuts the hat into pieces with the scissors Patrick has carefully brought, stuffs them into her bathing suit and swarms up the ladder in double-quick time, slips into her beach pyjamas and runs back to the hotel. Just time to have a quick bath, washing off the brown suntan application, and into her tennis dress. One other thing she does. She burns the pieces of the green cardboard hat and the hair in Linda's grate, adding a leaf of a calendar so that it may be associated with the cardboard. Not a *Hat* but a *Calendar* has been burnt. As she suspected Linda has been experimenting in magic—the blob of wax and the pin show that.

"Then, down to the tennis court, arriving the last, but showing no signs of flurry or haste.

"And meanwhile Patrick has gone to the Cave. Arlena has seen nothing and heard very little—a boat—voices—she has prudently remained hidden. But now it is Patrick calling. 'All clear, darling,' and she comes out and his hands fasten round her neck—and that is the end of poor foolish beautiful Arlena Marshall. . . ."

His voice died away. For a moment there was silence, then Rosamund Darnley said with a little shiver: "Yes, you make one see it all. But that's the story from the other side. You haven't told us how *you* came to get at the truth?"

Hercule Poirot said: "I told you once that I had a very simple mind. Always, from the beginning, it seemed to me that *the most likely person* had killed Arlena Marshall. And the most likely person was Patrick Redfern. He was the type, *par excellence*—the type of the man who exploits women like her—and the type of the killer—the kind of man who will take a women's savings and cut her throat into the bargain. Who was Arlena going to meet that morning? By the evidence of her face, her smile, her manner, her words to me—*Patrick Redfern.* And therefore, in the very nature of things, it should be Patrick Redfern who killed her.

"But at once I came up, as I told you, against impossibility. Patrick Redfern could not have killed her since he was on the beach and in Miss Brewster's company until the actual discovery of the body. So I looked about for other solutions—and there were several. She could have been killed by her husband—with Miss Darnley's connivance. (They too had both lied as to one point which looked suspicious.) She could have been killed as a result of her having stumbled on the secret of the dope smuggling. She could have been killed, as I said, by a religious maniac, and she could have been killed by her stepdaughter. The latter seemed to me at one time to be the real solution. Linda's manner in her very first interview with the police was significant. An interview that I had with her later assured me of one point. Linda considered herself guilty."

"You mean she imagined that she had actually killed Arlena?" Rosamund's voice was incredulous.

Hercule Poirot nodded. "Yes. Remember—she is really little more than a child. She read that book on witchcraft and she half believed it. She hated Arlena. She deliberately made the wax doll, cast her spell, pierced it to the heart, melted it away—*and that very day Arlena dies.* Older and wiser people than Linda have believed fervently in magic. Naturally she believed that it was all true—that by using magic she had killed her stepmother."

Rosamund cried: "Oh, poor child, poor child. And I thought—I imagined—something quite different—that she knew something which would—"

Rosamund stopped. Poirot said: "I know what it was you thought. Actually your manner frightened Linda still further. She believed that her action had really brought about Arlena's death and that you knew it. Christine Redfern worked on her too, introducing the idea of the sleeping tablets to her mind, showing her the way to a speedy and painless expiation of her crime. You see, once Captain Marshall was proved to have an alibi, it was vital for a new suspect to be found. Neither she nor her husband knew about the dope smuggling. They fixed on Linda to be the scapegoat."

Rosamund said: "What a devil!"

Poirot nodded. "Yes, you are right. A cold-blooded and cruel woman. For me, I was in great difficulty. Was Linda guilty of only the childish attempt at witchcraft, or had her hate carried her still further— to the actual act? I tried to get her to confess to me. But it was no good.

At that moment I was in grave uncertainty. The Chief Constable was inclined to accept the dope-smuggling explanation. I could let it go at that. I went over the facts again very carefully. I had, you see, a collection of jigsaw puzzle pieces, isolated happenings—plain facts. The whole must fit into a complete and harmonious pattern. There were the scissors found on the beach—a bottle thrown from a window—a bath that no one would admit to having taken—all perfectly harmless occurrences in themselves, but rendered significant by the fact that no one would admit to them. Therefore, they *must* be of significance. Nothing about them fitted in with the theories of either Captain Marshall's or Linda's or of a dope gang's being responsible. And yet they *must* have meaning. I went back again to my first solution—that Patrick Redfern had committed the murder. Was there anything in support of that? Yes, the fact that a very large sum of money was missing from Arlena's account. Who had got that money? Patrick Redfern, of course. She was the type of woman easily swindled by a handsome young man—but she was not at all the type of woman to be blackmailed. She was far too transparent, not good enough at keeping a secret. The blackmailer story had never rung true to my mind. And yet there *had* been that conversation overheard—ah, but overheard by whom? *Patrick Redfern's wife*. It was her story—unsupported by any outside evidence. Why was it invented? The answer came to me like lightning. To account for the absence of Arlena's money!

"Patrick and Christine Redfern. The two of them were in it together. Christine hadn't got the physical strength to strangle her or the mental make-up. No, it was Patrick who had done it—but that was impossible! Every minute of his time was accounted for until the body was found. Body—the word body stirred something in my mind—bodies lying on the beach—*all alike*. Patrick Redfern and Emily Brewster had got to the cove and seen *a body* lying there. A body—suppose it was not Arlena's body but somebody else's? The face was hidden by the great Chinese hat.

"But there *was* only one dead body—Arlena's. Then, could it be—a *live* body—some one pretending to be dead? Could it be Arlena herself, inspired by Patrick to play some kind of a joke. I shook my head—no, too risky. A live body—whose? Was there any woman who would help Redfern? Of course—his wife. But she was a white-skinned delicate creature—Ah, yes, but suntan can be applied out of bottles—bottles—a bottle—I had one of my jigsaw pieces. Yes, and afterwards, of course, a bath—to wash that tell-tale stain off before she went out to play tennis. And the scissors? Why, to cut up the duplicate cardboard hat—an unwieldy thing that must be got out of the way, and in the haste the scissors were left behind—the one thing that the pair of murderers forgot.

"But where was Arlena all the time? That again was perfectly clear. Either Rosamund Darnley or Arlena Marshall had been in the Pixy's Cave, the scent they both used told me that. It was certainly not Rosamund Darnley. Then it was Arlena, hiding till the coast should clear.

"When Emily Brewster went off in the boat, Patrick had the beach to himself and full opportunity to commit the crime. Arlena Marshall was killed after a quarter to twelve but the medical evidence was only concerned with the earliest possible time the crime could have been committed. That Arlena was dead at a quarter to twelve was what was told to the doctor, not what he told the police.

"Two more points had to be settled. Linda Marshall's evidence gave Christine Redfern an alibi. Yes, but that evidence depended on Linda Marshall's wristwatch. All that was needed was to prove that Christine had had two opportunities of tampering with the watch. I found those easily enough. She had been alone in Linda's room that morning—and there was an indirect proof. Linda was heard to say that she was 'afraid she was going to be late,' but when she got down it was only twenty-five past ten by the lounge clock. The second opportunity was easy—she could alter the watch back again as soon as Linda turned her back and went down to bathe. Then there was the question of the ladder. Christine had always declared she had no head for heights. Another carefully prepared lie.

"I had my mosaic now—each piece beautifully fitted into its place. But unfortunately I had no definite proof. It was all in my mind. It was then that an idea came to me. There was an assurance—a slickness about the crime. I had no doubt that in the future Patrick Redfern would repeat his crime. What about the past? It was remotely possible that this was not his first killing. The method employed, strangulation, was in harmony with his nature—a killer for pleasure as well as for profit. If he was already a murderer I was sure that he would have used the same means. I asked Inspector Colgate for a list of women victims of strangulation. The result filled me with joy. The death of Nellie Parsons found strangled in a lonely copse might or might not have been Patrick Redfern's work—it might merely have suggested choice of locality to him, but in Alice Corrigan's death I found exactly what I was looking for. In essence the same method. Juggling with time—a murder committed not, as is the usual way, *before* it is supposed to have happened, but *afterwards*. A body supposedly discovered at a quarter past four. A husband with an alibi up to twenty-five past four.

"What really happened? It was said that Edward Corrigan arrived at the Pine Ridge, found his wife was not there *and went out and walked up and down*. Actually of course he ran full speed to the rendezvous, Caesar's Grove (which you will remember was quite near by), killed her and returned to the café. The girl hiker who reported the crime was a most respectable young lady, games mistress in a well-known girls' school. Apparently she had no connection with Edward Corrigan. She had to walk some way to report the death. The police surgeon only examined the body at a quarter to six. As in this case the time of death was accepted without question.

"I made one final test. I must know definitely if Mrs. Redfern was a liar. I arranged our little excursion to Dartmoor. If any one had a bad head for heights, they are never comfortable crossing a narrow bridge over running water. Miss Brewster, a genuine sufferer, showed giddiness. But Christine Redfern, unconcerned, ran across without a qualm. It was a small point, but it was a definite test. If she had told one unnecessary lie—then all the other lies were possible. In the meantime Colgate had got the photograph identified by the Surrey police. I played my hand in the only way I thought likely to succeed. Having lulled Patrick Redfern into security, I turned on him and did my utmost to make him lose his self-control. The knowledge that he had been identified with Corrigan caused him to lose his head completely."

Hercule Poirot stroked his throat reminiscently. "What I did," he said with importance, "was exceedingly dangerous—but I do not regret it. I succeeded! I did not suffer in vain."

There was a moment's silence. Then Mrs. Gardener gave a deep sigh. "Why, M. Poirot," she said. "It's just been too wonderful—hearing just exactly how you got your results. It's every bit as fascinating as a lecture on criminology—in fact it *is* a lecture on criminology. And to think my magenta wool and that sunbathing conversation actually had something to do with it! That really makes me too excited for words and I'm sure Mr. Gardener feels the same, don't you, Odell?"

"Yes, darling," said Mr. Gardener.

Hercule Poirot said: "Mr. Gardener too was of assistance to me. I wanted the opinion of a sensible man about Mrs. Marshall. I asked Mr. Gardener what he thought of her."

"Is that so," said Mrs. Gardener. "And what did you say about her, Odell?"

Mr. Gardener coughed. He said: "Well, darling, I never did think very much of her, you know."

"That's the kind of thing men always say to their wives," said Mrs. Gardener. "And if you ask me, even M. Poirot here is what I should call a shade on the indulgent side about her, calling her a natural victim and all that. Of course it's true that she wasn't a cultured woman at all, and as Captain Marshall isn't here I don't mind saying that she always did seem to me kind of dumb. I said so to Mr. Gardener, didn't I, Odell?"

"Yes, darling," said Mr. Gardener.

Linda Marshall sat with Hercule Poirot on Gull Cove. She said: "Of course I'm glad I didn't die after all. But you know, M. Poirot, it's just the same as if I'd killed her, isn't it? I meant to."

Hercule Poirot said energetically: "It is not at all the same thing. The wish to kill and the action of killing are two different things. If in your bedroom instead of the little wax figure you had had your stepmother bound and helpless and a dagger in your hand instead of a pin, you would not have pushed it into her heart! Something within you would have said 'no.' It is the same with me. I enrage myself at an imbecile. I say, 'I would like to kick him.' Instead I kick the table. I say, 'This table, it is the imbecile, I kick him so.' And then, if I have not hurt my toe too much, I feel much better and the table it is not usually damaged. But if the imbecile himself was there I should not kick him. To make the wax figure and stick in the pins it is silly, yes, it is childish, yes—but it does something useful too. You took the hate out of yourself and put it into that little figure. And with the pin and the fire you destroyed—not your stepmother—but the hate you bore her. Afterwards, even before you heard of her death, you felt cleansed, did you not—you felt lighter—happier?"

Linda nodded. She said: "How did you know? That's just how I did feel."

Poirot said: "Then do not repeat to yourself the imbecilities. Just make up your mind not to hate your next stepmother."

Linda said, startled: "Do you think I'm going to have another? Oh, I see, you mean Rosamund. I don't mind her." She hesitated a minute. "She's *sensible*."

It was not the adjective that Poirot himself would have selected for Rosamund Darnley, but he realized that it was Linda's idea of high praise.

Kenneth Marshall said: "Rosamund, did you get some extraordinary idea into your head that I'd killed Arlena?"

Rosamund looked rather shamefaced. She said: "I suppose I was a damned fool."

"Of course you were."

"Yes, but, Ken, you are such an oyster. I never knew what you really felt about Arlena. I didn't know if you accepted her as she was and were just frightfully decent about her, or whether you—well, just believed in her blindly. And I thought if it was that and you suddenly found out that she was letting you down you might go mad with rage. I've heard stories about you. You're always very quiet but you're rather frightening sometimes."

"So you thought I just took her by the throat and throttled the life out of her?"

"Well—yes—that's just exactly what I did think. And your alibi seemed a bit on the light side. That's when I suddenly decided to take a hand and made up that silly story about seeing you typing in your room. And when I heard that you said you'd seen me look in—well, that made me quite sure you'd done it. That, and Linda's queerness."

Kenneth Marshall said with a sigh: "Don't you realize that I said I'd seen you in the mirror in order to back up *your* story. I—I thought you needed it corroborated."

Rosamund stared at him. "You don't mean you thought that I killed your wife?"

Kenneth Marshall shifted uneasily. He mumbled: "Dash it all, Rosamund, don't you remember how you nearly killed that boy about that dog once? How you hung on to my throat and wouldn't let go."

"But that was years ago."

"Yes, I know—"

Rosamund said sharply: "What earthly motive do you think I had to kill Arlena?"

His glance shifted. He mumbled something again. Rosamund cried: "Ken, you mass of conceit! You thought I killed her out of altruism on your behalf, did you? Or—or did you think I killed her because I wanted you myself?"

"Not at all," said Kenneth Marshall indignantly. "But you know what you said that day—about Linda and everything—and—and you seemed to care what happened to me."

Rosamund said: "I've always cared about that."

"I believe you have. You know, Rosamund—I can't usually talk about things—I'm not good at talking—but I'd like to get this clear. I didn't care for Arlena—only just a little at first—and living with her day after day was a pretty nerve-racking business. In fact it was absolute hell, but I *was* awfully sorry for her. She was such a damned fool—crazy about men—she just couldn't help it—and they always let her down and treated her rottenly. I simply felt I couldn't be the one to give her the final push. I'd married her and it was up to me to look after her as best I could. I think she knew that and was grateful to me really. She was—she was a pathetic sort of creature really."

Rosamund said gently: "It's all right, Ken. I understand now."

Without looking at her Kenneth Marshall carefully filled a pipe. He mumbled: "You're—pretty good at understanding, Rosamund."

A faint smile curved Rosamund's ironic mouth. She said: "Are you going to ask me to marry you now, Ken, or are you determined to wait six months?"

Kenneth Marshall's pipe dropped from his lips and crashed on the rocks below. He said: "Damn, that's the second pipe I've lost down here. And I haven't got another with me. How the devil did you know I'd fixed six months as the proper time?"

"I suppose because it is the proper time. But I'd rather have something definite now, please. Because in the intervening months you may come across some other persecuted female and rush to the rescue in chivalrous fashion again."

He laughed. "You're going to be the persecuted female this time, Rosamund. You're going to give up that damned dressmaking business of yours and we're going to live in the country."

"Don't you know that I make a very handsome income out of my business? don't you realize that it's *my* business—that I created it and worked it up and that I'm proud of it! And you've got the damned nerve to come along and say, 'Give it all up, dear.'"

"I've got the damned nerve to say it, yes."

"And you think I care enough for you to do it?"

"If you don't," said Kenneth Marshall, "you'd be no good to me."

Rosamund said softly: "Oh, my dear, I've wanted to live in the country with you all my life. Now—it's going to come true. . . ."